s h i n i g a m i

d j a n g o   w e x l e r

Silver Imprint
Medallion Press, Inc.
Printed in USA

Previous accolades for *Memories of Empire*:

"A swashbuckling epic fantasy."
—*Publishers Weekly*

"Wexler's first novel is set in a world that blends the trappings of Asian and Middle Eastern cultures to create a rich, exotic background for a group of unique and memorable characters. A good choice for most fantasy collections."

—*Library Journal*

"Django Wexler has a complicated fantasy world with not only humans and their problems, but also a spirit hierarchy that starts with hard-to-kill monsters and go to intelligent spirits with their own motivations. It is a world where intelligent spirits can manipulate whole armies to get at the treasure tomb of the Gods. Great stuff."

—*H. Lazarus, Independent Reviewer*

"Fantasy fans who enjoy stories with ultra-elaborate plot lines will absolutely love Wexler's debut offering, a novel with the rip-roaring action of Glen Cook's Black Company saga and the intricacies of Robert Jordan's Wheel of Time."

—*P.G. Allen, Explorations* – BN.com

"It is hard to believe that this is Django Wexter's debut novel because it is as well written and character driven as a Terry Brooks or Robert Jordan novel. Veil humanizes Corvus through her force of her personality changing him from an obsessed individual be a man who cares about others. The Imperials and the Khaevs are reminiscent of the Romans. Sword and sorcery fans will find MEMORIES OF EMPIRE a very enjoyable one sitting reading experience."

—*H. Klausner, Independent Reviewer*

DEDICATION:

For my parents, as always.

ACKNOWLEDGEMENTS:

People who helped make this book what it is,
in no particular order:

—*Konstantin "The Zombie" Koptev, who debated the world design with me and helped hammer the text into shape.*

—*Betsy Kolmus, who cheerfully took on the unenviable position of alpha reader.*

—*Dan Blandford, who slogged through an early version.*

—*Melanie Benkin, who talked me out of some really bad ideas.*

—*Write Or Die (WorD), my writing group, who helped me with my bad habits.*

—*Once again, Helen Rosburg and everyone at Medallion Press.*

Shinigami (noun, Japanese): Literally "Spirit of Death," often translated as "Grim Reaper." In traditional Japanese folklore, a spirit that collects the souls of the dead and ushers them into the next world.

part one
Creation

chapter one

SYLPH WALKER OPENED HER EYES WITHOUT REALLY feeling like she'd awoken. Her head was filled with cobwebs, still half-captured by dream.

"Miss Walker?" said a voice. "Are you awake?"

"Yeah." Sylph sat up and shook her head. Something loomed in her recent memory, something large and important, but she couldn't quite place it. What happened . . .

"I wouldn't try to think too hard just yet. This place isn't conducive to thinking."

"Where am I?" She blinked again, but everything remained maddeningly blurred. The source of the voice was a blue-and-white mass in a red-and-black landscape.

"Hard to explain. You won't be staying long, in any case. I just wanted to give you a gift, to help you get started."

"Get started?" It was a stupid question, but her mind still felt sticky-slow.

"Like I said, don't try to think too hard. Take this."

She felt something against the palm of her hand, smooth and cool.

"And remember," the voice continued, "you've fallen through a hole in the web, but the spider will still come for you sooner or later. Good luck."

"Lina!" Sylph's straggling brain had finally gotten around

to that point. "Where's . . ."

Then she was falling.

* * *

". . . Lina! *Fuck!*"

This last was because she'd sat up suddenly and banged her forehead quite hard against what felt like rock. She pressed her hand against the pain automatically and felt the slickness of blood.

Ow. She kept her left hand against her head, while her right hand explored upward. The ceiling was close and made of smooth stone, slick with moisture, and her back was pressed against the rock. *Ow, ow, ow.* Sylph opened her eyes, but it didn't seem to make any difference. She closed them again, just to be sure. Colored phantoms danced in total darkness behind her eyelids.

Okay, what the hell is going on?

At least her brain seemed to be working again; *maybe,* she thought sourly, *it was the sudden jolt.* She probed her recent memory as she might have probed a broken tooth with her tongue, knowing that there was something painful there . . .

The car. We were in the car, and that old man just stepped out into the road . . .

Lina had been driving. She'd swerved, slammed on the brakes, skidded on the inch-thick snowpack with an under-layer of ice. The Corolla had gone over the verge and down the side of the hill, end over end.

Jesus Christ! Sylph's heartbeat hummed. *I . . .*

Memory fragmented after that. She remembered Lina trying to say something, choked off in an awful gurgle; she remembered a funny feeling in her chest. When she put her hand to it, she found a shard of twisted metal . . .

Sylph slapped her hand to her breast, hard enough to sting. There was nothing but smooth, unbroken flesh. Her breath came fast.

. . . naked. Why am I naked?

A moment's examination confirmed this. Sylph took a deep breath, closed her eyes, and tried to think.

What happened? Lina put the car over the edge, and we crashed, and then . . .

There was a blank. *I must have passed out.*

Which means I'm in a hospital now? With no lights, and granite ceilings six inches overhead?

She'd felt her body give a little jerk, her hands tightening on the metal until it cut her flesh. *And then someone came and saved me?* Sylph shook her head. *No. Not possible.*

So either that was all some kind of a dream—which didn't go very far toward explaining her present state—*or I'm dead.*

I'm dead. She took this with a certain degree of equanimity—since there was obviously some part of her left to be doing the thinking, death was apparently not as final as she'd hitherto imagined. *I guess the priests and so on were right after all. Except I don't remember anybody mentioning caves, unless I've gone to Hell or something. Actually*—the thought came unpleasantly—*if the priests were right I probably would go to Hell.* Sylph had never been to church in her life, and hadn't given much thought to the existence of God. *I suppose it's too late now to change my mind?*

Sylph, you're panicking. Forget God, forget that crap, figure out where the hell you are. She winced at her choice of words. *Come on, come on. Move!*

A little exploring with her hands showed that she was in an angled pit in the rock. When she pointed her toes, she could feel granite, and there was no room to move to the left, right, or in front of her. Above her head, though, her groping hand found passage—the passage continued at about the same height and width.

Not much choice, then. Hell or not, she wasn't going to accomplish much at the bottom of a pit. Sylph inched her body upward, bracing her hands against the ceiling above her and earning a dozen scrapes on her back. There was no room to turn over, even if she'd wanted to, so she pushed herself up with her feet, inch by careful inch. The groove tended upward, more and more steeply, so before long it was less like sliding along and more like climbing a hill with her back to it. This made for extremely clumsy going, and Sylph was just starting to consider how she might contort herself into flipping over when her outstretched hand closed over a lip of rock and she pulled herself free into the open air.

She couldn't help emitting a hoarse whoop of victory, which she regretted immediately. *Idiot! You don't know who's listening . . .*

Sylph looked around. Her eyes had adjusted to the dark, but there was still little enough to see. The stars overhead were few and dim, and she recognized none of the constellations; a half-moon rode near the horizon, but that too seemed smaller and less brilliant. By its faint light, she could see the side of a hill strewn with boulders, and what looked like trees down-slope. *But no burning pits of sulfur thus far.*

"Sylph?" Her sister's plaintive voice was achingly familiar. "Sylph, is that you?"

"Lina?"

Lina. She'd been avoiding thinking about Lina, so skillfully that she hadn't even noticed. *If she's here, she must be dead too.* That gave Sylph a queer feeling, which she shook off angrily. *Idiot. She's as alive as I am, here, even if she's dead—God, this is confusing—*

"Lina? Are you there?"

"I'm here!" Her voice was coming from somewhere uphill. "Sylph, help! I'm stuck!"

Typical. "Keep talking! I'll see if I can find you."

Walking across the rocky hill was hell in the dark. Every little pebble felt like a rusty nail when she stepped on it, and there were a dozen places she nearly tripped and sprained an ankle, or worse. So she kept it calm and careful, despite Lina's frantic tone.

"Okay . . . okay, keeping talking . . ." Lina stopped for a

moment, then said, "Okay. I'm not sure what happened, but I remember rolling the car over the cliff and you screamed 'You idiot!' at me, and you're probably right, but I didn't get the chance to say anything before we hit the ground. And then . . . then I *tried* to say I was sorry, but I couldn't talk and I couldn't breathe and it hurt so much I thought I was going to die. And then I woke up and I was stuck in here and—"

"You can stop talking," said Sylph. She stood on a ledge above where Lina was trapped—an angled hole just like the one Sylph had been in. Lina, two years older than Sylph's fourteen and quite a bit taller, had tried to turn onto her stomach and gotten herself wedged in sideways. Sylph rolled her eyes and sighed, a familiar gesture that banished a little bit of her fear.

"Sylph!" Lina tried to turn her head and failed.

"Hold still." Sylph climbed down the boulder and touched her sister's hand; Lina's fingers contracted on hers with the grip of a drowning man. "I'm happy to see you too, but let go so I can get you out of there, okay?"

"Okay."

Sylph studied the situation for a moment by what light she had, noticing in passing that her sister was naked too. Finally she put her hand on Lina's shoulder and said, "Here we go. Breathe out and hold it."

Lina obediently did so.

"This is probably going to hurt," said Sylph, and before her sister could react she pushed, hard. Lina's arm came free from where it was jammed against the rock, Lina rolled onto her back and screamed, and Sylph grabbed her under the arms and braced her feet against the lip of rock to keep her sister from sliding all the way back down to the bottom.

"My *arm*, I think you broke my arm . . ." Lina sounded on the verge of tears.

"Just a scrape." Sylph took a deep breath. "Now come on, you're almost out. Just push a little bit."

It was more than just a little, but eventually Lina emerged

from her not-so-shallow grave. The skin near her elbow was torn up pretty badly; Lina wiped the blood away, nervously, and every time she touched the wound her eyes glittered with tears.

"There." Sylph sat back. "Come here, would you?"

She wrapped Lina in a sisterly hug. Despite the blood and the grime, it felt good. *I need to distract her before she starts bawling, anyway.* Sylph felt her sister shaking with released tension, and held her quietly until she stopped. Eventually Lina sat back against a stone, exhausted, and Sylph gingerly sat next to her. The rock was moist and cold against her bare skin.

"So, where are we?" Lina asked. "Why am I naked?"

"Dead," said Sylph. "And I don't know."

"What do you mean, dead?" Lina took a deep breath and put one hand over her heart. "I don't *feel* dead."

"Neither do I, but last time I checked I had a big metal spike coming out right here," Sylph touched her breast, "and people don't generally survive that. And *you* were trying to breathe with a ruined throat and a punctured lung."

Lina rubbed a hand along the skin of her throat. "But . . ."

"Maybe it was all a dream?"

"Yeah."

"Then where are we?"

"Maybe we were dreaming . . ."

". . . the same dream . . ."

". . . and then our friends decided to play a practical joke on us and took us out somewhere and . . ." Lina trailed off under Sylph's withering glare.

There was another moment of silence.

"Maybe we're *still* dreaming?" Lina suggested hesitantly. She yelped when Sylph pinched her on the shoulder.

"Maybe. But I don't think so." Sylph got to her feet. "Come on."

"Where are you going?"

"To find out where we are, and what's going on."

"You're just going to walk around naked?"

"I don't seem to have much choice."

❋   ❋   ❋

THE TOP OF THE HILL SEEMED THE LOGICAL PLACE TO GO. *Actually,* Sylph thought, *the logical thing to do would be to wait for morning.* But she couldn't bring herself to just sit and do nothing—the pressure of thought and inactivity felt like it would crush her into a tiny, sobbing ball. *Who knows if there even* is *a morning?* She closed her eyes for a moment and tried to drill that grim reminder into her brain. *I can't assume anything.*

Climbing in the dark was no fun, and Sylph skinned her knee on a particularly nasty rock, but eventually she and Lina sat atop a wide, flat boulder at the summit. When she finally pulled herself up, Sylph blinked in the light—it was only a weak glow, but much brighter than the moonlight. There was a sword lying at the center of the boulder. Sylph caught only that much before the glow winked out; she hurried to the spot while Lina struggled to pull herself onto the plateau.

A sword. Sylph felt a flash of recognition. *Just before I . . . woke up.*

"I wouldn't try to think too hard just yet . . ."

Something against the palm of my hand.

". . . you've fallen through a hole in the web, but the spider will come looking for you sooner or later."

"Is that a sword?" Lina breathed.

"Don't touch," Sylph snapped.

"It was glowing!"

"I know." That was a bit worrisome, to be honest. Never having died before, Sylph didn't know what to expect, but something about the situation smelled like a set-up. *Who was talking to me?* She could remember the *feel* of the voice, but not a face. *Was it just a dream? Unlikely.*

"A magic sword?" Lina sounded a little skeptical. "I mean, if we're dead, who knows—"

"Probably," said Sylph irritably. She'd reached the same conclusion, but she wasn't happy with it. "If it's so magical, what's it doing lying on a rock?"

"Maybe we were Meant to find it," said Lina, pronouncing the capital letter.

"That just means someone put it there for us to find."

"Who?"

"How should I know?"

It was hard to make out details by moonlight. The weapon's straight blade was about three feet long, sheathed leather. Silver glittered on the hilt.

"It's beautiful," said Lina eventually.

"It looks . . ." Sylph searched for a word. ". . . dangerous."

"Of course it's dangerous, it's a weapon."

"Not like that."

"I—" Lina was interrupted by a scream from below, high and inhuman.

Sylph scrambled to the edge of the boulder and peered down. Fire flickered at the base of the hill and she heard the rapid beat of horses' hooves. She got a brief glimpse of two women, dressed in cloaks and rough homespun, cornered against the base of the rocks by a semicircle of riders with torches. Naked steel glowed in the flickering light.

"Robbery?" Sylph whispered. *Or worse.* She was suddenly acutely aware of her unclothed state, and blushed. "Stay quiet. I want to see . . ."

She realized Lina was no longer at her side. Her sister had slipped clumsily over the side, sword tucked under one arm, and was picking her way down the slope as fast as she could.

"Jesus *fucking* Christ, Lina!" said Sylph. She rolled over the edge of the boulder, stubbed her toe and cursed again, and tried to follow.

✳   ✳   ✳

THE RIDERS HAD DISMOUNTED, EACH CARRYING A TORCH in one hand and a sword in the other. There was one woman among them—Sylph hadn't noticed, at first, because she was dressed the same as the others, mostly in leather with blackened metal plates over her chest, forearms, and legs. The two that faced them were little more than girls, not more than Lina's age. They were both armed, but with short-swords that looked like toys compared to the soldiers' blades.

Sylph caught up with Lina just at the edge of the rocks. By some miracle, none of soldiers had noticed their descent; their eyes were entirely on their prey. The four men had tightened the circle while the woman waited behind. They feinted to keep the girls on their toes; the victims looked scared, but not terrified, and handled their weapons with practiced ease.

More is going on here than we thought.

"Damn it, Lina!" Sylph hissed. "What the *fuck* do you think you're doing?"

"They're going to get killed!"

"So are you!"

"I can't just—"

The woman heard them, spun, and gestured with her torch. "Ambush! There's more of them—"

"Shit!" said Sylph, and then things started to happen very fast.

The two men nearest to her and Lina turned. Sylph shouted, "Lina, run!" and tried to get back up the slope, but a traitorous rock gave way and she lost her footing, falling heavily against an outcropping and bruising her shoulder. Lina stood, and the sight of her—possibly aided by the sight of her breasts, Sylph thought—was enough to startle the pair momentarily. Lina tugged the sword free of its sheath, which she tossed aside.

At the same time, the two girls who'd been cornered acted. The taller of the pair ignored the men on either side of her and charged the woman, sword flashing; there was a skitter of steel on steel, and then the girl danced back as the woman thrust the torch in her face. The other girl stuck close to her back, driving back the nearest soldier with a quick series of cuts. After a moment she was facing two of them, and was forced to give ground.

Sylph didn't have much time to watch the girls fight, because the other two soldiers were advancing on Lina. Sylph levered herself off the rock, shoulder in serious pain, and stumbled down-slope. *I have to do something . . . maybe I can distract them . . . I'm not even armed!* She stooped, on the way, and scooped up a handful of loose gravel. *Better than nothing. Lina and her stupid magic sword . . .*

Lina had no idea how to handle a sword. The first soldier cut at her, a lazy swipe that would have opened her throat; she got the sword up in time by dumb luck, and lashed out wildly after the impact. The soldier moved to parry, casually. *He's going to run her through.* Sylph closed her hand around the little rocks. *I'm not going to watch her die again . . .*

The swords connected with a single, ringing note, like the sounding of the purest of crystal. There was a flash of white light, which blinded Sylph for a moment; by the time she blinked away the green and purple afterimages, the soldier was *gone* and his companion lay motionless on the ground, missing his legs and half his torso. A cone of glowing rock started from where the man had been standing; it extended for a few feet and then faded out, as though the energy had fused the ground itself. Sylph realized her mouth was hanging open, and closed it with an audible click. All the other fighting had stopped.

A magic sword.

Then Lina's eyes rolled up in her head, and she folded up into a neat pile on the ground. The sword clattered from her hand.

The girls recovered first. The taller one pressed the attack against the female soldier, striking low and fast; the soldier tried to ward her off again with the torch, but this time the girl bulled through it. She brought her short-sword around in a strike that would have buried it in her opponent's gut, but the soldier twisted at the last instant and the short blade failed to bite, drawing a bright line across her breastplate. The soldier dropped her torch and grabbed the girl by the shoulder, pushing her away with one hand and drawing a sword across the girl's belly with the other. It all happened in a second or so—the girl tottered another step, then collapsed with a nasty wet sound.

The other girl was faster, twisting inside the reach of one of the pair facing her and striking low before he could react, opening a gaping wound in his leg that immediately started spurting blood. The man staggered drunkenly away from her, sword waving halfheartedly, as she engaged his companion. There was a flurry of blows too fast for Sylph to follow, and then the soldier was backpedaling and had dropped his sword, clutching his wrist. The girl dropped and swept his legs out from under him with a kick, and he went down hard.

In the meantime, the woman had recovered, holding her sword two-handed for a strike that would split the girl's skull from behind . . .

I, Sylph thought, *am* such *an idiot.*

"Behind you!"

Too late for the girl to get out of the way entirely, but she threw herself out of the crouch. The woman's strike took a good chunk of the fleshy part of her leg, and blood spurted, but the girl managed to bring her knife around and put it in her opponent's shin, just past the armor. The woman screamed and fell, her sword clattering in the dust.

Before she could retrieve it, the girl crawled closer and slipped her blade under her opponent's breastplate. The blade was now red to the hilt—the woman could do nothing but curse as the girl pulled herself the length of her opponent's body, leaving a trail of blood from the wound on her leg. The soldier made one attempt to toss her to the side, but the girl pinned her arm and with a last effort drove the dagger into the woman's eye. The soldier's body jerked and lay still, and the girl, apparently exhausted, put her head down on the woman's breastplate and closed her eyes.

And then there was silence, except for the sound of rapidly retreating hoofbeats. *One of them got away*, Sylph thought inanely. There was blood everywhere. She'd never seen so much blood—*except after the car went over the verge . . .*

Sylph shook her head. She wanted to vomit, wanted to faint like her sister had, wanted to run and run and run until all this was behind her. *I want to go* home, *and curl up on my crappy old couch and watch reruns of* Star Trek *until one in the morning.* Instead, she forced herself to her feet, wincing at a twinge from her shoulder, and looked around.

Lina. As far as Sylph could tell, Lina was fine. *Who knows what that thing did to her?* She patted her sister's cheek and got no reaction. But she was breathing, and not obviously bleeding, and that was good enough for the moment. The two men she'd—*I don't know* what *she did*—she'd killed were, well, dead. Sylph left them alone, but was unable to escape the stench of burnt flesh; it was like a barbeque gone horribly wrong.

The woman and the girls. One of the other two men had escaped, and the other lay perfectly still after bleeding enough to paint the ground beneath him red. *The woman's dead*—Sylph gulped nervously at the sight of the dagger hilt sticking out of her eye—*but the two girls . . .*

The shorter one, who'd killed the woman, was alive. Bleeding like a stuck pig, but alive. Vaguely remembered first-aid classes came back to Sylph—*pressure. Stop the bleeding, elevate the wound*—or was it *elevate the head?* She felt lightheaded and a little dizzy, but she bent over and found a corner of the woman's cloak. *She won't need it anymore.* It was a tough weave, too tough to tear—the thought of pulling the dagger out of the woman's eye was too much to bear, but a quick search revealed her bloodstained sword in the dust, and a little work with that produced a ragged strip of fabric. Sylph tied it around the girl's leg, as tight as she could, and then grabbed one of her limp hands, pulled her off the woman's body, and propped her legs up on the corpse. That done, she took the girl's heartbeat—it was strong, but much too fast, and Sylph couldn't remember if that was good or not.

The other girl. Sylph was exhausted. She didn't want to look. *I have to see if she's alive, at least.*

It was the work of a moment to confirm that she wasn't. Sylph nudged her onto one side with a shaking foot, and found that most of the girl's guts had spilled onto the ground. That, finally, was too much; Sylph fell to her knees and retched. Then she got up, on shaking legs, and stumbled back toward Lina. Sylph had just enough energy left to plant her back against the rock and sink down next to her sister.

Now what? She leaned her head against Lina's shoulder, absently. All the thoughts she'd hoped to ward off came crashing down. *I'm dead. I'm fucking* dead *and I'm naked and covered in blood.*

Christ, Sylph. You could be in Hell with some guy in red tights dissecting you with a pitchfork, count your blessings.

That didn't have the intended effect. She closed her eyes against welling tears. *So, now we're dead, just like Mom.* She thought back to the crash and tried to remember if it had hurt—she couldn't recall any pain. Just a sudden realization, like waking from a dream. *That's good.*

Sylph cried, but only a little. Crying never solved anything.

WARLEADER KARL VANTZ WAS ALERTED TO THE RETURN of his man by a sudden commotion at the edge of the camp, in the woods. He waited patiently, although his insides were roiling and his stomach felt like it was awash in acid. Vantz's riders had been involved in the campaign against the Circle Breakers for more than a year, and he'd been forced to replace his losses. But that meant that many of his men were from the villages west of the Rippers, with their harsh accents and olive skin, and he didn't trust them enough to show weakness in front of them.

The arrival was Gethor, one of Vantz's old guard who'd ridden with him since Bleloth. Vantz had sent him with Tyra to keep an eye on her, along with three of the westerners he trusted the most. *It's a bad omen that he returns alone.* But there was still hope, Vantz reminded himself. *Perhaps he's a messenger bringing me news of victory.*

Gethor was wounded in one arm, and his sword was gone. His mount, which bore signs of hard riding, was led away by servants and the soldier was escorted into his lord's presence by two of Vantz's easterners.

"Well?" the warleader snapped, too anxious to bother with niceties.

Gethor put his fist over his heart in salute. "Warleader, we pursued the two, as instructed—"

"You were instructed to bring them to me in chains."

"Yes, Warleader." Gethor lowered his eyes. "I must apologize—"

Vantz cut him off again. "Where is Tyra?"

Gethor paused. "I believe she is dead, Warleader. It is possible she was taken prisoner, but not likely."

Dead. The word thumped through his mind like the dull crash of a hammer. *Dead, dead, dead.* He licked his lips and tried to maintain his composure. "How?"

"We were ambushed. Warleader . . ." Gethor hesitated, and Vantz gestured impatiently.

"What!"

"Magic, Warleader. Two of our men were struck down by a flash of light."

"Impossible," said Vantz, rage serving as a stand-in for grief for the moment. "There are no Magi west of the Rippers."

"Yes, Warleader . . ." Gethor looked like he was about to add something, but Vantz's expression cut him short. He kept his head bowed.

"But," Vantz continued, "perhaps the Breakers have uncovered an artifact in the desert. That is a possibility, no?"

"As you say, Warleader," said Gethor nervously. "It's power—"

"Leave me."

"Yes, Warleader." Gethor saluted again and departed. Once he was gone, Vantz settled back in his chair and waited for Schwartz to present himself, which took only a few moments.

"Warleader," said Schwartz, his salute crisp and precise. Vantz's lieutenant had been with the riders since Bleloth, but Vantz still could not bring himself to fully trust the man. He was too . . . neat.

"What's our strength, Schwartz?"

"Forty-six men, Warleader, and seventy horses. Seventy-one if Gethor's survives. He was forced to turn the others loose."

Forty-six. Half of what I started with. That count didn't include Tyra or the men lost with her, he was sure—Schwartz was always careful about that kind of detail. "I want you to detail five men and ten mounts to get a message through to Highpoint."

"Yes, Warleader."

"I'll write it myself." There was another band of riders at Highpoint, one of the few permanent garrisons supported by Gargorian himself. Vantz and the warriors of the plains had always thought of it as a sinecure, a reward for tired old soldiers at the end of their careers. They'd passed through, on the ride west, and Vantz had exchanged pleasantries with the warleader there. *He seemed brave enough.* "Have them ready in an hour."

"Yes, Warleader. And the rest of the men?"

"Tell Gethor to come back."

Schwartz saluted and left. A few minutes later, the survivor was once again in front of his master, looking even more nervous than before. Vantz let him stew for a minute, running his fingers along the ornate scrollwork of his sword-hilt, then said, "How did she die?"

"Warleader?"

"How did Tyra die?"

"We were fighting the two Breakers when the others attacked. Fanoe and Gilep were killed instantly, but Tyra pressed the attack against the bodyguard and struck her a fatal blow. She was wounded, however, and fell in combat against Fah."

"Fah." *How that girl torments me.* "Thank you, Gethor."

"I am yours to command, Warleader."

"Go." Vantz sighed. "Tell the men we're riding west. If the Circle Breakers have obtained an artifact, it must be captured as soon as possible."

Gethor saluted. "Yes, Warleader."

Tyra, thought Vantz. He remembered practicing swordwork with her, the blade flashing almost as bright as her smile. The warmth of her afterward, and the pleasant smell of sweat. The little noises . . .

All gone. Dead and gone, food for the Lightbringer. His lip twisted. *Fah. When I find her, I'm going to have all the men fuck her bloody, then strangle her with her own entrails.* And even that, he decided, would be less than she deserved.

✳   ✳   ✳

LINA WOKE UP FROM A HORRIBLE DREAM.

God . . . I was naked and so was Sylph, and I had a magic sword, and there were people fighting and blood . . .

Naked was the clue. *You're naked all the time in dreams, like the one where you have to give a speech in front of the entire class and you realize your forgot your notes and your pants too.*

There was something else in the dream, a sound that was so deep she felt it in her gut rather than her ears; like a deep, horrible chuckle. It was laughter with no humor in it whatsoever.

She opened her eyes. *I've got a lot to do today, too.*

The night sky, slowly turning pink with the dawn. She was resting against a rock ledge—*naked*—and there were people lying everywhere . . .

"Sylph! Sylph, are you okay?" *Please be okay please be okay please be okay and tell me I'm dreaming.*

A hand shot out and grabbed her. "Lina! I'm fine!"

"Thank God." Lina was breathing too fast. "I woke up and I thought that something had happened to you and there's all these people and I think they're *dead* and you're still naked and I didn't know what to do."

"What else is new?" Sylph tried to move, but Lina's hand still pinned her shoulder to the rock. "Mind letting me up?"

"Oh! Sorry. You're really okay?"

"Banged my shoulder a little." Sylph rubbed her bruises gingerly. "I'll be all right. You?"

"I'm fine." *I think.* She examined herself quickly, just to be sure.

"Do you remember what happened? Slowly."

Not a dream? I guess not. "We woke up and didn't know where we were, and I found this sword. And then we saw some girls who were in trouble, and we went running to help them . . ."

Sylph's arched eyebrow said *We?*

". . . and then there were men with swords," Lina continued hurriedly, "and I swung that thing and . . ."

There wasn't much after that. She remembered a light, and a black smile like a hole in the world. And the laugh.

". . . and then I'm not sure. What happened?"

"A swordfight, obviously." Sylph got to her feet and looked around.

"Are they all really . . ." Lina lowered her voice. ". . . *dead*?"

"That's what happens in a swordfight, yes." Sylph pointed, and winced when her shoulder twinged. "But not *all*. One of the girls is still alive, or was last night."

She walked toward the bodies. Lina's legs didn't seem to want to follow, and it took her a moment to bully them into obedience. By the time she got there, Sylph was already kneeling by the girl with a hand pressed against her forehead.

There was blood *everywhere*. The girl was lying on top of a woman in soldier's clothing, her face twisted in a final agony. Nearby there was another girl, lying on top of the cut that had killed her. Her guts had spilled all over . . .

"Sylph, you can't—you don't know what you're doing—"

"She needs water."

Lina caught a whiff of charnel stench and it drove her to her knees, retching on an empty stomach. She convulsed helplessly until the dry heaves had subsided, and remained on her knees with her eyes tightly closed.

"I can't do this, Sylph, I—"

"Lina. We'll get her away from here, okay? Help me carry her."

"We shouldn't move her, we should call a doctor or something."

"Where exactly are we going to call a doctor from?"

Lina paused. "Oh. Right." *I forgot that we were dead.*

"Just get her feet."

"You're sure you know what you're doing?"

"No."

Lina picked up the girl's feet. The sisters carried her away from the battlefield, her arms trailing on the bloody rocks. They were in luck as far as water was concerned; a stream ran down the hillside, just around the corner from where the fighting had been. Sylph laid the girl out next to the water and tested it with a toe. She yelped.

"What's wrong?"

"Cold. Very cold."

Lina realized how thirsty she was. She scrambled over to the stream and drank from her cupped hands. The water was freezing, but felt wonderful going down. By the time she got up Sylph had found a knife on the girl's belt and slit the leg of her pants around the wound, unwinding the blood-soaked bandage before washing the cut in the stream water. The patient moaned, unintelligibly, but didn't wake. Sylph spread a little more water across the girl's forehead.

"Sylph?"

"Hmm?"

"What are we going to do for food?"

There was a pause.

"Sylph?"

"I'm thinking."

After a moment, Sylph started going through the girl's pouches. Lina watched uncomfortably.

"I feel like a thief."

"We're helping her, aren't we? Here." Sylph tossed a strip of dried meat to Lina, who bit into it eagerly, thief or not; it was tough and salty, like beef jerky. There was also a half a loaf of crusty bread, a needle and thread carefully tucked into a bit of fabric, and a couple of copper-colored coins Lina didn't recognize. Sylph returned all but the food to the pouches.

"I'm going back."

"Back *there*?"

"There might be more food, and we need something to wear." Sylph looked at her sister, and sighed. "You stay here with her, okay?"

Lina shivered. "Be quick, okay?" She hated herself as she said it. *She's always taking care of me, and I say things like that . . .*

But Sylph just nodded and disappeared around the corner. Lina sat next to the unconscious girl, chewing on the meat, naked and cold and miserable.

She's so . . . I don't know. Whatever the situation was, Sylph just dealt with it. It was an ability Lina envied. *Look at me. I'm two years older, and all I can do is throw up and make a fool of myself and . . .*

The girl groaned. Lina knelt beside her.

"Hello? Are you okay? Can you hear me?" Sylph rounded the corner, and Lina waved her over. "Come quick!"

Sylph had found more food somewhere, a couple of cloaks, stained with blood, and had the sword under her arm. Lina hadn't realized until that moment she'd left it behind, but she found herself strangely reluctant to touch the thing. Sylph laid it aside and moved to the girl's side just as her eyes opened.

"Hi." Sylph sat down. "Can you understand me?"

"I . . ." The girl swallowed. "I understand."

"Good." It hadn't occurred to Lina that the girl might not

speak English, but Sylph had obviously been worried.

"If you're going to kill me," said the girl, "please just get it over with."

"Right." Sylph rolled her eyes. "Because I always bandage and take care of people I'm going to kill."

The girl looked confused, so Lina cut in, "She's just kidding. We're not going to hurt you. My name is Lina, and this is my sister Sylph."

"Lina." The girl said the name as though it was significant. "You're a Magus!"

"I am?" said Lina.

"You killed two of Gargorian's soldiers with magic."

"I don't . . . I mean . . ."

Sylph jumped in to cover for her. "Do you have a name?"

"Fahlimini Horizt." She pronounced this in a way Lina could not hope to reproduce, and added, "But call me Fah. Everyone calls me . . . Fah." A thought seemed to strike her, as she said this last, and her face fell.

"What's wrong?" said Lina.

"Did anyone else . . . survive?"

Lina glanced at Sylph, who said, "One of the soldiers ran for it. Other than that, no."

Fah swallowed again. "You're sure?"

"I'm sure." Sylph held up the pouches and set them next to Fah. "Here. I'm afraid we helped ourselves to some of your food."

"Please." Fah waved a hand weakly, then gestured to the bandage. "I guess I have you to thank for this?"

Sylph shrugged uncomfortably, but Lina nodded.

"Thank you." Fah took a deep breath. "I didn't really expect to wake at all, except possibly for Vantz to torture me. I don't know who you two are, but . . . thank you."

"Don't mention it!" said Lina. Sylph sighed and cut in.

"Do you mind if I ask a few questions?"

"Not really." Fah tried to sit up, and managed to struggle onto her elbows. Lina hovered over her nervously. "But we can't stay here. If one of Vantz's people got away, he'll be coming here."

"What if he thinks you're dead?" said Lina.

"He'll come to make sure," said Fah. "I just killed his mistress, so I imagine he's not going to be very happy with me."

"You . . . you killed . . ." Lina glanced back in the direction of the bodies.

"Go where?" said Sylph.

"There's a village about a day's walk to the north." Fah pointed. "Some of my friends are hiding there."

"Can you walk?"

Fah looked, suddenly, a little scared, as though she'd just realized what she was asking of two total strangers. "No," she said eventually, "probably not."

Sylph looked a little hesitant, but Lina was already helping Fah off the ground.

"I can take her." She looked down at herself. "Can you fix up those cloaks . . . ?"

Sylph had already draped herself in the stained fabric, creating a toga-like garment. She did Lina's too; Lina shivered as the damp cloth touched her skin, and tried not to think about it. She draped Fah's arm around her shoulders.

"You forgot this, by the way," said Sylph, holding up the sword.

"I don't want it."

"I'm taking it along." Sylph put it under one arm. "It seems like the sort of thing that might come in handy."

chapter two

WE'VE FOUND THE BODIES, WARLEADER," SAID Schwartz.

Vantz straightened up. "And Tyra?"

"She's . . . there, Warleader. But it has been several days."

Vantz imagined her laughing, wonderful face covered in flies, eyes a roiling swarm of maggots. Her soft, supple limbs gone rigid; her—

"What is your command, Warleader?"

"Bury them."

"Even the Circle Breaker?" asked Schwartz.

"No. Leave her for the crows." His lip twisted into a death's-head smile. "How long till we make the village?"

"We've almost completed re-provisioning, Warleader. We should be ready to leave tomorrow morning—after that, two days through the woods."

"Good." *She's not going to escape me this time. Not after what she did.* His gauntleted hand curled into a fist.

* * *

"A DAY'S WALK" TURNED OUT TO BE AN OPTIMISTIC ESTI-mate. Sylph and Lina were shoeless—the thought of going back to the battle and trying to pull the boots from the dead soldiers was too much for Sylph, however practical an idea it might have been. Thankfully the woods around the hill were mostly pines, so there was a soft carpet of fallen needles to make the going easier; rocks lurked underneath it, though, and Sylph managed to cut herself quite badly in the first hour of hiking.

Fah was more suitably attired for a hike, but she couldn't put any weight on her leg. Lina chopped her a stick to use as a makeshift crutch, and lent her a shoulder for the rougher stretches. The three girls still had to take a roundabout route, circumventing ridges and rock outcroppings; every little stream they came to was a serious obstacle. Fah said they were making progress, but by the time the sun touched the horizon there was no village in sight.

They didn't talk much throughout the day. It was enough of a task for Sylph to scramble another few feet without injuring herself—she didn't have much attention to spare for conversation. Nevertheless, she found her mind racing in an inward spiral. *Figure it out. You can always figure it out, if you think hard enough.*

So, where are we? The forest wouldn't have been out of place where Sylph had grown up, in upstate New York. *On the other hand, I'm not exactly a qualified botanist.* There were pine trees, mixed in with a few leafy types she didn't recognize, and light underbrush consisting mostly of bushes and ferns. *Obviously a lot of things are the same—we can breathe, eat, drink, and so on. Fah looks human enough. Hell, she speaks English!*

But the constellations last night had been unrecognizable. Once again, Sylph didn't consider herself an expert, but she could normally at least pick out the Big Dipper and Orion. *We could be in the Southern Hemisphere, I guess.* But that didn't seem right. Sylph's gut instinct said she was no longer on Earth. *Where on Earth do they have swordfights like that? Not to mention what Lina did.*

So another world. Not exactly an alien world, but definitely someplace other. *Where does that leave us?* Unfortunately she couldn't think of a good answer to that question, besides "cold, sore, hungry, and scared."

Lina seemed to be bearing up fairly well. Having to help Fah along, Sylph thought, was actually good for her—needing to assist someone else meant she couldn't just withdraw into an inert ball, which was her usual response to adversity. She seemed to be able to pretend that this was like any other hike through the woods, despite the fact that she was wearing only a cloak taken from a dead soldier—*and that who-knows-who-else is waiting for us out there. Three girls, alone in the woods, two of them naked. It doesn't strike me as a safe situation.*

The next time they found a creek, Fah called a halt. "We're going to have to stay here for the night," she said, frustrated.

Sylph collapsed gratefully on one of the flat rocks by the water. She couldn't help but be impressed with Fah's stamina—Sylph's foot hurt worse with every hour she walked, and Fah's pain had to be much worse. She could see it in the strained lines of the girl's face when she sat down, but Fah hadn't complained. Lina looked equally happy to get off her feet; she put her back against one of the leaning pines and closed her eyes with a sigh.

There was a moment of silence.

"Fah," Sylph said after a while, "we're going to need a fire."

"I've been thinking about whether we should risk it," the girl said.

"Risk it?" said Lina. "What's the risk?"

"Vantz's people might be following us."

"Those are the ones who tried to kill you before?" Sylph asked. Fah nodded.

"It was cold last night. If it gets any worse, Lina and I might be in trouble."

"I know." Fah considered a moment. "Lina, can you get us some firewood? Just a couple of dry branches and some brush should do it."

Lina nodded wearily, staggered back to her feet, and walked into the forest. Sylph turned her mind to her own problems. She borrowed Fah's belt knife and cut another strip from her bloody cloak, then washed it in the bitterly cold stream water. Once it was clean, or at least some reasonable approximation of clean, she spread it on a rock to dry and dipped her injured foot in the water. Pain shot up her leg, but only for a moment; her skin was quickly numb with cold. She bent over and scraped out the little bits of dirt and gravel that had worked their way into the cut.

"Are you all right?" Fah asked.

Sylph nodded, her back to the girl. "I'll be okay. It's just a little cut." She turned around and started wrapping the bandage around her foot. "What about you? That must hurt."

"I'll live. Daana will clean it out when we get home."

There was another pause. What Sylph really wanted to say was, "What the *hell* is going on?" but she suspected it might not be wise. *I'd rather not reveal the depths of our ignorance.*

"Sylph," Fah said, "I hope you don't consider this rude— since you saved my life—but I'm curious about what the two of you were doing out there."

"Ah." Precisely the question Sylph had been dreading. *Stick as close to the truth as possible, but don't give it all away.* "I really don't know myself. I just sort of . . . woke up there, I guess? Lina too."

"With no clothing?"

Sylph blushed. "Y—yeah. It sounds crazy, I know."

"Your sister . . . she is your sister, correct?"

Sylph nodded.

"She is a Magus."

"I . . . don't know." Sylph didn't really feel like she was in a position to deny this.

"She is," Fah said. "And when a Magus is involved anything is possible. Where are you from?"

"I don't even know where we *are*."

"About a week's ride from the Rippers, south of the pass at Highpoint." Fah searched Sylph's face for some sign of recognition.

"We may have different names for things," she muttered.

"But I'm pretty sure we're a long way from home."

It doesn't sound *like Fah got here the same way we did.* At least, she hadn't mentioned waking up naked after dying somewhere else, which Sylph thought was the kind of thing one would talk about. *From the way she's talking it sounds like she just lives here.*

"My turn," Sylph said. "Who is 'Vantz'? And why is he trying to kill you?"

"Vantz is one of Gargorian's cavalry captains." When Sylph gave her a look of blank incomprehension, she said, "You've never heard of Gargorian?"

"I told you, we're a long way from home."

"You've never heard of the Archmagi? The Lady Fell, or Vilvakis?"

"No."

Fah's eyes widened. "You *are* a long way from home. Maybe from across the Moonblack Sea."

"I've never heard of that either, so it's possible."

"It's nice to think that there are places in the world where the Circles will never reach." Fah sighed. "Though I suppose that doesn't help you very much."

"What's a Circle? In fact," Sylph said, "why don't you start from the beginning?"

Fah smiled agreeably and found a long stick she could use to scratch pictures in the dust. She started with a line of upside-down "V"s.

"Those are the Ripper Mountains, that way." She pointed over her shoulder, then drew a circle in the middle of them. "That's the pass, Highpoint. There's a fortress there. We're over here." Fah tapped the stick on a spot to the left of the mountain range.

"Okay, with you so far."

Fah put another dot much father to the right of the mountains. "This is Bleloth, Gargorian's capital."

"Who's Gargorian? Some kind of king?"

"Gargorian is an Archmagus, the Magio Creator. But he

rules, if that's what you mean." Fah sketched four concentric circles with Bleloth at the center. The last one went through the spot she'd marked as Highpoint. "There are the Circles. Within that area his power is absolute—the Plague afflicts the people, and the only antidote is Gargorian's magic." Catching Sylph's worried expression, Fah said, "It's not an illness like sin fever or the pox. The Plague affects only newborn infants. But without Gargorian's help it's almost invariably fatal."

"If Gargorian goes around helping people—"

"He *created* the Plague," she spat. "It affects only the people inside the Circles. And he uses it like a club to keep the people in line—who can fight when he holds your unborn children hostage? So they do nothing, while he strips the land bare and sends their sons east to die in his wars with Lady Fell."

"Where do you fit in to all this?"

Fah looked pained. "I probably shouldn't tell you this . . ."

"You don't have to, if it's a problem."

"It hardly matters now. Our secret is out; that's what I need to tell everyone." She took a deep breath. "We call ourselves Circle Breakers. In Gargorian's last war, he won enough territory to the east to create the Fifth Circle." She sketched another ring on the ground, which enclosed most of the Rippers and the territory beyond. "The people here have already been bled dry. The Archmagus's legions visit yearly for fresh recruits, so there's barely enough hands left for the villages to feed themselves. Now he wants to wipe them out with the Plague and resettle the area with his easterners."

"And you're trying to stop him."

"Yes."

"Just you?" Sylph asked.

"Most people have given up and either accepted Gargorian's rule or fled farther west. Those of us who are left have nothing left to lose."

"Can you really hurt him?"

"We can slow him down. We don't entirely understand how

Circles are built, but it involves placing a series of nodes around the periphery. Gargorian sends teams to survey for good sites, and we make life hard for them. So he sends men like Vantz to try and wipe us out." She put on a thin smile. "He hasn't managed it so far."

At that point Lina returned, arms full of wood and dead ferns. She dropped them on the rock, and Fah clambered painfully to her knees. She arranged the kindling underneath the branches, pulled a piece of flint from her belt, and struck a spark off her dagger with a single practiced motion. It caught in the dry brush at once, and a few seconds later the little campfire was smoking happily. Sylph and Lina both pulled themselves closer; Sylph hadn't realized how chilly she'd been until that moment.

"Ahhh," Lina said. "That's much better."

Fah nodded agreement. "I've been trying to help your sister figure out how you got here."

Sylph shot her sister a "keep your mouth shut" look.

"Any progress?" Lina asked.

"Not really," Sylph said.

"I was just about to ask Sylph to tell me something about the two of you," Fah said. "It's not every day you get to meet a Magus."

"I'm not . . ." Sylph saw Lina look over at the sword, which had spent the day tied to Fah's belt and was now propped against a rock.

"There's not much to tell," Sylph cut in. "We're just normal." Somehow she didn't feel up to the task of explaining a world of cars, computers, and television to Fah. "Lina works, and I go to school."

"What about your family?"

"My father ran off before I was born," Sylph said. "And Mom died a few years ago."

I'm getting better at that; I rattled it off without even flinching. It still feels horrible.

"Ah," Fah said. "I'm sorry."

There was an awkward silence.

"I think," said Lina, "I'm going to try to sleep."

"Should one of us stay awake?" Sylph asked. "In case Vantz shows up?"

"If Vantz finds us," Fah said, "he'll kill us. Awake or not."

SOMEWHAT TO HER SURPRISE, LINA GOT A BETTER NIGHT'S sleep than she'd had in months. She settled down in a narrow space between a rock and a sticky pine tree; at first she was afraid to close her eyes, waiting for an armor-clad Vantz to spring up at any moment. Eventually sheer exhaustion won out, her eyelids drooped, and by the time she got up the sun had risen. Sylph was still asleep, curled up next to the ashes of the fire, but Fah was up and refilling her waterskin from the stream.

"Good morning, Magus," she said.

"Morning." Lina rubbed her face. "Please call me Lina?"

Fah nodded, and tossed her the skin. The water was nearly freezing, but Lina drank greedily. Afterward she and Fah breakfasted on some of the bread and dried meat, and Lina poked Sylph awake.

"Ah." Sylph sat up and stretched. "So, nobody found us after all?"

"There's nobody out here, except for Vantz and his men." Fah stood up and pointed. "We'll head that way. There's an old game trail that should make things easier.

They quickly settled back into the hiking routine. Lina's legs hurt, but after helping Fah past the rough spots and watching Sylph limp to spare her bandaged foot she didn't feel like she could complain. They found the game trail, which made the going a bit easier, but Fah still needed an extra hand from time to time. The sky had gotten cloudy overnight, which made it even chillier than before; Lina shivered and hoped it didn't rain.

Around noon they ate a bit but didn't stop walking, driven

by Fah's unspoken need for haste. Sylph limped along in front, putting one hand against a half-buried boulder to guide herself around a curve. A moment later she stepped back, both hands in the air, followed by another girl. The newcomer was dressed in leather and homespun, like Fah, and carried a bow whose curve stretched from above her head to below her knees. She had an arrow nocked and drawn, and the bowstring vibrated with tension. The tip of the arrowhead was only a few feet from Sylph's chest.

"Back away from her," the girl said to Sylph, "nice and slow." Her eyes flicked to Lina. "You, don't think about moving unless you want your friend to get skewered. Fah, come over here."

"She's my sister," Lina babbled, "and . . . and . . . Fah, do something!"

"Yahvy?" Fah held up her hands. "It's okay! They're friends."

This didn't produce an immediate effect. Yahvy kept the bow leveled, taking a step back so she could cover Sylph while glancing toward Fah. "Friends? Fah, you know you can't bring anyone here."

"It's hard to explain . . ." Fah began.

"What are we supposed to do with them now? We can't just let them go—"

"Yahvy! Listen for a second."

"What?"

"Vantz knows where we are. I think he captured someone and tortured it out of them. We were ambushed on our way back."

Yahvy let the bow sink until it was pointed at the ground, to Lina's relief; the girl's hand had been shaking where it held the arrow.

"Vantz knows?" Yahvy digested this. "*Fuck.*"

"I know—"

"He's going to come here to kill us!"

"I *know*!" Fah shouted. There were tears in her eyes. "Lady,

Yahvy. How about 'Hi, Fah, good to see you're still alive'?"

"I . . ." Yahvy let out a deep breath. "Sorry. I'm sorry."

"Safael is dead," Fah whispered. She wobbled on her feet, as though she was about to fall. Lina rushed to her side and steadied her.

"Oh. Fah, I'm so sorry . . ."

Fah wiped her eyes and looked up. "I'd be dead if it wasn't for these two. This is Lina, and the one you nearly shot is Sylph." She turned to face Lina. "This is Yahvy. She's a Circle Breaker too—"

"They already know about us?" Yahvy interrupted.

"They know more or less everything," Fah said. "I told you, it doesn't matter anymore. We have to warn everyone before Vantz catches up with us."

"Are we taking these two along?"

Fah looked at Lina for confirmation, and Lina looked at Sylph. Sylph nodded and said, "We don't have anywhere else to go at this point."

"I left Mel up the trail a bit," Yahvy said. "Come on."

Yahvy moved to take over the task of helping Fah along, which Lina was happy enough give up. She dropped back to walk with Sylph instead; once the two Circle Breakers had gotten far enough ahead, Lina said quietly, "Are you okay?"

"I'm fine." Sylph shivered. "Just surprised the hell out of me."

"Me, too." She glanced over her shoulder. "Fah talks like Vantz was right behind us."

"Maybe he is."

Sylph stayed quiet after that. Yahvy talked with Fah in low tones, occasionally glancing back at the two girls lagging behind. She was a little older than Lina had thought at first, probably seventeen or eighteen, with a dark ponytail and tomboyish features. Aside from the bow, she wore a short-sword at her hip and a quiver of arrows.

Around a bend in the trail, they came on the remains of

Yahvy's camp—flattened underbrush and a neat campfire. A much smaller girl—thirteen, if not younger—was sitting cross-legged and poking the still-glowing embers with a stick, sending up intermittent wisps of smoke. She jumped up at the sound of footsteps, and when Fah came around the corner she lowered her head and charged. Fah barely had time to raise her arms before the girl wrapped her in a fierce hug.

"It's nice to see you too, Mel," said Fah.

The girl said something unintelligible, pressed up against Fah's chest. Fah put one hand on her head and stroked her hair, gently, until Mel's grip relaxed enough to separate her.

"We thought . . ." She sniffed. "We thought you were dead."

Fah smiled. "Sorry to have worried you. This is Lina, and this is Sylph. They saved my life. This," she pointed, "is Melfina."

She wiped her eyes and gave Lina a little bow, then went back to hugging Fah. Eventually Yahvy had to pry her off.

"Vantz is coming, Mel. We've got to get home."

Melfina nodded and scrambled out ahead of the little party, agile as a monkey. Lina leaned close to Fah.

"Is she a Circle Breaker too?"

Fah nodded. "Hard to believe, isn't it? She's more danger-ous then she looks."

"Are you all—you know—girls?"

"Not all. But Gargorian's conscription crews round up most of the young men and some of the women. Like I said before, we're all that's left."

"What are you going to do when we get to the village?"

"Get everyone together and tell them about Vantz."

"And then what? Figure out a way to stop him?"

Fah shook her head grimly, but said nothing.

✳   ✳   ✳

MELFINA STAYED OUT OF SIGHT FOR MOST OF THE AFTERNOON,

usually a few minutes ahead on the trail. Despite what Fah had said to Lina, Sylph still thought Mel looked like a normal little girl. *I guess she's only a year younger than me, but it's been a long time since I felt like a little girl.* For her part, Yahvy was downright suspicious of the two of them, despite Fah's protestations. Sylph tried to stay close to the two Circle Breakers, and managed to pick up at least one exchange she probably wasn't supposed to hear:

". . . but where did they come from?" Yahvy was asking.

"According to Sylph, they just woke up out there."

"They just woke up? Naked, in the middle of nowhere?" Yahvy snorted. "I sincerely hope you're not buying that."

"I didn't feel like I could question it. She saved my life, Yahvy."

"Still. There's obviously something they don't want to tell you."

"There's another thing," said Fah. "Lina is a Magus."

Yahvy looked over her shoulder, and Sylph pretended to stumble and dropped back a bit, so as to be less obvious about her eavesdropping.

"*Her?* You're kidding."

"I saw her kill two of Vantz's men with magic."

"And after that you just invited her along?"

"We need her. Do you know what's going to happen when Vantz gets here . . ."

At that point, Melfina came back up the trail, and Yahvy cut off the conversation with a thoughtful nod. While the little girl chattered with Fah, Sylph fell in beside Lina and tried to think.

Okay. So Fah isn't completely altruistic or completely grateful—nothing wrong with that. She saw Lina blow those guys away, and she's going to want her help to deal with Vantz, somehow. What can we do about it?

There was depressingly little. Sylph felt, not for the first time, the frustration of helplessness. *God, we wouldn't even have anything to* eat *if it weren't for Fah. We're not exactly her prisoners, and I'm sure she wouldn't think of it that way, but we certainly can't wander away.* Fah might not know that, though. *We need to stay with her until we get back to some kind of civilization.* Unfortunately, that could easily mean having to address the Vantz problem first.

"Here we are," Yahvy said, bringing Sylph back to the here and now. She looked up and found herself at a rather abrupt tree line. Ahead was a grassy field, dotted with tree stumps and a few patches of leafy vegetables. Past that lay the village itself, which was not much to look at—maybe fifteen timber and stone buildings, none more than one story tall. The largest sported a lean-to that covered the business end of a forge.

A small figure sitting on the roof of one of the buildings shaded its eyes, peering at them, then waved and disappeared below the thatched roof. Melfina led the way toward town, winding through the stumps and little gardens. A few of the villagers were around, weeding between the rows or digging holes; almost all of them were old women, and they didn't look up as the Circle Breakers passed. Sylph caught the sound of quiet muttering behind them.

They were greeted at the edge of the village by a young woman—Sylph guessed her age at nineteen or twenty—wearing a sword and another of the enormous bows. She hugged Fah, and pulled back hastily when the girl winced.

Turning to Yahvy, the woman smiled and said, "When you said you were going to find Fah, I didn't realize you meant *today*."

"You were out looking for me?" said Fah.

Yahvy coughed. "Not my idea. The little one wouldn't stop talking about it."

Melfina retreated behind Fah, and the woman laughed. "You found her, at any rate. And some others?"

"Fah's idea," said Yahvy. "She brought them along."

"More like they brought me along," Fah said. "Lina, Sylph, this is Kiry."

"Welcome then, Lina and Sylph," said Kiry. She had a warm smile and long brown hair in a thick braid. "Do they know—"

"Yes," Yahvy interrupted. "Fah filled them in before I found her."

"We don't have a lot of time," Fah said. "Is everyone here?"

Kiry nodded. "Everyone except Vhaal. I'm afraid he wandered off again."

"I doubt we'll miss his input," Yahvy said dryly.

"Daana and Garot are inside," Kiry said. "Come on."

Yahvy hooked a thumb at Sylph and Lina. "Are they coming?"

Sylph was torn. *On the one hand, I'd rather not get involved in whatever they've got going on here. It looks dangerous, to say the least. On the other hand, we may not have a choice, and I'd like to have as much information as I can . . .*

"I'd like to help," said Lina. "If . . . if I can. I mean . . ."

Well, that makes that decision easier. Sylph sighed.

"Bring them along," Fah said. She led the way into the largest building, which consisted of a bedroom and another room with a firepit in the center and a circle of chairs. A fire was already burning, topped by a blackened kettle. Sitting beside it was a young man, with a redheaded girl hanging on his arm and resting her head on his shoulder.

"Fah!" said the young man, who Sylph assumed was Garot. "Thank the Lady. Yahvy found you?"

"Just a bit outside the village." Fah collapsed into a chair, the relief in her face betraying how much walking still pained her. The group arranged itself into a rough circle around the fire; Sylph sat cross-legged next to Lina and managed to grab her sister's attention for a moment.

"Stay quiet for a bit, okay?"

Lina nodded. She looked a little uncertain, and Sylph squeezed her shoulder reassuringly.

Fah said, "Okay. The good news is that I'm back in one piece."

"What about Safael?" said Daana.

Fah squeezed her eyes shut. "She's not. That's part of the bad news."

"There's more?" Kiry asked.

"Vantz knows where we've been hiding. He's on his way—

Safael and I were ambushed on our way back. Without these two I wouldn't be standing here." She gestured toward Sylph and Lina.

"Hi," said Sylph, feeling ridiculous. "I'm Sylph, and this is my sister Lina."

"I think you know everyone except for Daana and Garot," Fah said.

"If you've got the social niceties out off the way," Daana said, "can we focus on the fact that we have a *problem* here? If Vantz finds us—"

"We all know what happens if Vantz finds us," said Kiry.

"So, what are we sitting here for?" Daana said.

"We're trying to figure out what to about it," said Fah quietly.

"Do? We run, obviously. Vantz must have at least fifty men."

"It's not that simple," said Kiry. "When he gets here and doesn't find us, he'll ask the villagers. If he finds out they were helping us he'll burn this place to the ground."

"The village women know that," Garot said. "They wouldn't talk to Vantz."

"Torture," Yahvy said. "Everyone talks eventually."

"But what can we do about it?" asked Daana.

"We can fight him," said Fah.

"He'll kill us!"

"And probably leave the village alone," Fah continued.

"The villagers invited us," Garot said. "They knew the risks."

"They invited us after the conscription party came through." Fah sighed. "People do things in anger that they regret later on."

"The old women are definitely having second thoughts," said Kiry. "I think they'd have asked us to leave a while ago, if we hadn't been waiting for you."

"And now it's too late," said Garot.

"You can't seriously be considering fighting them," said Daana, with a note of panic in her voice. "That's suicide!"

"We're dead already, remember?" said Kiry. "We swore . . ."

Dead already? Sylph's ears perked up at that, but she decided

Kiry probably didn't mean it literally.

Everyone started to talk at once, until Fah gestured for silence. "Quiet, please. We need to think about this, and I for one
need to get some sleep. Vantz was at least a day's ride behind us,
probably two, so we've got until tomorrow evening at the earli-
est. Tomorrow morning will leave us plenty of time to get away
if we need to. When is Vhaal getting back?"

"Who knows?" Yahvy said. "We'd be better off without
him . . ."

"If he shows up, make sure he doesn't leave again." Fah glanced
at Lina and Sylph. "Is there somewhere these two can stay?"

"Plenty of empty beds," said Kiry. "I'll take them."

The argument started up again, despite Fah's best efforts.
Kiry rose to lead the sisters out; Sylph brushed past Melfina,
who'd been clinging silently to Fah's side as though afraid she
was going to disappear. Lina followed; as she passed Fah, the
girl gave her back the sword, which Lina took with the air of
someone accepting a live grenade.

After the cramped, smoky interior, the fresh air felt wonderfully cool. Kiry stretched like a cat and said, "Sorry about that.
You haven't exactly caught us at our best."

Sylph ran her hands over the bloodstained cloak that kept
her modest. "This isn't exactly our best, either."

"I can probably do something about that. Come on."

The sisters followed her across the village. Kiry stopped
a few times to talk to the local women, who responded more
warmly than Sylph had expected. The Circle Breaker caught
the attention of a hunchbacked crone tending an infant, who disappeared inside a house and returned with some clothes draped
over her arm. Kiry took them, stopped by the well for a bucket
of water, then led the two to another building. There was a rag
curtain for a door, and the inside was a single room furnished
with a cold firepit and a bed of straw in one corner.

"Nobody's using this at the moment," said Kiry, "so make
yourselves at home." She poured the water into a metal basin next

to the door. "I'll get someone to come by and light a fire later."

"What did you mean," said Sylph, "when you said you were already dead?"

"Fah told you what we are?"

"Circle Breakers. But she didn't explain very much."

"We've all sworn to fight the spread of Gargorian's Circles, to the death. Most of us are from west of here, and a lot of those people don't care about what we're doing. So everyone we know already thinks of us as dead. My family already held my funeral." She sighed. "I doubt they'll mourn much. A daughter—a second daughter, at that—isn't much use to anyone."

Sylph nodded thoughtfully.

"What about you?" said Kiry. "Where are you two from?"

"We're not sure, to be honest." Sylph tried to smile. "Mostly we're lost."

Whether or not Kiry believed that, she wasn't prepared to press the issue. "I'm sure you're tired too. Get some sleep. I'll come get you for breakfast in the morning."

Sylph nodded. After subsisting on stale bread and dried meat for two days, the thought of breakfast sounded extremely appealing. Kiry pushed the curtain aside and let herself out; Sylph waited a dozen heartbeats, then beckoned her sister close.

"Lina, listen to me."

"I feel like we're lying to them. You said—"

"I know. But don't tell anyone where we're really from until I say so, okay?"

"Why?"

"Do you have any idea how we got here?"

"No!"

"Neither do I. I'd rather be careful until I know how this place works. It certainly doesn't look like any of them died and showed up here."

Lina nodded hesitantly.

"Another thing," Sylph said. "Don't talk about the sword."

Her sister glanced at the weapon, which lay on top of the

bundle of old clothes.

"Sylph," Lina said, "they think I'm a Magus."

"I know. I'll figure something out."

Lina nodded again. Sylph smiled and patted the top of her head.

"You okay?" she asked.

"I . . . think so. I'm trying to convince myself I'm not terrified."

"You're doing great." Sylph gave her sister a quick hug. "Get yourself cleaned up and change clothes, okay?"

Lina pulled the cloak over her head and spent some time at the basin, trying to rub the grime off of her skin. Sylph lay back on the pile of straw, trying to ignore the tickling points.

So, now what? For better or for worse, they seemed to have fallen in with Fah and her Circle Breakers. *Lina won't want to leave them behind*—her sister was ridiculously sentimental—*and I doubt Vantz will just leave us alone. Though we could probably head out into the woods before he gets here.* Sylph thought she might be able to talk Lina into that, especially if Fah decided that a suicide stand was her best option. *But where does that leave us? Who-knows-how-far-from-anywhere with no food or water? I'm not ready to try living off the land, not to mention we'd probably get raped and murdered by the first gang of bandits we ran into.*

So then . . . what? Sylph closed her eyes and thought hard. All the evidence thus far pointed to people coming into this world in a more or less normal fashion. *Certainly nobody else remembers a life on Earth or anything like it. That makes us anomalies, and there has to be a reason. I'm not going to believe that the two of us just happened to drop in, somehow.*

And there was the matter of the sword. *Someone just left it there? Unlikely. The thing was planted there for us to find. Me, Lina, and the sword. Once is chance, twice is coincidence, but three times is conspiracy.*

If there really is someone behind this, I want to meet him. Unfortunately, none of that exactly helped with the short term.

"Sylph?" said Lina. "Are you asleep?"

"No. Just thinking." Sylph opened her eyes. Lina was dressed in what was clearly boy's clothing; rough cloth pants, a shirt, and a sleeveless leather vest. It hung a little long on her, but not too badly.

"Do you want to wash up?"

"Yeah."

Sylph stripped off the bloody cloak and tossed it in the corner. The water was ice cold; she splashed some on herself, and her skin pebbled to goose bumps. The other set of clothing was also a boy's, and also a bit too large, but wearing real clothes again felt remarkably civilizing. Lina had already burrowed into the straw, and Sylph snuggled in close to her to try and dispel some of the water's chill.

"Sylph?" Lina whispered.

"Yeah?"

"Do you think we'll ever get home?"

Get home? Sylph hadn't even considered it. *Usually when people die, they don't come back.*

"I don't know," she said. Lina squeezed her a little tighter.

"At least we're together."

"Yeah."

Sylph had expected to have difficulty getting to sleep, but once again exhaustion worked wonders; before she knew it the sun's rays and the smell of frying meat had disturbed her slumber. Lina, a notorious slugabed, had to be poked before she bestirred herself, but eventually the sisters wandered out into the village green. Yahvy and Melfina were tending a cast-iron pan over the firepit, which was the source of the aroma. Another pot boiled nearby and smelled of steam and cinnamon. Sylph's mouth watered.

"Morning," said Yahvy. Melfina was still skittish, staying quietly on the other side of the fire.

"Good morning," Sylph yawned. "Is this breakfast?"

"Squirrel," Yahvy said. "Garot checked the traps this morning."

Sylph opened her mouth to object, hesitated, and closed it again. Lina looked appalled but had the sense to look at her sister and stay quiet.

"Sounds good," Sylph managed.

"And oatmeal," said Melfina, gesturing to the other pot. "Help yourselves."

Sylph was hungry enough to do so without much trouble. *I've never had squirrel before.* It was actually quite good—a bit stringy, and fried in some kind of grease. Lina avoided the meat until Sylph forced to her try a few bites, but after that she wolfed it down. Yahvy and Melfina watched, amused, and Melfina giggled when Lina finished and looked around for something to wipe her fingers on besides her clothes.

"You didn't get the chance to tell us much about yourselves last night," said Yahvy. "All I know is what Fah told me—she met you at the edge of the woods, after Vantz's riders caught up with her. And that you said you just sort of woke up there." Her eyes flicked to Lina, and Sylph realized with a sinking feeling Fah had spread the idea that Lina was some kind of wizard. *I guess I should have expected that.*

"There's not that much more to tell," said Sylph. She'd devoted some time to thinking about this question last night. "We're . . . travelers, I guess you'd say. I'm not sure how we got here, but we seem to be a long way from home."

"Are you from across the Moonblack Sea?" Melfina piped up.

"I'm not sure. It's possible."

"And there really aren't any Archmagi there?" Yahvy asked.

"I'd never even heard of one until I got here."

Yahvy shook her head. "You must come from a carefree place."

Sylph thought back. *School, trying to keep Lina employed, bills, rent, never knowing whether there'd be enough money for food or when some druggie might bust down your door . . . but compared to this?* "I guess. I didn't think so when I left."

Yahvy laughed, and poked at the remaining bits of squirrel.

Lina leaned close to Sylph and said, "I'm going to go find Fah, okay?"

"Don't get lost. And please try to stay quiet about . . . well, you know."

"Right."

*   *   *

LINA WANDERED THROUGH THE VILLAGE FOR A WHILE UNTIL she found the larger central building the meeting had been in the previous night. She paused in the doorway, which was covered by another rag curtain, not sure whether to knock. While she hesitated, voices came from inside, speaking in quiet tones.

"What do you think about the others?" said Fah.

"Yahvy and Garot understand. And Melfina will follow you anywhere. Daana . . ." It was Kiry speaking, and she paused. "I don't know. And Vhaal's crazy."

"We don't all have to go," said Fah. "You—"

"I'm staying with you," said Kiry firmly.

"What about Melfina? Or Garot and Daana? We could send them away."

"Where? They'd just get captured by Vantz's riders. And afterward—"

"I know," said Fah. She hesitated. "You . . . I mean, you understand, right? You'll make sure . . ."

"They won't take any of us alive," said Kiry.

Fah sounded like she was getting choked up. "And you—"

"I don't fancy the thought of being shared around Vantz's campfire any more then you do. Don't worry."

"Good." Fah swallowed. "Then we'll meet at the feet of the White Lady."

There was a long pause. Lina blinked away tears. *They can't.* Fah was the first person she'd met in this world, not counting Sylph of course. *They can't all die.* She barely noticed when the rag curtain was brushed aside and Fah came out, eyes puffy and bloodshot. Lina put her hand to her mouth and ran, instinctively looking for her sister. *Sylph will know what to do.*

She found her sister where she'd left her, talking to Yahvy and Melfina. Lina skidded to a halt in a cloud of dust and grabbed Sylph by the shoulder.

"Sylph! You have to talk to Fah!"

"What?"

"They're talking about *suicide*! She says she's going to fight Vantz!"

"She's crazy," said Yahvy. "He's coming here with sixty men and she wants to *fight* him. Crazy. Come on, Mel." She stalked off in the direction Lina had come. Melfina followed, leaving the sisters alone aside from a few of the village women, who regarded them suspiciously from a distance.

"Slow down," said Sylph. "What did Fah say?"

"You remember when they were talking about the village being burned . . . ?"

"Shh!" Sylph looked around at the villagers. Lina swallowed and lowered her voice.

"You remember, right?"

"Of course."

"I . . ." Lina blushed, "I happened to overhear her talking to Kiry, and they're going to go and fight Vantz! Kiry said she'd make sure they wouldn't be taken alive."

Sylph rolled her eyes. "She *is* crazy."

"We have to stop her!"

"*We* have to stop her? Lina, I don't think we're really qualified."

"She's the only person I know here, and I don't want her to die!" Lina set her jaw. "Come on, Sylph."

"How? You heard what they said about the village."

"I . . ." Lina hesitated.

"You'd better not be thinking . . ."

But Lina was already running back toward the meeting room. She heard Sylph curse behind her, and start to run. By the time Lina stumbled in, out of breath, Fah and Kiry were looking at maps and Yahvy was in mid-shout.

". . . the two of you are insane. I expect this from Fah, but Kiry . . ."

Lina took a deep breath. "You can't do this!"

There was a moment of silence. Yahvy looked at Lina with hooded eyes. "With all due respect, I don't see what concern it is of yours."

"Don't you understand that you're going to die?"

"We swore," said Kiry. "And we've done our best. Gargorian's Fifth Circle would have been complete by now, if we hadn't."

"What if . . ." Lina hesitated. *Sylph isn't going to like this. But what else can I do?* "What if there was a way to beat Vantz?"

Yahvy sneered. "Why not? There's only fifty of them. If we each take one, that leaves just forty-two for you to handle."

"Lina is a Magus." Fah got to her feet.

"I'm not . . . it doesn't matter what I am! If we could beat him, everything would be okay, right?"

"For the moment," Yahvy said. "But Vantz isn't an idiot. I'm sure he sent a rider to the garrison at Highpoint, and from there word will get back to Bleloth. If he doesn't come back, Gargorian will send someone to break heads until he finds out why."

"Do you understand now?" said Kiry. "We swore, for the good of generations unborn. To keep the Circles and the Plague from our homes, at least for a little while longer. We're already on a suicide mission; whether we get there faster or slower doesn't matter, as long as we've given everything we can. It's something we have to face, sooner or later."

Lina stood in the middle of the room, her hands clenched into fists and her lip quivering. Tears dripped down her cheeks.

"Excuse me," said Sylph, stepping through the rag curtain. "I don't mean to be presumptuous, and I'm hardly well-informed. But the problem is this Gargorian person, correct? He's the tyrant behind all this."

"He's an Archmagus," said Yahvy. "One of the three who

are second only to the Lightbringer himself."

"Whatever. My point is, you just have to get rid of him, and all your problems are over."

Yahvy stared. "Get rid of him."

"Yeah."

Lina moved to one side to let Sylph walk past. Her sister wore a cocky smile, but Lina knew her well enough to see the signs of strain at the edges.

God. Sylph . . . I didn't mean—

"Of course," Yahvy deadpanned. "It's so simple. I can't believe we didn't think of that earlier!" She laughed. "And you call *us* crazy!"

"Gargorian's army is tens of thousands strong," said Kiry. "He lives in the fortress-city of Bleloth, which has never been taken. And he has the power of four Circles to draw on."

"I don't know about any of that. I'm just saying I think you're aiming a little too low."

"We don't have time for this," Yahvy snapped. "Fah . . ."

"Lina," said Fah, who had been silent to this point. "Your power."

Lina looked up. "What?"

"Will you help us? With your power?"

Lina felt the buzz of the sword in her hands, and the awful laughter that welled up inside her head. *I don't want to touch that thing ever again. But . . .*

"I'll try," said Lina quietly.

"She will," Sylph said.

"Sylph?" Lina stepped next to her sister and bent to her ear.

"Trust me," Sylph whispered, then looked back at Yahvy with a crazy grin.

"Insanity," Yahvy said. "This is what you're relying on."

"Since our plan at the moment is to die gloriously, I don't see the harm," said Kiry reasonably.

"You didn't see what she did," said Fah. "Magic."

"What would a Magus be doing this far west, wandering

around the forest?"

Kiry tilted her head to one side. "Does it matter? What do you have to lose?"

Yahvy pressed her lips together, muttered a brief "As you wish," and stalked from the building. Lina saw Melfina, who had been waiting on the other side of the curtain, scramble out of her way. Fah and Kiry look at one another and sighed.

"So . . ." Lina began.

"Any help you can offer," said Fah, "would be very much appreciated."

"Can I speak to my sister alone for a moment?" said Sylph sweetly. She grabbed Lina's hand and towed her back to their own room. Before the curtain had even swung shut, Sylph rounded on her sister; Lina had already started preemptively cringing.

"You have gone *out* of your *fucking mind*, you know that!"

"I . . ." Lina hung her head.

"You just met this girl! And now you're going to go out there and *kill* for her? Or much more likely get yourself minced trying!"

"I—"

"God." Sylph rolled her eyes. "We're already dead, and I still feel like keeping you alive for ten minutes at a time is an accomplishment. Or something," she added, as Lina's eyes crossed trying to think around the contradiction. "You're really planning to go through with this?"

"Yes," Lina said.

"Great. You know we don't even know for sure that sword will work again? Or where the hell it came from, for that matter."

Or what it does to me, Lina thought. *But . . .* "Someone gave it to us."

"I know that."

"And someone led us here. You feel it, don't you?"

"I feel like a goddamn puppet, is how I feel."

"I feel . . ." Lina searched for a word. "Right. This is right." *It is!*

"You *are* crazy."

"I'm sorry." Lina looked down again. "I didn't mean for you . . . I mean . . ."

"Relax." Sylph shrugged. "There's no way I'm going to leave you behind, so that means trying to keep you alive. But will you please start listening to me?"

Lina nodded. Sylph threw herself into the pile of straw and set her back against the wall. Lina couldn't help but picture the little gears in her head, turning furiously. *She'll think of something. She always does.*

✳   ✳   ✳

"How many men does Vantz have?"

Sylph sat in the large building, which she was beginning to think of as the command center, with Kiry and Fah. Yahvy had not returned, though Melfina had stopped in briefly to say that the two of them were going to shoot something for dinner. Garot and Daana were also nowhere to be found.

"Somewhere between fifty and sixty," said Kiry. "Unless—"

"We killed four," said Fah. "I don't know if he's replaced them."

"Fifty." Sylph tapped her finger on the map. "Fifty, fifty, fifty. And how many do we have? Just the six of you?"

"Seven," Kiry corrected. "Assuming Vhaal gets back in time."

"None of the villagers?"

"If they fight, Vantz will burn the place after he kills us."

"The point is to *win* the battle."

"Besides," said Fah, "Gargorian's army took all the men near fighting age last time they swept through."

"Ah." Sylph cleared her throat. "I was wondering about that."

"It's too much trouble to actually massacre these little westerner villages," said Fah bitterly. "Once he completes the Fifth Circle, the Plague will take care of things, and until then he'll just use them for whatever he can get."

"They won't unite against him?"

"Then he *would* massacre them. Mostly they prefer to keep their heads down and hope someone else does something. Those that don't . . . well, that's us." Kiry smiled. "So we're all we've got."

"So the seven of you, plus me and Lina." Sylph had no illusions about her own ability in a fight. "What are Vantz's people armed with? Any bows?"

"Not that I saw. Spears and swords, light armor."

"And how good are you with those longbows?"

"Pretty good." Fah shrugged. "Daana's probably the best shot, but we've all had practice. Melfina's not really strong enough; she prefers throwing knives."

"Is she really . . . you're really bringing her to the battle?"

"She's a Circle Breaker," said Kiry.

"I told you, she's tougher than she looks," said Fah. "She's killed probably a dozen men already."

A dozen men? That little girl? Sylph shook her head.

"So what exactly did you have in mind?" she said.

"Ambush. Split up, and when they get to about here . . ." Kiry tapped a spot on the map. ". . . start hitting them. We bring down a few, and they have to split into two or three groups to come after us."

"Two or three groups isn't good enough." Sylph stared at the map. "We've only got a chance if we scatter them."

"Vantz is a decent commander," said Fah. "He's not going to scatter if he can help it."

"I've got an idea." *Not a great idea, but an idea.* Part of Sylph cringed at the thought, but it couldn't be helped. "Look here."

Explaining things and hammering out the details took the better part of two hours, so it was getting close to noon by the time Sylph finished with Fah and Kiry. Fah had gone for the plan immediately, and while Kiry had been a bit more skeptical she'd eventually agreed. That left Sylph with one person to convince.

Me. I'm not sure I can do this. Lina could get killed. They could *all* get killed, actually, but somehow the former mattered more. She went to find Lina, and was directed to a clear space on the outskirts of the village.

Lina had stripped off as much clothing as she could, and her bare skin was covered in sweat. She had the sword out, and was practicing a few strokes in the air. Sylph could see the strain it put on her; when she set it down, her hands were shaking. *That's a damn heavy thing to be swinging around.*

"Hey." Sylph found a place to sit on a tree stump. "Any good?"

"I can feel it." Lina put a hand on the hilt of the sword. "It's tingling. Like it's eager."

Sylph reached out and put her hand on the pommel; it felt like cold metal. "I don't feel anything."

"I don't think it will work for anyone else."

"How do you know?"

"I just . . ."

". . . know," Sylph finished. "Lina, Fah and I have worked out a plan."

"Great."

"It's dangerous. For you especially. You could get killed."

"If we don't do anything, they're all going to die. And we're dead already, remember?"

"I'm thinking, I'm breathing. I count that as alive, and I'd rather keep it that way."

"What else can we do, Sylph?"

Sylph could think of a dozen things. But there was an odd light in Lina's eyes, and Sylph knew her sister well enough to know what she was thinking.

We were Meant to be here. To fight this battle.

Bullshit. Someone's just pulling strings.

"I just wanted to give you a gift, to help you get started."

She felt something against the palm of her hand, smooth and cool.

"And remember, you've fallen through a hole in the web, but the spider will still come for you sooner or later. Good luck."

Sylph put her palm against her forehead. *What's wrong with me?* There was something important, hiding just out of reach. *I can't remember.*

"Sylph? Are you all right?"

"Fine. Just a little nervous."

"Me too." Lina laughed. "Of course I'm nervous."

"Lina—"

She was interrupted by shouting from the other end of the village. For a horrifying moment Sylph thought Vantz had already found them, but there were no screams and after a moment all she could hear were voices raised in argument.

"What's going on?"

Sylph got to her feet. "Let's find out."

It was a quick walk across the village to where a small crowd had gathered on the green. An unfamiliar young man had arrived, who Sylph assumed was the missing Vhaal. He was carrying three heads—two women and a man—by their hair. They were fresh enough that all three still leaked blood, and their expressions were horrific. He tossed them carelessly to the grass of the village green, as though in challenge, and stood waiting.

Fah and Kiry eventually emerged from the meeting room. Fah saw the heads and her face twisted in disgust; she looked up at Vhaal, eyes flashing.

Sylph kept a discreet distance, among the crowd of villagers. Several mothers were ushering the younger children away from the grisly scene. As long as she didn't look right at the edge, Sylph felt in no imminent danger of losing her breakfast, but Lina had already gone back to her sword practice, looking green. Sylph focused on Vhaal instead. *At least he's easy on the eyes.*

He was handsome, certainly. Yahvy's age, eighteen or nineteen, more man than boy; he was six feet and well-muscled, dressed in a chain-mail shirt over dark leathers and a black cloak with a high collar that gave him an almost priest-like look. His hair was black and cut short, and his eyes—*it's his eyes that bother me.* They were blue, and curiously *intense*. She got the sense he was judging everything he looked at, and very little measured up.

"There," he said. "Another of Gargorian's Circle survey teams won't be reporting back."

"Things have been happening," Fah grated, "while you've been roaming the woods."

"I'm glad to see you're still alive," he said with a mocking smile. "You didn't happen to bring Safael back with you?" He watched her face; Fah took it like a physical blow. "Pity."

"You swore to be a part of our band," said Kiry, "not wander around taking heads."

"I swore to fight Gargorian's soldiers." He gestured at the heads. "You don't approve of the job I'm doing?"

"Vantz is coming here," said Fah.

"Good." Vhaal smiled. "I've been wanting to cross swords with him."

"Don't you understand . . ." She stopped and looked around at the villagers. "Don't you understand what that means?"

"Does it matter? We'll be dead."

"Damn it, Vhaal."

Kiry cleared her throat. "We have a plan."

"To fight fifty men? I look forward to hearing about it."

"All we need is for you to play your part."

"As long as my part involves killing Gargorian's men."

Fah turned on her heel and strode back to the forge. Vhaal laughed, turning to Kiry. "Is it me, or does she get more stuck up every time she gets one of us killed?"

"You're an ass, do you know that?"

Vhaal bowed. "At your service."

Kiry walked away. Vhaal looked around at the crowd, smiled, then kicked one of the heads toward them. It rolled across the grass spraying blood, and the village women scattered. The black-cloaked swordsman laughed again and turned away.

So that's Vhaal. I can see why Yahvy's not fond of him. They couldn't afford not to use him, though. *Seven. Eight, with Lina. I wonder if he can fight, or if it's all just bravado?*

I guess we'll find out tomorrow. Oddly, Sylph found herself looking forward to it.

chapter three

HOW MUCH FARTHER?"

"Over the next ridge, Warleader, and then another five miles. Another few hours at most."

Vantz nodded. They were riding through the woods two abreast, following a game trail. The head of the column bristled with steel, while the riderless remounts brought up the rear. It wasn't great terrain for his riders. No room for a charge, and plenty of places to hide.

"How many outriders do we have out?"

"Six, Warleader."

"Make it fifteen."

Schwartz hesitated. "Our main strength . . ."

"I'm more worried about an ambush. We can reform once we get to the village."

"As you wish, Warleader."

Vantz spurred his mount toward the head of the column and touched the hilt of his sword, a nervous gesture he'd never been able to shake. The men who'd come with him from Bleloth shouted as he passed, and he acknowledged them with a wave; the western sell-swords rode in silence. They weren't happy in the woods, and truth be told neither was he. *But she's here. I'll have her head on a pole.* Maybe that would ease the aching pain in his gut.

More scouts peeled off, riding ahead and to the sides of the main column.

* * *

THEY'D SPLIT INTO TWO GROUPS FOR THE APPROACH: KIRY, Yahvy, Garot, and Daana had gone the long way around, circling the ridge. Fah had kept Vhaal with her—more to keep an eye on him, Sylph suspected, than because she enjoyed his company—and Melfina refused to leave her side. Plus Lina, looking uncomfortable in a hastily fitted sword belt. *And me.*

"I've got them," Melfina called quietly. As soon as they'd picked a spot, she'd scrambled up a tree, nimble as a monkey. As Fah had predicted, the sobbing little girl from yesterday had been replaced by . . . something else. She had a bandolier of thin knives over her shoulder, and a couple of longer fighting daggers at her belt. Fah had her longbow and sword, and Vhaal still bore the chain mail and paired blades Sylph had seen yesterday. For her part, Sylph had considered taking a sword and ultimately decided not to. *I'd just hurt myself.*

"How many?" said Fah.

"Three . . . four. I can't see the main group, so they must be scouts."

Fah turned to Sylph. "The others should be set up by now."

Sylph glanced at her wrist, where her watch should have been. The gesture puzzled Fah.

"They should be."

"Lina, are you ready?"

Lina nodded. Her hand was already on the hilt of the sword, gripping it so tightly her knuckles had gone white. When Sylph touched her shoulder, she jumped.

"Sorry." Lina shivered. "Just—"

"I know," Sylph said.

"Okay." Fah turned to Vhaal. "If they make it to us, you're on."

He bowed, sweeping his cloak aside with a flourish. "As you command."

Sylph caught Fah's eye. The girl took a deep breath. "Here we go."

She drew the bow and stood in a single motion, taking only a moment to pick a target. The deep *thrum* of the release was followed by gurgling scream. Sylph and the others stood as well; she could see the four riders at the bottom of the ridge, one of them toppling as his mount reared. One of the remaining three pointed and shouted something; he and one of the others dug in their spurs and headed up the slope, while the last turned and trotted in the direction of the main body of Vantz's men, somewhere to the south. The other two drove their mounts up the hill.

"Perfect." Fah pulled an arrow from the ground, where she'd staked it in preparation, and fired again. It was a harder shot. Both soldiers ducked instinctively, but the arrow went wide. The horsemen kept coming.

Melfina, in the tree, held her knives until they had almost crested the ridge. One dagger thunked solidly into a man's shoulder, while another missed and opened a cut on his horse's rump. The animal screamed and bolted forward, almost immediately becoming entangled in tree roots and toppling in a flurry of limbs. The man cursed as he hit the ground.

That left one. Fah had another arrow drawn and nocked, but the soldier was on top of them before she could fire; she stepped aside as he passed, and he could do no more than take a wild swipe with his sword. Vhaal stepped into his path, steel flashing in each hand.

Idiot! Sylph couldn't help but gasp. *He'll be—*

Before she could finish the thought, the black-cloaked boy thrust and spun away, one blade trailing blood. The horse's breath gurgled through a ruined throat and it stumbled a few more steps before collapsing. The rider hit the ground rolling and managed to land well; he got his sword up in time to stop

Vhaal's first attack, but was no match for the Circle Breaker's speed. There was a moment of blurred, ringing steel, and then the soldier's blade went flying and he sagged with one of Vhaal's swords through his chest.

The other rider had landed badly. By the time he struggled to his feet, another of Melfina's daggers caught him in the chest; he staggered backwards, and the next one found his eye. The soldier crumpled on top of his still-thrashing mount.

And that was it. Sylph's mouth was dry. The whole engagement had been finished in seconds. Vhaal was wiping his blade clean on his victim's cloak, and Fah had gone down to put the broken-legged mount out of its misery. The horse's screams made Sylph shiver; they sounded almost human, like wailing children.

"One of them got away," said Vhaal, sheathing his swords with a metallic whisper.

"That was the plan," said Fah.

"Vantz will bring his men over the ridge to find us."

"That's also part of the plan," sing-songed Melfina.

"That's where your secret weapon comes in?" said Vhaal dryly, glancing at Lina.

"Yes," said Fah.

"Well," Vhaal murmured, "at least I don't have to run around a lot before I die."

Sylph leaned close to Lina. "You okay?"

"I . . . I don't think so." Her voice was a whisper.

Sylph put a hand on her sister's shoulder. She was shaking. "Come on, Lina."

"I can't do this. I can't . . . this is crazy . . ."

"You can. Look at me." Sylph made Lina turn until she could see her eyes, filled with tears. "Trust me, Lina. You can."

Lina was silent for a moment, then nodded.

Vhaal chuckled. "Looks like our Magus has got cold feet."

"Do it," Sylph whispered, "just to prove that asshole wrong."

Lina gave her a shaky smile.

✳   ✳   ✳

A LONE SCOUT GALLOPED UP TO THE COLUMN.

"Warleader! Bowmen on the ridge!"

"We can't charge up that slope, Warleader," said Schwartz. "Better to dismount."

"No. They'll be long gone by then. Send someone after the scouts, and everyone double-time up the ridge."

"Warleader—"

"I've dealt with this kind of thing before." Vantz put on a cold smile. "They fight from ambush because they have no stomach for a battle. You've got to sting them hard, make them think twice about trying the same trick again. If we wait to dismount they'll be long gone." He drew his sword and raised it over his head. "With me!"

The roar from behind him was less than wholehearted, but it was the best he was going to get. He put his heels to his mount and headed up the trail.

✳   ✳   ✳

"HERE THEY COME!" MELFINA SANG OUT.

"How many?"

"A lot."

"This is it, then." Fah looked over her shoulder. "Lina?"

"Ready."

The horses pounded up the ridge, losing speed as they gained height. The front rank had six-foot spears, leveled like lances; those in the rear had already drawn their swords. It was a *lot* of men; Sylph had the sudden urge to grab Lina and get the hell out of the way, but it was already too late. Lina drew the sword and stood at the top of the ridge, looking absolutely ridiculous. And then . . .

. . . an arrow sprouted from the throat of one of the riders, throwing knives whistled overhead, Vhaal drew his blades with a flourish, and the lead rider lowered his lance contemptuously to spit Lina like a pig . . .

Lina swung the sword.

This time, forewarned, Sylph had the sense to put her hand in front of her eyes. For a moment she could see the bones of her fingers, outlined against orange flesh, and there was a colossal hum that seemed to resonate with something in the pit of her stomach. It was repeated twice more, and the silence that followed was quickly broken by screams of agony.

Sylph blinked and took stock. Waves of brilliant energy had seared their way down the hillside, annihilating the first few riders in line. What was left was horrific; arms and legs strewn about, the back half of a horse, neatly severed, its legs still kicking reflexively. The scent of roasting meat was strong in the air. Only six or seven men had actually gone down, however, and there were still dozens on the path.

If they had been on foot, spectacularly well disciplined, and willing to throw their lives away, Vantz's men could have pressed the charge home. Half of them looked like they wanted to try, but none of them had any choice. The horses wanted to get as far away from the killing light as they could, and what had been an organized column turned into a panicked rout.

The other four Circle Breakers, who had positioned themselves to the rear of the ridge, rose from cover and opened fire. The screams of the horses were joined by shouts and curses from the men.

Sylph scrambled up to the top of the ridge where Lina had fallen, letting the sword slip from nerveless fingers. Her eyes were rolled up in her head, and her breathing was fast and shallow. The heat coming off the ground was palpable, and the blade itself was steaming where it lay in the damp earth.

Lord Almighty. What is *that thing?*

Vhaal and Fah followed her up and then charged after the fleeing riders. Sylph put Lina down and watched them. *This is the key.* Getting them to run was good, and the archers would do some damage, but if Vantz managed to rally even a dozen . . .

He was doing just that, Sylph saw with sudden horror. One rider, adorned with shoulder epaulets and a black cloak, had struggled off his horse and was encouraging others to do the same. While most of the soldiers struggled to control their mounts, the one Sylph assumed was Vantz shouted for an advance on foot.

"Let the horses run, you cowardly bastards, and get back here! The Magus is *down*, we have them!"

"Vantz!" Fah tossed her bow aside and drew her sword. "You want me, come and get me!"

It seemed like insanity, but it worked. Vantz spun at the sound of her voice and roared like an enraged bull, powering up the slope and leaving his men behind him. Fah readied herself to meet the charge, but Vhaal stepped into the soldier's path, swords flashing. Vantz's longer blade rang against the boy's for a moment before Vhaal had to sidestep one of the other riders, leaving Vantz clear to disengage. Fah blocked a vicious horizontal cut and fell back, unable to find a moment to riposte.

Arrows *thrummed* again, this time into the men on foot. Two of the soldiers pitched and fell, and another pair half-turned to see what was going on. Vhaal took advantage of the distraction and threw himself into their midst, stepping *between* the two men he was fighting. He stayed close to one, too close for the man to strike, and knocked aside the sword of the other before running him through. Then he ducked, with perfect timing, under a decapitating slash; the one he'd been pressed against had to dance backward, and Vhaal spun in a crouch and removed his leg at the knee with a nasty crunch. The man screamed and fell, and the boy kicked the legs out from under one of his two remaining opponents before springing backward and parrying the desperate assault of the last.

Sylph's attention was distracted by Vantz, who continued to attack Fah with one of his men at his side. The girl was outmatched; she parried frantically, but already bore a cut on her leg and another on her shoulder. Vantz was wounded on the hip, but didn't seem to notice. He hacked at her defense with a savage fury, both swords ringing with each impact. Fah parried, spun, and got tangled in some brush; she stumbled across the slope and finally fell backwards.

Vantz's man leapt toward her, triumphantly, only to be struck down by an arrow from downhill; Vantz himself took a shaft in his left shoulder. He raised his blade, determined to finish his enemy, but before it could fall Vhaal came charging up the hill and caught the warleader in the stomach with his shoulder.

Blood spattered from Vantz's wounds, and his sword flew from his hands; before he could recover, Vhaal spun and removed his head from his shoulders with a two-handed stroke. Twin jets of blood spurted briefly skyward, and then the cavalry leader's body fell motionless to the soaked earth. The head landed nearby. After cleaning his blades and carefully sheathing them, Vhaal picked it up by the hair to admire.

And it was over, as fast as that. Horses were still audible, fleeing into the distance, and one or two of the soldiers still groaned. Otherwise the battlefield was still. Sylph blinked, and tried to remember what it was she should be feeling. *We won. Didn't we?* Vantz was dead, his men slaughtered—blood *everywhere*, it was worse than the movies—*so we won.*

There was a rustle behind her and Sylph turned to find her sister staggering to her feet. Lina tried to start down the slope and stumbled, and Sylph hurried into her way to prop her up.

"God. Are you all right?"

"Yeah," Lina mumbled. She didn't *look* all right: Her face was drawn and pale as a ghost, and her eyes were as sunken as though she'd missed a week of sleep. She leaned heavily on Sylph as they walked together toward Fah, who was back to her feet despite the gash on her thigh.

"Magus?" she said. When Lina didn't answer, she turned to Sylph. "Is she . . ."

"I think she's just exhausted. She passed out after . . . after the last time." She'd almost said "the first time," but Sylph had just enough rational thought left not to reveal information like that.

"M'okay," said Lina groggily. "Fah? You're bleeding."

"I'll live," said Fah. "Where's Melfina?"

"Right here!" The girl dropped from her perch and landed neatly in a crouch. She surveyed the destruction with an experienced eye and smiled. "It looks like we won!"

"Let's go find the others."

That turned out not to be very difficult. Daana and Garot were standing together, while Yahvy had already busied herself pulling arrows from the body of the dead. Garot bore a wound on his arm, and Daana was busy wrapping it; the boy stood as Fah approached.

"Fah . . ."

"Where's Kiry?" Fah demanded. Garot's hesitation made the answer obvious, and Fah's eyes filled with tears. "Where?"

He pointed, wordlessly. Fah followed, and Sylph left Lina with Daana and went with her. Somehow, she felt, she had to see. *My plan. It was my plan.* The fact that they had all been planning to kill themselves was a mitigating circumstance, but . . .

Kiry was pinned to a tree by a spear, struck with such force that the wood had cracked up and down the trunk. Her bow had slipped from her fingers and landed at her side, and her hands were clenched around the shaft through her chest. Her head drooped, long hair just brushing the haft of the spear.

Fah's jaw trembled, and she couldn't bring herself to approach. Sylph thought about putting a comforting hand on her shoulder, but Yahvy beat her to it.

"She was shooting at Vantz, thought she had time for one more before getting out of the way." Yahvy closed her eyes, looking exhausted. "Obviously not."

Fah's fists clenched. "She's dead."

"So is Safael. And Atham. And how many others before them?"

"Fuck you."

"We're at war. We're lucky any of us survived."

Yahvy turned to look up the hill, where Lina sat at rest. Sylph couldn't read her eyes. Fah was silent for a moment, then turned and trudged back to the rest.

Sylph hesitated a moment. "What are you going to . . . do with her?"

"Garot and I will get her down and bury her," Yahvy said quietly.

"Good."

"Your sister . . . that was amazing. We'd all be dead without her."

"I know." Sylph shook her head. "I know."

SYLPH WANTED A MOMENT ALONE WITH HER SISTER, BUT SHE didn't get one. Lina zombie-walked back to the village and tumbled into her straw bed the moment she got there, sleeping with the dedicated snores of someone who didn't intend to wake up anytime soon. Daana and Garot retreated to their own hut—*probably* not *to rest*—and Fah shut herself in the forge and didn't seem like she wanted any company. Sylph wanted to curl up next to her sister and go to sleep, but her body wouldn't let her; she felt like she was in some kind of post-adrenaline stupor, slightly dazed but unable to sit still. She found a few of the village women tending the main cooking fire, and accepted some soup, boiled meat, and water. Then she wandered to the outskirts, picking her way past tree stumps and stacks of split wood.

We won. We won the fucking battle—I won the fucking battle. They were ready to march into Hell and I came up with a plan and we won. So why do I feel like I want to vomit?

She'd gotten almost halfway around the village when she came across Yahvy and Melfina. The latter was cleaning her knives; she had a small pile of dirty ones, extracted from the bodies, and a bucket of sand and water. Yahvy had her longbow out and a dozen arrows sticking into the dirt in front of her, and was sending them one by one toward a lone pine tree fifty yards downrange. There were already a half-dozen shafts sticking in the trunk.

Sylph stood silently for a moment, watching. Yahvy put another arrow into the tree, just where one of the limbs met the trunk.

"Couldn't sleep?"

"Honestly?" Sylph said. "No. I feel . . . I don't know. Jittery."

"Was this your first real fight?"

Sylph didn't feel like she could deny it. *Why is my first instinct always to lie to everyone, anyway?* "Yeah."

"It's a good time to get laid." Yahvy ignored Sylph's blush. "Not a lot of opportunity for that here. I suppose Vhaal might be willing."

"Please." Sylph shook her head.

"Sorry. Just a thought." She pulled another arrow from the dirt and examined it carefully.

"You've been in a lot of fights, I guess?"

"Fights, yes. Fights like that, no." Yahvy shook her head. "I was sure our number was up this time."

"Yeah." Sylph shifted uncomfortably.

"Most of the time," Yahvy continued, "fight's over before it really starts. We've been playing this area for a couple of years now—at least I have—" She glanced at Melfina, who didn't look up. "—ambushing Gargorian's Circle teams and so on. Always five or six or seven of us. Most of the time they're just walking along, we jump up and feather them, and that's the end of it. Only had to draw my sword every once in a while, to finish some poor wounded guard."

"Did you get used to it?"

"To what?"

"Killing people." Sylph shivered. "After we were done, I . . . I don't know. I wasn't sure what to think."

"We do what has to be done. Every one of those soldiers

threw in their lot with Gargorian, and like it or not that means they want to kill us and our families and everyone who isn't willing to knuckle under. Everyone lying out there deserved what they got."

"Except Kiry," said Melfina.

"Except Kiry."

There was a moment of silence.

"You've done that before too," said Sylph. "Lost friends."

"Of course," Yahvy said. "We're already dead. Sooner or later it catches up with us."

"But—"

"You're going to ask whether it bothers me. Of course it does. I just have to find ways of dealing with it."

"It doesn't bother *me*," said Melfina. "'Cause my friends are with the White Lady now. And when I get killed, I'll be there too, and I'll see them again."

"You," said Yahvy, "were crying pretty hard when you thought Fah wasn't coming back."

"That's different." Melfina sniffed. "And besides, I thought Vantz would carry her off to Bleloth to be tortured to death, and then when she died she'd go into the Circle and the Spider would get her and carry her off and bury her forever."

"Hmph." Yahvy nocked the arrow, drew, and fired. The shot whistled wide of the tree by a yard.

"Sorry," said Sylph. "I guess I'm distracting you."

Yahvy shrugged. "I'm just trying to clear my mind, you know?" She half-turned, suddenly. "Can I ask you something?"

"Sure."

"All that stuff you said before, about going all the way to Bleloth and taking down Gargorian. Do you really believe it?"

Sylph chuckled. "I didn't think *you* did."

"Doesn't matter. Do you?"

"Maybe." Sylph sighed. "Where I come from, it's very different. There are different rules. Now I'm here and I don't know what the hell is going on. So, if you're asking whether I believe I *can* do it, I don't know."

"But are you really going to try?"

"Is the alternative to sit here and wait for him to come kill us?"

Yahvy tilted her head. "I never thought of it that way."

"I mean, we killed this batch of soldiers. Maybe they were bad people, maybe they weren't. But he'll just send more, and then we have to kill them too. And on, and on, until we finally give up and die." Sylph took a deep breath. "So, if it's a choice between *that* and trying something impossible, I know what I'd say."

"The two of you don't have to stay with us."

"We do now. A bunch of soldiers rode away from that ambush, and someone was bound to have gotten a look at us. Besides, I can't just wander around the woods. What would we eat?"

"Squirrels!" said Melfina.

Yahvy smiled. "Sometime you'll have to tell me exactly how you made it this far."

"Sometimes I'm not exactly sure." Sylph paused. "Mel, can I ask what you meant about the Circles and the White Lady?"

Yahvy snorted. "She's nuts."

"I am *not* nuts!" Melfina snapped. She put on an offended face. "I learned from my grandmother. She said that only people outside the Circles get to go to the White Lady when they die!"

"The White Lady? She's a goddess?" Sylph asked.

"We're too far away for the gods to see us," said Melfina, "so for a long time there was nothing here but smoke and darkness. Then the White Lady came, and she made the world for the people to live in. And then she died and went down to Heaven, and everyone was happy because they knew they'd get to go with her when they died."

"What happened?" asked Sylph.

"The Lightbringer came," said Melfina, lowering her voice. "The *Spider*. He and the Archmagi keep the people from getting to Heaven—"

"Quit it, okay?" Yahvy shook her head. "I know the story."

"*She* doesn't!"

"You don't want to bore her."

"It's not boring," said Sylph.

"I was done anyway," said Melfina, looking sulkily at Yahvy. "And it's not a story. Grandma told it to me."

"So did mine, before she died and my dad threw me out. She didn't look like she was going to Heaven, and neither did Kiry."

"They *are*, and the White Lady—"

"Dying's real. The Plague is real, Gargorian is real. The rest of it . . ." Yahvy spread her hands.

"I think," said Sylph, "I may be able to sleep after all. Sometime, Mel, I'd like to hear the rest of the story."

"Really?"

"Sure."

Yahvy rolled her eyes, but said nothing. As Sylph got up, she raised a hand, then hesitated.

"What?"

"I . . ." Yahvy shrugged again, a little nervously. "I just wanted to thank you. For what you did."

"You should be thanking Lina."

"I think we'd be dead without you too."

"In that case, I graciously accept." Sylph bowed, which made Yahvy giggle. "You're welcome."

"Thanks!" said Melfina brightly.

"You're welcome too."

"If you run into Fah," said Yahvy, "tell her I need to talk to her."

Sylph nodded. She walked back to her own hut, and tunneled into the straw beside Lina, who mumbled something in her sleep and rolled over. Sylph closed her eyes and tried not to think.

The Plague. She thought back to Fah's explanation, newborn infants who died without ever taking a breath. It sounded, well, horrible. *I can see why they're fighting.* It wasn't that Sylph had thought much about having children—*I'm only fourteen, for Christ's sake!*—but she could see the principle.

She didn't remember going to sleep, but the next thing she knew someone was shaking her and the sun was much lower in the sky; by the shadows, it was getting on toward evening. She opened her eyes to find Melfina poking at her shoulder.

"I'm up." Sylph blinked crumbs away. "What's going on?"

"One of Gargorian's soldiers showed up and said he wanted to talk. Vhaal almost killed him, even though Fah told him not to, but Garot and Daana wouldn't let him. So now they're talking, and Fah sent me to get you. Should I wake up Magus Lina?"

"She's not . . ." Sylph sighed. "No. Leave her, I think she's worn out."

"Okay!" Melfina jumped to her feet. "Follow me!"

They passed a scowling Vhaal on the way to the forge; he brushed by without a word. Sylph pulled the rag curtain aside to find Fah sitting across the fire from a young man dressed in the leather and mail of Vantz's riders. He was unarmed, and Garot and Daana stood on either side of him with their weapons ready. The man's arm was bandaged, crudely, and she could see a bit of skin where the leather had been hacked away.

"Sylph." Fah rose. "Sorry to wake you."

"Don't worry about it. Who's this?"

The man got up, smoothly, and bowed. "My name is Heraan." He raised one eyebrow. "Are you the Magus?"

"My sister is sleeping," said Sylph evenly. "I'm Sylph Walker."

"She's one of the leaders here," said Fah. Sylph shot her a surprised look.

"I see." Heraan sat back down, cradling his injured arm. "You'll forgive me if I'm a bit brief. I had one of your arrows pulled through my arm a few hours ago."

"Of course. Sylph, sit down."

She did, keeping her eyes on Heraan. He was hard to read; his expression was guarded, but it didn't look like the face of someone who had come to beg for mercy. *He's not bad to look at either, minus the bandages and the stubble*, Sylph mused.

"So what are you doing here?" said Fah.

"I . . . to be honest, I'm not entirely sure this was a good idea, but we couldn't think of what else to do."

"Who's we?" said Sylph.

Heraan seemed taken aback. "Me, Gaav, Corian, a few of the others, maybe ten of us, all told? All westerners. We've been riding with Vantz for six months or so, since he hired us at Highpoint."

"Mercenaries," said Fah coldly. "Riding against your own people?"

Heraan held up his hands. "We didn't have a choice! Ever since the war ended, work's been scarce for a sell-sword. It was either sign up with Vantz or cross the mountains and head down toward Bleloth, and none of us wanted to do that."

"Go on," Fah said.

"After the fight I collected all the westerners I could, mostly my friends, and tried to figure out where to go next. Vantz is dead, and his easterners took our baggage train with them when they ran for it, so we don't have much in the way of supplies. It was either try to make it to Highpoint with what we've got, and then hope someone else is hiring, or come here."

"You're not here to ask for a *job*?" said Fah.

"Sort of, yeah."

She rolled her eyes. "First of all, even if I wanted to pay you, we don't have anything to pay you with. And second, what makes you think I'd trust a bunch of sell-swords?"

"That's the other thing," Heraan cut in. "The Magus. When I saw that, I thought . . . I mean . . . is she the next Liberator?" he finally blurted.

"Lina?" said Sylph.

Fah stayed quiet, thinking. Eventually she looked up and said, "Garot, Daana, do you mind taking our guest outside?"

Garot nodded. "Come on."

Once they were alone, Sylph leaned close to Fah and whispered, "What's a Liberator?"

"A holy man," said Fah gravely. "A Magus. The last Liberator was named Jaen, and he overthrew Tyramax, the Archmagus who ruled here before Gargorian. He abolished the Circles and let the people rule themselves."

"What happened?"

"Eventually he marched his army east to try and destroy the Lightbringer, and never came back. When Gargorian showed up, he just took over and started everything up again."

"When is all this supposed to have happened?"

"It really happened. Six hundred years ago, more or less. And he promised there would be another."

Figures. "So this guy thinks Lina is a new Liberator?"

"Or he's making this up as he goes along." Fah's eyes narrowed. "Sylph, you don't think we should keep him around, do you?"

"He might stab us in the back," Sylph conceded. "On the other hand, if we tell him to get lost, he might jump us in the woods. And if we kill him his friends might do the same. It might be worth having them where we can see them. Besides . . ."

"Besides?"

"What were you planning to do next?"

"I haven't the faintest idea," said Fah. "I was planning to die this morning, remember?"

"If you really want to take the fight to Gargorian . . ." Sylph shrugged. "I don't know. Having more swords around seems like a good idea."

Fah nodded, and called to Daana to have Heraan come back in. The soldier sat down again, outwardly unperturbed, but Sylph could feel his nervousness. *He's not that much older then Lina. Nineteen, maybe?*

"You're willing to come with us?" said Fah. "To fight against Gargorian?"

He nodded eagerly. "Of course."

"Why now, and not before?"

"We never had a Magus before. Only magic can fight magic . . . but if this girl really is the Liberator . . ."

"Enough." She held up a hand. "You know we can't afford to pay you."

"My friends and I will settle for food and water. And," he smiled crookedly, "a share of the plunder."

Fah sighed. "You can have all the plunder, as far as I'm concerned. How far away are your friends?"

"Not far." Heraan leaned forward eagerly. "But we have to move fast. Vantz's men will make for Highpoint, and once they get there they'll send for reinforcements. If we don't take Highpoint before that happens, we're finished."

"Take *Highpoint*?" Fah said. "Are you crazy?"

Heraan smiled.

＊　＊　＊

"THIS IS A TRAP," SAID YAHVY.

"It could be," said Fah, "but then again . . ."

"I just don't see what he has to gain from a trap," said Sylph. "If he really is still working for Gargorian, he doesn't have to risk himself like this. You said yourself eventually they'd send enough troops to squash us."

"He could kill Lina," Yahvy retorted. "Whoever kills the Magus would gain favor with Gargorian."

"But he's coming with us," Fah mused. "He volunteered. He has to know we'd kill him if he turned his coat again."

"Once a traitor," Yahvy said, "always a traitor. He deserted Vantz and Gargorian when things went against him, he'll turn on us when things go sour."

"Even if we trust him," said Fah, "does it do us any good? He said he can get us inside the walls, but there are at least two hundred men in the Highpoint garrison. Not conscripts, Gargorian's elite. It's the only decent pass for a hundred miles. I can't believe we can take it with just the six of us plus however many of Heraan's friends come along."

"I've been thinking about that," said Sylph. "I think it could be done."

They both looked at her. Eventually Yahvy said, "Do you want to enlighten us?"

"I'm not sure yet. I need to see the place, first, and talk to Heraan some more. But, if it's possible . . ."

There was a moment of silence.

"If it's possible," said Fah, "if there's a chance, we should take it. One of the nodes of the Fourth Circle is in Highpoint. If we can destroy that, it would do more damage to Gargorian then we could ever hope to achieve out here."

"I still think it's a trap," said Yahvy. "But if you say it can be done . . ."

When did my opinion become so important? The thought was sobering. "I *think* so."

"Let's do it," said Fah.

Yahvy nodded. "What about the others? Melfina would follow you anywhere, and Vhaal will come along if he thinks there's blood in it."

"Garot was listening, back in the forge," said Sylph. "He looked excited."

"And Daana will go with him," Fah concluded. "Easy enough. Yahvy, can you look at getting our food wrapped and ready to go?"

"Got it. When are we leaving?"

"Dawn or so." Fah turned to Sylph. "Sleep if you can."

Sylph doubted she'd be able to. She felt keyed up, full of energy. *They're really going to do it.* March to Highpoint, fight Gargorian, take on the world. *We're crazy. We're all crazy.*

Their little huddle broke up, and Sylph went back to the hut she was starting to think of as home. Lina was still in the straw, but she opened her eyes and looked up as Sylph entered.

"Hey."

"Hey, yourself." Sylph knelt next to her. "How're you feeling? You crashed pretty hard after we got back."

"Fine." Lina yawned. "Good, actually."

"That's a relief."

"Anything happen while I was sleeping?"

Actually . . . Sylph suddenly realized what she'd signed Lina up for. *Christ. I didn't even ask her.* "S . . . sort of."

Sylph explained, hesitantly, and Lina took it all in with enviable calm. When she was finished, Sylph waited for her sister to explode, or more likely break down in tears. *She never gets angry at me, not openly, but I can see it.* But there was nothing like that in Lina's face.

"Okay," Lina said. "We're leaving for this Highpoint place tomorrow?"

"Y . . . yeah." It was picking at a scab; she couldn't help but ask. "It's okay with you? All this?"

Lina shrugged. "If you think it's the best way to go."

Sylph checked a sigh of relief. *This would be an inconvenient time for her to develop a mind of her own.* "Heraan seems to have convinced himself you're some kind of saint."

Lina laughed. "I'm sure that won't last."

Sylph laughed too, but her thoughts had been diverted to a new track. *Maybe it will, maybe it won't.*

4

chapter four

HERAAN INTRODUCED HIS FRIENDS, BUT THE NAMES didn't stick with Sylph. They seemed like a pretty nasty lot all told, and there were a few leers directed at Lina, Fah, and even Yahvy. They snapped to quickly enough when Heraan gave the word, though, and didn't complain much when he told them their horses were going to be used for carrying supplies instead of riding. And Sylph had to admit that they *looked* more professional than the ragtag band of Circle Breakers. Heraan put scouts out, two men ahead and two behind, and they ghosted through the woods with the ease of long practice.

The mercenary leader himself stayed with their little column. He walked with Yahvy and Sylph, probing discreetly but firmly for information. Sylph tried to maintain a charming demeanor while not actually giving anything away, but as the day wore on she was increasingly convinced that he had figured out there was something abnormal about her. She quickly cast about for new topics of conversation.

"What made you become a mercenary?"

"Money." Heraan laughed. "I guess it's a bit more than that. I had two younger brothers, and after my father died there was no one but me to support us. So I learned to use a sword and started selling myself as a bodyguard around Highpoint. Eventually you just get used to it."

"What happened to your brothers?"

"The army, what else? They got rounded up the last time Gargorian's slave-drivers came through. Marched off to the east, and like as not I'll never see them again."

"That's awful."

He shrugged. "It's not such a bad life in the army, if you can make a space for yourself." He cleared his throat. "How about you? Have you always been following the Liberator?"

Yahvy snorted, but said nothing. Sylph picked her words carefully.

"As long as I can remember. She's my sister, after all."

"You're doing an amazing job for a little girl."

She colored. "I hate being called a little girl."

"Ah." Heraan shook his head. "Sorry."

They rode in silence for a while, until Fah glanced at the sun and announced it was time to stop. Heraan's scouts found a flat, dry spot to camp, and Daana and Melfina got a fire going in short order. Garot, Yahvy, and a few of the men vanished into the woods, looking for game. Sylph sat on the bedroll she'd borrowed from Fah and looked at the bustling activity, not sure what to do.

"Everyone seems to be avoiding me." Lina sat down next to her.

"They think you're a saint, I told you. And a wizard." *I don't blame them, especially Heraan's people.* The soldiers made a point of keeping a safe distance from Lina and the sword at her belt, as though she might explode into sorcerous fury at any moment. "You holding up?"

"My feet hurt." Lina sighed. "And I'm hungry. Aside from that, yeah."

"Mine too." The boots she'd been given didn't *quite* fit, but Fah assured her they'd break in after a while. She knew there'd be blisters by tomorrow. "Dinner should be soon."

"Probably squirrel again."

It turned out to be deer, actually, courtesy of an alert

cavalryman with a short-bow. Sylph had never been a fan of venison—*back in real life, anyway*—but carved fresh and roasted over an open fire, juices popping and dribbling when she bit into it, it had a certain appeal. *Not to mention I'm starved.* A full day of walking had worn her out most satisfactorily, and she dropped off to sleep immediately.

In the days that followed, Sylph decided the best thing for her and Lina to do was to acquire some rudimentary combat training. She had a quiet word with Fah, and since game was plentiful Yahvy stopped going hunting and started trying to teach Sylph enough not to chop off her own foot. Lina was enthusiastic, despite waking up with aching wrists. *Good. If she's going to be the next Joan of Arc or whatever, she'd better know how to fight.* They didn't practice using *the* sword, of course; Lina leaned it carefully against a tree stump and borrowed a shorter blade from Yahvy. By the end of the six-day journey to Highpoint Sylph felt like all she'd done was plumb the depth of her ignorance; Yahvy assured her she was making quick progress, but the smooth movement that seemed so natural to someone like Vhaal felt all but impossible.

Vhaal, for his part, had taken the new plan with studied indifference. He stayed with the camp at night, on Fah's orders, and occasionally came with a lazy sneer to watch Sylph and Lina practice. Heraan stopped by occasionally too, and was much more supportive. Sylph felt herself trying a bit harder when he was around, and laughed at herself when she thought about it.

All in all, the days were exhausting and the nights peaceful. There was little to break the routine. Garot and Daana snuck away from camp every night, and once Sylph saw them while she was walking through the woods, their lips entangled and Garot's hand under the girl's leathers. She fled, red-faced, and had a hard time talking to Daana the next morning. Surprisingly, the cavalrymen behaved themselves, although one of them propositioned Yahvy and got a black eye for his trouble. He took it cheerfully, and from then on smiled at her whenever she passed.

Sylph spent quite a bit of time interrogating Fah and came away frustrated. It seemed to be common knowledge that Gargorian was an Archmagus, the source of the Plague, and ruler for the past six hundred years; whenever Sylph tried to press deeper, Fah had to admit she didn't know the answers. *Like what exactly makes an Archmagus, and how he's lived for so long?* There were two others, apparently, along with a mythical being called Lightbringer. Melfina had referred to the latter as a mythical evil figure, but Fah insisted that he was a real, physical being who ruled over a blasted land far to the east.

Even more frustrating were the curious *gaps* in the Circle Breaker's knowledge. Fah explained the difference between easterners and westerners: the latter were the descendants of the primitive tribes who'd originally inhabited the area around Bleloth, while the former came from a more advanced people who had been pressing east for generations. But when Sylph asked whether they had originally used different languages all she got was a blank stare.

"Languages?" Fah said. "What do you mean?"

"Did the easterners speak a different language than the tribes that were there already?"

"I'm not sure what you mean by language."

Sylph thought for a moment. *Maybe my English and hers don't match up exactly?* "Like . . . when one person speaks differently than another, and they can't understand each other?"

Fah shook her head. "If one person speaks clearly, how could someone else not understand?"

"But if one of them comes from a completely different place . . ."

"I understand *you*," Fah pointed out. "And you come from across the Moonblack Sea."

Sylph had to admit that was true. *They don't even understand the* concept *of another language.* It made Sylph wonder what would happen if she spoke to Fah in French or German. *Would she understand me just as well?* Curiosity was almost enough to make her wish she hadn't dropped her language classes to leave more time for war games before lunch.

On the morning of the seventh day, the scouts reported the tree line just ahead. Sylph and Lina hurried on, but there wasn't much to look at; the land had been sloping gently upwards since they'd left, but past the point where the woods had been logged back it turned into an actual hillside. At the very top Sylph could see the walls of what looked like log cabins, much larger than the little huts of the village.

Fah and Heraan joined the sisters. Fah said, "Are we going to have any trouble getting into the village itself?"

"Not if we don't make ourselves too obvious," said the mercenary. "Gargorian's people don't much care what happens on the west side of the walls."

"Where's the entrance to your passageway?" asked Sylph.

"One of the inns near the fort. The last warleader had a taste for whores, and a friend of mine used to smuggle them in."

"Will it be locked on the inside?"

"Possibly, but we should be able to break down the door."

Not without noise, Sylph thought.

"So," said Fah, "what's the plan?"

"Even if we can get inside the walls, we can't just rush them."

"I'm sure the Magus . . ." Heraan began.

"She has power," said Fah, "but it is exhausted quickly."

That wasn't a fact Sylph had wanted broadcast. *Oh well.* "In any case. I once asked a . . . a teacher of mine"—actually it had been Fred, after he'd roundly trashed her in the tournament at WarCon '02—"what to do if a battle involved attacking an impenetrable fortress."

"And?" asked Fah.

Sylph smiled. "He said, 'Make sure to be the one on the inside'."

✲   ✲   ✲

IT TOOK A FEW MINUTES TO EXPLAIN THE PLAN, AND THE
better part of an hour to iron out the difficulties. The biggest obstacle was the lack of good timekeeping devices. Sylph was used
to wearing a watch, and got a bit nervous when Fah started talking in terms of counting heartbeats, even though the girl assured
her it would be accurate enough.

"Are you sure you want to do this, Lina?" Sylph asked, while
the camp picked itself up around her. Heraan and three of his
men were pulling the supplies off of their horses and readying
the animals for combat.

"It would be a shame to come all this way for nothing."

"We could wait. I could try and think of a better plan . . ."

"It's a good plan." Lina took a deep breath and picked up
the sword, belting it tightly around her waist.

"Your part is too dangerous."

"I'm not sneaking into the fortress! Besides, I've got this."
She patted the blade. "You just take care of yourself."

"I'll do my best."

Lina paused for a moment. "I'd better go mount up."

Sylph nodded. That was another sticking point: Heraan had
picked the horse with the friendliest disposition for Lina, and
there was nothing tricky for her to do. *But if things go wrong . . .*

Sylph wandered over to the mercenary. "Heraan," she said
quietly.

"Yes?"

"You're sure about the tunnel? And about—"

"Relax," he said, and grinned. "I'll take good care of your
sister."

"G . . . good. Take care of Fah too."

"Orbaa here will take care of you." He nodded to one of his
men, a lean-faced youth with a ponytail and arms like knotted
lengths of cord. "If he knows what's good for him."

Orbaa smiled and put a hand on Sylph's shoulder, protectively. She shook him off and went in search of the rest of her team.

Melfina, Garot, and Daana were the best riders among the Circle Breakers, so they were going with Lina; Vhaal insisted on going into the fortress, of course, and Yahvy detested horses.

"Besides," she said to Sylph, "someone has to keep an eye on that lunatic."

"I heard that," Vhaal said cheerfully.

"You were supposed to," Yahvy snapped. "Are we ready to go, Sylph?"

Sylph glanced over her shoulder at the horsemen. "Looks like it." She turned to Orbaa, who was leading the rest of Heraan's men: a half-dozen in all, in leather and mail. *Not much of an army.* "We're headed out. Lead the way."

"Good luck!" Fah called as they started to climb the hill. Sylph didn't shout back, for fear of being heard. *Good luck. Lina, try not to get killed.*

The slope up to the town was hard going, and everyone was puffing before they got to the top. By the time they reached the outermost of the buildings, it was getting close to noon. Orbaa leaned close to Sylph, to whisper in her ear.

"Let me do th' talkin' if we run into anybody." He had an odd accent, halfway between a southern drawl and a Hollywood pirate.

Sylph nodded, and Orbaa led his half-dozen up the street with a practiced swagger, the cavalrymen keeping Yahvy and Sylph in tow. He got some nods and a few cursory greetings, but the merchants of the town hadn't woken up yet. Sylph found that she collected a few strange looks. Once she realized what she must look like, a lone little girl in the company of all these armed men, she turned red and did her best to stay next to Yahvy.

"Nervous?" said the Circle Breaker.

"Not exactly. Hard to explain."

"We're almost there," said Orbaa quietly. They'd been threading their way through log and thatch houses, laid out according to no particular pattern bordering an open area that was a street only by consensus. The land was still sloping upward, and when Sylph looked up she found she could see the wall of the fortress, black, square, and smooth, gleaming coldly in the sun. *Wait a minute. What the hell is it made of?*

"That's it," said Orbaa, indicating a two-story building. A sign outside had concentric red-and-white markings, like a bull's-eye.

"Good timing," said Yahvy. "Here they come."

✳   ✳   ✳

LINA HAD RIDDEN A HORSE EXACTLY TWICE DURING HER LIFE, both during the same vacation; they'd bused to the North Carolina shore and spent a week on crowded beaches and even more crowded boardwalks. The horseback riding had been one of the attractions; those horses had been slow and friendly, accustomed to a life of trudging slowly around a fenced-in square.

This horse was not like that. It was a high-spirited horse, eager to run and jump and do back-flips. Heraan swore it was the friendliest and calmest beast he had, but Lina still held the reins tight and worried the thing might bolt at any second.

Some of that had to do with what she was about to try, of course. *Crazy. I'm crazy.* She put one hand on the hilt of the sword, lightly, and felt distant laughter in the back of her mind. *I'm crazy to even touch this thing again.*

Fah, riding alongside, touched her hand gently. "Don't worry."

"I'm . . ." Lina looked up at her, and shook her head. "I *am* worried."

"You'll be all right." There was an odd look in the girl's eyes. "You're a Magus, after all."

Lina stifled the urge to scream that she wasn't, that it was all a sham. Instead she said, "What about Sylph?"

Fah hesitated. "It's dangerous for all of us."

"Here we go," said Heraan. "The fortress is up ahead. Fah, remember to hang on to Lina's reins."

"I remember." Fah had already slid out of the saddle and

was pulling the longbow from her back. Lina had watched her string the thing earlier; that alone was no mean feat. Heraan's three men dismounted as well, along with Melfina, Garot, and Daana. Heraan stayed on horseback, trotting slowly toward the fortress.

The fortress. Lina could see it now. The wall had to be forty feet high, black as sin and flashing in the sun as though it had been glazed. It didn't look like any kind of stone she'd ever seen. The closest comparison she could come up with were the black glass-lined skyscrapers of Manhattan. *And those weren't all one piece like this.* The wall stretched from one edge of the pass to the other, pierced by a single gate of ordinary wood. Two towers, of the same strange black stuff, rose behind the wall where they could oversee the gate. The doors were open, and through them Lina saw a squat stone building beside the road.

There were four men on guard, dressed similarly to Heraan and his mercenaries, leather and mail, though these soldiers wore red gloves and boots. One of them sauntered forward, either to question Heraan or deny him entrance; the mercenary leader twitched his reins and shifted his feet, and his horse was suddenly rearing. The soldier staggered backward. Lina's grip on the reins tightened when she saw the man's face had been kicked into a red ruin by a steel-shod hoof. *I can't do this. The blood . . .*

The other three guards shouted and drew steel. The little square in front of the fortress gate, which hadn't been heavily trafficked when they arrived, was suddenly completely empty. Heraan controlled his horse with one hand and snatched a mace from his saddle with the other, concealing the latter movement with the body of the animal. The closest guard got a solid steel ball with spikes to the side of the head; he fell and didn't move. The horse lashed out again, teeth snapping at a man who had come too near. Both the guards and Heraan backed away, the soldiers still shouting for help.

Fah patted Lina's shoulder again, then stepped next to Garot and Daana and put an arrow to her bow. The guardhouse must have been just on the inside of the wall, because a wave of soldiers came boiling out of the gateway like ants. Heraan was already riding away, but there were at least twenty men following, about half of them armed with long spears.

"Now," said Fah quietly. The three Circle Breakers raised their bows and fired from a distance of perhaps sixty feet. Three men in the front row stopped as though they'd hit a brick wall, the force of the arrows pushing them backward into their fellows. Then Heraan's horsemen fired, their smaller bows having a less devastating effect but still drawing blood. Heraan himself was still riding, but the mass of men faltered under this new threat.

It was enough time for Fah and the others to draw and fire again. More men fell, one staggering away from the group with an arrow through the eye that emerged from the back of his head. Lina clutched at her own eye and almost gagged. *God. I can't do this.* Another group of soldiers emerged from the gate, including one wearing a helmet of polished bronze. He pointed and shouted something that sounded impolite, and the hesitant guards drew their swords and charged.

By this point Heraan had reached the rest of the group. The Circle Breakers fired again, aiming for the leader. He ducked sideways at the last moment, but the man next to him was impaled on two shafts and dropped to the dirt, soaking in a pool of red. The horsemen fired wildly and drew their swords, and Garot and Daana tossed their longbows aside and reached for hand weapons; only Fah kept her bow, serenely confident, firing another arrow at point-blank range that dropped yet another man. Melfina threw her knives, once the guards were close enough, and sank both of them into the stomach of a pimply faced young man in the front rank who tripped and was nearly trampled by his comrades.

There were at least fifteen soldiers left. *I can't do this. Fifteen of them, against three girls and five soldiers. I can't.* Lina took one last breath to silence the nagging voice of doubt and stepped in front of Fah. She drew the sword. It felt a little more natural, now, but the background buzz of the blade intensified to the point where her vision blurred and her teeth rattled. That lasted only a moment before settling down, but she could *feel* the thing at the end of her arm, soaked in power like a cloth bathed in blood.

The soldiers were almost there. One of them, the bronze-helmeted leader, lowered his sword to impale Lina on the charge. He was a middle-aged man, she saw at the last moment, with a jowly face and white sideburns. A nice enough face. *Not the kind of person I'd expect to see screaming for my head.*

She swung the sword in a flat arc. White energy flared, screamed, and rippled outward in a semicircle. The leader didn't even get to shriek before he was vaporized, his blood hissing into puffs of steam. The man behind him fell too, cut neatly in half, and a guard to his left reeled away clutching the stump of his arm.

The rest of the guards couldn't stop moving; they couldn't react fast enough. Lina swung again, as if she were swatting at ferns with a stick, and more soldiers went down or vanished entirely. They were running now, skidding to a halt on the bloody ground and running for their lives. Garot grabbed one who had jumped aside, dragging his head back by the hair and pulling a sword across his throat before letting him fall. Fah fired again, and one of the fleeing men took the arrow in the back and dropped face down in the dirt. Then they were past the gate, and . . .

Laughing. The voice echoed in her head. *He can't stop laughing . . . high and fast and* mad—

"Lina!" Fah shook her shoulder. "Are you all right?"

That was much easier than last time. Lina looked down at the sword wordlessly, then slammed it back into its sheath. She turned to Fah and nodded.

"Fine. I'm fine."

Heraan and his men were still standing with their mouths open, staring at the swath of destruction. Heraan looked at her, closed his mouth, blinked, and then said, "Holy *shit.*"

The others chorused agreement. Lina looked down, embarrassed, and shook her head. *It's the sword, it's just the sword. I don't really do anything.*

"Okay," said the mercenary leader finally. "That has to have scared whomever's in command in there. The only question is how long we have to wait before they come out and get us."

"Archers on the walls!" someone shouted, a moment before the air was alive with the deep *thrum* of arrows.

There was a scream somewhere to Lina's right, and a moment later she felt a sting on her leg, as though a bee had gotten her. She slapped her hand against it, automatically, and it came away wet with blood. *My blood.* She looked down, felt suddenly faint, and would have fallen over if Fah hadn't steadied her with a strong grip on her shoulder.

"Magus! Are you . . ."

"Fine," Lina gasped. "I'm okay."

Garot and Daana were already firing back, side by side. A body toppled from the wall, and there was an odd ringing sound as arrowheads struck the black whatever-it-was. There was another scream, this one from inside the fortress. More arrows flew.

Heraan and one of his men knelt by their wounded companion, while the third fired his short-bow toward the wall. The one on the ground had taken an arrow in the belly, and he moaned piteously.

"Heraan . . ."

Heraan went for his blade, a single quick thrust under the ribs and into the heart. The man stilled, and the cavalry leader got up and swung onto his horse.

"Come on, we're getting out of here!" An arrow *zinged* past, a few feet from Lina's head, but she stood motionless.

"You *killed* him!"

"Magus, *please.*" Fah dragged Lina toward the mounts. Daana fired a last arrow at the battlements before climbing onto her own steed; Garot was carrying Melfina under one arm, lifting her onto her horse despite her feeble protestations. Lina saw half an arrow shaft protruding from the girl's side. Finally Garot mounted up, as another trio of arrows zipped into the dirt nearby, and they were off. The one riderless horse trailed behind them.

"They're coming!" Heraan shouted. Fah was holding the reins, so Lina could spare enough attention to look back; cavalry was thundering through the Highpoint gate, past the black walls and in hot pursuit. A half-dozen of the bronze-helmed sergeants had the vanguard, and in the lead was a huge black stallion bearing a warrior in elaborately worked silver plate.

"Old One-Eye himself," said Fah breathlessly. "We must have touched a nerve."

"There must be a *hundred* of them," Lina said, forgetting for a moment about the pain from her leg.

"Just don't stop, and hope . . ."

✳   ✳   ✳

"What I'm sayin' is, I'm a friend of Heraan's, if you know what I mean."

"No," said the fat woman with floury arms who stood in the kitchen doorway, "I don't."

"Are you sure this is the right place?" said Sylph.

"Course I'm sure," said Orbaa. "Right where Heraan pointed out. He said to ask for Mistress Magphy."

"My aunt's dead," said the woman stoutly. "Has been for a year now. I'm her niece, Dora Magphy, and I've taken over the business."

"Oh," said Sylph quietly. Heraan had promised the innkeeper would be on their side, and give no trouble about using the secret passage in her basement, but that put an entirely new face on things.

"Well . . ." Orbaa hesitated, looking back at Sylph, who was thinking furiously.

We could force our way past. But if we leave her behind, and she raises the alarm, we're finished.

Outside, the distant sounds of fighting were drowned out by a mind-numbing hum that Sylph recognized. *Lina! We're out of time.*

Dora rushed to the door. "What in the name of the White Lady . . ."

That was as far as she got. For a moment she stood mouthing noiselessly like a landed fish. Vhaal pulled his sword from her back with a wet, squishy sound; she half-turned, one finger raised to berate him, then crumpled like a puppet with cut strings. Vhaal was already cleaning his blade with a black cloth.

Sylph felt her mouth hanging open. "V . . . Vhaal . . ."

"She wasn't going to let us through." The black-clad swordsman shrugged. "And she might have raised the alarm. We're running out of time, Sylph."

Orbaa looked back at his companions—even the professional mercenaries seemed a little discomfited—but eventually they all looked to Sylph, who swallowed her bile and nodded.

"Through the tunnel. Come on." She tried to avoid looking at the woman's staring eyes as they filed past.

"Someday," Yahvy hissed as Vhaal passed, "they are going to find *you* with a sword in your back."

"Someday I'm going to sneak into your tent in the middle of the night and find out if you're really a girl or not."

Yahvy's went to draw her sword, but Vhaal was already laughing and walking away.

"Christ," Sylph said, when she and Yahvy were the only ones left upstairs. Yahvy's hands opened and closed, and she took deep, deliberate breaths.

"Come on," said Sylph. "Let's go."

Heraan's information was good, at least as far as the tunnel went. It was in the root cellar dug out of the earth underneath the inn, a wooden trapdoor sealed with a stout chain to prevent anyone from coming out. Orbaa had already untied it and opened the trap, revealing a length of stone-lined tunnel.

"I'll go first," Vhaal said. "Follow, but not too close."

He jumped down before anyone could stop him. Sylph nodded at Orbaa, who waved his men through. He went last, followed by Yahvy and Sylph. Underground it was damp, cool, and dark. Sylph blinked as her eyes adjusted, but the tunnel was only a few hundred feet long; Vhaal was already standing by the trapdoor at the other end. Sylph squeezed past the mercenaries until she was at the head of the line.

"Locked?" she said curtly. Vhaal nodded.

"Close enough. Take a look." He pushed the trap open. The tunnel went up a couple of steps and then emptied into a tiny cell, cordoned off from a larger room by a curtain of vertical bars. *A jail cell.* She stepped into it, cautiously; there was a torch flickering on the wall opposite, past the bars, and she saw several more cells adjacent. A quick push confirmed that the door was locked from the other side.

The bars had the same strange, black quality as the outer wall of the fortress; they seemed to be made of the same stuff. Sylph ran her hand along it. *It feels almost like . . .*

"Orbaa?"

"Yeah?" he said, after he'd worked his way past everyone. Vhaal stood behind him, watching silently. The mercenary surveyed the situation and said, "Ah."

"What are these made of?"

"Obsidian. Same as the outer walls."

Sylph blinked. "That's not possible. You could never get obsidian so smooth."

He gave her an odd look. "Gargorian raised this fortress himself, by magic."

By magic?

Sylph turned back to the bars, ran her fingers across them. They seemed solid enough. *Magic?*

"We'll have to break it down." Orbaa turned back to his men, who had brought along an iron-headed hammer to deal with inconvenient locks. They passed it forward. *But that will take time, and make noise. We're dead if they catch us in here.*

And there was . . . something. A tickle under her fingertips. She closed her eyes and opened them again, quickly, and for a moment it was as if the bars weren't there, like they'd drifted away when they were out of focus. She caressed the smooth glass, somehow feeling the structure of it, atoms locked in serried ranks. *It must be close to a perfect crystal.*

"Sylph? You need to get out of the way."

There was an edge, a trailing string, like the little piece of a scab a fingernail can just get underneath. Sylph had a scar on her knee from a scab she'd torn off too many times; she could never resist. *Pull right here, and the whole thing . . .*

. . . the bars dissolved into glowing streamers of light, then vanished entirely . . .

. . . *unravels.*

She opened her eyes.

What the hell just happened?

It had taken only a few moments. Orbaa turned around with the hammer to find the bars gone. He shook his head, bemused.

"What did you do?"

Sylph turned around. "I don't . . . I mean . . ."

She caught Vhaal's expression, one eyebrow raised with a look that said, *Interesting.* Her fist clenched.

"I opened it," Sylph finished firmly. "Are you guys ready to move?"

"Sure." Orbaa laid the hammer aside, carefully. "Bens, Corian, take the left side. Veck, with me."

They spread out with professional precision; left turned out to be a blind alley, but right led to a narrow guard room, where two of Gargorian's soldiers loafed at a table. Sylph didn't blame them—guarding empty cells was hardly enthralling work—but their swords were leaning against the wall and they didn't have a chance. The mercenaries surrounded them and silenced them with a few quick thrusts. Another door, this one unlocked, led to a stone staircase lit by more torches.

The trick with the bars was still preying on her mind. *It was just there. Obvious. I just touched it . . .* Sylph shook her head. *Focus. Come on.*

From the distance they had traveled, she knew roughly where they were; underneath the left-hand guard tower. Orbaa opened the door and motioned for silence; Sylph listened attentively, but heard nothing. Vhaal tapped his foot impatiently.

"Assumin' everythin' has gone well," the mercenary said, "this place should be on a skeleton crew. We make sure of these two towers and the wall; that's all that really matters."

"What about the barracks?" asked Sylph, nodding in that direction.

"Shouldn' be much left. We've got to take these towers fast. I'll go with the three of you and the rest of you finish here. Got that?" he said over his shoulder to a chorus of affirmative grunts. "Follow me."

The ground floor of the tower was clear, and the door unbolted. Orbaa nodded toward the stairway and his men filed quietly past. In the meantime, Vhaal led the way outside. They crossed the forty feet of open ground between the towers at a walk, with Sylph feeling horribly exposed every second. *They must be watching, from the barracks, or the tops of the towers.*

But no arrows flew toward them. The sound of massed horses was disappearing into the distance, but whatever action was taking place out there had everyone inside the fortress straining for a look. Vhaal reached the door to the right-hand tower, kicked it open, and skewered the surprised soldier inside without breaking stride. The man died with a squeak; Orbaa headed for the doorway while Yahvy closed the door behind them.

"Two more floors," Orbaa whispered. "Sounds like two on the next."

"I'll take it," said Vhaal, stepping in front of the mercenary and bounding up the stairway. Yahvy cursed and ran after him, and Sylph followed Orbaa up the stairs, once again feeling like useless baggage despite the sword hanging from her waist. *It's my plan*, she reminded herself. *And I opened the gate.*

There was a ringing of steel on steel, and a hoarse shout from above them. Orbaa cursed.

"Idiot! Now they know we're coming."

They burst onto the second floor to find one soldier dead and Vhaal dueling another up the next staircase. There were no windows, only arrow slits and a torch on the wall, and the pair of them danced frantically in the flickering light until Vhaal managed to bat the man's sword aside and bull into him with his shoulder, knocking the soldier off balance and sending him sprawling against the steps. The boy finished him with a thrust through the neck and kept running, taking the stairs two at a time. The other three hurried after him, past the groping hands of the dying man.

The group on the top level had been watching the battle outside, but after their comrade's shout they'd arrayed themselves around the top of the stairs. Vhaal came in low and fast, rolling past their initial strikes and toward the edge of the circular room. Two of them turned to deal with him, while the other two confronted Yahvy on the staircase. Orbaa drew his sword, but was unable to pass in the narrow space. Yahvy gave ground frantically, parrying as her opponents advanced until one of them was squeezed out.

In the meantime, Vhaal held off both men with a spectacular display of swordsmanship. He was nearly skewered a dozen times that Sylph could see, but one of his twin blades was always in the way at the last moment, pushing the opponent's sword aside just far enough. It was only a matter of time until he missed, though, and one of the soldiers' swords scored on the meaty part of his thigh. Vhaal sagged, and they pressed their advantage . . .

. . . *it's a bluff*, Sylph thought wonderingly . . .

. . . the young man popped up like a jack-in-the-box, the wound not nearly as severe as he'd been pretending. He laid a long cut on the arm of one enemy, who dropped his sword and backed away while Vhaal pressed in on his suddenly out-matched opponent.

Orbaa had gone back down the stairs, and Sylph found Yahvy backing right into her, grunting with the effort of turning the sol-dier's blows. The man grinned, striking with savage strength, and Sylph felt her head ring with each impact. But Yahvy's at-tention seemed to be elsewhere; Sylph followed her gaze to the fourth man, who'd left the fight at the stairway to close on Vhaal from behind. Yahvy locked blades with her opponent, giving her a moment to watch as the soldier raised his weapon.

She's not going to tell him! The girl was grinning.

"Vhaal, behind you!" Sylph heard herself shout.

Vhaal spun with the reflexes of a cat, ducking low. His blade caught the soldier in the back of the knee and took off the lower half of his leg, leaving the surprised man to topple forward into the guard Vhaal had been fighting. The boy thrust into his chest before he could recover, and the soldier sank to the ground with his maimed companion on top of him.

Yahvy cursed, fell back to one side as the soldier pushed her forward, and took a heavy clout to the side of the head from his off hand. She staggered.

"'Scuse me," said Orbaa. Sylph moved aside automatically, and the mercenary thrust a torch he'd scavenged from the wall into the guard's face. The soldier screamed and clutched at his eyes, and Yahvy ran him through.

And that was it. In the room above, a moan trailed off into a gurgle as Vhaal finished one of the wounded men. Sylph felt her heart beating like a tom-tom, and sweat had reduced her hair to a tangled mess. But she was high on a rush of adrenalin, and felt like she could take on the world.

I didn't even draw my sword. Didn't even have to.

"Come on," said Orbaa. "There may be more on the battle-ments."

*　*　*

"We . . ."

The man was stammering, and sweating under his chain mail; he clearly didn't relish the prospect of presenting his commander with bad news.

Falk One-Eye grunted impatiently. He already knew what was going to be said, but there was value in making the man say it and demonstrating the consequences. Falk was not sweating, despite the afternoon sun and the weight of his plate—he wasn't capable of sweating anymore—but he still drummed his fingers on the haft of his battleaxe impatiently.

"We lost them, Warleader," the soldier managed to get out. "Somewhere in the village. I've got men searching now . . . we picked up their horses, but there's no sign—"

"How," Falk growled, "do you *lose* a half-dozen armed men?"

"They were excellent riders, Warleader, with good knowledge of the terrain. One of them led us into a blind alley, and it cost a few minutes to get turned around—"

Falk cuffed him on the side of the head, a heavy blow that picked the soldier up and tossed him a dozen feet to lie bleeding in the dirt. He didn't rise; the left half of his skull had been squashed like an overripe fruit.

I didn't mean to do that, Falk thought, and grimaced inside the safety of his armor. *To chastise him, perhaps.* He clenched one gauntleted fist. *No matter. It will encourage the others.* He looked up at his four remaining captains, picked the bronze helmet off the ground and tossed it to one of them.

"Choose one of the men to replace him," Falk growled.

"Yes, Warleader." The man bowed smoothly. "And what of the attackers?"

The attackers. Only a lunatic would attack a fortress like Highpoint with a handful of archers; a lunatic, or someone with an ace in the hole. *Those* lunatics *killed twenty men before we got there.* And one of them was apparently a Magus.

Falk snatched a torch from his saddlebag, lit it with a prac-ticed strike of a flint against his axe, and waved it until it burned merrily. Then he tossed it, whirling end over end, into the thatch of the nearest roof. The dry straw caught instantly, and seconds later the building was ablaze.

"They couldn't hide," he said, "without the help of someone in the town. Burn the place to the ground if you have to, but I *want them found.*"

The captain swallowed. Screams came from inside the torched house.

"I understand, Warleader."

"*And*," Falk continued, "once they are found, report in im-mediately. I will have no disappearances, understood?"

"Yes, Warleader." The captains saluted as one, then turned back to their troops. Within minutes the village was full of shouting men in groups of four or five, and the air was full of smoke and the merry crackle of burning thatch.

The peasant village on the western side of the fortress wall had always been an inconvenience, Falk mused. It had provided services to the garrison, which helped while away the long dull peaceful days, but it should never have been allowed to grow so large. *I should have had all the mercenaries rounded up and killed.* But they were always too useful . . .

He had to admit it, at least to himself. Falk One-Eye, one of an elite few chosen personally by the Archmagus Gargorian, was afraid.

Thirty years ago, he had been an ordinary man, albeit a large and ferocious one. His first taste of combat had been against Lady Fell's *auxilia*, poorly trained conscripts who were no match for Gargorian's legions. He'd cut a bloody trail through their ranks until the Second Battle of Blistering Pass, where the hard core of Gargorian's army had finally met the Lady's leg-endary Clockwork Legion. While Gargorian's men held the field afterwards, the pass was choked off by corpses.

Falk had covered himself with glory during the battle, but

the wounds he received had been mortal. Gargorian himself, walking the field afterward, had come upon the dying young man. Falk had smiled, despite the pain, and his last words were, "I regret that my service to you is at an end, Archmagus."

Something about the scene had tickled Gargorian's fancy. He had commanded that Falk be healed, and spent a day and a night personally crafting a suit of silvered armor that grafted itself to the warrior like a second skin and provided him with supernatural strength and prowess. If he still had flesh, it was buried deep under layers of steel, and the only pleasure he felt was in battle.

And then the wars had ended, and Falk had been left to amuse himself by hunting down the pathetic renegades who were trying to stop the Fifth Circle. He'd waded into every fight without fear.

Until now. He had never faced a Magus. *What magic has made, magic can unmake.* The mindless bravado he'd known in his youth had abandoned him. *I've grown soft, locked in this steel cage fighting worms.* Thirty years since he'd faced the jagged claws of the Clockwork Legion, and there had been nothing like them since.

The air was starting to grow uncomfortably hot, though Falk didn't feel it. Civilians were running for the forest; a few tried to stand in the way of his soldiers, and were butchered for their trouble. Most of the village was ablaze.

The men don't like it. Without the village, there would be no inns at which to carouse, no whores with whom to pass the lonely nights. Falk saw more than one grumbling when they thought he wasn't looking. *I don't like it either. Thirty years ago I would have stood in the gateway and dared them to come for me. Now . . .*

He shook his head with a clatter of armor.

"I want them *found*!"

"Warleader!" One of his captains pointed.

There was a small group of people making a run across the dirt square in front of the fortress. At first he thought it was another bunch of civilians, perhaps mistakenly thinking they might find shelter inside the obsidian walls; then he recognized the mailed mercenaries, and the little girls carrying bows taller than they were. And one with a sword that pulsed in his vision with a stained white light, while matching pain flared just behind his eyes.

"They're *attacking* the fortress?" someone said incredulously.

"Idiots." One of the captains chuckled. "The archers will cut them down. Falk left orders . . ."

I left orders for no one to be admitted. He stared. *They're well within bowshot by now.*

"To horse!" he screamed. "After them!" Men scrambled to obey, vaulting into their saddles and pounding after the little group without thought of formation or strategy. Falk led the charge, his huge black stallion passing the others despite his great weight, his battleaxe held out before him like a lance.

All for naught. The last of the mercenaries passed through the gate before he had made it to the square, and before he could cross the muddy field the lines securing the doors were cut. Ingeniously balanced counterweights fell, chains rattled, and the obsidian passage was blocked by several tons of wood and steel.

Falk's troops pulled up short, slowing their gallop just in time. They milled about in a confused rabble, and Falk himself had to work to stop his stallion's mad charge. He knew what would come next. Before he could rally his men, arrows flashed from the towers, men screamed and fell, and the square dissolved into bloody confusion.

"To me!" Falk shouted, riding away from the fortress and out of bowshot. His voice seemed to draw fire, which he contemptuously ignored; three arrows struck home and shattered against his enchanted plate. Gradually, his men regained control of their mounts and retreated in good order, minus six or seven left moaning in the square in front of the fortress.

"Warleader!" one of the captains shouted as he rode up. "What in Lightbringer's name is going on?"

"We've been betrayed." It was the only explanation; High-point's wall could not be breached. "There can't be many of them, or we'd have noticed their approach."

"But what do we do?"

Falk stroked his battleaxe. "Start looking for ladders. If you can't find enough, build some." *I'll kill whoever thought of this trick. Slowly, and in great pain.* But the fear remained. *There's a node of the Fourth Circle in there,* locked underneath an impenetrable dome, to be sure, *but if they have a Magus, it's not really impenetrable, is it? Whatever was made by magic can be unmade.* And if the Fourth Circle was broken, even for a few hours, the mercenaries would not be the only ones dying in great pain.

"Ladders!" Falk shouted.

chapter five

FAH HAD BEEN HELPING LINA WALK, EVER SINCE THEY'D left the horses but she'd had to manage the last run by herself. Lina collapsed almost as soon as she was clear of the gate, the cut on her thigh pulsing white-hot daggers up and down her leg. Fah rushed to her side immediately.

"Magus! Are you . . . ?"

Lina wanted to scream. She couldn't think of any good reason not to, so she cut loose with a shriek that squeezed tears from her eyes. Afterward, when Fah stepped forward again, Lina said, "I'm . . . I'm okay. In pain. Running hurts."

"I'm sorry." Fah shook her head. "It was the only way—"

"Fine. It's fine." Lina took a deep breath. "Find Sylph. Make sure she's okay. Please?"

Fah nodded and ran toward the black glass towers. Lina lay on her back, staring straight up with her hands tight around the wound. The pain was just beginning to subside.

"Lay her down," said someone nearby. Lina turned to find Garot and Daana carrying Melfina, though it hardly took both of them to hold the girl's tiny frame. They put her down carefully; her arms flopped limp and nerveless, and her eyes were closed. Lina's throat felt choked.

"Is she . . . ?"

"Not yet," said Daana without looking up. "Garot, lend me

your sharp knife. The head's still in there, and I can't force it through."

"You're just going to cut it out?" Lina said.

"It's grating when she breathes. If I leave it in she'll be dead within the hour."

"But . . ." *No anesthesia. No* sterilization, *nothing. You're just going to cut it out, here in the yard? We really are in the dark ages*, Lina realized. She closed her hands a bit tighter around her own cut. *This could get infected. They might have to chop off my leg, or . . .*

Christ! There's a little girl dying *over there, and that's all you can think about?*

She looked over in time to see Daana cut Melfina's tunic down the side and toss it away, baring her chest for all the world to see. *She doesn't even have* breasts *yet, and she's going to die—*

"Lina!" Sylph came running across the yard. "Lina, are you okay?"

Yahvy followed her at a jog but broke into a run when she saw Melfina. "White Lady. Mel!" She dropped to her knees, just short of Daana. "What . . . ?"

"Shh!" Daana was sweating. "Quiet!"

"Lina!" said Sylph. Lina, who had been watching the surgery, turned to her sister.

"I'm okay. Just a scratch." Sylph looked upside down, but uninjured. "How was the plan?"

"I'm still alive, so it must have worked." Sylph knelt by Lina's side and nodded at Melfina and her anxious bystanders. "What happened?"

"They decided to shoot at us for a while before sending the cavalry out." Lina closed her eyes. "Sylph, they were burning the town. Killing everyone."

"I know. We could see from the towers." Sylph put her hand on her sister's forehead. "There was nothing you could do."

But it's my fault. Lina didn't say it. Sylph dug through her pouches until she came up with a strip of bandage, gently moving her sister's hands aside and pulling it tight around her leg.

"That'll do for a bit. I'm going to want to clean that out later."

"You should look at Melfina."

"Daana's better at this sort of thing than I am, I'd imagine." Sylph took a deep breath and hugged Lina fiercely. Lina hugged her back as best she could, lying on the ground.

"I'm glad you didn't die," Lina whispered.

"Me, too." Sylph pulled away, and they both laughed a little. There was a flurry of movement near Melfina, and Sylph looked up.

"What's happening?"

"Daana got the arrow out," said Garot. "They're wrapping her up now."

"Do you think she's going to die?"

"I have no idea." Sylph shivered. "Maybe. No antibiotics or anything." She glanced down and must have caught Lina's worried look, because she continued, "I'm sure we can come up with some substitute for you."

"I'll be fine," Lina repeated, hoping that repetition could make it true.

"What about Heraan? Is he okay?"

"Yeah." The mercenary captain had gone straight up to the battlements, where most of his men were waiting with their short-bows to discourage Gargorian's soldiers from rushing the gates.

"Good." Sylph caught Lina's look again, and said, "We need him. He's the closest thing we've got to a professional."

"Yeah."

"Sylph!" a male voice called from across the yard. Lina turned her head and saw Vhaal. "The barracks are clear."

Sylph looked a little ill, but said, "Any problems?"

"Nothing I couldn't handle." Lina could *hear* him swagger. "There was a door I couldn't open, but I don't think anyone was inside. Everyone alive over here?"

"I counted Heraan's men and came up one short. And . . ." Sylph nodded at Melfina.

Vhaal looked and shrugged. "I'm surprised someone wasted

an arrow on our little stray cat."

"Shut the *fuck* up," said Yahvy, jumping to her feet. "If you say one more *gods*damned word I swear I'm going to castrate you and leave you for the crows."

Vhaal's hands dropped to his swords. "You talk a lot, don't you?"

"I'll show you talk—"

"Stop it!" said Fah, hurrying back. "Lady preserve us! There's an *army* outside the wall, if you haven't noticed."

Vhaal shrugged and let his hands fall. Yahvy nailed him with a killer glare, which he ignored.

"What's past the barracks, on the east side?" said Fah.

"Nothing." Vhaal shook his head. "The road, going down through the pass to Bleloth. No wall, no defenses."

"It figures," said Sylph. "If I were Gargorian I wouldn't want a place like this being used against me."

"Fah?" Daana broke in. "She needs to be somewhere warm. Is that barracks safe?"

"Vhaal?"

"Yeah, I was just there."

"Come on," said Sylph. "Can you walk, if I help you?"

Lina gritted her teeth. "Probably."

✳   ✳   ✳

SYLPH GOT LINA SETTLED IN WHAT HAD BEEN THE BARRACKS common room, next to a roaring fire Garot and Yahvy had built by the simple expedient of breaking furniture until they had enough wood and kindling. She managed to steal a moment of Daana's time, and was again reassured that Lina's wound was nothing to worry about. Then she went in search of Heraan.

The barracks was very simply designed—a common room at the front, then sleeping quarters, then a corridor leading to what were probably private rooms for the officers. There were four or five bodies in the sleeping quarters, two still in their bunks. They were unarmed and unarmored, but looked like soldiers. Sylph hoped they had been soldiers; the thought of Vhaal slaughtering helpless servants or cripples was not exactly appealing. She moved through that room quickly and found the mercenary leader in the corridor beyond, coming out of one of the smaller chambers.

"Heraan! I've been looking for you."

He nodded. "Just looking for anything useful."

"Did everything go okay out there?"

"Aside from them getting a chance to shoot at us before we ran for it." He sighed. "Is the kid going to live?"

"I think so," Sylph said, with more optimism then she felt. "Daana's still working on her."

"And your sister?"

"She'll be fine."

"Good." He broke into a lopsided smile. "We took the fortress at Highpoint with, what, twenty men?"

Sylph chuckled weakly. "We haven't really taken it yet. They're still out there."

"And I imagine old One-Eye is pretty irritated right now."

"One-Eye?"

"Falk One-Eye, the garrison commander. One of Gargorian's elites. He wears a suit of magic armor, I'm told, and supposedly no normal man can stand against him."

"Great." Sylph shivered.

"I wouldn't worry about him," he said, and clapped her lightly on the shoulder. "Not unless he's got wings. We've got forty feet of obsidian between them and us."

"Not good enough." She shook her head. "Heraan, we don't really have enough people to man the wall."

"My men are out there now."

"Your men are going to need to sleep, and then what? And what are we going to do when they come at us with ladders or grappling hooks or whatever else they can find?"

Heraan shrugged. "I kind of assumed we wouldn't be hanging

around. It'll be a while before they can manage any of that; plenty of time to slip out the back."

"And then what?"

His expression made it clear he hadn't thought that far ahead. Sylph shook her head again.

"Never mind. Did you find anything?"

"Not really. A little bit of coin. I'll save a cut for you and your friends."

Good. Heraan's men were mercenaries; a little loot would help keep them loyal. "Don't worry about me and Lina. I'm not in this for the money."

"Neither are we," he reminded her. "This is crazy, remember?"

"Right." She looked around; all the doors were open but one, a heavy iron-banded slab of oak at the end of the hall. "What's in there?"

"Not sure. It's locked. Treasury, maybe? I can get the boys to take an axe to it when we get a moment."

"I'm not sure that would help." The door looked remarkably solid. *I'm sure they'd get it down eventually, but you could wear out a dozen axes against that iron.* But there was something about it that looked—*felt*—familiar. "Let me take a look."

Heraan stood wordlessly while Sylph went up to the door and put her hand against it. She didn't feel anything special, not at first, but there was an odd tingle at the ends of her fingers. *Just like before.* Sylph closed her eyes. She could hardly feel the door itself, layers of iron and hardwood, but there was something behind it. *A bar, or something, locking it into the wall.* She pushed and felt no give at all, but it was almost as though her hand went *through* the barrier until she grabbed the bar beyond. Sylph hastily opened her eyes to make sure her hand was still there, and in the process lost the feeling. She took a deep breath and started over.

Okay. What am I really doing here? It was hard to say, exactly; it was like seeing with her fingertips, looking deep into things until she could see their most basic nature. *I wonder why it doesn't work on the door itself?* She could only feel the bar, which she realized was a single carbon crystal, impossibly large and regular. *A diamond. Who would use a diamond to bar a door?*

And, like before, she could feel the edge. *Just a little pull, and the whole thing falls apart.*

This time there was nothing to see. Sylph opened her eyes and gave the door a push; it ground inward a quarter of a inch, hinges groaning from years of neglect.

"Heraan, help me with this?"

"Wait a minute." He frowned. "I could have sworn that door was—"

"Just help me."

He nodded and put his shoulder into it. Together they managed to move it a couple of feet before the hinges seized up entirely; that was enough to squeeze into the space beyond.

There were no windows, but the tiny stone room was lit from within by an arcane glow, flickering from blue to green and back again and throwing weird shadows on the wall. Heraan made an odd gesture as soon as he saw it, pressing two fingers of his right hand against his heart.

In the center of the room, hovering a few inches off the floor without visible support, was a glass globe the size of a basketball. The source of the glow was inside, a dozen or more tiny points of green and blue light that circled one another in shifting, unpredictable orbits. Sylph felt her mouth hanging open, and closed it firmly. Both of them stood and stared for a moment.

Magic. It was one thing to be told that it exists, even to see evidence—*if Lina's sword isn't magic, I don't know what is*—but that didn't have the eldritch weirdness of something like this. Sylph's skin broke out in goose bumps, and she shivered.

"What is *that*?" Heraan breathed.

"I . . . can take a guess." Sylph swallowed. "Highpoint marks the boundary of Gargorian's Fourth Circle, right?"

"Yeah . . ." He stopped. "You think this is part of it?"

"He has to build something around the Circles, right? I think this is one of the nodes."

"I've never heard of anything like it. He built the Circles through towns and fortresses, but no one's ever seen something like this."

"I imagine he keeps people away." Sylph took a deep breath. "This one was pretty well protected."

"Yeah." He shot her an odd look, but didn't press the matter, much to her relief. "What do we do with it?"

"I'm not sure." Sylph reached out a hand.

"Be careful."

She nodded, mouth dry, and laid her hand on the surface of the globe . . .

*   *   *

. . . IT WAS A WHIRLPOOL, A WIND-CHOPPED OCEAN UNDER an utterly black sky that spat thunder and forks of lightning.

Sylph found herself hovering bare feet above the spray, every wave drenching her legs with foam. The ocean whirled round, rippling like the walls of a tornado or water in a draining bath. But this was larger, unimaginably larger, so big she couldn't see the other side. And the center was definitely lower then the edges, as if the ocean itself were draining away into infinity.

Over the waves and the lightning, it took Sylph a moment to hear the screams.

There are people in the water . . .

Dozens of people. Hundreds. Bobbing heads as far as the eye could see, gasping for air and shrieking at the top of their lungs as they spun into the abyss. Other things, too. She caught a glimpse of something large and green, swimming powerfully but unable to fight the current. An eye larger than she was blinked once, on the edge of the central funnel, then disappeared.

What's in the center?

Hunger. She felt it, something that drank and drank and

could drink the whole ocean and not be satisfied. She felt it shift, turn its attention toward her, like a spider reacting to its web being shaken by a doomed fly. She felt it . . .

. . . AND SYLPH RAISED HER HAND, SHAKING VIOLENTLY.

"Are you all right?" Heraan took her shoulder. "Sylph?"

"I . . ." She licked her lips. "I just saw . . ."

"What?"

"The Circle, I think." She groped at her side. "Stand back."

"What are you . . . ?"

He scrambled out of the way as Sylph drew her sword, clumsily. Before Heraan could shout she swung it at the center of the glass globe. There was a high-pitched whine, a moment of strained space, and the air rippled and distorted. Then, with a last flash of green and purple, it was gone. Shards of glass rained to the floor.

There was a long silence.

"Sylph," said Heraan, "what did you just do?"

"I'm not sure." Sylph let out a long breath and carefully sheathed her sword. "The right thing, I hope."

TAK TAK TAK TAK TAK TAK TAK TAK TAK TAK.

The floor of the Diamond Tower was elaborately decorated marble, an abstract swirl of black and white polished to a fine sheen. Vesh, the Keeper of the Tower, had taken to wearing metal-toed boots; he was fond of the sound they made when he walked, like the perfectly regular tick of one of Lady Fell's clocks. It also meant that any listeners could tell when Vesh was nervous by paying attention to his pace; since Vesh's moods usually corresponded to his master's, it helped give the other denizens of the Tower fair warning.

Tak tak tak tak taktaktaktaktaktaktak . . .

"*Vesh!*" boomed the Archmagus, clearly audible in every room of the Tower. Ringing echoes filled the silence that followed. Vesh skidded around the corner so fast he practically raised sparks, went through the huge double doors at a run, and flopped to his knees in the august presence of the Archmagus Gargorian, Lord of the Western Rim, Magio Creator, and Master of the Diamond Tower. Vesh's brilliant crimson robe flopped down around his ears as he bowed his head.

"Vesh," Gargorian rumbled. "Rise."

The Keeper obeyed. Gargorian shifted his bulk on the diamond throne and looked down at him with red, piggy eyes. The Archmagus was a huge, wheezing mass draped in velvet and silk. His hair was braided into many tails, each of which was adorned with a dangling, clinking mass of gold ornaments. A short, bristly black beard did little to hide his wobbling chin.

To his left sat the Magus Rathmado, a thin, well-dressed character of uncertain provenance. No one seemed to be quite sure where he'd come from, but he'd risen high in Gargorian's confidence over the past year and was now privy to the Archmagus's innermost councils. At first Vesh had feared that the foreigner was after his position, but Rathmado had demonstrated a singular disinterest in court politics. Why Gargorian kept him around was frankly baffling, but it did not do to question the Archmagus.

Diamond Guards lined both walls of the room, for appearances more than anything else; no potential assassin could get this close to the Archmagus. Though they did have a secondary function, when it amused Gargorian to call on them.

Vesh glanced nervously at the soldiers with their glittering armor and their heavy axes, then back to his lord. Gargorian remained silent, obviously enjoying watching the Keeper squirm, but finally he waved a hand.

"Get out, all of you."

The guards filed away, filling the room with the sinister click of crystal. When they were gone, and the double door sealed behind them, the Archmagus leaned forward.

"Vesh," he said, "I don't suppose you have an explanation."

"My lord . . ." Vesh's lip twisted unhappily. "I'm afraid the facts only admit of one, my lord."

"Facts? My Fourth Circle has been broken; that is the only *fact* available to us. The gathering of *facts* falls under your purview, does it not?"

It did. The Keeper of the Tower, among many other responsibilities, was responsible for keeping the Archmagus informed of everything of import that went on in his domain. Gargorian had ruled, ageless and undying, for more than six hundred years; in that time he had gone through two dozen Keepers. As far as Vesh knew, none of them had died of natural causes. But the position was the pinnacle of power, as high as someone could rise under the iron hand of the Archmagus.

"My lord, I can only assume the involvement of one of the other Archmagi. Lady Fell, for a certainty, or an agent of Vilvakis."

"An odd choice for sabotage, wouldn't you say?" said Rathmado genially. "They can't hope to hold on to the node, after all, and we will have a replacement in a week or less. An inconvenience, but hardly worth the life of an agent."

"And we can assume," Gargorian rumbled, "that whoever did this did not get away with it?"

"Of course," said Vesh, sweating. "I have the utmost confidence in Warleader Falk."

"Who allowed this to happen in the first place." Rathmado put his chin in his hands. "Interesting."

Enough, Vesh decided, was enough. "My lord, is it entirely wise that he be here?"

Gargorian smiled, his flesh rippling. "Entirely, Vesh. Rathmado, tell him what you told me."

Magus Rathmado cleared his throat. "The seventh Liberator has arrived."

The was a long silence.

"What?" said Vesh eventually.

"The seventh Liberator," Rathmado repeated patiently. "She has arrived to destroy the tyrannical Archmagi and free the lands from bondage, et cetera, et cetera."

"Did you say *she*?"

"Indeed. This Liberator is a woman."

"A girl, really." Gargorian shook his head, braids jingling.

"How do you know this?" said Vesh.

"I have my methods," said Rathmado haughtily.

"Really, my lord—"

"His word is not for you to question," the Archmagus said. "I believe him, and that is enough. The Liberator is responsible for the failure of the Fourth Circle. I want her crushed, Vesh. Take the Second Army and see to it."

Rathmado smiled. Vesh bowed again, gritting his teeth. "As you wish, of course."

"And Vesh . . ."

"Yes, my lord?"

Gargorian licked his lips. "Bring her to me alive, if possible."

"As you wish, my lord."

✳   ✳   ✳

"Magus," Fah said quietly. Lina's eyes snapped open and she shook herself out of a light doze, already dreading whatever the news was.

"What?"

Fah looked taken aback. "I was just wondering if you were hungry."

Thank God. Hopefully that means nothing horrible has happened. "Starved, actually."

"Let me help you up."

Lina leaned on the smaller girl's shoulder, noticing as she did that someone—*probably Daana*—had re-bandaged the cut on her leg. The pain was much more tolerable. They passed Melfina, who was curled up next to the fire and heavily wrapped in blankets.

"Is she going to be okay?" Lina whispered.

"If her wounds don't become inflamed, Daana thinks so."

"That's good to hear." Melfina was an odd little girl, but the idea of watching her die made Lina shiver.

"Through here."

Lina limped through a doorway and into what had been an officer's private quarters. There was a table, which was laden with food presumably raided from the barrack's storehouse. Cold meat, grapes, bread, and flagons of water looked like an absolute feast to Lina after the last couple of days, and she dug in with a will. Fah smiled and sat down next to her, pouring herself a glass of water but otherwise abstaining. Lina paused, a slice of meat in one hand and her cup in the other, and said, "Don't you want some?"

"I ate before I woke you."

"Good enough for me," said Lina. She went back to eating and kept it up until she started to feel stuffed, then gulped down a whole cup of water and sat back, refreshed. There was a pause, during which Fah did nothing but stare; she'd been doing it the whole meal, and Lina was beginning to feel uncomfortable.

"What? You're looking at me like I've grown wings or something." She checked, quickly, to make sure she hadn't. *You never know around here.*

"Magus . . ." Fah hesitated.

"Please don't call me that." Lina shook her head. "It's not like that. I just—"

"You come out of the west," said Fah. "Like Jaen. You've declared war on Gargorian, all alone."

"Not declared *war* so much as, well . . ." Lina remembered Sylph's "simple" solution. *I guess we* have *declared war. At least, it's him or us.*

"And you destroy the enemy with the slightest sweep of

your sword."

Irrationally, Lina felt her ears burning. She'd never been comfortable with praise—*I never thought I'd hear myself being described as a great warrior*—

"Sylph comes up with the plans. I just do what she says."

"Lina," Fah said firmly, "you are the Liberator."

"The what?"

"The Liberator. Someone sent to free the world from the rule of the Archmagi. A holy woman."

Sylph mentioned this. "You've got to be kidding."

"Of course not!" Fah looked like the very thought scandalized her. "Magus, you have no idea what this means to us."

"Fah, listen for a second. I'm just a normal person. Just like you. Well . . ." Lina recalled that Fah had abandoned her home to fight a suicidal battle. "Maybe not like you. Not as brave, not as strong, not as *anything*. But I'm not holy and I certainly haven't been sent by anyone."

Haven't I? whispered a sly voice in the back of her mind. *What are we doing here, anyway? Someone* gave *me the sword, I said it myself. Someone made sure we were in the right place at the right time, made sure we found Fah, made sure . . .*

That's just paranoia. Reverse paranoia, maybe? What's it called when there's someone secretly looking out for you? But the minute I start relying on that, I'm dead. That, in Lina's experience, was how the world worked.

Fah just smiled. "You *are* the Liberator, Lina. You took Highpoint with twenty men. Did you know the fortress had never fallen until today?"

"Heraan told us about the secret passage. And Sylph and the others actually took the place."

"The sooner you accept it," Fah said serenely, "the better off we're going to be. The legend of the last Liberator runs deep around here. Gargorian remembers, for certain, and he won't take this lightly."

"I think we have other things to worry about first."

As though the words had been a summons, Garot burst into the room.

"They're coming."

* * *

IT WAS GETTING ON TOWARD EVENING AND THE SUN DREW Falk's men as long shadows against the wall. Lina shaded her eyes and counted four crude ladders made of raw timber and boards and lashed together with whatever the soldiers had been able to find. Eight men carried each one, and another score rushed forward and dropped to one knee, aiming short-bows at the defenders on the walls.

Heraan's men fired back, and soon the air was full of the *zip* of arrows and the *crack* of metal on stone. The range was long for the small bows both sets of soldiers carried, and Heraan's men were protected by a waist-high lip of obsidian at the top of the wall or the arrow slits in the towers. On the other hand, the attackers wore heavier armor and had twice as many bows, forcing their opponents to keep their heads down much of the time. The ladders closed with the wall as the archery duel continued.

Fah pounded up the steps two at a time, reached the top of the wall and then dropped flat behind the protective lip as arrows sailed overhead. Lina climbed up more slowly, favoring her good leg. Below, Garot grunted as he bent and strung a longbow, then tossed it up to Fah. She caught it, drew an arrow from her quiver, and leaned briefly over the battlement. The bow *thrummed*, and one of the approaching soldiers flopped to the ground. The girl dropped back as Falk's men replied.

Lina was impressed in spite of herself. Fah moved like she knew what she was doing. Garot strung another bow and handed it to Daana, who had come running out of the barracks; she took it with one hand, pressed herself against him, and gave him a kiss that lasted so long Lina felt like she had to look away. Garot eventually detached himself and bent his own bow, and

Daana climbed to a position on the walls. Lina checked her scabbard and made sure the sword was in place, in case Falk's men reached the rampart.

It quickly became obvious that this was not going to happen. The three Circle Breakers were taking a murderous toll; their arrows carried immense force at such close range, and they had the advantage of cover. Heraan's men concentrated their fire on the ladder-bearers as they approached, and before long Falk's soldiers were retreating from the field in good order, taking their wounded with them but leaving behind a dozen bodies.

Sylph, Yahvy, and Heraan came up to the rampart only after the action was over. Sylph put her hands on the wall and stared over, then turned to Fah and said, "How many?"

Fah blinked. "What?"

"How many were there?"

"Fifty, maybe?" said Orbaa from the wall. "Could be a bit less."

"Falk should have a good hundred-and-twenty men left," said Heraan. "Maybe some of them deserted?"

Fah nodded slowly. "And where was he? From the stories I've heard he doesn't sound like the type to lead from the rear."

"Just a test," Sylph said. "He knows we can't afford to ignore him, but he didn't know how many men we have. Now he does." She looked up. "Anyone hurt?"

The call went up and down the wall, and came back negative. Chain-mail shirts and obsidian had protected the defenders from Falk's arrows.

"Good." Sylph glanced at the sun, which was almost touching the horizon. "I want everyone to get as much rest as they can."

"You think he'll attack again today?" said Fah.

"Tonight. He'll come over the walls in the dark." She shook her head. "I would."

✳   ✳   ✳

"How many?" Falk rumbled.

"A dozen, if that," his captain said, kneeling on the ash-stained ground.

If I'd known we were going to have to stay out here, I wouldn't have been so quick to burn the place. There wasn't much food left, and his soldiers were getting hungry. *We're taking that wall tonight, or we're going to die trying.* He shifted his grip on his battleaxe.

"A dozen?"

"They were excellent archers, Warleader. Most likely the Circle Breakers Warleader Vantz wrote of."

Falk grunted. "Distribute whatever food we've got to the men. No alcohol. And make sure everyone knows the plan; over the wall and *take that gate.* Understood?"

"Yes, Warleader." The captain hesitated. "What about the Magus?"

Falk shouldered his axe with a clatter of armor. "Tell them to leave the Magus to me."

✳   ✳   ✳

"Vhaal?"

"Yes?" Vhaal looked up from where he was lying on an officer's bed, hands behind his head. "Oh, it's our little general. How did the battle go?"

"We're still alive," said Sylph, edging into the room. "The question is, where were you?"

"Right here, taking a well-deserved nap."

"Vhaal . . ."

"You know any sane commander would wait for dark. Falk may not be quite sane, but he's no fool. It follows that this attack was a diversion, and I can't be bothered with shooting sticks at people."

"What if they'd made it over the wall?"

He smiled thinly. "I'd have been very disappointed in you. But that's neither here nor there, is it?"

There was a pause. Sylph stared at him, steadily, and the

attention seemed to discomfit the boy. He sat up with a sigh and said, "Anything else? Perhaps you want me to service you before the battle?"

Sylph did her best to keep a straight face, and not to blush. "Why, Vhaal?"

"Well, because you're supposed to enjoy it."

"Why did you join the Circle Breakers?"

His eyes narrowed. "Why the sudden curiosity?"

"I'm your little general, and I like to know the men under my command."

"First of all," Vhaal said, "I am *not* under your command. I happen to be helping you because I have as little love for Gargorian as any of the others, but don't make the mistake of thinking I'm on your side."

"Not likely."

"Good. And second, if you must know, it was boredom."

"Oh?"

"Killing people it just about the only thing that really relaxes me." He yawned. "I killed my first man—boy, I suppose—when I was fifteen." Vhaal's smiled turned wicked. "Afterward I found his house and it turned out he had two younger sisters waiting for him to come back. So I took them and—"

"Stop," said Sylph, her fists clenching involuntarily.

Vhaal shrugged. "You asked."

She spun on her heel and walked back into the common room. *Well, that was a mistake.* She'd thought she could sound him out—*since we're certainly going to need him*—but there seemed to be nothing to the boy but venom and bravado. She wondered if the story about the man and his sisters was true, or if he'd made it up on the spot to irritate her. *Neither would surprise me.*

The sun had sunk, first below the wall and then below the horizon. Almost everyone was in the barracks, lying in the bunks with their eyes closed at Sylph's suggestion, but she doubted if any of them were actually asleep. Lina certainly wasn't; she kept tossing and turning, trying to find a comfortable way to rest with the bandage on her leg. Sylph passed through the barracks quietly and made her way to the wall, where two of Heraan's men were keeping watch. Every half hour or so, they tossed another burning brand into the square. *At least it's not such a wide area to defend. They're not going to be able to sneak up on us.*

Heraan himself materialized from the darkness at the base of the wall and nodded to her.

"Couldn't sleep?" said Sylph.

"Of course not." He laughed. "I've never been able to sleep before a battle. Not a great trait for a soldier. Did you talk to Vhaal?"

"Yeah."

"And? Will he fight?"

She sighed. "Probably."

"Great." He shook his head. "Falk is going to have our heads on pikes by morning."

"Smaller armies than this have defended walls."

"Once in a while. More often they die, and nobody hears about it."

"You seem remarkably cheerful, considering," Sylph said.

"Ha." He shrugged. "Even if my mind is sure we're going to die, my body won't believe it."

"Maybe Lina will pull off another miracle."

His face went suddenly serious. "There is that."

"What's wrong?"

"I was just thinking. If she really is the Liberator, she'll win this fight. And if she dies here, she's not the Liberator. It'd just be nice if I had a way of finding out without ending up on the spike next to her."

Sylph smiled. "We're not going to end up on spikes, Heraan."

"Oh? You have a plan."

"I have a plan." She shrugged. "But mostly I don't think Falk could get any spikes into that obsidian wall. More likely we'd be drawn and quartered."

This time he laughed. "I've said this before, but . . ."

"You're crazy?"

Their shared smile lasted for only a moment, broken by a cry from above.

"Here they come!"

Sylph barely remembered scrambling to the top of wall; it seemed like she blinked and was looking down at the blood-stained square of the demolished town, lit only by the burning brand. Shadowy figures were sprinting for the wall, casting long, twisting shadows, first a few at a time, then a whole group together with a ladder. In the darkness it seemed like there were hundreds of them.

"Up!" Heraan was screaming. "Everyone on the wall! Don't let them get those ladders up!"

There was a rush of people from inside the fortress, Heraan's men and the Circle Breakers together. The two men already on the wall were firing into the darkness, but it was impossible to see if there was any effect. *At least they're not shooting back this time.* The first of the ladders had almost reached the base of the wall. *In fact . . .*

"There!" Sylph pointed. The top of a ladder had just appeared. Heraan and one of his men rushed to the spot just as an armored soldier put his hand on the top of the wall. Heraan kicked him in the face and sent the ladder tumbling backward with a hard shove. Something flashed up from below—an arrow—but it skittered against the wall and spun into oblivion.

"Over here!" someone yelled—it sounded like Yahvy—and there was the sound of steel ringing on steel, too far off for Sylph to see in the gloom. A moment later a descending shriek and a thud revealed another ladder had been pushed from the wall.

It's not going to work. We don't have enough men. Sylph's heart sank. The defenders were concentrated around the gate and the towers, and it was hard for the ladders to get a foothold, but there was plenty of wall for them to scale and not enough people to walk it. *They've got to be getting up on either side.*

Heraan had apparently had the same thought. "Orbaa,

Gaav, Corian, with me! I'll make sure the north side is clear."
The four of them charged off into the darkness. Sylph looked
back into the fortress and saw Lina making her painful way to
the top of the wall, followed by Fah. Back at the barracks, Vhaal
had emerged, spreading his arms in a leisurely stretch before
sauntering to the stairway.

"Another one!" shouted one of the men Heraan had left
behind. A moment later it turned into a scream, as a gauntleted
hand reached over the parapet and grabbed him by the ankle,
yanking hard enough to send him toppling over the edge into
the milling mass of enemies forty feet below. The soldier scrambled to the top of the wall; Fah met him with blade in hand, and
sparks flew. Suddenly Garot appeared from the darkness, and as
the attacker turned to meet this new threat Fah kicked him in the
stomach and sent him staggering backward into empty space.

The ladder. Sylph darted forward, drawing her sword but not
entirely sure what to do with it. She reached out for the wooden
spars, but before she got there another snarling face appeared
over the obsidian lip. She thrust with the sword, purely on re-
flex, and the point went into his cheek and buried itself in the
back of his skull. Blood welled, and the shock of impact made
her squeak and drop the blade. She cursed at herself. *You sound
like a little girl!* Luckily the man gurgled and lost his grip on the
ladder, falling backward, and the next moment Fah and Garot
grabbed the spars of the ladder together and tossed it back into
the night.

Sylph giggled hysterically when she realized the man had
taken her sword with him. *It wasn't much good anyway.*

"Garot!" someone screamed. *Daana.* She was backing
away on the south side of their little island of light, dueling with
one of Falk's men while a half-dozen more pressed behind. *They
must have gotten a ladder up on the south wall.* There wasn't room
for more than one to attack, but Daana was overmatched; before Sylph could react she took a cut to her off-arm and tripped.
The soldier gave her a casual boot to the shoulder to roll her

out of the way, down into the courtyard. Her scream ended in a dull thud.

"Daana!" Garot rushed forward, but a black-cloaked figure blocked his path. Vhaal was smiling, hands on his swords, walking to meet Falk's men as if he was headed to a night on the town. Garot moved to push past him, but Sylph had enough presence of mind to catch his shoulder.

"Garot! Go help Daana!"

He nodded and sprinted for the stairway. Fah had caught another ladder before it could get a foothold on the wall, spitted one of the men, and kicked it away. The leader of the little group from the south lifted his blade and screamed something unintelligible, then charged Vhaal.

Sylph gaped. She'd never seen anyone move so fast. Vhaal's swords flashed from their sheathes when the soldier was half a step away, slicing him twice across the midsection. The man was moving too quickly to stop, but the boy simply dipped a shoulder and slipped him neatly off the wall. Then he sprang at the others, batting aside the wavering blade of the first and sinking a sword into his stomach before chopping his legs out from under him with a kick. As the soldier toppled with a roar, Vhaal sprang up and impaled the next man under his jaw. He died, silently, and the two remaining soldiers hurriedly backed away.

Unbelievable. Sylph shook her head. *How does he do that?*

"Sylph!" Lina had finally made it to the top of the wall. "Are you okay?"

"We're not going to hold it," Sylph said. "Lina, we've got to get out of here. I was wrong, we can't keep them off!"

"We can't leave everyone!"

"If we don't we're going to get killed!"

Lina set her jaw and drew her sword, smooth metal glittering in the flickering light. *The sword.* A few swings of that might buy some time, but Sylph had seen how exhausted Lina was after only a couple of seconds. *There's too many of them, and they're not going to run. It's not going to work this time.*

There was a metallic clank as a heavy gauntlet grabbed the edge of the obsidian wall.

✳   ✳   ✳

LINA SPUN AT THE SOUND, SWORD RAISED, AND FOUND HER-self facing a man in a full suit of silver armor, covered from head to toe. One hand held a short-hafted battle axe, with a pair of blades like steel crescents. She recognized him as the one who'd led the charge, at the beginning of the fighting in the morning. *What did Heraan call him? "Old Falk One-Eye"?*

Whoever he was, Fah and the others did not intend to give him purchase on the wall. She and one of Heraan's men stepped forward, swinging at his head and chest. The armored figure ignored the blows, which ricocheted harmlessly off his silver pro-tection, and bulled forward. He flat-palmed Fah in the chest with a sound like a sack of meat hitting the floor, knocking the wind out of her and leaving her reeling on the edge of the wall. Lina darted in and snatched at her flailing hand, drawing the gasping Circle Breaker back from the brink. In the meantime, Falk spun and bashed the mercenary's parry aside by sheer force, the axe cutting his torso nearly in half and sending his broken body to plummet to ground outside.

Lina took a deep breath and let go of Fah. *Showtime.* Before Falk could turn, she swung the sword.

The familiar flash of white light enveloped him, but Lina could feel almost immediately that something was wrong. The sword's normal background hum flickered and intensified, like a car whose engine was failing, and the solid ball of white resolved into a mass of tiny lightning bolts, crawling all over Falk's silver armor. *Like insects*, Lina thought, *looking for a way in.*

They didn't find one. Within seconds the brilliant energy had dissipated, leaving only green and purple afterimages. Falk still stood, his armor steaming in the chill night air; a big chunk of the obsidian rampart behind him had been obliterated.

Oh, Lina thought, surprisingly calm. *It didn't work.*

Then Falk raised his axe, and her calm evaporated. *Oh, shit!* He swung it a horizontal arc, and Lina held out her sword as a kind of prayer, without expecting it to actually stop anything. *Shit, shit, I'm gonna die . . .*

Instead there was the ringing impact of steel on steel, and Lina felt her arm shiver under the strength of the blow. The sword's hum redoubled, and she felt it traveling up her arm. It was a creepy sensation, as though it was a living *thing* at the end of her arm sending invisible tendrils into her core, and Lina tried desperately to block it out. Somewhat to her surprise, that seemed to work, and the hum subsided.

What the hell is going on?

The parry had taken Falk by surprise, but she'd been too busy to riposte. He feinted left, and she swung her sword clumsily to parry; it missed by half a foot, and Lina had to step backward to avoid his next swing. The hum from the sword redoubled, so strong it made her teeth chatter. *It's almost like it's trying to say something.*

Let me. The words were suddenly clear, in the midst of the vibration. *Let me.*

Falk raised his axe for a blow she knew she would never stop, and there was nowhere left to run; she felt the edge of the wall under her foot.

Let me. Let me.

Lina wanted to scream. *Fine!* And she let go.

"LINA!" SYLPH SCREAMED.

Her sister paused, on the very lip of oblivion, as Falk raised his axe over his head for the finishing blow. Sylph rushed forward—*to do what, I don't know*—her sword was gone, and she didn't have the time to draw a knife from her belt. *Maybe I can distract him*—

The axe came down before she could get there. *Lina!*

There was the scream of tortured metal, and the axe crashed into the obsidian. Lina spun to one side, her sword sliding smoothly from parry to attack. In less than a second she rang blows off of Falk's helmet, arm, and midriff, white energy wreathing the sword in crackling flame. Falk staggered backward, but was apparently unharmed; he swung his axe in horizontal sweeps to keep her away, then returned to the offensive. Lina parried, nimbly slipping to the side when she was unable to deflect the full force of the blow. She hit him again, with similar lack of effect.

What the hell is going on? Sylph shook her head. *Where did Lina learn to fight?*

It doesn't matter! Magic or not, she can't hurt that thing.

The sounds of fighting had nearly stopped elsewhere, as both sides watched the duel. Falk pressed on with a tireless strength, and Lina's attacks were getting more desperate. *She's still going to lose.*

Sylph blinked. *Unless . . .*

She ran forward and laid a hand on the back of the armored figure. *Quickly, quickly*—the tangled weave of metal armor, somehow melded into the flesh beneath—*there it is*—the trailing end that would unravel the whole . . .

Sylph pulled, and Falk screamed, high and inhuman. His armor shifted and rippled like quicksilver. In that moment, Lina struck. The sword flashed white fire, cutting through with a horrible ease, and his entire body dissolved in crackling white lightning that left nothing behind but dust.

What followed was a long and pregnant silence. Lina was breathing hard, but her sword was still raised. Sylph took a step back from Falk's smoking remains, shivering.

It was Fah who first regained her presence of mind. She held up her sword and shouted:

"She is the *Liberator*!"

chapter six

UMBRELLAS WERE APPARENTLY AN UNKNOWN TECH-
nology in the afterlife; Sylph had accepted a heavy leather
cloak and tented it over her head, but the storm was drenching
her anyway. At least it was a warm rain. And given that Sylph
hadn't expected to live long enough to see the dawn, the fact that
she couldn't actually *see* it did little to dampen her mood.

*Unbelievable. Fucking unbelievable. I just touched him, and then
Lina took him apart.* It still gave her shivers, the good kind. *We
actually beat them!*

Well, not quite. After Falk's death and Fah's spectacular decla-
ration, the battle had kind of petered out. Falk's men had pulled
back or run away, no one was really sure which, and the battered defenders were happy to let them stay out of sight. Then,
at dawn, there had been a rider with a white flag.

They want to meet. Sylph's palms were tingling. *They want to
meet. Why? A trap? It doesn't seem likely; they even agreed to stay within bowshot of the wall.* Garot and a few of Heraan's people were
up there now, being conspicuous. *Not that they'd be quick enough to
save us.* But Sylph somehow wasn't afraid. *It seems like things are
going our way.*

Yahvy, Heraan, and Vhaal accompanied her, the former
pair to help with any negotiations and the latter as a sort of
bodyguard. To Sylph's secret disappointment, Vhaal had made

it through the night without a scratch. The same could not be said for most of the others. Yahvy walked with a limp from a minor wound, Daana had broken her arm and was lucky not to have broken her neck, and a number of Heraan's people were in the barracks-turned-infirmary, or covered by blankets in the field next to it.

And me? Sylph hadn't taken any wounds, but it felt like something had changed. *I killed someone. Is that it?* That image had haunted her during her brief, exhausted sleep, the soldier clawing at his ruined face as he fell backward into the darkness.

Enough. She rubbed her eyes. *Stay alert, Sylph. Just a bit more, and then maybe I'll get a chance to nap.*

"Here they come," said Yahvy. She, Sylph, and the others were standing in what had been the town square, now a blood-stained ruin surrounded by wet ashes. Sylph was grateful Falk's men had carried away their dead before the rain turned the place into a morass of mud and puddles.

Two riders were approaching from the cover the tree line, the first carrying the same white flag he had in the morning. Once they got close, they dismounted; both were armored and, Sylph noticed, still armed. *They must not trust us, either.* She glanced over her shoulder at Garot, who waited forty feet above with an arrow at the ready.

"Hell of a day for it," said the soldier cheerfully. He approached, while his companion waited with the very unhappy looking horses. "Nearly got stuck on my way back."

He was a big man, with broad, honest features and short black hair under a bronze captain's helmet. Between his expression and his tone, Sylph felt a bit friendlier immediately; the thought that it had been men like this she'd been stabbing the previous night gave her a sudden turn.

"Hell of a day," Heraan agreed.

"My name's Captain Marlowe." He smiled wider. "Which one of you is the Liberator?"

Yahvy and Sylph looked at each other, and Yahvy nodded.

Sylph said, "She's still in the camp."

"I suppose I can't blame you." He shrugged. "Then who do I have the honor of addressing?"

"I'm the . . . the Liberator's younger sister, Sylph. This is Yahvy and Heraan, and the brooding one is Vhaal."

"I'm not brooding," Vhaal muttered, "I'm wet. And bored."

"Sisters, eh? Interesting." He took a deep breath and said, "I'm here to inform you, Sylph, that my men and I belong to the Liberator, if she'll have us."

Sylph kept her face straight with an effort. "Really. All of you?"

"We had a bit of a discussion about it last night, see. A lot of the guys from Bleloth, or the east, thought it was bull, but those of us from around here," he tapped the side of his helmet with a clank, "we know."

"And you convinced them?"

"Some," he said bluntly. "The rest won't be botherin' us anymore. Since I was the only captain left, I was kind of elected leader by default, and they sent me over to see if her ladyship needed us."

"Let me be blunt," Heraan cut in. "How can we trust you?"

"Well, that's hard to say." He scratched the side of his nose. "But burning the town, that didn't sit well. A lot of us had girls there, or friends, or what have you."

"And why should the Liberator forgive you?" asked Yahvy. "I've lost count of the number of my friends Falk and Vantz cut down."

"She doesn't have to. If she tells me to leave, I'll leave, though I can't speak for all of the boys. But we'd rather tag along."

"May I talk to my companions for a moment?" asked Sylph.

They huddled some distance from the pair, with the exception of Vhaal who stayed in a wet, miserable world of his own.

"Is it me," said Sylph, "or is everyone here crazy? Why do they keep wanting to *join* us after we kill a bunch of them?"

"Well firstly," said Yahvy, "nobody really *likes* Gargorian.

Until recently it seemed like there just wasn't any alternative, except maybe to sell out to Lady Fell. But she's even worse. And secondly, people like to be on the winning side."

"How are we the winning side? Even if we take them on, we'll have what, sixty or seventy men? How many does Gargorian have?"

"Probably six or seven hundred riders all told, plus the four field armies at two thousand infantry each. Plus anything that he doesn't make public."

"Crazy," Sylph muttered. "Heraan, do you think we can trust them?"

"You trust *me*, don't you?"

"I do after last night."

"I don't know." He shook his head. "This Marlowe seems earnest enough, but I'd be willing to bet a lot of his 'boys' just didn't like the idea of storming a fortress wall in the dark. That kind is going to go sour real fast if we can't pay them."

"We can pay them," Yahvy said, "for a while, anyway. We got ahold of Falk's treasury when we took the fortress."

"I say we take them," said Sylph impulsively. "We're going to need all the help we can get."

"Shouldn't we wait for Lina to wake up?" asked Heraan.

"Lina trusts our judgment." *Besides, I have no idea when that will be.* There didn't seem to be anything *wrong* with Lina, but she had slept—restlessly—since her duel with Falk. *The sword, of course. It leaves her drained.* Sylph hoped that was all.

LINA WAS RUNNING, NAKED, THROUGH THE SNOW.

It was a dream and she *knew* it was a dream, but that didn't seem to help. The snow was not dream-snow, all fluffy and white and not at all cold to the touch. It was the freezing, bitter North Atlantic coast snow with which she was intimately familiar, crusted over with a thin layer of ice. Every time she put her foot down it crunched, and slivers of ice raked her skin. When she dared to look behind her, she saw a trail of bloody footprints stretching back to infinity.

She was pursued, though by what she didn't know. He was there, just out of sight and waiting for her to tire. She could hear his faint, mocking laughter and feel his eyes on the back of her neck. She couldn't let him catch up, so she ran and ran.

But there was nowhere to run *to*, just an endless waste of snow and ice. Once she glimpsed something huge and black in the distance, and she turned toward it, looking for a place to hide. Before she'd gotten there it had moved away on four massive legs, thick fur heavily matted down with water and snowflakes. She hadn't pursued.

And, eventually, her strength failed her. Lina tried to put one foot in front of the other but didn't lift it high enough, catching on the jagged rim of ice. A new cut opened on her ankle, and she fell face first into the powder.

It was almost warm, with the falling snow forming a blanket across her naked back. *I could just lie here and die. It doesn't matter if you die in dreams.* But he was coming. *I have to get up . . .*

Too late. Lina rolled over to find that her pursuer had overtaken her. His black boots crunched through the snow behind Lina's bloody footprints. The man—if it was a man—was swathed head to toe in a black wool cloak, with a deep hood that hid his face in shadow. His hands were gloved in crisp black leather.

It's just a dream. *This isn't happening, not really.* She blinked and tried to focus. *It's not real!*

The figure knelt beside her in the snow. Lina wanted to jump to her feet, but her cold-numbed body refused to obey. She was suddenly absurdly aware of her nakedness. She tried to cover herself with her hands, tried to even scream, but only a thin rasp emerged and she lay as motionless as though she were already dead.

There wasn't even the outline of a face under the shadow of

the hood. He reached out and let one hand rest on the bare skin of her stomach; snow settled on the black leather glove and did not melt. Lina felt his touch only distantly as his fingers traced a path up her ribs and cupped her left breast, his palm directly over her heart.

It's not real, Lina repeated to herself. *He can kill me or rape me or whatever he wants, and it doesn't matter because it's not* real. *I'll wake up and I'll be in my bed, and Sylph will be there . . .*

There was an instant—just an instant—of terrible violation. Something *flowed* from the man's hand, crawling into her flesh; she felt tendrils writhing under her skin and wrapping themselves through muscles and bone. The numbing cold was suddenly gone, and the cuts didn't hurt anymore. The man stood and Lina sat up.

Run, she willed, *run for my fucking life and never come back. This is a fucking* nightmare *and it can't be real, it can't be real, it can't be . . .*

Instead she got to her feet and stood before the black-cloaked figure, and he reached back to remove his hood. The pale light glinted on polished bone; there was nothing there but a skull, covered in creatures of decay. Centipedes twined their way through his eye sockets, and maggots writhed where his nose and mouth had been. From the hollow of his breastbone she saw the red, staring eyes of a nervous rat. He took a step forward, and flies rose from him in a black, buzzing cloud.

Lina took a step forward. She screamed at her body, but it simply wouldn't listen. She held up her hands and clasped his fingers, feeling smooth bone under the gloves. Lina closed her eyes and tilted her head back, waiting. Her lips touched bone, smooth as a cue ball, and then she wrapped her arms around him and pulled him close. She pressed her tongue into his mouth, and in return maggots crawled into hers. She bit down, and felt one of them crunch between her teeth.

And then . . .

✳   ✳   ✳

"*No!*" Lina sat bolt upright, her heart jackhammering in her chest as though it wanted to tear through her ribs and escape. Her pulse pounded in her ears, and it took her a moment to focus on her surroundings.

She was in a bed in the Highpoint fortress, with the door closed and the window tightly shuttered, but she heard the drumming hiss of rain outside. Distant thunder rumbled.

A dream. She put a hand on her chest. *Just a dream. A nightmare. Calm. Be calm, it was just a dream and it was* just *a dream and oh God I* kissed *that thing . . .*

She leaned off of the bed and found a chamber pot conveniently positioned. Everything she'd eaten in the last day welled up, and she rolled back into bed with an empty stomach and her mouth tasting of bile.

Nightmare. A nightmare. She tried to chuckle and got a dry wheeze. *No wonder, right? It's been a pretty traumatic few weeks. I've never killed anybody before. Never used a magic sword before . . .*

She looked around, automatically. Someone had propped the sword in one corner. Just the sight of it made her shiver.

"My lady?" said Fah, peering in after opening the door a crack. "Are you all right?"

"Yes." Lina coughed. "I mean, no. I'm not sure."

"May I come in?"

"Sure." Lina waved at her weakly. "Can you get me some water?"

"Of course." She had a whispered conversation with someone outside, then slipped into the room.

"What happened?" said Lina. "Did we win?"

"Sort of. After you killed Warleader Falk, his men pulled back and decided to negotiate. Sylph is talking to them now."

"Sylph's out there by herself?" Lina struggled to rise. "They might kill her!"

"Relax." Fah pressed her shoulders gently back into the bed. "She took Vhaal and Heraan to guard her. She'll be fine."

Lina closed her eyes and nodded. Fah pressed a cold mug of water into her hand, and she drained it with long, greedy gulps. Lina wiped her mouth with the back of her hand and said, "What about the others? Is everyone okay?"

"A couple of Heraan's people didn't make it, and Daana broke her arm when she fell. She'll live."

"Good. Thank God." She took a deep breath. "Now what?"

"Now, if you feel up to it, I'll bring you some breakfast."

"Please. But I meant . . . I mean . . . what do we do now?"

"First we see how Sylph's negotiations work out. Then," Fah shrugged, "I'm sure you'll think of something."

"*Me?*"

"Or Sylph."

"But—"

"You *are* the Liberator, Lina," said Fah, deadly serious. "I know you'll succeed. You're destined to."

"Destiny?" She glanced again at the sword. *I was Meant to have it. But . . .*

Breakfast arrived.

*   *   *

HUNCH OR NO, SYLPH AGREED WITH THE OTHERS THAT letting sixty heavily armed men through the wall was an invitation to disaster. Marlowe suggested that he and a few of his companions come inside to fetch food for the rest of his troops, and Sylph readily agreed; given the losses Falk's men had suffered, the fortress was stocked with enough to last both soldiers and Circle Breakers for some time. Marlowe returned to the tree line and came back leading a troop of ten or so, on foot. The rain still poured, and by the time the soldiers reached the wall they were covered in mud. Yahvy shouted up to Garot, who ran down to open the gates.

"By the Lady," said Marlowe, "it'll feel good to get out of this damned rain. All our gear is in there, you know, tents and capes and suchlike. You lot really caught us with our pants down!"

There was an awkward silence, until Marlowe roared with laughter. Hesitantly, Sylph and Yahvy joined in. Heraan remained quiet, and Vhaal, for his part, had long ago retired to the warmth of the barracks. Sylph watched Marlowe's men as they filed through the gate after Heraan. They were bundled up tight, looking cold and miserable. She and Yahvy waited until the last of them was walking through . . .

There was a quick flurry of action, too fast to follow; Yahvy sprang forward and drew her sword, lunging for the last man in line. He barely got his weapon up in time, and steel slipped and shrieked against wet steel. One of Marlowe's men shouted, and then swords were out on both sides. Sylph's heart skipped a beat as for a moment it looked like a fight would break out after all, but the cavalry captain filled his lungs and stopped the action with a bellow.

"All of you, *stop*!" Such was the force of his voice that even Yahvy paused; she'd just disarmed the soldier, and his blade was sinking slowly into the mud of the courtyard. The other cavalrymen kept their weapons out, but froze as she leveled her blade at his throat.

"Yahvy, what the hell are you doing?" said Sylph.

"It was him." She was breathing hard. "He . . ."

Marlowe peered at the man. "Schwartz? What in the Lady's name are you doing here? I told the rest of you to wait at the camp."

"Don't let her kill me, Captain!" Schwartz's throat bobbed. "I just wanted to get in the warm for a while, I swear!"

There was a muttering amongst the other men. Sylph was paying more attention to Yahvy, who was glaring daggers at Schwartz.

"Yahvy, tell me what's wrong."

"This . . ." She swallowed, and brushed wet hair from her eyes with her off hand. "This is the man who killed Kiry. One of Vantz's."

"Is that where he came from?" Marlowe frowned. "I was never quite sure. He's not one of mine; turned up a few days before you people did. We gave him a place to stay and all, but . . ."

"What do you mean, but?" Sylph turned back to Yahvy. "Let him go."

"No." Her sword trembled. "I'm going to kill him. I swore it."

"Captain," Schwartz said, "please!"

Marlowe looked over the rest of his men. Most of them had sheathed their weapons, and one or two were smiling under their helmets and heavy coats. Apparently Schwartz was not well-liked by Falk's garrison.

"Yahvy . . ."

"Sylph, don't push me."

Marlowe harrumphed. "As far as I'm concerned, if the girl's got a vendetta to settle, she can settle it. I'm not going to play champion for one of Vantz's easterners." His men muttered approvingly. "Since she demonstrated her ability to beat you in a fair fight—"

"No, Captain, please! You've got to do something!"

"Get inside," Marlowe roared, "the lot of you!" He looked down at Sylph. "If you feel like you have to stop her, you're welcome to try. It makes no difference to me."

The big cavalryman followed his men into the fortress. Sylph stared at Yahvy, and shook her head.

"Do what you like."

Before Schwartz could move, Yahvy leaned forward and put the point of her sword through his throat. He gurgled and fell back against the wall, and the Circle Breaker stood watching until his thrashings had ceased. Then she turned on her heel, without a word, and stalked back inside. Sylph stared mournfully at the corpse before going through the gate. *Not a good note on which to start an alliance, easterner or no.*

❊   ❊   ❊

INSIDE THE BARRACKS WAS A CONFUSION OF WET ARMORED men. Marlowe established some kind of order by sheer volume, organizing his people to head to the supply sheds and get their rain gear and food. Sylph retreated from the confusion, finding sanctuary in the small section they'd cordoned off as an infirmary. Daana was on her feet already, talking animatedly with Garot; Melfina lay in a corner bed, curled up but with her eyes open. Sylph took a seat on the bunk next to her, feeling like she should make some effort to be comradely. Melfina glanced at her, but said nothing.

"Hey," Sylph said eventually.

"Hey," Melfina answered in a small voice.

"We won," said Sylph after another pause.

"I know. I heard Garot talking." She nodded at the soldiers. "And now they're switching sides?"

"So they claim."

"Just like Heraan." Melfina yawned and sat up, wincing a little.

"You feeling better?"

"Better than right after I got shot?" The girl rolled her eyes. "Much, thanks."

"Sorry. Stupid question." Sylph looked at the floor. Something about talking to Melfina was like pulling teeth, but she couldn't help feel like the girl really *wanted* to talk.

"I'm sorry." Melfina sighed. "I'm just . . . I didn't get much sleep. Lying here and listening, wondering if they were going to kick down the door and kill me for real this time."

"Yeah." Sylph hadn't thought about that. "Sounds awful."

"Not as awful as actually fighting." Melfina smiled weakly.

I'm not so sure about that. Being helpless would be worse, straining to hear the screams of your friends in the dark. Sylph shivered, and they sat in silence for a while.

"Fah's okay, isn't she?" asked Melfina.

"Absolutely." Sylph looked at her. "Why?"

"Just worried. She didn't come and see me afterward."

"She's been busy with my sister."

"I figured."

Sylph saw something in Melfina's eyes she couldn't quite place, but it was gone in a moment, replaced by a brittle smile.

"What was wrong with Yahvy, anyway? She ran through without talking to anyone."

"Where'd she go?"

"Back to the rooms. Daana said she'd locked herself in and didn't want to be bothered."

Great. "I'd better go and find her."

"Do you know what happened?"

"Yeah." Sylph hesitated. "I'll tell you later, okay?"

The little girl nodded. "Okay."

"How long until you're out of bed?"

"A couple of days. Daana says nothing's inflamed."

"Great." Sylph rose. "See you later on."

It wasn't hard to find the room Yahvy had locked herself in; two of the four doors were open and one other was Vhaal's, and it was hard to imagine the two of them being in a room for more than five minutes without killing each other. Sylph looked in on her sister—Lina was eating breakfast, and she waved cheerfully—before making her way to Yahvy's door and rapping as loudly.

"What?" came Yahvy's muffled voice, after a moment.

"Just wanted to talk to you."

"Go away." It was hard to tell, but it sounded like she'd been crying. Sylph shook her head.

"Yahvy, we're going to need you. There are things that need to be decided."

"You and Heraan and Fah can handle it. Just leave me alone."

Sylph sighed and put her hand on the knob, which refused to turn. The keyhole looked primitive, which meant the lock would probably be easy to pick. *That would be a help if I knew how to pick locks.* After a moment, she started fumbling for the little trailing thread she'd used to pull apart Falk and the locks on the node room door, but found nothing.

What is that, anyway? She hadn't thought much about her odd power. *I've barely had five minutes to myself since yesterday. Magic, I guess?* It didn't seem like much of a spell, though she was starting to understand how it worked. *Diamond and obsidian; no way stuff like this is natural. Heraan said Gargorian built this fortress himself. So I guess whatever he built, I can pull apart?* Creating diamond would be pretty easy, as such things went. *Just convince all the little carbon atoms to line up in a row.* But the barracks and the other buildings had apparently been built of non-magical material, so there didn't seem to be much she could do.

Hmm. She kept her mind in the state it took to look for the little thread—this was far from easy, like trying to keep her eyes from refocusing—and instead poked at the wood itself. It didn't have the utterly simple feel of the diamond lock, or even Falk's armor. All she felt was a kind of gray mass. *But that's something. Unless I'm just going nuts.* She pressed further in, fighting a headache building around her temples, and found that she could just about resolve the gray down to lots of little colored pieces . . .

Not really colored. She wasn't really *seeing* any of it—her eyes were tightly shut—but that was apparently how it mapped into her mind. *Little colored balls on springs. I wonder . . .*

A brush, and one of the springs shivered. Sylph pushed harder and felt it snap, along with a dozen of its neighbors. She grinned without opening her eyes. *So, let's give this a try.*

She gave the metal bolt a harder shove. Bonds snapped and the little pieces scattered in all directions, smashing apart as yet unaffected structures like bowling pins. A few more prods and the whole thing was falling to pieces. Sylph opened her eyes and found that the entire lock had melted out of the doorframe in a kind of gooey mass, running down both sides of the door.

Cool! was Sylph's undeniable first thought. Before she could ponder the implications, the door swung silently half open, and she could see Yahvy lying face down on the bed. Sylph padded into the room; a floorboard creaked, and Yahvy hastily sat up.

Sylph tried not to look guilty.

"Sylph!" Yahvy sounded like she'd been strained to the breaking point. "I thought I told you—"

"I'm sorry. I didn't really mean to come in." Yahvy's eyes were red and her pillow was stained with tears. "What's wrong?"

The older girl hesitated. Sylph sat down on the bed next to her. *As long as I'm being amateur psychiatrist, I might as well play it to the hilt.*

"I don't really know," said Yahvy slowly. "I mean, I guess I *know.* I miss . . . I miss Kiry."

It took Sylph a moment to place the name; the girl who had died in their skirmish with Vantz. Once she remembered, she felt awful for forgetting. *It's hardly my fault. I only knew her for a day or so.*

Yahvy continued, to fill the silence. "After Fah got back, I felt like I was ready to die. We were *all* going to die. There was no way out, and that made it . . . kind of okay, you know? There was nothing I could do." She took a deep breath. "Do you understand?"

"Yeah," said Sylph, who didn't really. She found it hard to imagine just completely giving up hope. *There's always a way out, if you look hard enough.*

"After we killed Vantz, and she died, I was just in shock. And then you said we were going to Highpoint, and I figured we were going to die after all. I mean, this was crazy. Just fucking crazy. And then last night, I thought we'd finally had it. But after you and Lina killed Falk . . ." She shook her head. "It just hit me this morning."

"Schwartz?"

"He *killed* her. He stuck a fucking spear in her belly and left her to hang, so I cut his throat. But when I got back here . . . she's still dead. And now we might get to live a little bit longer. If I'd just gotten her past that one little fight she'd still be *here.* But she's dead, and what the fuck do I do now? Just keep fighting until someone kills me too?"

"You don't have to," said Sylph. "If you want to stay behind . . ."

"What's the point?" Yahvy flopped back on the bed. "What do I have here? I could go home and let my father make me into a whore, like he wanted to in the first place. Although I doubt he'd even take me now. Too skinny."

"What about Gargorian and the Circles? The Plague?"

"I know, I know." Yahvy sounded resigned, which made Sylph feel a bit queer; she didn't care as much about the Plague as the Circle Breakers did, or were supposed to. "We're doing a good thing, right?"

"Absolutely," said Sylph, with as much certainty as she could muster.

"I guess that should be enough." She shrugged uncomfortably. "Daana has Garot, and Fah hasn't left your sister since the battle. Vhaal is . . . Vhaal, Melfina's hurt and maybe dying, and Kiry's dead. What's left for me?"

"Melfina's not dying," said Sylph. "She's awake and getting better, Daana says."

"Thank the Lady," Yahvy murmured. "That's something, anyway." She sighed, and for the first time seemed really aware of who she was talking to. "Sorry to unload all this on you."

"I asked, didn't I?" Sylph smiled.

Yahvy nodded and sat up, looking a little cheerier. "It just got to me."

"Are you sorry you killed Schwartz?"

Her expression went hard. "No. Whatever *I* feel about it, he killed Kiry."

Sylph backed away from that line of conversation and changed topics. "In any case, we're going to have a planning session in the barracks in a few hours, once Marlowe's men have gotten their supplies. I'd like it if you'd come."

"Sure." Yahvy sniffed and wiped her eyes. Sylph got up and headed for the door. "Sylph?"

"Yeah?"

"Thanks for breaking the door down."

"No problem." Sylph left before Yahvy realized exactly *how* she'd broken the door down, which might engender awkward questions.

THE MEETING OF WHAT SYLPH WAS STARTING TO THINK OF as the War Council was fairly rocky at first. Lina was nominally in charge, as the Liberator, but she seemed more than happy to sit back and let Sylph run things. Fah had faded into the background at Lina's right hand, but the presence of Yahvy on one side and Heraan on the other reassured Sylph quite a bit. They were joined by Marlowe and two of his men.

Everyone was talking at once and Sylph didn't have the voice to shout them all down, so she waited for the noise to wear itself out. One by one she got their attention. Once she'd captured everyone, she said:

"Okay, firstly, I want to make a few things clear. Most important is what we're all here for."

"Breaking the Circles," said Fah.

"Getting rid of Gargorian," said Heraan.

"You lot don't think small, do you?" said Marlowe, with a raised eyebrow.

"In addition to the fact that my sister is the Liberator," she could say it with barely a twinge, now, even though she still didn't believe it, "I have reason to think that Gargorian knows who I am, at least in general terms, and wants me dead. I'm not going to be able to rest easy until he's no longer in charge." She cocked her head at Marlowe. "Are we clear?"

"Of course. That's what the Liberator is *for*, after all."

Lina winced a little. Sylph didn't think anyone else noticed. She cleared her throat and said, "I just wanted to make sure you knew what you were signing up for. The next order of business is figuring out how to do it. Marlowe, how much do you know about Gargorian's disposition?" He didn't seem to understand that, so she clarified. "Where are his armies?"

"Oh, aye. Three armies in the city; since it's summer, the harvest around Bleloth is coming in soon. He'll have the Third Army dispersed to take care of bandits and so forth. The First Army is supposed to guard the walls, and the Second is still getting up to strength after spending a year or so smashing the western tribes." He glanced at Yahvy and Fah. "No offense meant, girls."

"None taken," said Yahvy, grinning wide enough to show her teeth. Marlowe ignored her.

"The Fourth'll be on the eastern front, probably east of Orlow by now. Last I heard things were pretty quiet between Gargorian and Lady Fell, but you never know when it'll start back up again. Mind, the Lady got cut to bits in the last war. If not for the Clockwork Legion we'd be marching on Stonerings right now."

"Three armies. How many men is that?"

"Six thousand, more or less. Plus the Diamond Guard at Bleloth, that's another five centuries."

Sixty-five hundred men. Sylph couldn't help but cringe inwardly.

"If I may, miss," said Marlowe, "I'd like to lay out a plan."

"Feel free, but don't call me 'miss.' My name is Sylph."

"As you like." He cleared his throat. "We have the advantage of the Highpoint wall. Assuming you didn't let anyone escape from the fortress . . ." He looked for and got a confirming nod from Sylph and Heraan. "And assuming we keep a tight lid on things, Gargorian won't know we're here for some time. There's a lot of people in these parts who aren't happy with the Circles, especially just east of the mountains. All we have to do is find them. Maybe send someone to the western tribes."

Sylph cleared her throat uncomfortably. "Unfortunately, our problem runs a little bit deeper than that."

"Oh?"

"There was a node of the Fourth Circle here."

"I know." Marlowe stopped. "What do you mean, was?"

Yahvy and Heraan were both staring at Sylph, open-mouthed. Sylph swallowed. "I destroyed it. The Fourth Circle is broken."

There was a long silence.

"That's not possible," Marlowe said at length. "Gargorian constructed that room himself; diamond layers in the walls, diamond bars on the door. And the node itself was supposed to be unbreakable."

"What was made by magic," said Fah from the back, "can be unmade."

Interesting, thought Sylph.

"You're a Magus?" asked Heraan incredulously.

"It seems that way," Sylph admitted. "If that's what you want to call it."

"Sylph, are you *serious*?" said Lina. "When did you find this out?"

"Pretty recently."

Lina leaned forward and wrapped her arms around Sylph. "My little sister's a wizard!"

"If we can get back to the *point*," said Marlowe, "what does this mean?"

"It means we're winning!" said Yahvy. "One of the four Circles broken—no one has ever done that except for an Archmagus. You've stripped Gargorian of a fourth of his power at a stroke!"

"Seven-sixteenths of his power," said Sylph absently, "assuming the Circles are evenly spaced."

"It means," said Heraan quietly, "that Gargorian probably knows we're here."

That brought on another silence.

"Is that true?" asked Marlowe.

"I'm not sure." Sylph shook her head. "I think so. I could feel . . . when I broke the Circle, it felt like it set a wave racing around the edge. I'm sure Gargorian felt it. Unless he wasn't paying attention or something."

"He knows," said Heraan. "The Circles are like a spider's web. He's sitting in the middle, and he feels every little twitch."

"When did you do this?" said Marlowe.

"Yesterday afternoon."

"That means we don't have time to recruit like you wanted to," said Heraan. "Gargorian's army is probably double-timing it here from Bleloth."

"How long does that give us?" asked Sylph.

"Depends how long it takes them to get organized. Ten days minimum, probably two weeks."

"Ten days!" Marlowe roared. "What can we possibly do in ten days? Even if we scrape up some defenses on the other side of the wall and try to demolish the stairways, we couldn't possibly hold the fortress against so many men."

"That's what they told me when I wanted to take it from you," said Sylph.

"True." Marlowe seemed taken aback. "But if Gargorian knows we took this place, he'll have siege equipment. A hundred-and-twenty cavalry is one thing, but two thousand men with scaling ladders and battering rams . . ."

"Not to mention," said Yahvy grimly, "if Gargorian is really serious he could come out here himself. The wall is his creation; I'm sure he could pull it down around our ears."

"Stop." Sylph held up her hand. "You're all right. We can't defend Highpoint."

"Then what?" said Marlowe. "Fall back to the woods? We're mounted; we can certainly lead him a merry chase, but that'll be tricky."

"I don't think we should abandon it, either." Sylph allowed herself a smile. "We need to make sure that army never gets here."

"You're going to have a hard time waylaying two thousand men, Sylph," said Heraan.

"Two thousand conscripts." Sylph grinned wider, and caught

Lina's eye before she turned to Marlowe. "This is what we need to do. Pick ten fast riders that you can trust . . ."

✳   ✳   ✳

Tap, tap, tap. Vesh's finger bounced up and down on the parchment map, on which every forest and every rise and fall of the ground had been carefully hand painted. Highpoint was a stylized fortress with exaggerated battlements, rising above the jagged peaks of the Rippers.

Twelve days to march to Highpoint. It was a conservative esti-mate. There was a good road most of the way, which meant they were making excellent time despite the downpour. *Damn the rain.* It was hard to coax the scouts to go out in bad weather, and they couldn't range far afield. *I feel blind.* The road was clear, any-way. *If there was an army between here and there, I'd know about it.*

Twelve days to march, nine to ride there and back. It was the eve-ning of the tenth day, and the messengers he'd sent to Falk and his garrison had not returned. *Falk always had more fury than sense. Could he have been taken?* It seemed unlikely. Even if the western-ers had somehow put an army together, a hundred men could hold Highpoint against any conceivable force. *Short of an Archma-gus. Now there's a cheerful thought.* That too, was unlikely. *Sabotage, it has to be sabotage. Someone snuck into the fortress and destroyed the node. Which is impossible.* But all the other explanations were worse.

"My lord Vesh," a voice came from outside. Vesh recognized Falschim, General of the Second Army and overall military commander of the expedition. He and the general were not on good terms; Falschim was not used to the immediate presence of a superior. The Second had spent a year on the plains, beat-ing the fight out of the tribesmen; most of the men had rotated out since then, of course, but there was a culture of arrogance among the officers that had remained that troubled Vesh. He'd resolved to have a private word with Gargorian on his return. General or no, Falschim needed a reminder of who was really in charge.

"Let him in," said Vesh reluctantly. A moment later the general entered, accompanied by a Diamond Guardsman in his sparkling armor. Vesh had brought a dozen of Gargorian's elite to serve as his personal guards, and he was beginning to feel sorry he had not asked for more. *I could dispense with Falschim and his staff, for starters.* That was an idle dream, of course; Diamond Guardsmen were not trained for command, only obedience and discipline.

"Well?" Vesh said. "Any word from the messengers?"

"No more than yesterday." Falschim talked around a large and impressive moustache, the tips of which he seemed to be in constant danger of accidentally swallowing.

"They've been taken," Vesh said, a sour taste in his mouth. His finger tapped once again on the map. "And the scouts?"

"Of the twenty men I sent out this afternoon, twelve had seen nothing and eight have not returned at all."

"I thought I told you to send them in pairs. I'm tired of these disappearances."

"With respect," Falschim said, "I did send them in pairs. This is no longer a matter of desertion or lame horses. Someone is out there."

"It's not possible." Vesh shook his head. "There's no way the tribesmen could have taken the fortress so quickly."

"I can think of one," the general said quietly. "Treachery."

"For all his faults, Falk is not a traitor. I can't believe—"

"It doesn't have to be him. Perhaps his second in command. All it takes is a few men, to open the gate in the middle of the night and—"

"All right!" Vesh frowned. Reinforcing the Highpoint garrison until the node could be repaired was one thing, and open battle against an unknown enemy quite another. "If the rain would clear . . ."

"The rain has not cleared, and the longer we sit the more time they have to slip past us."

"What do you suggest?"

"Continue the march. If Highpoint has fallen, recapture it and cut off the westerners' lines of supply. There may be a few raiders loose in our rear, but they can be easily dealt with."

"Mmm." Vesh stroked his chin. "Too risky. Highpoint is deep in the pass; it's perfect for a trap. I won't march without knowing what we're up against."

"My lord . . ."

Vesh stood from his map table. "Order a reconnaissance-in-force; send a regiment to Highpoint, with a squad of messengers attached. Make it clear that their orders are to observe and not to engage."

"If it is a trap, they'll be massacred," snapped Falschim.

"So be it. Even a massacre will leave enough survivors to report on the enemy. Better a regiment than an army."

The general's lip twisted, but he nodded. "I will give the orders."

"Good. I want them off in the morning. The rest of the men are to begin work on a palisade, in case the enemy steals a march on us. I want patrols in all directions, not just west, and send the men in groups of four this time. No more disappearances, do you understand?"

"Yes, my lord."

"Go."

The Diamond Guardsman escorted Falschim out, expression invisible behind his glittering mask. Alone again, Vesh turned back to the map and began marking his army's position with a quill pen. *I'd gladly spend a regiment for decent intelligence.* He smiled thinly. *They're only conscripts, after all. I guarantee we have more men to spend than they do.*

chapter seven

THEY CAME IN A LONG SNAKE, FOLLOWING THE ROAD
from the west, a formation five or six men wide and perhaps
forty men long. *So two hundred, give or take.* That was the size of a
regiment in Gargorian's army, according to Marlowe. *Only one.*
Despite the assurances she'd given the others, Sylph had worried
that Gargorian's commander might deploy more. *He has to know
that whatever he marches in here is at risk. And he won't want us to get
away, so he can't afford to take his time.* A commander moving at
his own leisure might advance slowly up the road, clearing the
bluffs on either side as he went, but that would give the rebels
plenty of chances to escape.

There were banners at the head of the regiment, red and blue
pennants heavy with the weight of water and hanging limply on
their poles. The rain had continued more or less uninterrupted
for nearly a week; it cut visibility and would make accurate missile fire difficult. *Thankfully, accuracy is not what we need.*

"Get ready," Sylph said, peering down into the valley and
marking the advance of the column of soldiers. Orbaa, who had
accompanied her, was checking his equipment. With him was
Yahvy and half the archers Marlowe had split off from his force
of cavalry. The other half were with Heraan and Garot on the
other side of the valley, where another set of bluffs rose.

Perfect for an ambush. To the west the slope was gradual, but here the road followed an old riverbed between the paired cliffs. Drainage ditches carried the water away and protected the road from being washed out. *Too bad we can't arrange* that. She shook her head. *Pay attention. He has to* know *it's a good place for an ambush, and he has to know that we know that he knows, and . . .*

"Almost there," said Yahvy. She had her bow bent and ready, the string carefully oiled to keep it from stretching in the rain. A half-dozen arrows were planted in the ground at her feet. "They still haven't sent any scouts out."

"Marlowe's been picking off their scouts for a week," said Sylph quietly. There was really no need to whisper since the enemy was much too far to hear them, but it felt right somehow. "They probably don't want to risk any more. Remember, they're still not sure we took the fortress."

"They will be after today," said Orbaa, and smiled viciously. He was in a good mood. "Should I give th' signal?"

"Not just yet." Sylph squinted. "Another few seconds . . . wait . . . now."

Orbaa reached under an oiled cloak and took a burning torch from its bed of coals. He waved it back and forth over his head, and fire flickered on the other bluff in answer. Word spread up and down the line of archers, and they went into a brief flurry of preparation. Marlowe's men impressed Sylph; they were competent and professional. *Falk must have done a good job keeping them trained. We'll have to keep it up.* On the other cliff, Heraan's contingent was also getting ready. Sylph and Yahvy counted together.

". . . seventeen, eighteen, nineteen, twenty, twenty-one . . ."

"Ready," said Orbaa. Ten bows creaked.

"Twenty-eight, twenty-nine, thirty."

"Fire!"

Bowstrings slapped and the arrows whispered into the air. A moment later Sylph caught a flash of motion from across the valley—the other team had opened fire. Most of the first volley landed well short, but the archers were already firing a second,

aiming higher, and soon arrows were falling amongst Gargorian's soldiers. Given the rain it was impossible to hit any specific
target, but lobbing shots into the body of men had the desired
effect. They broke their close formation, some knots of men remaining together as officers strove to maintain order while other
groups ran for the cover of the scraggly trees that lined the valley floor. The archers kept shooting, directing their fire toward
the largest remaining groups. Sylph saw a few soldiers already
down, dead or pretending. Some of Gargorian's men carried
short-bows and tried to fire back, but the slope and the rain defeated them. A shaft rattled through the trees over Sylph's head,
but she refused to be distracted.

Another count of thirty. She whispered the numbers under
her breath—Yahvy was too busy firing, her great western longbow outranging the weapons of Marlowe's troops. *Twenty-eight,
twenty-nine . . .*

Then—a bit early, by Sylph's count, but close enough—the
thunder of hooves became audible over the rain. A moment later
Marlowe and his riders crested a rise in the path and pounded
down the other side in a line, sticking to the relatively solid road-
bed and avoiding the patches of mud. Each one carried a spear,
all leveled together into a mass of deadly points.

Sylph felt her throat catch. Lina was down there, well in the
rear with Fah to guard her, but still amidst the charge. It was
necessary, but Sylph had to fret. Lina hadn't been herself for the
past few days; it didn't seem like she'd been sleeping well, and the
dark circles under her eyes had become a permanent feature.

Marlowe's cavalry was hardly mighty Teutonic knights; they
carried infantry spears, not lances, and wore mostly leather and
mail instead of plate. A solid block of spearmen could have stood
off the charge, and a well-drilled square of pikes would have
made mincemeat out of them. But Gargorian's conscripts were
neither well-drilled nor well-equipped, and Sylph's relatively
small volleys of arrows had a disorganizing effect disproportion-
ate to the actual damage inflicted.

There was nothing close to a solid formation left able to receive the charge. The largest remaining group of soldiers, still
in the roadway, boiled as an officer tried to get his men to form
up; at the last minute, however, Sylph saw soldiers breaking and
running, and Marlowe rode over the group with barely a pause.
His men cut through Gargorian's army like a well-honed blade,
and the disorganization turned into a general rout, with soldiers
dropping their weapons in their haste to get out of the valley.

"Now," Sylph whispered.

As though Lina had heard her command, a white light
started to grow. Before long it had become an actinic flare, too
bright to look at, and all through the valley her soldiers took up
the cry:

"Liberator! Liberator! Liberator!"

Sylph smiled and leaned back against a wet tree trunk, feeling her heart pound in her chest and trying to will it to relax.
*Let them take that message back to whomever's in command. Your worst
fears are realized.* The men would convey her message, no doubt
about it; not just to the enemy commanders, but to the rest of the
soldiers. Marlowe's scouts had reported an entire army on the
march, two thousand men, and news like this would rip through
their camp like wildfire.

Perfect. So much for part one. She yawned and stretched, the
weight of the sword she'd taken to wearing on her hip feeling a
bit less awkward with each passing day. Heraan had become
her tutor, and he had her wear the thing at all times for that very
reason. *Didn't even have to draw it this time.*

The flare of light had faded away. *Time to go and make sure
everyone's okay.*

✳   ✳   ✳

LINA STUMBLED OFF OF HER HORSE; HER FOOT GOT CAUGHT
in one stirrup and she had to perform a little hopping dance to
try and get it out. When the horse, perversely, decided to take a

step toward her, Lina tumbled backward and would have hit the ground rather painfully if Marlowe had not been there to catch her. He supported her shoulders with one hand and disengaged the offending stirrup with the other, then returned her gently to her feet.

"Thanks." Lina squeezed her eyes shut for a moment; they still ached, and the rush of the battle was still fighting with a bone-deep weariness. "Riding isn't exactly my thing."

"I noticed," he said dryly. "Are you sure you want to do this? If you don't mind my saying so, you don't look so good."

"I just haven't gotten enough sleep."

"Some young man keeping you up late?"

"I . . ." Lina went crimson. Fah, who had dismounted in the meantime, shot Marlowe a venomous look.

"Joke, girl. Just a joke."

I wish it was something so simple. How can I explain that every time I close my eyes I see a death's head? The first dream had been the worst, but it seemed like every night she woke up cold and sweating, and all she could remember was staring into maggot-filled eyes of that horrible skull . . .

"Anyway," said Lina, "Sylph said I should be down here."

"And she does seem to be in charge around here," said Marlowe.

"Lina is the Liberator," said Fah protectively. "It's important that she be seen."

"As you wish. I'd just like to be on record as saying this is a bad idea. The aftermath of a battle is never a pretty sight."

"I can deal with it," said Lina, and Fah nodded. Marlowe shrugged and trudged down the road. The rain had abated somewhat, to a kind of airborne mist; everyone was damp, all the time, which wasn't particularly pleasant. The floor of the valley was a morass of waterlogged plants, mud, rocks, and blood. Marlowe picked his way through, and Lina couldn't help wincing as something squelched under his heavy boots. She hoped it was just muck.

"Still," said Marlowe over his shoulder. "Your sister is something else, Lina. Everything happened like she said it would, down to the last detail. Magic, you think?"

Fah scoffed. "There's no such magic."

"You're an expert on magic now—"

"I don't think it was magic," Lina cut in. "Sylph's just smart—very smart." That had always been true; Lina had a hard time remembering a time when she hadn't had to deal with the fact that her sister was a certifiable genius, with a genius's quirks. "And she reads a lot, and . . ." She paused. 'And she plays a lot of war games' might not go over particularly well.

Marlowe shrugged again and turned back to the trail. "It's almost enough to make a man believe we've got a chance."

"We have the Liberator on our side," said Fah, "and we have more than a chance. We have Destiny on our side."

"Destiny, eh?"

"Yes!"

The argument trailed off because they'd reached the edge of the battlefield. Most of Marlowe's men had retired back to their camp outside Highpoint, but a few remained behind to sort through the debris. Half a dozen had their spears leveled at a small knot of prisoners, perhaps thirty in all, who had already been stripped of their weapons and armor. Another half-dozen had the unenviable task of dragging the dead to a pit they'd dug near one of the drainage ditches. Lina wanted to look away, but forced herself not to. She felt somehow responsible. *It's not exactly my* fault, *since they came here to kill me, but still . . .*

"Why are there so many women?" She'd heard that Gargorian conscripted without regard to gender, but seeing girls heaped among the piles of corpses was still a shock.

"Man, woman, Gargorian doesn't care," Marlowe said. "All he needs are warm bodies to fill the ranks, and with the Plague taking so many he has a hard enough time getting them."

The soldiers ranged from fuzz-cheeked boys and gawky girls barely older than Lina to middle-aged faces she wouldn't have been surprised to see running a corner store back home. Marlowe's men had barely started clearing the dead, and bodies were everywhere. The searchers stripped the fallen of anything useful and carried the wounded over to the prisoners. *Some* of the wounded; Lina saw one man approach a boy with a spear standing practically vertical from his stomach, his hands still scrabbling at the mud. The soldier reached down and cut his throat with one swift motion, then waited for his thrashing to cease.

"It's a mercy," said Marlowe, who must have caught something in Lina's expression. "A belly wound, lying in the mud for this long—he'd fester and die, no question. This way is cleaner."

She nodded, striving desperately to breathe. The big soldier had fallen in behind her, so Lina led the way through the killing fields. It wasn't long before they were noticed by the survivors, and a chorus of whispers followed her.

One woman in her twenties stepped forward, before the guards could stop her, and stood in Lina's way. Her expression was defiant.

"*You're* the Liberator? A little girl like you?" The woman laughed. "Got yourself a magic pig-sticker and you think you're going to beat the Archmagus?"

Fah stepped into her path, along with one of Marlowe's guards, but Lina held up her hands and stopped them. The woman took this as license to continue.

"You westerners are all the same. All this talk, liberation and bringing down the tyrant, and all it means is more of us in the grinder. And when you get killed it'll all be for nothing!"

"She won't be killed," Fah retorted. "This isn't some petty rebellion; she's the Liberator, and this time we'll bring Gargorian down."

"You did a great job of 'liberating' everyone here!" said the woman, waving her hand at the field of corpses.

Fah hesitated. "Sacrifices are necessary . . ."

The woman's hand cracked across her face, and Fah stumbled back. Marlowe's guard moved in before the woman could get in another blow, catching her in the stomach with a gauntleted fist and knocking the wind out of her.

"Sacrifices?" she wheezed. "That's my *husband* out there, and my daughter out behind the trees, and you're talking about *sacrifices*?"

The guards quickly muscled her back into line. Fah fell in behind Lina again, looking a bit chastened; Lina, who'd been silent the whole time, turned to Marlowe.

" 'Behind the trees'?"

"Ah . . ." The soldier hesitated. "I'm not sure I should . . ."

"Show me." Lina felt her voice go cold. For a moment she thought Marlowe was going to object, but he finally looked down and appeared to deflate.

"Follow me."

There was indeed a line of trees at one end of the valley, and Marlowe started in that direction. Lina followed, her hand dropping unconsciously to the hilt of the sword. Fah hurried to keep up.

"You have to understand," Marlowe was saying, "men who've just gone into battle . . . they're not quite civilized. You need to let them burn off—"

He was interrupted by a high-pitched scream from the trees, accompanied by coarse laughter. Lina broke into a run, plunging through the brush and ignoring the branches that whipped across her face. She tasted blood, and realized she'd bitten her lip. *They can't be . . . these people are on* our *side, they can't be . . .*

She burst into a clearing where three armored soldiers surrounded a girl hardly older than Sylph. She was wearing what was left of Gargorian's uniform, with the top cut away; she'd crossed her arms over her breasts and backed against a tree trunk. One of them men had his sword out.

There were others, she was vaguely aware: an older, buxom girl sat with her knees drawn up to her chin, weeping silently, and another soldier was buckling his armor back on next to the shaking form of a third captive. But by this point Lina was blind with rage; she didn't recognize her own voice as it cracked across the clearing.

"All of you stop this. *Now!*"

The soldiers turned to look at her, then swiveled to face Marlowe, who emerged from the brush at her side. He leaned closer and whispered:

"I'm not sure that's a good idea. It's like . . . rights, see? After a battle. When there's prisoners, or . . ."

Lina drew the sword. White fire crackled along its length, and it began to hum in the expectation of mayhem. It didn't feel awkward anymore; Lina held it naturally, as though it were a part of her arm. She leveled it at the nearest soldier's throat. He froze, swallowing, as tiny arcs of lightning jumped from the tip of the blade and earthed themselves on his armor.

"Do not," she said, "make me repeat myself."

"Easy, girl," said Marlowe. "Easy."

She twitched the tip of the blade. "Get out, all of you."

The soldiers needed no encouragement, piling out of the clearing as though faced with the devil himself. Marlowe hesitated until Lina rounded on him.

"You *allow* this?"

He spread his hands. "I have no choice. Warleader Falk used to—"

"Warleader Falk is *dead*," Lina snarled. "Let me make myself perfectly clear. If I find any more *rapes*"—she spat the word—"going on, I will personally execute whoever's involved. If that means I have to fight every one of you, *so be it.*"

There was a long moment of silence. Even the crying girl had gone quiet. Eventually, Marlowe gave a stiff bow.

"As you wish, Warl . . . ah . . . Liberator."

"Get out of my sight."

Fah made it into the clearing just as Marlowe was leaving. She watched the big soldier go, then looked at Lina questioningly.

"Is he gone?" Lina whispered.

"I think so." Fah looked after Marlowe, then nodded. "Yeah."

Lina collapsed to her knees, letting the sword fall from her hand. She hugged herself so tightly her arms shook. Fah knelt at her side.

"Liberator?"

"Don't . . ." Lina shook her head weakly. "Don't call me that. Please."

"Lina? Are you all right?"

"No." Her stomach felt like it was filled with bile, and a week of lack of sleep had just smashed into the back of her skull. "I'm . . . I don't know."

Fah put her hand on Lina's shoulder, tentatively. Lina let it remain.

"Did you know about this?" Lina said quietly.

"I . . . suspected." Fah shook her head. "It's the kind of thing that happens. Disgusting, but I didn't think there was anything we could do."

Lina gave a hollow laugh. "Nothing we could do. You're probably right. The old woman was right. These are the people we're supposed to be *helping*, and this is what happens."

"You made them stop," said Fah.

"A little late!" Lina shook her head. "Too late."

In the meantime, the girl who had been crying shuffled over to the one who seemed nearly unconscious. The other, whom the men had been tormenting at the end, had struggled back into her jacket and wrapped it tightly around herself until she was nearly modest. This done, she sat down cross-legged across from Lina. Lina took a better look at her.

She had short hair and a boyish look, especially in cloth trousers and a leather jacket. The girl cleared her throat, then hesitated, as though thinking about what to say. Just before Lina spoke up, she decided on, "Thank you."

"I'm not sure you should be thanking me. We were the ones who attacked you in the first place."

"Only because we were coming for you. If anyone is to blame, it's the men who sent us here. And in any case, I thank you for saving me from . . . that."

Lina nodded, too exhausted to argue. The girl continued:

"They called you the Liberator. Is it true?"

"Apparently."

"Lina!" Fah said, shocked. "You *are* the Liberator, and it is your destiny—"

"To destroy the tyrant, I know."

"And you really intend to bring Gargorian to battle?" the girl pressed.

"If we can," said Fah, when Lina seemed disinclined to speak up. "One step at a time."

The girl got up, awkwardly, and then back down on one knee, head lowered. "Then I am yours, Lina, if you'll have me."

Lina blinked. "What?"

"I've dreamed of this my whole life. They took my whole village into the army. My mother and brother died, and my father lost an arm and was sent to the fields. They told me I was the lucky one, since I lived to see the end of the campaign. We spent a year in Bleloth, waiting and drinking and whoring," she blushed, which made her look somehow ridiculous, "and then all of a sudden they marched us out here and told us we were going to fight the westerners again."

Lina nodded, not sure what to say. The girl's eyes were slowly filling with tears.

"And I thought, I'm going to get out of it this time. Run away. Even if they kill me, even if I end up starving to death on the plains. Every night I said I'd wake up and make a run for it, but I never actually did it."

There was a pause.

"Gargorian," Fah said quietly, "deserves a lot worse than we could ever give him."

The girl nodded, then bowed further, pressing her head nearly to the ground. "Please, Liberator. Accept me?"

"I . . ." Lina hesitated, caught by surprise. ". . . of course. I mean, if you want to fight with us, of course I accept. What's your name?"

"Myris. Thank you, Lib—"

"Call me Lina, please."

"L . . . Lina. Thank you."

"We'll follow you too," said the crying girl, who was no longer in tears. She was still naked, having wrapped her cloak around her companion and propped her against a tree, but this fact did not seem to bother her.

"But . . ." Lina felt a lump rise in her throat.

"It won't . . ." The girl took a deep breath. "You won't let this happen again. So we're better off staying with you than anywhere else, right?"

"What about Kari?" said Myris, nodding at the third young woman who still seemed catatonic. "Are you volunteering her too?"

"She's got nowhere else to go."

"How many," Fah said, "how many of you are going to want to do this? We're not going to hold you captive, you know. At least," she looked at Lina, "not longer than necessary."

"I'm not sure," said Myris. "The new recruits might want to go home. The rest of us don't really have anyplace to go back to."

"We did some awful things back on the plains," said the other girl. "Worse than this. I owe Gargorian for making me into someone like that."

Lina nodded, feeling a little numb. *Now what am I going to tell Sylph?*

✴ ✴ ✴

"ARE YOU SURE YOU SHOULD EVEN BE OUT OF BED?"

Sylph was packing a knapsack she'd pilfered from Marlowe's stores. Her costume was already complete; the brown leather of

Gargorian's soldiers felt uncomfortable across the shoulders. At least she was getting used to the weight of the sword on her hip.

Melfina sat on a nearby rock, swinging her legs quietly. She was also dressed in Gargorian's uniform, though Sylph could see the bulge of the bandage under one side of her armor.

"Daana says I should be okay, as long as we don't get into any real fighting," the girl said.

"You're aware that real fighting is a distinct possibility."

"Please." Melfina rolled her eyes. "If it comes to that we're all dead anyway, but I'm sure it won't."

"You're awfully confident."

"Everything you've planned has worked so far." She shrugged. "I'll put my money on the winning horse."

Sylph forced a smile. *This is just the latest crazy scheme in a long line of crazy schemes.* The others didn't understand that—she was starting to see *trust* in their expressions, which was crazier than she even had words for. *They don't get it. I have to scheme and plan and cheat so that we have a chance, a tiny chance—that's the best I can do!* But on that chance, Yahvy and Melfina and the others were apparently prepared to march into Hell.

I forgot. We're already in Hell. Sylph sighed. "Look, Mel, it's up to you."

"I know you're going to need people you can trust in there. And I don't look very dangerous; for once being a kid will come in handy."

Sylph laughed at that one. "*Normally,* being a kid is pretty good. Most kids don't have to fight wars. At least I didn't, when I was your age."

Yahvy appeared, clad in leathers that hung loose on her skinny frame. She'd picked up one of Gargorian's spears and had it slung over one shoulder.

"It's almost time to go."

"Melfina's coming with us," said Sylph, half expecting an argument. Yahvy just looked at the little girl, shrugged, and said, "Okay. Who else?"

"Orbaa and a couple of Marlowe's people found uniforms that fit." Sylph hesitated. "And Vhaal."

"You are *not* bringing him."

"We need him, Yahvy. If things go sour . . ."

"I can't believe you put that kind of trust in him!"

"It's not trust. You've seen him fight, haven't you? He's an . . . an *asset*, and I intend to exploit him. That's all."

Yahvy's lip twisted, but she just shook her head.

"Go and make sure the horses are ready," said Sylph. "I'll be there in a few minutes."

"As you wish." She stalked off.

"What about Lina?" said Melfina.

"Lina's not coming," Sylph replied. As a matter of fact, Lina hadn't even been told about the plan, and with a little bit of luck—

"Lina's not coming *where*?" said Lina, walking up the ridge with the ever-present Fah at her heels. She took in her sister and Melfina, dressed in enemy armor, and reached the logical con-clusion. "You're not going—"

"Lina, we have to."

"Then of course I'm coming!" She folded her arms. "You think I'm letting you go over there *alone*? You're nuts!"

"I won't be alone," said Sylph. "I'll have Mel and Yahvy and Orbaa with me." She didn't mention Vhaal, since that would likely not be reassuring. "Besides—"

"If you say one *word* about how I'm more vital to the cause than you are and I shouldn't place myself at risk, I'm going to smack you." Lina shook her head violently. "You know none of this means anything if you don't come back."

"What I was *going* to say," Sylph interrupted, "is that you're a terrible liar. And don't try to deny it."

Lina looked at the ground, but said nothing.

"So this kind of thing is not your forte. Leave it to me—you stay here, with Marlowe and the others, and be ready when we send for you. Okay?"

Lina hesitated. "You know . . ."

"What?"

"You know what I'm going to do to you if you get killed, right?"

Sylph smiled. "I'm afraid to imagine."

✳   ✳   ✳

VESH STARED AT THE UNFORTUNATE SERGEANT ACROSS steepled fingers. The man was the highest ranking survivor of the Seventh Regiment, since his captain had gone down under the cavalry charge and the lieutenant was missing and assumed dead or a prisoner. There were an awful lot of missing men, more than the sergeant's story could explain; Vesh suspected a good number had taken the opportunity to quietly melt away. *It doesn't matter.* They'd already served their purpose.

"Forty horsemen, you said?"

"Yes, my lord. And the Liberator."

"You said that as well." Vesh's smile faded. "Who is he?"

"Beg your pardon, my lord, but it's she. A girl, beautiful like you've never seen but cold as ice, with a sword that flashes like the sun. It's true, my lord, ask anyone. We all saw her."

"Saw" being a relative term. Vesh had no doubt some of the men had gotten a glimpse of the self-proclaimed Liberator, but he was wearily familiar with the tendency of stories to grow in the telling. No doubt the campfires were crowded with anxious renditions. *Damnation.*

"Your men have already returned to their camps?"

"Yes, my lord."

Pity. It would have been nice to keep them separated. "Very well. You're in charge of what's left of the Seventh, though I doubt I'll deploy you for combat. See if you can get me an accounting of what's left." *Information for the next recruiting drive. Details, details.*

The sergeant nodded and bowed his way between the two sparkling Diamond Guardsmen. Vesh gestured to them and said, "Get me Falschim."

The general entered soon after, barely able to contain his rage.

"An ambush. The Seventh has been destroyed."

"As expected," Vesh sighed. "Sacrifices can be useful, General."

"Captain Adrian has served with me for ten years, and he was your *sacrifice*."

"He will be missed, I'm sure." Vesh yawned. "Now, we need to discuss our disposition for tomorrow. You've heard the report?"

"I have." The general tried to regain his composure. "I suggest a slow advance into the woods along the bluffs—fortify our camps and make sure none of them sneak behind us, so we can march to Highpoint without interference."

"Unacceptably slow. Besides, chances are we will be unable to engage the rebels."

"The rebels are of no consequence," said Falschim. "Once we have the fortress . . ."

"One of them is apparently known as the Liberator."

Falschim snorted. "Don't tell me you believe in—"

"It doesn't matter what *I* believe, General, only what *they* believe." Vesh waved his hand to encompass the sprawling camp beyond his tent. "We have no choice now. This girl must fall in battle, and soon, or things will only get worse."

"Girl?"

"So I am told." Vesh shrugged. "In any case, the First and Second Regiments will advance into the valley, presumably causing the enemy to reenact their trap. At that point, the Third and Fourth will attack the south bluff, and the Fifth and Sixth the north. The rest of the army will form our reserve."

"That will expose our leading units."

"I'm aware of that, General. From the sergeant's account I suspect there are only thirty or forty archers at maximum, and perhaps thirty cavalry. If our formation holds—and it will this time, I trust—we should be able to stand them off until the archers are cleared from the walls."

Vesh looked in Falschim's eyes and saw defeat. The general nodded and said, "As you wish, my lord. May I have your leave to go prepare?"

"Go."

Falschim departed, but he was immediately replaced by another of the Diamond Guardsman, who gave a crisp salute. Vesh nodded.

"Yes?"

"More of the Seventh has been trickling in, my lord. Did you want them separated?"

Vesh toyed with the idea. He wasn't comfortable with defeated soldiers spreading the story of the Liberator all across his camp, but since that was already happening confining some of the survivors would only hurt morale. *Besides, the bigger her story becomes, the more effect it will have when we kill her in the morning.* He shook his head.

"Go ahead and let them in. No point in closing the barn door once the horse has escaped."

The Diamond Guardsman bowed, his helmet sending glittering sparks from the candles all over the tent. "Yes, my lord."

✳   ✳   ✳

SYLPH WAITED UNTIL THEY WERE CLEAR OF THE OUTER cordon of sentries before she risked whispering to Orbaa.

"Who's the guy in the sparkling armor?"

"Diamond Guard," the soldier replied in a whisper. "Heard of 'em but never actually seen one before. They're the elite of the elite, Gargorian's personal troops."

"He looks pretty, anyway." Sylph tried to keep smiling; her heart was pounding and her breath came fast. *There's so many of them.*

She'd been afraid Melfina wouldn't fit in well enough, but the army included the usual leavening of camp followers, prostitutes, and enterprising businessmen to serve its needs, and that meant there were quite a number of younger children around. The six of them attracted no real curiosity as they walked down one of the main aisles between the neat rows of tents, but Sylph felt like every last soldier was watching out of the corner of his eye. It made her want to whirl around and check, an urge which she had to constantly suppress.

She was also beginning to wonder if bringing Vhaal along had been wise. *I'm sure he'll come in handy later, but he certainly doesn't look like a conscript.* Even armored in the relatively crude leathers of Gargorian's soldiers, the Circle Breaker had retained his twin blades and moved like a hunting cat on the prowl. He looked deadly; most of the genuine soldiers just looked tired.

Once they reached the first intersection, Sylph pulled her little band into a brief huddle.

"Okay. You two go south . . ." She pointed at the two soldiers from Marlowe's group who'd accompanied them, men he'd sworn she could trust. ". . . and Yahvy, Orbaa and Vhaal will take the north side. Mel, you stay with me. Meet back here just before midnight, and try not to loiter. Understood?"

Everyone nodded.

"Good luck."

They broke up, strolling away as though they'd simply been having a casual conversation. Mel hurried to keep up with Sylph. The two of them struck out to the east, made a few turns into the tent city at random, and started looking around for a place to start.

"How about that?" Melfina pointed to a group of soldiers who'd just sat down to dinner, a couple of birds roasting in their own juice above a crackling campfire.

Sylph nodded. "Follow my lead, okay? And remember to break off if you see anything that looks like an officer."

"Got it."

She took a deep breath and started over. There were seven soldiers in total, five men and two women, and all of them looked up as she and Melfina took seats around the fire. It was all Sylph could do to keep calm. *If I missed something, we're going to be awful dead awful fast . . .*

"Seventh, huh?" said one of the men, nodding at the insignia on the shoulder of her stolen armor. "I heard you guys got your asses handed to you."

Sylph gave him a big smile. "Course we did. Marched in there with no flank cover, damn westerners in the trees shootin' at us—arrow came *this* close to my head!"

"You're lucky," said a tall man morosely. "They always shoot at me."

"You ain't dead yet," said one of the women.

"That's only 'cause I got a thick skull."

"*I* heard," said the first man, "that there were only a couple of dozen of 'em. What in the name of the White Lady happened?"

Sylph shrugged. "We got halfway up the pass when they started shooting arrows at us. Everybody split up, even though Adrian wanted us to stay in formation." She'd gotten the name from one of the prisoners.

"Fuckin' right," said the other woman. "Let him stick his own damn neck out. When the arrows are flying you need somethin' to hide behind."

A general chorus of assent went around the circle.

"He got something stuck in him, anyway," Sylph said. "I saw it all. The captain was blistering everyone pretty good when the Liberator herself rode up on a big white horse and took his head clean off. One swing, damnedest thing I've ever seen." She could feel herself slipping into character. *This is fun!*

"Lady's name," said one of the women.

"Did her sword glow the way everyone says it did?"

"Bright as th' sun. Though you understand I didn't stick around for a closer look."

"Course not!" There was much laughter.

The conversation went on for some time, segueing onto unrelated matters such as the merits of the local whores; this made Sylph a bit uncomfortable, but didn't seem to trouble the two women in the slightest. Eventually three of the men excused themselves, possibly to take their comrade's advice, and Sylph glanced at the so-far-silent Melfina and nodded. *Let's see if this is actually going to work.*

"How long have you been with the army?" she said, trying to sound casual but ringing false in her own ears. None of the others seemed to notice.

"Two years," said one of the women with a sigh. "Since before the western campaign."

"And nothing to look forward to but dying in battle, or maybe if you get really lucky a festering wound'll get you something long and lingering." The soldier spat into the fire with a crackle.

"Why don't you do something about it?" Sylph held her breath.

"You gotta be careful with that kind of talk." One of the women looked around. "You won't even make it to dying in battle, they'll string you *right* up."

"Let her talk," the man said. "Nobody to hear."

"But what can we do?" The woman shrugged. "Run? Gargorian'd hunt you down in the end, he always does."

"What if the whole army turned on him?" Sylph smiled to herself. *They're listening.* "Then who would do the hunting?"

"Not gonna happen. Reason being, nobody is stupid enough to think Gargorian would actually lose, and everyone has family inside the Circles. Even if every last soldier went against him, he could just wall himself up inside the Diamond Tower and wait for us to die. What's a hundred years to an Archmagus?"

"He can't do that if the Circles are broken."

The man laughed. "We can't—"

"The Liberator can. Why do you think we're out here? She broke the Fourth Circle at Highpoint."

There was a stunned silence.

"You're serious?"

Sylph nodded and put her hand on Melfina's shoulder. "This girl was at the fortress when they took it. Tell 'em, Mel."

"I saw it happen," Melfina said in just the right nervous tone. "They opened the node room with axes, and then the Liberator smashed it with her magic sword. We could *feel* it."

"We're outside the Plague right now?" said one of the women.

"I'll fuck you if ya want, but it'll take nine months to find out." The man laughed nervously, then silenced under the glares of his companions.

"You *are* serious."

"Let me tell you something else," Melfina cut in. "The Liberator is coming here tonight."

"Tonight?" the man said, incredulous.

"You don't think she's just going to sit around and wait for us, do you?" said Sylph. Everyone shook their heads. "She's a Magus to match Gargorian, and that means she's going to go through this camp like a hot knife through butter. I, for one, plan to be on the winning side, you know?"

"If she loses, they'll hang us all."

"If she loses, they'll just find someone else for us to fight until everybody's dead. But she's not going to lose."

"You haven't seen her fight," added Melfina. "It's unreal."

"I don't need to hear this," said the quiet woman. She stood up and stalked away from the fire.

"She won't tell anyone," said the other. "I'll go talk to her afterward." She leaned closer and lowered her voice. "Is there a plan?"

"Meet at the central crossroads just after midnight, and wait for word that they're attacking. And tell as many others as you can."

The two soldiers who were left both nodded. Everyone stood up together, shared a last knowing glance, and headed out into the gathering darkness.

"Not bad," Melfina murmured as soon as they were safely away. "You're good at this, Sylph."

"You're pretty good yourself," Sylph returned. "But we're just getting started."

And so it went, group after group and conversation after conversation. The longer Sylph talked, the less respect she had for Gargorian; the army was *ripe* for rebellion, and only resignation kept the men and women in their places. *It's been this way for a long time.* Marlowe had said the best guess was—hard as it was for Sylph to believe—Gargorian had been around since just after the time of the *last* Liberator, almost six hundred years. Archmagi, it appeared were not as mortal as everyone else.

The sun set, though the camp still glowed with torches and campfires. The groups became smaller and the conversations more furtive, which Sylph felt worked to their advantage; people were willing to listen to more in private. There was one bad moment: she'd just finished her revelation on how the Liberator had broken the Fourth Circle when the woman she was talking to got a very cold look in her eye.

"You're from the Seventh, you said?" She put her hand on her sword. "I think we should go see—"

That was as far as she got; Melfina moved, and a knife sprouted as if by magic in the soldier's throat. She stumbled back beside a tent, trying to scream but not succeeding. Sylph watched her twitch without expression. When she was fairly certain the woman was dead, she backed out of the little alley they'd been talking in and set off down the aisle between the tents at a fast walk.

"Think they'll find her?" said Melfina quietly.

"Not soon." Sylph tried to calm herself down. The knife had made a nasty whistling sound as it ripped past her ear. "Not soon enough, anyway."

"Good. It's almost midnight."

"Yeah." Sylph shook her head. "Time to meet up with everyone."

They turned toward the crossroads.

"Melfina?"

"Yeah?"

"T . . . Thanks."

8

chapter eight

THE MAGIC MIRROR REQUESTED ATTENTION WITH A gentle chime. Gargorian had built it that way, but he still found it immensely irritating. *Probably because they only use it for bad news.* He'd considered building another, with a different tone, but the things were fantastically expensive in terms of power and he was feeling hard-pressed as it was.

The Archmagus sighed and waved one meaty hand, and a pair of servants wheeled the circular mirror with its gilt frame in front of the throne. For a moment he was looking at his own reflection—draped in silver and gilt cloth, and so bulky that he filled his chair—then the surface of the mirror misted over and cleared to reveal an anxious General Karl Roswell, of the Fourth Army. He bowed, hurriedly, and said, "My lord Archmagus, we are under attack."

Gargorian's lip twisted. There was no need to ask by whom; only Lady Fell possessed the gall. Instead he said, "How many?"

"We engaged a force of at least two thousand, and victory seemed imminent when her heavy cavalry arrived on our flank. At least another thousand men, my lord."

"Lady Fell doesn't *have* a thousand heavy cavalry left." Gargorian's chins jiggled. "You told me so yourself."

"I . . ." Roswell swallowed. "I must have made an error, my lord. Our intelligence indicated she could not train so many so quickly, but—"

"How many men did your error cost me?"

"We lost perhaps three hundred in the battle and more in the pursuit. I have approximately six regiments left here in Orlow, plus whatever local guards I can press into service."

"What about the Clockwork Legion?"

"We've seen nothing of them, my lord."

The Archmagus harrumphed. "I need to think for a moment." Turning to a servant, he snapped, "Get me Rathmado, now."

Magus Rathmado must have been nearby, because he appeared in the throne room with very little delay. He bowed deeply to Gargorian and offered the general a condescending nod.

"Magus," said Gargorian. "We have a problem. Lady Fell—"

"I know." Rathmado smiled. He seemed to know everything before it happened, and one of these days Gargorian was going to teach him that it was possible to know too much. *Once he's not so useful.* "Lady Fell has got the Fourth Army bottled up in Orlow, correct?"

"We're not bottled up," Roswell protested. "I was discussing our next sally with our officers only an hour ago."

"Then you're more of an idiot than I thought," Gargorian growled. "She has you outnumbered two to one without committing her most powerful unit."

The general fell silent, and Rathmado continued. "The whereabouts of the Clockwork Legion should, therefore, be our primary concern. If she has not committed them against Orlow, it follows that her primary objective is not the Fourth Circle node there."

Gargorian nodded, but Roswell seemed confused.

"But . . . if she doesn't destroy the node, she's risking her army inside the Archmagus's Circle!"

"She's apparently prepared to take that risk," Rathmado said smoothly.

"Enough." Gargorian slashed his hand at the mirror. "You will hold Orlow until instructed otherwise. No sallies are

necessary unless it appears her forces are departing. Understood?"

"Yes, my lord!" The general bowed again, and the glass
misted over once more before returning to normal. Gargorian
waved for the servants to take it way. When they were gone he
turned on Rathmado.

"You know something."

"Only following a train of logic, Archmagus." He smiled
wider.

"Speak, then."

"Roswell is correct; the Lady would not risk the Clockwork
Legion deep inside the Fourth Circle, for fear you would confront it personally."

"You know the Fourth Circle is broken."

"And, therefore, so does she."

Gargorian slammed one hand on the arm of his throne.
"Damn her. This was exactly what I was trying to avoid."

"She has risked much, my lord, by leaving the node at
Orlow in our hands. There is an opportunity here—if we can
reestablish the circle at Highpoint, we will be able to catch the
Clockwork Legion and the rest of Lady Fell's army exactly as
Roswell suggested. She must try to break the Third Circle be-
fore that can happen, and we can make that quite difficult."

"What do you suggest?"

"The Third is still dispersed, correct?"

"Yes." Gargorian shifted on his throne. "There have been
more bandits then I feel comfortable with of late." *Why is it that
I feel put out when he asks a question like that?*

"Begin recalling them. In the meantime, send the First out to
the Circle line and garrison the forts at Silverlake and Brookhold."

"If the Clockworks should attack . . ."

"The Legion is not suited for siege warfare," said Rathmado.
"They won't be able to take the nodes. The Lady will have to
move up human troops, and that will take time. And then when
the Fourth Circle is reestablished . . ."

"We'll have them all," Gargorian finished.   He nodded slowly.   Something about the plan made him uncomfortable— *leaving Bleloth without an army? I'll still have local forces and the Diamond Guard, and the Third Army will only take a few weeks to gather. It's only for a short time. And Rathmado is right; if we can break the Clockwork Legion, Stonerings will be mine within the year.*   No one had ever done that before, conquered the domain of another Archmagus; not Lady Fell with her metal monstrosities or Vilvakis with his demon horde. *Not even the Lightbringer.*

The Archmagus nodded curtly. "I will give the commands."

"Excellent, my lord." Rathmado bowed and withdrew. Gargorian shook his massive head. *If only he wouldn't* smile *like that.*

THE INITIAL RENDEZVOUS WENT AS SMOOTHLY AS SYLPH could have hoped. Yahvy and the two soldiers were waiting in the square, with Vhaal a few feet away. Orbaa was nowhere to be seen, which was also part of the plan.

The calm that had come to Sylph as things had started falling into place was evaporating. *We really don't know anything.* How many of the soldiers would believe what they were told, how many would care? What would happen once the fighting started?

Sylph nodded to Yahvy as she approached, and kept her voice low. "How did things go?"

"Surprisingly well." Yahvy shot a glance at Vhaal. "Though he wasn't much help."

"I didn't expect him to be. Do you think the story got through?"

"It certainly sounded like it. Gargorian must be getting lazy; I heard he used to shuffle people around to make sure there were a reasonable number of veterans in each unit, but this army is almost all recruits."

"That's good."

Yahvy nodded. "They'll be eager to get out of here."

"Did you find out where the commanders are?"

"Officer's section, over that way." She pointed. "There are a few Diamond Guards, but not enough to make a difference. Maybe a hundred professional soldiers all told."

"Good. If we can hit that, we've got this won. How long is Orbaa going to wait?"

"I told him a quarter of an hour. We want to give everyone a chance to get here."

And, Sylph noticed, people were arriving. Most were not obvious about it, but little crowds were gathering in the aisles around the intersection. Sylph and her companions were attracting an increasing amount of attention, which she wished she could have avoided, but there was nothing to be done. *Now, we just have to hope that no one notices before Orbaa pulls his trick.*

Too late. She had a few seconds warning—one of aisles was suddenly full of shouting, pushing people, and the soldiers quickly cleared aside to make way for a new party, a gang of tough-looking men in black leather and chain. At their head was a short, stocky man with a mustache; the insignia Sylph had hastily memorized made him a captain—a regimental commander. From the looks the rest of the soldiers were giving him, he wasn't a well-liked one.

"What," the newcomer growled, "in the name of the Lady is going on out here? What is this disturbance?"

There was a good deal of mumbling from nearby troops, but nothing coherent. A few at the back took the opportunity to slip quietly away.

"This isn't good," Yahvy whispered. "Orbaa might be too late—they're not going to just ignore this guy."

"I'll try to handle it. Get Vhaal over here."

"Vhaal?"

Sylph eyed the captain's guards; there were six of them, all a good head taller than she was. "Just do it." She took a deep breath and stepped forward.

"Captain!"

The man whirled. "Who are you?" His eyes narrowed. "The ringleader of this little organization, perhaps?"

"Something like that." *Stall. Stall for time.* "I'll take responsibility."

"You and everyone else here. I'm going to see to it that General Falschim is informed." He raised his voice. "I'll be back in five minutes, and anyone still here is going to be *very* sorry. We have a rebellion to crush tomorrow!" He turned on his heel, guards following after, and headed for one of the streets.

I can't let him go. "Don't let him through!" Sylph shouted.

There was a strained moment; the crowd in front of the captain shuffled and for a instant looked as though it were going to break, soldiers slipping to either side to stay out of his way. Enough people remained, though, to keep him from just pushing through. Once it became clear that a stand was being made, others filled in behind them. The captain stopped, drew in his breath for another shout, then thought better of it and turned back to Sylph.

"I see how it is." He smiled nastily. "You're an enemy agent."

True enough. "I'm no one's agent, Captain. I'm just here to tell the truth."

"Lies, you mean. And to incite treason, which I need not remind you is punishable by death." He crossed his arms. "I give the rest of you one last chance to leave, but this girl is coming with me. General Falschim and Lord Vesh are going to want to hear this."

More muttering. Sylph tried, but she couldn't make out the words. Almost no one was moving. The captain's smile faded, and he gestured angrily at Sylph. "Take her!"

The guards moved as a body, drawing their swords. Six shards of flashing steel advanced in a semicircle. Sylph kept her knees from shaking by sheer effort of will, and leaned her head at Vhaal and the others.

"Kill them all."

A hush descended over the intersection. It lasted for only a split second, and then the Circle Breakers were moving. Vhaal drew both his swords with an almost musical *tzing* and charged the center of the semicircle, and Melfina moved faster than Sylph could have believed, her knives just appearing in her hands. The leftmost guard grunted as a dagger sank into his belly and another found his shoulder.

One man charging six was madness, and the guards knew it; it took them just an instant too long to realize that Vhaal wasn't going to stop, and move to defend themselves. The one to his right parried, while the one on the left chased after a feint and screeched as Vhaal's sword laid open his side. The boy spun away as the guards turned to follow, and in the next instant Yahvy and Marlowe's men had drawn their swords too. The remaining left-hand guard charged Vhaal, while the others hesitated for a crucial moment. Steel flashed and sparked. Without support, Vhaal's lone attacker was down in a matter of seconds, allowing him to step up and run Yahvy's opponent through from behind. The last two were quickly overwhelmed, and less than a minute after the first sword had been drawn all six guards were lying dead or wounded in the dirt.

Sylph had kept her eyes on the captain, watching the color drain from his face as the fight progressed. His sneer was still arrogant, but she could see the fear behind his eyes; he knew his chances of escaping were slim. *And where the hell is Orbaa, anyway?* She took a step toward the captain, and put her hand on her own weapon. *Let him think we're all as fast as Vhaal.*

"I think, Captain, that we won't be accompanying you after all."

"You'll hang for this." He shook his head violently. "All of you! Do you realize what you've done? Standing by while an enemy agent bares steel against an officer!" He pointed. "Kill her! Kill them all!"

More murmurs, and here and there someone drew a weapon. But there was no massed rush, and Sylph let herself smile.

We've got them.

"Enemy attack!" Even at a distance, she recognized Or-baa's voice along with the sound of a horse at a gallop. "The enemy is raiding the camp! To arms! Enemy attack!"

"The Liberator is here!" Sylph shouted. "The Liberator!"

And a cheer went up from the assembled crowd.

❋   ❋   ❋

"WHAT IN THE LADY'S NAME . . ."

Vesh rushed to the entrance of his tent, pushing past the Diamond Guardsmen. The distant shouts were barely audible, but whatever it was was spreading through the camp like wildfire.

The enemy? They must be mad.

"Sir!" A sergeant was running toward the camp, waving furiously. "My lord Vesh!"

"What's going on?" Vesh snapped.

"Some sort of riot, my lord. We can't get any good information."

"Not the enemy?"

"We're not sure! We've had conflicting reports."

"Find General Falschim. Tell him the enemy stole a march on us and he's to form up as many regiments as possible around the commander's hill, understood?"

"Yes, my lord!" The sergeant dashed off. Vesh turned on his heel and pointed at one of his guards.

"You, get all the other Diamonds to report here. If you see anyone getting organized bring them along. We'll reform the army here."

The man bowed, glittering, and set off down the hill at a jog. Vesh swept back into his tent and started sweeping masses of parchment into their traveling chests. *We may have to move, no harm in being prepared.*

❋   ❋   ❋

"THE LIBERATOR IS COMING!" SYLPH SCREAMED. *MY VOICE
isn't going to last much longer.* "Either stand with her, or be destroyed!" She pointed uphill, dramatically. "We will break our
own chains!"

God, that came out sounding cheesy. It seemed to be working regardless. The mob started to move, slowly at first but gathering
momentum. The captain who'd been so brave moments before
had taken advantage of the distraction to vanish. Sylph grabbed
the others in her small group and kept them close so they wouldn't
be pulled apart in the tumult.

"Sylph, this is unbelievable!" Yahvy shouted, barely audible
above the roar of the crowd.

"Not finished yet!" She leaned closer to Marlowe's men,
who seemed just a little in shock. "You two know what to do?"

That seemed to wake them. One nodded and the other said,
"Yes. Go and tell Marlowe that he should ride."

"Make sure he brings Lina along!" *I think we're going to need her.*

"Yes, sir!" said the soldier, automatically. He and his companion broke away, fighting the press. Sylph stared after them
for a moment—*who addresses a fourteen-year-old girl as "sir"?*—and
then turned back to the others.

"Come on, we've got to make sure this doesn't bog down."
She tried to be certain no one had gotten separated, keeping
an especially close eye on Vhaal. The presence of so many
armed men was making him twitchy. With Yahvy clearing a
path and Vhaal watching the rear, the four of them moved faster
than most, and gradually they approached the wavefront. The
crowd was like a living thing now. Sylph doubted she could have
stopped it if she'd wanted to. The power of what she'd unleashed
was a bit frightening. *Everyone was ready for this to happen. It just
needed a little spark.*

"Stop this at *once!*" The voice that rang out was so loud,
so drenched with the air of command, that Sylph found herself
obeying involuntarily. She shook her head and pushed her way

into the front rank of the crowd, off to one side so as not to attract attention. Once she got there, her heart sank. Arrayed on
the main road was a block of soldiers, all with insignia from the
First Regiment. They were armed with spears and packed into
tight formation, and the orderless mob shied away from the solid
wedge of bristling points. Behind them, mounted on a black
charger and spectacularly armored in silver and gold, was a tall
man bearing the marks of the army general. *Falschim*, the prisoners had named him, famous for his prowess in battle as well as
his leadership. *This is trouble.*

"The camp is under attack by the enemy; we do not have
time for this *foolishness*. Form up in regiments, on the double!"
It was a voice the soldiers had been hearing day in and day out,
many of them for years; obedience was instinctive. Some of the
raw rage began to fade, and Sylph could hear people starting
muttered conversations. *Shit, shit,* shit—*we almost had it*—but a
rush onto those spear-points would kill dozens, and she couldn't
think of a way to make it happen.

Unless . . .

"Mel!" Sylph hissed. "Can you hit him from here?"

"The general?" Melfina gauged, then shook her head. "Too
much in the way. It'd be pure luck."

"Try it."

"But—"

"Just do it!"

The girl swallowed and gave a hurried nod, slipping her
hand inside her armor and coming out with a balanced throwing knife. The line of spearmen had advanced a step, and that
opened up the line-of-sight a little. Melfina took a deep breath,
brought her arm back, and whipped the dagger forward just as
Falschim opened his mouth to issue another tirade.

Sylph wanted to close her eyes, but it happened so quickly
she didn't have the chance. One moment the general was sitting on his horse; the next the animal was rearing and he was
collapsing backwards, spurting blood from a ruined throat. A

number of spearmen turned to see what was happening. *Now's our chance.*

"For the Liberator!" Sylph screamed. At the same time she grabbed Melfina by the collar and backpedaled hurriedly, shouldering men aside in her haste to get back into the press. It was just in the nick of time; the front rank of spearmen, having heard the cry, pressed forward to get to the source. They weren't about to ground their weapons, and there wasn't room for the mob to clear a path. The street was suddenly full of jostling, shouting men and women, and with steel already drawn that could only go on for so long.

A woman in the front rank screamed as a fed-up soldier thrust his spear into her belly. She stumbled and sank to the ground, her hands wrapped around the shaft; a man who'd been standing next to her drew his sword with a scream of rage and charged the unfortunate spearman, shattering his skull with a single blow. Before he could get any further a pair of spears jabbed him, in the leg and the shoulder, and he fell beside his victim. Another heartbeat, and the spearmen charged; screams and curses went up and down the line as they drew blood from the front of the mob. Sylph, holding on to Yahvy with one hand and Melfina with the other, struggled desperately to stay in one place as the soldiers surged forward, breaking the line of spearmen by weight of numbers and pulling them away from one another to be pummeled or gutted in desperate, close-quarters fighting.

Falschim's stand was done, his body trampled by a crowd of men and women driven into a murderous rage. Blood was in the air, and Sylph knew there would be no stopping them now. They packed the street like a river, heading for the officers' tents. Another captain, backed by only a dozen or so guards, tried to make a stand; his men abandoned him before the mob reached him, and he was cut down before he said a word. Sylph thought she caught a glimpse of Vhaal at the forefront, finally unleashed and doing what he did best.

It was a few minutes before the largest part of the army had passed them by and it was quiet enough for conversation. Sylph looked around carefully. There were scattered groups of soldiers visible, engaging in a little looting during the confusion, but no one close enough to threaten them. She let out a deep breath.

"I think . . ." Her voice was hoarse from screaming, and she cleared her throat. "I think we did it."

"Unbelievable." Yahvy shook her head, slowly, then let out a wild whoop. "Un*fucking*believable! Sylph, you are a Lady-damned *genius*."

"Not really," Sylph protested, before she was smothered under Yahvy's hug. Sylph had to wait until she let go to gasp for breath; Yahvy turned to Melfina and wrapped an arm around her shoulders.

"And you! What a shot!"

"Mostly luck," said Melfina, but without force. She smiled as Yahvy shook her.

"It's amazing what a little luck can do, then!"

"It may be a bit early to start celebrating," Sylph said. "We still have to get things moving our way, once this burns itself out."

Yahvy nodded and took a deep breath. "I know. I'm just not sure I believed this would work—do you realize what we've *done*?"

Sylph held up a hand. "Later. Let's go find Orbaa and the others."

"What about Vhaal?"

Sylph looked up at the hill, where fires had already been started. The night sky had started to glow a smoldering red. "If he wants to take off on his own, there's not much we can do for him."

"My lord!" the sergeant protested. "We don't have the men! The general is dead, and—"

"Idiot!" Vesh whirled on him. "I told you to take everything you have and *hold that street*. Were my instructions unclear somehow?"

"But I haven't got even a regiment's worth ready to follow! There's more than a thousand men out there. My lord, it can't be done!"

Vesh snapped his fingers and pointed. The sergeant turned, but before he could draw one of the Diamond Guardsmen thrust his sword into the man's belly. He groaned and collapsed, bleeding all over Vesh's expensive fur rugs.

It can't be helped. Going to have to leave it all . . . it doesn't matter if I can't think of someway to explain this to Gargorian. He tossed the last of his papers into a trunk and slammed it shut. *The Diamonds should be able to cut a way out of here, in any case. They don't have anything like proper leadership.* He looked around irritably. *Of all the times for the servants to run off!*

"You!" He pointed at one of the Diamond Guardsman. "Find me someone who *will* hold that road. And while you're at it, send some men to carry my things."

The man saluted and ducked out the tent flap. Vesh had just turned back to his packing when he heard a nasty squeal, like fingernails on glass, followed by a gurgling shriek. *What in the name . . .*

The two remaining Diamonds already had their weapons out, slashing at a cloaked figure that burst through the tent flap. The attacker stopped one strike with his blade and took a cut on the shoulder, diamond blade biting through chain mail and drawing blood. Despite this, the man kept coming, rolling toward the guard who'd wounded him and coming up from a crouch sword-first. It caught the Diamond Guard just below his impenetrable breastplate and drove up into his stomach. He sank without a sound. The other guard lashed out at the figure's back, but the attacker had abandoned his weapon and leaned forward, so the diamond sword glanced off the chain mail under his cloak.

"Kill him!" Vesh shrieked, but no one was paying attention. The attacker had relieved the dead guard of his weapon and was dueling with the Diamond Guard, crystal blades flickering too fast to follow. There was a horrible screech as the Guard's blade scraped along the figure's side, but the thrust left him wide open; the attacker leaned in and sank his sword into the Guard's throat, below his chin-guard. His corpse joined his partner's and the sergeant's on the rug, and the attacker spun to face Vesh.

"Y . . . You . . ." Vesh sputtered for a moment before regaining his composure. "Who do you think you are? What do you plan to accomplish? All you're doing is assuring yourself a long and painful death when Gargorian catches up with you. Let me go, and I may be able to get you a pardon; otherwise when he finds you, you'll live for *weeks* in the dungeons, I promise you . . ."

The figure reached up and pulled back its hood, and Vesh was taken aback. *I* know *that face.* "Steelbreaker." He thought frantically. "You must be . . . Vhaal, yes?"

Vhaal nodded, smiling ominously. He took a step forward, and Vesh backed away.

"The prodigal son. Who would had though I'd see you here?" He shook his head. "Your father's dead, you know, and your sisters aren't happy with you. But we can leave here. Come with me, and Gargorian will reward you."

Vhaal shook his head, still smiling. Vesh barely had time to throw up his hands as death lunged across the tent for him.

LINA RODE UNEASILY TOWARD GARGORIAN'S ARMY. SHE was beginning to suspect she'd never have the same easy grace on a horse as, say, Marlowe; the clumsy feeling his bulk lent him vanished when he was mounted, and he rode as though he'd been born in the saddle. She was starting to get a little more comfortable with the idea of having this *thing* underneath her with a mind of its own, one that might suddenly take it into its

head to run very fast or roll over; that helped with the nervousness, but didn't make her any less sore.

It wasn't much consolation to see that her escorts weren't
having things much better. Fah was a competent rider, nothing
more, and none of the other three seemed totally at ease.

The other three. Myris, Kari, and Zaya, whom she'd saved
from rape at the hands of Marlowe's soldiers. She'd tried to put
the episode out of her head; Marlowe rode at her side and acted
as though nothing unusual had happened, but she couldn't let
it pass so easily. The cavalry commander had been true to his
word—there'd been no more rapes while they rounded up the
prisoners, and if there had been grumbling from the men it had
been handled out of her sight. *Still.*

Myris, Kari, and Zaya had insisted on accompanying her
to the camp, despite their bruises. "Insisted" was probably the
wrong word, truthfully; they had simply refused to leave her side
under any circumstances. Lina wasn't willing to order Marlowe to get rid of them, despite the misgivings he and Yahvy had
expressed. Not that she minded the company. Kari and Zaya
stuck close together most of the time, and Myris seemed to have
established a fast friendship with Fah, the two having spent most
of the ride talking in low tones. There was just something in the
eyes of all three that made Lina uncomfortable.

"Comin' up," said Orbaa. He rode at Marlowe's side, preen-
ing over his role in the plan. Marlowe grunted assent and gave
a hand gesture that sent scouts dashing ahead. One returned, a
minute later, to report that no resistance was expected.

"Lady be praised," Fah whispered. "It actually worked?"

"Of course it worked," said Lina, suppressing a sigh of relief.
"Sylph's plans always do."

Marlowe smiled at her, but said nothing. The little band of
cavalry made its way to the encampment, a wide ring of tents
in orderly rows spread around a central hill. On the hilltop,
something was burning; a plume of black, heavy smoke rose in
a twisted pillar into the sky. Almost no one was visible on the

outskirts. A group of soldiers piled out of a tent, but fled deeper into the camp when the horsemen approached.

"Lady Almighty," Marlowe swore. "What did you sister *do* to this place?"

Lina nodded, feeling a little ill. While the rows of tents were mostly still standing, here and there they were crushed with spars sticking from the cloth like broken bones. There were bodies everywhere, all in Gargorian's armor, and the cries of the wounded rose from every direction. Marlowe led, picking his way around clusters of corpses and scattered cookfires. Lina followed, with her four bodyguards.

"Where's Sylph?" she said.

Orbaa shrugged. "She told us to meet her here."

She'd better not have gotten . . . hurt, or anything like that. Lina clenched her jaw. *Damn her . . .*

"That's her!" It happened so quickly—a dozen soldiers rounded a tent, one woman pointing in Lina's direction. They were all armed and armored, and only Marlowe and Fah were between them and Lina. Steel shivered as the cavalry commander drew and bellowed for support—Gargorian's soldiers rushed forward, and . . .

. . . threw themselves onto their knees, bowing.

Marlowe's cavalry pulled up short, which was no easy thing on horseback, and Marlowe stood over the prostrate soldiers with sword in hand. It took Lina a moment to get anything from their confused babble, but there was one word she could pick out.

"Liberator! The Liberator!"

"It's her!"

"Lina! The Liberator!"

"Quiet!" Marlowe roared, and was obeyed, much to Lina's relief. He gestured to one of the men with his sword. "Get up, slowly. What's going on here?"

The man obeyed, dusting himself off and regaining some of his composure. "The camp's been thrown into confusion, my lord . . ." He hesitated.

"My lord will do," said Marlowe.

"Yes, my lord. The general ordered us into regiments to crush the traitors, and when no one listened his men attacked the crowd! Afterward things fell apart completely. Almost everyone went up to the hill to kill officers, but there are a few wandering around stealing or just lost or hiding. We've been trying to find them and bring them here—"

"Waiting for you," one of the women cut in. "My lady, the Bane of Gargorian." She bowed again.

Lina felt too stunned to speak, though she'd known at least some of this had been a part of Sylph's plans. Marlowe cleared his throat and said, "What's happening now?"

"I don't know, my lord. There's still fighting on the hill, and fires, but it seems to be mostly over. I saw some sergeants trying to form up their squads to wait for the . . . for you, but some of the men weren't listening to them. Sometimes they were killing them."

"Chaos, in other words."

"Yes, my lord."

Marlowe took a deep breath, let it out slowly, and turned to Lina. "My lady."

"Don't . . ."

He leaned closer and whispered, "Appearances, my dear. Just don't let it go to your head." Then, in a more normal tone, "Do I have your permission to establish control of the situation?"

"Yes." She nodded vigorously. "Of course."

"Good." He turned and bellowed at his men. "Veiz, Krauz, Dellwood!" He got back a chorus of acknowledgements. "Take ten men each and spread out. Tell anyone who'll listen to meet us here, and that we'll guarantee their safety. Tell them the Liberator is here to protect them, understand?"

"What about anyone who won't listen?" asked one of them.

"Leave them alone. They're free to leave if they want. Make sure you send people back in groups, and bring along any wounded who look like they can saved. Understood?"

"Yes, Warleader!"

"Good. Get going."

"Warleader," said Orbaa, as the three squads rode away, "are you sure that's wise? Even with desertions and so on, there's enough men here to squash us flat."

"Doesn't matter how many there are," said Marlowe. "Discipline's shattered. There's no way they'd try to take us on."

"And even if they did," Fah put in, "Lina would dispatch them."

Myris nodded fervently. Lina, personally, felt a bit less confident. She had the sword—she touched the hilt at her side, just to be certain it was still there—but she didn't know exactly what it could do. *Or how safe it is.* Its presence was certainly reassuring. She'd been wearing it more and more; it seemed to focus her mind on the matters at hand, and keep her from revisiting her nightmares during the day.

It wasn't long before soldiers started trickling in, mostly in small groups. They stopped to gawk at Lina as soon as they noticed her; she was starting to wish she'd worn something a bit better-looking that her usual leathers. Marlowe had his men establish a perimeter and start organizing the new arrivals into details. Some he set to clearing away the bodies, some to digging graves, and some to removing enough tents to leave a large open square.

"What's the point?" Lina whispered to him, after he returned to her side.

"Keeps 'em busy," Marlowe said. "First thing you learn about commanding men—never let them sit around and think, it's bad for morale."

"But you're not commanding them," Lina said. "They rebelled against Gargorian."

"And now they're working for you, they just don't know it yet."

Lina shifted uncomfortably. "Are you sure about this?"

"We're going to need an army, aren't we?"

"Yeah." She shook her head. "Just remember—anyone who wants to leave can leave, no questions asked."

"Try not to say that too loud."

"I'm not imprisoning people here, Marlowe. If they want to help fight, that's fine, but if not—"

He held up his hands. "I get it, I get it. I'll make sure they know."

"Good." She settled back, feeling a little better. *Now where's*—

"Sylph!" said Fah, pointing. Marlowe's bellows quickly cleared a path for Sylph, Yahvy, and Melfina. It was obvious to Lina that Sylph was exhausted—it was getting close to dawn, and she hadn't slept—but she was grinning like the cat that got the parrot.

"Sylph!" Lina restrained herself until her sister got through the cordon of soldiers. Then she ran over and hugged her, despite the odd looks it drew from everyone. *I don't care. She's my little sister.* "Are you okay?"

Sylph nodded. "We did it!"

"I know. Marlowe's been gathering everyone here. I'm so glad you're all right. Did any of the others get hurt?"

"Not a scratch, except for Vhaal. He wandered off and we haven't found him yet."

Lina nodded. She couldn't force herself to feel much worry for Vhaal, though it was awful to think so. Instead she hugged Sylph again and said, "You have to tell me what happened. There's bodies everywhere!"

"Later." Sylph disentangled herself. "I have to talk to Marlowe before I collapse from exhaustion."

"Oh." Lina took a step back. *Stupid, you can see how tired she is, what are you getting in her way for?* "He's over there, go."

Sylph nodded wearily. Yahvy followed her, and Melfina seemed almost asleep on her feet, leaning on the older Circle Breaker's arm. Fah exchanged a brief nod with her companions as they stumbled past.

Marlowe was barking orders as soldiers poured into the

square. Lina looked at them, and tried to smile. More men arrived bearing wounded; those members of Gargorian's forces with any first-aid training were pulled out of the ranks to tend to them. The army was putting itself together in front of Lina's befuddled eyes, men and women who'd been in the same regiment naturally seeking one another out and then obediently sitting in neat ranks as Marlowe or one of his sergeants got to them.

"I feel kind of, I don't know, useless," Lina said to her bodyguards. Fah smiled at her.

"There's no shame in leaving things to Marlowe. He knows what he's doing."

"What should I do to help?"

Fah shrugged.

"You could wave," Myris suggested.

By the time the War Council reconvened it was well after noon. Sylph had barely managed to assure herself that Marlowe had things under control before lack of sleep and adrenalin backlash overwhelmed her; she awoke hours later, curled up under a blanket some kind soul had pulled over her. On waking, she'd done a more considered evaluation of the situation and decided the world could manage without her for a little while longer. So she rolled over and went back to sleep, and didn't get around to convening the leaders until afternoon.

Heraan had returned, she was glad to see. He'd ridden off to try and restore some order to the camp, and privately she'd been a bit concerned for his safety, but he hadn't taken a scratch. He'd placed himself at Sylph's right hand, and adopted the manner of some kind of executive assistant. Lina was accompanied by Fah and three other girls, whom she'd apparently rescued from something or other; Sylph wasn't particularly happy about their inclusion but didn't have the energy to argue. They seemed to be content to sit quietly, in any case.

Orbaa sat in Marlowe's seat. The big cavalry commander was still out with the men, making sure everything was in
place. Under his direction the camp was coming apart; the tents
folded up, the giant supply wagons that accompanied the army
re-hitched and reloaded with food and water. And the graves, of
course, which were being filled as fast as they could be dug. He
was letting the troops sleep in shifts, so that some would always
be occupied.

Yahvy sat on Sylph's left. She'd also gotten a few hours
of crash-sleep and was looking much better; Melfina was still
snoring. By Sylph's request, Garot had joined them. He was
normally content to follow orders, and Sylph normally wouldn't
have bothered him. *But I think I'm going to need him.* Daana, as
usual, was with the wounded.

This time, when Sylph cleared her throat, she didn't have
to wait very long for silence. She kept a straight face, but somewhere inside she was giggling madly.

"First things first," she said in her most businesslike tone.
"Orbaa, want to give us an update?"

"We've got the camp cleared, more or less, and everybody
back under control. After they trashed th' officers' tents on the
hill things got a little confused. There was some . . ." He glanced
at Lina. ". . . unpleasantness over in th' camp followers' section,
but we sent some people over there to keep an eye on things. Not
too bad, all in all. A lot of runaways, of course, but a surprisin'
number of them came back in the mornin'."

"The military lifestyle," said Heraan. "Once you get into
the habit of obeying orders, it can be hard to stop."

"Marlowe agrees with you," Orbaa continued. "We're letting anyone go who wants to go, of course, but most of them
seem pretty happy to do what they're told."

"How many?" said Sylph.

"After desertions, and countin' the prisoners from earlier,
about fifteen hundred."

"What about the commanders?"

"The general was this Falschim," said Orbaa, "and we know how he died. Apparently some henchmen of Gargorian's named Vesh was along as well. I'm not sure what he was up to, but he's dead now; somebody cut through half a dozen Diamond Guards to get to him."

"Somebody?" Heraan raised an eyebrow. "You think one person did that?"

"Could've been a gang of soldiers, but if so they carted off their losses and did a good job cleanin' up afterward. In either case, we got Vesh's papers, some good maps of the city and the Circles, and some other stuff we're still lookin' through."

"Good." Sylph nodded to him. *This isn't so hard after all. Just listen to what people say, and nod, and maybe give the occasional order.* She stopped herself from giggling aloud. *I always wanted to be a general!*

"Now what?" asked Lina.

All eyes turned to Sylph, and she swallowed. *Okay. Maybe not* easy. "First we start moving. I'd rather not camp right here if we can avoid it. Orbaa, how's our supply situation?"

"Pretty good. We got Falschim's stores almost intact, and he had enough to support th' entire army for a month or so. I'd say we have six weeks, give or take, an' here on the plains water shouldn' be a problem."

"Let's move a couple of days east. How far to Bleloth?"

"Two weeks," said Heraan, "for an army this size."

"And that's where we have to go?" Lina asked.

"Gargorian's there," Orbaa said. "An' whatever magical gewgaws he uses to maintain the Circles. If you can break that you'll end th' Plague once and for all."

"The countryside would rise for you," said Fah eagerly. "Without the Plague, if he can't just murder the children of anyone who opposes him, Gargorian's lost his most important hold on the people."

"She's right," said Heraan. "Even if Gargorian sees us coming and flees the city, if we take the Diamond Tower the war's as good as won."

"What about Gargorian himself?" Sylph asked. "Can we expect anything from him during the battle, fireballs or something like that?"

Heraan shook his head. "Gargorian is the Magio Creator, the Archmagus of Creation. His magic is chiefly concerned with building things; none of the others could have put up the Tower, for instance. But I doubt he'll even show himself until this is done, one way or the other."

"That's one less thing to worry about. Still, I think we may be getting a little bit ahead of ourselves here," said Sylph. "Gargorian's still got two armies at Bleloth, right? Four thousand men, plus his local garrison and the Diamond Guard. Why should he flee?"

"The Diamond Tower's never been taken," said Orbaa, "not even in the bad ol' days before Gargorian cemented control."

"Nobody ever got one of his armies to turn on him, either." Heraan smiled. "We'll think of something."

That was the phrase that kept ringing in Sylph's ears as the meeting broke up. *We'll think of something. He means* I'll *think of something.* Not that she minded the vote of confidence, but . . . *well, maybe I do mind. What if I can't think of something?*

There had been a few more details to sort out. The regiments needed commanders; the vast majority of the officers had been killed overnight, and those few who hadn't had fled with the morning. The sergeants, drawn from within the ranks of the conscripts, seemed solid enough; still, Sylph hesitated to put anyone she didn't know in command.

With that in mind, Marlowe (through Orbaa) had recommended a reorganization of the army into five regiments, under Orbaa, Yahvy, Garot, Heraan, and Fah. Daana had already declined to command, preferring to remain with the healers. Garot nodded and accepted the order, and the others all seemed pleased except for Fah, who flatly refused. Her place, she'd insisted, was by Lina's side. That left command of the

Fifth Regiment up in the air, but Orbaa said that Marlowe could manage it for the moment.

Sylph had been glad to escape from the confines of the tent and take a breath of fresh air, wet with the smell of the rain. Almost everything had been packed away, and all that was left of the camp was a vast patch of turned earth, scorched black here and there and mounded up along the edge. *Graves.* She didn't like to think about that.

All Sylph really wanted was to find a place on one of the supply wagons and curl up, but it was not to be. A runner from the healers found her, and before too long she was in another tent, watching a pretty blond girl wrapping Vhaal in bandages. She was taking more care than Sylph would have. The boy had taken off his shirt, and Sylph admitted he was well muscled and perhaps handsome in a cruel sort of way, but that was no reason to . . .

Enough. She cleared her throat, and realized she didn't know what to say. *I can't really welcome him back, can I?*

Vhaal solved that problem for her. "I wanted to thank you, Sylph, for what you've done over the past few weeks."

She gritted her teeth. "It wasn't for your sake."

"My thanks stand nonetheless. And I also thought it would be courteous to inform you that I'm leaving, as soon as my wounds have healed sufficiently for me to ride."

"Leaving?" She blinked. "To go where?"

"Home."

Sylph realized she knew next to nothing about where Vhaal had come from, besides the awful stories he'd told. To cover her confusion, she shrugged.

"As you like. It's not my concern."

He nodded, as though that had been the answer he expected, then suddenly grinned. "Do me a favor. Tell Yahvy—"

"I'm not doing you any favors, and you can deliver your jibes yourself. Just be careful she doesn't give you another decoration to add to these."

His smile remained, but he said nothing. Sylph shook her head.

"Was there anything else?" When he was silent, she turned to go. As she reached the tent flap, he spoke again.

"One thing. Where exactly *are* you from, Sylph Walker?"

She almost stumbled. Rather than answer, she kept walking, slipping into the fresh air as though she hadn't heard. Behind her, Vhaal chuckled softly.

*　*　*

"THAT," SAID HERAAN, "HAS GOT TO BE THE MOST PREPOS-terous thing I've ever heard."

"The man swears it's true," said Orbaa.

"Do you believe him?" Sylph asked.

"I think so. His markings are Third Army, sure enough, and he looks like he's been running a long way."

"It's a long way to go, just to give us some news."

"He didn't come to give us news," said Fah. "He came to serve the Liberator, because he believes in ridding our land of the Tyrant."

"What does this mean?" said Lina.

"If Gargorian sent the First Army easterly, it can only mean Lady Fell has decided to toss the dice again." Heraan shook his head. "And the Third is scattered, chasing bandits. It seems too good to be true."

"Did this man say if Gargorian knew of the Second Army's rebellion?" said Sylph.

"No. But if rumors have already reached the city, we can assume he knows all about it," Heraan said.

"Too bad we couldn't keep everyone here," Sylph mused. "It would have been nice to surprise him."

"We're not holding people against their wills," Lina said firmly.

"I know. I'm just thinking." Sylph closed her eyes. "Even

if Gargorian called in the Third as soon as he sent the First east, he won't have his full strength concentrated at the city for some time."

"Two more weeks, the man said." Orbaa looked eager. "If we strike now, all he's got to man the walls are the Diamond Guard and whatever bits of the Third that have arrived! A thousand men at most."

"Certainly sounds better than four thousand," said Sylph, "but—"

"We're not ready." Heraan shook his head. "Give me a month, maybe, and I can have my regiment in shape to fight a battle. We're trying to make conscripts into real soldiers. They believe in the cause, but it still isn't easy. Now you want me to take them up against a fortress wall? We won't have a chance."

"We won't have a chance anyway," said Sylph, "unless . . ."

"Unless?" Heraan leaned forward expectantly. So, Sylph noticed, did everyone else.

"Let me think," she said, to buy time. "In the meanwhile, if Gargorian already knows about us, there's no harm in marching to Bleloth. He doesn't have the strength for a field battle, we hope, which means we can always leave again."

"Unless it's a trap," said Yahvy gloomily.

"We'll have scouts out," said Orbaa. "We'll see them coming, don't worry."

Sylph closed her eyes. *Something clever. Come on, Sylph. Time to reach into the magic box and pull out something clever.*

chapter nine

IAM OZYMANDIAS, KING OF KINGS. LOOK UPON MY works, ye Mighty, and despair."

"Hmm?" said Yahvy.

"Nothing," Sylph muttered. "Just thinking."

The Diamond Tower, lit by the sun rising behind it, rose like a single bolt of pure white light from the heavens, or the blade of an enormous spear jutting up through the earth. If Yahvy hadn't assured her of it, Sylph wouldn't have believed they were still a few days march from the base. It was easy to be deceived by the sheer size of thing until she noticed the city clustered around its base like an afterthought. It wasn't a single perfect diamond, either; subtle internal flaws sent glittering spots of light the size of a village crawling slowly across the landscape as the sun toiled across the sky.

"How does he get *up* there?" Sylph shook her head. "High-speed elevator?"

"High speed what?" Yahvy asked curiously.

"From what I've heard," said Heraan, "Most of the Tower is just solid diamond. Gargorian and his people live around the base, and above that they have some dungeons and interrogation chambers and so forth. The spire is just for show."

"Someone's compensating."

Lina giggled, but no one else seemed to get the joke. *Oh,*

well. Sylph continued, "How far to the city?"

"If we pushed we could make it by sundown tomorrow," said Marlowe.

"No, take it nice and easy. I want scouts out, but no engagements until I give the word. Just because we've got them outnumbered doesn't mean they'll just sit inside the walls and wait for us. Make sure there's nothing nasty in the valley."

Marlowe nodded. "As you wish."

Sylph looked up and down the immensity of the Tower and shook her head again. *How in God's name are we supposed to take something like that?*

WITH THE FIRST ARMY MARCHING TO THE AID OF THE Fourth, and the Second having turned its coats—Gargorian ground his teeth—that left only the Third to defend the Tower. The commander of the Third Army was named Viigo Harenson, a dutiful enough man but not one who had gone out of his way to draw attention to himself. He'd risen through the ranks by being careful, and the thought of having to take charge of his master's physical defense was clearly too much for him. So, somewhat unwillingly, Gargorian had sent for the always-helpful Rathmado. *My own private genie.* He rubbed the soft skin of his forehead with one ring-covered hand.

"My lord . . ." Viigo began.

"Wait." The door to the throne room opened, and Rathmado entered at a brisk walk. Gargorian nodded to him and received a bow in turn. "Magus."

"My lord. General." He gestured to the map table. "Shall we begin?"

Viigo nodded firmly. "Let's begin with the central problem. We have too much wall and not enough men to hold it. With the Diamond Guard, and stripping the city absolutely bare, we can field perhaps twelve hundred. Bleloth's walls are more than twelve miles around, and over the years the city has grown considerably beyond them. With numbers like that, it will be much too easy for the attackers to gain a section of wall, clear it of defenders, and force us into a house-by-house fight."

"All of which is irrelevant," Rathmado said, "since clearing the city of guards is out of the question. If anything, we need more security to protect us against traitors."

"Conscript more men," Gargorian wheezed. His fingernails clicked on the arm of his throne. "Take every man, woman, and child in the city and put them on the walls, and hang anyone who disobeys."

There was a moment of silence, after which Viigo cleared his throat. "With respect, my lord, I don't think that will produce the intended result. There are more than a hundred thousand civilians in the city; we couldn't arm them all even if we wanted to, and if they turned on us we would be overwhelmed."

"Though the idea has some merit," said Rathmado. "Go to the nobles and take their household guards."

Good idea, indeed. The nobility owed everything to Gargorian; they were chiefly composed of his closest followers and their families, along with a few wealthy merchants. More, they knew it would be their heads on the block if the city fell. "Have it done," the Archmagus rumbled. A servant rushed to obey.

"In any case," Viigo continued with a little less certainty, "we must consider a second option."

"Such as?"

"Dispatch my men, with riders, to gather the rest of the Third Army outside the city. Pull the Diamond Guard and the rest of the auxiliaries inside the Tower, and send messengers to recall the Second. Once we have that force, we'll have the strength to crush the rebels whether they hold the city or not."

The Archmagus's lip twisted, like a petulant child.

"Out of the question," said Rathmado.

Viigo glared at him. "With all due respect, Magus . . ."

"What you don't understand, General," rumbled Gargorian,

"is the . . . the . . ."

"Political," Rathmado suggested.

"The political aspect of the situation." Gargorian shook his head. "What will the people of the city think if we hide in the Tower?"

"Not to mention Lady Fell," said Rathmado quietly.

"If I am treed by a *rebel* it will do damage that will take years to mend."

"My lord," Viigo said, "let the peasants think whatever they like. The Diamond Tower is impregnable, and if you let the Plague take them all soon enough they will be clamoring for your return. This is a minor setback, nothing more."

"And if Lady Fell retakes Orlow in the meantime?" Rathmado demanded.

"Orlow can be retaken," Viigo said. "What I've suggested is our only valid course of action."

"I have another," the Magus said calmly.

Gargorian took a deep, raspy breath to calm himself. One hand reached automatically to a bowl on his left and popped a grape into his mouth. "Speak."

"We should meet them in the field."

"Are you *mad*?" Viigo sputtered. "We know they have at least seventeen hundred, probably more!"

"A small force."

"And ours is smaller! Five hundred of the Third and another five hundred—"

"Numbers are not everything, General. Five hundred of ours are the Diamond Guard, the finest fighting men in the world. With the least bit of support from your men I'm sure they'll be *more* than a match for a swarm of rebels."

"The Diamond Guards are trained for personal combat, not field operations."

"And you think the rebels will have adequate training?" Rathmado sighed. "The decision is simple: we cannot risk a siege, and we dare not fight inside the city. Therefore, we must fight outside it."

"This is insanity." Viigo turned to Gargorian. "My lord, this man is not a soldier. What does he know of these matters?"

"Enough." Gargorian's face twisted. "Rathmado."

"Yes, Archmagus."

"You are certain the Diamond Guard will be sufficient to defeat the rebels?"

"Of course, my lord."

"My lord . . ."

"Do not interrupt me, Viigo," Gargorian rumbled. "You will do as Rathmado orders. I am placing him in command of Bleloth's defense. Is that understood?"

"I . . ." The fire of resistance, never strong, died behind the general's eyes. "As you wish, Archmagus."

"Good. Now leave me."

The two bowed and made a quick exit. Gargorian plucked another grape.

They will be crushed, Gargorian thought. *They* will *be. And that will leave the Second Army free to deal with Lady Fell.* He feared the Clockwork Legion more than some ragtag band of rebels.

His fingers drummed a tattoo on the crystal throne.

THE STRANGER PULLED BACK HIS COWL, REVEALING YELLOWED bone. Vermin crawled and writhed inside his head, and flies were dense on the gobbets of blackened flesh that still remained. When he moved, they took off in a buzzing swarm that surrounded Lina in a cloud of winged specks. She was stuck, frozen in place, and could do nothing as skeletal fingers gently wrapped themselves around her hips and pulled her close.

"Lina?"

Lina rolled onto her back, her hair drenched in sweat, desperately trying to breathe. The dream faded slowly, and it felt as though the stranger were still with her; she could almost feel the prickle of centipedes crawling across her skin, and hear the drone of the flies.

"Lina? Are you awake?"

The voice—Sylph—was coming from outside the tent flap. She heard Myris answer.

"She's asleep, as I told you. You'll have to wait until the morning—"

"I'm awake!" Lina shouted. "Let her in, Myris. I'm awake." She stumbled out of her cot, dragging the bedclothes halfway across the tent before she got disentangled. Myris opened the tent flap and bowed, holding it aside for Sylph to duck under.

"Hi."

"Hi," Lina said. "Myris, if my sister ever wants to see me, you let her in. Understand? Tell the others too."

Myris nodded. "Yes, my lady." She let the flap fall, leaving the sisters alone. There was an awkward silence.

"Are you planning to fight someone?"

"What?" Lina said.

Sylph indicated the sword. Lina didn't even remember picking it up. She'd taken to keeping it by her bedside, since it seemed to help with the nightmares. She shook her head and laid it next to the cot.

"You just . . . startled me."

"You still not sleeping well?"

"Bad dreams." Lina shivered. She cast about the tent for somewhere to sit and ended up flopping back onto the bed. Somewhat to her surprise, Sylph flopped down next to her, curled into a tight ball.

Lina took a deep breath. "What's up? It must be three in the morning."

"I couldn't sleep," said Sylph in a small voice. "And I thought . . . I've barely seen you in the past couple of weeks. You know?"

"You've been busy. We've all been busy." That was true enough. Lina couldn't have imagined, a week previously, the amount of work that went into just keeping an army fed, watered, and pointed in the right direction. Thankfully, Marlowe and Heraan had risen to the task; just watching made her feel overwhelmed.

Sylph lay on her side, in silence. Hesitantly, Lina reached out and touched her shoulder, but stopped as her sister flinched away.

"Sylph? What's wrong?"

"I can't."

"You can tell me."

"I can't."

"Sylph . . ."

"I can't take it." She curled a little bit tighter. "They want me to think of something. Everyone says that, Heraan, Yahvy, everybody. 'You'll think of something, Sylph.' I can't . . . I can't *talk* to anyone anymore."

Lina stayed silent, not sure what to say.

"And no matter what I think of," Sylph continued, "people are going to get killed. These are real fucking people, and tomorrow they're going to do what I tell them and some of them are going to die. I was sitting in my room with the map and a pen and thinking to myself, 'Well, if we hit one section of wall with two regiments, we'd probably only lose three hundred men and we'd have our breach.' And I realized I'd made them all into fucking *game pieces* to move around on the map, and . . . I just felt . . ."

She was crying, Lina realized. Quietly.

"I'm such an awful person. A g . . . goddamned frozen hearted b . . . bitch. I just c . . . couldn't take it anymore . . ."

Lina had heard enough. She rolled over and wrapped her arms around Sylph, fighting off her sister's feeble attempts to stop her.

"Leave me alone!"

"Shhh." Lina felt lump in her throat. "Listen to me. We both know that's not true . . ."

"It *wasn't*. Now it is. It's this place. We're in Hell, Lina, we've died and gone to Hell and there's no way home."

"We're not in Hell," said Lina, a little surprised at her own certainty.

"How do you know?"

"If we were in Hell, we wouldn't be together."

That brought on an altogether more comfortable silence. Sylph relaxed a little, huddled under her big sister's arms. Lina rubbed the top of her cheek against Sylph's head, the simple gesture carrying with it a host of memories. She realized it had been weeks since she'd even thought about her life before she'd plowed the car through the barrier. *I was getting ready for my new job. Sylph was getting ready to go back to school—she was bitching about the end of summer, but I could tell she was getting bored. She and Apple wanted me to drive them to the mall on Saturday to shop for school stuff.* She squeezed Sylph a little harder, and felt her sister squeeze back. *God. It already feels like none of that ever happened.*

"I thought . . ." Sylph swallowed. "I think Mom would hate me, the way I am now."

Lina closed her eyes. "Mom would love you no matter what. You know that."

"Maybe she thought so, but she never knew what would happen . . ."

"No matter what," Lina said firmly. "She might be worried about you, but she'd never hate you."

Sylph said nothing. Lina rubbed her cheek against her sister's head again and said, "You *do* know that, right?"

Sylph gave a jerky nod. She lay silent for a moment longer, then said, "I wonder if she's somewhere like this. Some other world."

"I hope it's a little nicer than this one. Though," Lina giggled, "she'd probably be Emperor or Archmagus or whatever before long."

"Yeah."

Sylph wiped her eyes on the sheet and snuggled a little closer. Lina smiled.

"I just can't talk to anyone else," Sylph said eventually, in a more normal tone of voice. "They . . . I mean, nobody treats me like a little girl. And that's great, but I can't talk to anyone like this because I'm afraid they might start. Generals aren't supposed to cry for their mothers the night before a battle, right?"

"Well," said Lina, "you never have to worry about *me* treating you like a grownup. At least not in private."

Sylph giggled. "Thanks."

After a while, Lina said, "Are you going back to your tent?"

"Mph," Sylph mumbled. "No. It's warm and soft here."

"It's a sleepover, then?"

"Do we get to gossip?"

"If you like."

Sylph nodded eagerly. "Let's see. I think Marlowe likes you."

"Seriously?" Lina wasn't sure if that was supposed to be a joke.

"Seriously. Sometimes he looks at you while we're riding, and . . . it just looks like it, you know?"

"Odd."

"Odd? That's all you have to say? What do you think of him?"

"*Me?* I don't . . . I mean . . ." He was *handsome* enough, but it just wasn't something she'd considered. "I never thought about it."

"That's my Liberator. Ever observant."

"Quiet, you. Time for sleep."

Sylph obligingly shut up. Lina savored the warmth of her sister, the feel of her. She closed her eyes and let out a long breath, trying to relax. *Maybe now the stranger will leave me alone.*

Eventually the rhythms of quiet breathing were all that could be heard in the tent. Sometime later, though, Lina's hand broke from Sylph's embrace and groped along the side of the cot, sliding up and down until it found the hilt of the sword.

✳   ✳   ✳

"Why?" said Sylph. She squinted in the early morning sun; the rain had gone, thankfully, but it had taken the clouds with it and the air was warm and getting hotter. She could already tell the day would be a scorcher.

"Who knows?" said Marlowe. His horse took a nervous step forward, and he pulled back gently on the reins. He too, had one hand up to shade his eyes against the sun.

Their little group had claimed the top of a hill, the edge of the gently sloping valley in which Bleloth was situated. From there they could look across a couple of miles at the city and the Tower itself, which now stretched far overhead. And, outside the city, an army was forming up in ranks.

"There," Heraan said, and pointed. "See the sparkle? That's the Diamond Guard. Looks like all of 'em, or damn close."

"That," Marlowe grumbled, "is going to be trouble. We're not ready, Sylph. This lot is getting better, but I wouldn't send them up against the Diamond Guard. We'll be fine as long as things go well, but if something goes wrong they're going to break."

"What worries me more," said Yahvy, "is that this whole thing is a trap. Sylph's right—it makes no sense at all! Why would Gargorian deploy for battle when he's got the city wall to hide behind?"

"He may not want to risk house-to-house fighting." Heraan shook his head. "That could get ugly real fast."

"Especially if the civilians join in," Sylph said. "Much harder to turn traitor on an open battlefield. After what happened to the Second Army, just Lina's reputation may be frightening."

"Or," Yahvy said again, "it could be a trap."

"Ten to one he's got cavalry waiting out of sight along the wall," Marlowe said, "but with the numbers he's got that's not much a trap, especially if we deploy to meet it."

"Assuming our numbers are right," Yahvy retorted.

"It seems like neither one of you likes the looks of this,"

Sylph said. She stared down at Gargorian's army. A thousand men was small as armies went—at least for Earth—but it certainly looked impressive enough. "But what option do we have? We can't go around them, and if we fall back to Highpoint it just gives him the time to finish gathering his forces and come finish us off."

"We could hold Highpoint for some time, even against the entire Third Army. That's one damned big wall, and we've got the men to defend it." Marlowe sounded doubtful, though, and Heraan shook his head.

"We won't have the army for long. We wouldn't be able to feed them . . ."

"The westerners might be able to help with that," Yahvy put in.

". . . and more importantly, these people signed up to fight Gargorian. They're not going to stick around for a siege."

"So it seems like we have no choice but to attack." Sylph's lip twisted doubtfully.

"I don't like it," Marlowe repeated. "When we have no choice, that means he knows what we're doing. He's got to have something planned."

"It's a pretty safe toss of the dice for him," said Yahvy. "At worst, he can just bar the Tower doors and wait us out. That's diamond, and its lousy with magic; I doubt we could even scratch it."

"One thing at a time." Sylph forced herself to smile.

"I still think the Diamonds are going to be our biggest concern," said Marlowe. "Whoever we put against them is going to get slaughtered, and even if we get through to them eventually, morale is going to take a beating."

"I've got an idea about that," said Sylph. "Tell the regiments to form up, I'm going to talk to Lina."

"Yes . . ." Marlowe shook his head irritably. "What do I call you, anyway?"

"Call me Sylph."

"I mean officially." He gave her his half-smile again. "Appearances. Gargorian's chief officers are 'general,' so that's out, but 'warleader' is pretty generic. Can I—"

She held up a hand. "I'll think about it."

* * *

Lina was just getting off her horse when Sylph got to the base of the hill. The army was forming up around her, sergeants shouting their men into place under the fairly loose directions Sylph had given the captains. Lina had ended up taking charge of the Fifth Regiment herself, with Fah as a kind of executive officer, so something like three hundred men and women were getting ready to follow her right down the center of the line.

Myris, the odd girl Lina had rescued, gave Sylph a nod as she passed. Sylph nodded back, feeling a little uncomfortable. She didn't know Lina's bodyguards as well as she probably should have. *Lina seems to trust them, but that's no help. She trusts everybody.*

"Hi, Sylph." Lina had borrowed some mail from the stores. Sylph felt funny looking at her; it was like a picture of a medieval warrior, with the head cut off and her sister's face inserted. She shook her head.

"Hey."

Lina stepped closer. "You feeling any better?"

"Much." Sylph took a deep breath. "But . . . I'm not quite sure how to say this."

"What?"

"We talked about the battle yesterday, and you agreed to keep yourself out of the fighting."

"Yeah." Lina looked uncomfortable; she had a hard time asking people to do things she wasn't willing to do, and getting that promise out of her had taken a lot of work.

"I think I may have to ask just the opposite," Sylph continued hastily. "The Diamond Guard is out there, and Marlowe is worried if we hit them head-on we'll take too many losses. The only thing I could think of that might help . . ."

". . . is this thing," Lina finished, patting the sword at her hip.

"Yeah." Sylph looked down. Trying to convince her sister *not* to fight was one thing; it was quite another to send her purposely into harm's way. "I can't . . . I mean, you don't have to. We can think of something else . . ."

Lina shook her head. "I'll do it."

I knew she would. That somehow made it worse. "We're trying to keep the plan as simple as possible. You and your people hit the Diamond Guard as hard as you can, while Garot and Yahvy engage the enemy wings. We'll have Heraan and Orbaa on the ends, watching for tricks—Marlowe thinks Gargorian probably has some cavalry waiting in the wings."

"I heard the plan, Sylph." Lina smiled. "We'll be fine, don't worry."

"Good." There was a lump in Sylph's throat. "Don't get yourself killed."

"How many times have you said that to me now?"

"Too many."

"And have I ever gotten killed?"

Sylph had to laugh. "Not yet."

"So trust me!" Lina swung herself back onto the horse and started toward the troops. Her riding was still awkward, Sylph noted, but she was actually becoming a passable imitation of a horsewoman. *She'll still have to get off before she fights. Controlling a horse in battle . . .*

Myris stepped forward, interrupting Sylph's wandering thoughts. "You care for her."

"She's my sister." Sylph looked up at the girl and her two companions. Unexpectedly, Myris smiled.

"She will survive. Before she is even wounded, you will find our bodies piled on top of her."

That's not exactly comforting. Sylph decided to take it in the spirit it was meant. "Thanks. You be careful too."

✳   ✳   ✳

LINA FELT AS THOUGH THE STRANGER WAS RIDING WITH HER, just behind her shoulder. She could *feel* his hand on her hip, his hot breath in her ear. She had to stop herself from constantly brushing the back of her neck, where centipedes and uglier things seemed to crawl.

*It's a god*damned *dream.* A nasty one, but a dream. *Concentrate on what you're doing, Lina, or you really will get killed.* She put a hand on the sword, and felt the stranger retreat, just a little. *Concentrate.*

"My lady," said Fah from behind her. "We've received the signal to advance."

Lina nodded. The Circle Breaker's formality felt a bit uncomfortable. *It's all well and good in front of the troops, but I feel like she means it.* For all that Fah proclaimed her the Liberator, she didn't *feel* any different. *Except for that thing in my dreams.*

"Let's get moving, then."

The sun climbed in the sky, and the day was starting to get hot. Lina's nerves started to thrill as soon as her regiment—Fah's regiment, really—started their haphazard march across the battlefield. The majority of the soldiers were armed with spears and short-swords, and armored only in leather. While marching, they didn't bother to maintain formation; instead, each squad was a loose group around its sergeant, so they advanced in clumps of twenty or thirty men. Marlowe had said their training was as good as could be expected, under the circumstances, but somehow Lina had thought they'd be a bit more . . . *martial, I guess. This is like a bunch of kids heading off to a picnic.* There was chatter and even laughter from the more recent conscripts, but the veterans of the western campaign maintained a stony silence. Fah had organized the lead squads so they contained the highest proportion of men that had been "blooded." *More likely to hold. Makes sense.* She found herself feeling a little giddy. *Do I count as "blooded"?*

"Enemy ahead!" someone called from the front ranks. "Two thousand feet!" He paused, then shouted, "It's the Diamond Guard!"

Excited murmurs ran through the soldiers. In a way Lina was glad Sylph had matched her against Gargorian's elites; while her troops might have second thoughts about killing men who were, after all, only conscripts themselves, there would be no such reservations here. *On the other hand, we're much more likely to get killed.*

She kicked her horse, carefully, and made her way to the front of the loose formation. The enemy army looked small compared to the stone walls of Bleloth and even smaller against the bulk of the Diamond Tower, but she could already see sparkles of light from their gemmed armor. She glanced to either side; the army was advancing in a phalanx with her regiment at the tip. *Just great. Just great.*

"My lady," said Myris quietly, "you should dismount. We're forming ranks."

Lina reined up her horse, dry-mouthed, and almost fell as she tried to swing out of the saddle. If her bodyguards noticed, they didn't comment; a boy led the horse away, toward the rear.

"I need to be in the front," she said.

Myris and Fah looked at each other, then back at her. Fah opened her mouth to say something, but Lina cut her off.

"The front! Understood?" *Before I get so nervous I start running.*

Myris smiled at Kari and Zaya. "She is the Liberator."

Sylph asked me to, Lina thought as the formation assembled around her. Fah's veteran squads formed the lead rank; they looked fierce enough. Fah herself took a position at Lina's right hand, fitting an arrow to her massive longbow. Gargorian's armies were woefully under-equipped with missile weapons, since training a conscript to use a bow was generally considered a waste of time.

"One thousand feet," said the young man whose job was

apparently to announce such things. *I know so little about this army.* She could make out the Diamond Guard, huge men made small by distance and decked with armor that shattered the light. On some unseen command, they drew their swords as one, and a cheer went up from Gargorian's ranks.

We're going to fight that*?* She felt as though her legs had turned to jelly, and grabbed at the hilt of the sword like a drowning man clutching a life preserver. It lent some comfort. Absentmindedly, she realized the nervousness had almost made her forget the dream-figure that hovered a step behind her.

Concentrate, Lina! Come on!

"Five hundred!" shouted the young man. Fah dropped briefly to one knee and sent an arrow winging into the enemy ranks. It struck one of the Guards dead on, shattering against his helmet; the man fell, but was helped to his feet a moment later by his comrades. Up and down the line, the Circle Breakers fired what bows they had, the shafts proving deadlier against the lightly armored regular troops.

"It would be best," Fah murmured, "if you gave the order."

"What order?" said Lina.

"Charge."

This is crazy this is crazy this is crazy *God damn it what am I even doing here . . . ?*

She drew the sword and shouted in a hoarse voice.

"*CHARGE!*"

"HERE THEY COME," MARLOWE COMMENTED. "LOOK WEST. See the dust? Cavalry."

Sylph's lip twisted. She and the burly cavalryman were well back from the front line, on the slopes of the hill and surrounded by a few handpicked horsemen. *I should be watching for surprises.* But she couldn't take her eyes off the center regiment, closing rapidly with the Diamond Guard.

"That's Orbaa's troop," said Marlowe, misinterpreting her nervousness. "We expected this; he'll handle it, don't worry."

Sylph nodded. A sudden pain told her that she'd bitten her lip, and she sucked up the salty taste of blood. Dust obscured the regiment as three hundred men broke into a run. Sylph wanted to reach out across half a mile and pluck her sister out of harm's way.

Fuck the rest of them, screw everything else. Please, please, please. Lina—

*   *   *

THE FIRST CONTACT, FUELLED BY THE MOMENTUM OF THE rebels' run and five hundred years of pent-up rage, was deadly. Steel *screeched* against diamond as spears found their targets; the heads couldn't punch through directly, but the men tried to aim for the weak spots in their opponent's plate. Two Guards to Lina's left took the points in the throat, spears smashing aside the thin material of their gorgets; all along the line, Gargorian's soldiers went down, wounded or simply bowled over. The rebels couldn't have stopped then if they'd wanted to; their speed flung them bodily against the second line of Guard, who met them with swords in hand. All at once, the fighting front dissolved into a confused brawl.

Lina swung the sword once, just before the line made contact with the enemy. Pure white light burst forth, scything into the tightly packed Guard in a deadly arc and vaporizing soldiers, diamond and all. Her own men, who'd been warned of the Liberator's sorcerous talents, stayed well clear and raised a cheer of their own.

But the discipline of the Guard was superb, and they closed in almost as soon as light had faded. Lina whipped the sword back and gave them another taste, and searing fire scorched the earth black. But each effort took something out of her; two in a row left her feeling like she'd been punched in the gut, gasping for breath.

The wild burst of magic had won her a brief respite, how-ever, and the Guard hesitated to approach. They concentrated their efforts on the rest of the line, where—as Marlowe had predicted—things were not going well.

While the initial rush had taken its toll, the Guards had not broken. The spearmen drew short-swords as they pressed in closer, but steel and leather were proving a poor match for diamond plate and unbreakable long-swords. The Guards advanced, heedless of the weapons which for the most part glanced off their unbreakable armor, and hacked down rebels with savage abandon.

It's not going to be enough. Her power had unnerved the Guards, but they weren't going to run. For the moment men and women rushed forward to replace those that were chopped apart, but that wouldn't last. Lina saw a Guardsman hit one of her soldiers just above the ear, and his head practically exploded, helmet and all. A woman fenced with her enemy, but on her first attempt to parry he lopped her sword in half, then took off her hand at the wrist on the backswing. Blood spurted, and she fell back scream-ing. A girl no older than Lina charged a Guardsman twice her height; he simply extended his sword and spitted her through the stomach. The girl made not a sound, simply latched on to the pommel of his weapon with a grim determination; a moment later two men swarmed past her and chopped the Guard's legs out from under him. Only then did she let herself fall.

One more. Lina forced her attention back to her immediate surroundings. *I can do one more, and then I'm going to fall on my face. Going to* die. She took a panicked breath and stepped forward, swinging the sword at the surprised Guardsmen. The white fire, weaker now, cut a half-dozen of them in half; Lina dropped to one knee, using the sword as a crutch. The Diamonds ad-vanced, cautiously; Lina heard shouting from her own ranks, but only her bodyguards made it to her side in time.

Fah threw herself against the first of the Guard in a furious attack, using her shorter weapon's speed to good advantage against the ponderous diamond blade. He stepped back, fouling his comrades' advance; in that moment, Myris lowered her spear and placed the point right below a guardsman's breastplate, twisting the point in his guts. He shuddered and fell, and she let the spear go with him, drawing her sword as two more advanced.

Lina struggled to rise. *They're dying. My men. We're all dying.* She was dimly aware of shouting on either side of her, but couldn't muster the energy to think what it might portend.

Fah had wounded her opponent and was now fighting another; the first limped away from the battle, blood ruining the finish of his crystal armor. Myris parried the blade of the first man to reach her, and Zaya ducked between a pair of them to drive her sword into his side. He staggered but didn't fall; the other turned to follow the girl, but found Kari thrusting wildly at him and had to step back to parry. Zaya spun, sword raised, and took a chop from behind that cut her waist almost to the navel. The girl looked at Lina and blinked—*big, blue eyes, I never noticed that before*—then died without a sound.

Kari's opponent bulled into her, letting her sword glance off his diamond armor; he thumped her in the chest with his knee and stepped aside as she went down, then thrust his sword through her and into the ground with a nasty wet sound. Kari screamed, flopping like a wounded fish. Myris threw herself at the man before he could get his weapon free and managed to find a chink in his protection; he fell, clutching his stomach. Moments later, she was engaged by two more Diamond Guards.

Dying. I saved them, and they are dying. Kari's screams were drowned out by the general furor of battle, but they echoed off the inside of Lina's skull. *There's nothing I can do, nothing I can* fucking *do . . .*

Her hand curled around the hilt of the sword. She felt the stranger, close behind her, his breath rustling the hair on the back of her neck.

I . . . I can't . . .

What are *you?*

She could see his face, crawling with vermin, now half-covered with rotting flesh that distended and tore and oozed with pus as his mouth tried to form words.

Rahmgoth.

White fire flared.

*   *   *

GARGORIAN WAS STILL EATING. IT WAS A NERVOUS TIC WITH him, as another man might toy idly with a pencil. He popped hot strips of roast boar into his mouth from a steaming pile on a platter beside him; his fingers were slick and greasy with the juices. Most of the Archmagus's attention, however, was elsewhere.

As soon as the throne room doors opened, he snapped, "Report!"

"Ah . . ." said the luckless servant. "Battle has been joined, my lord."

"I can hear that, fool. What's happening?"

"The Diamond Guard engaged the enemy command regiment, and our superiority was telling, but . . ."

"I knew there was a 'but'." His hand tightened on the arm of the throne. "What happened?"

The servant took a long time working out the precise phrasing. "The . . . Liberator, Archmagus. The girl the peasants call the Liberator. She intervened with magic."

"That's not possible," Gargorian growled. "No magic can pierce the heart of my domain, inside the Second Circle!"

"N . . . Nonetheless, my lord, she was able to destroy many of the Diamond Guard. When I left, the battle hung in the balance. They were mounting a charge that was sure to overwhelm her, and if she falls the rebel army will come apart."

"So what are you doing here?" Gargorian shouted. His hand twitched, knocking the platter of meat all over the floor.

"You sent a message. You wanted to be appraised of any developments . . ."

The Archmagus's lip twitched. "Come back when you have a victory to report, not sooner."

The servant's head bobbed with relief. "Yes. Of course, my lord."

The Archmagus reached out automatically for another mouthful, and only then noticed the food wasn't there. *Damnation.* Gargorian looked up, but the servant had already gone. His other hand closed around a decanter of red wine, which he drained in a single gulp.

"Rathmado!" His shout shook the throne room. "Get in here. Rath*mado*!"

*　　*　　*

"LINA!" SYLPH'S VOICE. "LINA!"

"R . . . Rahm . . ."

Lina opened her eyes. She could see nothing but glittering light, and a weight on her chest made breathing difficult.

"Sylph?" she managed, the effort taking most of her breath. "Sylph!"

"Lina! Down there!"

She felt the weight shift, then slowly roll off of her. There was an explosion of daylight, and a ring of worried faces. Sylph, Yahvy, Marlowe, Heraan, Melfina.

Not dead. Or still dead, or whatever. What happened to me?

"Get her legs, Marlowe." That was Daana, spouting orders. Gauntleted hands gripped Lina's wrists and ankles and lifted her gently into the air, moved sideways a few feet, and laid her down again. Lina lay on the grass in a pleasant fog, not sure what she should do or say. She felt Daana prodding her, touching her head and then lightly along her side, probing for injuries.

"Lina? Can you hear me?" Sylph sounded on the verge of tears.

"I can hear you." Lina blinked and tried to sit up, but Daana put a hand on her chest and stopped her. Lina couldn't have disobeyed; she felt weak as a kitten. "What happened?"

"You don't remember?" Sylph asked, looking concerned. Lina shook her head.

"We were losing. I tried to break them, like you said, but it wasn't enough . . ."

"You broke them, all right," said Marlowe. He was grinning. "I've never seen anything like it."

"I don't remember." Lina closed her eyes. *I fell to my knees, and . . .*

"You got up," Sylph said, "all of a sudden, and started fighting like a demon. Faster than anyone I've ever seen. And that sword went through diamond like it wasn't even there. They couldn't touch you, couldn't even get close. We'd beaten the Third Army, and Yahvy and Garot were turning the Guard's flanks, but it looked like our center wasn't going to hold long enough. But after you got up . . ." Sylph shrugged. "They broke, tried to get back into the city."

"Except there were civilians on the walls, watching the battle," Marlowe said. "A gang of them stormed the gatehouse from behind, and we got the Diamonds almost to a man."

Lina raised her head with an effort and looked around. What had been piled atop her, and indeed laid out all around her, were corpses: the Diamond Guard was a ruin of sparkling crystal and blood, hundreds of them mixed with the more plainly dressed bodies of the rebels. A double ring of soldiers, from her own regiment, held at bay a crowd of civilians in bright colors. There was scattered cheering but mostly just silence, as though a thousand people were holding their breath.

"Are you okay?" said Sylph.

"I . . . think so." Lina took a deep breath. "I feel okay. Weak, like I always do, but . . ."

Sylph nodded hurriedly. "It's just . . . there are a lot of people waiting to see if you're alive or not. I think it would be a really good idea for you to stand up."

"Oh." Lina shook her head, trying to clear it. "I can try. Give me a hand, Marlowe?"

The big cavalryman, surprisingly gentle for all his armored bulk, took one of her hands in his. With that to balance on, she managed to clamber to her feet, holding up her other hand to wave to the crowd.

Fah was the first to respond; she was mounted, sitting with the regiment who were preventing the mob from reaching their fallen leader. "The Liberator!"

The soldiers echoed the cry, then the civilians. It became a roar that took on physical force, shaking and reverberating until it seemed like it would topple the Diamond Tower by sound alone.

"Liberator! Liberator! Liberator!"

Lina blinked.

"This is the part," said Sylph right in her ear, "where you ride into the city in triumph."

Lina looked at her little sister; Sylph was smiling, and she wiped away the pooling tears with the back of her hand. Lina smiled back at her. She took a hesitant step, with Marlowe close by, and managed to retrieve the sword from where she'd left it among the fallen. Lina held it aloft; as though it knew what was expected of it, the weapon responded with a gout of pure white fire that speared into the sky and outshone the afternoon sun. It managed to silence the crowd, but only temporarily. A moment later they burst into another cheer, even louder than before.

*　　*　　*

"Where is she now?"

"At the best inn in the city. The owner insisted."

Heraan and Sylph walked side by side across the empty courtyard. They were trailed at a distance by a group of Heraan's men, for security's sake.

"You've got someone watching her?"

He laughed. "Plenty. Fah and her people, plus a couple of mine. Daana had to practically tie that girl Myris to the bed."

"Is she going to be all right?"

"Seems like it."

Sylph sighed, and Heraan tilted his head inquisitively.

"Lina's troops took an awful pounding from the Diamond Guard," she said.

"It worked."

"I know. I just can't help wondering whether there was a better way."

"That kind of second-guessing will drive you crazy." He shook his head. "You won, Sylph. Everyone in the city is lining up to thank you."

"We haven't won yet." She stopped walking and looked up, and up, and up. It was late evening, and the Tower caught the reddish light and glowed as though it were full of blood. She and Heraan were walking in the large clear space that surrounded it, a killing field for archers lodged in the more mundane fortifications that guarded the entrance.

Gargorian's remaining forces had abandoned those, though, and closed the Tower doors tight behind them. There were no arrow slits in the Tower itself, no way in or out except for ventilation gaps, almost a thousand feet above the ground. Inside the impenetrable fortress the Archmagus sat with somewhere between one and two hundred men. A pittance, compared to the army Sylph had destroyed, but enough.

Heraan was also looking at the Tower. "You're right. There's no way we can take that place by storm. And since Gargorian can create his own food and water, we can't even starve him out."

That had been Marlowe's assessment too. Sylph pursed her lips, trying to think. "If we break all the Circles, maybe he won't have enough power to do that."

"Maybe. Who knows? But knowing Gargorian, if it's at

all possible he'd have a reserve. I don't know anything about magic."

"Neither do I."

"You're the wizard."

"Not much of one." Sylph walked forward until she came to the very base of the Tower. The diamond plate dove underground, and preliminary digging had shown that it curved inward to meet itself, sealing off yet another avenue of attack. She put her hand against the wall; it felt oddly warm, as though heated from within.

"At the same time . . ." Heraan shrugged. "We might have to just leave him in there."

"I don't like it. He could leave, rally his forces. We can watch the front gate, but who knows what other ways in or out he might have."

"True enough." He craned his neck back. "Damn impressive, isn't it? I suppose he is the Magio Creator, after all."

Sylph nodded. *I'm so tired.* It had been, to risk a truly colossal understatement, a long day. She closed her eyes and leaned against the wall.

The wall.

She could *feel* it. The whole gigantic edifice was a single crystal, force-grown *ex nihilo* by the power of Gargorian's sorcery. There was more there than just neatly aligned carbon. She felt the threads of something else, something *other*; not matter and not quiet energy, just an odd presence that led inside the Tower and into something at its base. *It doesn't look stable, like something real. There must be an energy source in there maintaining it.* Heraan had speculated about a reserve. *Like a pool of magic. God, there's so much I don't know.*

A tiny germ of an idea sprouted, in the back of her mind.

By magic done, by magic undone.

The *other*, the pure sorcery, was wrapped around the more mundane elements of the Tower in such a way that it created self-reinforcing grid. It tied off what Sylph thought of as the loose thread that had allowed her to tear apart the gate at Highpoint, or break through Falk's armor. *But what about the grid itself?*

Her brow furrowed in concentration. *It's there, it has to be there.* It was a complex web of strands, one leading to the next and the next. *But it can't be a circle; one end goes to that power source, whatever that is, so where's the other? Tied up in the structure somehow.*

"Sylph?"

"Shh." She spared Heraan only that much concentration. Minutes passed. Sweat appeared on Sylph's brow and started to trickle down her face and drip off her chin.

He's good. She couldn't help but admire the intricacy with which the warding was put together. *Very good. But . . .*

Got it!

When she tapped the threads, there was the slightest bit of motion. *Of resonance.* And from that she could feel where the ward ended, the loose end that would give her the leverage she needed. *And from that, all we need is one good solid pull.*

"Heraan," Sylph said quietly. "Run."

"What?"

She was already halfway across the courtyard and accelerating. *"Run!"*

✻ ✻ ✻

Gargorian sat alone in his throne room. The remnants of yet another meal lay in front of him; he'd demolished the chicken like it was an opposing army. He emptied another goblet of wine and settled back on his throne as the big doors opened, revealing a tremulous servant.

"What?" Gargorian snapped.

"My lord Archmagus . . ."

"You said you would return only with news of victory." Gargorian leaned forward, voice low and dangerous. "Is that what you bring?"

"Not . . . not *exactly*, my lord . . ."

Gargorian smiled, like a lizard. "Kill him."

Nothing happened. The Archmagus glanced at the corners of his room, where his Diamond Guard usually stood; they'd been sent out with the rest. His expression twisted into disgust as the servant turned and beat a hasty retreat, shutting the doors behind him.

Just a setback. The Archmagus shook his head ponderously. *A temporary setback. I can outlast them, if necessary. The Diamond Tower is invulnerable, and I have power for a hundred years. My other armies . . .*

There came the most peculiar sound, the tiniest musical note at the upper end of the scale. Gargorian looked around until he spotted the source; a change in the character of the light from the ceiling, almost as though the pure gemstone had fractured.

Again, and louder this time. Another crack ran the length of the floor and hit one of the pillars, which crazed like a broken mirror. Gargorian stood up in alarm, his legs protesting his massive bulk, and started shouting.

This is not possible. No one can undo my wards short of Lightbringer himself! Gargorian paused. *Could he be here? At the heart of my domain?*

"Rathmado!" *Where is he when he'd be useful?* "Rathmado!"

The floor shifted with a lurch, and for a moment the whole Tower seemed to hold its breath. Gargorian steadied himself against a pillar and screamed:

"*Rathmado!*"

The ceiling shattered into a million glittering, deadly shards.

✳   ✳   ✳

SYLPH DID NOT GET A FIRSTHAND VIEW OF THE COLLAPSE of the Diamond Tower. She was too busy running away from it. She and Heraan managed to get to the ring of buildings that surrounded the courtyard by the time the thing came down.

Chunks of diamond the size of a man's head fell from the sky, with edges like razors; thankfully most of the pieces rained down on the grounds of the Tower itself as its entire structure collapsed inward. The upper part dropped straight down as the hollow lower levels collapsed, as though the fortress were descending into Hell. Sylph came to rest against a stone bulwark, gasping for breath and fighting cramps in her side, with Heraan a short ways behind her.

"Sylph Walker?" said a voice.

She looked up.

"My name is Magus Rathmado," the man said, and smiled. "At your service."

part two
Mutation

chapter ten

*A*ND REMEMBER," THE VOICE CONTINUED, "YOU'VE FALLEN *through a hole in the web, but the spider will still come for you sooner or later. Good luck.*"

Sylph was convinced, by the time she'd bathed, dried, and clothed herself, that the voice belonged to Magus Rathmado.

Being able to bathe, at this point, seemed like an incredible luxury. She hadn't had a real bath since they'd left the village of the Circle Breakers, what seemed like an eternity ago; the closest she'd gotten to clean was when it rained, or what little washing she'd been able to grab on the march. But the best inn in Bleloth, "Liberator's Alcove" (hastily renamed from "Gargorian's Alcove"; the paint was still fresh on the sign) had a full bathtub in each room, and servants to carry buckets of hot water from the cisterns in the basement. Sylph felt guilty, but only a little. *I deserve a bit of luxury.*

It had been twelve hours since the Fall, as the common folk were calling it. Almost miraculously, no one outside the Tower had been hurt when it came down, another act of Fate they were attributing to the Liberator. Everyone inside had been killed, of course, in such a thorough way that only the strongest-stomached citizens were willing to go and look. The entire city had cast itself into increasingly drunken festivities, and the lowliest boy from Sylph's army was swimming in free drinks and come-hither looks from comely young maidens.

Marlowe was maintaining order, of sorts. He'd built a corps of the hardest-headed soldiers and set them to patrolling the streets, just to maintain a presence, and manning the exterior walls. Units of the Third Army were still straggling in, but they were met with overwhelming force when they reached the city. Most were happy to hear the news of Gargorian's demise; those that weren't had the sense to keep their mouths shut.

"Good morning," said Heraan when Sylph opened her bedroom door.

"Morning." Sylph yawned. "Where's Yahvy?"

"At the end of the hall. But . . ."

Sylph had already knocked—the door was unlatched and swung open at her touch, revealing Yahvy drying herself off with a towel but otherwise not wearing a stitch. It didn't seem to embarrass her, though Heraan immediately turned away; Sylph looked long enough to recognize Orbaa asleep in the bed before she turned bright red and looked at the floor.

"What's with the two of you?" Yahvy wrapped herself in the towel.

"When you've got some clothes on," said Sylph slowly, "we're having a meeting downstairs. In an hour or so, along with breakfast."

"Sounds good." Yahvy shut the door, and Sylph let out a long breath. She looked up at Heraan, who raised an eyebrow but said nothing.

Yahvy and Orbaa? She shook her head as she made her way down the stairs. The inn was luxuriously appointed; stone walls covered with colorful tapestries to muffle the chill in winter, fine carpets edged with gilt on the floor. It felt like a palace, which was presumably the point.

They were greeted at the base of the stairs by a positively obsequious servant, who directed them to the main dining room. The hotel's other patrons had all left, leaving the whole inn for the use of Sylph, Lina, and their commanders.

And, apparently, Rathmado. He was sitting at one of the fine hardwood tables, leaning his chair back on two legs and resting his boots on the tabletop. One of the servants, in the background, was desperately trying to figure out a polite way to get him to stop; Sylph suppressed a giggle. The Magus smiled when he saw her, and stood up so fast the chair thumped down hard enough to dent the floor. The servant winced.

"Miss Walker! So good to see you up and about."

Sylph smiled back, cautiously. She'd been exhausted the previous night and hadn't gotten much of a chance to talk with Rathmado on the way back to the inn. He clearly knew who she was, and just as clearly had something to say, but she'd decided it had to wait. *Maybe not the wisest decision, but I wasn't exactly rational.*

"Good morning, Magus."

"Call me Rathmado, please." He had a remarkable smile: pure white, reflecting the light as though his teeth had been glossed. His clothing was equally immaculate, dark gray trousers and something resembling a cross between a suit jacket and a cloak, clasped at his throat by a pair of pearl-and-gold hooks. His hair was short, dark, and exceedingly well-behaved. If she had seen him back on Earth, Sylph would have pegged him for a salesman or a priest; he had the right self-assured, thrusting air to him.

"Rathmado, then. I'm sorry I ignored you yesterday."

"Please, don't worry. It's not every day one topples a Archmagus, after all, and you're entitled to a good night's sleep afterward. And besides, I relish the opportunity to enjoy the hospitality here."

"And I've got some questions for you."

"I imagine you do." He smiled. "Might I suggest that we talk in private?"

"I'm afraid not," said Heraan over Sylph's shoulder.

"If it has to do with Gargorian or the war, Heraan will hear about it anyway. So . . ."

"While I'm sure your questions bear on those subjects, there are more central matters to be discussed."

"Such as?" said Heraan.

"Something about a car and a hillside," Rathmado said. Heraan gave him a look of bland incomprehension, but Sylph felt like she'd taken a small caliber round between the eyes.

It was him . . . the voice I heard. And he knows . . . he knows everything. She met the Magus's friendly eyes and perfect smile; utterly motionless, as though his face was painted on a mask. Sylph swallowed and pulled Heraan aside.

"I need to talk to him alone."

"I don't trust him."

"Neither do I, but I don't think he's going to assault me, if that's what you mean. He's not armed."

"He's still just a *bit* bigger than you. And he's a Magus."

"So am I, remember? We'll use one of the rooms upstairs; you and the guards wait outside. If he tries anything, I'll scream."

"Sylph . . ."

"Heraan, I have to."

He nodded. "As you wish."

Sylph turned back to the table and gave Rathmado her best smile.

*   *   *

"OKAY," SHE SAID, AS SOON AS THE DOOR HAD CLOSED BE-hind them. "Question the first. How the hell do you know who I am?" She paused. "Scratch that. Do you know what happened to us?"

"I do." Rathmado began an aimless circuit of the room, examining the furnishings.

"And?" Sylph gritted her teeth.

"You died." He looked back at her. "Smash, crunch, cute little body all twisted and mangled. No more Sylph. Except, of course," he waved a hand, "here you are."

"*Where* am I?"

"The Veritas named this place Omega, because they thought it was the lowest world there was. Turns out they were wrong, of course—Vilvakis knows all about that—but the name has sort of stuck. Call it Omega."

"It's another world?"

"Of course."

"But how did I *get* here?"

"You died."

"There's got to be more to it than that."

"It's not the *fact* of your arrival that's remarkable so much as the *manner* of it," Rathmado said, examining a tray of grapes some servant had left as a snack. He popped one off the vine and tossed it into his mouth. "Mmm. Specifically, that you arrived awake, aware, and possessed of a body that resembles the one you left behind. You have me to thank for that, by the way, and I hope you're properly grateful. I could have made you twelve feet tall with two heads and six breasts."

"You could have . . ." Sylph spluttered to a halt. "Wait. Wait a minute."

He favored her with his smile again. "Am I going too quickly for you?"

"You . . . arranged . . . for me and Lina to come here?"

"To come here as you are *now*. You had no choice but to come here, it's like water rolling downhill, but most people don't retain any memory. The two of you, you might say, are having your cake and eating it too."

"Why?"

"Because," he said, and his voice suddenly became deep and ponderous, "it is your Destiny."

Sylph gave him a flat look. Rathmado raised one eyebrow.

"Was that a bit too much?"

"Just a bit."

"It's true." He took another grape. "Destiny."

"I," said Sylph with mounting impatience, "do not believe

in Destiny. That just means someone else is deciding where you go and what you do."

"That is a little bit true, and a little bit untrue. Untrue in the sense that there is something *special* about you, but quite true in the sense that it becomes Destiny only when certain powers take an interest."

"Who's taking an interest?"

"I'm not at liberty to reveal that information. Suffice to say it's a being or group of beings of sufficient caliber that the manipulation of destiny is fairly trivial."

"What are *you* doing here?"

"*I* am playing the agent of Destiny, if you will. I'm here to make sure it all happens properly."

"If it's my Destiny," Sylph said sarcastically, "doesn't it have to happen properly? Isn't that the whole point?"

"The problem is that there are a number of definitions of 'properly,' in this case. What you might call my job is to make sure we end up on the right branch."

"Can you tell me what happens?"

"Of course not. If I told you . . ."

". . . we'd end up on the wrong branch?"

"Or at a paradox or something equally unpleasant. In any case, I don't know, because they—'they' being my all-knowing but not quite all-powerful boss or bosses—don't tell me these things, because then I might be tempted to tell you. I'm only human, after all."

Sylph collapsed into a chair. "This is a joke, right? Some kind of sick joke."

"I'm afraid not. It's been working out so far, right? The sword and so on."

"That *was* you. I remember . . ." Her brow furrowed. "I don't *really* remember, but you were talking to me."

"You were in transit between life here and life there, which is not a very natural place for a human mind to exist. It's no wonder you don't recall properly."

"So, where have you been?"

"Here, advising Gargorian." He smiled wider. "I don't think I did a very good job."

"And that was all part of the plan?"

"It's not so much a plan. I play things by ear, maybe give them a nudge in the right direction." He shrugged. "Things went okay, didn't they?"

"Barely."

"Destiny is funny that way."

"I don't believe any of this, you realize."

"Of course you do. I'm the only person you know here who's making any sense at all."

"That's certainly true," Sylph muttered. To Rathmado she said, "In that case, oh genie of the lamp, what do I do next? I've got the city, but what do I do with it? Settle in and become queen?"

"Of course not. You go west, where the population labors under the lash of an even greater tyrant: Lady Fell, the Magio Mutator."

"Why?"

"The suffering of innocents isn't reason enough?"

"We've got plenty to work on here. I told the Circle Breakers I would kill Gargorian because he was going to kill me otherwise. I did. I'm not out to conquer the world."

"Yes, you are."

"Because it's my Destiny?" Sylph snapped.

"Because there's a very important question that you haven't asked."

✳   ✳   ✳

Despite all of Fah's protestations and Marlowe's advice, in the end Lina had been unable to stay away. She hadn't been watching during the Fall, but she remembered the sound: crack after brittle crack rising and blurring together into an inhuman scream, as though the building itself were shrieking in agony. It was a horrible sound, and even in her exhausted state Lina had clamped her hands over her ears and curled up around the sword, waiting for it to end.

Now she'd come to pick through the wreckage. Giant shards of diamond had embedded themselves in the turf, lending the whole place a weirdly alien air; in between the house-sized chunks were smaller fragments, pieces of pillar or glass-like sheets miraculously undamaged by the fall, along with tiny splinters and shards. It reminded Lina of a bus stop behind her school, where teenagers had gone to drink and then hurl their beer bottles into a dark corner, creating a garden of broken glass.

She was glad that she'd taken at least one piece of Marlowe's advice; steel-plated boots and thick leather clothes. She'd scraped herself a dozen times in the first ten minutes, and some of the little pieces were as sharp as razors. A quartet of guards kept a polite distance behind her; Fah was otherwise occupied, assisting Marlowe's attempts to keep order, but she'd chosen protectors who would be no less vigilant. *At the moment we've no shortage of enthusiastic converts.*

Somewhat to Lina's surprise, she wasn't alone in the ruins. Small groups of civilians, decked out in protective gear, were combing through the rubble. At first she assumed they were looters; diamond wasn't worth much, but there had been other furnishings in the Tower and a few had survived the fall. She saw people making off with whatever they could find: an elaborate gold-chased strongbox; half of a gorgeous tapestry, trailing thread; a painting and its elaborate wooden frame. A few others took only fragments, bits of furniture or diamond that would serve as souvenirs of the most important event in the history of the city.

There were others that she didn't understand until she saw them find what they were looking for. Two women, one old and one young, struggled to move a diamond shard and finally unearthed the blood spattered body of a young man. The older one dug him out with quiet efficiency, while the other fell to her knees and cried. One of the boy's arms was missing; the old woman found it a few yards away, severed cleanly by a falling crystal razor. She helped the younger woman to her feet, and the two of them bore their grisly burden away.

There were other bodies, dozens if not hundreds. Lina made her circuit in silence, and those who caught sight of her stayed quiet until she was out of earshot. A storm of whispers arose in the Liberator's wake.

They were soldiers. Somehow she felt better about that. Most of the bodies wore armor, carried weapons; they had been the men of Gargorian's army, ready to die in his defense. *And they did. At least we gave them a chance to surrender.*

But the others . . . *there are others.* A girl just a bit older than Sylph in a maid's uniform, apparently unwounded except for the massive diamond pane that had bisected her at the waist. Two men in the rough clothing of kitchen servants, mutilated by flying shards until they were just a tangle of limbs and blood. And on, and on. *They cooked his meals, set his table, took his money,* Lina thought. *But they weren't ready to die for him.* She turned away, one hand on the hilt of the sword for the comfort it lent her.

We won the battle, she had to keep reminding herself. *They were cheering in the streets. Sometimes losses are inevitable; Sylph did the right thing. How many would have died if we'd had to storm the gates?*

There was something different ahead, a clear space in the crystal garden. It was roughly circular; tiny shards were piled high around its edges, as though a giant broom had swept up a bit after the Tower had fallen. Lina clambered over, curious. Diamond scraped against the bottoms of her boots, and little pieces crunched together under her weight. Inside there was nothing special, just a flat expanse of diamond that must have been part of the Tower's bottom level. In the center . . .

Lina shivered. It *looked* like a metal sphere, about the size of a grape, but what she felt made it seem somehow more sinister. A cold wind blew from the tiny thing in waves, cutting right through her clothes and making her skin pebble into goose bumps. The little marble was perfectly smooth and reflective, so as she walked close she saw a funhouse-mirror version of herself on the curved surface. Lina gave the thing a tap with her foot, and it rolled away across the diamond until it came to rest against one of the heaps of shards at the edge of the clear space.

This is important. Her instincts told her that much, but she found herself reluctant to pick the thing up. She checked the sword to make sure it was still at her side—*in case it releases a demon or something like that, you never know. But Sylph will want to see this.*

Slowly, Lina bent and retrieved the metal sphere. It was slightly cold to the touch, even through her gloves, but otherwise felt like an oversized ball bearing. She glanced over her shoulder at her guards, none of whom had entered the cleared section.

"Where's Sylph? Still at the inn?"

A woman bowed, then said, "As far as I know, my lady."

I'll never get used to all this bowing and scraping. "Let's head back there, then."

"As you wish."

✳   ✳   ✳

"A question . . ." Sylph trailed off, and Rathmado waited in expectant silence, one hand poised in the act of twisting off another grape. She closed her eyes and thought, then shook her head. "I'm not playing word games, Rath."

"If you could have anything you wanted, what would you pick?"

"Getting myself out of this place? And Lina too, of course."

"And?"

"What do you mean, 'and'?" But there was something else—she felt it, a tiny worm of doubt, gnawing at the base of her mind.

"I thought you were smarter than this. Or perhaps,"

Rathmado smiled, "perhaps it is the subconscious that rebels. If you could convince Omega to give up her dead, Sylph, is there not one other you would bring back with you?"

Another? She blinked, and got it; just a flash of a smile and silky red hair. *Mom. But . . .*

"She's dead." Sylph gritted her teeth. "She's dead . . ."

"And that means she's here." Rathmado waved a hand. "Somewhere."

"You said that people don't wake up here. Only the two of us . . ."

"Correct. The rest are either reborn, or slide down the strands of the Circles into the repositories of the Archmagi."

"Repositories . . ." And suddenly, as though the clouds had parted, everything made sense.

The Circles and the Plague. Dead newborns—they were never alive to begin with, because they had no—might as well call it a soul. Because Gargorian was collecting them! She pictured the Circles by night, from far above, spread across the land like a spider's web. *Or a net. Only the ones who slip through, or those he chooses to* allow *through . . .*

Sylph realized she'd been silent for a few long seconds. Rathmado stared at her attentively.

"But," she said, "what does he *do* with them?"

The Magus popped the grape into his mouth. "With the people? Nothing. But the energy they carry is like life's blood to an Archmagus. So they are imprisoned, stacked like so much cordwood and their power used to fuel his ambitions."

"Imprisoned where?"

There was a knock at the door.

"Ah," Rathmado said, "perfect timing."

"Sylph?" came Heraan's muffled voice. "Your sister's here."

"Let her in," Sylph called back. A moment later the door opened. Lina looked a little tired but worlds better than the last time Sylph had seen her; she smiled and was in the midst of a cheerful greeting when she caught sight of the Magus and stopped. Rathmado bowed politely.

"Oh. Lina, this is Magus Rathmado. This is . . ."

"Lina Walker, of course."

"N . . . nice to meet you, Magus." Lina turned to Sylph. "Can I speak to you privately, Sylph? I have something to show you."

"I can assure you," said Rathmado, "that you need have no secrets from me."

"Because you already know everything?" Sylph glared at him, then looked back at Lina. "He can stay, but shut the door."

Lina did so. Then, with a nervous glance at the Magus, she dug in her pouch and produced a cloth-wrapped ball. She placed it on the table, carefully, and pulled the cloth back. A breath of cold air filled the room, as though someone had opened a window onto a chilly night, and the metal sphere glittered in the candlelight as though it had been oiled. A moment later Sylph felt something else; *power* radiated from the steel marble, so much so that it glowed like a furnace in someway unrelated to actual light. She couldn't help but take a step back, and Lina looked alarmed, dropping one hand to the hilt of her sword. Only Rathmado remained perfectly calm, maintaining his smile.

"I thought you'd find it," he said. "Or, perhaps, the other way around."

"What is it?" Sylph asked, trying to regain her composure.

"It is called a *geist*. You asked where Gargorian stored those who came to him. The answer is he kept them in there, along with their power. But the geist predates him; there are only three in the world. In a way," the Magus mused, "it is the geist that make the Archmagi. Certainly not the other way around."

Lina looked from Sylph to Rathmado, clearly confused. Sylph held up a hand, motioning her to wait. "Can I touch it?"

"Of course."

"And nothing horrible will happen?" *You have to be exact, when it comes to Rathmado.*

"No." He shrugged. "Although you may find the experience a bit unsettling at first."

"Sylph, I'm not sure you should—"

Before Lina could finish her sentence, Sylph had taken a deep breath and put her hand on the sphere. The Magus and her sister vanished and the room spun away, leaving her floating alone in a vast space.

What the hell?

She twisted wildly. Above her, in the middle distance, was a flat plane dappled with tiny bumps. Sylph stared, trying to make them out, and she found herself moving toward it at a fantastic speed. Perspective flipped, and she suddenly felt her stomach trying to escape via her throat. *I'm falling . . .*

The specks—no bigger than grains of dust at first—got larger as she approached. She'd been farther from the wall than she'd originally thought, thousands of feet up. *If distance means anything here.* Freefalling, Sylph fought the urge to squeeze her eyes shut. She was seconds from being a sticky mess down amongst the whatever-they-weres, and the fact that she was already dead wasn't much of a consolation. At the last instant, she could no longer stop herself from screaming . . .

. . . and she stopped, without the slightest sense of acceleration, a few feet off the "ground."

Tentatively, Sylph stretched out and touched the surface. It felt like metal, solid and cool underfoot. She could see the specks, ranged in neat rows all around her: bodies, corpses as far as the eye could see. All were naked but whole, and they ran the gamut from tiny babies to old men and everything in between. She walked to the nearest, fighting the feeling that it would have been quicker to fly—*I've done enough flying!*—and found a young man, hands crossed on his chest, his expression at peace. Hesitantly, she bent and touched his skin, and was surprised to find it just slightly warm. *Not dead, then?* But his chest wasn't moving. *Not alive, either.* She took a hissing breath. *These are the souls inside the geist.*

Inside . . .

Sylph looked up. The corpse-studded plain stretched away

in all directions, as far as the eye could see. She let her eye follow the pattern; *does it go* up, *as it runs into the distance? It does!* She looked straight up, and squinted. There was no sun to interfere, and she could almost convince herself that the sky's steel-gray color was the same as the ground's. *A sphere. I'm* inside *the geist. And if these are the souls . . .*

Her jaw sagged.

. . . there must be . . . billions . . .

"Sylph?"

Between blinks of the eye, the world shifted and she was back in the inn, with Lina shaking her by the shoulder.

"Sylph, are you okay?"

"I'm fine." Sylph took a shaking step to a chair by the table and fell into it. Rathmado gave her a sympathetic look.

"You saw them, didn't you?"

"Saw *what*?" Lina asked.

"Inside that thing." Sylph gestured. "Gargorian used it to collect the souls of the dead."

"Gargorian, and all the Magio Creators before him," Rath said.

"They're all there." Sylph looked at Rathmado. "All the dead from Earth?"

"From Earth and elsewhere," the Magus confirmed. "Of course, there are two more geists. And the largest repository is in the Black Keep, where the Lightbringer waits. His web is largest of all."

"People who die here must get trapped too," said Sylph. "Remember what Melfina said, about not wanting to die inside the Circle?"

"I remember," said Lina, "but I still don't understand."

"Neither do I, really." Sylph shook her head. "But I'm starting to feel like I will, now that Rathmado here is giving me some straight answers."

"Forgive an old man his sense of drama," Rathmado said.

"You don't look like an old man," Lina pointed out.

"Appearances," he replied, "can be deceiving."

"Sylph, can we talk? Alone?"

Before Sylph could answer, Rathmado bowed. "I believe I've given the younger Miss Walker enough to think about for one day. Sylph, my lady Lina, I remain at your service should you require me."

He walked to the door, pausing to take one last grape before he went. Lina was vibrating by the time he was halfway across the room, hand twitching on the hilt of her sword; as soon as the door had shut behind him, she turned on Sylph.

"Sylph, who *is* he?"

"I'm not really sure." She leaned back against the chair's padded headrest. "But he knows things. He knows . . ."

"Too much, for my tastes! You can't seriously be trusting him."

"Of course not. But . . ." She glanced at the geist, sitting innocently in its nest of cloth. "He was right about some things."

"We have no idea what he wants from us!"

"He told me, at least the first step."

"And?"

"He wants us to take the army against Lady Fell, to the west."

"No." Lina shook her head violently. "No, Sylph. We can't."

"But—"

"*No.*"

There was a pause. Lina walked slowly to the bed and sank down among the cushions, her head in her hands.

"Lina? Are you all right?"

"No." Lina's voice was muffled. "I'm not. There's something wrong with me."

"What's wrong?"

"I'm turning into something awful."

Sylph got to her feet, still feeling a bit shaky, and made her way across the room. "What do you mean?"

"I went down to the Tower. That's where I found that . . . thing." Lina took a shaky breath. "But I went . . . I don't know.

I had to see."

"See what?"

"There were people in there when it came down. Just ordinary people, not Diamond Guard or anything. Maids and cooks and butlers and . . . whores, I guess, or whatever you'd call Gargorian's harem. They all died."

Sylph, still standing, closed her eyes. "I know."

"You killed them all, Sylph. How do you feel?"

How do I feel? She thought for a moment. "I feel like a murderer. But it had to be done, Lina, you know . . ."

"I know!" She shook her head again. "I'm to blame as much as you. I led the army here; Zaya and Kari died because they were trying to protect _me_."

"You had to do it," said Sylph. She reached out and put a hand on Lina's shoulder. "Things are going to be better."

"That's _not_ the point!" Lina brushed her sister's hand off. "You know what I feel? Come on, ask me!"

"What?"

"_Nothing._ Not a god_damned_ thing. I watched them pick this one boy up, his father had to go and get a _bag_ to carry all the pieces, and I felt _nothing_. It was like . . . I reached inside myself, and there was nothing there. Nothing left." Lina doubled over, hugging herself tightly, eyes streaming tears. "What's _wrong_ with me?"

Sylph said nothing. Truthfully, she could think of nothing to say. _She's been through so much._ She sat down beside Lina and hugged her, and this time Lina let her arms remain, leaning down to muffle her sobs on Sylph's shoulder.

It seems like we take turns, Sylph thought after Lina quieted. They lay together in the too-soft bed. Lina looked awkward, on her side atop the sheathed sword, but Sylph didn't have the heart to move her. _I guess it's my turn to be the strong one._

I think I understand Yahvy. It's nice to have someone to hold you, until your muscles stop shaking. It helps you remember that you're still alive, whatever else happened.

Or not alive, as the case may be. If Rath is telling the truth, then we're all dead. Maybe this really is Hell.

She closed her eyes. *No. He said that Mom is here, and that means it can't be Hell, right?*

He wants me to try to find her. Lina's right; he must have his reasons. Her instincts rebelled. *I always hated being manipulated.*

But . . . I have to find her. I have to tell her I'm sorry.

I have to.

Eventually, Sylph fell asleep, her head filled with plans for the next war.

*   *   *

THE NEXT DAY DAWNED BLESSEDLY CLOUDY; AN OVERNIGHT shower had cut down the heat and lent a wonderfully fresh feeling to the dusty air. Lina woke and dressed, planning to spend the morning working on her swordplay with Fah—a pleasantly mindless task—but her hopes were dashed when she opened her door to find Marlowe waiting, with Fah and Myris behind him.

"Good morning, Lina." He looked her over and nodded appreciatively. "Nice to see you without armor, even if you are still dressing like a boy."

She colored. Myris had acquired the new clothes for her, much more comfortable than leather and chain, but Lina felt suddenly self-conscious. At least the belt still had a sword-loop, from which the sword dangled. *I've worn the damn thing so much I don't feel comfortable without it anymore.* Fah and Myris were still dressed as though they were going into battle, but Marlowe had also traded his armor for something more fitting.

"Good morning," Lina said. "I take it you've come to get me?"

"We have indeed." He gestured. "Some of the local bigwigs are here to talk to you and Sylph about what happens next for the city."

Lina shook her head. "I have no idea what should happen next . . ."

"Nevertheless," Fah put in, "having the Liberator present lends weight to whatever decisions are made."

"I figured."

Sylph was already in deep discussion with the civic leaders when Lina and the rest arrived. There were two of them: a pale-faced, bespectacled man with the look of an accountant, and a hugely fat merchant with gaudy clothes and a tremendous laugh. They both stood, with some effort on the part of the merchant; Lina waved them down as quickly as she could and took a seat next to Sylph.

"My lady," said the merchant, "I am Belladon, and my companion is Corio. Between us we represent the majority of the merchants and landowners in the city."

"Greetings," said Lina, with what she hoped was appropriate gravity. "I am Lina Walker."

"First," said Belladon ponderously, "let me convey our sincerest thanks for freeing us of the burden of the Archmagus. Without the Plague, I have no doubt that Bleloth and the surrounding lands can become more prosperous then they have ever been . . ."

He went on, and Lina found herself tuning out automatically. Phrases like "inherent dignity of the working class" and "welcome redistribution of property" rolled past. Lina glanced at Sylph, who seemed both sincerely interested and a bit irritated. Sylph must have noticed her sister's attention, because she leaned close and whispered, "What a windbag. Follow my lead, okay?"

Lina nodded gratefully. Sylph held up a hand, cutting off Belladon in mid-sentence. While he gasped for breath, she said, "And whose property would you be redistributing, Belladon?"

"Those who had grown fat under the old order, of course. The nobility are mostly ex-soldiers and Gargorian's former servants; if their estates are broken up, all will rejoice."

"Except for them, presumably. And is it your intention to oversee this breakup personally?"

"I . . . I would of course be willing to attend to the details, with my lady's permission." He looked at Lina, but it was Sylph who answered.

"I see. And Corio, what are you here for?"

"I've come seeking guarantees," he said, with a slight lisp. "Since you have cast down Gargorian, I assume you intend to install yourself as the ruler of Bleloth?"

"We intend to install someone," said Sylph. "The Liberator has more important things to intend to."

"I would be happy—" Belladon put in, but Corio cut him off.

"It should be done sooner rather than later, my lady. Gargorian had agreements with the merchant companies who travel the road to the east. Currency agreements, rules against the simple creation of coin, for example. His minister Vesh handled the details."

"I understand." Sylph smiled. "You want to know if we're playing by the same rules."

"Not for my own sake," Corio said. "Uncertainty helps no one. Already the price of grain has doubled, and unless you make a public announcement, I fear the worst is yet to come. A word from the Liberator would mean a great deal."

"You have my assurance that there will be no wholesale creation of coin. The rest will have to wait."

"About my redistribution . . ." said Belladon plaintively.

"Any redistribution will be handled ourselves, Belladon, but thank you for the offer. Now you'll have to excuse us. The Liberator needs to confer with her advisors."

"My lady!" said Belladon in protest, ignoring Sylph. "Do you—"

"Sylph speaks with my voice," Lina snapped. "She has my absolute confidence, do you understand? Any promises she makes, I will abide by."

The merchant looked taken aback. "I understand."

"I'll leave you to your deliberations," said Corio, rising. Marlowe and Myris escorted the pair of them out, leaving the sisters alone with Fah for the moment.

"I feel," said Lina, "like I've had a glimpse into my future. I'm not sure I like it."

"Belladon's just a jackal," said Sylph. "As for the other, I'm not sure. But fear not, I wasn't kidding when I said you had better things to do."

"Someone has to deal with all this."

"I imagine someone will." Sylph sighed. "And I'm sure there'll be wars and coups and assassinations to beat the band. I don't plan on sticking around for any of it."

"What do you mean?"

"Do you remember when we first came here? You got that sword, and you said you were Meant to have it."

"Yes . . ."

"It turns out you were right. Literally right; the fact the we won here is the proof."

"You said that you didn't believe in any of that."

"I'm not sure I do, but it seems to have some meaning here." Sylph turned to Fah. "What happened to the last Liberator, Fah?"

"According to legend," said the Circle Breaker, "he spent no more than a month in the city before striking out for the east. Lady Fell ruled then, and she rules now, so we can assume he was unsuccessful in defeating her. But no one really knows."

"That doesn't exactly thrill me," said Lina. "This is your plan, Sylph? More war?"

"I'm not sure we have a choice." Sylph reached into her pocket and produced the geist, which she set on the table with a click. Lina let out a hiss.

"You're carrying that thing around?"

"Can you think of a better way to keep it safe?" Sylph challenged.

"I . . . don't know."

"This belonged to Gargorian. Rath says it made him what he was, and that Lady Fell and this Vilvakis each have one as well." She closed her eyes and took a deep breath. "I think we're here, Lina, to take them away. Not to rule some little city."

"If I may speak . . ." said Fah hesitantly.

"Go ahead," said Lina, her eyes still on the geist. Her reflection looked back at her, reversed and upside down. *I remember when Fah was in charge of things.* Something in the girl had changed. *She found what she was looking for.*

"I think Sylph is right. You are the Liberator, and your purpose is higher than the mere command of armies and cities. Breaking the rule of the Archmagi—"

Lina stood up abruptly. "I am going for a walk," she said.

"A walk?" Fah shook her head. "Let me assemble a guard."

"No. Leave me alone, please. I need to think." She fumbled at her belt. "Sylph . . ."

"Yes?"

"Keep this here for me." She drew the sheathed sword out of its loop and set it on the table. Letting go of it was harder then she expected, almost a physical wrench, but once it was gone she felt different. *Almost . . . lighter. It's not just the sword, but everything it represents. All the pain.*

Sylph nodded. "Are you going to be all right?"

"Yeah. I just need a little bit of air."

She turned to Fah, who stepped out of the way only reluctantly. But she did step aside, and Lina left the room and the inn behind her as quickly as she could.

Free!

*   *   *

SYLPH SAT BACK IN THE NOW-EMPTY ROOM AND CLOSED her eyes.

I hate, hate, hate lying to my sister.

Not even lying, exactly, but . . .

No. Don't beat around the fucking bush, Sylph. I don't believe we were meant for anything. And if I had the chance to take Lina back home and live happily ever after, I think I'd leave everyone here to burn in a second.

But if Rath is right, and Mom is really here somewhere, then I don't have much of a choice.

Lina wouldn't understand. Lina hadn't been there when their mother had died. *She doesn't know.*

But it's not like what I told her isn't true. *The geists are horrible; the people here will be better off once the Circles are broken. Just because I have an ulterior motive . . .*

She sighed as the door opened to admit Marlowe and Heraan. The latter raised an eyebrow.

"Something wrong?"

"Kind of."

"I hear our Liberator has gone off by herself," said Marlowe.

"She should be okay. Half the city's in love with her."

"Some of them, the nobles especially, are less in love then they claim to be." He shook his head. "In any case, I've got some people following her. Discreetly, of course."

"Probably a wise move," Sylph agreed. "Sit down, we've got things to discuss."

The two men took seats across from her, Heraan listening attentively while Marlowe slouched in his chair.

"First question: What are you planning to do now?"

"Do now?" Heraan looked confused.

"We won the war, in case you hadn't noticed. Gargorian's dead, his army's a shambles, the Circles are broken. Now what?"

They were silent for a moment; Heraan spoke first.

"I think it depends on what you and Lina do, Sylph."

That was the answer Sylph had been expecting, arrogant as that assumption seemed to her. She couldn't help but ask, "Why?"

"I can't speak for Marlowe, but . . . Lina's the Liberator, and you're a Magus."

"I didn't figure you for a believer . . ."

"Believer or not, the two off you accomplished something

no one has been able to do for six hundred years. If you're going to keep going, I'd like to tag along and see what happens."

"That's remarkably cavalier of you." Sylph smiled and turned to Marlowe. "What about you?"

"I'm with you," he replied immediately. "Being an officer is the only thing I've ever been any good at."

"Excellent. I think I'm going to need both of you."

"I take it," Marlowe said, "that you're not planning to stick around Bleloth?"

"Only for a little while."

"And then?"

"East."

"Lady Fell. And Vilvakis, after that." Heraan smiled crookedly. "Have you been reading old legends, Sylph?"

"Something like that. Still interested? Lina could probably set either of you up as king here in Bleloth."

They looked at each other, and both men burst out laughing.

"No offense," said Marlowe after a moment, "but if Lina set me up as king and then left, I doubt I'd live out the month. Those merchants might come over all pious when you're looking at them, but I wouldn't want to have them at my back."

"True enough." Sylph nodded, relieved. "On to more important things. I think we can be fairly sure Lady Fell is not going to just hand over her geist and walk away. Marlowe, if we announce we're going to march, what kind of an army are we going to have?"

"A pretty damn big one, if I'm any judge. A lot of the young idiots—present company excluded, of course—worship the ground your sister walks on. If she tells them to go, they'll go."

"Give me a number."

"Maybe two thousand with military training, and another two or three without? Assuming you can provide food and water for them all."

"That shouldn't be a problem," Heraan put in, "at least for the moment. We got Gargorian's main storehouses; thankfully, they weren't in the Tower itself."

"So call it four thousand, half former conscripts and half civilians. How long to make a decent army out of them?"

"A couple of months just to teach the basics. After that . . ." Marlowe shrugged. "It's hard to predict when a unit will acquire real discipline, and training isn't always enough. On the other hand, a bunch of them have already been blooded out beyond the walls. That counts for a lot."

"We may not have that long, but we'll do what we can. What about weapons?"

"We've got plenty of spears and short-swords from Gargorian's stores," Heraan said, "and not much else."

"Longbows," Sylph mused. "How many?"

He raised an eyebrow. "A couple of dozen? Maybe more if I buy some in the market. Those are really a western weapon."

"Fine." *As long as we're training an army from scratch, might as well do it right.* Gargorian's conscripts were intended to be little more than warm bodies on the walls and bandit-fighters; Sylph knew at least a little about what a professional army should look like. "Marlowe, I want you to start organizing as soon as you can. Go through the people that came into the city with us first, see if you can find some trustworthy ones to use as sergeants. Then set up some recruiting stations and camps outside the walls for everybody who joins. Get all the longbows you can, and separate out anybody who claims to have training or looks strong enough to be a decent shot. Have them practice in shifts."

"How many bowmen do you want?" Marlowe objected. "I don't see the point in training more men than we have bows . . ."

"I'll work on that," said Sylph, who had the germ of an idea. "We're going to train the rest as pike-men. Do you know what a pike is?"

She got a pair of blank looks.

"Like a spear, but longer—twelve, fourteen feet long—a nice point and a sharp blade at the end?"

"Sounds a bit unwieldy to me," said Marlowe. "Gargorian—"

"Gargorian never had any infantry worth a damn," Heraan said. "Is that how they fight where you come from, Sylph?"

"Yeah." *Eight hundred years ago, anyway.* "It takes some training to get right, but I think we can manage it."

"We don't have any 'pikes' either," Marlowe pointed out.

"Use plain wooden poles for now. I'll work on getting some heads made."

The big soldier shrugged. "As you say. You'll have to come show me what you want done with them." He smiled at her. "To be honest, I was always a cavalryman; this business of slogging about on foot is new to me."

"That's the other thing. Heraan, your job is going to be to get us some cavalry. Get whatever decent horses you can; buy them, commandeer them in the name of the Liberator, I don't care. Pick some likely men from Marlowe's recruits and start working with them. Sound possible?"

"It'll be a pleasure," said Heraan.

"Great." Sylph gave them both a big smile and tried to conceal her own trepidation. *What the hell do I know about running an army?* "Let's get to it, shall we?"

NEWS OF THE RECRUITING SPREAD QUICKLY THROUGH THE streets. All the local businesses seemed to have decided that this was some kind of festival, and everything was closed except for food vendors and wine shops, which were doing record sales. The streets were therefore packed, and as Marlowe had predicted young men and women flush with victory were eager to sign up. The graves, conveniently outside the city walls, seemed to have been forgotten. Sylph watched the unruly lines snaking back from the square and shook her head.

I need them, but it still feels wrong somehow.

A runner found her with the news that Lina had returned, and Sylph threaded her way back to the inn, which had turned into the unofficial headquarters of the Liberator's army. She saw, as she pushed her way through the crowds, that Marlowe had posted guards at the doors. *I don't think we need much guarding, not here, but it's a nice image.* The two by the door spotted her and saluted crisply. *Must be some of Marlowe's veterans.*

"The Liberator is waiting for you in the dining room," said one, and Sylph acknowledged with a nod. Lina was, indeed, waiting, though she was also snacking on a meat and cheese tray that had been left by some thoughtful servant. Sylph was relieved to see her sister wave her over enthusiastically.

"Feeling better?"

"Much," said Lina, who was in the midst of stuffing herself with cold chicken. "Have you been out on the streets at all?"

"A little, yeah."

"They're so *happy*." Lina gave her sister a big smile. "I was just walking along, and I could feel it. Everyone's a little scared, maybe, because they don't know how things are going to turn out. But they know they're not going to have to knuckle under to a tyrant just to save their children's lives, and that counts for an awful lot."

"It's true." And it was, mostly. While a few nobles who'd risen high under the Archmagus might grumble, for the most part Gargorian's demise came as a near-miracle. "You did it, Lina."

"*You* did most of it, Sylph. We'd have been dead a long time ago if not for you."

"Either way. I think it was worth the price we paid."

"I know." Lina shook her head. "I'm sorry about this morning. Something about the Tower just . . . got to me, you know? I just needed to clear my head."

"You certainly seem a bit livelier."

Lina grinned and stretched like a cat, wincing when her shoulders popped. "If a bit sore."

"I've got Marlowe recruiting . . ."

"For the army. I heard, it's all anyone's talking about."

"Lina . . ." Sylph hesitated. "I need you to be with me on

this. If you're not . . ."

Lina bounded from her chair and wrapped her sister in a hug. "Of course I'm with you. You were right, you're always right, why should this time be any different? Those people *need* us."

Sylph closed her eyes, leaned on her sister, and tried to hold back both laughter and tears.

chapter eleven

THE DAYS WENT BY SO QUICKLY THAT SYLPH THOUGHT about inventing a new aphorism: "Time flies when no one's trying to kill you."

The city of Bleloth had settled into an uneasy peace. After the civic leaders convinced themselves that Sylph honestly didn't mean to rule the city, they fought a covert power struggle. It stayed covert because Sylph had asked Marlowe to spread the word that wholesale violence in the streets would be frowned upon. So for the most part the merchants stuck to scheming, wheeling, and dealing. A few bodies were found floating face-down in the reservoir, most notably the bloated windbag Belladon; when things settled down, a council of the most powerful merchants and nobility were more or less running things. Prices came down a little, which helped keep order on the streets.

Marlowe was the busiest, trying to forge the army of the Liberator into something like a real fighting force. He'd ended up with around four thousand fighting men and women, split between infantry, archers, and a relatively small force of medium cavalry Heraan was putting through its paces. Everyone Sylph felt she could trust had been drafted as a regimental commander: Garot, Melfina, Yahvy, and Orbaa. The latter pair continued to spend every spare moment in one another's company and behind closed doors. Fah and Myris had outfitted a regiment of handpicked soldiers with heavy plate and diamond swords left over from Gargorian's elites and were building a special guard to make sure Lina's person was never threatened again.

The Liberator herself spent most of her time out with the army, either helping Marlowe with his efforts or practicing her own swordwork. She didn't use *the* sword, for fear of incinerating a hapless partner, but she reported she felt as though she could at least defend herself. All in all, Lina was happier than Sylph had seen her since they'd arrived, which was another burden off her mind.

For her part, Sylph had been trying to fulfill the promises she'd made to Marlowe. He needed pikes, more than the city's blacksmiths could manufacture, and enough longbows to equip a force of archers larger than Gargorian had ever conceived of. The only way to get those supplies was by magic, and Sylph set to the task with a will.

If Gargorian could churn out all those suits of armor and swords for his Diamond Guard, I should be able to make a few pikes. Admittedly, Gargorian had a half a millennium of experience and was an Archmagus to boot, but Sylph felt her newly discovered magical talents had to be good for something.

Her first efforts had been encouraging. Sylph sat alone in her room, with the door locked and the windows shuttered, and just concentrated. She could feel the table she was sitting at, and the chair, and the air that swirled around both. Her own body, for that matter, a riotous confusion of organic compounds and structures. She took a deep breath and started with something simple. *Diamond—just a nice carbon matrix, nothing fancy.* The gemstone was incredibly simple chemically. *Probably why Gargorian used so much of it.*

She found that she could build it quite literally out of nothing, layering energy in the right patterns, over and over, until she had a finished product in the shape she wanted. After a few tests, she set about creating a pike-head, a kind of spear-point with an axe-like blade at the bottom. It was the kind of work it was easy to get lost in, carefully sculpting the final form like a potter working with clay. When Sylph sat back and opened her eyes, she was delighted to find a perfect weapon sitting on the table in front of her, its edge so sharp she dared not touch it.

Sylph blinked and yawned. She pushed her chair back from the table, tried to stand up, and found herself unaccountably lying on the floor. Her arms twitched, as though she'd been holding up heavy weights for hours, and her legs gave all the support of lengths of cooked spaghetti. Every breath was an effort, and her chest ached abominably. Within moments she was covered with sweat.

The clatter brought the servants rushing in. Sylph convinced them to put her to bed and say no more about it; she awoke almost twenty-four hours later, feeling a bit stiff but refreshed.

Energy. Sylph ran her hand across the glittering pike-head. She could feel the energy she'd invested in it, a little piece of herself in every layer of carbon. *No wonder it took so much out of me.*

Further experiments confirmed it. Even making a tiny gemstone left her winded, and manufacturing something the size of a pike-head knocked her off her feet for a day or more. Once she tried making two at once, but only once; while it was easy to duplicate the pattern in more than one place, the world went suddenly black before she was halfway finished. Sylph spent the next couple of days shivering in her bed, fighting off the bowls of warm soup that her sister insisted on bringing her. *I just don't have enough energy.*

Finally, reluctantly, she turned to the obvious solution.

The geist, perfectly smooth, glimmered almost malevolently in the candlelight. Sylph had set it on a cloth, and donned a light jacket because of a chill; outside the sun was shining, but in her private space it felt like the dark of the night. She took a deep breath, closed her eyes, and reached out to the thing. The barest brush of her fingertips against it sent a swell of power rushing through her, as though she'd stuck her finger in an electrical socket. Sylph gasped.

Within minutes she'd created a dozen pike-heads on the table, all perfectly identical. Sylph wasn't even sweating. She stacked them carefully in the corner and materialized a dozen more, watching them take shape out of nothing with a bemused astonishment. Power flowed *through* her, from the geist into the products, with unbelievable ease. More, the reservoir of power in the little metal ball seemed limitless. She felt as though it was a well from which she could drink forever, until the sheer depth of it consumed her. Sylph took care to move slowly, manufacturing the weapons in expanding lots, but with the geist under her fingers it felt as though she had no limitations at all.

This is blood-magic, she reminded herself. *Blood power. Those are* souls *in there.* But without the Circles—"unplugged," as it were—the geist seemed benign. She didn't feel any pain from those imprisoned, just a numbness; the power had already been stripped from them and placed into the geist's vast reserves. Gargorian had surrounded it with Circles, in order to capture more souls and gain ever more power, but there was already enough to last a lifetime. *I would never capture someone's soul. But using the power that's already there . . . until we figure out how to free the souls within . . .*

That was something she'd tried, and failed, to accomplish. Rathmado insisted that her mother was somewhere in Omega, but Sylph's searches through the inside of the geist had come to nothing; her attempts to extract one of the imprisoned souls had been met with cold indifference, as though she were scrabbling against a glass wall. Nothing she did made a mark on the chilly metal shell of the geist. And the glib Magus admitted he knew nothing of such matters, which left Sylph feeling frustrated. *She's probably not in there anyway. He said Lady Fell has more souls, and Vilvakis more still. And the Lightbringer . . .*

Bows had proved to be a bit harder than pikes, but not intractably so. Diamond obviously wouldn't do, so Sylph played with alloying metals until she got a shape and stiffness that Marlowe pronounced satisfactory. Once she started using the geist,

magic was *fun*; she could poke and prod at the very fabric of creation, creating objects from their fundamental building blocks in
a way a scientist could only dream of. After a while, she started
to suspect that Gargorian for all his power had been ignorant;
he hadn't even scraped the surface of what could be created. *Of
course, he never had high school chemistry.*

With the army getting close to being outfitted, Sylph had
to start thinking of what to do when the time came to march.
There were a thousand details to manage, only some of which
she could hand off to Marlowe. Food, transport, clothes and
boots, flags and colors and trumpet calls; Gargorian's officers
had solved all of these problems, but the solutions had to be
found and expanded on. She was starting to feel like she and
Marlowe had gotten things under control when news arrived
from the east.

✳   ✳   ✳

Marlowe walked into her room and said, "I've got
someone you need to talk to."

"Oh?" Sylph looked up. She'd been toying with some more
complicated chemicals, making slow but steady progress. "Who?"

"One of Gargorian's people, a messenger. It'll be faster to
talk to him than explain."

"Are we in a hurry?"

"I'm not sure."

Sylph got up, popped the kinks from her shoulders, and followed him down to the inn's basement. It had originally been a
wine cellar, and still served that purpose, but Sylph had set up a
table down there for meetings that needed to be a bit more private. Despite the cleaning staff's efforts, it smelled of dust and
spilled, sour wine.

Sitting at the table, between a pair of guards looking particularly smart in their gray-and-white uniforms, was a man
dressed in the leathers of Gargorian's armies. He was looking

a bit overwhelmed, and didn't seem to register Sylph's arrival until she sat down opposite him. Then he blinked and shook his head.

"You? You're the Liberator?"

"Actually," Sylph said, "the Liberator is my older sister. I sort of handle the details."

"You're just a kid!"

"Tell me," Marlowe rumbled in his best frightening voice, "if you want me to break his arms."

The prisoner looked up at the big cavalryman, swallowed, and kept his eyes glued to Sylph thereafter. She smiled at him, though that didn't seem to help his nervousness. *Small wonder. He rides back into town to find out the world's fallen to pieces while he's been away.*

"What's your name?"

"Max. I mean, Max, sir."

"Don't bother with 'sir,' my name is Sylph. What are you doing here?"

"I was . . . I mean, I'm assigned to the First Army. Now under General Roswell. I was given a message for the Archmagus."

"The Archmagus is dead," Marlowe put in.

Max looked as though he didn't know what to think about that. Sylph said, "What's the message?"

She could tell he was thinking about objecting, but decided against it. After a moment he nodded and said, "G . . . General Phaelas was killed in the first day's fighting. He deployed the First for a field battle once our scouts made sure the Clockwork Legion wasn't close. Lady Fell came to meet us; she had more men then we thought, a lot more. The general said he thought it was two or three thousand just in the infantry. But we were holding, and it was a close thing until . . ."

He swallowed again. Marlowe leaned forward. "Until?"

"Riders, sir, on black horses the size of oxen. All in black. I've never seen anything like it. It was like trying to stand up to an avalanche, doesn't do nobody no good. The general got us off the field in good order, and we were falling back to Orlow when someone got to him."

"Got to him?" Sylph said.

"We don't know how, sir . . . Sylph. Just that he wasn't with us. General Roswell, that's the Third, he took command. He's got the town walled up tight, but she's got us surrounded and there's not much food left. Roswell told me to tell the Archmagus . . . he said, give him my compliments, and tell him I will hold Orlow for another month. He said if he's not relieved by then he won't be able to guarantee the town's safety."

"There's a node in Orlow," Marlowe said quietly. "Lady Fell's wanted to take it for years. That's the Fourth Circle; if she breaks it, she could knock Gargorian all the way back across the Kev. Never thought she had the manpower for a serious try, not without risking that Legion of hers in Gargorian's territory . . ."

"But . . ." Max halted. "You said Gargorian's dead?"

"Yes." Marlowe smiled. "So we don't particularly care one way or the other."

"That means there's not going to be any relief?" Max shook his head. "It's just that I have friends in the Third, sir. And there's a girl, in Orlow."

"I understand," said Sylph. She got up from the table and added, "Marlowe, join me for a moment?"

They reconvened upstairs. The cavalryman, bending so he could whisper closer to Sylph's ear, said, "Well?"

"There have to be a couple of thousand soldiers left in Orlow."

"Gargorian's soldiers." Marlowe frowned. "This isn't the time to be feeling sorry for them."

"They didn't ask to be there. And in any case, I'm not feeling sorry for them. I want them."

"You think a whole army's going to roll over, just like that?"

"One army has already. Besides, we're going to be saving them from certain death."

"Interesting." Marlowe tilted his head. "That's got possibilities. And if you wanted to take on Lady Fell . . ."

"Better to hurt her while those men still have her attention. With any luck we'll catch her army between us."

"Risky, but I think I like it."

"Do you think we're ready?"

"That's the question, isn't it?" He scratched his chin. "A month ago and I wouldn't have laid odds, but . . . maybe. A lot of these boys and girls are itching for a fight, but I'm not sure how well they'll cope with one."

"Only one way to find out, right?" Sylph gave him a smile full of confidence, which in truth was not far from the way she felt. *I'm not sure why.* Magic, possibly. The sheer joy of creation lasted all day, afflicting her with a kind of euphoria. *I feel like I could take on a whole army myself.* "I'll have to talk to Lina, but my gut says to go for it. Start getting us ready to march. How far to Orlow?"

"A week to the ford at Hornfork, a day to cross, then perhaps another week. Depends on the weather."

"We'll get there just in time, then."

"Assuming this Roswell can hold out as long as he thinks he can."

"There's that too." Sylph frowned. "Get them moving as quickly as you can."

He smiled and saluted crisply. "Yes, sir!"

✳   ✳   ✳

LINA HAD LONG AGO DISCARDED HER LEATHER TOP AND wore only a thin pair of shorts and a kind of slip, both of which were absolutely soaked in sweat and stuck to her skin like suction cups. Her arms had passed through pain and into numbness, so the sword felt like a steel bar in her hands and her fingertips tingled. She bore a half-dozen bruises, courtesy of the morning's lesson from Yahvy, but the pain from those had faded as well as she stood alone in the clearing.

Just me and a sword. Not *the* sword, which was tucked under the mattress in her room at the inn. *Not that sword.* But there was something simple about exercising, swinging a thin, pointed piece of metal over and over until her arms shook and the tendons in her wrists stood out like steel cables. She swung, and tried to forget what she was practicing for.

Sylph was right. She repeated it with each swing, like a mantra. *Sylph is right. We are right. And all of this*—she followed through a swing, letting the sword bury its tip in the ground, then stood panting—*all of this was Meant to happen.*

What was frustrating was how little she understood. *Not that I've ever understood much about this place.*

The stranger was just . . . gone. Gone from her dreams, as though he'd never been. *But not quite. I can't help shake the feeling that he's standing behind me.* She'd come to think that swinging the sword—*the* sword—took more out of her than just energy. *I feel different.*

It may not be important. The army was close to being ready, and the Liberator's magic might not matter so much anymore. Lina prayed silently that she wouldn't have to swing the sword again.

"Lina?" said Melfina curiously. "You okay?"

"Yeah." Lina stood up, wobbling a bit on shaky legs, but managed to turn around without falling over. Melfina was wearing her uniform, the crisp gray-and-white Sylph had helped design. It made her look older, which Lina supposed was the point. "Just a little tired."

"Aren't we all?" Melfina smiled and sat down on a stump. Lina collapsed against a tree across from her, wiping sweat from her forehead.

"How's the training going?" Lina asked.

"Okay." The girl shrugged. "I still don't feel like they're taking me seriously. It's not as though Sylph expects me to actually make any decisions, just get people to do what they're told."

"You'd be surprised. Sylph trusts you."

Melfina nodded, unconvinced. Lina leaned back against the tree, rubbed an itchy spot on her back against the bark, and finally said, "I think we need to do something fun."

"What?"

"Fun. You remember what that is?"

"I know what fun is, but . . ."

"The army can run itself for a day."

"But what do you want to do?"

Lina blinked. "I'm not sure. What do you usually do for fun?"

"I don't often get the chance."

"What about before you joined the Circle Breakers?"

"I got kicked out of my village when I was ten. So it was just kid stuff, races, bucket-ball, you know." She looked embarrassed.

"Nothing wrong with kid stuff." Lina shrugged. "How old are you now?"

"Thirteen, as of last week."

"Really?" Lina jumped to her feet, just before her muscles reminded her that this was a bad idea. She overcompensated and ended up hugging the tree for support. Melfina smothered a laugh.

"Yes, really."

"We should celebrate."

"Celebrate what?"

"Your birthday?"

Melfina seemed at a loss. "Why?"

"You don't do that here?"

"Do what?"

"On . . . where I come from," Lina said carefully, "you have a celebration on someone's birthday."

"Why?"

"We just do." She grabbed Melfina's hand. "Come on. There has to be something to do in this town."

* * *

SYLPH HAD OBTAINED A MAP FROM MARLOWE, AND WAS looking it over. She was surprised at how primitive it was; she hadn't been expecting a satellite photo, but this was just the rough outlines of mountains and rivers painted onto a roll of thin leather. Bleloth was off to the left, so the center of the map was the land between Gargorian's domain and Lady Fell's; an expanse of grassland, cut through by three roughly parallel rivers and broken by small forests. According to the map it was also dotted with fortifications; the war had been going, off and on, for quite some time.

The town of Orlow stood prominently near the center, next to a not-to-scale bridge over the river Akyso. The thin line of Gargorian's Fourth Circle, the one she'd broken at Highpoint, reached its easternmost point there. *No wonder Gargorian was so set on defending the place.*

Further east was another river, labeled as the Whiteflow, and then a big blank space until the map's eastern edge, which displayed Lady Fell's seat at Stonerings. *We're going to have to get better maps, or make our own; there has to be* something *between here and there.*

There was a knock at the door. Sylph said, "Come in," and looked up.

"Sorry to bother you." It was Daana, one of the original Circle Breakers. She and Garot had been so wrapped up in each other Sylph felt like she knew neither of them particularly well. Garot had fought at her side, and she'd found nothing to complain about in the way he'd put his regiment together, but he'd always seemed just a bit afraid of her and Lina. And Daana . . . Sylph shook her head.

"Don't worry about it. I'm just killing time until Marlowe gets everything ready to march."

"He's really gotten everything in hand, hasn't he?"

"I don't know what we'd do without him." Marlowe had confided that he hadn't been at his post under Falk very long, and hadn't intended to remain; he was career military, climbing the ladder toward a regiment or even an army of his own. He'd joked that working for Sylph was an unexpectedly early promotion. *I'm still not sure I like the way he looks at Lina.* "The regimental commanders are doing a good job too . . ." Sylph caught Daana's expression. "What's wrong?"

"To be honest, I have a favor to ask you."

"Sure."

"Garot . . ." She hesitated. "He won't make much of a difference to your war, will he?"

Your *war*, Sylph noted. She said, "I need all the trustworthy people I can get, but—"

"Tell him he can't go with you," Daana blurted. "Please. Order him not to."

"Why? What's wrong?"

"Nothing's *wrong.*" Daana sat down heavily in a padded chair. "It's just . . . we were fighting Gargorian, and now he's dead. By some miracle he hasn't been hurt badly so far, and I just broke my arm." She flexed it, and winced with remembered pain. "But what about next time? What if he ends up like Kiry or one of the others?"

"There's certainly a chance."

"I'm sorry." She was almost in tears. "I know you just want to help everyone, Sylph, and I've *tried* and tried to tell myself that it'll be okay, but I just think about him getting hurt and I can't stop. How much longer is this going to go on? Would it really be so bad if the two of us just stayed here, found a house, had a . . ." She sniffed. "A *normal* life?"

"Have you talked to Garot?" Sylph asked.

"I tried. I just suggested it, but . . . he *believes*. In Lina, the Liberator of Bleloth. He's so convinced what you're doing is right he barely even notices me anymore. Half the nights he comes home and he's too tired to even . . ." She broke off, looking at the floor. Sylph felt herself blush.

"So he said no."

"He didn't even let me ask."

"And you want me to . . ."

Daana nodded miserably.

Sylph blew out a long breath. "I might be able to talk to him, Daana, but I'm not going to *order* him to stay if he really doesn't want to."

"I see." She stood up, too suddenly.

"I'm sorry," said Sylph hurriedly. "I mean, I'll give it a shot . . ."

"Never mind." Daana wiped her eyes. "Forget I asked."

"But . . ."

"I've got to go get ready to march." She spun on one heel and headed for the door, slamming it behind her. Sylph sighed and settled back in her chair.

They never tell you about this kind of thing in war games. All the little pieces just go where the dice tell them. She glanced down at the desk, where the map was still unrolled. *Stonerings. And past that, who knows?*

✳   ✳   ✳

LINA SAT AT A HEAVY OAK TABLE IN A TAVERN, FEELING A bit morose. *Note to self: Asking certain types of people where I can have a good time is not a great plan.*

"Are you sure it's okay for us to be here?" asked Melfina, for what seemed like the tenth time.

"What's wrong with it?"

"Well, I mean, you're . . . you."

"Nobody's recognized me yet," said Lina quietly.

"I still think we should have told Marlowe or somebody."

"I can fend for myself for one night without Marlowe's guards looking over my shoulder. Besides, how many knives are you carrying?"

"Eleven, but—"

"But nothing. That should be plenty to protect me, don't you think?"

Melfina shrugged and sank back in her chair, watching the bustle. This particular tavern was identified by a painted sign depicting a tipsy-looking frog, and had a good amount of clientele, mostly men of the middling-to-wealthy variety, judging by their clothes. It was only a bit after midday, but there was already some serious drinking going on. A barmaid in a barely decent skirt bustled past; she glanced at Lina, who shook her head.

"So this is what people do for fun around here?"

"Seems like it." Melfina's eyes followed the barmaid for a moment.

Screw it. I'm a long way from New York. "I think I'll give it a shot. Have you ever gotten drunk before?"

"Not really. I never had much opportunity."

"Neither have I." Lina took a deep breath. "No time like the present."

"You've never gotten drunk?" Melfina looked skeptical. "How old *are* you?"

"Sixteen. Where I'm from you're not supposed to drink alcohol until you're twenty-one—"

"That's the stupidest thing I've ever heard!" Melfina giggled. "You wouldn't be able to drink the cheers at your own wedding!"

"Things are different."

"It sounds like a strange place."

The barmaid, noticing Lina's raised hand, stopped at the table on her way back to the kitchen. "What can I get you?"

"I'll have . . ." Lina thought desperately, came up short, and improvised. "Whatever's best."

"Me, too." Melfina giggled again, and the two shared a conspiratorial glance. The barmaid returned a moment later with two pewter mugs, big enough that Lina might have misidentified them as soup bowls. They were filled with something thick and brown, so hot it was still bubbling.

"Take care not to burn y'rself," the server drawled, then disappeared into the crowd. Lina stared down into her drink, caught Melfina's eye, and smiled.

Like I said, why the hell not? She blew across the top and took a cautious sip, then a longer gulp. It tasted like apple cider, maybe a little bitter, but when the warmth hit her stomach it just spread out until she felt a pleasant tingle all over. Melfina watched—*waiting to see if I topple over?*—and then sipped her own.

"It's good."

"Better than I expected," Lina agreed. She downed some more. "Somehow I thought this stuff would taste vile."

"If it tasted bad you'd think it would be less popular."

"It's amazing what people will drink to get drunk."

"True. There's a drink out west made from fermented cactus juice and horse's blood. I used to make it for my father."

"Yuck." Lina stuck out her tongue. "How did it taste?"

"I never tried it." Melfina savored a bit more of the whatever-it-was. "Not like this, though."

They passed a while in silence. Lina finished her mug, ordered another, and wondered if she was drunk yet. She was definitely feeling a bit . . . odd, but without the apparent idiocy she'd always associated with drunks.

"Still perfectly coherent, right?"

"Mostly," said Melfina.

"Not bad at all," Lina said. "Should do this more often."

"I imagine you could do it whenever you want."

"That's the problem, really." She blinked, and swayed a little. "I mean, what am I doing here? Really?"

"Drinking?"

"Not *here* here. You know, here. This place."

"You mean in Bleloth?"

"The world. Whatever."

"Oh, that here." Melfina shook her head. "We're here because the White Lady put us here."

"The White Lady." Lina looked down into her glass.

"You don't believe?"

"I . . ." Lina hesitated.

"It's okay." Melfina leaned back in her chair. "Not everyone believes anymore. She created this place, and she comforts the souls of the dead. But people are always, you know . . ."

" 'What have you done for me *this* week?'—right?" Lina laughed. "Where I'm from—"

"What's it called, your country?" Melfina interrupted.

"New York." Lina continued. "We've never heard of her. I never heard of the White Lady until I got here."

"What do you believe?"

"Some people believe in God, but . . ." She shook her head. "I don't know."

"You don't have to believe in gods," said Melfina. "They're real. They just live too high up, they can't reach us."

"Then what's the point of them?"

"The point?" Melfina wobbled a little. "I'm not sure there is one."

"The point," said Lina, "is this. I mean, this. I told Sylph we were Meant to be here."

"We're all meant to be where we are."

"I mean, we had a purpose. Right?"

"To defeat the Archmagi?"

"Or something. I didn't know. This was before I met Fah, before I found you all. I *knew* there was a purpose. But when she said it back to me . . ." She blinked and tried to focus on one of the two mugs in front of her, but it seemed to slide out of her line of vision. "I just . . . couldn't make myself believe it."

"The White Lady sent you here." Melfina gave Lina a shaky smile. "To save us."

"Then why is it so *hard*?" Lina had somehow ended up with her cheek on the table, staring at the wall. "Why do people have to die? Why did she send *him*?"

"Who?"

"Rahm . . ."

The door of the tavern opened with a bang, loud enough to startle Lina off the table. She tried to focus, gave up, and slumped back in her chair. *Drunk. I think I'm drunk.* She tried to count the mugs on the table. *I didn't think I had that many.*

"Lina?" said a quiet voice. *Fah.* "Are you okay?"

"'M fine. Just a little . . . you know . . ."

"Drunk," said Melfina. "Me too. Just a little."

"Figures," said a heavier rumble. *Marlowe.* "This is phers-cut; tastes like apples but kicks back like a mule."

"It tastes like apples," Melfina confirmed. She didn't sound incoherent, just dreamy.

"Fah," said Marlowe, "do you think you can help Melfina? I'm going to have to carry Lina."

"I think I can walk," said Melfina, and pushed back her chair. Once she got too far away, she turned into a vague blur, which stumbled and collided with another vague blur. "Maybe not."

"Got her?" Lina felt someone's hand under her shoulders, lifting her up as easily as a man lifting a child. "Come on, Lina. We're heading home."

The trip passed in a blur, though the jolts did bad things to Lina's inner ear. She didn't even realize they were inside until she felt Marlowe walking up the stairs; then there was the creak of the door and he laid her down on the too-soft bed. She kept her eyes closed, since opening them made her want to be sick.

"Lina? Are you awake?" Marlowe's voice was very quiet.

Not really. She felt like she was spinning.

His kiss was so light, so hesitant, that at first she didn't re-alize what was happening. Just a brush, at first, his lips against hers. Then he pressed down more firmly. She could feel the scratching of his beard against her chin.

Marlowe! What the hell are you doing? Except that she didn't say it. Not that she could, even if she'd wanted to. *I want to! Don't I?*

She felt the bed shift as he put one hand on it, and her heart pounded. A moment later, he pulled away. Lina could hear him muttering as he walked to the door.

"Stupid. Stupid, stupid, stupid . . ."

The creaky wood slammed shut. Lina opened her eyes and thought, *Something really important just happened, and I should pay attention to it.* And then she was asleep.

* * *

"YOU HAVE BEEN KEEPING ME WAITING," SAID THE STRANGER. His face was almost whole, now, but his skin was still marred by great sores that leaked colorless puss. Hair had sprouted; a thick, unruly black mop. "That's not polite, Lina Walker."

She was lying in bed—or in something soft—paralyzed, naked and helpless.

"What do you want?" All she could do was speak.

"I want you," he said.

Her body shivered of its own accord as his finger touched her skin, running from her knee up the length of her leg, then back to trace a careful circle on her inner thigh. He smiled, and his skin split in a fissure along one of his cheeks. Thick black blood leaked down to his chin.

"I want you," he repeated. "I want to know the inner secrets of your body and your soul. And I will."

"I won't." She gasped for breath. "I won't let you."

"You have no choice." He leaned closer, close enough that she could smell the stench of decay that wafted from him. His face was inches away from hers. "Because, Lina Walker, you *need* me."

Then he kissed her, his flesh cold and clammy. His tongue worked its way between her lips like a frigid, writhing worm, sheathed in its own slime. She tasted him, and gagged; he slipped a bony knee between hers.

You will be mine, his voice echoed.

* * *

SHE WOKE UP WITH THE BED IN A TANGLE, THE COVER kicked off entirely and the sheets wrapped around her like an overly affectionate octopus. Lina panicked for a moment before she realized her attacker was just a piece of cloth; she disentangled herself, with some difficulty, and rolled onto the floor. This turned out to be a poor plan, as the sudden movement made her head explode. It felt like it had, anyway, and after a few moments more she was beginning to *wish* it had.

God. I always thought they were kidding about hangovers. Her mouth felt like it had been scrubbed with carpet. Thankfully there was a basin of cool water on the nightstand. Lina took a greedy gulp and then plunged her face into what was left. *That's a little bit better, anyway.*

Once she was clean and dressed, she felt almost ready to face the day. The events of the previous night were fading in her memory already; she was too embarrassed to think about them, mostly. *I hope Melfina's okay.* The nightmare had been awful, but she was almost accustomed to that now. *Though I was hoping I'd shaken them. Maybe the liquor stirred something up.* She stretched, buckled on her sword—the mundane one—and headed down to the main floor of the inn.

"Morning, Lina." Sylph was surrounded by a swarm of uniformed men, moving things—mostly bags of food—out of the inn. "Feeling okay? No pink elephants or anything like that?"

Lina rolled her eyes. "Just a headache. You heard . . ."

"From Fah."

"Sorry," Lina said. "I just . . ."

"You don't need to be sorry. We all need to relax. Besides," Sylph winked, "I might join you next time."

"Sylph!"

"I'm older then Mel, right?"

Lina groaned. "Is she okay?"

"She's fine. Apparently hearing that their commander can tie one on made her regiment proud of her."

"That almost makes sense, in a strange kind of way." Lina gestured at the bustle. "What's going on?"

"You didn't hear? We're marching today."

"*Today?*" Lina was incredulous. "Why?"

"An opportunity. I'll explain on the way."

Marlowe entered through the front doors. "Sylph? I've got the last of the grain wagons loading now, but . . ."

His gaze passed over Lina, and his expression flickered. It was only a minor lapse, and Lina would have missed it if she hadn't been watching. He continued with barely a pause.

". . . we're going to need another team of horses. Have you seen Heraan?"

Oh. So that part wasn't a dream. She brushed a hand against her lips, unconsciously. *Marlowe . . .*

"My lady?"

Lina looked up to find Fah bowing. "Morning, Fah."

"Good morning. Your army is waiting for you."

"Yeah." Lina shot a last glance at Marlowe, who was deep in conversation with Sylph. "Let's go."

Fah paused. "Is something wrong?"

"Nothing. Just a little leftover from last night."

"Ah," said Fah carefully.

Lina shook her head. "Come on."

* * *

STONERINGS GOT ITS NAME FROM THE CITY'S WALLS, WHICH had expanded outward as the urban area did, forming a series of concentric circles that mirrored the Circles themselves. Unlike Bleloth, whose massive citadel had been assembled from nothing by Gargorian, Stonerings had grown, slowly, from humble beginnings. The fortress at its center had none of the majesty of Gargorian's Diamond Tower; instead of growing *up* it had burrowed into the ground like the roots of some strange plant, forming an overlapping complex of tunnels of which only Lady Fell knew the full extent. Sometimes, the servants whispered, one could hear them shifting in the middle of the night, as new routes formed of their own accord. And there was an old, old story of a young man who'd woken up to find his room had no exits at all.

Lady Fell dwelt in the center of this vast construction, moving between the small suite of rooms in which she lived and the much larger complex that housed her experiments. She was, after all, the Magio Mutator, master of constant change and alteration. It was in the pits under Stonerings that the Clockwork Legion had been born, and it was there that its members ultimately returned.

When Leila Verdun arrived, Lady Fell was in her primary laboratory. It was a huge, dank room, with only a shaft to the surface to let in outside air. A half-dozen metal plates provided illumination, manipulated by the Lady into shedding a reluctant reddish glow; the furnishings were four massive steel tables, empty at the moment but bearing stains, claw-marks, and other disfigurements from past experiments.

Leila paused at the doorway and waited patiently. Lady Fell's attention was focused on the table in front of her; something was glowing white hot, and there was a rapid high-pitched *scree* that rose to a crescendo, then ended abruptly with a wet pop. Blood spattered across the table and white-jacketed figure of the Archmagus. She sat back in her metal chair, and her clothes squelched.

Only then did Leila approach. She did her best not to look at the end of the table, where what had once been a rabbit or a squirrel or some other small creature had been turned messily inside-out. Lady Fell was staring at it as though it had personally offended her.

The Archmagus, standing, was a bit more than six feet tall and as thin as a rail. Her frame was gaunt, eyes sunk deep in her head, stringy brown hair raggedly cut short, mouth thin and constantly twitching as though worrying some difficult problem. She wore the white coat she always wore, which came down to her ankles more for protection than modesty.

Leila, on the other hand, was short and compact, her uniform spotless down to her shiny black leather shoes. She raised

her hand, palm out, in the traditional salute; Lady Fell acknowledged it with a nod. Leila had been serving her master long
enough that she did not take this as license to begin speaking,
and after a moment the Lady said:

"Demons, you see, are inherently more malleable than what
you might call 'organic' creatures. I purchased a few from Vilvakis, at a frightful cost, and the extent of the change that can
be wrought to their systems is astonishing. Whereas the human
body *objects* to the slightest improvement like growing an extra
limb. So I thought, what if the principle of malleability might be
transferred from a demon to a more natural creature?"

"Did you achieve success?" asked Leila, politely. All those
who came in contact with Lady Fell quickly learned that there
were certain parts of a conversation they were expected to fill
in, not because the Lady cared, but because it helped the flow of
her monologue. It was a necessary prerequisite to her descending from whatever arcane plateau she was currently occupying
to deal with more mundane matters.

"No." The lady gestured at the remains of the rabbit. "No,
I'm afraid the test subject reacted poorly to the introduction of
demonic essence. Perhaps in the future I may happen on a method to suppress this reaction . . ." She trailed off, then looked up
at Leila and said, "What are you doing here?"

"I have information, Archmagus, from our agents in Bleloth."

"And?" said Lady Fell eagerly.

"The rumors are confirmed, my lady. Gargorian is dead."

"I knew it!" she cackled, pumping one bony fist in the air.
"He'd lived beyond his time, that one. Once they go to fat it's
only a matter of years until a Liberator comes along to bump
them off. Gargorian." She wiped her hands on her bloody coat,
which achieved the opposite of what she'd presumably intended.
"I knew it. About time."

"There's more, my lady."

"Of course! The disposition of our dear Liberator. Has he
assumed Gargorian's title and claimed his realm?"

"She, Archmagus. And apparently not. She has been busy assembling an army, and the latest report has them marching in our direction."

"Of course. If she doesn't settle down, we're the only logical alternative." Lady Fell smiled. "I assume the local commander has been instructed to deal with her?"

"Indeed." Leila bowed.

"Good. If she's really determined, that won't stop her. We'll need the Legion for that." She focused on Leila. "Recall everything we have near the capital, and make sure it's ready to march at a moment's notice."

"To the relief of the forces besieging Orlow?"

"No. No, no, no. They'll either break the Liberator or be broken by her, and what of it? Orlow is nothing without Gargorian. If she makes it this far, we'll be ready for her. Oh, yes."

"As you wish, Archmagus. I must inform you that Kurai has already departed for the front."

"He would, wouldn't he." She waved a hand. "Let him go. If that insufferable lunatic gets himself killed, so much the better."

"Yes, my lady," Leila said, her tone conveying sincere agreement.

"But Gargorian is dead. He's *dead*, and the Liberator declined to assume his mantle. Most intriguing. Once she's broken and bound at my feet, it seems the west will be ripe for the taking. Can't take the geist, of course, *he* won't allow it, but the people . . . oh, yes. And if Vilvakis objects we'll see how well his precious demons fare now that we have *his* favor."

"Do I have your leave to depart, my lady?"

"Go. Return as soon as we know more."

"As you wish." Leila bowed and made her exit, Lady Fell still muttering unintelligibly behind her.

272

chapter twelve

SYLPH WALKED THE LAST FEW DOZEN FEET TO THE TOP of the hill. She'd been getting more comfortable with horses, though she'd never lost the feeling that the horse only went along with the program for lack of anything better to do, but she didn't trust her skill on the rocky scree of the hillside. Heraan and his men had already proclaimed the summit safe; he was waiting for her, while a dozen gray-and-white uniformed men held the perimeter.

"How does it look?" Sylph said. She was pleased to find that the short climb had barely winded her. *I was never in great shape back on Earth, but it's amazing what tramping around the wilderness for a couple of months will do for you.*

"See for yourself." Heraan gestured to a rock outcropping that commanded the best view, and Sylph scrambled to the top and looked east. It was just after noon, and the day had dawned crystal clear with a steady wind to take the edge off the heat. She shaded her eyes. *I should build myself a telescope.* The equations for lenses were buried in her mind, somewhere. *Nothing I can't coax out with a little bit of trial and error.*

The river the map named the Kev was wide and flat, gently winding its way between the hills. According to Marlowe, it was deep enough that crossing would be a serious hazard—except here. The ford was called Hornfork, for fairly obvious reasons;

a huge granite monolith reared out of the flow, creating a little rocky island behind it. It really did look like the horn of some great beast, punching out of the ground. Upstream of that, the water was shallow enough that Sylph could see it rippling over stones in the current.

So it was here that Lady Fell's army had chosen to make its first stand against the army of the Liberator. She could see them, milling around like so many ants whose nest had been kicked over. They were forming into regiments on the near side of the river, which was something of a surprise.

"I expected them to try and contest the crossing," said Sylph.

Heraan nodded. "They must be getting good intelligence; we've got more bows than they do, and your new metal long-bows outrange them considerably. If they deploy on the other side and we refuse to engage, they'd have to charge across the ford to get to us."

"Mmm," said Sylph, considering. Charging across the ford did not seem a pleasant prospect. "What are they up to, then?"

"Frankly, I'm not sure." Heraan squinted, then shook his head. "I see three thousand men, and that's being generous. We've got the numbers to turn their flanks, and with their backs to the river it won't be pretty if we do. Not to mention our range advantage."

Sylph had been talking to herself, really, and now she answered her own question. "Think about it from his point of view"—referring to the unnamed enemy commander—"and what he's got to work with. He's been ordered to stop us, and he knows he can't do more than harass the crossing. What advantage does he have?" She shrugged. "He knows our men are undertrained recruits, and most of his are veterans, at least of this most recent campaign. A cautious commander would already be falling back, looking for better ground, but a bold one would throw the toughest units he's got right down the center and hope we crack. We're looking at a bold commander."

"Interesting," Heraan mused. "Unless he's got something

we haven't thought of."

"There's always that." Sylph grinned. "That's what makes things exciting."

"What's the plan?"

"See the cavalry there, in the center?" She pointed out a block of horsemen, sitting stolidly amidst the mass of moving soldiers. "That's the tip of the lance. Tell Marlowe this is what I want: the first two pikes in center, with two more behind them. One regiment of archers on the left and the rest on the right, with another couple of pikes in front of them. Keep your cavalry behind the right-hand archers until the enemy is committed, then take the right flank and get between them and the river, understand?"

Heraan nodded. "Makes sense. Who do you want up front?"

Sylph thought through the commanders of her pike-men: *Yahvy, Orbaa, Fah, Garot, Gelman, and Metz.* The last two were Marlowe's men, survivors of what had once been Falk's company. He'd sworn they could be trusted, and they seemed competent enough. *How do I pick which of my friends to send into harm's way?*

"Tell Marlowe to decide. Lina and Fah in the rear, and make sure Melfina's with the right."

"Understood. Will you be staying here?"

It was tempting. High above the fray, away from the screams and the stench of blood and carrion. *But we're too high. It'd take forever to get a message down.* She shook her head. *Maybe someday I'll be able to make myself a radio too.* "I'll join Lina. Let's go."

They wound their way back down, Sylph mounting her mare at the halfway point, and rode with their silent escort to where the army was unfolding into blocks, like a steel snake spreading diamond fangs. Ranks of pikes caught the light and glittered in the afternoon sun. Heraan caught sight of Marlowe, who was using his booming voice to good effect haranguing troops into position, and delivered the battle plan. Sylph let him go, looking for Lina. She found her with Fah and Myris, at the head of a nearly assembled regiment of pikes.

Lina raised an arm, weakly, in greeting. Her sister's appearance worried Sylph; Lina was nearly gray, as though deathly nauseous, and her eyes looked as though she hadn't slept in weeks.

"Are you . . . ?" Sylph looked around and waited to finish until she got close enough she could whisper. "Lina, are you all right?"

"Fine." Lina closed her eyes for a moment, then opened them with a jerk. "I'm fine. It's just . . . a little nervous, you know?" Her hand was on the hilt of her sword—*the* sword, Sylph saw—gripping it so tight her knuckles had gone white.

"If everything goes right, you shouldn't even have to draw the thing," said Sylph reassuringly.

Lina gave her a tight nod. "Let's hope."

"I certainly am, because I'm staying with you." Sylph patted the sword at her side. "I haven't exactly gotten much practice."

"We will be glad to defend you," murmured Fah. Myris nodded agreement.

"Like I said, we'll hope it isn't necessary."

It was the better part of an hour until the regiments were ready to march. *Too long. Assuming we win, we'll have to drill.* Sylph took a deep breath, admitting to herself her own nervousness. Despite everything—numbers, new weapons—she felt like the whole enterprise might go to pieces as soon as it ran into something hard. *It won't. And ultimately we'll be better off; the army will be blooded by the time we get to Orlow.*

From somewhere up ahead a trumpet sounded, brazen and brave. Sylph caught sight of Marlowe, a huge figure on the back of his massive stallion, cloak whipping around him in the wind. He gestured, and the trumpeter played again, the signal to advance.

Sylph pressed her hand in Lina's for a moment before letting Fah pilot her sister to the front of the regiment. The Circle Breaker drew her sword and shouted for an advance, with a louder voice than Sylph would have given her credit for.

Four thousand men and women moved forward as one

body, at a measured pace. Archers, their bows already strung, tested the pull and sighted as they walked; the pike-men talked amongst themselves in quiet voices, as though they didn't want to attract attention. Those in Lina's company were silent, their eyes glued to the Liberator.

A cadre of messengers, mostly young girls mounted on fast horses, walked a few steps behind Sylph. She beckoned one of them close and said, "Tell Marlowe to halt the advance once we're within bowshot. Start firing in volleys; target cavalry until they get close, then have regiment commanders fire for effect. Archers should withdraw if their position is in danger."

"Yes, my lady," said the girl. She ducked her head and galloped in search of the cavalryman.

It's not what I expected. Even mounted, it was hard to see. Sylph let her horse walk beside the block of pikes and peered at the river, looking for the enemy. By the time she saw them, the trumpets were already calling for a halt; someone else apparently had better eyes.

A messenger trotted up, bowed, and said, "They're coming. Right down the center, except for a few on either side."

I figured. As she'd told Heraan, there wasn't much else the enemy commander could do. Lina's regiment and the block to the west of it comprised the second line; Sylph rode to the head, until she could see the flags of the two regiments in the first line snapping in the wind. Beyond that boiled the enemy, at this distance an undifferentiated horde, except for the larger, darker splotch of the cavalry.

Getting close. One of the things they'd done during training was measure the effective range of the alloy bows she'd crafted, and drilled the commanders until they could estimate that range accurately. Sylph had learned to do it pretty well herself. *Three, two, one . . .*

A volley of arrows took off with admirable timing, a thousand shafts rising with a soft whisper. The wind took them at the height of their arc, but most of the missiles still plunged down amongst the enemy. Distance muted the screams and made the effects invisible, but Sylph didn't have to strain hard to imagine.

Again. It was a maddeningly long time before more arrows rose. Firing a longbow quickly was a skill that couldn't be built in a month of training, no matter how intensive. More shafts were fired, in smaller groups as the regimental commanders called for volleys. The enemy cavalry was close enough that Sylph could see a few of them stumble and fall as arrows struck home. On the flanks of the enemy charge, archers ducked to one knee and sent volleys back—not nearly as many, but just as deadly. *They're faster too*—a second volley was in the air before the first had landed. Sylph watched the arrows, foreshortened into a hail of points, with a bemused sense of detachment until rapid *zip-zip-zips* and screams sounded nearby. The lead pike regiment was bearing the brunt; men and women crumpled where they stood, or stumbled out of line wounded and bleeding. The commander's voice sounded from the front rank, and Sylph recognized Yahvy.

I wouldn't have put her there. The enemy cavalry were less then thirty seconds from contact. She could hear the hooves pounding, watched the armored horsemen lower their lances.

"My lady," said the voice of a messenger. "Heraan requests permission to attack."

Damn it. She'd forgotten about him completely. *I'm supposed to be in* charge *here, not just watching.* "Go! Tell him to go!"

The girl saluted and rode away, and Sylph turned around just in time to watch the charge hit home. Ranks of pikes, leveled at chest height on the horses, provided a formidable barrier—*but only if it holds*—

It wasn't going to hold. The pike-tips were already wavering when an expertly timed volley of arrows landed just ahead of the cavalry. As men in the front rank fell, panic spread; the neat row of pikes disintegrated as men scrambled to get out of the way of the oncoming juggernaut. Sylph backed her mount away, involuntarily, and tried to see Yahvy in the confused mob.

Dear God . . . what the hell was I thinking . . .

The cavalry weren't stopping, taking advantage of the gap created by the disintegrating block of pike-men. That meant they were bearing down on Sylph and Lina, and the pounding of their hooves was louder than she could have possibly imagined. Sylph was frozen by it, staring down the horsemen like a deer caught in the headlights of an oncoming semi. *I should run . . . ride away . . . come* on, *Sylph!* But her legs wouldn't move.

"Fix pikes to receive charge!" Fah shouted. Men and women from Yahvy's regiment were streaming past. They were the lucky ones; dozens had simply been ridden down, though the riders had avoided fouling their lances. The armored wedge gathered speed, and Sylph could saw pikes once again start to waver.

"Hold the *fucking* line!" Lina shouted. She'd unsheathed the sword and held it skyward, and white light crackled forth. The line of pikes leveled.

The collision was cataclysmic. The pike-men had driven the butt end of their weapons into the ground to receive the charge, and the diamond spearheads stretched further than the cavalry's lances. This may have become clear to a few amongst the chargers, at the last moment; Sylph wasn't sure whether the horses that shied away did so of their own accord. But it was far too late.

Sheer momentum carried the cavalry into the wedge of spears, and an unholy clatter of armor mixed with screams. Dozens of horses were down, men and women fighting to get free of a sea of kicking, dying, screaming beasts. The luckier ones had managed to pull up short, seeing the fate of the first rank, but now Lina slashed downward with the sword and the pike-men charged forward with a roar, running over the corpses of the fallen. Without the momentum of a charge, the horsemen didn't have a prayer; it was only a few moments before they were galloping back toward the river, leaving nearly half their number dead or injured on the field.

Sylph gasped for air—she hadn't dared breathe since the

charge hit—and kicked her horse forward, toward where the cavalry had fallen. Fah was working to pull her pursuit up short, since the infantry had no chance of catching the horsemen in any case. On the right, a quick witted archery commander ordered another volley into the fleeing soldiers, and more men and horses fell. Sylph shaded her eyes, trying to see past the dust to the back of the line. Just for a moment, a chance gust of wind cleared a path and she saw exactly what she wanted to see: Heraan's charge had overwhelmed the thin screen of infantry on that side and crashed into the lightly defended archers, who broke and ran for the ford. The enemy's right had completely collapsed.

On the left, Lady Fell's infantry had been goaded into an attack by the rain of arrows. Orbaa and Metz had met them half way, and the shock of the pikes' charge had been devastating. Whoever was in charge there was competent enough to extract what was left of his unit and order the archers behind him to retreat; these were the only parts of Lady Fell's army left in good order, covering the rout over the ford. Even as Sylph watched, the infantry was crumbling under a concentrated barrage from all of her archers. Before long they were running too. Another minute, and Heraan's charge reached the ford, trapping all the enemy left on this side of the river.

And that was the end. Lady Fell's troops were surrendering in droves, throwing down their weapons and kneeling at the feet of the cheering pike-men. Sylph became aware there was a messenger asking for her attention.

"My lady?"

"W . . ." She shook her head. "What?"

"Marlowe wishes to inquire if we are accepting prisoners."

"Of course. Make sure they're stripped of weapons and set up a place to keep them for now. Assign guards, and—"

"It will be taken care of, my lady." The girl saluted and galloped away. Sylph spun to another and said, "Gather everyone you can. We have to find Yahvy."

"My lady, it's dangerous—"

"*Now!*"

Without waiting for a reply, Sylph slipped off her horse and sprinted to where the first pike regiment had broken, searching for a familiar mop of blond hair and at the same time praying she wouldn't find it.

The smashed bodies of those ridden down in the charge were interspersed with the corpses of the enemy felled in the counterattack. Wounded, from both sides, were screaming or whimpering or dying with any variety of awful sounds. Sylph tried to blot them all out, stumbling over the blood-slicked grass and looking . . .

Yahvy! A flash of blond and familiar armor. Sylph's heart was pounding so hard she thought it would burst as she ran to her friend's side, shoving aside the corpse of an armored cavalryman. Yahvy lay underneath, spattered head to toe in blood; Sylph froze for a moment, until she saw the girl's chest move. Her breathing sounded *wrong*, though, harsh and bubbly. Sylph rolled her over to find that one of her cheeks was gone—it had been laid open from the ear down to the chin, trailing a ragged scrap of flesh and skin. The white of bone was visible in the red mess that remained.

Sylph threw up. She couldn't help it; she only just managed to get clear of Yahvy. It was all she could do to remain on her knees, trembling. She saw other soldiers in white-and-gray moving amongst the dead and wounded. A phalanx of men in armor, headed her way; she focused her will and forced herself to raise her head. Heraan, in the lead, ran to her.

"Sylph! Are you hurt?"

"No," she forced out. "Fine. Yahvy. Help Yahvy."

He looked down and hissed. "Someone! Over here!"

Men hurried over. Heraan reached down and took Sylph's hand, his gauntlets cold and hard. He helped her to her feet, though it was only by leaning on him that she was able to stand.

"Yahvy." Sylph mumbled. "Help . . ."

"They're helping her." He put an arm around her shoulders

and started walking her away from the field. "It's okay, Sylph. It's okay."

It's not okay. But for the moment, she could believe the comfortable lie. "Okay." Nausea returned in force, and she stumbled against him. "Over. Is it over?"

"Yes. Lady Fell's army is in full retreat."

"Then I think," said Sylph, "that I'm going to pass out now." And then she did.

LINA, FROM HER POSITION IN THE FRONT RANK OF THE INfantry, had an excellent view of the rout of the enemy archers and Heraan's capture of the ford. She looked down at Fah, who was watching the battle with a tight, satisfied smile. The pikemen around her were less restrained; when the enemy started to surrender, they gave a cheer that grew and grew until Lina wanted to cover her ears. She didn't. *It wouldn't look right.*

Instead she sheathed the sword, keeping her hand on the hilt. Sylph's promise that she wouldn't have to draw it hadn't come true, but Fah had made sure none of the enemy got close enough to her Liberator that she had to swing it.

Not this time, came a thought, and she knew it was his. *But you will. The next time, or the next.*

Shut up. She squeezed her eyes tightly closed. *Go away! You're a dream!*

For now, Rahmgoth purred. *Only for now.*

Lina released the hilt and took a deep, cleansing breath. Men and women were cheering all around her. A wedge of soldiers fought their way through the press, with Marlowe at the head.

"My lady Liberator," he said formally, "we are victorious."

I can see that, Lina thought, but put the thought down as impolite. Instead she said, "Is my sister all right?"

Marlowe nodded. "Heraan is with her now."

Good. Some of the weight lifted from her shoulders. "And

everyone else?"

"Things are still a bit confused. We've got Daana and the other healers setting up a field to work on the wounded, so we should be able to sort things out in a few hours."

Lina glanced to her right, where the majority of the archer regiments were positioned. Melfina had been over there, and those companies had been untouched. *So she's okay, at least.* She looked back at Marlowe, at a loss.

What do I do now?

Marlowe seemed to grasp her situation. He extended his hand and said, "Come with me. You need water, and something to eat. So do I, for that matter. Winning battles is thirsty work."

"We won?" She shook her head. *Of course we won!* "We won."

"We won," Marlowe repeated, taking her by the hand. "Come on."

The supply wagons had been circled a safe distance behind the line of battle. Runners were already setting up casks of water and distributing bread and dried meat to the soldiers who walked back from the field. Aside from a few troops Marlowe had commanded to hold the ford, order seemed to have disintegrated. The cavalryman looked displeased.

"Have to work on that," he muttered. "Still, can't be too hard on everyone now. Let them have their moment."

"Hmm?" Lina, having regained her balance, let go of his hand.

"Just talking to myself."

A half-dozen runners, having recognized Lina, raced to be the first to offer her bread and water. She accepted gratefully. By the time she'd quenched her thirst, a crowd was forming around her, more cheering, shouting soldiers.

"I didn't . . ." She looked at Marlowe. "You and Sylph ran the battle. I didn't *do* anything!"

"You're the Liberator," Marlowe said with a smile. "They're here to fight for you." A moment later, he was swept away by the press.

Lina watched the crowd with something approaching panic. She raised a hand and waved, tentatively, and the soldiers answered with a roar.

✳   ✳   ✳

". . . SO OUR LOSSES WEREN'T BAD AT ALL, CONSIDERING," said Marlowe. He handed Sylph some papers, which she glanced at and laid aside. "Yahvy's people had it hardest, of course, but even there I think we got lucky."

"Good," said Sylph. They were sitting in her hastily erected tent, on the east bank of the river. She and Marlowe had agreed that it was in their best interest to make the crossing before nightfall, so they'd moved everything over and set up camp on the other side of the ford. Heraan's cavalrymen ran patrols in all directions, but there was no sign that the enemy army intended to mount a counterattack. "What about the prisoners?"

"Nine hundred or so, mostly from the infantry and archers."

"I mean, what do we do with them?"

Marlowe thought for a moment. "That's always a tough question."

"We don't have the manpower to just guard them forever. I suppose I could send them back to Bleloth, but I'd rather not hold them indefinitely. These are the people we're supposed to be liberating, after all." She gave the word a heavy spin.

"First let me comb through and see if I can find any officers. They're most likely to go back to the army, and we might be able to get something useful out of them."

"Agreed. But I don't want them treated too badly."

He nodded. "As for the rest, I think we can just turn them loose. Most of them probably have homes to go back to. And, frankly, some of them will want to join up. I get the impression Lady Fell's people are about as fond of her as Gargorian's were of him."

"Make sure we hang on to their weapons and so on."

"Of course."

"How about our supply situation?"

"Excellent for the moment. They tried to burn whatever they couldn't carry away, but we got a lot of it anyway. And there's plenty of fresh water from the river."

"Good." Sylph closed her eyes for a moment. She could feel a pounding headache coming on, and knew from experience the only way to avert it was sleep. But there was too much to be done for her to sleep yet. "What next?"

"Orlow." Marlowe unrolled the map. "I don't expect any major engagements between here and there. There's not a lot of good ground, assuming we go around the woods here." He pointed.

"That'd be an awful good place to raid us."

"True."

"Pikes won't be much good on that kind of ground, either." Sylph thought for a moment. "Have one of the unit commanders start pulling together people with wilderness experience. We'll keep patrols out as long as we're in the forest."

"I'll put Orbaa on it," said Marlowe. "He's got a fair amount of that kind of experience himself."

Sylph nodded. "Anything else?"

"Get some sleep," the cavalryman said. "You look exhausted."

"I plan to, as soon as I hear from Daana about Yahvy."

Marlowe nodded. "She'll be okay. She's too stubborn to let something like this stop her."

"Probably." Sylph laughed halfheartedly. "I'll see you in the morning."

He stood, saluted, and ducked out the tent flap. Sylph leaned back in her chair, one hand over her eyes, and tried to think about something other than the spikes of pain behind her eyes.

I haven't talked to Lina since the battle. The Liberator needed to be with her men, Marlowe and Sylph agreed on that. But it was an unsatisfying decision. *I want to crawl into someone's arms and fall asleep.* But there wasn't much to be done about that.

The tent flap rustled, and Sylph looked up—too fast, her head pounded—hoping it was a runner with word from Daana. Instead, she saw the silk-draped form of Rathmado, smiling his usual perfect smile. *Great. Just the thing for a headache.*

"Congratulations, Miss Walker," said the Magus. "I'm impressed. Very impressed."

"That means a hell of a lot to me," said Sylph sarcastically. "Where have you been, anyway? I haven't seen you since we left Bleloth."

"Just attending to a few matters."

"I'm sure. I thought . . ." She lowered her voice. "I thought I was the one doing your dirty work?"

"I hope you don't find the work 'dirty,' Miss Walker."

"Whatever." The thought that the Magus might have other people out there working in his name was vaguely disquieting.

"Have you had any luck with the geist?"

It took her fogged brain a moment to remember. "Looking for Mom? No. There's so many people in there, I barely know where to start."

"If I might make a suggestion?"

"That would be a welcome change."

"While the interior of the geist appears vast, it is not in fact a physical location. Rather, it is more of a metaphor, an information space designed to accommodate a frankly huge amount of data. Looking through it 'by hand' is probably not an efficient method for traversing this space."

"*What* should I do?"

"It's difficult for me to say, exactly. But when you next attempt the geist, try thinking of it in terms of metaphor rather than reality."

"God," said Sylph, with feeling. "I'm too tired for this. Was there anything else?"

"Just a warning. An individual who calls himself the Black Magus has apparently joined Lady Fell's besieging army at Orlow. He appears to be a warrior of considerable prowess."

"Great. I don't suppose you want to tell me how you know this?"

"I'm afraid I can't."

"And you don't have any *useful* information? Like how many troops she's got, or where the Clockwork Legion—whatever that is—has gotten to?"

"No."

"I thought not." Sylph closed her eyes again. "I'm sorry. It's been a long day."

"Of course." Rathmado bowed. "I shall withdraw, Miss Walker, and we can discuss this further on the morrow."

He stood to leave, and the tent flap rustled again. This time it was the runner Sylph had been waiting for, a girl who spared only a glance for Rathmado before saluting Sylph and saying, "Daana says that Yahvy is conscious. You asked to be informed . . ."

"I'm on my way," Sylph growled. "Magus . . ."

"On the morrow," he said, still smiling.

✳   ✳   ✳

"Yahvy?" Sylph edged closer to the cot the healers had set up. "They said you were awake."

"Sylph?" Yahvy opened her one visible eye. Her speech was clipped, since talking obviously caused her some pain. "You okay?"

"Am *I* okay?" Sylph blinked. "I'm fine."

"Lina?"

"She's fine, Yahvy. Everyone's okay."

"Not everyone." Yahvy's voice was a croak.

Walking through the healers' tents had been an ordeal. It was one thing to watch men and women go down on a battlefield; Sylph felt like she'd grown numb to the sight shockingly quickly. But looking at the aftermath, each bed representing someone who would probably never be whole again . . . she kept her eyes down, and even still couldn't help but catch the stares of the soldiers. A man with only one arm, his other shoulder wrapped in cloth strips; a woman clenched over a belly wound she would almost certainly die of.

She'd been ready for recriminations, even disgust. *I sent them there, after all.* But they'd just stared, and finally the man had led a salute—with the wrong hand—and everyone in the tent had followed suit. And that, somehow, was worse. *They all think it's for a good cause.* It is *for a good cause, but . . .*

"No," Sylph agreed quietly, "not everyone." She shook her head. "But forget me. How do you feel?"

Stupid question. She regretted the words as soon as they left her mouth—*how do I* expect *her to feel?*—but Yahvy apparently did not take offense. She said, "Like a horse bit half my face off. Otherwise okay." And then she smiled, with the half of her face that was visible past the bandages. Sylph wanted to scream.

"Is . . . that what happened?"

"Yeah." Yahvy shifted. "Sylph . . ."

"What's wrong?" Sylph leaned forward. "Should I get Daana?"

"No." Yahvy's wiped her eye, scratching at the bandages with her other hand. "I wanted to say . . . I'm sorry." Tears started, despite her efforts. "White Lady, Sylph, I'm sorry."

"But . . ." Sylph stared at her. "Why?"

"We were supposed to hold the center. You told us to. And we . . . I . . ."

"They were recruits, Yahvy! They'd never been in a battle before, you can't—"

"Doesn't matter!" Yahvy shouted, then doubled over clutching her jaw under the bandages. Tears flowed freely down her unblemished cheek. "Should have trained them better. Should have led them better. Should have done *something.*"

Sylph had lowered her eyes to the floor, hands clenching into fists of their own accord. *I don't deserve this. Any of this.*

"I'll understand," Yahvy said, "if you won't forgive me. Give my men to someone else. I understand."

"No." Sylph couldn't think of anything else to say. "Please don't say that. Of course I forgive . . . I mean, there's nothing to forgive! You tried, stood there with a hundred goddamn horsemen bearing down on you. You did the best you could."

"Best is sometimes not enough." Yahvy raised a bitter smile. "Usually not enough."

"Stop. Don't apologize to me, understand? As your commander, I forbid it." Sylph's hands clenched tighter. "Please?"

There was a long silence.

"Yahvy?" Sylph looked up, tentatively. The bandaged Circle Breaker met her eyes, then nodded slowly, and Sylph let out a breath she hadn't realized she'd been holding.

"I understand."

"I need you," said Sylph, as the tension drained away. "So get better quick."

"Do my best," Yahvy said. "Daana says, I'll live. Not pretty, but I'll live."

"God." Sylph hadn't even thought about that. *We're not on Earth; no reconstructive surgery and skin grafts and who knows what. She's going to look like that for the rest of her life.* "I'm sorry."

"You don't apologize, either." Yahvy closed her eye. "Things happen. War."

But it's my war. "Has Orbaa been by?"

"Briefly." Yahvy smiled briefly. "Didn't stay. Didn't think he would."

"But . . . you two . . ."

"Just for fun. He understands, I understand." She took a deep breath. "He'll live too."

✳   ✳   ✳

LINA FOUND HERSELF ONCE AGAIN GETTING DRUNK.

She felt a little more in control of the process this time. Her companions were Marlowe, Melfina, and a dozen men and women they had invited. Two of them, both impressively large women with forearms as thick as Lina's neck, were from Melfina's regiment and sat on either side of the girl. They seemed to look on her as some sort of pet, or mascot; every time she drained a mug, they raised a cheer and replaced it with another. After a few rounds of this Melfina was definitely wobbling, but with a smile on her face.

The rest of them were ranged in a rough circle around the fire. Marlowe sat next to Lina, naturally enough, and the were sharing a jug of something strong and spiced between them. It wasn't too long after sunset that they'd degenerated into telling stories, and of course each one had to top the last.

"You saw 'em out there," said one of the big women. Her name was Dora, or possibly Nora; Lina hadn't quite caught it. "Enough to cover the ford with plenty left over. And while you were havin' all that trouble with the little horsies, they were *shootin'* at the rest of us, right?

"There was a company across from us, they'd managed to sprint into range. With their little bows that meant we could practically spit at 'em, right? And I could see the guy in command, a big one-eyed son-of-a-bitch, looked mean as a bulldog and twice as vicious. He's shoutin' and carryin' on, and he gets 'em to open fire fast as greased lightning. We start firing back, o' course, and pretty soon arrows are fallin' like rain on both sides.

"I was in the front—they always put us in front, on account of wanting to hide behind us—" At this some of the other soldiers hooted derisively. "We took the worst of it. Guy next to me, little kid barely done playing with his toy soldiers, took one in the throat and just dropped where he stood. They got me in the arm," she displayed the wound, already stitched up, "but it didn't bother me none. Just kept pullin', and everyone else too. And the commander here right in the front, firin' with the rest of us."

Melfina bobbed her head nervously as everyone's attention focused on her, but she didn't seem to be coherent enough to manage words. Dora continued.

"So this one-eyed bastard, right, he sees the commander and figures out she's in charge. Take her down, and the rest'll run. So they start aimin' for her, and she's still standin' as cool as you please while the arrows stick all around her. They couldn't get a shot within a yard of her, and one-eye was gettin' pretty pissed, let me tell you. Finally he grabbed a bow from one of his men and took his own shot. And man, it was a beaut. Up and arcin' down, right where it would've made the commander a third eye." She poked Melfina in the middle of her forehead. "But the commander, she stood her ground and *caught* the damn thing in one hand! Right here!"

The level of intoxication was high enough that this passed without comment, though Melfina's wandering gaze found Lina and the girl managed to raise a shaky eyebrow.

"And then," Nora said, "she took a shot back, and damned if it didn't put out that bastard's *other* eye!" She looked around. "Lady's truth, I swear. I was standing right there."

The soldiers around the fire roared their appreciation. Lina smiled. *I think Mel's troops have accepted her after all.* That was one minor worry off the pile, leaving only countless millions to go. *But progress is progress.*

She'd stopped in to visit Yahvy in the afternoon, but the Circle Breaker hadn't woken. Marlowe insisted on Lina's presence at these informal gatherings. Lina wondered, somewhat blearily, how much of that insistence came from legitimate military concerns and how much from . . . other areas.

Every time he looked at her, she felt like there was something else in his gaze. *That might just be hypersensitivity.* It made spending time around him slightly uncomfortable, but also somehow exciting. *He did kiss me that night. Why?*

On Earth, Lina had suffered through the occasional attentions of boys her own age. Their clumsy advances inevitably left her feeling repulsed; she couldn't think of any reason she'd want to spend *time* with a hormone-driven high school jock, much less become romantically involved with one. And anyone older seemed to know better. Besides, friends had been hard to come by; her life had consisted chiefly of work and spending time with her sister, whose social circles were similarly lacking. Ever since their mother had died, it had been Lina who kept the pair of them fed and clothed. Sylph was too young to get a real job. *And besides, Mom would have wanted her to finish school. She's too smart to waste her life working behind a counter.* They'd often joke that Lina was only working until Sylph figured out a way to get rich, and truth be told Lina had put more credence in that idea than it probably deserved.

She shook her head and took another drink from the mug. *Wandering. It's hard to think.* But that wasn't so bad. *The point, Lina. There was a point.*

Oh, yes. Boys. Marlowe didn't seem to fall into that category. *How old is he, anyway? Too old for me, for certain. But he kissed me.* And for some reason it hadn't felt as awful as the ridiculous come-ons of some drunken teen. *He thought I was* asleep, *for God's sake! That's kind of creepy. More than kind of.*

But still.

She was vaguely aware that another story had started.

"It was a quiet night, right, and the captain had given me a patrol with this recruit Quelas. She was from some village in the south—you know what those southern girls are like, right?" The man, from Heraan's cavalry unit, smiled in recollection. "Big hips, big tits, just a fuzz of red hair on her head and eyes the color of Nithan apples. I'd been watching her since she was assigned to our regiment—along with half the other men, right—but I saw a buddy of mine get cut down so badly he spent two nights under a bottle. So I figured she already had a boy somewhere, or maybe a girl—she looked the type, right?"

Lina shifted, uncomfortably, but less than she would have thought. *It's just how soldiers talk. Maybe I'm getting used to it.*

"We were on patrol, and all of a sudden it starts to rain like the Lightbringer himself is pissin' down on us. I mean, I couldn't see a foot in front of my face. We'd passed an old traveler's shelter, so we hightailed it back there and managed to start a fire with some wood they had stacked up. But of course we were soaked, right, so I suggested we strip off our leathers so they could dry by the fire. Otherwise I might get sick, right, and that would be no good . . ."

He was hooted down, and there were a few moments of confusion before the storyteller could restore order. Finally he continued, "Anyway, being the gentleman that *I am*," he shot a glance at the others, "I said that I'd sit in one corner, looking one way, and she could sit in the other. But she said that since we had the chance, we might as well use it, and that pretty much put an end to my being a gentleman. So I was introducing myself to her *other* fuzz of red hair, right, when some traveling girl shows up. She walks into the shelter an' finds two soldiers butt-naked and intimate, and you know what she does?"

He paused, for dramatic effect. The others leaned closer.

"She puts down her pack, never says a Lady-damn word, just strips off her cloak and the rest of her things and joins in. So we pass a pleasant hour or two . . ."

"More like ten minutes!" someone jeered.

". . . and when we're done, the rain's stopped, and she gets up and dresses and leaves without a word. Quelas and I look at each other, and for some reason we can't stop laughing. It took us another hour to get back to camp, we were laughing so hard."

"An' what did Kira do to you, when you got back to Bleloth?"

He smiled. "She kissed me and called me a liar, what else?"

Lina spoke up. "And what happened to the recruit?"

The circle got quiet for a moment too long, which told Lina that she'd stepped in something awful. The storyteller sighed and said, "Patrolling, while we were fighting the bandits up north. She and her partner were late coming back, an' we found them the next day hanging from a pine tree."

"Ah." Lina paused, at a loss. "I'm sorry."

"That's war," said Dora. "We hung plenty of bandits too."

The chatter resumed, if anything louder to cover the lapse. Lina stayed silent. *That's war.* It was an awful thing to say, all the more awful for its truth. *It's the only way to deal with it. Seal those things off, push them to one side and say, "That's war." God.* Her semi-drunken good mood had fled, and she looked at the mug in her hand doubtfully. *What the hell am I doing here?*

Out of the corner of her eye, she saw Marlowe staring at her. Not staring, not exactly; stealing a glance, as often as he could without being so obvious she'd have to notice.

Without really thinking about it, she leaned sideways, until her shoulder was pressed against his. The big cavalryman started, as though he'd been pinched, and then settled down; before long, he'd worked his hand around and put his arm across her shoulders. Lina felt closed in and warm, shielded by him and the fire from a cold, uncaring universe.

I need a hand on my shoulder, that's all. And Sylph is busy. And . . . I don't know. I'm drunk. She smiled, just a little. *That's all.*

✳   ✳   ✳

THE SUN HAD SET BY THE TIME SYLPH LEFT THE HOSPITAL tent; she took a deep breath of fresh night air, untainted by the putrid scent of gangrene and stale blood. She was surprised to find Heraan waiting for her. He held up a lazy hand in greeting.

"Something up?" she said.

"Nothing in particular. Everyone's celebrating, and for some reason I didn't feel like joining them." His eyes flicked toward the tent. "How is she?"

"She'll live, but . . ." Sylph sighed. "I'm having a hard time getting over it." She looked up at him. "Maybe I'm not fit for this job, you know? No matter what happens, no matter how good we are, things like this are going to happen. How many people died today? How many were hurt much worse than Yahvy? They weren't my friends, and it's not like I don't *care*, but . . ."

Heraan smiled. "You need to get some sleep."

"I know." Sylph yawned. "I just hope I'll be able to."

"Come on, they've set up your tent. I'll show you the way."

She padded along behind him, silent for a few moments. Then Sylph said, "Do you think it's worth it, Heraan?"

"What?"

"What we're doing here. All these people are going to die . . . for what?"

"To get rid of a tyrant. Topple a system where people have to ask *permission* to have children, and anyone who goes against the Archmagus's will just gets shut out of the next generation."

"But they've lived with it for a long time; everyone seems to have survived."

He paused. "It hard to explain, hard to understand for someone like you. I was stationed in the west, and we talked to the people from the tribes outside the Circles. It was like the difference between a stuffy room and one with a draft—they *did* things, made progress. There was a sense that things were getting better, or would have been if not for Gargorian's incursion. But inside . . ." He shook his head. "Gargorian ruled for six hundred years, and nothing changed. How could they? With that fat worm in the Diamond Tower, sucking the life out of the people. He left us just enough to survive, just *barely* enough except for a couple of his favorites. And then you came along . . . White Lady knows, Sylph, you and your sister are the best thing to happen to Bleloth since . . . since the last Liberator. And it'll be the same for Stonerings, and everything past it."

She regarded him silently. "You really believe that, don't you?"

"I wouldn't be here if I didn't." He put his head on one side. "You don't?"

No. "I'm . . . not sure. But Lina does, and that's enough for me." The lie rolled easily off her tongue.

He shook his head. "You know, I think you're the bravest person I've ever met."

"Wha . . . why?"

"Lina's the Liberator, chosen by the White Lady. But you . . . she just said one morning, 'Hey Sylph, let's conquer the known world!' and you went ahead and made it happen!"

"It wasn't *exactly* like that . . ."

"You get my point."

"I guess."

They'd arrived at the tent Sylph shared with her sister. Heraan looked down at her with serious eyes. "It *is* worth it, Sylph. No matter what. You may not be one of us, and you may never understand, but for us it *is* worth it."

She managed a smile, for his sake. "Thanks, Heraan."

There was an awkward pause, as though he wanted to say something else but couldn't find the words. Finally, he saluted.

"Tomorrow, then."

"We march," she agreed. "Orlow awaits."

chapter thirteen

LEILA FOUND HER MISTRESS TOURING THE FIGHTING pits, a huge complex of interlocking chambers and walkways that occupied considerable space under the Stonerings fortress. It was in the fighting pits that Lady Fell's most infamous—and most successful—creations had been born. While Leila had seen the results, she had never before been privileged to walk with her mistress and observe the process that had created the Clockwork Legion.

She and the Magio Mutator stayed above the actual fighting floor, on a narrow stone walkway edged with metal. Below was a labyrinth of corridors, lit by occasional torches. Aside from their crackle, it was almost silent. A sudden crash and screech of metal on metal made Leila jump, which earned her a bemused smile from the Archmagus.

As usual, Lady Fell started her lecture somewhere in the middle.

"The latest crop, you see, is just not measuring up. It's a process I've been worried about for years; each successive generation is better than the last, yes, inheritance of successful traits and competitive examination, but I'm afraid that diversity has suffered. I've had to introduce more and more randomness to counteract the tendency toward convergence, and that means correspondingly less progress. Really I'm afraid we may have hit the limit of this technique."

"I . . . Interesting, my lady," said Leila, looking nervously off the walkway. Somewhere in the dark, two metal bodies thrashed against one another and raised a shower of sparks.

"Hence my experiments into the demonic, you see. If it were possible to add an organic component, counterintuitive though that might seem, we might be able to achieve a new plateau in deadliness. On the other hand, that would add yet more randomness, and at the moment their tactical cohesion is about as high as I've been able to refine it. My tests show cohesion is more important than raw speed at a ratio of—"

She was interrupted by another shriek of tortured metal. Something broke with an awful snap, and a chunk of sharpened iron the size of a fist ricocheted off the ceiling and embedded itself in the walkway. It bore two claws which gleamed like liquid silver, and twitched for a moment before stilling. Lady Fell smiled down into the darkness.

"Someone is having a good day," she said, then looked up at Leila with clearer eyes. "Did you have something for me?"

"A report from Kurai. He's reached Orlow and rendezvoused with what's left of Keldon's army. Apparently, the Liberator beat them rather badly at the ford."

"As expected, as expected." Lady Fell cackled. "But what did we learn in the process?"

"Something of her disposition; she apparently has acquired an inordinate number of metal longbows and employs them to good effect, along with diamond-tipped spears . . ."

"The power of the Magio Creator, of course. She's a Liberator."

"Yes, my lady. In any event, Keldon reports that her troops have shown considerably more discipline than expected."

"I imagine their spirits are high, having just defeated Gargorian. What's Kurai's assessment?"

"He's confident of victory."

"Of course he is, he's always confident of victory. What

about Keldon, did he have an opinion?"

"Apparently not, my lady. Kurai has taken charge."

"Insolent." She waved a hand. "Well, I shall forgive him if he brings me this Liberator's head. And if not, it hardly matters, does it?"

"No, my lady." Leila hesitated. "Kurai writes that he intends to use the Shadowcore knights en masse . . ."

"Oh, and wouldn't that be a sight to see!" Lady Fell clapped her hands together.

"It has occurred to me—that is, to us—that this represents something of a risk."

"Risk?"

"Our new ally might not take kindly to our spending his troops recklessly."

"Do you really think the Lightbringer cares what happens to a few armored horse?" The Archmagus shook her head. "Please. They're just humans; there's always more where they came from. Let Kurai do as he wishes."

Just humans? Some of us still think of ourselves that way. Leila bowed. "Yes, Archmagus."

Orbaa bowed his way into the tent and said, "You wanted t' see me?"

"Just an update on the forest patrols," Sylph said. She didn't look up from her map. It was unfair, but since the battle she hadn't been able to look at Orbaa the same way; Yahvy was recovering, but he'd clearly ended whatever relationship had existed between the two of them. She didn't seem to take offense, but something about it bothered Sylph. *Just for fun or not, there are times when you stand by someone.*

"We rounded up a few stragglers this afternoon," said Orbaa. "Mostly deserters, runnin' away from the retreatin' army. Th' general is apparently someone named Keldon, and the consensus seems to be he'll keep fallin' back till he gets to Orlow."

"Good. Once we're clear of the woods, I'm going to need you to take a few squads forward to see if you can figure out what we're up against. Maybe even try to make contact with Roswell, though I doubt they'll make that easy for us. Think you can manage?"

Orbaa scratched his chin. "Most likely. Though if he's got outriders coverin' his retreat we might be in for a scrap."

"Take what you need. Heraan's handling the new recruits from Lady Fell's people, and you might want to borrow some of them. There might be a few who know the terrain."

He nodded. "I'll look into it."

"That's all."

Orbaa bowed again and let himself out. If he sensed her coldness, it didn't bother him. She looked back to the map.

Four days. They'd reached the midpoint between the Kev and Akyso rivers. As they got closer to Orlow, the outriders began to report signs of civilization: outlying farmsteads, streams diverted to serve neatly tilled fields. Many had been abandoned at the news of Lady Fell's oncoming army, and quite a few had been looted and burned. Sylph forbade her own army such pursuits, and every smoking ruin fueled the desire for vengeance amongst the troops.

Odd. Lady Fell's people didn't look particularly different from their neighbors; they were all what the Circle Breakers would call "easterners." *The only thing that divides them from Gargorian's is which tyrant rules. The tyrants are universally detested, but the people are still willing to kill one another at the drop of a hat.* In the end Sylph assumed it was simply human nature. *Gargorian ruled for six hundred years. That's long enough for his victims to achieve a separate identity, I suppose.*

The sun was setting, lending the walls of her tent an orange glow. Sylph leaned back, felt something pop in the back of her neck, and sighed. *I've been putting it off long enough.* One hand dug into her pocket and found the geist; contact with the little metal sphere was as always both creepy and, in an odd way, comforting. Power pulsed just under her fingertips, eager to be drawn forth and shaped into whatever she might desire.

Instead, she focused her attention inward. The sphere of the geist expanded with breathtaking speed, until she found herself floating once again in the artifact's vast interior space. *But it's not a space.*

Rathmado had been conspicuous by his absence in the past few days. She'd considered sending runners to hunt down the elusive Magus, but she had the uneasy feeling that he wouldn't be found if he didn't want to be. *He's not telling me everything, not even close. But I suppose there's no harm in trying what he does tell me, as long as I keep that in mind—*

So. Not a space, but a metaphor. She closed her eyes—not that her "body" was any more real than the space around her—and tried to do as Rathmado had suggested, to sense the interior of the geist for what it really was. *Information storage.* She could feel it, just out of her mental reach; *a metaphor is necessary, I can't parse it on my own . . .*

She opened her eyes to find herself adrift in a world of glowing letters, flashing past in blurred streams. In front of her, close enough that she saw every sickly yellow-green pixel, was a blinking command prompt.

Sylph had to laugh. *A new metaphor.* Apparently the geist had pulled something more appropriate from her memory, or else her subconscious had supplied it, complete with the bad special effects from a hundred hacker movies. *I think it'll work.* She'd never considered herself a computer buff—science and history had always seemed more fun—but she knew enough to find her way around. *Since this is the world my mind has apparently chosen, I'll deal with it.* She set to work.

By the time she returned her attention to reality, the sun had long since set. Someone had delivered a meal, which had grown cold in the interim. Sylph reached for a chunk of bread anyway. She looked down at the geist; it looked no different from the outside, but she imagined its interior buzzing with activity. Her simple avatars, replicating and recursing through the vast, cold ranks of souls, searching for someone Sylph already suspected wasn't there.

Rathmado knows. He wouldn't have given me a hint, wouldn't have helped me search, if he thought I would find what I was looking for. After all, he still needs me to lead this army. By his own admission, the Magus had reasons for wanting to see Lady Fell crushed, and presumably Vilvakis as well.

I hate playing his game. But what else can I do? He knows who I really am. How he'd come by that knowledge was something she kept meaning to bring up. *Though I'm sure he'd have some clever evasion.* He always seemed to.

RUMORS HAVE A WAY OF FLYING THROUGH AN ARMY, AS THEY fly through any tightly packed group of people. Lina found herself hearing about what she'd done. No one was bold enough to tell her to her face, of course, but she caught whispered conversations. And there were the looks on people's faces when she walked the camp, particularly when Marlowe was at her side.

The Liberator has taken a lover, they whispered, after she was gone. Gossip spread like wildfire.

It wouldn't be so maddening if I was sure where I stood with him. It felt as though something had passed between them, but Lina couldn't be sure it wasn't entirely in her own imagination. Certainly he seemed happy to ride with her, or to tour the camp after sunset, but since she was nominally in charge of the army he might just be doing his duty. That left Lina trying to read his cryptic smile.

I should really just ask him about it. If it's truly what I want, anyway. That was another thing she was undecided about. *I mean . . . I don't know what I mean.* She felt nervous, which frankly was a ridiculous way for someone with four thousand armed soldiers at her back to feel about talking to some *man*, but Lina couldn't help it.

What if I ask him, and he doesn't want anything to do with me? Then what? He runs this whole army, it's not like I can avoid him. Hell, if I distract him I might get someone killed. On the other hand, maybe he'll be distracted if I don't talk to him about it. Maybe I'll be distracted . . .

She was grateful, at least, for something else to focus on. The dreams had not recurred, but she couldn't shake the image of the stranger—*Rahmgoth*, she felt sure that was his name—smiling through his torn face. Since Sylph was in overall charge of the army and Marlowe took care of the details, Lina was left without anything to really *do*. She'd taken it upon herself to move through the camp at night and talk to people, or just let herself be seen. It seemed to make the soldiers happy, which to Lina was still a bit inexplicable. *But as long as it works, I can do it.*

Yahvy was already out of the healer's tent, after only four days of rest and against Daana's advice. She was working hard to put her battered regiment back together; they'd taken in a lot of the new recruits from among Lady Fell's soldiers, many of them veterans of the wars against Gargorian. Though they'd been trained as sword-and-shield fighters they quickly saw the advantages of the pike, and Yahvy had them drilling and practicing long after the other companies had settled down for the evening. Lina was coming up on their section of the camp; torches and a central bonfire cast dozens of shadows from each sweating body, the soldiers running through a few basic maneuvers with the diamond pikes until they performed them to Yahvy's satisfaction.

Lina was thinking about looking in on the practice—she wasn't sure if that would be helpful or just a distraction—when a voice spoke up behind her.

"Miss Walker."

Lina spun. For some reason her heart was pounding. *What am I so afraid of?* Rathmado—she'd almost forgotten the name—was indistinct in the torchlight. He bowed low, and she nodded back to him.

"You're . . . Magus Rathmado, right?"

"Indeed."

She'd seen him around the camp a few times. Sylph consulted him occasionally, and he'd accompanied the army since Bleloth. But they'd never been properly introduced. "You obviously know who I am."

"Of course." He smiled. "How could I not? We're here for your sake, after all."

"I like to think we're here for everyone's sake." Lina shrugged. "It's not really my war."

"It seems to be yours as much as anyone else's."

"Except Sylph. And maybe Marlowe."

Rathmado nodded. "There is that."

There was a pause. "Did you want something?" Lina asked, finally.

"Nothing in particular." He smiled again, which made his eyes twinkle in the torchlight. There was something off about his eyes; they had a peculiarly penetrating quality that made his stare difficult to stand. "I just saw you wandering and thought I would introduce myself, since I don't think we've ever really met."

"I see," said Lina, who didn't.

"And now that I have," Rathmado continued smoothly, "I'll be on my way. Good night to you, Lina Walker."

He turned and walked away, fading into the darkness as he left the circle of firelight. Lina stared after him for a while, then shook her head.

What an odd person.

He's dangerous. The second thought was decidedly not her own.

Rahmgoth. She shivered. *Get* out *of my head! You're not even real.*

Rathmado is dangerous, the stranger repeated. *You will stay away from him.*

I'll do whatever I want without you *telling me anything!* Lina almost screamed, right in the middle of camp. *God, I'm going crazy.*

Oh, yes, thought Rahmgoth, and she felt his anticipation.

Lina started to walk blindly, passing through Yahvy's practice session and ignoring the Circle Breaker's greeting. She kept going, moving too quickly, paying no attention to the bows and salutes of the soldiers on her path. She was fleeing, she realized, trying to get away, but Rahmgoth sat in the back of her head like a toad at the bottom of a pond, and no amount of walking could dislodge him. *He's in my* mind *and I can't get rid of him.* The thought made her want to vomit.

By the time she came back to herself, her steps had taken her all the way to the other side of the camp, where her own tent and those of the other commanders were. Sylph's light was still burning. *Probably hard at work on her maps, or planning supplies, or something.* She wanted to go, to tell her sister about the stranger and her dreams and the fear that preyed on her, but something stopped her. *I can't. I can't put this on her, on top of everything else. I just—can't.* Instead she turned the other way, not quite realizing what she was doing until after she'd done it.

Marlowe's tent was the same gray fabric as all the others, slightly larger to accommodate the table of paperwork that seemed to follow him around like some kind of curse. Lina had been inside, to talk about plans and routes of march, but this seemed somehow different. She only hesitated briefly, however, before sweeping the flap aside and ducking through. The big cavalryman was sitting on his camp bed, finishing his nightly ritual of caring for his weapons and armor.

He looked up as she entered, and blinked. "Lina?"

There was a horrible moment when she realized she didn't have anything to say to him, followed by relief when she decided she didn't have to speak. Instead, she crossed the tent in two quick strides, bent over, and kissed him. Their noses bumped; Lina was inexperienced but energetic, fueled by desperation. Marlowe tried to push her away for a stunned moment; then he wrapped his arms around her and pulled her close, sitting her on his lap like a little girl and pressing her body close.

After a second, she pulled back to breathe. Marlowe relaxed

his grip while she panted. He said, "People are going to talk, you know."

"People are already talking. They think they already know."

"So why not make the rumors true?" Marlowe raised an eyebrow.

Lina pulled her legs out from under her, so that she was straddling his waist. She took his hands by the wrists and placed them on her breasts.

"Shut up," she said, to the sarcastic cavalryman and the voice in her head. "Just . . . shut up."

✳   ✳   ✳

A TELESCOPE, SYLPH HAD LEARNED, WAS A SLIGHTLY MORE complicated thing than it at first appeared. She'd managed to build one none the less, scratching out the basic principle on paper—a tube with a lens at either end—then simply playing with the shape and width of the lenses until she got something that served. Trial and error, but when each trial was just a second's worth of reshaping the instrument via the geist it was an easy way of doing things. Once she had one working, she manufactured another for Marlowe and a few more for the archery commanders. The cavalryman accepted it, bemused, as one more example of Sylph's magic.

Magic. I suppose it is, at that.

Lina was hanging from Marlowe's arm, which was something Sylph preferred not to think about. The rumors about the Liberator and her lover had reached such a pitch that she'd been on the point of asking Lina about it, but the way she'd been acting proved it for all to see. *And, I suppose, she has every right to do what she wants. Yahvy had Orbaa, after all, and Daana has Garot. Melfina . . . I don't know. I hope she hasn't.* The thought made her uncomfortable. *She's younger than me.*

She shook her head and raised the telescope to look east. The sun was behind her, and a cool wind whipped up from the

Akyso valley toward her vantage point on a hill covered with scraggly pines. She could see all the way to the other side of the valley with the aid of her new instrument. The river was a winding series of crescents, shining in the afternoon sun. Orlow itself consisted of a double handful of tall stone buildings surrounded by a larger number of small wooden structures, which in turn were surrounded by another of Gargorian's diamond walls. A no-man's-land slightly more than one bowshot across separated the outer wall from the besieger's camp, a vast sprawl of tents and temporary shacks that wrapped itself around the town like the red ring of infection around a wound.

Orlow's back was against the Akyso, and its docks extended into the river. Lady Fell's army had archers watching, however, and several burned-out hulks north of the town attested to the fate of ships attempting to bring in supplies. Rising from the bank of the river was a massive double-arched bridge, constructed of solid metal and presumably built with Gargorian's magic. The far end was held by the attackers, who had raised a wooden palisade to prevent sorties by the army under siege.

What interested her most, though, was Lady Fell's army. Discounting the force cut off by the river, it was still considerably larger than the one they'd already beaten, numerically almost equal to Sylph's forces. *But they can't be ready for combat after this long of a siege.* And the opposing general—this "Black Magus," if Rathmado was to be believed—would have to spare enough troops to blunt a supporting attack from inside the town. Unlike the last army, she saw only a few horsemen; the preponderance of Lady Fell's force was medium infantry, armed with sword, shield, and javelin.

So that's what he's showing me. What kind of surprises can we expect? The approaches would be contested; while the enemy didn't dare fight *en masse* within bowshot of the valley wall, the set of narrow defiles leading to the flood plain were too good to pass up. *A few troops with bows or rockfalls, hit-and-run attacks as we descend; it won't stop us, but it won't be good for morale. Nobody likes fighting someone they can't hit back.*

What else? There was a mass of woods north of Orlow, on both sides of the river, enough to hide another army the size of the one she was facing. *I don't think he has that many troops, but he could have easily left something in there.* She couldn't do much about that, at the present.

Sylph slipped the leather cap onto her telescope, to protect the lens, and turned to her messengers. Her brown hair whipped back in the wind, and she brushed it out of her face in irritation. She hadn't cut it since she'd arrived, and it was nearly long enough to pull back into a tail. She was still undecided whether to let it grow or hack it all off. She'd noticed Lina trimming hers back to just below her ears. *I wonder if Marlowe told her to . . .*

"You, find Heraan. You, Marlowe. You, Rathmado. Go." She didn't have much hope for the last, but it didn't hurt to try. The three girls saluted and ran off; one of them returned with Heraan almost immediately.

"I was on my way," he explained. "What do you think?"

"Could be better, could be worse." Sylph gave him a half-smile. "I'm afraid I'm going to have to give you the dangerous part again."

He rolled his eyes. "You know I live for danger." That got a laugh from Sylph. "What do you need?"

"Do you still have that group you patrolled with in the forest?"

"I could get them back together quickly enough."

"Good. In fact, after this I may make them a permanent formation, rangers or outriders or something like that. In any case, I need you to sweep the approaches and clean out any surprises our friends down there had waiting for us."

"Hmm." Heraan peered down the slope. "Makes sense. All of them?"

"We'll just be taking the southernmost. And be ready to pull back into cover if their regular army starts to move. I'll have Marlowe leave some archers on at the top. That should discourage them a little."

"Consider it done. When should we start?"

"Now. I want to do this tonight, if possible."

"Understood. I'd best get started." He bowed and strode off. Sylph watched him go, thoughtfully. More and more, she was coming to rely on him as her right hand. While Marlowe had displayed an undeniable gift for logistics and organization, there was something about Heraan that made her certain he would get the job done or get killed trying. *Maybe I should take him into my bed, just for symmetry.* This wasn't a serious thought; he'd never displayed any interest in that direction. *I don't exactly have much to offer.* She glanced down at herself. *No hips, not much of a chest . . .*

The clatter of Marlowe's armor as he saluted brought her back to herself. She acknowledge him with a nod, and said, "We're starting the descent. I'm sending Heraan ahead to clear the path as best he can. Which of the pike blocks can get itself sorted out the quickest?"

"Probably Lina's," he replied after a moment's thought. "Fah's, I mean."

"Send them down the path first—Lina stays up here—and then some archers. I want us formed for battle at the bottom as soon as possible."

"You think they'd come and fight at the cliffs?"

"Given the advantage that would give our bows, I imagine not, but if I were in his place and had some cavalry hiding somewhere, I might try a quick raid or three. Either way, I want to discourage him."

"Understood. What happens when we're all on the plain?"

"Start sliding east, one unit at a time, until we can put our right hand against the river. He won't be able to stop us; he's got to keep the bulk of his force between us and the town."

"I see." He smiled at her. "Very clever."

For some reason this annoyed Sylph intensely. *Something about his attitude.* "Thank you," she said, trying not to show it. "Let's get moving."

"What about Lina?"

I'll take care of Lina. "Keep her up here until we're well em-placed at the bottom. I don't think they're the type to try a suicide charge to get to her—"

"I'm sure the Liberator can handle herself."

"Let's not tempt fate."

"As you wish." Marlowe bowed again. "Anything else?"

"I'll let you know if I think of anything."

He left, leaving Sylph once again alone with her thoughts. *Was he always this annoying? I feel like he's smirking at me.* She slipped the cover off her telescope and went back to studying the enemy lines, paying particular attention to the woods north of town. Several times she caught flashes of movement, enough that she was certain something was hidden there. *But what?*

"My lady," said a messenger into the stillness, "Heraan re-ports he's engaged several enemy patrols of uncertain size. They seem to be breaking. Fah's pikes are starting the descent."

"Good." She recapped the 'scope and turned. "I'd better find my damn horse."

*   *   *

THE TRAIL DOWN TO THE VALLEY FLOOR WASN'T AS CLEAR-cut as it had seemed from on high; less of a trail, actually, and more of a scramble down a long rocky slope dotted with clusters of trees. Sylph had units of archers pause whenever there was a clear spot, to cover the movement of the rest of the army. Mes-sengers came and went; they were halfway down, most of the pikes already reforming their squares at the bottom. The enemy hadn't moved, other than a screen of outriders keeping tabs on her movement. Apparently, the Black Magus was content to let his opponents descend. *Or Heraan spoiled his plans . . .*

Arrows whistled through the air, and pain bloomed along Sylph's side. Another volley *thrummed* out as the first struck the ground with a solid *thwap-thwap-thwap*. Sylph turned, trying to locate the shooters, but before she found them her horse let out a terrified scream as two shafts stuck in its ribs in rapid succession. It reared, and Sylph snatched desperately at the reins.

Someone was shouting. A lot of people were shouting, in fact, but someone was shouting her name. Sylph felt curiously calm as the world wheeled around her. The horse reared again and her boots tore free of the stirrups, the desperate strength of the dying animal proving too strong for the leather straps. Nearby, a cluster of archers had gotten their bows up and were shooting back into a wooded clump just up the hill, where someone fell from a tree limb with an awful crunch. Sylph felt herself lifting free of the saddle. She felt afraid for the first time, not of the arrows, but that the horse might crush her in its flailing. *I never liked horses . . .*

The moment stretched, then broke. Someone caught Sylph around the midriff and lifted her bodily into another saddle, prompting a wave of pain from where an arrow had grazed her side. She looked up to find Heraan skillfully guiding his mount to a stop, a safe distance from Sylph's own; he was accompanied by a half-dozen cavalrymen, who'd obviously been riding hard up the incline.

Sylph started to speak, but her breath failed her. Arrows continued to fly between the woods and her own archers, who had broken up to take cover. A score of pike-men were swarming up the slope, casting aside their long weapons in favor of the short-swords at their belts. The would-be assassins held their fire until the last minute, and two soldiers staggered back and started rolling the way they had come. The rest plunged into the trees.

"That was . . ." Sylph twisted in Heraan's grip. *Close* didn't seem adequate, but it would have to do. "Close. Could you put me down, please?"

"It's not over." He swung her back on his horse, spinning in a wary circle. All Sylph could see were her archers, rising from their hiding places. *Everyone else went off to chase them . . .*

Oh. Shit.

A row of black-clad figures rose from the grass at the edge of the trail, storming forward in total silence. The archers barely saw them coming; the closest, a woman, had time to look up and shout a warning before she was gutted like a fish. Most of the rest were cut down in a few seconds, and the last few ran past Sylph. The assassins ignored them, spreading out into a semi-circle and closing in on Heraan and his horsemen.

"Form wedge!" he shouted. "Break through, down-slope!"

Risky, Sylph thought, analytical despite it all. She clung to Heraan's back as hard as she could. *No room for spears, not enough speed* . . .

The cavalry responded beautifully, three of them swinging in front of Sylph and Heraan in a flying wedge. The other two took the flanks, but the men in black ignored them. All the confirmation Sylph needed, if she'd been looking for it, that they'd come for her in particular. They knew how to deal with horsemen too; knives flashed, humming through the air and glancing off the cavalry's chain and leather. One found a throat or an eye, and the rider on the right toppled; the line of assassins parted to let his horse through. Four of them closed with Heraan and Sylph, while the others engaged the rest of the party.

"Try to hold on . . ." Heraan managed to get out as he dug his spurs in hard. One of the assassins reached for the reins and got a hold, but the mount jumped at its rider's command and the man got an iron shod hoof in the shoulder. Two of his companions had drawn nasty looking short blades, and they laid the horse's belly open on both sides as it passed. Blood gushed, and Sylph cringed as the animal's front legs crumpled on landing. Fortunately, its body shielded the two of them from the brunt of the impact, but she lost her grip on Heraan and rolled off into the dust. The horseman struggled to free himself from the straps of his saddle as one of the black figures closed. Two more were coming for Sylph, who got to her feet just in time to scramble out of the reach of their short-swords.

I'm trapped. To turn and run was a invitation to a knife in the back, but she couldn't fight them. *Heraan . . .*

"Charge!" The voice came from behind her, harsh but familiar. Sylph felt someone pull her aside as armored figures rushed past, pikes leveled. The two assassins had nowhere to dodge on the narrow trail, and both were impaled on spear-points. A second line of soldiers rushed past with swords to finish the job.

"Nick of time," said Yahvy. Half her face was still wrapped in bandages, so she kept her speech short and to the point. Sylph had never been gladder to see her. "You okay?"

Sylph pressed a hand to her side. The cut there bled, but not badly. "I'm fine. Scratched by an arrow. Heraan . . ."

"I'm okay." He had managed to get to this feet, she saw, and duel the woman facing him to a standstill until the pike-men had rushed forward to impale her on half a dozen swords. Sylph counted the bodies in black and came up with eight. *I guess we won't be asking them any questions. Not that there's much to ask about.*

"What happened?" Yahvy snapped. "This was cleared."

"I know." Heraan nodded wearily. "We walked into it. There were some groups of skirmishers, and we got a little involved with them. When they pulled back I had my people follow. It occurred to me that we might not have gotten them all, but I was thinking in terms of an attack on the army and not something like this." He shook his head. "I'm sorry, Sylph."

"It's okay." It was all she could think to say. She still felt in shock, detached from the world.

"Not okay," said Yahvy. "Sylph's important. Need to take care of her."

"I know," said Heraan. "Damn it . . ."

A messenger ran up, accompanied by more pike-men. "The Liberator wants to know what's going on."

Sylph looked to Yahvy, who nodded and said to the girl, "Assassination attempt. Stopped it, everyone okay. I'm taking Sylph down."

"Got it." The messenger dashed back up the slope.

"We should pull back," Heraan said. "There could be more of them."

"No." Sylph shook her head, gradually returning to herself. "No, we're already halfway down. Pulling back now would leave us in chaos."

"But . . ."

"I'm fine, we stopped them, we move on." She smiled at him. "I was worrying too much about the army and not enough about myself. You stick close until we get there."

Heraan's eyes were unreadable, but he said, "Good." He turned to a messenger standing nearby and added, "Get me a status report from Garot and Metz at the bottom."

Someone offered Sylph a horse as the formation started to move again, but she waved it away. Yahvy fell into step beside her, while a squadron of pike-men formed a bristling ring. Heraan and the horsemen held the outer perimeter.

"You really okay?" Yahvy murmured as they picked their way down-slope.

"Yeah." She put one hand over the wound on her side. "I'll have to get this bound. Speaking of which, should you be up?"

"All right if I keep it wrapped." Yahvy shrugged. "People dying. Can't just sit in bed."

"You don't have to keep doing this. You've done enough, more than enough."

Yahvy just nodded and kept walking. There were no more assassins hiding in the brush, and at the bottom the army was spreading out into an orderly front line of pikes backed by archers. The cavalry was on the east side of the line, scouting the path toward the river; messengers reported that the Black Magus's troops hadn't moved.

"He's still expecting us to come straight in," Heraan observed.

"Or waiting to see if I'm still alive," Sylph said, impressed with herself for being so blasé. "Start sliding east before he has a chance to change his mind. He'll have to reshuffle or risk us getting through to the town and linking up with Roswell. Where's Lina?"

"Here!" said Lina, waving to Sylph. She hurried over, followed by Fah and Myris. "Sylph, are you . . ."

"I'm fine." Sylph shook her head. "We don't have time. Lina, you're going to be the reserves. Take your people and keep marching east till you hit water. We'll leapfrog the rest of the line in front of you. Heraan, once she gets there I want your people back here guarding our open flank."

"Got it," said Heraan. "Those are going to be some tired horses."

"I know, but hopefully we won't need them for anything else. Go with them."

He saluted and swung into his saddle, riding after his men. Sylph turned back to Lina, irritated to find her still standing with her mouth gaping. *She looks like a fish.* "Lina, *go.* If we don't get to the river before they do they'll turn our flank and this will all fall apart."

The Liberator shut her mouth with a click and nodded. "I'm on my way."

That left just Yahvy standing next to Sylph, along with the usual gaggle of young female messengers. She picked one at random and said, "Find Marlowe and tell him his job is keeping the pikes and the archers straight. I want the line reformed as soon as humanly possible. And if they start to move toward us, I want to know *yesterday*, understood?"

The girl, slightly terrified, ducked her head. "Y . . . Yes. I'm on my way."

"What about you?" said Yahvy.

"I'll stay with you," said Sylph. "This'll be the third to last block in line, I think . . . Garot and Gelman on your left. As good a place as any." The valley floor had an irritating lack of high ground; she'd give anything to be able to command from the heights and *see* what was going on, but as it was she'd have to rely on runners and shouted reports. *Hopefully, this won't get too complicated.*

LINA WAS STARTING TO FEEL LIKE AN OLD HAND AT THIS, striding into battle with Fah on one side and Myris on the other, surrounded by ranks of leveled pikes. Like the last time, the enemy was a distant blur; the walls of Orlow reared up behind them, and the men were a milling crowd at their base. Sylph's eastward slide had thrown off whatever plan they'd had, and the new dirt palisades were being hurriedly erected as the Liberator's army oriented itself on the river and marched across the open ground.

This time there was a human wall between Lina and the enemy. Her regiment was a few dozen steps behind the main line of pikes, which was thickest in the east and trailing in the west. Immediately behind the line marched small clumps of longbowmen, alloy bows already strung and waiting. The gap between the two armies was closing quickly, and Lina could see why Sylph had been in a hurry. There were wood-and-dirt fortifications covering the western approach to the city, trenches dug out with the dirt piled behind them to form a barricade. But they didn't extend to the river, and Lina could see—when gaps in the pike formations allowed—the enemy commanders pulling their men off of digging and getting them formed up in ranks.

"Almost to bowshot," said Fah.

Lina nodded, not trusting her voice. *Sylph has a plan.* Sylph always did, but this time Lina didn't feel like she understood it. *She said she'd tell me what to do, but we're stuck here* behind *the line, and I can't see anything.*

It didn't help that she felt Rahmgoth waiting in the back of her mind. She had the sword on—*I can hardly* not *use the thing*— and the impending battle made the stranger eager. He felt closer, sitting right behind her eyes. In unguarded moments, she found herself looking at something she hadn't meant to look at, as though her unwanted passenger were directing her. The thought made her want to dig him out of her skull with a butter knife.

"Now," said Fah, and touched Lina on the shoulder. She stopped walking, along with the rest of the unit, as the line of archers dropped to one knee on the shouts of their commanders and sent a coordinated volley arcing into Lady Fell's lines. Lina caught sight of Melfina, half the height of her burly subordinates but shouting orders nonetheless. The flight rose with a deadly whisper, falling among the soldiers across the field; the range was long, and most of the men threw up their shields in time, but a few cries were audible even at a distance. The pike line started advancing again as the archers lofted another volley over the heads of their comrades. They managed to get in one more before the distance between the two sides had shrunk to the point where arrows might drop amongst the pike-men.

The line was deforming, presumably in response to Sylph's orders. Lina had a very good view of her *own* soldiers; Orbaa's troop was tightly packed on the bank of the river, with Metz's just to the left of it. Those two were pushing forward of the rest at a gentle trot that broke into a full-fledged charge with weapons leveled. They were faced by a barrier of interlocking shields, behind which some of Lady Fell's archers waited. Arrows were starting to fall among the attackers too, although not many and none on Lina's unit, behind the line. Melfina and the other archery commanders directed their fire to the east, away from the charging pike-men; Garot, who had the far eastern end, had held his men back far enough that the nice straight line had become a curve.

I think I understand. The pikes on the right were the hammer; *the rest of us just have to hold until they break through, I guess. But what are* we *doing here?*

Blood, thought Rahmgoth. *I smell blood.*

The pikes made contact. The wall of shields shook with

their momentum and buckled in a dozen places. The second rank attacked the breaches, as they'd been trained to do, widening the gaps and forcing their opponents back from a wall of spear-points. The third rank's task was to deal with any enemy who tried to force his way forward; a few brave swordsmen batted aside the shafts and tried to reach the pike-men, but they quickly died on the blades of the waiting reserves. The relentless forward pressure was crushing the shield wall, and before Lina could take another breath the enemy had broken, their organized line disintegrating into a panicked rout in which the pikes cut down foes by the score.

The enemy archers, behind the line, fired a volley at close range into the advancing pikes; their shots were mostly fouled by their own fleeing troops, however, and Lina didn't see much effect. Orbaa kept advancing, pushing the fleeing soldiers away from the river and driving a wedge to Orlow's walls.

A few cheers went up from Sylph's own troops, but more action had drawn their attention. The second pike block, Metz's, had made contact with another enemy unit, this one armed with spears. The more densely packed pikes were pushing the spearmen back, but something was happening right at the center of the combat that Lina couldn't see; the pike-men immediately around whomever-it-was were running, pushing their way back through the press of their companions. Something lofted into the air, a soccer ball–sized object with a long tail; before it landed, Lina realized it was a woman's head.

What the hell is that?

Blood! thought Rahmgoth gleefully.

The whole unit was wavering, and Metz was nowhere to be seen. Lina glanced at Fah.

"Should we—"

"Lina!" The scream was Marlowe's, and Lina whipped around at once. The cavalryman was riding in her direction, his horse tired and blowing, waving a blood-tipped sword over his head. "Lina, go!"

"What? But . . ." Lina looked for Sylph; last she'd seen, her sister had been with Yahvy's troops, but that pike square was hunkered down as the longbowmen behind it exchanged flights with Lady Fell's archers. *She said she'd send a messenger when she wanted us to move.*

"Lady, Lina, get your people *in* there or it's all going to break! Go!"

But Sylph said . . . She forced herself to stop. *Be honest, Lina. You don't want to go because . . .*

. . . you know I'm waiting for you, Rahmgoth finished. *Eventually you will submit to the inevitable.*

No! She looked at Fah and the rest of her soldiers. *They need me. People are dying. They need* me, *not you.*

The stranger was silent. Lina shook her head. "He's right, Fah. Move!"

"Advance!" Fah shouted, and the call was echoed across the regiment. Pikes clattered, and the archers in front of them parted to let the block through. Fah found a runner and grabbed her. "Tell Metz we're coming to relieve him!"

The girl gulped, nodded, and sprinted ahead of the advance. Lina kept one hand on the hilt of her sword and hoped she'd done the right thing. She looked back to Marlowe for reassurance, but he was already galloping toward the right. *But people are dying . . .* It felt like a thought she'd had before. *We can't just stand here.*

"ORBAA REPORTS RESISTANCE ON THE RIGHT IS COLLAPSING," said the messenger. "He's broken through to their light infantry."

Sylph nodded with a slight grimace, glancing sideways at Yahvy. Her friend might not have any problems with Orbaa, but Sylph still felt like Yahvy had been betrayed. *Best not to think about that now.* "Get back to him," she said. "Make *sure* that when they break he doesn't pursue. His regiment is to turn and help roll up the line, understand?"

"Yes, my lady!"

"Go."

The runner sprinted away. Sylph turned her attention back to her own side of the battle, which was going well. The enemy archers had broken under a withering hail of longbow fire, and their comparatively light weapons hadn't done much damage to her pike-men. Now the bows were raining fire on the enemy spearmen, and she could see the officers losing control as men ducked for cover. They'd either break or be goaded into a charge—soldiers hated to be under fire with no way to respond—and either way they'd be easy prey for the pikes.

She kept one eye—*metaphorically speaking, anyway*—on the woods to the north of town. Garot's pikes on the extreme left were facing it, thus far unopposed. *If he has a surprise waiting there, he's running out of time to spring it.*

As though triggered by her thoughts, riders started streaming out of the woods. They were kitted out in black and red, reforming into a solid mass impressively quickly and pounding across the open ground at a trot. In their lead was a solid black banner with no device. There seemed to be no *end* to them, more men pouring out of the woods than she'd have thought they could have held. There were already five hundred riders on the plains, and still more were arriving.

And those are heavy cavalry, she thought with a chill. She could already make out armored forms on the horses, with ten-foot lances edged with flashing steel. Sylph leaned toward one of the runners. "Tell Garot to set for charge. He just has to hold them for a few minutes, and we'll take them in the flank." While the column was deep, it wasn't very wide . . .

"Sylph!" Yahvy said, and pointed. The spearmen had apparently decided they wanted to be brave after all, and were streaming across the field in a disorganized mass toward Yahvy's pikes. Sylph spat a curse. *We can't turn without exposing our side to them . . .*

"You!" She collared another runner. "Go to Lina and tell her to support Garot . . ." Sylph was turning as she spoke, toward where Lina's regiment was waiting in reserve. Her heart skipped a beat when it simply wasn't there. "Where the *fuck* is Lina?"

"I . . . I don't know . . ." said the hapless messenger.

"*Find* her, fast, or we're going to lose this whole flank!"

"Yes, my lady!"

"Yahvy," Sylph said, "finish this fast."

"On it," Yahvy replied tersely. "Set to receive charge!"

Sylph turned back to Garot. Some of the archers had started directing fire into the oncoming cavalry, and a few horse-men faltered or fell, but for the most part their heavy armor and shields protected them. Garot's men had locked their pikes into the ground, presenting a wall of deadly points; *if they're not well-trained, cavalry's going to hesitate before charging that.*

There was no hesitation at all. The lancers hit a full gal-lop two hundred feet out, throwing themselves at the pikes with no regard for their own lives. There was a horrible drawn-out crash of metal and flesh, the screams of the men drowned out under those of the terrified horses. The front line of lancers went down, skewered on the diamond spear-points, but the second line was actually leaping over the bodies to press the charge home. Pike-men were falling, and the line wavered; Sylph caught sight of Garot, half covered in blood, trying to get the front rank out of the way to present a fresh line to the enemy. For a moment it hung in the balance, and then some unseen command pulled the cavalry back, leaving a pile of corpses both friendly and enemy in front of the pikes. An archery regiment behind Garot moved up, eager to pepper the retreating lancers, while the pikes strug-gled to reestablish order.

In the front ranks of Yahvy's own regiment, the pike-men received the enemy charge. Most of the spearmen, faced with the longer weapons, halted at the last moment to edge forward carefully; without a charge's momentum, the line of pikes was butchering them. It would only be a few moments before they were broken. *And then we can get turned around and help over there.*

Sylph looked back to the cavalry and was horrified to see that they had already reformed, and another charge was bearing down on Garot's battered regiment. Heraan, holding the left flank, had seen what was going on and pulled his own riders in; the few that dared get between the heavy cavalry and their target, however, were simply swept aside.

This time there was no stopping them. The dark-armored lancers smashed through the thin line of pikes with unstoppable force, and within seconds an organized block turned into a mass of fleeing, dying men, scrambling to avoid being ridden down or skewered. The horsemen plunged onward, into the lightly armored archers behind, and Sylph had to look away. *Slaughter.*

"Yahvy! Get us turned around *now!*"

The spearmen were broken and Yahvy's pikes were giving chase, eager to pursue; their commander's shouts brought them up short.

"*Stop!* Reform rear. Hold ranks!"

Where's Lina? She was supposed to be there to stop this . . .

✳   ✳   ✳

THE ARRIVAL OF FAH AND HER PIKES STEADIED WHAT HAD been about to become a full-scale rout. Lina left her side and pushed forward through the milling ranks until she arrived at the scene of devastation. A line of corpses marked where the spearmen had first made contact with the pikes, but closer still her own soldiers lay in heaps, gray-and-white armor liberally spattered with gore. The stench of death hung over the battlefield, strong enough that Lina gagged.

In the center of the destruction was a slim figure, splashed in blood. He bore no visible wounds, so Lina had to assume it wasn't his. At his feet was a large man she recognized as Metz, one of Marlowe's companions, tall and blond, with a remarkably peaceful nature given his profession. He wasn't moving.

The man looked up at her, curiously. He had dark hair cut back to a tennis-ball fuzz, and a soft, almost feminine face with large, liquid green eyes. In each hand he held a weapon of a kind Lina had never seen before, an outward-facing crescent of steel, with a recess in the center for a grip. At the moment his hands hung at his sides, and blood dripped from the points of the crescents.

Lina was aware of a murmur amongst her own troops as she pushed her way to the front.

"The Liberator . . ."

"She's come to save us!"

She swallowed and tried to put on a brave face. Myris, who'd followed her through the press, stayed by her side when she stepped forward to confront the apparition; Lina pressed her back. *I won't have her getting killed like the others.* Dozens had already flung themselves against this man to no apparent effect. One more would make no difference.

They stood facing each other for a full minute. Lina wasn't sure what she was supposed to *do*, exactly—*just draw my sword and cut him down?* Her hand twitched on the hilt. *It seems . . . I don't know . . .*

Do it, thought Rahmgoth.

No! Lina thought, automatically. She licked her lips, then said, "Who are you?"

The man tilted his head to one side. "My name is Kurai," he said in a silky voice, "sometimes called the Black Magus. And you?"

"Lina Walker," Lina answered. "Sometimes called the Liberator."

"Ah!" he said with a childlike grin. "The lady herself. They told me you were a Magus."

I can't just kill him. Not without any kind of warning. "Leave," she said. "Or—"

"We both know I'm not going to leave." He shrugged. "Lady Fell asked me to kill you. She's scared of you, I think. I came because it sounded like a challenge, and I do love a challenge. So far . . ." He gestured at the bodies. "This has been disappointing."

"A challenge?" Lina gritted her teeth. "Try this, then."

She drew her sword as Marlowe had taught her, slashing across her body. While she was still five or six feet from her opponent, white fire echoed the gesture with a rumble like thunder. The power rolled out, obliterating everything in its path, bodies, blood, and Kurai all in one. Lina felt the now-familiar ache settling into her bones, but she managed a smile.

"Is that," said Kurai's voice once the fire had passed, "the best you've got?"

The ground where the magic had passed was red hot, fused by the immense heat into clay. Shadows flowed across it, building a man-shaped figure from the feet up, as though a black liquid were being poured into a human mold. Once complete it hardened and the shadows fled, revealing an unblemished Kurai. Even the blood that had marred his tight-fitting blacks was gone. There was a gasp from the ranks of pike-men.

"A challenge," Kurai continued, "but you'll have to do better than that."

Lina raised the blade in front of her, desperately trying to think. *Now what the* hell *do I do? Last time Sylph helped, but this is different.*

The Black Magus shrugged. "Let's try this, then."

She'd thought she was prepared, but Kurai's speed made her best efforts seem clumsy. He pushed off into a run, feinting at her face with one of the moon-shaped blades. When Lina pulled the sword around to block, the Black Magus ducked underneath, spun, and struck. Lina felt a sudden cold sensation; when she look down, the tine of his weapon was embedded under her left breast, curving upwards into her heart.

"No," said Kurai, as Lina took a last bubbling breath, "not much of a challenge at all."

14

chapter fourteen

R a—" said Lina, before her mouth filled with blood.

Rahmgoth.

Twice now, you've invoked me, the stranger thought. *I told you you'd have to.*

Kurai pulled his weapon from her chest and let her fall forward, first to her knees and then face down in the dust. The silence from the army behind her was so loud as to drown out the noise of battle; she could feel them waiting, feel the fragile moment where things hung in the balance. She felt a sensation of incredible cold where she'd been wounded, as though someone had pressed an icicle against the raw flesh. After a few moments the cold lessened, and with it the pain.

"So much for the Liberator," said Kurai. "Is there anyone else?"

Lina's hand groped out, found the hilt of the sword. She could tell where the Black Magus was standing by the sound of his voice.

First strike needs to stop him. Lina wasn't sure if the thought belonged to Rahmgoth or not.

She took a deep breath, pushed off with her right hand, and rolled toward him. Once she got her left hand underneath her she stiffened it to stop herself and let the sword swing around.

She felt it bite, and the wonderful, forgotten taste of warm blood once again filled her. Kurai grunted as Lina got her feet under herself; there was a stain where her wound had been, but the flesh underneath was whole.

Behind her, the army let out a collective sigh. Lina smiled.

The Black Magus had a hand pressed against his side as he backed away. After a moment, he raised his weapons. The cut bled, but it wasn't deep enough to be fatal. His expressive face was twisted with rage.

"Interesting," he said. "I see that your talents include coming back to life."

Lina shrugged. The Black Magus's hands clenched, his knuckles going white.

"Very well. Let's see if you can do it once I cut you to pieces."

She'd expected a charge, but instead Kurai simply disintegrated in place, bits of shadow flying in all directions. Lina spun, able to *feel* somehow the emanation of sorcery from which he would reemerge a split second before he actually did. Steel met steel as she blocked his strikes in rapid succession, one, two, three, four, then interrupted his rhythm with a horizontal swipe that forced him to jump backward. The sword burned with white fire, hot enough that Lina felt the scorched air move over her as he closed; he parried her first cut with both blades, raising sparks from his weapons, then pulled the disappearing trick again to leave her stumbling forward. Lina ducked as both crescents whistled over her head, then spun once again. This time Kurai barely dodged; he stumbled away, breathing hard.

Lina straightened. "Are we having fun?"

He smiled beatifically. "Oh, *yes.*"

Shadows descended once more, and the Black Magus's form blurred. He came at her, preternaturally fast, but Lina found her hands weaving their own defense. She moved as though the sword were made of aluminum instead of steel, sparks flying from every parry. Finally she found an opening, stepping aside and letting his momentum carry him past her. By the time he

got turned around she was the one on the offensive. The ringing of the blade sounded like church bells, timed to her relentless
assault. Finally Kurai had no choice but to catch her blade on
both of his as she chopped downward, and Lina felt his strength
faltering. She smiled wider, and white fire exploded; the steel of
his crescent blades went cherry red, then white, and the weapons started to sag. All at once resistance was gone; he dissolved
once more into shadows, leaving his weapons behind. They fell
to the clay and smoked.

The Black Magus regained his form a little ways away, behind the line of corpses, trailing wisps of smoke from his hand.
His exertions had worsened the wound in his side, and blood
flowed freely.

"Lina . . ." He shook his head, as though in wonder, then
vanished into flowing shadows. Lina's smile twisted; she raised
the sword over her head and screamed. It was answered by a
hoarse shout from the men behind her, and when she swept the
blade down they charged. The remnants of Lady Fell's army
fled before them.

Before Lina could even lower her arm, Fah and Myris were
at her side. She let the sword drop, feeling a sudden, unutterable
weariness; when her bodyguards arrived, Lina stumbled forward into their arms, closed her eyes, and let darkness take her.

Twice, thought Rahmgoth. *Once more, and you are finished.*

THE WALLS OF SYLPH'S TENT GLOWED WITH THE MORNING
light. She pulled the thick quilt over her head, as though shutting out the sun would shut out the necessity to get out of bed;
alone in the soft, warm darkness, Sylph curled into a tiny ball
and tried not to cry.

Lina saved the day, again. The Black Magus had been beat-
en, if not killed, and the Liberator's legend had added another
verse. Her sister's return from the dead had been recounted by

everyone who had been watching. Sylph had a healer examine Lina on her return, but there was nothing wrong with her that anyone could see. She was sleeping, as she'd slept the previous time. *Using the sword takes a lot out of her. But she saved the day.*

Except . . .

Except the day hadn't really been saved. Militarily, the battle had been a disaster. The heavy cavalry that had appeared so suddenly had broken through the army's left flank and delivered a terrible slaughter. Sylph had watched them cut down nearly an entire regiment of archers after smashing Garot's pikes to bits. Yahvy and Gelman, who'd been next in line, had gotten their units turned around shortly thereafter, while Heraan's cavalry cut off any line of retreat. The red-and-black armored soldiers had died to a man in the fighting that ensued, but they'd given a good account of themselves. Gelman's troops in particular had been badly mauled, and an impromptu charge had come close to breaking through.

They died in the end. And everyone feels like we've had a victory, which I guess is the important thing.

Garot was dead, ripped open by a lance while trying to rally his men. *He believed in Lina.* Sylph had sent a runner to tell Daana before retreating to her tent for the night, feeling like a coward. *I sent him there, I should be the one to tell her.* But she just couldn't face it, couldn't face the thought of trying to find words. *Besides, he's not the only one who died.* Metz had fallen to the Black Magus, and the total casualties were probably going to reach one thousand. The healers were doing their best with the wounded, but there would inevitably be men and women too badly hurt to fight on. *And what am I supposed to do, send them back to Bleloth?*

"Sylph?" Yahvy's voice. Sylph sighed, tossed the quilt off, and sat up.

"I'm awake, I'm awake."

"Meeting with Roswell in thirty."

"I know." Sylph shook her head. She'd slept ten hours, but felt as though she could crawl back into bed and sleep for ten more. *Pull yourself together. A victory is a victory. I'm alive, Lina's alive, and Lady Fell's army is in tatters. The only thing standing between us and Stonerings is the Clockwork Legion, wherever it's gotten to.*

She washed with the tepid water from the basin and dressed quickly in the half-light, emerging into a day that had dawned clear and windy, a welcome relief from the heat. Yahvy was waiting. She gave Sylph the half-smile that was all she was really capable of, and Sylph smiled back. The healers had pronounced Yahvy out of danger, but she still wore bandages over half her face. Despite this she seemed cheerful, which for Sylph was a welcome relief.

"Morning," Yahvy said. "You sleep?"

"Like a rock. You?"

"A little. Found a lad, now a man." She smiled again. "Told you, best thing after battle."

Sylph shook her head. "Maybe you're right."

"Course I'm right. Find you somebody soon. Heraan seems willing."

"Heraan?" Sylph looked up at Yahvy incredulously. "Come on."

"Serious. He respects you, watch him." Yahvy shrugged. "Lina has Marlowe. Why not?"

Marlowe. That was another worry. By all accounts, he'd been the one who'd ordered Fah's regiment to support the center. *So what do I do? If I say nothing, he'll feel like he's justified, but I can't exactly chastise him, since the army practically worships Lina because of what he did.* She pushed that thought to one side. *Later, when we're in private. He needs to know who's in charge around here.*

"Ready to go?" said Yahvy.

Sylph felt in her pocket for the now-familiar metal sphere, and cool power burned under her fingertips. "Ready."

*   *   *

SYLPH HAD HOPED TO RIDE INTO ORLOW UNDER RATHER

different circumstances. If everything had gone as planned her
army would have been mostly intact, and she'd be bargaining
from a position of strength—*we would have had the power to crush this
place if we had to.* Now she wasn't sure. At the very least her troops
needed to rest and recover before another major engagement,
while the regimental commanders rebuilt their ranks. General Roswell was still worried—the fact that there were a score of
guards lining Orlow's gate as she and Yahvy rode in attested to
that—but he wasn't as frightened as he might have been.

*No sense worrying about what might have been. We'll just have to
deal with him.*

The inner walls were stone, assembled the hard and painful way instead of wished into being via magic. They were lined
by Gargorian's soldiers, still in uniform; quite a crowd had assembled to watch their entrance, both soldiers and civilians. A
squad of horsemen met them in the main street, and their sergeant gave a stiff formal salute.

"My lady," he said. "If you'll follow me?"

Yahvy and Sylph fell in behind them. The scars of battle
were evident in the architecture of Orlow; every house seemed
to be built on the ruins of another, so the style of the foundation
stones clashed with that of the first floor, or three walls didn't
match the fourth. Every window had heavy wooden shutters,
and every door opened outward and was larger than its frame—
harder to kick in, Sylph mused. The citizens of Orlow had obviously
gone through sieges before. She revised her earlier estimate. *If
the people support them and not us, there's no way we could take this place.*
It would be a nightmare of house-to-house fighting for which her
pike-and-arrow army was ill-prepared. *But Roswell obviously doesn't
mean to offer battle, at least not now. We'll have to see what he wants.*

Soldiers lined the route to the citadel, saluting as Sylph and
Yahvy passed.

"More discipline than I expected," Sylph said quietly.

"First Army," Yahvy replied. "Picked from the conscripts
for strength, courage. Stupidity, maybe. More training than

the others."

"Do you know anything about Roswell?"

"He fought Lady Fell in the last war. Otherwise, no."

The citadel was hardly worthy of the name—a fortified bunker was more like it, one story and low to the ground with thick stone walls faced with metal. The massive wood-and-iron doors were open, and the horsemen dismounted and waited for their guests to do the same. There were more guards inside; oddly enough, Sylph didn't feel nervous. *It would make no sense for him to hurt us. The army—and the Liberator—are still outside, and he can't be that confident of his strength. At the very least it would be a bloodbath.*

There was an audience chamber, of sorts, with a square table behind which two officers were seated. The room was too small for their escort to stand comfortably with them, so Sylph and Yahvy were left alone with the pair. *A gesture of trust? Or just expedience?*

The man on the right was in his forties, with graying hair, a serious expression, and the indefinable air of authority that came with his position. He wore the uniform of a general. On his right sat a younger woman in a captain's uniform. She had long blond hair, tied back in a severe braid, and stared at Sylph as though she was already suspicious. It was enough to take Sylph aback; she cleared her throat, then hesitated.

The general stood. "Let me do the introductions. I'm Karl Roswell, and this is my assistant Loquiana."

"My name is Sylph Walker," said Sylph, "and this is my companion Yahvy. You'll forgive her if she doesn't say much. No insult is intended."

Roswell smiled, just barely, and gestured. A pair of servants hurried in with chairs. "Sit, please." He resumed his own seat, then said, "I take it the Liberator won't be joining us?"

"She's exhausted, General, from yesterday's battle. But I can speak for her."

"A pity. At some point I'd love to meet her."

"I'm sure you will," said Sylph cautiously. *How do I get him to get to the point?*

"What do you want from us?" Loquiana snapped, apparently no longer able to restrain herself. Roswell leaned back, waiting for Sylph to answer.

"Gargorian is dead," Sylph said. "We've beaten his armies and set them free, and now we march to Stonerings."

"I don't see free men," Loquiana said, "I see yet another army."

"Here by choice," Yahvy murmured.

"So your goal, then, is the destruction of all tyrants?" said Roswell.

My goals are none of your business. But Sylph nodded. "The Liberator believes that people deserve to be free, or at least have the chance to be."

"Presumably, then, if you succeed in defeating Lady Fell you'll keep marching east? To Adriato? Or to the Black Keep itself?"

Sylph let herself smile a little. "I try not to get too far ahead of myself, General."

"Of course. But you haven't answered Loq's question."

"What do we want of you?" Sylph shrugged. "The same thing we wanted of the others. Orlow is now free to govern itself as it chooses. You must offer your men the option to leave the army and return to their homes, without fear of retribution."

"No purges?" said Loquiana. "No arrests of senior officers?"

"Loq," the general said warningly.

"No." Sylph shook her head. "Lina is only the Liberator, not a judge. What was done under Gargorian's orders is done. We're only here to remove what's left of his influence. And," she added as an afterthought, "anyone who wishes to join our cause will, of course, be welcome."

"Ah." Roswell thought for a moment. "Let me speak plainly, Sylph Walker. The First Army, of which I am now the head, is not the Second or the Third or any of the others. My men will follow my orders. Oh, I'm sure a few might desert, but not enough to make a difference. I should, by rights, lead them into battle against your army as revenge for my master's death."

Loquiana looked incredulous. Roswell continued, "But, I confess, we have little love for Gargorian here on the border. We've always fought for him, but only because the other option was even less palatable. So with his downfall, that leaves my army at . . . loose ends."

Sylph nodded. "So what do you want, General?"

"Power, alas, is addictive." He settled back in his chair. "After commanding like this, who could go back to being a farmer or a craftsman? And I have a responsibility to these men. To fulfill that I must keep them together, find a source of food, money, supplies, everything an army needs. For that I need a city."

"Bleloth is yours for the taking," Sylph said.

"Most likely not. I'm sure by now the merchants have shared it out amongst themselves, and liberating it again would be a costly business. No, what I want is Stonerings." He smiled like a predator. "I will admit too, that having fought against Lady Fell for so many years I'm eager to see her final downfall. So that's my price—my men and I by your side, in exchange for the authority to rule Stonerings once we're done. I'm happy to bend my knee to the Liberator if that's what's required, but the city will be mine."

Sylph nodded, and spent a moment in calculating silence. Then she said, "Done."

Roswell blinked. "Just like that?"

"Just like that. The Liberator's battle is with the Archmagi; who rules the city afterward is not our concern. I have only three conditions. First, we still require that you give your men the option to go home. If they are as loyal as you say, that shouldn't be a problem."

"Granted." Roswell waved a hand. "What else?"

"I remain in overall command of the army until Stonerings falls. You and your men obey my orders."

"The general has more experience—" Loquiana cut in.

Roswell cut her off. "Also granted." He caught his subordinate's eye. "It's a matter of expedience. The Liberator's army will not accept my authority, and we can't do this without them. And a divided command can be fatal." He turned back to Sylph. "I trust I'm still welcome to offer advice?"

Sylph nodded. "Of course."

"And what is your third condition?"

"After the battles . . ." Sylph hesitated. "There will be no executions and no rapes. The Liberator has made her will in this matter quite plain."

Roswell steepled his hands. "It may be difficult to restrain my men."

"Find a way," Sylph snapped.

The general nodded. "As you wish."

"In that case," Sylph said, "we have an accord."

"How can we trust you?" said Loquiana.

"Likewise," said Yahvy.

"Enough." Roswell looked at Sylph, and she saw a new respect in his eyes. "If she says it is done, it is done."

Sylph nodded. "You'll need supplies, presumably. Luckily we have more than enough at the moment. You—"

Roswell waved a hand. "I'll send my clerks over. Many matters of organization to attend to, so you'll have to excuse me. I'm sure you'll have a lot to do as well." He stood up. "Come, Loq."

Loquiana shot Sylph a last glare, then followed her superior. Sylph and Yahvy got up, bowed, and headed for the door where their escort was waiting. Once they were mounted again, they began the ride back to camp.

"Easy enough," Yahvy commented.

"Surprisingly," said Sylph, and sighed.

"Problem?"

"Not exactly . . ."

"Lina won't be happy."

Sylph nodded. "But she understands the necessity. After yesterday, we need him more than ever."

* * *

ONCE AGAIN, BILLOWING WHITENESS, LIKE LYING IN A CLOUD or a room full of cotton. It was soft, and warm, and felt good against Lina's skin when she moved. She was naked, as usual, but she could feel the scratchiness of cloth underneath her. She twisted her head—her body seemed reluctant to move—and found the stranger staring down at her. His skin was clean and unbroken, his eyes a brilliant sky blue. She might have mistaken him for a normal young man, even a handsome one, until he smiled at her. His teeth were dark and rotten, his breath smelled of decay, and maggots still squirmed where his tongue should have been.

She was lying on top of him, Lina realized. His hands, no longer bony, ran up and down her arms, trailing long, supple fingers.

"Hello again," said Rahmgoth.

Lina closed her eyes. *It's not real.* But she'd stopped believing that long ago. He *was* real, if not in a physical sense then in someway she didn't really understand. And here he *felt* real. She shivered as he picked up her limp arms by the wrists and set them delicately at her side.

"I find my patience returning," he said, and traced a path with his fingers up her shoulders and over the hollow of her collarbones. "I had grown frustrated with you, Lina Walker, but as I've come back to myself I think I am enjoying the . . . pleasures, of the chase."

"Who . . ." Lina swallowed and continued weakly. "Who *are* you?"

"It would be long in the telling," he said, "and pointless as well, since everyone involved is long since dead. There was a pact and a betrayal, the usual sordid business. They moved on, I did not. I *waited*. It is a hard thing, waiting."

Lina suppressed a gasp as his hands slipped lower, to cup

her breasts. He rolled one nipple between thumb and forefinger, while sliding his finger teasingly around the other. When he finally brushed against it, Lina felt as though a shock had run through her body. She shivered again.

It's wrong. This is wrong. Rahmgoth was a . . . *I don't know what he is, but I don't* want *him here.* The building pleasure was a betrayal, the flesh giving way. She tried to fight it, but didn't know how. *I can't move . . . I can't . . .*

"Please . . ." It came out as a whimper. "Don't. Please."

That's not me. I sound so . . . pathetic.

He didn't reply, but his hands kept moving. Before long, her breath came quickly.

"Rahmgoth," she managed.

"Hmm?"

"W—" He pinched her nipple, and she squeaked. "Why? Why me?"

"You're the beginning, Lina, and I'm far from done with you. Sooner or later, you'll see—the fun we'll have, together."

His hand left her breast and slid down the flatness of her stomach, past the soft thatch of her pubic hair, and found the spot of wetness between her legs. Lina closed her eyes and clenched her teeth, determined not to make a sound, but she felt her hips jerk involuntarily.

"Ah," said Rahmgoth. "Stubborn. It's for the best, really."

He pressed his lips to hers, tongue running along her teeth. She felt the maggots crawling.

❋   ❋   ❋

Sylph! Lina awoke with a scream that was not entirely terror. *Sylph . . . I need Sylph. I need help . . .*

"Lina!" Not Sylph's voice, deeper. *Marlowe.*

Lina sat bolt upright. Someone had undressed her, leaving only the damp cotton undershirt. She was in a tent, at night, surrounded by cool darkness; Marlowe sat by the side of her camp bed, a hulking, immobile form in the gloom.

"Sylph," Lina got out. Her heart was pounding, and her breath came much too fast. "Where's Sylph?"

"Lina . . ."

"Find Sylph," she said. "Please."

Marlowe shook his head. "She's in the city, Lina, in negotiations with General Roswell. I can't get her. What's the . . . ?"

"I . . ." Lina felt her body shaking. *Sylph. I need . . .*

"Are you all right?"

She threw herself at him, pressing her lips frantically against his and wrapping her arms around his wide shoulders. Marlowe resisted only for a moment. Then he was kissing her, pressing her back onto the camp bed. She was already fumbling at his shirt. It didn't take long before her legs were wrapped around him, her back arching in desperate need. He was warm and heavy on top of her, and his hands gripped her shoulders tightly before he shuddered and lay still. Lina lay underneath him, panting.

It wasn't enough, not for the release she needed. It didn't erase the memory of Rahmgoth's hands, or the insects squirming against her tongue.

*　　*　　*

BY THE TIME SHE WOKE AGAIN, LINA WAS FEELING BETTER. Finding Marlowe still in bed helped a lot—she felt calm, almost safe in his arms. He was awake, and when she shifted he hugged her shoulders.

"How do you feel?"

"Better." Lina sat up, thought about pulling the sheet to cover herself, and decided not to. Being naked in front of another person—*a man, no less*—was a shock, but somehow a pleasant one. It wasn't something she would have dreamed of doing before.

Before I died. Lina shook her head, trying to drive away the morose thoughts. *I'm here, now. Marlowe's here, Sylph is here, there are people who need me.* She took a deep breath, held it, then let it out slowly.

I should tell Sylph about Rahmgoth.

"We should probably get dressed," Marlowe said, climbing out of the bed himself. "Sylph will want to get underway before too much longer."

"How long was I asleep?"

"A day and a half, give or take. We're getting ready to march east."

Always east. "What about Roswell?"

"He's coming with us. Your sister talked with him."

Of course. Sylph had come up with some clever solution, as always. Lina found a basin of water and started wiping the sweat off her skin. Someone had laid out clean clothes, which she slipped on as Marlowe was getting ready. The tent flap was tied shut; Lina emerged to find Fah waiting for her.

"My lady!" she said. "You're feeling better?"

"She hardly left your tent," said Marlowe, from inside. "I think someone's in love."

"She's the Liberator," said Fah. "Sent by the White Lady . . . of course I worry about her . . ."

"I'm fine," said Lina. She noticed a recently bandaged wound on Fah's shoulder and added, "Are you all right?"

"Just a scratch."

"What about everyone else?" Lina realized she had no idea how the battle had ended. *Obviously, we won.* "Melfina?"

"She's fine." Fah hesitated. "Garot . . . his unit was over-run. He died trying to rally them."

Lina nodded. She felt like it didn't really sink in. *I never really knew him.* Fah had, though. "Poor Daana. Have you—"

"She hasn't spoken to anyone, really. She's in the healer's tent, working on the wounded."

I'll have to go and see her, Lina resolved. Being the Liberator carried responsibilities. *But first*—"Where's Sylph?"

"Over with Heraan." Fah pointed. "He's taken over some of the logistical stuff while Marlowe was—ah—taking care of you."

Lina blushed. "Thanks." She started walking, and Fah fell in beside her. "You're coming along?"

"I've been waiting for you to wake up. Our people are already breaking camp."

"I see." Lina half-turned. "Marlowe, I'm going to find my sister. I'm sure they need you for the army, so I'll see you later?"

"Absolutely," he said with a smile, and let the tent flap fall.

Fah led the way through the camp, passing soldiers and servants in the process of getting ready for yet another day of marching. Those that saw Lina stopped and stared, often straightening up and putting their right hand over their heart, palm down.

"What're they doing?" she asked Fah.

"It's a gesture of respect for the White Lady. It's sort of been spreading through the army lately."

They really do think I'm a saint. "What do I do?"

"Just nod and keep walking."

She did, and felt awkward. Lina found Sylph at the center of a knot of messengers and unit commanders, with Heraan and Yahvy at her side. The former was deep in conversation with Orbaa; Yahvy still wore the bandage on her face, but she looked up and smiled faintly when she saw Lina coming.

"Lina. Sleep well?"

Lina nodded. "Very."

"Not *too* well, hopefully?"

Lina blushed again, just as Sylph sent another messenger away and turned toward her. It had been a long time since she'd really *looked* at her little sister, Lina realized, and Sylph was changing in the role she'd chosen for herself. She'd never lacked self-confidence, but there had always been a shyness to her; now she wore her uniform, edged in gold, as though she'd been born to it. She accepted the soldiers' deference with ease. But, Lina was glad to see, she still looked like a little girl when she smiled. Lina wanted to hug her, but refrained when Sylph made no move in that direction. *Decorum, I suppose.*

"Morning, sleepy," said Sylph. "Everything okay?"

"Fine. You know how that wears me out." *I should tell her about Rahmgoth. But . . .* Lina looked at the dozen men who were already waiting for Sylph's attention, and couldn't bring herself to add yet another worry to her sister's pile. *Later. When things calm down.*

"I figured. We needed the day just to get things in order here."

"I heard you sorted things out with Roswell?"

"Sort of." Sylph looked uncomfortable.

"What did he want?"

"He wants us to set him up as lord of Stonerings when we're done."

Lina blinked. "But—"

"He's not an awful person," Sylph said hastily. "And he can't be worse than the Archmagus. Some sort of ruler is inevitable, but at least he won't have the Plague and all the powers the Archmagi had."

Lina nodded, slowly. "But—"

"We need him, Lina." Sylph lowered her voice. "He knows this place, he's been fighting Lady Fell a long time. And with two thousand men at his back, we can't just leave him here."

"I know." Lina sighed. *Something clever.* "I get it."

"Good." Sylph sounded almost pleading. "We're going to be leaving soon. Are you ready?"

"No." Lina paused. "I'd better go pack up."

✳   ✳   ✳

Yahvy waited until the Liberator had gone, Fah trailing behind her like a puppy.

"Could have gone better."

"It could have gone worse too." Sylph shook her head. "It's hard for her; it's all well and good to have ideals, but reality tends to get in the way."

"Easy for you?"

Sylph gave her friend a crooked smile. "Apparently."

✻   ✻   ✻

GETTING THE ARMY ACROSS THE RELATIVELY NARROW bridge at Orlow had been a bit of a trick, but a comfortable command structure had developed with Sylph in overall command, Marlowe leading the infantry and keeping track of the supplies, and Heraan in charge of the scouts and outriders. Sylph realized she'd been avoiding Marlowe; the rumors about him and Lina were obviously more than just rumors, and while she didn't resent it—*not exactly, anyway*—she wasn't quite sure how to act around him. Once they were forced to work together, however, Marlowe solved the problem by being as thoroughly professional as he always had. *Just as though he wasn't sleeping with my sister.*

That was odd. Just the idea, not the reality. Sylph had a hard time imagining Lina in that light. *But I guess she's good-looking. She's got breasts and so forth. I'm just—I don't know.* She still owed Marlowe a chewing out, but under the circumstances she couldn't bring herself to do it. *He seems to have accepted my authority. That's good enough for now.*

Roswell's army brought up the rear, in better order than Sylph had expected considering they'd just gone through a siege. The general obviously ran a tight unit. He'd spent a fair amount of time reorganizing his force, which consisted of the mauled remnants of two of Gargorian's original armies. They marched as eight separate regiments of spearmen, each with its own attached archers. It wasn't how Sylph would have split the troops up, but clearly Roswell wanted to do things his own way. *He doesn't have the luxury of spending weeks retraining, either.* While on the march, she kept the bulk of his men together as a rearguard, with one regiment up front with the pikes.

As Roswell had predicted, only a few had taken the offer to return home, mostly those who were from Orlow originally. There were practical considerations, Sylph was sure; it was more than a hundred miles to Bleloth, and some of the conscripts had even farther to go. *That's a long walk.* She felt a little bad about it, but it meant more men under the Liberator's banner.

Roswell's people had also helped to fill in the map. They'd crossed the river Akyso at Orlow, so the next obstacle was the Whiteflow; according to Roswell's cartographer, it was low enough to cross on foot and wouldn't be a problem. Beyond that was cultivated land, the heart of Lady Fell's domain; the White-flow marked the edge of her Third Circle, and the extent of her power and her Plague.

The Plague. She knew the source, or at least thought she did. Souls intended for newborns were instead caught in the Circles and funneled into the geist, where they remained while the Archmagus put their power to use. *I only have Rathmado's word for a lot of that.* It rang true with what she saw when she looked inside the metal sphere, though, and made a certain amount of weird sense. *So people die on Earth and they end up here. Like me, except not—Lina and I weren't reborn, we just* appeared. Rathmado had, as usual, evaded questioning on that particular topic. *He has something to do with it, I'm certain.* The Magus knew too much not to be involved.

The Liberator's army crossed the Whiteflow a week and two days after they'd left Orlow, in the pouring rain. It was a thoroughly miserable experience for all concerned; everyone was soaked to the bone, Sylph included, and there was no drying out during the downpour. On top of that, a supply wagon broke an axle in midstream, forcing the men to pull it out with ropes and horses. It took one full day and the better part of another to get everyone to the east bank, and by the time they were finished Sylph was starting to wonder why Lady Fell's army hadn't contested the crossing. *It wouldn't have taken much to slow us down a lot. Unless she really does have nothing left?*

Excepting, of course, the Clockwork Legion, the whereabouts of which had become the topic of polite but heated debate between Roswell's people and Sylph's. The general was of the opinion that the Archmagus had pulled her elite force back to defend Stonerings, now that her main army had been broken. Sylph didn't think so—it was hard to put into words *why* she didn't think so, but it just felt wrong. *A bold commander.* That's what she'd told Yahvy, back before the battle at the ford. *Lady Fell is a bold commander. She's not just going to squat in her fortress and wait for us.*

So there were outriders flanking the army the whole way, regardless of the strain it put on Heraan's cavalry. They were enough to provide a warning a few moments before the Clockwork Legion descended.

✳ ✳ ✳

LINA WAS RIDING WITH MARLOWE, AS HAD BECOME HER custom, just behind Fah's regiment. A compromise between the two people who wouldn't leave her alone. *Although at least Fah hasn't tried to sleep in my tent.* The weather had cleared since the awful river crossing, and the soldiers seemed to be in generally good spirits; the long, snaking column was abuzz with conversation and marching songs.

Marlowe was in a good mood too. He kept his horse at a walk, content to pace alongside Lina's mare, and he'd removed most of his armor and left it with the wagons. He seemed to be basking in the sun, which was pleasantly warm since the storms. Autumn was on the way, he'd told her, and it was only another week or so till Stonerings.

She couldn't help but watch him, in the dreamy Zen-like state induced by riding for hours at a time. Eventually he noticed and looked back at her, curiously.

"Something the matter?" he said.

"Not really. Just thinking."

"What about?"

Lina paused, then said, "Where are you from?"

"What?" Marlowe looked bewildered. "Why?"

"No reason in particular. I was thinking that I barely know you, in some ways."

"There's not much to tell." He shrugged. "I'm from a village called Quen, about forty miles north of Bleloth. I got drafted when I was sixteen, went and fought against Lady Fell for a while. After the war they let us go, but I got to like being a soldier. So I stayed, and eventually they made me an officer. Somewhere along the way I met Falk, and he liked me, so when they sent him west, I went with him."

Lina nodded. "What was your family like?"

"A normal family, I guess. My dad served in the previous war. Came back alive, obviously, and started his own little farmstead. Mom was a city girl he met on the way, I think."

"It was just the three of you?"

"Since I can remember. Anne, my older sister, got married when I was six or seven, I think. We'd see her on holidays."

"That's nice," Lina said. "Do you still see them?"

"Not for years. Maybe I'll go back once all this is finished." Marlowe looked at Lina curiously. "Why the interrogation?"

"Just curious."

"I hardly know anything about you, either."

"Yeah." She felt suddenly guilty. She'd never questioned Sylph's policy of keeping their time on Earth a secret, but it hardly seemed to matter anymore. "I'm sorry, I just—"

"Don't worry about it." He waved a hand. "You've got your reasons, I'm sure. You're the one who was chosen by the White Lady and all that."

"Yeah," Lina repeated.

They rode in silence for a few moments.

"Can I ask you one other question?" she said eventually.

Marlowe chuckled. "Go ahead."

"Have you ever had a . . . a girlfriend before?" Lina was trying furiously—futilely—not to blush.

"Someone like you, you mean?"

She nodded.

He leaned back and sighed. "I mean, I've had my share of women through the years, you know how the army is. But . . ." He looked over at her. "Someone I really cared about? No."

Lina's blush spread further, but there was a warm feeling underneath it. "Oh."

"And turnabout is fair play. What about you?"

"Of course not!" She stopped and shook her head. "I mean . . . I don't know. Obviously I've never had a . . . lover, or anything like that. Back then it was just me and Sylph. She needed me, and I didn't have time for anything else."

"That's hard to imagine." Marlowe shaded his eyes and looked at Sylph, who was with Yahvy's group on the other side of the column. Lina followed his gaze; her sister was chatting animatedly with Yahvy and Melfina, whose archery regiment was adjacent. She rode her horse with more assurance than Lina felt, and her sword swung easily at her side. "She doesn't seem the type who'd need a lot of taking care of."

It was the other way around, more often than not. But . . . "Things were different back home. Since we've come here, she's . . ."

"Blossomed?"

"I was going to say changed, but I guess so."

"They say that's the way it is, with Magi. You never know how the power is going to affect them." He glanced at Lina. "I suppose that probably applies to you too."

Lina's hand fell automatically to the sword at her hip. It had been days before she'd dared wear it again, but the voice in her head had fallen oddly silent. He was still there, she was certain—she could feel Rahmgoth when he was paying attention—but he seemed content to leave her be.

"Can I ask *you* a question?" said Marlowe.

"Go ahead. Although I reserve the right not to answer."

"What—"

He was cut off by screams from the other side of the column. Two horses came over a ridge to the south, only one with a rider. It was one of Heraan's people, shouting and gesticulating madly.

He didn't slow a bit as he approached, taking the slope at a full gallop and plunging in among the troops. The other horse was galloping too, and Lina could see a splash of blood on its flanks.

They were followed, scant seconds later, by a monster that put Lina in mind of some sort of horrible crab. Or possibly a lobster, she thought with odd clarity. It had a metallic shell and eight multi-jointed legs, and four arms that ended in wicked blades. There was no head, no obvious eyes, but the creature was following the horseman at a startling speed, its limbs a blur as it tore down the slope. It was followed a moment later by another, similar beast; then a half-dozen smaller things crested the ridge, each a random assemblage of thin, powerful limbs jutting from a compact, cylindrical core.

The outrider's warning had been met with panic at first, but enough soldiers ran toward the things that Yahvy and Sylph were able to whip them into some kind of order. One of Roswell's regiments of spearmen was double-timing from the south in an organized block, and in the meantime a block of pikes was forming up. Melfina's archers scrambled backward, desperately stringing their bows once they were safely behind the pikes.

The first of the crab-things crashed into the line, and the screech of diamond blades against its metal shell was audible even from where Lina was standing. A dozen or more men stabbed at it, to no visible effect; pincers snapped and clicked, chopping the pike-men to bits where they stood. The smaller things followed it, using the gap it had created in the line to get close to the soldiers. Then they attacked, almost too quickly for the eye to follow. Lina saw one sink a razor-edged limb into a woman's gut and open her like a fish, then scramble up her body as she fell to her knees. She collapsed bonelessly into the dust and the creature used her as a springboard, jumping a dozen feet and landing with its limbs wrapped around the upper torso of another pike-man. When it unfolded, like some horrible flower, it left him in pieces.

The other crab had crashed into the regiment of spearmen, and from the sound of it they were faring no better. More of the metal monsters were coming over the ridge. Arrows flew from the army, but not in any great number, and the creatures simply shrugged them off.

"This is bad," said Marlowe. "Lina . . ."

She was already gone, galloping around the wagons toward the fighting. Three of the crabs, in tight formation, were charging down the slope at Sylph.

A HORSE WAS NOT LIKE, FOR EXAMPLE, A BICYCLE. LINA found she couldn't exactly skid to a halt, so she overshot and rode past Sylph before she managed to get the thing to slow down enough that she could jump off. By that time the crabs had reached the thin line of soldiers and broken bodies were flying through the air. The little stickmen were pressing through, cutting down anyone in their way; they were intent on Sylph's little group, where Yahvy had already drawn her sword and stood waiting. Sylph had her hand on her sword, but looked like she didn't quite know what to do with it. As Lina ran and got ready to draw her own blade . . .

Rahmgoth.

Twice, he said. Once more . . .

Then there was no more time for thinking. She reached Sylph at almost the same time as the metal creatures, two of them, splitting up to circle around Yahvy. One feinted at her head, while the other reached in to casually slash open her hamstrings—it would have, at least, if Lina hadn't brought her sword down on what passed for its head. White fire flared, and the thing flew apart into droplets of liquid metal, hissing as they ate their way into the turf.

The other backed off for a moment. A thrown dagger clattered off, to no effect. Yahvy took advantage of the lull and charged it, while Sylph backed away.

"Behind me!"

"Yahvy!" Lina shouted. "Over here!"

Yahvy's thrust scored the metal cylinder and left a bright mark, but didn't slow the creature down. It counterattacked, swinging beweaponed arms with deadly grace. The attacks didn't have much force behind them, but the blades were razor sharp and faster than a human could manage. Yahvy gave ground, parrying desperately, and Lina hurried to stand beside her. She brought the sword around, white fire crackling expectantly, but the creature cleared her head with a standing jump, balancing on Yahvy's shoulder's with two limbs. Yahvy thrust upward, this time aiming for where the leg met the body, and managed to snap the brittle joint. The thing was already falling toward Lina; she managed to avoid getting skewered but ended up with the creature on top of her, pinning her to the ground . . .

. . . and then it fell to dust as Sylph darted forward and put her hand on one of its legs.

"Lina," she said anxiously, "did you . . . ?"

"I'm fine." Lina struggled to her feet. "Let's get out of here."

"Have to stop them," said Yahvy. "The army . . ."

Fah was on her way, with her entire regiment behind her; most of them had abandoned pikes and formation in order to sprint. Closer still, two of the giant crabs were closing after dealing with what was left of the infantry.

"That trick—" said Yahvy to Sylph.

"I need to touch them." Sylph was breathing hard. "I can't . . . not from here . . ."

"Trouble, then." Yahvy raised her sword.

"Get behind me."

"Lina?" Sylph said.

"Do it!"

I should have told Sylph about Rahmgoth. I should have figured something out, some way . . .

No way out, thought the stranger.

I know.

The third time . . .

She cut him off. *I* know!

She had a sudden flash of the white nothingness, his oh-so-handsome face. He was reaching toward her, toward her breast—she clenched her teeth, but his hand passed *through* her flesh to close around her beating heart.

You're mine, Rahmgoth thought.

✳   ✳   ✳

SYLPH WATCHED AS LINA PAUSED FOR A MOMENT, ON THE verge of turning, as though there was something she wanted to say, but she'd forgotten. Then a white glow sprang from the sword and ran up and down her body, engulfing her in an actinic aura almost too bright to look at.

The Clockwork beasts didn't stop coming. Two of the little ones launched themselves from the back of one of the crabs, both aiming at Lina. She intercepted one in midair with the sword while stepping lithely out of the path of the other; the thing she'd hit exploded, scattering metal droplets like rain. The other landed and spun, but despite its awesome speed Lina was faster, the sword slashing through metal like vapor.

The big crabs slowed, but couldn't stop in time. One of them lashed out with its blade-arms; Lina ducked and came up swinging, removing all four in a businesslike fashion before stepping onto the carapace and driving the sword into its midsection. The white glow spread from the blade to engulf the creature, which slumped into a pool of metal a moment later. The other crab was already backing away, and the little stick-things flung themselves in Lina's path to slow her down. She simply smashed them aside and managed to get close enough to chop off one of the crab's rear legs, which left it trying to limp up the hill. Before it could turn she bisected it into two twitching sections.

All along the line, the strange creatures were retreating,

pulling back over the ridge from which they'd come. The humans made no attempt to pursue; the dead lay in heaps, up and down the line, and there were only a handful of smashed Clockworks besides the ones Lina had destroyed. Roswell's spearmen had managed to upend one of the crabs and crack it open, but they'd paid a fearful price; it was surrounded by dozens of corpses.

Sylph realized she was shaking. She tried to stop, but couldn't seem to manage it. Up on the hillside, Lina let the sword slip through her fingers. The white glow faded, and she collapsed into unconsciousness in the now-familiar aftermath.

Familiar. That was something Sylph could cling to. *But I've never seen her do* that *before.*

"Lina!" Marlowe was riding to the scene. Troops poured in behind him, restoring order and setting up a defensive line. Sylph desperately wanted to collapse, to curl up into a ball and let someone else take charge. *I can't, though. They need me.* She staggered toward Yahvy, who was reforming what was left of her regiment.

"Okay?" Yahvy said.

"Yeah, but that was close."

"Not over yet. What happens when they come back?"

That, Sylph thought, *is a very good question.*

❋   ❋   ❋

THERE WAS, OF COURSE, NO QUESTION OF MAKING FURTHER progress that day.

Sylph retired to her tent as soon as she'd gotten things under control. Her hands wouldn't stop shaking, even after she collapsed onto the camp bed. She sat on them, frustrated.

What's wrong with me? Something about the Clockwork Legion . . . *no, I don't think so. I've been nearly killed so often I'm used to it.*

Lina. She'd seen her sister wield the sword before, even seen it grant her speed and strength. She hadn't been there to watch

her come back from the dead, thankfully, but even witnesses to
that event hadn't mentioned anything like what had happened.
She'd moved like something inhuman. When Sylph thought of
her sister, she got an image of Lina laughing, smiling, looking
embarrassed—it was impossible to reconcile with the creature of
white fire that had torn the Clockwork beasts to shreds.

But if not for her I'd be dead. Maybe we'd all be dead.

There was a rustle at the tent flap.

"Who's there?"

"Heraan."

She breathed out. "I was worried you'd gotten yourself
killed."

He slipped into the semidarkness. "I was on the other side
of the column. We got here just as they were leaving. You're
not hurt?"

"No." Sylph shook her head. "But we lost a lot of people."

"I know."

"How's the camp?"

Heraan waggled his hand. "So-so. A lot of the ones who
weren't in the fighting are saying the Liberator saved us again,
but people who got to actually see it happen aren't so sure. If
Lina were up and talking to them it would help a lot."

"She's unconscious. She always is, after she uses her power
like that."

Heraan gave a tired nod. "It'll hold together. For the moment,
anyway. Marlowe's working on getting things reorganized."

"Yeah," said Sylph dully.

Heraan paused. "Do you mind if I sit down?"

"Feel free."

There was only the bed to sit on, and Sylph didn't turn as
he sank down next to her, gingerly. There was another moment
of silence.

"You don't like Marlowe?"

"It's not . . ." Sylph hesitated. "It's not that I don't *like* him.
I don't think I trust him."

"Oh?"

"He's helpful—he's always helpful—I just feel like he might be too ambitious. I worry about Lina. He might be using her just for—I don't know, power and wealth and all that. I worry."

He nodded.

"Not going to tell me I'm just worrying too much?" she said.

"Would it help?"

"No."

"How about this, then: you have better things to worry about than Marlowe?"

"Such as?"

"You want a list?" Heraan held out a hand and started ticking off points. "What to do about the Clockwork Legion when it returns. How to take Stonerings and how to hand it over to Roswell. How to deal with Lady Fell herself. Where the hell those heavy cavalry came from . . ."

"The group at Orlow? I thought they were part of Lady Fell's army."

He snorted. "She doesn't have any heavies worthy of the name, and those weren't plains horses they were riding. Those men were from further east. Mercenaries from Vilvakis, maybe? What worries me is that there might be more of them."

"Oh." Sylph sighed. "That's quite a list."

"Sorry. I just think that Marlowe is a pretty small issue."

Sylph nodded. They sat in companionable silence for a while, and then she stood, the bed creaking.

"Time to get to work on that list. I need you to play errand boy for a bit."

"Sure."

"Go and find me the pieces of the ones we killed. Don't bother with whatever Lina carved up. Bring the biggest chunks you can find."

"Got it."

"Then find me Rathmado, I need to talk to him."

"Understood."

"Where is Marlowe now, anyway?"

"With Lina." Heraan paused. "I mean . . ."

"It's fine." Sylph waved a hand. "Once you've done that, go to Roswell's cartographer and get me the most detailed map of this area he's got."

"Anything else?"

"Probably, but that's all for now."

"Then I'm off."

He ducked out, the tent flap falling shut behind him. Sylph sat on the ground, cross-legged, and fished the geist out of her pocket. She hadn't used the thing in days. *Because my program is probably finished, and I think I know what it says.* She took a deep breath and dove in, green-and-black metaphor space opening around her. The report was, as expected, waiting.

She's not here. Mom's not here. She left the geist and shivered. *There are still two more geists, and one of them is waiting in Stonerings. Time to concentrate, Sylph.*

*   *   *

LEILA STOOD IN THE CORNER OF THE WORKSHOP, WATCHING the Black Magus. *It's not a good time to disturb the Archmagus, but I don't think Kurai understands—*

"My lady," the Black Magus said, with the radiant smile of a cherub.

"Kurai," Lady Fell said with uncharacteristic abruptness. "You've returned?"

"Yes . . ."

"With this Liberator's head?"

There was a long silence. Finally the Black Magus bowed. "No, my lady."

"I see." Lady Fell picked up a cloth from the workbench and began wiping the bloodstains from her hands. "I was under the impression that I had employed you to complete this task."

"Matters have become complicated."

"You mean she is a Liberator in truth. An Archmagus."

"No, my lady."

Lady Fell spun. "Then *why* the failure?"

"She is receiving aid, my lady. It has a demonic scent to it, but it is nothing I have ever seen before. The creature possesses both power and enormous . . . subtlety."

"Demonic?"

Leila shivered. Demons had infested Stonerings of late, minor imps and oozes that had escaped from the Lady's experiments. She'd been buying the things from Vilvakis by the score, paying in precious souls. The pace of her tests had increased as the rebellious army drew nearer and news of the defeat at Orlow trickled in.

"So," said Lady Fell after a moment, "you suspect our dear neighbor to the east?"

"That is not for me to say, my lady. Vilvakis has been unleashing demons on his opponents for thousands of years, and inevitably a few of them escape. Or, it could have made its way here of its own accord."

"Unlikely," the Archmagus mused. "Up the energy slope . . ."

"It has happened," Kurai said. "But the important question is how we deal with it."

"Luckily, you needn't concern yourself. Consider your employment terminated."

"My lady?"

"I've deployed the Legion to finish the problem."

"There's the matter of my payment . . ."

"You led my army to be slaughtered, not to mention the Shadowcore which was so kindly lent to us. It's fortunate for you that I'm feeling generous, or else you wouldn't leave here with all of your limbs, much less your payment."

Leila cringed, waiting for the explosion, but Kurai just bowed. "As you say, my lady. Excuse me." He walked out, black cloak flapping behind him.

"My lady?" Leila ventured.

"What?" Lady Fell snapped.

"Ah . . ." She swallowed. "There are plans, Archmagus, for the defense of Stonerings. They require your approval."

"The defense of Stonerings? Why? The Legion is smashing the enemy even now."

"In the case of . . . a contingency. My lady."

"Contingency." Lady Fell's face twisted. "Contingency?"

It was all Leila could do to stand her ground. "Just for the sake of . . ."

The Archmagus took a deep breath, then let it out. "Consider them approved. You make any necessary arrangements."

"Y . . . yes. Thank you, my lady." Leila scrambled out, holding the plans to her chest. Behind her, Lady Fell chuckled as she turned back to her work.

"Contingency. Ha."

chapter fifteen

BY THE TIME RATHMADO ENTERED, SYLPH HAD THE Clockwork beast torn to bits on the floor of her tent. She'd snapped off all its limbs, leaving only the cylindrical torso. Sylph had pulled off a rectangular slice to reveal its inner workings. The whole inside of the cylinder was filled with delicate filigree, like a three-dimensional frost pattern made of metal, and tiny lights ran along the myriad fractal protrusions. Sylph stared at it in a trance, leaving her hands at her side and probing entirely with her mind. Any physical contact would have crumbled the fragile structure like a sand castle.

"Good evening, Miss Walker," said the Magus after a moment. "Are you achieving success?"

Sylph blinked and looked up, rubbing her eyes. "This thing is amazing. I mean, look at it." She gestured at the exposed workings of the creature. "It's not *alive*, not really, but it has organic complexity. And they're all different, every single one they brought in!" She pointed, delicately, to a section. "Sensoria and communications, feeding decision-making—some kind of a tactical planner—they *talk* to each other, you know. It's like a work of art instead of a war machine."

Rathmado peered down, then shrugged. "It certainly looks impressive."

"What I can't figure out is where it *comes* from. No way

Lady Fell built this by hand—figuratively speaking—it would take her a hundred years just to put one together, much less a legion. I couldn't do it if you left me alone for an eon. I know she's been around a bit longer, but she can't be *that* much better." Sylph looked up again. "Can she?"

"From the story I heard . . ." Rathmado paused.

"What?"

"She creates crude versions and lets them loose in the fighting pits under Stonerings. The survivors of each *battle royale* are used as templates for the next generation, and so on. The current Clockwork Legion is the end result of more than a thousand years of this process, and so they are very deadly indeed." He shrugged. "Or so the story goes."

"Forced evolution." Sylph nodded. "That explains a lot. It would take forever, but I suppose an Archmagus has time to waste. That doesn't help me figure out how to kill them, though."

"I have confidence in you."

"You and everyone else, but I can't think of *anything*. Two dozen of them slaughtered more than a hundred men this morning, and half of them escaped. Arrows won't faze them, we can't distract them—fire, smoke, water, none of that makes a difference. They lock on to life energy like a shark and don't let go until someone tells them to. I suppose they're vulnerable at the point of command, but all the leader needs is one to relay his orders." She shook her head, still talking mostly to herself. "They talk by infrared. It's line-of-sight but fast, so it's easy to set up relays and hide the commander. Maybe cut the relay line? If they have any sense there'll be more than one . . ."

"Sylph," said Rathmado gently. "You wanted to see me?"

"Yeah." She looked at him again. "Sorry. I haven't slept. I've just been staring at this thing."

"What did you want?"

She blinked tiredly. "I searched the geist."

"Already?"

"Choice of metaphor is important." She smiled. "Mom isn't

in there."

"I mentioned that might be a possibility. The two remaining geists are larger still, and then . . ."

"And then? I don't think you ever finished that statement."

Rathmado shrugged again. "The Lightbringer himself possesses the majority of the souls that fall to Omega."

"The Lightbringer." She'd heard the name mentioned, but . . . "Who, or what, is the Lightbringer?"

"No one really knows. The oldest of the Archmagi, perhaps? He's been there since time beyond memory, supposedly since the White Lady created this world from chaos."

"Enough." Sylph held up a hand. "We can leave the mythology lesson for later."

"I agree." The Magus smiled. "I'll leave you to work on more immediate problems."

"I don't suppose you can *help*?" Sylph said.

"My poor powers are not of the sort that would be any use to you," Rathmado said. "But you are the chosen agent of Destiny, so I have no doubt you'll succeed."

With that he left the tent. Sylph muttered to herself in his absence.

"Chosen agent of 'Destiny' my ass—this is ridiculous." She stared at the impossibly complex innards of the Clockwork beast. "How am I supposed to deal with this?" *I expected an army, I could handle an army, but this magic is not something I can ask soldiers to fight. We might be able to beat them, but they'd wipe us out in the process. So there has to be another way. If I had . . .*

She paused, trying to hold on to a thought that threatened to melt away like a will-o'-the-wisp. *If I had. If I had.*

Slowly, Sylph reached for the geist.

"FAH! ARE YOU IN HERE?"

Sylph pushed her way into Lina's tent without waiting for

an answer. Fah was, as expected, sitting by Lina's bedside; Melfina had been asleep on a cot in the corner, but she sat up at Sylph's greeting.

"Oh. Sorry, I didn't think anyone would be asleep." Sylph moved to Lina's side, pacing back and forth excitedly.

"'S fine." Melfina rubbed her eyes. "I just wanted to be near Lina when she wakes up."

"She's gone pretty far this time," said Fah.

Sylph blinked. "Is she going to be all right?"

"I think so, but it may be a while before she wakes up. We kept her hand on her sword; she doesn't seem to want to let go."

Sylph looked down. Lina's face, even sleeping, was screwed up as though she were about to cry. *Poor Lina. I should have come to visit before.*

"Is something wrong, Sylph?" said Melfina. "You look . . ."

The girl trailed off. *Energetic*, Sylph thought, *would probably be the appropriate word.* She'd just spent hours with the geist, and having the stored power of billions of souls flowing through her was exhilarating. She felt keyed-up, as though sparks should be flying from her fingers whenever she touched something.

"I think I figured out what we need to do."

"To do?" said Fah.

"About the Clockwork Legion."

"I assumed the Liberator would protect us, as she did before."

Sylph shook her head. "You said yourself it might be a while before she wakes up. It's hard on her—she can't fight them all by herself. And if they attack while she's asleep we're all going to die. It's a miracle they haven't come back already."

"Maybe they don't know she's asleep," said Melfina.

"Probably." Sylph did another lap around the bed. "In any case, we've got to work fast. I've got a plan, I've got Heraan working on the first part of it, but I needed . . ." She stopped, and took a deep breath. "There's another part, and it's going to be very dangerous. I need volunteers."

"I'll do it," said Fah at once. "In service to the Liberator."

"Thanks, but no. You're a regiment commander and Lina's right hand, we can't afford to lose you. But I need you to find people for me. Twenty of them, good riders and good shots with a short-bow."

"Of course." Fah turned to leave. "I'll go at once."

Sylph caught her shoulder. "Tell them," she said, "what I told you. That it's dangerous, and I need *volunteers*. Understand? This isn't . . ." She hesitated. "This isn't the kind of thing I can order someone to do."

Fah removed her hand. "I understand. We serve the Liberator, and if we die in her service the White Lady will cherish us all the more."

Sylph tasted bile at the back of her throat, but said nothing. *If she wants to believe, let her. It's better this way.* Fah slipped out of the tent into the predawn gloom.

"Lina's been restless," said Melfina after a moment. "She called for you."

Sylph laid a hand on her sister's forehead. "I'm . . . sorry."

Melfina gave her a brave smile. "She understands. You're trying to save everyone."

Almost everyone. Sylph smiled, but she felt her gut twist. "Where's Marlowe?"

"He was here until a few hours ago. Fah finally convinced him to get some sleep."

"Good. We're going to need him tomorrow if something goes wrong." She sighed. "I have things to do, Mel. Can you . . . ?"

"Go. I'll stay with her."

"Thank you." She touched Lina again. *I'm sorry.*

"Good luck!" Melfina called after her.

✳   ✳   ✳

THE SUN HAD JUST PEEKED OVER THE EASTERN HORIZON when Heraan returned. Sylph saw him coming and ran out to meet him on the outskirts of camp; he swung off his horse, which was clearly exhausted.

"Did you find it?" said Sylph, before he could speak.

"Right where the map said it would be."

Thank God. That had been one potential sticking point; Roswell's men had fairly detailed maps, but she'd learned that mapmaking on Omega was not exactly reliable. "And it looks okay?"

"Just like you wanted. I've got the men working now, though I'll admit I don't understand any of this."

"Don't worry about it." *Let me worry about it.* There was plenty to worry about. *There was no time to test anything.*

"We should have some men there, just in case." Heraan shook his head. "We'd be able to do some damage with bows, or even rocks, if your magic fails."

"Trust me, Heraan, that would be a very bad idea."

"As you say." He shrugged. "Now what?"

"Fah's assembling the team on the north side of camp. I've got to go brief them."

"I'll come with you."

"You've been working all night."

"I want to see how this ends," said Heraan with a sly smile. "Thus far your magic has been impressive, Sylph."

"Come with me, then." She started walking, and he fell into step alongside her. "How long until the canyon is ready?"

"Another hour at the most."

"You passed my instructions to the men."

"To the letter. They know what to do."

Run like hell. There wasn't much more to the instructions.

The camp was waking up around them, tired sentries making their way inward as the shift changed. Roswell's army was encamped to the south, in orderly rows. Sylph's force, by contrast, threw up their tents by regiment around their commanders. *I should establish a doctrine or something.* She shook her head. *Distractions. There's always distractions.*

Fah was waiting just outside the ring of sentries, accompanied by twenty-three men and women standing quietly in a double line. A string of horses waited nearby.

God, it's mostly girls. It made sense, they were better riders, usually, but . . . *I can't do this. I can't do this.* She took a deep breath. *They signed up for it, all of them. Come on, Sylph.*

"Good morning." Sylph paused, trying to find words. "Before I continue, if anyone's having second thoughts now's the time to back out. Understand?"

No one moved, not that Sylph had really been expecting them to.

"I see." She walked up the line and back down again. Two middle-aged men, a woman who could have been Sylph's mother, two girls not much older than Lina who looked so much alike they had to be related. *I can't do this.* She wanted to vomit.

"This morning," Sylph said, finally, "we're going to destroy the Clockwork Legion."

HERAAN HAD FOUND A GOOD PLACE TO OBSERVE, A WOODED hilltop about a mile from where the Clockwork Legion had made camp. Not that there was any camp to speak of; the Clockwork beasts simply froze in place, waiting for their human masters to make up their minds. *Still worrying about Lina, beasties?* Sylph, observing through her telescope, favored them with a tight smile. *You took too long.*

It had taken some work with the cartographer to find exactly the terrain she needed. Centuries ago there had been a river here, possibly large enough to match the Whiteflow, but some shift in rains had reduced it to a mere stream winding a placid course through the bed of the once-mighty torrent.

The creek's origin was a spring on top of a hill. When the river had existed, it had carved a gully through which the stream now ran. It plotted a twisty course through perhaps half a mile; the far end, where the walls had been highest, had long since collapsed to block the path in a mountain of jumbled rock.

In other words, perfect. She turned her attention back to the Clockworks. There was, as she'd predicted, a single tent amidst the sea of unnatural creations. One man stood outside it, sitting at a folding table and writing a letter. A lone horse stood nearby.

And—she turned—riding closer across the plain, Fah's handpicked twenty-three. They all carried short-bows, small enough to be used from horseback. The Clockworks had no outriders, no scouts—what would be the point, since engaging the monsters was practically suicide—and so they didn't respond until the horsemen were almost on top of them.

"There will be one human with them," Sylph had said. "He goes down first, no matter what it takes. Understand?"

They'd understood. Two dozen bows twanged—inaudible at this distance, but Sylph could imagine—the shafts all arcing down on the poor man at his writing table. He had time to look up and shout something before he was hit by four or five arrows and flopped to the ground.

Now, Sylph willed. *Run.*

The Clockwork beasts were quick to react. While they normally didn't act without orders, there were certain circumstances under which they were allowed a free hand. *Such as when they're attacked.* Sylph hadn't been sure, but any other design would leave the Legion vulnerable to a surprise assault.

The giant crabs shifted on their eight legs, rotating in the direction of the horsemen and beginning their strange, shuffling run that carried them forward deceptively fast. The little spindly ones bounded around them, some riding on their larger cousin's carapaces while others fanned out ahead. They moved through the grass so fast they were a blur, leaving ripples in their wake.

The horsemen had already turned, galloping away from the enraged constructs. A human would have known that it was a simple spoiling attack, and detached a few units to chase down the raiders; but the only human was down, choking on his own blood, and the Legion had been bred in the fighting pits where the only success came from destroying the enemy. *They're strong, tough, fast, and tactically perfect, but they lack strategic vision.* So the entire Legion—Sylph counted at least two hundred crabs and innumerable smaller beasts—unfolded like a silver river and gave chase to a handful of terrified cavalry.

There's bound to be another agent of Lady Fell's nearby, ready to take charge. But the Clockwork beasts could keep up with a galloping horse, so assuming command would be difficult. *Once they run down the riders, they'll stop. He'll be waiting for that.*

The horsemen thundered toward the entrance to the gully. It was mercifully close, no more than two or three miles away. Sylph watched through the telescope, her heart in her mouth.

She realized with a start that the crabs, at a dead run, were *faster* than a galloping horse. They were gaining. *If they catch up too soon . . .*

The slowest of the riders made the mistake of looking back, just as two spindly beasts launched themselves from the back of a crab and landed on him. Man, horse, and beasts went down in a bloody tangle, from which only the Clockworks rose. They grabbed the shell of the next passing crab and resumed the chase.

Sylph wanted to close her eyes, but she had to watch. *As though I can do any good now.*

The riders had spread out, the best horses outdistancing the rest, and the oncoming tide of the Legion engulfed the stragglers one by one. Some of the riders tried to veer at the last minute, and one brave fool turned and drew his sword; all were crushed underfoot with barely a pause by the inexorable rush of metal. Before long only four horsemen remained, in a ragged line at what had been the head of the pack. The mouth of the gully loomed ahead.

Just a little bit farther. Now Sylph did close her eyes, willing strength to the flagging horses. *Please.*

One animal stumbled on the rocky ground, breaking a leg and tossing its rider into a bone-snapping roll. Both were buried by the rush of Clockworks seconds later. A spindly beast launched itself, managed to get close enough to a galloping horse to sever its hind leg with a lucky swing. Two riders remained, and the silver river streamed into the gully. The tail end, the slowest of the Clockworks, was shrinking as the leaders disappeared into the canyon. *Just a little bit farther . . .*

And the last of them went inside.

"What I wouldn't give to be up there dropping rocks on them," said Heraan in a tight voice. "I don't care how tough they are, we could squish one or two . . ."

Now. Up on the cliffs, one of Heraan's men had dropped a torch and, if he was obeying instructions, run like all the demons of Hell were behind him.

The moment of truth. Does it work?

They were far enough away that Sylph saw the detonation before she heard it. Red and black bloomed all along the cliffs, bits of rock and scree flying in every direction. Heraan stared, uncomprehending, as Sylph silently counted the seconds. *Ten, eleven, twelve . . .*

Boom. The sound rolled over them, a single staccato blast followed by a drawn out roll of thunder, loud enough to be uncomfortable even miles away. Sylph kept her telescope trained, straining to see through the spreading smoke; the rocky walls of the cliffs *folded*, undermined along their base, and the entire gully crumbled. Ten thousand tons of rock came crashing down like the hammer of a vengeful God.

Sylph smiled. *Let's hear it for high school chemistry.*

BY THE TIME SYLPH STRAGGLED BACK INTO HER TENT, IT was only midmorning; she still felt like flopping down on the bed and going to sleep for a week or so. It didn't help. All she could see when she closed her eyes was the ragged double line of volunteers, ready to give their lives for the Liberator.

I warned them. I told them it was dangerous. But that didn't cut it. *Dangerous means you* might *come back. That was certain death.*

The worst part was that they probably would have volunteered anyway. *For the Liberator. Why do they do that for Lina? Although, to be fair, it's not exactly for Lina. They're dying for a legend that she happens to resemble.*

After an interval, Yahvy slipped into the tent and cleared her throat.

"What?" said Sylph from the bed.

"What happened? Everyone's curious."

"It's done." Sylph closed her eyes. "We killed them all."

"Good news. Any losses?"

"The squad we sent in." *As bait.*

"All?"

Sylph nodded, mutely.

"You okay?"

"No," said Sylph, "not really."

"Heard what you told Fah. Volunteers."

"I know." *But it doesn't matter.*

"What now?"

"Take the day to celebrate, bury everybody. Then on to Stonerings tomorrow morning. It's less than a week's march by the map."

"Roswell wants you."

Tell him to fuck off. "Tell him I'm on my way."

"Understood."

After Yahvy ducked out, Sylph rolled off the bed and onto the floor. It was still gritty with fine gray powder, left over from her frantic experiments the night before. Getting the size and composition of the grains right had been the hard part, but the quick trial-and-error nature of the geist had helped a lot. *I should probably clean this up. Kind of a fire hazard.* A moment's concentration, and the magically created material unraveled and dissolved.

I should have thought of this a long time ago. Pikes and longbows— that was the best I could do? The power of the geist could take her a lot farther than that. *Take all of us. No more losing men against these little armies. I just need some time to work on it, that's all.* Not a luxury she was likely to have until after Stonerings fell. *Damn it.*

Roswell's section of the camp was surrounded by guards from among his own troops, but Sylph was expected—a couple of spearmen escorted her to the largest tent, where she found the general having a late breakfast with his chief of staff. *Loquiana, I think?* Sylph gave him a nod and received one in return.

"You wanted to see me?"

"Yes." Roswell had half a roll in one hand and spread butter across it as he spoke. "I thought we should meet regarding our disposition. I know something of the tactics normally employed in combating the Clockwork Legion. They're quite formidable, but we've been fighting Lady Fell long enough to have learned a few tricks. I'm more than willing to have my men teach yours . . ."

He hasn't heard. "It won't be necessary."

Roswell paused, then put the roll down. "Sylph. If I may speak plainly, this is not a time to let pride get in the way of victory."

"I mean it won't be necessary. We destroyed the Legion this morning."

Sylph had to admit she took a certain perverse pleasure in letting that drop and watching the expression on their faces. Roswell tried ineffectively to conceal his surprise, while Loquiana glared daggers. *She really doesn't like me for some reason.*

"Was there anything else?" Sylph said, after a few moments.

"No," said the general faintly. "I think that will be all."

*   *   *

LADY FELL WAS LOATH TO LEAVE HER SANCTUARY UNDER the fortress at Stonerings. In the best of times, she could stay down there for weeks without seeing the light of day. But these were not the best of times.

She'd left Leila to prepare the defense of her city. Not that it would do much good against the Liberator's army, but without the Legion other choices had to be made. *Other . . . contingencies.* She almost laughed at that.

The camp was a small one, a score of primitive tents around a central bonfire. Two or three dozen men and women sat in a rough circle, warming themselves and talking to one another in low tones. They were dressed in rough fabric and patchy leather, dyed black and then streaked liberally with ochre mud. Most of them, particularly the younger men and women, wore the mud in patterns on their faces as well. The flickering light made them look inhuman.

Lady Fell picked her way down the slope, one hand holding her skirt up so that she wouldn't trip and the other extended for balance. One of the old men, relegated to the outskirts of the fire, noticed her approach first; he got to his feet and grabbed a spear.

"Who are you?"

"I'm invited," said the Archmagus. Inwardly she seethed. *Once I'm done with the Liberator, there will be a reckoning.* "I must speak with the Steelbreaker."

"The Steelbreaker is expecting only one guest," said the old man. A half-dozen of his companions had gathered around to watch. "And you do not look like her."

"And what do I look like to you?"

"An old woman in need of a good time!" one of the youths called out. There was laughter around the circle.

Enough. Lady Fell's hand shot out and grabbed the spear below the tip. She reached out to the geist, safe under the fortress but projecting its power through the Circles, and concentrated. The wooden shaft of the spear was suddenly too hot to hold; the old man cursed and dropped it, and Lady Fell let it fall. It burned with a blue-white fire, and the metal head turned cherry red and started to lose its shape. The warriors stared in awe.

"I am the Magio Mutator," the Archmagus said. "And I believe I am expected."

A young man had emerged from one of the tents. He gestured, and the others cleared a path; then he bowed, deeply.
"Indeed, you are."

"You're younger than I expected, and the wrong sex besides."

"My father recently passed away." He straightened and
gave her a glittering smile. "As did my older sister."

Lady Fell nodded. Her memory for details was, as always,
impeccable. "In that case, you must be Vhaal."

He bowed again. "At your service."

* * *

Two days to the city. Somehow, Sylph had expected
Lady Fell to just roll over and die with the defeat of the Clockwork Legion; it was, after all, the centerpiece of her power. That
had been a bit naïve, in retrospect. *You don't get to be a thousand
years old by giving up easily.* Somewhere, the Archmagus had found
new allies. *She must have favors to call in, influence to sell.*

The new arrivals called themselves the Steelbreakers and
apparently came from a single fierce, if primitive, tribe. The first
warning Sylph had was when her outriders started disappearing,
first one at a time, then in twos and threes. She increased the
pickets, sent them out in larger groups. When a squadron of
twenty horsemen happened on a raiding party of six mounted
savages, the tribesmen fled and drew the cavalry into pursuit.
The soldiers rode into an ambush, forty or fifty men on a hillside
with short horn bows, and only a half-dozen got away. At the
same time, another large band slipped through the gap this action had left in the patrol lines.

That was the night Sylph got her first sight of the new enemy.
She awoke to the sounds of screams and wild war-cries; when
she dashed to the tent flap, the night was lurid with flames. As
she watched, another flight of fire-arrows took to the sky, landing amongst the army's supply wagons. Pike-men were running
everywhere, but no one seemed to be organizing a coherent

defense. Sylph shouted for a messenger, but succeeded only in attracting the attention of a trio of riders.

They were a bit shorter than the men of Bleloth and Lady Fell's domain, with pale skin and flat features. One was a woman, breasts bound up in a wrapped cloth and reddish mud streaking her temples, while the two men wore only leathers and war paint. The woman pointed and shouted something unintelligible, and the three of them charged. Sylph ducked back inside the tent, reaching for the sword she'd left beside the bed; she managed to draw and turn in time to make the trio pull up short just inside the tent flap.

They bore short wooden clubs with nasty looking sharp rocks and glass set around the tips. The woman gestured the men forward, and they split up to circle around her. Before she could order an attack, the point of a sword emerged from her belly; she wrapped her hands around it and groaned. The men spun as she fell and Heraan stepped into the tent, followed by Yahvy. Trapped, they bellowed another war-cry and attacked together. Heraan parried the strike while Yahvy neatly side-stepped and drew her blade across the man's gut. He fell with a gurgle, and she turned and ran the other through as he tried to force Heraan back.

It occurred to Sylph that she'd come very close to dying— *again*—but there didn't seem to be time to worry about it. The three dashed outside, but the attack was already ending. The raiders extricated themselves from the camp, leaving fifty of their own and twice as many of Sylph's lying dead. More importantly, half of the big wagons that carried the army's supplies were in flames. Despite the fervent efforts of the soldiers, most of them were destroyed. Sylph surveyed the destruction grimly. *There's enough to get us to Stonerings, but after that . . .*

The next morning she reorganized her defenses: standing units of archers, ready to string and fire in the event of an attack, and a regiment of Roswell's spearmen kept together as a quick-response team. The cost was strained, tired soldiers, but Sylph paid it gladly. The next time, the outriders ignored the decoy attack and faded away from the main thrust, bringing warning to the camp in plenty of time; the tribesmen were met at the border by a murderous hail of missile fire and two hundred spearmen ready to counterattack, and the raid was decimated. That bought her a day of peace.

Since then it had been a deadly cat-and-mouse game, with the tribesmen constantly probing the circle of outriders looking for a weak point. They'd slipped through a couple of times, though once she managed to get a unit of pike-men astride their escape route and chop their band to flinders. The problem, however, was that there simply weren't enough outriders to maintain a full screen twenty-four hours a day. Sylph put them where she thought they'd do the most good and pushed the army forward as quickly as possible, eager to reach the city.

There were two days left, and everyone was exhausted. Heraan, in command of the screening troops, had been run ragged; she'd finally outright ordered him to get some sleep and commandeered Orbaa as a replacement. Yahvy's pikes camped around Sylph's tent, and there had been no repeat of the first night, but everyone slept fitfully and waited for the whistling sound of the barbarians' arrows. Sylph herself divided her time between planning their defense and her own experiments with the geist; she was making progress, but not as much as she would have liked. *If they'd just leave us alone for a week . . .*

But that was a foolish hope. *We don't have supplies to camp for a week anymore. If we can't take Stonerings within the next few days, we'll have to retreat.* She and Marlowe had laid private plans for that contingency; there were a few villages nearby that would probably be undefended and provide at least part of what she needed. But Sylph had privately decided it would be disastrous. *Desertion will destroy us. These people are here because they believe the Liberator's victory is inevitable, and if that faith is shaken they won't hold.*

Worry about Lina was another worm twisting in her gut. Her sister wasn't wounded or feverish, and showed no obvious signs of illness. But she hadn't woken once in the week since the battle against the Clockwork beasts. Fah practically lived at her bedside, making sure she got food and water; in the meantime, she prayed to the White Lady. Melfina spent a lot of time there too, and Marlowe when his duties didn't take him away. Sylph went to see her as often as she could, but her desperate tinkering with the geist consumed what free time she had.

Heraan slipped into her tent shortly after dawn and found Sylph already awake, her latest creation torn to shards of blackened metal on her workbench. Sylph took a moment to notice him.

Spring goes here, that should be easy—receiver above that—but how do I keep the damn thing from spinning all the way around?

"Sylph?"

"Hmm?" She looked up. "Good morning."

He looked at her project. "I'm not even going to ask what kind of magic this is."

"It's not really magic." She folded a thin cloth over the gathered pieces. "I'm trying to remember how to build something."

He nodded, a little skeptical. "There's someone in the healer's tent you should see. I think she's the leader of the raiders; we caught a big group of them last night, managed to get close and get a volley in before they ran for it. We picked her up afterward."

"We need to get on the road."

"Marlowe will handle that. You need to come and talk to her."

"Why? Is she badly hurt?"

"More or less. They're working on her, but we don't know . . ."

Sylph climbed to her feet. "Let's go."

They had the woman in a separate tent from the rest of the injured, for which Sylph was grateful; she didn't feel up to walking through a graphic demonstration of the horrors of war so early in the morning. Two healers, both young women, were waiting; Sylph did a double-take when she recognized Daana. *I haven't seen her since Garot died.* The Circle Breaker looked as though she hadn't slept since then; there were dark bags under her eyes, her hair was dirty and had been inexpertly hacked short, and she'd lost quite a bit of weight. She turned away as they entered and busied herself in one corner, refusing to meet Sylph's eyes, and after a few moments Sylph turned her attention to the patient. *Daana will have to wait.*

The woman on the cot was older than Lina, somewhere in her early twenties, with short brown hair and pudgy features. She wore only leathers and a few wrapped strips of cloth, and most of the war paint had been washed from her skin; without it, she didn't look as fearsome. There were bandages around her stomach and thigh; the former wound seemed superficial, but the latter was deep and still bleeding enough to stain the wrapping.

As Sylph moved to her bedside, the barbarian's eyes opened; they were full of pain, but lucid.

"You," she managed. "You are Sylph?"

Sylph nodded.

"And this . . . this is your army?" The woman gestured weakly.

"Technically, it's my sister's, but I'm running it at the moment."

"Ha." The barbarian lay back. "I had heard rumors, but no one believed them. That there was a *child* in charge here— beaten by children." She gave Sylph a wan smile. "I think I am glad I will not get to face the Steelbreaker again."

"Who are you?"

"My name is Saar," the barbarian said. "My family is Crackrock, of the Steelbreaker tribe. When you write of your worthy enemies, Sylph, I hope that you count me amongst them."

"I'll have to."

"That is good." Saar closed her eyes. "We were foolish. I didn't count on those Lady-damned bows; I didn't believe what we heard about their range. I have never seen the like."

"They come from the west." Sylph didn't add that they were like no other bows in the world, manufactured in a single piece from composite alloy.

"So we concluded." Saar gave a raspy cough. "The victory is yours. The Crackrock family has failed; my brothers, sisters, cousins and grand-cousins lie dead around your camp."

"I'm sorry," Sylph said quietly.

"For what? Winning? You would have been sorrier had you lost, I assure you." She shrugged, as best she could on the cot. "It matters little now."

"Can I ask a question?"

"You can ask, though I may not answer."

"Why did you attack us? I had never heard of the Steelbreaker tribe a week ago. What have we done to earn such hatred?"

Saar shook her head firmly. "No hatred. We go where the Steelbreaker wills. He directed my family and I to stop you, and so we made the attempt."

"But who is the Steelbreaker? A servant of Lady Fell's?"

"The Steelbreaker serves no one," Saar said firmly. "The Archmagus requested his aid, yes, but the tribe was already on its way."

"Why?"

Saar looked surprised. "For you, Sylph. He came here for you."

Sylph paused. "What do you mean, for me?"

The barbarian took a deep breath. "Some time ago, when his father Yzail ruled, the Steelbreaker-to-be fled the tribe. We thought he had left forever; when Yzail died, his eldest daughter Morgan became the Steelbreaker in his place. Those were years of peace; it made the women happy, but the young men of the families grew restless and disputes within the tribe multiplied.

"Then Morgan's younger brother returned from the city. He challenged her rule, as was his right."

"Challenged how?" Sylph asked.

"A duel, of course."

"He killed his sister?"

"Yes. And then he became the Steelbreaker, and proclaimed that the tribe would march to war. He had found his bride while he traveled though the lands of the Archmagi, and he needed the might of the tribe to claim her."

"And you said he's coming for *me*?"

"Yes." Saar sounded puzzled. "You did not know?"

"If he wants to *marry* me, why did you attack us?"

"You are a chieftain, with an army at your back," the barbarian said. "We assumed he had asked for your hand and been rejected. In such a case, his only hope for winning you is in battle."

"This is insane," said Sylph. She looked up at Heraan. "I haven't rejected any proposals recently, have I?"

"Not that I remember," he said. "What's the Steelbreaker's name?"

"It is stripped from him on his ascension, and only returned on his death," said Saar.

"Can you tell us what it *was*?" Sylph asked.

Saar nodded. "Vhaal, of the family Lashsnake. Son of Yzail, and brother to Morgan."

"Vhaal." Sylph turned back to Heraan. "You think that's our Vhaal?"

"I assume so, since he seems to know you."

"So you did journey with the Steelbreaker," Saar said. "He mentioned as much."

"I did," said Sylph. "But he never gave any indication he wanted me to . . . to do anything like that."

"It is not given to me to know the Steelbreaker's mind. But since I have failed, he will be waiting for you outside the Archmagus's city."

"Waiting for us?" Sylph didn't like that sound of that. "With how many men?"

"All the families of the Steelbreaker tribe."

"How many is that?"

Saar coughed. "Three, perhaps four thousand. Assuming all have answered his summons."

Three or four thousand? Sylph felt numb. Saar's five hundred or so raiders had wreaked havoc on her army. *How am I supposed to deal with four thousand of them?* The Liberator's army could barely field five thousand men, even if Roswell's troops were included. *We were hoping Lady Fell didn't have more than a few hundred left. If Vhaal makes us fight house-to-house in Stonerings it'll be a nightmare.*

We have to talk to him. He'll see reason, or we'll buy him off somehow. I don't know what Lady Fell's promised him, but Vhaal's not the type to refuse to negotiate. Unfortunately, Sylph remembered, he *was* the type to order his army into battle out of sheer bloodlust.

One of the healers came over as Saar's cough worsened, coaxing the barbarian into accepting a pitcher of honeyed water. Afterward she said quietly to Sylph, "She needs to rest."

"Will she live?" asked Sylph, once she was sure she was out of earshot.

"Maybe." The healer gave an exhausted shrug. "We may have to take off the leg, and that far up it's difficult."

"I'm going to need to talk to her again."

"Come back tomorrow. After that, I can't promise anything."

Sylph nodded and beckoned to Heraan. The two of them headed back through the tent city, which was once again in the process of packing itself up.

"Four thousand," said Heraan. "You think she was telling the truth?"

That hadn't occurred to Sylph. "Do you think she was lying?"

"I'm not sure she has a reason to. She must know she's not going to scare us off."

"Yeah," Sylph agreed grimly.

"What are you going to do?" Heraan kept his voice low. "We're run ragged, Sylph. If he really has four thousand horsemen like that . . ." He made a so-so gesture. "Not good odds, and it'll be bloody either way."

"And even if we win, he can retreat into the city and make us pay for every street."

"Exactly. What's the plan?"

"Talk to him." Sylph shook her head. "Then I'll think of something. Hell, if nothing else comes to mind, maybe I'll just have to marry the bastard."

The look on Heraan's face, Sylph thought, almost made the whole situation worthwhile.

* * *

TWO FIGURERS MATERIALIZED IN THE BLANK WHITE SPACE of Lina's dreams. It was like watching a movie; Lina drifted through nothingness while the same scene played itself out over and over. Closing her eyes or turning her head didn't make a difference; it unfolded inside her skull, like a memory. It was worse than a movie; Lina *felt* the shock of the white-robed figure as his companion ran him through, the horrible cold of steel in his belly and the damp stain that glued his clothes to his stomach.

Somehow he found the voice to speak.

"Why?"

The one opposite was nothing more than a shadow, a pale blur of roughly man-shape. It shrugged. "I need your power."

"But . . ." The robed figure staggered back against a boulder, the sword point protruding from his back scraping the rock. "We . . . would have won."

"Yes," said the shadow.

"You would have had . . . *everything.*"

"Not everything." The shadow stepped closer. Lina felt her limbs going numb. "You never understood, Rahmgoth. I never wanted to crawl back in, pull myself hand over hand up the slope. And for what? There's nothing left for me there. I have *nothing* without her."

"But . . ." Rahmgoth's eyes widened. "You can't. It is . . . forbidden."

"I know."

"You can't . . . leave me here . . ."

"Don't worry," said the shadow. "I'll be there to catch you, when you fall."

"You can't have her." A bubble of blood burst between Rahmgoth's lips. "You'll never have her."

The shadow pulled the sword out with a gush of blood and slammed it home again, through the heart. He gave it a vicious twist, and Rahmgoth's body jerked. His lips parted for the last time.

"For . . . bidden."

Then Lina's vision faded to white for a moment. The two figures materialized, and the scene began again. She tried to scream.

THE STEELBREAKER TRIBE WAS ENCAMPED ON THE WIDE plain before Stonerings's western gate, just as Saar had said. Long ago there had been a forest, but only a few trees and scattered stumps remained as evidence now. What was left was a few miles of rolling grassland between the hills to the north and south of the city, perfect terrain for the hit-and-run tactics of the barbarian cavalry. *We can make them pay for it*, Sylph thought. *Our bows outrange theirs. But there are so damn* many *of them.* The strip of ground outside the wall was aswarm with Steelbreakers, little clusters of tents presumably denoting the various families that made up the tribe.

Sylph, telescope in hand, turned her attention to the wall itself. It was nothing like the perfect, magical constructions of diamond or obsidian Gargorian had favored. This was a stone wall built by long decades of painful labor. It stood thirty feet high, with wooden palettes adding a few more feet and providing cover for Lady Fell's archers. The only heartening thing about it was the scarcity of defenders; the Steelbreakers apparently felt it beneath their dignity to man a wall, and Sylph saw only a handful of archers wearing Lady Fell's colors gathered beside the gatehouse to watch the impending battle.

If not for the barbarians, we could do this. Though, granted, three or four thousand tribesmen was rather a lot to dismiss.

"Sylph?" said Heraan. She looked up. He was already ahorse and fully armored. "We've gotten a response to your message."

"Will he talk to us?"

"Vhaal says he'll meet us halfway between the armies. You're to bring a troop of archers, and he'll do the same. They'll wait close enough that no one will be able to abduct anyone."

"That could get ugly if it turns into an ambush."

Heraan nodded. "Do you want to risk it?"

Her stomach turned. "We don't have much of a choice, do we? Don't answer that. Any word on Lina?"

"Still sleeping peacefully."

Sylph took a deep breath. "Okay. Let's see what he has to say."

Her horse was waiting, and Sylph strapped on her sword and rode to the fore with Heraan following. There were a few halfhearted cheers, but most of the soldiers were busy gawking at the size of the enemy formation. Lina's continued absence had not been good for morale, either. On the right General Roswell and his men were deployed in disciplined ranks.

Sylph's heart fluttered in her chest; she felt a little bit irritated, actually, that after everything that she'd been through she was still frightened. *I wish Lina were with me. Or Yahvy, or even Melfina.* But her friends were all with their regiments. Heraan's presence was reassuring, but he had to drop back as they neared the meeting point. She saw two dozen barbarian horsemen approaching with strung bows; they pulled up short, except for one. Sylph got to what she judged was the middle and slid from her saddle, and he did the same a moment later.

Vhaal. He looked much as she remembered him: well-kept black hair, slick, too-handsome features embellished with a few tiger-stripes of war paint on the cheeks. The grin was the same too, the nasty smile that was all the more irritating because it was backed by unmatched skill at arms. *And now an army to boot.*

She was willing to bet that hadn't helped his over-inflated ego.

"Vhaal," said Sylph gravely as they drew close.

"Sylph." His grin widened. "I wasn't sure you were going to come yourself."

"I invited you," she said. "I could hardly refuse."

"You've gotten braver, then."

"I've got two dozen longbows at my back too."

"I suppose," he said, as though he hadn't noticed.

Sylph ground her teeth, her patience fraying. "Vhaal," she managed, "what the *hell* is this about?"

He tilted his head. "You don't know? You didn't seem surprised to see me, so I assumed . . ."

"I talked to Saar. She said you were here to *marry* me."

"And so I am."

"Pretty funny way to go about it," she said, gesturing at the barbarian horde.

"I didn't think you'd appreciate it if I left a wreath on your door. Besides," he leaned forward, "this way's more fun."

"Fun." Sylph had to take a deep breath.

"Let's be plain about it, shall we? At the moment, we both have armies, but if you retreat from here yours won't last. No supplies, and my men raiding you every night—you won't have a soldier left. Roswell certainly won't stick around if it looks like his victory's slipping away. My army, on the other hand, is generously provisioned. So you either give battle today or tomorrow, give up and slink home, or . . ." He grinned again.

"Why? What do you want with me?"

"You're the Liberator's sister," he said. "You beat the Archmagus. It's been six hundred years since that happened. And with my help we can beat this one, and the next. That's power, and once we're wed it'll be mine."

"Why not Lina, then?"

Vhaal rolled his eyes. "Give me *some* credit for taste, Sylph. Your sister, well . . ."

"Stop." Sylph felt her hands clenching into fists. "I'm going to kill you, you realize."

"You're going to have a hard time managing that without getting skewered yourself."

"Maybe I'm angry enough."

"Maybe. But that doesn't sound very much like you, does it?" He shrugged. "In any event . . . return to your camp. You have a day to make your decision. If I don't hear from you by noon tomorrow, I'll assume it means battle." He nodded politely. "Until then?"

Sylph said nothing. Vhaal spun on his heel and walked back to his horse, and the barbarian party returned to their ranks. Heraan approached once they'd reached a safe distance, with Sylph's horse in tow.

"How bad is it?" he asked.

"Bad enough." Sylph let out a deep breath. *Think.*

"You're not going to marry him, are you?"

She glanced up at him, and he looked so worried she had to laugh. "Of course not."

* * *

"Saar," Sylph said quietly. "Are you awake?"

"I am," the woman said. "Has there been a battle? I have not heard one."

Outside the tent it was dark. The two armies had settled into uneasy restfulness with only a length of open field between them; Sylph had told her men that negotiations were proceeding, but not the details. She'd spent the day closeted in her own tent.

"No battle. Not yet. I'm trying to avoid one."

"You think you will lose."

"I don't know," Sylph said truthfully. "But either way it will be a slaughter. My men—your families—will die. Do you want that?"

"We die where the Steelbreaker commands."

"The Steelbreaker would spend your lives to no purpose."

There was a long silence.

"What do you want from me?" the barbarian asked.

"I have an . . . idea. I need to know if it's going to work. I need to know more about the Steelbreakers."

"My family," said Saar, "would think me a traitor for even talking to you."

"Saar—"

"My family is dead," she cut in. "If I help you, do you swear that you will try to avert the battle?"

Sylph nodded eagerly. Saar sighed, and closed her eyes.

"The battle would have been glorious. But I would not have seen it in any case . . . not long, I think, until I feel the White Lady's embrace."

"Our healers are doing their best," Sylph said. "But . . ."

"Ask," Saar said tiredly.

✳   ✳   ✳

"Heraan?"

He stuck his head out of his tent after a moment, blinking in the light of the torch Sylph carried. "Sylph? What's the matter?"

"I need to talk to you."

He looked around. "It's before dawn."

"We've got no time. I'm planning something idiotic and I need your help."

"Ah." He gave her a bleary smile. "Well, when you put it like that, how can I refuse?"

16

chapter sixteen

As dawn approached, Sylph's bone-weariness departed, replaced by a kind of manic energy. It wouldn't last, she knew from experience. *If it gets me to noon—if we're still alive by noon—I'll be in good shape.* She'd left Heraan on their makeshift training ground outside the camp, and by the time the sun showed over the horizon Sylph was already back among the tents looking for Marlowe. She found him, not unexpectedly, in the healer's tent where Lina was still sleeping.

"Marlowe!"

"Sylph," he said, and yawned. *I guess I wasn't the only one who had a long night.* "She's still sleeping, although she was mumbling to herself just after midnight." He peered at her. "Are you all right? You look a little . . . scorched."

That was true; Sylph's skin had a definite gray cast, and her hair had picked up quite a bit of ash and smoke. "There was an accident, but I'm fine. I need you to get the army ready."

"Vhaal gave us until noon. I've got scouts out, if he tries anything we'll see him coming."

"We may not have till noon, if this goes badly. Get everyone up *now* and formed in ranks as soon as you can."

"I . . ." He caught her expression. "As you like. Anything else?"

"I've got to find Yahvy."

"She's still asleep, as far as I know."

"Thanks!" Sylph was already running, leaving the cavalry-man scratching his head behind her. Yahvy's tent wasn't far, and Sylph pulled up short outside the closed flap.

"Yahvy? Are you up?"

"Wait," came the voice from inside. A moment later Yahvy opened the flap, still in her nightshirt. "Sylph?"

Sylph blinked and stared levelly. "That . . . that's really un-pleasant-looking."

"Oh." One of Yahvy's hands went to her cheek. Sylph had never seen it without the bandages; it was a mess of raw, red flesh, with just a hint of ivory bone and teeth peeking through. Yahvy retreated back into the darkness. "Sorry. Forgot."

"It's okay. You just surprised me."

"Thought the battle was later?"

"I'm hoping there won't be one. I need a third person. Her-aan's coming already, and—"

"Let me dress."

Sylph smiled. "Don't you want to know what we're doing?"

"Something clever. Right?"

"Right."

"Be right out."

A few minutes later they were jogging back to the outskirts, where Heraan was waiting with the horses. He still had some-thing of a dazed look, either from lack of sleep or because he still couldn't believe what he'd been talked into doing. *Not that he required much talking.* Sylph looked from him to Yahvy. *They must really trust me. I wonder how that happened?*

They saddled and mounted in silence, and Sylph led the way after exchanging greetings with Marlowe's outlying pickets. East, toward the city and the barbarian lines. Once they were away from the camp, Yahvy said, "So what's going to happen?"

"I talked to Saar," Sylph said. "She thinks a lot of the Steel-breakers are unhappy with Vhaal—"

"—everyone is—" Yahvy muttered.

"—and that means that if we can convince them they should find a new leader, we might be able to get out of fighting them entirely. They're all here because of him."

"He really wants to marry you?" said Heraan.

"Sort of." Sylph shook her head. "He thinks that if I marry him he'll be able to use me to control the Liberator's army."

"Lina listens to you," Yahvy mused. "Don't think you'd obey orders, even married."

"Some women might," Heraan said. "Maybe that's how it works for the Steelbreakers."

"In any case," Sylph continued, "I don't want to marry him, so I'm going to kill him."

"Good." Yahvy half-smiled. "About time someone did."

Heraan rolled his eyes. "Wait until you hear how."

"How?"

Sylph shot Yahvy a sly grin. "I'm going to challenge him to single combat."

"That's crazy!" Yahvy said. "Vhaal's good. Very good. You saw—"

"I know. Trust me."

"Not many other options," Heraan muttered. "It's magic. I'm not sure I like it."

"It's not really magic." *But it's too complicated to explain.*

A pair of barbarian riders, both women, had seen them coming and rode up with short-bows at the ready. One of them recognized Sylph—*apparently my description has been circulated*—and lowered her weapon when none of the three made a move for theirs.

"What do you want?" she said.

"To talk to the Steelbreaker, of course." Sylph struggled to maintain her smile. "As you can see, we've placed ourselves in your power."

The woman nodded. "He's been expecting you. Follow me."

✷   ✷   ✷

LINA'S BODY OPENED ITS EYES, BUT THERE WAS ANOTHER being peering through them. Rahmgoth blinked, trying to re-member how to focus.

I . . . He closed his eyes again, feeling the steady *thump-thump* of the girl's heart and savoring the body's myriad tiny move-ments. *I am alive.*

There are some things you don't miss until they're gone. Having a heartbeat was one of them. The sheer comfort of the sound, with its constant reminder of continued existence, and the blood that sloshed around the body in waves. Alone in the Pit, there were times when he'd wondered if he'd finally achieved oblivion and hadn't noticed, his thoughts chasing themselves round in ever-smaller circles. *I was mad.* That hadn't taken long; months, maybe years, since there was no way of knowing how much time had passed. As the decades wore into centuries, and the centu-ries into millennia, Rahmgoth had achieved a kind of discipline; passed through madness and into perfect clarity.

There are always constants, and patience is always rewarded. He opened his new eyes again and saw the roof of a tent, patchy and bright in the morning sun. He couldn't move—the body's limbs felt as though they were made of solid steel—but that would come, in time. *All I need is power.*

Rahmgoth smiled to himself.

VHAAL HAD JUST FINISHED DRESSING WHEN THEY ARRIVED, dismounted and accompanied by two dozen armed tribesmen.

The hide tents of the Steelbreaker encampment seemed to stretch for miles in every direction. Vhaal's was huge, elaborate-ly decorated with woven cloth and painted fabric. Dressed in his tight-fitting blacks amidst the barbarians in leather, he looked like he was from another world.

"I thought you would come to see me," he said as they

approached, "so I took the liberty of being prepared." He took his swords from a waiting attendant and buckled them around his waist. "It's good to see you again, Yahvy. I wouldn't have thought it possible for your appearance to have improved, but I see someone managed."

The half-smile Yahvy gave him in return was dangerous, but she said nothing.

"And Heraan too. Still taking orders from a little girl, I see."

"Vhaal," said Sylph patiently.

"You've returned," he said, "before the deadline expired. So I can only assume you mean to agree to my request?"

"Not exactly." Sylph took a deep breath. This was the part Saar had coached her on. "You want me to do as you say, you said it yourself. You want a servant, not a wife."

He gave her a lazy smile. "And if I do?"

"Then I take offense." She pointed. "I challenge you, as is my right."

Vhaal's eyes narrowed. "You challenge me as a Steel-breaker, then?"

"If you like." She watched him carefully.

"And you know the rules?"

"We fight until one of us dies, gives up, or is rendered unconscious. In the latter two cases, the loser becomes slave to the winner."

"If you lose, you won't even be my wife, you'll be nothing. Do you understand?"

"I do."

"And still you challenge me?"

"Yes."

There was a murmur from the tribesmen. News was spreading fast, and Sylph could see the crowd growing. She kept her eyes forward.

Vhaal shook his head. "You're a Magus. It's not allowed—no magic is permitted."

"We're inside Lady Fell's Circle. No Magus can draw power

without her permission, which I certainly don't have. And . . ." Sylph pulled the geist from her pocket. "You know what this is?"

He did, she could tell. He watched it hungrily. *It represents the accumulated power of Gargorian, over six hundred years; even if he's not a Magus, he can auction the stored energy to the highest bidder.*

Slowly, Sylph rolled the smooth metal ball in her fingers. Then with a sudden motion she tossed it to Yahvy, who caught it and tucked it into her pocket.

"No magic, Vhaal."

He closed his eyes. "As you wish. You may choose your own weapon."

"I already have."

"Then clear us a circle." He gestured at the tribesmen, who hurried to mark out the bounds of a dueling area. Sylph could hear a dozen muttered conversations; she was trying to listen in when Vhaal stepped close to whisper in her ear.

"I don't know what you're playing at," he growled, "but it won't win you anything. I would have made you my queen. Now, if you're lucky, I'll kill you."

"If I'm lucky," Sylph said, "I'll kill *you*."

Vhaal sneered and stalked to the dueling circle. Sylph followed, with Heraan and Yahvy close behind her; Yahvy's expression was unreadable, but Heraan looked from face to unfriendly face with increasing anxiety. Sylph wanted to whisper something comforting, but there wasn't time and she wasn't sure he had the wrong idea in any case. She took a deep breath and found that it didn't help much.

Once he reached his end of the circle, Vhaal spun and drew his swords with a flourish. Sylph's position, as indicated by the onlookers, was about thirty feet away. *Perfect.* Her hands were sweating, and she wiped them on her shirt. *We're only going to get one shot.*

"No sword?" Vhaal said. "I don't understand. Would it really have been so bad?"

He thinks I'm killing myself. She wanted to laugh. "Probably."

"I would have been kind to you." His smile glittered, like ice in the sun.

"I doubt it."

Vhaal shot a glance at one of the older tribesmen, who'd pushed his way to the edge of the circle and seemed like he planned to act as referee. The man turned to Sylph and said gently, "Are you ready?"

"Absolutely. Get on with it."

"Very well." He stepped back. "Begin."

Vhaal took his time, practically sauntering forward. *After all, I'm not even armed, and he's the best swordsman I've ever seen.* She reached to the small of her back, drew her pistol, and aimed.

He stopped, still smiling. "And what is that supposed to do?"

Sylph pulled the trigger. The gun almost jumped from her hands, but Vhaal flew back as though he'd been kicked in the chest by a horse. She'd been expecting the sound, and even so it was startling; the assembled tribesmen flinched *en masse.* Several looked up as though they expected to see lightning to match the thunder. Once the echoes faded away, there was a moment of silence, broken only by Vhaal's feeble scrabbling.

"Magic!" A young woman burst from the crowd, her bow leveled at Sylph's chest. "He was struck down by magic!"

Another god-awful bang and she staggered back a step, dropping the bow and clutching her chest. Blood welled in a massive gush, and the barbarian fell to her knees, then full-length on the ground. She didn't move. Heraan had his own pistol drawn, held in two hands like Sylph had taught him, with the tiniest curl of smoke rising from its barrel.

And let's hope that's all, because I'm not sure how well these work as repeaters. It was simple enough in theory, particularly when she was free to work with components made of solid diamond or other exotic materials that could be as strong as required, and springs that would bear the harshest loads without complaint. The hardest part had been the powder, and getting the rifling right on the barrels. *Only because I'm an idiot. I should have been working on this weeks ago. Got stuck thinking in medieval terms.* She was aware that her thoughts were wandering; she was waiting for the Steelbreakers to decide if they were going to live or die. *Even if the gun works perfectly, we'll never stop them all.*

The old man, who'd officiated the duel, took a step forward. "He . . . is also a Magus?"

"Me?" Heraan snorted. "I'm no—"

"He is not," Sylph cut in.

"Then how?"

"Not magic." She began to feel a sliver of hope. "This is a weapon, a new weapon. Vhaal said I could choose."

"I heard," he said. "We all heard."

"Is he dead?" she asked.

One of the younger tribesmen, who'd rushed to his master's side, looked at her and nodded.

"Then the business of the Steelbreakers in this land is concluded. I would not have you as enemies if it could be avoided; my quarrel, and my sister's, is with Lady Fell. So now my friends and I will return to my army, and at noon we will march on Stonerings. I respectfully suggest that you get out of the way."

It was the hardest thing in the world to turn her back on all those spears and bows, but somehow she managed. Heraan gave the old man a last look and followed, gently towing a stunned Yahvy by one hand.

"Kill her!" someone shouted. "Kill her, and take her weapon!"

Sylph held out her hand to Yahvy, who handed the geist back. As her fingers closed on the little marble, Sylph let the tiniest fraction of its power bleed through and crackle like heat lightning in the air. She had the pistol in her other hand as she turned, putting on her best evil grin.

"You're welcome to try."

After that the barbarians parted like the Red Sea, and in another minute the trio was saddled up and riding back toward their own lines. Sylph let out a long breath and slumped back in the saddle, and Heraan leaned closer anxiously.

"Are you okay?"

"Fine." She closed her eyes for a moment. "I just can't believe that worked."

"Me either," said Yahvy. "Might have warned me."

"Sorry." Sylph giggled. "I think I have a flair for the dramatic."

"Terrible flaw." Yahvy shook her head.

"You should have seen Heraan when I showed him how it worked and told him I wanted him to fire one."

Heraan rolled his eyes.

"Really not magic?" Yahvy asked.

Sylph shook her head. "I used the geist to manufacture it, but after that . . . no. Just steel and brass, a little bit of diamond, and some chemicals."

"This thing," Yahvy nodded at the gun, "also common where you come from?"

"We call it a pistol, and yes."

"Will it work for me?" There was an eager gleam in Yahvy's eyes.

"It'll work for anyone."

"Show me?"

*　　*　　*

THE TENT FLAP RUSTLED, AND RAHMGOTH OPENED HIS EYES again. He could hear someone moving about, and managed to turn his head enough to catch a glimpse—*Fah*. He'd watched her, through Lina's eyes. Her faith in the Liberator burned like a driven flame. *Fah*, he thought again, and ran his tongue across dry lips. *Fah*.

Fah set a bowl of honeyed water down on a bedside table and sat on a stool beside Lina's bed. She started to talk, not expecting anyone to hear, and her tone was bright.

"She did it! Sylph, that is. I don't know how . . . I heard she and Vhaal had a duel, and she beat him somehow. But he's dead, or run off, and the Steelbreakers are going to let us into the city. Lady Fell must be furious." Fah leaned closer, a water-soaked cloth in her hands. Carefully, she dribbled a stream of sweet water between Lina's lips. Rahmgoth savored every drop. *It has been so long.* The sensation was almost too much for him, after an eternity of empty darkness.

"We're really going to do it," Fah continued. "There's noth-ing to stop us now. Nobody doubts that you're the Liberator, and the stories are already spreading. The army will be twice as big after Stonerings as before, you'll see." She squeezed the cloth again. "Once you wake up, the world is yours."

The world is mine. Rahmgoth wanted to laugh. *I don't need the world.*

"Lina." Fah shook her head. "Why won't you wake up? Don't you want to come back?" She leaned closer still. "We *need* you. I need you . . ."

The lure of warm flesh—of sensation, in the raw—so close was too much for Rahmgoth to resist. He reached one arm around Fah's shoulders and pulled her close; she managed a sur-prised squeak before Rahmgoth pressed his lips against hers, drinking in the scent of her and the rasp of her teeth against his tongue. Fah resisted only a moment, and it was a long time be-fore she pulled away.

"L . . . Lina?" she said, eventually.

Rahmgoth nodded, not trusting himself to speak. Fah sat back a little, and he managed to pull himself into a sitting posi-tion as well.

"You're awake. You're awake! You . . ."

"Shhh." Rahmgoth put a finger to his lips. "Please."

"Sorry." Fah's eyes went wide. "I'm sorry! For kissing you, I mean . . . I didn't mean to . . ."

"Fah," Rahmgoth said. "You wanted to, didn't you?"

Fah lowered her eyes. "Yes," she said, so quietly it was prac-tically inaudible. "I wanted to. Almost since I met you. After Safael died, I was so lonely. There was no one I could . . . touch."

She looked up again. "But I didn't think you understood. You and Marlowe . . ."

"I understand." Rahmgoth leaned toward her, but to his surprise Fah backed away.

"I can't. You're the Liberator . . . you have everyone to think about. I can't let you do something like this, just for me."

"It's not for you." *It's for me. For six thousand years in the Pit.* "I also need someone . . . to touch."

"But . . ." Fah's objection was only partially voiced. When Rahmgoth leaned forward, she kissed him eagerly, pressing herself against Lina's body as though desperate for warmth. The sensations this engendered were strange; he tugged the blanket from between them and found himself dressed in nothing more than a nightshirt. Fah pulled herself onto the bed, sitting in Rahmgoth's lap with her arms wrapped tightly around him and her breasts squashed against Lina's. She was already dressed for battle, and the hard leather belt and buckle pressed painfully into Rahmgoth's thigh, but that too was sensation to be savored. He felt Fah's heart beating against his own, felt the power of her soul that was barely contained by her flesh.

"Lina," Fah murmured. "I love you."

"I know," said Rahmgoth, and kissed her again. He ran his hands down her back, across the uncured leather, until he came to her belt. Fah shifted, wrapping her legs around Rahmgoth's midsection and squeezing. Her breath came short and fast.

Rahmgoth ran his hand along her belt, past the tied pouches and the buckles, until he found the sheath for her dagger. She didn't notice when he drew it, running his other hand lovingly along the bumps of her spine until he found just the right spot. Fah shivered deliciously and pulled her lips from his, just as Rahmgoth plunged the razor-sharp stiletto between her shoulder blades. The girl gasped.

"Lina . . ." The word caught in her throat. "I . . . love . . ."

Rahmgoth put his hand behind her head and kissed her again, his tongue dancing with hers. Her legs squeezed him tightly, and shivers ran up and down her body; her hips bucked, suddenly, and then again before subsiding. Her arms, wrapped behind his back, raked bloody trails across his shoulders before falling limply to her sides. Rahmgoth tasted the pain and reveled.

A last shiver, a last breath passing from her mouth to his, and Fah went limp. He let her go, and she slumped backward nervelessly onto the bed; he rolled her over carefully and removed the dagger, which was coated in blood. Delicately, he brought it to his lips and ran his tongue along the length, tasting the salty sweetness. Power flowed through him.

Some things remain constant. Like blood.

LEILA HAD TURNED THE CHAMBER JUST INSIDE THE MAIN aboveground hall of the Stonerings citadel into her war room. She'd spread a map of the city on a hastily assembled table, and attendants were busy marking it with slips of paper. Leila glanced at their progress from time to time, but for the most part she knew what was being written. *In substance, as least. Not enough of us, too many of them.*

She had perhaps five hundred soldiers at her disposal, the dregs of Lady Fell's army, men too infirm to march on the campaigns, men who'd served loyally and were given garrison duty as a sinecure, along a smattering of survivors who'd returned after the defeats. And their numbers were getting fewer all the time. Everyone knew the battle was a foregone conclusion, and one by one the soldiers had the bright idea of throwing off their colors and melting back into the crowds. *After all, they say this Lina forbids rape and despises pillaging. She may keep her men in line.* Leila had her doubts—she'd seen what victorious armies did to captured cities—and her immediate future, even if she survived, was not likely to be pleasant. But she was a soldier first and foremost, so she pushed that to the back of her mind and concentrated on the moment.

And, at the moment, she was faced with a decision. *If we abandon the outer wall and the outlying districts, I can pull enough men back to the citadel walls to make a fight of it.* The alternative was to stay on the outer walls as long as they were viable and then retreat through the city fighting house-to-house. *We won't have enough left to hold the citadel once we get here, but we can make them pay a high price.*

She was still considering when the inner doors opened, revealing Lady Fell and a pair of her private guards. They were big, silent brutes in black leather and mail, all nearly identical and absolutely loyal to the Archmagus's orders. *We could use them on the walls.* But, of course, Lady Fell refused to release any of them.

"Leila," she said. "How goes the deployment?"

"As well as can be expected. My lady," said Leila, "I respectfully suggest that it may be time for some sort of negotiations."

"Negotiations!" The Archmagus's voice was shrill. "Have they made offers to negotiate?"

"No, but I'm sure—"

"Nor will they! She wants me dead, Leila, just like the others. That's the only thing that will satisfy them."

"Yes, my lady." Leila knew when not to push her luck.

"All I need is time, a little more time. You and your men *will* hold, do you understand? If Lina comes knocking on my door I expect to find you dead at her feet. Nothing else is acceptable!"

"Of course, my lady."

"Good." Lady Fell cast about for a moment, then said, "I return to my preparations."

Leila watched her go. Once the doors had closed, she turned to Vicarl, her immediate subordinate. He was a deceptively boyish-looking man whose sleepy eyes held a vicious intelligence; more to the point, Leila knew he was no fanatic. He caught her eye, and she beckoned him into a corner.

"Give the order to change the deployment," she said without preamble. "We'll make our stand at the citadel."

"Respectfully," he murmured, "the Archmagus asked for time. I think we would keep them away longer if they had to fight their way through the city streets."

"Stonerings falls today," Leila said. "An hour or two, either way, is not going to make much of a difference. If we fight at the citadel, we can minimize civilian casualties."

There was a long moment while he considered, but Vicarl finally nodded. "As you wish."

She watched him go. Minimizing civilian casualties was certainly a laudable goal, but it wasn't the only reason for her decision. *If we make our stand here, it should be easy to surrender once the walls are breached.* The Archmagus wouldn't like that. But Leila was, first and foremost, a soldier; her duty was not only to Lady Fell but to the men under her command. *They didn't ask to be here, and I won't have them slaughtered to no purpose.*

Thus resolved, she turned back to the maps. *Who knows? Maybe the Steelbreakers will decide to fight after all.*

THE TENT FLAP RUSTLED AGAIN, AND RAHMGOTH LOOKED up in a sudden panic. The flood of power he'd stolen from Fah's soul had shed light on parts of his mind that had lain quiescent for centuries, and he'd been engaged in trying to put himself back together. Now he realized he was alone in the tent with a dead girl on his bed, a situation which could prove difficult to explain.

Before he could do anything, however, a man entered. Rahmgoth didn't recognize him until he spoke; it was a voice that had haunted him, tortured him, and brought him back from beyond the brink of madness in order to exact his revenge.

"I see you've awoken," the man said.

"Rathmado," Rahmgoth growled. "You don't look like I expected you to."

"And what were you expecting?" said the Magus, with a

pleasant smile.

"Something more . . . imperious."

"I'm sorry to disappoint." Rathmado made a slight bow. "It's a pleasure to finally meet you."

"The pleasure is mine, to be certain."

"However . . ." He flicked his eyes to the corpse.

Rahmgoth grunted. "She was here when I awoke. After so long . . ."

"I understand. But you'll be more . . . discreet . . . in the future, yes?"

He nodded. Being chastened by a mortal—Magus or no—would once have sent Rahmgoth into a rage. But six thousand years had altered his priorities. *Revenge, first and foremost.* Rathmado had delivered him from unending damnation, and Rathmado promised that vengeance would be forthcoming. *So I do as he asks, until the day he decides to betray me.*

"The body is suitable?"

"Yes," Rahmgoth said. He put a hand on one of Lina's breasts and let it bounce. "Odd, but suitable."

"Good. We've discussed what you are to do."

"Maintain the ruse, that I am this Liberator?"

"Yes."

"We have discussed it." Rahmgoth shook his head. "What I don't understand is why. We know where he is; why not go there directly?"

"All in good time, my friend." Rathmado smiled. "He has had a long time to prepare, and his defenses are not inconsiderable. We must gather all the power we can."

"As you say." Rahmgoth sat back down on the bed, suddenly weary. The motion made Fah's head loll, her empty eyes staring at the ceiling.

"Did you observe Lina long enough to learn what you need?"

"Most likely." He shrugged. "These mortals practically worship the girl. I doubt they'll notice anything."

"Probably not," the Magus agreed. "But to be on the safe

side, try to stay away from Sylph. She'll be the most difficult to fool."

"Sylph." Rahmgoth licked his lips. "There's power there."

"Stay away from her," Rathmado snapped. "We need her, for the moment."

"As you say."

Rathmado glanced back at the tent flap. "I believe they are coming to see you. I'll take care of the mess, this time, but remember what I said about being discreet."

"I remember," Rahmgoth said. "I'm not a child, Magus."

"Of course not," Rathmado said soothingly. "Let me take my leave."

There was a swirl of golden light and the crackle and spit of magic, and both Magus and body vanished. Thankfully, only a few drops of blood had stained the bed sheets; Rahmgoth leaned back and settled in to await his followers.

∗   ∗   ∗

MARLOWE'S OUTRIDERS HAD FOLLOWED SYLPH IN, SO THE cavalryman was waiting on the edge of the camp when the trio dismounted.

"What happened?"

"Vhaal's dead, and I don't think the Steelbreakers are going to get in our way," said Sylph.

"You don't *think*? We're taking an awful risk."

"I know, but I don't think we'll get a better shot at this. They're confused, now; if we let them regroup who knows what they'll do. Get the army moving. I want us in bowshot of the walls in an hour."

The cavalryman snapped to attention. "As you wish!"

Sylph smiled. "What about Lina? Any change?"

"I haven't checked recently, it's been chaotic around here."

He was cut off by a cheer from inside the camp, a sound that began as a distant murmur but built and built until it became a roar. The carefully ordered ranks were dissolving, soldiers breaking into a run and joining the mob that trailed like a comet's tail behind its leader. Sylph had only a moment to gape before it was on top of them.

Lina was in the lead, dressed in her old leather-and-mail with the sword swinging at her side. Myris, Fah's second-in-command, followed a step behind her; there was no sign of the Fah herself.

"Lina!" Sylph had to jog to keep ahead of the crowd. "You're awake! Are you okay?"

Lina gave her a broad smile. "Fine, Sylph. I'm fine."

"But . . . should you be up like this?"

"I'm better than fine. I feel great. Had a nice long nap."

"A *nap*?" Sylph cast about for Marlowe or Heraan, but they'd gotten separated in the press of cheering soldiers. She saw Yahvy a little ways away, shouting a group of her pike-men into a rough square. "Lina, what are you *doing*? We can't just charge the walls like this, we'll get slaughtered at the gate . . . damn it . . ." *She's crazy!*

Lina stopped for a moment and put an arm around Sylph's shoulder, pulling her surprised sister in a momentary embrace. "I don't think Lady Fell herself could stop me right now."

"But . . ."

"Just trust me, all right?"

Sylph didn't have much choice; she could keep up with the press or be swept aside. So she jogged along with Lina, watching the walls come closer and fighting off visions of enfilades—*or boiling oil, or rocks, or worse.*

At least the Steelbreakers were not moving to engage. The army-turned-mob was paced by a few of the barbarian horsemen, but that seemed to be out of curiosity more than anything else. The great mass of tribesmen had withdrawn, leaving a clear path to the main gatehouse which loomed above the great stone wall like a fortress in and of itself. The gate was sealed tight, a twenty-foot monster of wood and banded iron.

Sylph tugged on Lina's shoulder. "We're going to need a battering ram. Siege ladders. Even if they're not shooting at us . . ." *And I can't think why.* There had been soldiers on the walls earlier, but none were in evidence now; not a single arrow or bolt lofted toward the attacking army. The Liberator's soldiers piled up around the walls, leaving Sylph and Lina a clear path to the gate. Lina strode forward, unhesitatingly, and Sylph hurried to keep up.

"Lina, what are you going to *do*?"

Lina chuckled. "I'll pull the walls down with my bare hands if I have to. But . . ." Her hand dropped to her sword. "I don't think that will be necessary. Stand back for a moment, would you?"

Sylph took a long step back, and motioned for everyone else to do the same. Lina took a deep breath, drew the sword, and concentrated; tiny tongues of white flame ran across her body in a torrent, beginning from where her hands held the steel and expanding into a nimbus of power. She lowered the blade as though sighting along its length, and the fire lashed out like a closed fist, punching a hole in the center of the gate. Wood and iron flashed to vapor, and the rest of the massive door shattered into splinters and shards. The entire gatehouse shook, and the troops at its base were pelted by a hail of small stones and loose mortar.

Oh, Sylph thought.

When the dust started to clear, Lina stood triumphant amidst the ruined entryway, the main street of Stonerings visible behind her. It was a clear run up to the looming bulk of the citadel at the center of the city; the street had been cleared of civilians, though Sylph could see a number of curious onlookers hurriedly closing and bolting their shutters.

The army was silent for a shocked moment. Then someone raised a cry.

"The Liberator!"

And the sound became a roar, a *sea* of noise. Lina flicked her blade at the city and the army poured through the breach, advancing up the main road and spreading out through the close-packed alleys. Lina herself followed, surrounded by a kind of bubble of awed troops not willing to get too close.

"Sylph!"

Hearing her name called at close quarters shook Sylph from her daze. She looked up to find Yahvy, Heraan, and a double handful of pike-men they'd managed to corral.

"Sylph," said Yahvy again. "What are we doing?"

Sylph closed her eyes and tried to think. *Think. Come on.* "We have to get to the citadel; I have to get to the geist. Obviously Lina's got—something—maybe she finally mastered her sword. But with the geist behind her the Archmagus has got to have a few nasty tricks up her sleeve."

"What makes you think we can stop her?" said Heraan.

"Because I have this." She produced the geist from her pocket. "Best chance we've got, anyway."

"The citadel," Yahvy agreed. "But it has gates too. Problem?"

"I think," said Sylph, "not for very much longer."

✳   ✳   ✳

A COLUMN OF SMOKE WAS RISING FROM THE MAIN GATE, and as far as Leila could tell from her vantage the walls hadn't slowed the Liberator's army at all. *Good thing we didn't make our stand there.* Though the ease with which they'd penetrated was worrisome. *Magic, maybe? That could get bad.*

The citadel covered a much smaller area: a simple circular wall, with two towers flanking the gate. Behind that was the keep, which was really just a barracks, since most of Lady Fell's personal chambers were underground. Its defenses were minimal, so Leila had concentrated her men around the two towers and along the facing wall. The enemy would be eager to get to grips—any sane commander would, in the midst of a hostile city—and Leila doubted they would spend the time to circle and probe for a weak spot.

Her instincts were apparently dead on. She could see a tight knot of men—commanders, presumably—advancing at the head of a vast mob of flashing pikes. Apparently they'd lost their discipline in the rush through the outer walls. *Good for us, anyway.* Another minute would bring them into bowshot, and the scattered enemy bowmen wouldn't be able to put together effective return volleys. *For an army that's conquered half the world, they don't seem very bright.*

She nodded to the commander of archers on the left-hand tower and hopped down the spiral stairs two at a time. The bulk of her infantry was formed up in squares in the main court-yard. Judging by what had happened at the city wall, the assault would come through the main gate; a determined counterattack against that limited front was her best chance of buying time.

And, though she hardly dared think it, it was the one chance she had of winning the battle outright. *If this so-called Liberator is foolish enough to lead from the front, and she should happen to go down in battle . . .*

"Fire!" came two screams, almost simultaneously. The ar-chers on the walls loosed as one, a cloud of shafts arcing high before rattling down amid the enemy. The arrows were pitifully few, and while enemy soldiers fell they weren't nearly enough, like fly bites on the hide of a great beast. The Liberator's army surged forward, and closed the distance with the gate in the time it took to fire two more volleys.

Leila had joined the infantry, finding some comfort in positioning herself behind a solid shield wall. *As solid as we've got, anyway.* A number of the men in front of her had seen too many summers, or not enough. They were arrayed facing the gate, and more archers waited on either side to catch whoever first stormed through in a deadly enfilade. Another *thrum* from the towers—*now there's nothing to do but wait, until they break the gate down*—

She'd been expecting a battering ram, or maybe even some sort of magic; Lady Fell could have taken the gate down by working on the hinges, altering the iron until it would no longer bear the weight of the wood. Either way they would have fallen gradually; instead, half the wooden planks vanished in a spray of dust and splinters while the others sprayed into the keep like so many matchsticks. A ten-foot timber skipped end over end before crashing into the formation of infantry, crushing a half-dozen men. Dust and smoke billowed outward, obscuring vision; from the sound of it, her archers had barely gotten off a shot before the enemy infantry swarmed through the gates and slaughtered them. Screams and the rasp of diamond on steel filled the courtyard.

This is hopeless. Leila shook her head and pushed her way toward the front of the unit. *We can't stand against power like that. This isn't a battle, it's a massacre. Lady Fell . . . no one could fault me for surrendering now. I can't just let my men die for nothing.*

"Leila!" shouted someone from behind her, but she didn't stop. She pressed through the last rank and motioned frantically to the unit captain to stay put, then walked out alone toward the slowly spreading smoke. There were figures visible, just reaching the edge; the first to emerge was a girl, younger than Leila and clad only in leather and chain. She had a naked blade in one hand and a vicious smile on her lips.

"I'm the commander of the garrison here," Leila shouted as the girl approached. "It is enough; we wish to negotiate terms of surrender . . ."

This last was cut off when as the girl strode forward without pause and jammed her sword to the hilt in Leila's gut. Dimly, Leila felt pain and the hot gush of blood; her legs gave way, and she was suddenly falling forward.

My men . . . she can't . . .

She heard the girl shout, before a gout of white fire crackled up the sword and reduced Leila's body to ash.

"*Kill them all!*"

✳   ✳   ✳

"Lina!" Sylph and her followers had waited for the smoke to clear before moving into the citadel. By the time they got through, the courtyard was clear of living foes and covered with drifts of bodies, both Lady Fell's soldiers and her own. The sounds of combat came from the flanking towers, and from around the sides of the keep.

"Some of them were trying to retreat," Lina explained. "And the archers have barricaded themselves in the tower. We'll take care of them."

"Good. I'm surprised they decided to make a fight of it."

"Me too." Lina jerked her head toward the keep. "Is that next?"

"Yes, but let me go in first. If Lady Fell's down there, I need to deal with her."

Lina hesitated a moment, then nodded. "Of course. We took the entryway—some of them tried to retreat that way too—but nobody's gone inside."

"Good." Sylph gestured to Yahvy, who motioned her block of pike-men forward. "We'll be back soon."

"I know you will." Lina smiled, a sight which made Sylph infinitely happier. *It feels like she's been asleep for ages.* "I'll have things settled out here by then."

"Right."

Lina turned on her heel and headed for one of the towers, while Sylph and Heraan hurried to catch up with Yahvy. Her men had stacked their pikes outside the entrance, since they weren't much use in close quarters, and drawn short-swords. They slipped in through the wrecked doors, and Yahvy poked her head out to motion Sylph and Heraan forward a moment later.

Inside was a wide corridor, lit by a few remaining torches. Side passages forked off at intervals, but Sylph kept the group heading straight until the corridor dead-ended at a switchback staircase, leading down. There was still no one in evidence.

"What do you think?" said Heraan. "Down there?"

"I guessed as much. This building isn't big enough above-ground to be much of a palace."

"Could be a maze," Yahvy mused. "Could hold out a long time."

"Only one way to find out."

Yahvy nodded and gestured her men forward, with Sylph and Heraan just behind the vanguard in a box of drawn steel. They descended three flights before reaching a vaulted chamber, also lit by torches, that had a corridor in the center of each wall.

"This is what I was worried about," sighed Heraan. "I doubt Lady Fell designed this place for us to find our way around."

"Could be another way out," said Yahvy. "Secret passage."

"Shhh." Sylph closed her eyes. "One moment."

She reached out, deliberately blocking out the feeling from the geist in her pocket. Lady Fell's Circles were a definite presence—a faint one, since their power was locked away, but this close to the geist she felt them. *And Lady Fell's geist has to be at the exact center of the Circle, gathering power. It means she's still here too; she wouldn't abandon the geist. So we need to go . . .*

"That way." Sylph pointed to one of the corridors.

"Sure?" said Yahvy.

"Reasonably. I can feel the center of Lady Fell's power."

"Any idea if she can feel you too?"

"Good question," said Sylph. "I have to assume she can."

"Waiting for us, then." Yahvy smiled. "Ah, well."

They threaded their way down that corridor, and through a few more branches; each time Sylph closed her eyes and felt her way forward. Floor, wall, and ceiling were all the same bare stone; the tunnel system had dug into the bedrock like the roots of some monstrous plant.

The feel of the geist was definitely getting stronger, de-spite the twists and turns they'd taken. Eventually, the corridor straightened and widened into a room, and Yahvy's soldiers proceeded cautiously inside. Two of them ducked through the doorway, and another pair stood guarding Sylph while the rest waited behind.

"Looks like there's some kind of a pit," one man reported. "It goes all the way across the room. Let me see how deep it is—"

He was cut off by a deep double-*thrum*. Bolts flashed across the room, pinning one soldier to the stone wall like a butterfly. The other took the bolt in the shoulder and lost his footing; Sylph saw his torch disappear into the pit, but it was three or four seconds before a distant *thud* indicated he'd hit the bottom.

She could see the near half of the room, illuminated by the soldier's dropped torch. The shots had come from the far half, still shrouded in gloom. Yahvy's men surged forward to protect their leaders, but had to pause at the doorway—more *thrums*, and one soldier groaned and collapsed. A bolt struck the wall nearby and clattered off, raising sparks.

"Get rid of the damn lights!" shouted Heraan.

They flung their torches across the gap, trying to reach the opposite side of the room, but all the flames vanished into the pit. Without them it was utterly dark. Another pair of bolts reached out, and someone muttered a curse, but after that there was silence.

Damn.

"Quick thinking," said Yahvy from beside Sylph.

"Only natural if they know we're coming," Heraan whispered. "Probably four men on the other side of the pit; two to fire, two to load. Those are heavy crossbows. They sit in the dark and wait for us to make ourselves targets."

Sylph nodded, realized he couldn't see, and said, "Yeah. So now what?"

"Sylph, can you make a light?"

"Yes." *Easy enough. Just give some air enough of a kick that it glows.*

"Good." Heraan touched her shoulder. "You take the left side, I take the right. After fifty heartbeats, make a light and shoot. If you miss don't just stand around unless you want to get skewered, understand?"

Heraan's plan unfolded in Sylph's head. "Right."

"Ready?"

"Go."

Sylph put her hand out to touch the left wall and followed it toward the doorway. Halfway there she stepped on one of the men who'd fallen; something squished, and he made no sound. She swallowed and edged past him, around the corner and into the room just short of the pit. Once there she drew her pistol and waited, counting heartbeats.

Thirty-one, thirty-two . . .

The last of the torches had guttered out, and the darkness was absolute. Sylph closed her eyes, then opened them, and it didn't make a bit of difference. She was reminded of her arrival on Omega, stuck in a shallow cave with her mind still reeling from a car accident. It felt like another lifetime.

Forty-eight, forty-nine, fifty.

She reached out to the geist and let power flow from her hand, infusing the air until it turned cherry red, then tossed it across the chasm. It wasn't much, but it cast long shadows, enough to see two figures kneeling and two more behind them. At the same time, Sylph took a long step to her right and brought her gun to bear. She fired twice at the figure on the left, recoil jamming the weapon painfully against her palm. At almost the same time two crossbow bolts passed through the space where she'd been standing, bouncing off the rock with a clatter. Another roar and flash from the other side of the room marked Heraan's position. Both kneeling figures sprawled backward, and Sylph saw the other two beating a hasty retreat.

She kept the power flowing, and the light gradually strengthened until they could all see again. The room was square and bisected by a chasm that ran from wall to wall. On the other side were two men in black uniforms, one lying motionless and the other curled up and shaking. A door on the opposite wall matched the doorway where they'd come in.

"Nice shooting," said Heraan.

"Likewise."

"Want one of those," said Yahvy.

"I'll make you one as soon as we're done here and I get some sleep." Sylph put her hand in her pocket, touching the geist, and concentrated; carbon coalesced out of the air into a neat matrix, and a diamond bridge assembled itself. One of the soldiers who'd been hit was still alive, and Yahvy detailed another man to carry him back to the surface. The rest crossed with Sylph and Heraan.

"They're going to be waiting for us behind this door too," said Heraan.

"Likely," said Yahvy.

"Let's hope they don't have a whole stockpile of bows down here," said Sylph. "Stay out of the way." She brushed her hand against the hinges; she didn't bother with a change in composition this time, just a big chunk of power dumped into each one so that they glowed and started to lose their shape. Heraan gave the door a solid kick and it flew inward, scattering droplets of molten metal and crashing into a black-uniformed figure who'd been waiting just behind it. Behind him were a half-dozen more. There were no bows in evidence, but all six had drawn swords.

Yahvy's men poured through the door before the guards could move up, and there was a short, brutal swordfight. By the end all the black-uniformed guards were down, along with three of Yahvy's men. The rest spread out, cautiously, and Sylph advanced the light into the chamber so they could see what they were doing. She had to stifle a gasp of surprise.

"What in the name of the White Lady . . . ?" Heraan breathed.

The chamber they'd entered was huge. A darkened lower level, thirty feet or more below where Sylph stood, was criss-crossed at regular intervals by arched bridges, forming a grid. Each intersection was furnished with a dim brazier, so a pattern of faint lights extended out into the darkness.

A movement caught her eye; she saw something big and silver scuttling from one arch to another down below. A moment later another creature jumped on it from hiding; there was a screech like the sound of a monster bird, and one of the two moved on carrying pieces of the other in its jaws.

"Odd," said Yahvy after a moment.

That's an understatement. But Sylph knew what she was looking at, thanks to her earlier vivisections. *The fighting pits, where the Clockwork Legion is born.* Here Lady Fell set each generation of constructs against itself as a part of her quest to build the perfect fighting machine. *I wonder how many of them are left?*

"Where do we go?" said Heraan.

"I think," Sylph said, "across."

"Carefully," Yahvy added.

Heraan nodded vigorously.

"The rest of you can stay here," said Sylph. The soldiers tried to hide their relief. Heraan leaned close.

"Are you sure that's wise?"

"If we have to fight one of those things, the only chance we'll have is magic or the guns. I don't think they'd be much help."

"That's nice to know." Heraan turned to the men. "Stay here and make sure we don't get cut off, and one of you go back to the surface for reinforcements."

Sylph led the way across the bridges. It felt more dangerous than it actually was; the catwalk was solid stone and four or five feet wide. Only the knowledge of what lay on either side made her breath come fast. *Or, rather, lack of knowledge.* The thought of *something* pouncing out of the shadows left her mouth dry.

Yahvy followed, glancing curiously down as they passed, and Heraan brought up the rear. Lady Fell's geist was close enough now that Sylph sensed it without even closing her eyes; she led the trio on the most direct path she could. Some of the bridges were missing, others broken by some long-ago collision with a particularly nasty beast. They threaded their way around any that looked too rickety; when Heraan dislodged a stone that started a minor rockfall, Sylph nearly had a heart attack, but in the end they made it across without incident. The grid ended at another vertical rock wall, this one sporting nearly a dozen doors. All were locked, but only one had the geist behind it; Sylph put her hand to the wood and twisted it until both hinges and bar shattered. Heraan looked on approvingly.

"You're handy to have around, you know that?"

"I aim to please," said Sylph, trying to hide her nervousness. She was starting to feel like they'd been too hasty. *Why I am so sure that I'm Lady Fell's match? We should have waited for Lina and some of the others.*

"Come on." Yahvy led the way past the destroyed door, down another short corridor that opened out into yet another chamber. This one was lit from within by an odd pale radiance; Yahvy hadn't taken more than a step past the threshold when something big and silver hit her from the side.

She hit the ground, hard, and the Clockwork beast turned its head to Sylph with a mechanical roar. It was vaguely feline in shape, with a long body and six legs, plus a head that seemed to be almost entirely teeth. Its mouth was hinged where the ears on a normal creature would be, and opened so wide it looked like a bear trap.

"Down!" Heraan shoved Sylph out of the way as he drew his gun, firing from a clumsy one-handed grip. One shot hit the thing in the flank and *spang*ed off in a shower of sparks, while the rest missed entirely. The creature yowled and charged down the corridor, and Sylph flattened herself against the wall as it bore down on Heraan. She pulled out her own weapon as soon as it was past and opened fire; at such close range she could hardly miss, and by sheer luck one of her bullets caught the Clockwork under its left front shoulder joint. The limb twitched and collapsed, throwing off the beast's charge and sending it careening into a wall so hard the impact sent out flying splinters of rock.

Now's my chance. It was hard for Sylph to even think of approaching the creature, but she managed to force her body into action, closing the distance and laying a hand on its flank as it struggled to right itself. The metal was warm against her skin; she closed her eyes and hastily felt her way into the Clockwork beast's structure, ripping and tearing at its complex innards. It gave one last complaining yowl before it staggered and collapsed; a moment later its whole body evaporated like so much smoke as Sylph undid the magic that had created it.

"Heraan?" she managed. "You okay?"

"Fine. Sylph . . ."

Sylph was busy; she rushed to Yahvy's side. The Circle Breaker had somehow avoided taking the full weight of the Clockwork beast, but its talons had still drawn bloody trails through the leather on her stomach. She was getting to her feet when Sylph arrived, wincing at every move.

"Yahvy? Are you all right?"

"No," she croaked. "Think I'll live."

Sylph nodded and helped her up. The room was a relatively small one after the fighting pits, a circle only fifty or sixty feet in diameter. All the light emanated from the center, where a thick diagram had been drawn in powdered silver around a tiny metal sphere. *The geist.*

A figure stepped in front of it, features nearly invisible in the backlighting. It was female, and it didn't take much to guess her identity.

"Lady Fell," said Sylph, getting off her knees.

"It's not possible," the Archmagus mumbled. "You can't . . . I mean . . . it's *not* possible."

Sylph took a step forward. "You know what I'm here for."

"You can't interfere with my creations like that. Not inside my First Circle. It's not *possible!*" Her voice rose to a screech. "Vilvakis *himself* couldn't do that! *Who are you?*"

"I'm Sylph Walker," said Sylph. "My sister's the Liberator."

"Your *sister?*" Lady Fell laughed, high and devoid of sanity. "No Magus could do that—no one! They've all tried to pull me down. Gargorian, that fat fool, and Vilvakis with his *demons* and his little mustache—they've all tried!"

Sylph took another step closer. "Get out of the way."

"You *dare*?"

Lady Fell was surprisingly fast; she darted forward before Sylph could step back, one of her claw-like hands locking around Sylph's wrist. The Archmagus cackled, triumphant.

"I am the *Magio Mutator*, you little slut. You think you can defeat me . . ."

Sylph felt the Archmagus's cold fingers twisting at the core of her being, trying to turn living flesh into something dead and rotting. Silver pain lanced from her heart with every breath. She reached out to Gargorian's geist and extended her own grip, grabbing the tendrils Lady Fell had extended and pressing them back to their point of origin. There was a momentary battle of wills, and Sylph bore down hard; a moment later resistance crumbled and the Archmagus was stumbling away, clutching at her right hand.

"You . . . you . . ."

The flesh on that hand had changed, turning into thin, papery ash that crumbled and drifted away as dust. Lady Fell sank to her knees, sobbing; soon only the bones of her hand remained, clenched in a skeletal fist.

"I told you." Sylph swallowed. *I wish I didn't have to watch that.* "Get out of my way."

"You can't have it," Lady Fell whispered. "It's not . . . it's not fair." Suddenly she surged once again to her feet. "It's not *fair*!"

This time Sylph was ready, her pistol drawn and extended less than an inch from the Archmagus's face. Lady Fell's expression froze.

"Back," Sylph ordered. After a long moment the Archmagus obeyed, shuffling a few steps away from the circle. Keeping her gun trained, Sylph stepped forward, knelt, and picked up the geist; it was as easy as though it had been a marble in truth. She dropped it in her pocket with the other, and the two met with a metallic click.

Then, to her astonishment, Lady Fell dropped to her knees

and began to cry.

Heraan was at Sylph's side a moment later. "White Lady, Sylph. What did you *do* to her?"

"She did it to herself," Sylph said.

"Are you . . . I mean . . . is everything okay?"

"Yeah." Sylph sighed. The fact that she hadn't slept in more than thirty-six hours was starting to press home rather urgently. "We won."

"You won," Lady Fell giggled. "You won, but you'll have no peace. No victory. You'll not have my secrets. I burned it all, the laboratories, the library, everything. Ashes, now." She clutched the bones of her hand. "All turned to ashes."

"I don't want your secrets."

"Of course you do," the Archmagus crooned, half to herself. "They all do."

✳   ✳   ✳

FROM THE HIGHEST SPIRE OF THE KEEP, A LONE FIGURE IN black watched the last of the fighting subside. Kurai had paid special attention to Lina; he was pleased at the chance to observe her new powers in person, though he was less than happy with the results.

Demonic, for certain. And it appears to have abandoned subtlety. Forcing a confrontation, he concluded, would not be to his advantage. Shadows sprang from nowhere to wrap the spire, and when they cleared the Black Magus was gone.

chapter seventeen

IT'S AMAZING, **SYLPH THOUGHT,** *WHAT A LITTLE METAPHOR can do.* The green-and-black world of the geist was gone, replaced by an endless sandy surface. The vault of the sky was studded with stars, each tiny point representing a soul. There were billions and billions, and the result was a panorama almost solid with light.

Sylph stood on the sand with a pair of tiny, winged creatures, featureless little things like fairies or cherubs. They were metaphors too, another way of looking at the recursive search she'd built the last time. Lady Fell's geist was larger than Gargorian's, so the search would take longer. Sylph concentrated on the strongest image she had of her target; oddly enough, it came from a photograph she'd stuck in an old album and looked at all of twice. A vibrant, smiling woman in her mid thirties, with the long red hair she was so proud of and which neither of her daughters had inherited. A transparent version took shape, on the sand, so like Sylph's memory of her mother that she had to fight off tears.

Find, she ordered the cherubs. *Find her.*

They flitted upward, splitting as they went, as though she were suddenly seeing double. Two became four, then eight, then sixteen. By the time they were out of sight they were a swarm.

Sylph wiped her eyes and returned to her body to wait.

*　*　*

LADY FELL'S LIBRARY, WHEN THEY FINALLY FOUND IT AFTER
more than a day of searching, was extensive; it occupied another
huge chamber in the underground complex and housed not only
books but stacks and stacks of carefully indexed pages, organized between metal plates and labeled according to a scheme
Sylph didn't even try to understand. It was all ashes now, in any
case; as Lady Fell had gloated, her minions had put the collec-
tion to the torch even as Sylph and her friends had broken into
the geist's chamber. The loose sheets had burned fiercely; as
far as Sylph had been able to divine from the scraps that were
left, they had comprised a complete record of Lady Fell's experiments in the creation of constructs and the beginnings of her
work in demonic fusion.

Since Sylph had no desire to recreate any of this, she considered the destruction of that part of the library no great loss. It
was the other, smaller sections for which she mourned. In particular, there was a stack of history books in one corner, stacked
carelessly as though they were of no great import. Only the
bottom one had survived, and not intact; the ponderous tome's
cover labeled it simply *Chronicles*, and perhaps three-quarters of
the pages had been converted into charcoal. Nonetheless it was
the most interesting thing Sylph had been able to find. She'd
conjured up some unblemished paper of her own and set about
copying out the interesting portions. This was necessary since,
half the time she turned a page, it cracked or simply fell to dust.

The book was in a single hand, but Sylph suspected it had
been copied out before. If the dates were to be believed, it had
to have been. *This first section talks about Tyramax in the present
tense.* According to Fah she had been the Magio Creator before Gargorian's ascension, a little over six hundred years ago.
And while Lady Fell and Vilvakis were mentioned as Archmagi, there were other names Sylph had never heard before: *Golaic*,

Herodot, Keston. She turned the crumbling pages, idly. *And Vilva-kis, always Vilvakis.*

"The Liberator's army met the forces of the Magio Creator on the banks of the river and fought for an hour and a quarter. Herodot, knowing his realm was in the balance, personally led his Companions in a charge for the Liberator's center. Hayao and the Archmagus met in single combat, and the Liberator emerged victorious. With the Plague broken, Hayao marched into Lastfort in triumph. Afterward"—the book was scorched for a score pages or more, and only fragments were readable— "the Lady Fell, and an army of magical monstrosities"—"Hayao fell by the banks of"—"passed to Golaic, the Fifth Magio Creator, who set about enlarging Lastfort—"

Some parts of the book were staggeringly mundane—the section that followed that was practically a brick-by-brick account of the rebuilding of some ancient city—but Sylph was fascinated despite herself. She flipped forward as carefully as she could, flicking away the flying ash where it got on her paper, and copied out intriguing fragments.

"—the Magio Mutator had raised an army of half-man, half-beasts—"

"—the power of the Magio Obliterator destroyed Que-Li and her army, leaving only an abyss—"

"Vorgeh, who had forsaken the Plague, handed power to the Liberator—"

"Erik defeated the Magio Mutator, and drove her slaves before him like cattle—"

Sylph hesitated. She was nearing the back of the book, and a whole block of pages had been fused together. She pushed at them as forcefully as she dared, and was delighted to find a few scraps intact.

"With the Magio Obliterator's body cooling on the field before him, the Liberator declared himself content. He tasked Garveh and Sulian with the creation of a new empire, stretching from Adriato to the edge of the Bone Sea.

"But the Liberator's Magus was not content. Hatred had long ago poisoned his heart, and he whispered in Erik's ear that his victory was incomplete as long as the true ruler of Omega drew breath. Sulian argued long and hard, but in the end Erik had grown greedy for further conquest. He turned his eyes to the east, to the Black Keep, and at Rathmado's urging entered the lands of the Lightbringer—"

Sylph sat back, blinked, and reread what she had just penned.

"—and at Rathmado's urging entered the lands of the Lightbringer—"

"—at Rathmado's urging—"

When was this? She glanced at her notes. There was no fixed system of dates; instead the book simply prefaced each section with, "Six hundred years previously," or the equivalent. One or more of those captions might have been destroyed, but even so— *two thousand years. Maybe longer.* She shook her head. *Rathmado was an advisor to a Liberator—two thousand years ago?*

What happened next? She flipped back, but the clear section ended there and there was nothing but char for a hundred pages. A few, tiny fragments:

"—the Lightbringer—"

"—the War had ended, and—"

"—love beyond death—"

"—forbidden—"

"—consigned—"

And then nothing. Sylph let the back cover fall closed with a thump that raised tiny whirlwinds of ash, and sat back on the floor. Her skin was covered in gray, and her breath had grown raspy, but she noticed neither.

The pattern was pretty clear. The Liberator arose in the west and began to conquer, first the Magio Creator, then the Magio Mutator, and finally the Magio Obliterator. All but one, as far as she could tell, had been defeated somewhere along the way. Erik, the oldest of whom *Chronicles* spoke, had beaten all three Archmagi. *And then he went after the Lightbringer.*

Love beyond death.

Whose *love beyond death?* She poked at the block of charred pages but only succeeded in flaking off more ash. *I need to know what happened.*

She'd always been aware that Rathmado was using her to achieve his own ends; his explanation of why he did what he did was too vague to make sense. *And I certainly don't believe all that claptrap he spouted about Destiny.* But to *what* end had become a pressing question. *What happened to Erik? He went after the Lightbringer—Rathmado keeps saying that Mom might be with the Lightbringer—and then, what?*

Presumably he got killed. The Lightbringer's still around, after all. But Rathmado must think we have a chance of winning, otherwise why do this at all? Unless he gets something out of us all getting killed.

"Damn it." She closed the book with a snap, inwardly cursing Lady Fell's decision to burn her library. *I didn't want any of her damn experiments anyway.* Sylph put *Chronicles* under one arm and waved her way through the ash to the exit. The pair of pike-men on guard saluted sharply, and she gave them a nod in return.

Let's have a little chat with the Archmagus. Then I have to visit the hospital to see how Yahvy and Saar are doing, then track down Lina and find out what's going on with Roswell. And the Steelbreakers. Sylph sighed. *Better a complicated life than none at all, I suppose.*

❋   ❋   ❋

LADY FELL SEEMED AT HOME IN THE DARKNESS. SHE COWered in the most shadowy corner of her cell when the guard raised the lantern. Her hand had been wrapped in bandages, to guard against infection, and her fine robes were growing brown and patchy from neglect. Sylph had been to see her once or twice, since the battle; the Archmagus's sanity had apparently abandoned her with the loss of the geist, and she was able to answer only the simplest of questions.

A simple answer is all I need.

"Here you are, Magus," said the guard. "I'll be outside when you're finished."

Sylph nodded and set the lantern on a shelf. The former Archmagus backed into a corner of the tiny room as though trying to escape by sheer force of will. The arrogance was gone from her face, replaced by wide-eyed disbelief. Sylph couldn't help but feel sorry for her, and had to remind herself of the countless wars and atrocities Lady Fell was no doubt guilty of. *You don't remain Archmagus for thousands of years by being kind to people.*

Still. "It's okay," Sylph whispered. "I'm not going to hurt you. I had some questions for you."

"Questions?" Lady Fell looked up, the sharpness of her tone indicating that perhaps she was not entirely gone after all. "What questions?"

"This book." Sylph held up *Chronicles.* "Have you read it?"

"Some," she muttered. "Some."

"Do you remember it?"

"I'm in it," she crooned, run her good hand across the charred cover. "Lady Fell. Not real of course, not my real name, it's the image that's important." Her eyes narrowed. "Why do you want to know?"

"My sister isn't the first Liberator to get this far."

"Of course not." Lady Fell snorted. "The fourth."

"What happened to the others?"

"I killed them." The Archmagus giggled. "Hayao had this girl, some little whore he'd picked up. He thought he was in love with her. I had her strangle him. It didn't take much, you know? Not much at all. Hee. I killed them all."

"What about the one before you came to power?"

"Que-Li. Ha. She strung up old Keston, mounted his head on her battle flag. I was at the last battle too—not Lady Fell, then. Someone else. He blew them away, blew them right out of the universe. Off the slope entirely, no souls to wing their way downward. Oblivion. He's the Magio Obliterator, he should know, right?" She giggled again.

"And . . ." Sylph paused. "What about Erik?"

"Don't know. Nobody knows. Everybody who knew is dead. All dead, long dead, except maybe the Lightbringer and he's not telling."

"Someone knew. It was written in this book."

"No more books," said the Archmagus, and cackled. "You'll have nothing of mine . . . all burned . . ."

"*This* book," said Sylph. "Is there another copy?"

"Another copy?" Lady Fell looked sly. "And why should I say?"

Sylph clenched her fist. After a moment, she took a deep breath and glanced down, deliberately, at Lady Fell's bandaged limb. The ex-Archmagus blanched.

"There is another copy," said Sylph. "Where?"

"I don't . . . I . . ." Lady Fell hesitated, and finally blurted out, "Vilvakis! He has it. Mine is a copy of his. He *collects* things like this, you know, it's like a way of keeping score. When you've lived as long as he has I guess you forget . . . need books to keep your memory in . . ." She looked up at Sylph, wide-eyed. "That's it. I've lost my memory. Lost . . ."

"So I'll have to take it from Vilvakis."

"You'll never have it," she snapped. "Never, never, never. He loves his books, more than his life. He'd die first. He'd *burn* them first. Like me. Except I didn't care about the books, just my experiments. You can't *have* them. You—"

Enough. Sylph stood and took the lantern. The shifting light made the prisoner scrabble wildly, trying to stay in the darkness. Once the creaky iron gate had closed behind her, she headed to the barracks Daana and the others had converted to serve as a hospital, already mulling the beginnings of a plan.

"Sylph!"

Sylph paused and waited for Melfina to catch up. The girl

jogged across the still-stained courtyard. Out beyond the citadel walls, the city was beginning to wake from its stunned
silence—armies had needs, after all, and the primary purpose
of Stonerings was to export grain and meat to the rich lands
to the east. Sylph had set her quartermasters to rebuilding her
army's stores, with a considerable safety margin built in. *I'm not
going to get caught again.*

"Good morning, Mel. You look . . ." Sylph searched for a
word. "Tired."

Melfina nodded. "I didn't get much sleep. We spent most
of yesterday sorting the regiments out again, and then last night
. . . Sylph, have you seen Fah?"

"Since the battle?" Sylph thought back. "I can't say that
I have."

"Neither have I. Neither has anyone I've asked."

"Do you think something might have happened to her? I
assumed she was with Lina. She always seems to be."

"I tried to ask Lina about it, but she's been so busy meeting
with Roswell and the people from the city, I haven't been able to
find a moment to talk to her." Melfina paused. "Fah's regiment
is scattered all over the place. Her second-in-command, Myris,
took an arrow during the battle."

"Ah." Sylph hesitated. "Is she going to be okay?"

"No."

Sylph was silent a moment. "I'm going over to the citadel
in a bit," she said eventually. "I'll ask. I'm sure Fah's just been
busy too."

"Thank you. Are you here to see Yahvy?"

"And Saar." The barbarian woman had lapsed into unconsciousness shortly before the battle, and Daana had been
removing the poisoned flesh from her leg in stages, as much as
she thought the Steelbreaker could stand. The penultimate operation had been last night.

It was a little strange seeing the hospital in an actual *building*,
rather than a tent. It had originally housed some of Lady Fell's

troops, so there were plenty of beds, linen, and other necessities. Walking down the halls, Sylph was struck by how few wounded there were. Lina's spectacular displays had mostly broken the morale of the enemy before the fighting had even begun. *It seemed rash to me, but at least it worked. And to be honest Lina's approach might be better.* Sylph would have carefully laid siege to the city, and casualties would almost certainly have spiraled.

"Yahvy!" Melfina dashed ahead. The Circle Breaker was sitting up in her bed, her side bound and bandaged. She looked to be good spirits, and raised a hand in greeting.

"Sylph, Mel."

"Are you okay?" Melfina piped.

"Fine." Yahvy smiled. "A scratch."

"And lucky for you," Sylph commented. "I thought that thing was going to crush you. How long until you're up and about?"

"Today sometime."

"That soon?" said Melfina. "Shouldn't you take a bit . . . ?"

"I'll be fine." Yahvy yawned. "Getting bored here."

"Good," said Sylph.

Yahvy eyed Sylph for a moment. "Got another idea?"

"Sort of."

"Crazy?"

"Of course."

"Good," echoed Yahvy. Melfina rolled her eyes.

"Speaking of which," Sylph said, "where do they have Saar? I wanted to thank her."

There was an uncomfortable silence, then Yahvy said, "Dead. Last night."

Sylph blinked. "Dead?"

"Daana said too much poison, too much bleeding."

"O . . . oh."

Sylph looked down; she felt Melfina put a hand on her shoulder, distantly, but she was lost in thought.

Dead. From some silly infection, for the lack of some penicillin or something like that. It was an uncomfortable reminder. The healers that followed the army were remarkably advanced in some ways, much better than a lot of the pseudo-mystical claptrap that Sylph associated with medieval doctors. But there was still a great deal that was beyond their capabilities.

And mine. She'd tried manufacturing drugs, via the geist, but it was a hopeless task. Diamond was simple, just rows of carbon, and even alloyed metal wasn't much harder. Gunpowder had been a triumph, but even that had been more trial-and-error than anything else; she wasn't entirely sure the formula she'd ultimately come up with was the one she vaguely remembered from chemistry. But even a relatively simple organic like penicillin was monstrously complex, and trial-and-error was impossible with no good way to test it. *Maybe if I had a few years, and some animals or something to experiment on.*

She looked back up at Yahvy with new eyes. *Every time she gets hurt for me, she tosses the dice.* The careless banter of a moment before felt distant.

"Sylph?" said Melfina. "Are you okay?"

"Yeah." Sylph wiped her eyes. "Just kind of caught me by surprise."

"Sorry," said Yahvy.

"Do you want to talk to Daana?" the girl asked.

"No. I need to go to the citadel and see if I can find Lina." *And if Saar's dead, what is there to talk about?*

✳   ✳   ✳

A FEW MOMENTS HAD PASSED, OR ELSE A THOUSAND YEARS; Lina wasn't sure. She felt solid ground underneath her, and instinctively recoiled; all sensation led to the same memory, the same horrible scene of betrayal. *I don't want to watch it again.* Lina curled into a ball. *Don't make me watch it again.*

She'd seen it a thousand times, ten thousand, until it was burned into the back of her skull. She felt that it was burned into this *place*, wherever it was, as though sheer rage, crystallized by the weight of millennia and unable to lash out, had infected everything around it. For a time she thought she'd been going mad, but instead she became numb, drifting without purpose and drowning in a sea of anger. Slowly falling.

Until, finally, she touched bottom.

It took her a long time to realize that something else had happened, to remember that there *could* be something beyond Rahmgoth and a shadowy figure, the flash of steel, and a few muttered words. But there was dirt underneath her, and light enough that her skin felt warm. She could hear the moaning of the wind, and feel it rasp over her face.

Cautiously, Lina opened her eyes, and found herself staring toward a blood-red sky. She was surrounded by old, dead trees, reaching upward with a thousand stick-fingers; whenever the wind gusted, they rattled like tumbling bones.

Where . . . am I?

She tried sitting up, and was surprised to find herself fully dressed, not in the leather she'd been wearing what seemed like a lifetime ago, but in well-remembered blue jeans and a hooded sweatshirt. My *hooded sweatshirt*, she thought, incredulously. It was black fading to dark blue after a hundred washes, and giving out at the left elbow. She wound one of the strings around her finger and popped the end into her mouth, a nervous gesture so achingly familiar it gave her chills.

Think, Lina. Her mind didn't want to work after so long in the empty whiteness, with only Rahmgoth's phantom for company. *Before that. What do I remember?*

Those metal things . . . I went to save Sylph.

"You're mine."

"Rahmgoth," she whispered. *It has to be.* "What the hell did he do to me?"

Lina stood, stumbled, and ended up sprawled against one of the sinister looking trees. She felt a scream welling up inside her, despite everything she could do.

"What did he *do to me*?"

Something—a movement, a slight sound—made her turn. There was someone else, standing on top of a boulder between two trees. Lina took a moment to focus. It was a little girl, dressed in an olive coat that was much larger than she was; she was filthy, face smeared with grime and ratty red hair falling past her shoulders in a tangle. She'd obviously been startled by the scream, and was staring at Lina wide-eyed. Once Lina turned and raised her hand, the girl bolted, jumping off the boulder and scampering into the forest. The sounds of crashing brush marked her retreat.

"Wait," Lina said, much too late. "Wait . . ."

"She won't listen to you," said a deep, resonant voice behind her. "She doesn't listen to anyone."

Lina spun and found herself facing a huge figure, resplendent in elaborate armor so white it seemed to glow. What wasn't enameled steel was flowing white cloth, and long blond hair hung like a glittering curtain down its back. A sword longer than Lina was tall stuck out over one shoulder. It was impossible to tell whether the thing was male or female; its features shifted from moment to moment.

A moment passed in silence. Lina's mouth hung open.

The thing said, "I've frightened you. I'm sorry. Look the other way, would you?"

She had enough self-possession to do as she was told. There was *pop*, like the sound of a helium balloon breaking, and then the voice said, "How about now?"

The figure in white was gone. In its place was a young man in a gray suit, with dirty-blond hair tied back in a ponytail. He gave her a thin-lipped smile—he looked as though he were unused to smiling—and dug in one pocket until he came up with a crumpled pack of cigarettes. He tapped it expertly against his hand to extract one, hesitated, then offered it to her.

Lina shook her head. "No. Thanks."

He nodded, popped the cigarette in his mouth, and passed

his hand over the tip; it glowed red for a moment, and he took a long drag.

"Filters," he said, apropos of nothing, "are wonderful things. It's hard to see how we could do without them. I mean, we can't do without them, they're kind of built in. But you have to ask yourself where they come from. I mean, how do I know that the words I'm saying over here mean the same thing as the words that are arriving over there?" He gestured for emphasis with the cigarette.

"Because they're the same words?" Lina suggested.

"You *think* so. You assume so. But how hard would it be for me to fuck with that? Not me, I mean, not now, this is more like some abstract me . . ." He paused, watching her face. "You have no idea what the fuck I'm talking about, do you?"

"Not really," said Lina. "Sorry."

"It's not important. I was just trying to give some, you know, some fucking *context* to my apology, 'cause otherwise it doesn't mean much. I mean, for all you know I hang around here scaring people for fun, right?" He waited a moment, and when she didn't respond he prompted, "Right?"

"Right!"

"Fuckin' right." He took another long drag. "You'll have to forgive me if my language has decayed somewhat. It has been a fuckin' . . ." He paused. "A *very* long time since I had anyone sane to talk to." He looked suddenly suspicious. "You are sane, aren't you?"

"I am," said Lina, still slightly in shock. "At least I think I am. I mean I was before I got here."

"You seem sane to me, so if you seem sane to you that pretty much settles the matter. I mean, there's fuck-all for anyone else around here to say you're wrong, right?"

"Right?" said Lina.

"Right." The young man appeared to have temporarily run out of things to say, or at least stopped for breath, and Lina used the opportunity to jump into the conversation.

"Where *is* here?"

He lowered his hand and blew out a puff of smoke. "This is, like, His personal icebox. Where He keeps things He wants to hang on to for one reason or another. We call it the Pit."

"The Pit?"

"Yah. I'm Molochim, I imagine you'll get around to introducing yourself eventually, and are you sure you don't want one?"

Lina shook her head. Molochim shrugged.

"Suit yourself."

✳   ✳   ✳

"Excuse me?"

Loquiana gave Sylph a condescending smile. "The Governor is meeting with the Liberator right now. They instructed me to admit no one."

"I . . . see." *No, I don't.* She tapped her foot on the scarred marble of the citadel floor. "Is there any way . . . ?"

"I'm afraid not." Loquiana leaned down, closer to Sylph's level. "You did a fine job running the army, but now that the war is over the traditional, civilian authority needs to be rebuilt. The Governor is very busy and—"

"I don't care about the Governor"—*he was a general until a few days ago anyway*—"I need to talk to *Lina.*"

"As I said, the Liberator is assisting the Governor. Given her position she obviously needs to play a role in rebuilding the city."

A role. I see. Sylph looked around; she saw a big square of pikes drilling in the courtyard. Her first instinct was to call them over and have them cut Roswell's arrogant assistant down to size, starting at the knees. Her second instinct was to draw her pistol from its newly crafted holster and do it herself. *But I suppose neither of those would be very useful.*

"Tell Lina," Sylph said, "that I wanted to see her."

"I'll certainly pass the message along when she has the time."

Loquiana's superior grin made it clear she thought she'd won. Leaving the older woman the last word was almost too much for Sylph. She managed one more question.

"And tell me, have you seen Fah?"

Loquiana arched an eyebrow. "Who?"

"Never mind." Sylph spun on her heel and walked back to the main corridor, headed out through the citadel's ruined doors. *Maybe she's telling the truth, maybe Lina really is busy.* That certainly didn't seem likely, since the Lina of old would hardly have dared *meet* with Roswell without her sister's advice. *But she's hardly the same. She's changed. Hell, I've changed.* Sylph took a deep breath. *Calm. Just be calm. Some assistant of Roswell's just wants to be a bitch, that's all. I'm not going to let it get to me.*

She passed a familiar figure in the hall almost without realizing it; at the last minute Sylph looked back and found Rathmado giving her a knowing grin before turning around the corner toward Roswell's offices. Her heart-rate doubled in that moment, and she stood stock still for a second afterward.

He knows. There was something in the Magus's eyes. *Or rather, he knows that I know. About him and the other Liberators. Suspect* was probably a better word. As far as Sylph could tell, only the Archmagi were immortal; ordinary Magi got old and died just like the rest of the poor mortals. *Which means Rathmado has to be more than he says he is. Or, there's someone in the book with the same name, but how likely is that?*

She was rethinking her first panicked assessment. *How could he possibly know? I didn't show the book to anyone except Lady Fell, and no one gets to see her without my say-so.* And, on second examination, a knowing grin was what the Magus always wore. *I'm jumping at shadows.*

Her reaction had made clear, however, that at least in her own mind Sylph no longer trusted the soft spoken Magus. *More like, now that I know he's not telling me the whole story, I'd rather find out the whole story from some other source before confronting him about it.* She had the feeling that he wouldn't approve of her current plan,

either. *So I just won't tell him about it. But I have to tell Lina.*
Let's see if Heraan thinks it's even possible. One thing at a time.

✳   ✳   ✳

RAHMGOTH LEANED BACK IN HIS SEAT AND YAWNED AS SOON
as Roswell had left the room. He wasn't alone for more than a
moment before the door opened to admit Rathmado, who shot
him a critical look.

"Is your patience wearing thin, my friend?" the Magus asked.

"May I assume nobody's listening?"

Rathmado smiled.

"Then, yes, it is. All I do is smile and nod anyway."

"If you weren't here, Roswell would think he was getting
away too easily. He'd suspect a trick."

"So what? Why not leave the pompous bastard here and let
him run the city?"

"It's not the city we want, it's his army. It's a long way from
here to the Black Keep, and I doubt you want to fight the Shadowcore single-handedly."

"Of course not." Rahmgoth rolled his eyes. "I'm going
along with the plan. I just don't have to like it. I haven't killed
anything in *days.*" In the Pit, he'd dreamed of the smell of blood
for six thousand years; now that he was surrounded by it, he
found it harder and harder to restrain himself. The mortals
were *everywhere; surely no one would miss one or two . . .*

"Rest assured, there'll be blood enough."

"When?"

"Another few days."

"*More* waiting," Rahmgoth snarled.

Rathmado sighed.

"I know!" Rahmgoth threw up his hands. "I know. You
got me out, so I'm yours." *For the moment.* "This charade is just
getting harder."

"It will only be necessary a while longer. By the time we

dispose of Sylph, you'll be dug in far enough that no one will challenge you."

"Dispose of her? You seem to have invested a great deal in the girl."

"Once she takes the third geist from Vilvakis . . ."

"Ah." Rahmgoth smiled wider. "I'd appreciate it if you'd turn her over to me for . . . disposal." He indicated Lina's body with one hand. "The idea has a certain poetry."

"I'll consider it."

"What do I do about Marlowe?"

"What about him?"

"His attempts at intimacy are becoming unpleasant."

Rathmado frowned. "I don't suppose you'd consider indulging him? Your body, after all—"

"No."

"Then what do you suggest?"

"Let me kill him."

The Magus sighed. "Is that your answer to everything?"

Rahmgoth smiled. Not for the first time, he wished he'd been able to keep his fangs.

✳   ✳   ✳

HERAAN, TO HIS CREDIT, TOOK IT WELL.

"You're crazy."

"Possibly," said Sylph. "But do you think it could be done?"

"I still don't understand *why*. What has he got that's so important?"

"On that you'll just have to trust me." She hadn't thought of a good way to tell Heraan and Yahvy about the *Chronicles* without explaining too much. *I still hate saying that.*

"So you want to walk through miles and miles of enemy territory until you get to Adriato, then just waltz in to the Archmagus's fortress and . . . what?"

"Steal some of his books."

"And you want to do this *alone*?"

"Well," said Sylph, "I was sort of hoping the two of you would come with me."

Yahvy chuckled. Heraan threw her a furious glare, then turned back to Sylph. "It's too dangerous."

"But is it possible?"

"How should I know? This is the furthest east I've ever been. Who know what Vilvakis has in terms of security?"

"Should work," Yahvy put in. "Nobody knows who we are. No faces, no names even. Shouldn't be able to find us."

"Yes, but if they do . . ."

"If they do, we have these." Sylph drew her pistol and set it down between them, then fished in her pocket for the geists. "And I have these." The little metal balls clicked against one another.

"True," Yahvy agreed.

Heraan sighed. "I still think it's reckless. If you get yourself killed . . ." He trailed off.

Sylph grinned at him. "Worried about the cause?"

He looked away, and for some reason Sylph felt a little warmer inside. There was a silence, which Yahvy broke by standing up.

"Going to pack. When are we leaving?"

"Tonight. I'd like to sneak out of our own camp if at all possible. The fewer people who know where we're going, the better."

Yahvy thought for a moment. "I left some things in the hospital. Might have to talk to Daana."

"That's not a problem." Sylph waved a hand. "Daana we can trust. I just don't want gossip."

Yahvy nodded and slipped out of the tent.

"I'll get my kit packed," Heraan growled.

"Thanks."

"I still say it's too dangerous."

"I know," said Sylph. "I'm sorry. You don't have to come along. I'm sure Yahvy and I can manage."

"That's not the point." He snorted. "I can't very well let you walk into enemy territory without me, can I?"

With that he stomped out. Sylph leaned back against her bed. In spite of Heraan's bluster—or perhaps because of it—she felt oddly content. *This will work.* With the power of the geists and handguns to back them up, only the Archmagus himself would be a serious threat. *And why would he bother with three anonymous travelers?*

Certainly the army can look after itself. Her expression soured. *Lina seems like she's taken things well in hand.*

"Sylph?"

Speak of the devil. Sylph jumped to her feet and beckoned her sister inside. "Lina! I've been looking for you all day!"

"Sorry." Lina rolled her eyes. "You know Roswell. He just wouldn't shut up."

"I figured it was something like that. What's he up to?"

"Setting himself up as a petty tyrant, looks like. But he'll be no worse than most."

Sylph nodded. The sisters looked at each other for a moment, and then Sylph said, "It's good to see you. I feel like we haven't gotten to talk in forever."

"I know. I'm sorry."

"My fault too," Sylph said hastily. "I've been busy, but I should have made more of an effort. Are you feeling all right? Before we got to Stonerings you were out for a long time."

"I'm fine," said Lina. She grinned. "Better than fine. I think I've finally mastered this thing," she stroked the hilt of the sword at her hip, "so it won't knock me out every time I use it."

"I noticed," said Sylph. "At the gates . . ."

Lina looked embarrassed. "Think I went overboard?"

"Just a little. But it all worked out in the end, right?" She paused. "I really missed you."

"Sylph . . ."

"It's just . . . I don't know," Sylph said hurriedly, "there doesn't seem to be anyone else I can talk to, who remembers that I'm human."

"I remember," said Lina quietly.

There was a pause.

"Lina," Sylph said, "I . . . I'm going away for a bit."

"Going where?"

"Adriato. Vilvakis's capital."

"Wha . . . I mean, why?"

Sylph took a deep breath. "Lady Fell burned her library—you remember, right? I found a book that didn't quite get destroyed. It talks about the past Liberators, and what happened to them. But it was incomplete. I need to read the rest, Lina. I need to find out—"

"And Vilvakis has another copy?"

"He has the original, according to Lady Fell. But if we're winning the war I doubt he'd let it fall into my hands."

"So you're going to steal it." Lina thought for a moment. "Who's going with you?"

"Heraan and Yahvy."

"Good." She smiled, suddenly. "You'll be fine."

"Lina . . ." Sylph felt herself tearing up, and at just the right moment—as always—Lina leaned forward and wrapped her in a hug. Sylph hugged her back, fiercely, savoring the warmth of the contact. Lina rested her chin on her sister's shoulder.

"You'd better be fine, understand?"

Sylph nodded.

A long moment passed.

"I should probably go meet Heraan," Sylph said. After another moment, "That means you should probably let go."

"Sorry." Lina disentangled herself and pulled away. Sylph wiped her eyes and got to her feet, collecting the two geists and the gun.

"If everything goes well, I'll get back to you after a couple of weeks."

"I'll get the army moving as soon as I can," said Lina. "It'll take us a lot longer, but maybe if we put some pressure on Vilvakis he'll be less likely to find you."

"Good. I don't imagine you'll have any problems, either."

Lina put her hand on the hilt of the sword. "I doubt it."

"One more thing," said Sylph. "We're trying to keep this quiet . . ."

"Of course."

"But." Sylph took a deep breath. "*Especially* don't tell Rathmado."

"Why?"

"It's hard to explain. I'm not sure I trust him, and until I know more I'd rather not—"

"Understood," said Lina. "Don't worry about it."

"Thanks." They shared a last glance, and Sylph wiped her eyes again. "I'll see you later."

Lina nodded, and Sylph slipped out through the tent flap. It wasn't until she was well outside that she remembered she'd forgotten to ask about Fah. *Melfina will ask Lina tomorrow, and I'm sure they'll find her.*

❋   ❋   ❋

A FEW MINUTES LATER, THE FLAP RUSTLED AGAIN TO ADMIT the Magus.

"You heard?"

Rathmado nodded. Since the sword—the gate to the Pit—was his creation, as best Rahmgoth was able to tell he could sense everything that went on around it.

"Well?"

"I think," said Rathmado, "that Sylph has solved a number of our problems for us."

"Oh?"

"With her out of the camp, the danger of you being discovered is minimal."

"True." Rahmgoth hadn't considered that. "But now she doesn't trust you."

"She doesn't have to trust me, as long as she continues on the course. She'll defeat Vilvakis and claim his geist, and that is enough."

"I suppose," Rahmgoth grumbled. His thoughts were elsewhere. "So you're going to let her go?"

"Yes." The Magus yawned. "Was there anything else?"

"No."

"The plan is set for the day after tomorrow. Make sure you're ready."

"I'll be ready."

"Excellent." Rathmado slipped out as quietly as he'd entered. Rahmgoth sat on the camp bed, arms crossed below Lina's breasts. He closed his eyes, trying to recreate the moment. *Her body pressed against mine, slim, and young, and so perfectly trusting.* His desire had very nearly overcome him at that moment. *Not just a dagger in the back, that's much too quick. Tie something around her throat, and make love to her while she thrashes and dies. Feel her last little twitches . . .*

Rahmgoth snarled and got to his feet. *Damn Rathmado and his waiting.*

✳   ✳   ✳

DAANA WAITED IN THE TENT SHE'D ONCE SHARED WITH GArot. There was a bed big enough for two, and a wooden trunk at the other end of the room with its latch still closed. She hadn't been able to bring herself to get rid of it, so the porters had been faithfully loading it onto the carts and bringing it from campsite to campsite. As though his memory were following her, clutching at her ankles, refusing to let go.

She took a deep swallow from a wineskin and sank lower in her chair. *Not my fault. None of it is my fault. I asked Sylph, I asked her, and what did she do? Nothing. Her mistake, and I'm punished for it. Now and forever.*

There was a rustle as someone scratched at the tent flap. She took another drink and said, "Come in."

A man entered. He was tall and blond, with a nondescript

face and a winning smile, which he flashed her. Daana didn't smile back. She gestured with the wineskin. "Sit."

He took the other chair. Before he could speak, Daana said, "I know what you're thinking."

"Oh?"

"This must be the way you normally operate; pick up some girl at a bar, talk to her until she invites you back to her place, do your unpleasant duty, then hope she says something once your prowess has loosened her lips." She raised the skin to her mouth and drained the last few drops, then tossed it aside. "Am I right?"

"I'm not sure what you think I am . . ." He didn't sound offended, and there was dark amusement behind his confused expression.

"I think you're a spy. For Vilvakis, I assume."

There was a long pause. "And what makes you think that?"

She noticed the way one of his hands crept into his sleeve. A paranoid would think there was a weapon hidden there, and in this case would probably be right. It occurred to Daana that what she was doing was quite dangerous, but even that didn't make her leaden heart beat faster. Nothing had, since that comparatively insignificant battle . . .

"Relax. I don't plan on turning you in, so you won't have to kill me. I just wanted to make it clear that we could drop the pretenses."

He nodded, but didn't release his grip on the hidden weapon. "What do you want from me?"

"First, to make it clear I'm not going to fuck you. Second . . ." She hesitated. "I have information that you need."

"Such as?"

"Sylph—you know who she is? The Liberator's sister, the brains of the operation."

"Yes." He tipped his head to one side, considering. "Why should I trust you?"

"Because I died at Orlow. My corpse is just still walking."

And because she should suffer the way I have. It's not fair.

"And what do you want?"

"Out of this hellhole, for starters. Somewhere to live in the city. Money, I suppose." She hadn't really thought about what happened afterward. In some sense, she didn't really feel like it would happen. Daana's world had already ended.

"That can be arranged."

"So, we have a deal?"

"It'll be some time before I can get you out."

"Understood." She didn't particularly care. "Sylph is gone."

"I was starting to suspect that. Where?"

"She's gone to steal something important from the Archmagus Vilvakis." Daana retrieved the wineskin and raised it to her lips before remembering that it was empty. She tossed it away, further this time. "Adriato. She's gone to Adriato."

part three
Oblivion

18

chapter eighteen

IT WAS NICE, WATCHING THE SUN SET AND LISTENING to the gentle crackle of the campfire burning down. East of Stonerings the land was flat and prosperous, crisscrossed with tiny wandering streams the horses were easily able to wade across. According to Heraan's map, they all joined up at a great basin to the south, which marked the edge of the Lady Fell's territory in that direction; from there a mighty river flowed to the sea. On the direct route to Adriato, however, there was only one sizable river, labeled the Zhine; they'd crossed that three days out, walking the horses carefully over the wooden bridge. There was a hut for guards, but they'd apparently fled. News of events at Stonerings was traveling fast.

Every night, they found a place to camp by the side of the road. Heraan collected sticks and brush until he had enough for a fire, and Yahvy produced a battered kettle to make stew. After a full day of riding this always tasted surprisingly good, and Sylph was usually happy to drift off to sleep soon afterward, curled up under her blanket. By unspoken agreement, Yahvy and Heraan took turns standing guard. Sylph thought about arguing with them and demanding her own turn, but somehow she never got around to it.

If not for that little detail—the need to set a guard—it would have felt exactly like being on a campout back home. Sylph's memories of vacation all featured camping out. She'd realized, later, that it was just about the only outing her mother had been able to afford. Whenever the girls had a week off from school, she'd toss some battered old sleeping bags into the back of the car and drive out to the nearest state park.

Sylph remembered, when she was seven or eight, being a little bit annoyed by this. She'd been just old enough to realize that her friends from school all got to go to Disneyland or some other licensed theme park, and that she and Lina never did. But Lina never complained, so neither did Sylph. And pretty soon afterward there was no more opportunity for complaints.

She opened her eyes. The blanket was a warm little bubble in the cool night; the sun had set, the fire had died, and all that was left was the faint light of the moon and the odd, unfamiliar stars. Heraan was lying under his own blanket, snoring faintly, and Yahvy sat by Sylph in the shadow of a mossy boulder.

Sylph didn't think she'd moved, but her breathing must have changed enough for Yahvy to notice.

"Can't sleep?"

Sylph nodded.

"Something wrong?"

"Not wrong, really," Sylph said.

"Worried about Lina?"

"Maybe a little."

"I worry about Melfina."

"Yeah." Sylph closed her eyes. "But that's not it."

"Then what?"

"Memories."

"Bad?"

"Sort of." Sylph rolled over, so she could look at Yahvy. "What were your parents like?"

Yahvy was silent for a moment.

"Sorry. If it's too personal . . ."

"No," Yahvy shook her head. "Just remembering. Not much to tell, really. Lived in my grandfather's house with my father and mother. Two little sisters too, both much younger. One died before she was two. Other about ten by now, I think?"

Sylph nodded.

"Grandfather ran an . . . inn, you'd say in the east. Place for travelers. Did well at it right up until he died. My father was not so good. Drank too much, drove away custom, drank more the worse we did. My bed was under that stairs. Listened to them, every night, father shouting and mother trying not to cry.

"At fourteen, he wanted me to 'help.' Be a whore, for the good of the business." Yahvy kicked idly at the remains of the fire. "Paid good money to Gargorian to have me, he said. Time to start earning it back. Told him I'd do anything else—cook, clean, anything—but not that. I was in love. Little boy a bit older than me, rich family. Said he loved me too, wanted to get married. I knew he wouldn't marry a whore."

"What happened?"

"Father . . ." She winced. ". . . insisted. I said no, ran away to my boy. He wouldn't let me into his house. After that it was either be a whore or a mercenary. Decided I'd rather choose who I got to fuck. Eventually met up with Fah. Guess something about what my father said, about how he had to pay for me, made me angry. So I stayed with the Circle Breakers."

Sylph paused. "Your dad," she said eventually, "sounds horrible."

"Probably." She shrugged. "Drank a lot. Could be nice at times. I remember one night, I had nightmares. Spiders or something. Father let me take a sword from downstairs and keep it under my bed, help keep them away. It worked too."

"What about your mother?"

"Sad," said Yahvy matter-of-factly. "Sad, all the time. After grandfather—her father—died, she had nothing left but father. So she held on, and he just got worse and worse."

There was a long silence. Sylph gripped the edges of the blanket tightly, deep in thought.

"I don't remember my father," she said. "I think he left before

I was born. Lina doesn't remember him either—she'd have been four or so. Mom didn't keep any pictures of him or anything, and she never talked about him. I never asked her, either."

"Must have been hard, a woman with two children and no husband."

"It's a little bit easier for a woman to live alone where I come from, but not much. She worked a lot." *Two jobs, with barely enough time between them to sleep. And weekends, half the time. So that Lina and I could go to school and not worry.* "But, yeah. It was hard."

"She did a good job."

She did better than that. She did a fucking perfect *job. And just when things were turning around I screwed it up.* "She did."

"You sound like you're missing home, tonight."

"Yeah." Sylph swallowed past the lump in her throat. "I think I am."

"Going back? Once all this is done."

I can't go back. I don't even know where I'd go back to. "No." Sylph cleared her throat. "Mom . . . died, when I was eleven. Lina's the only family I have left."

"Ah." Yahvy paused. "Sorry."

"Don't be." Sylph rubbed her eyes. "I'm the one dredging up old memories."

She wanted to just tell Yahvy the story, the secret truth she'd never told anyone. *Even Lina.* But of course it wouldn't work; there was too much context, too much Sylph would have to explain. *And I don't think I could say it, either.*

Yahvy reached over and scratched Sylph's head, as though she were a cat. "Sleep. We've got places to go tomorrow." She stopped a moment, then said, "Even if you can't go back, you have friends here."

Sylph nodded and pulled the blanket back over her head.

She's right. It wouldn't be so bad, staying here. As long as I can find her. Lina and Mom and I—we could probably set ourselves up as kings, if we wanted to. Though Sylph doubted the appeal would last. *We'll just find a place to live, get rid of the geists, and be happy, Earth or no Earth.*

She closed her eyes, and for some reason found the dusty pages of *Chronicles* floating behind her eyelids.

"*—love beyond death—*"

"*—forbidden—*"

"*—consigned—*"

"*—Rathmado—*"

FOR LACK OF ANYTHING BETTER TO DO, LINA WAS WALKING through the forest. Molochim paced along beside her, puffing on his cigarette that never seemed to get any shorter. Nothing much changed, just more woods, more trees like broken-backed old men clawing at the night sky.

"So, say that again. This place is like 'his' icebox? Whose?"

"Him. You know." He took the cigarette in one hand and mouthed, "Lightbringer."

"Li—"

"Shh!" The young man waved frantically. "Fuckin' . . . you can't say that name around here."

"Why not?"

"Just trust me, okay?"

"If you say so." Lina tried to get her thoughts back on track. "So where *is* it?"

"What do you mean?"

"Which way is . . ." She cast about for place names. "Bleloth. Stonerings."

"Never heard of them."

"But—"

"It's not like that. There's not a direction you can *point* to and say, 'That way's home,' unless you're some kind of weird motherfucker with arms that bend through six dimensions. This is, like, some tiny-ass universe that He appropriated to keep people in. It's probably a couple of inches across, if you could look at it from the outside, which you can't."

"You're not making a lot of sense."

"Fuckin' filters again. I could explain it better if you spoke Veritas, but of course it doesn't work that way."

"How did I *get* here?"

"How the fuck should I know? Presumably He sent you here. Do you remember getting killed by a particularly scary looking motherfucker?"

"I don't remember getting killed at all." She thought for a moment. "Well, not recently. I had a magic sword, and every time I used it I could hear this voice in my head. He called himself Rahmgoth."

"Wait." Molochim held up a hand. "Wait wait wait. Rahmgoth?"

"Yeah."

"And this was up . . . I mean . . ." He jerked his thumb at the sky.

Lina shook her head. "I don't know what you're talking about."

"He talked to you through a *magic sword*?"

"Yes!" Lina rounded on him, annoyed. "Why? What?"

To her amazement, Molochim was laughing. "A *magic* . . . I mean . . ." He shook his head. "Somebody fucked you over, girl. Fucked you over *big* time."

"Why? *What happened?*"

"Finish the fuckin' story. You heard Rahmgoth. Then what?"

"He seemed to get stronger every time I used the thing. Until eventually . . ."

"Eventually?"

"I don't know. I blacked out. I was just kind of drifting, and then I started seeing things."

"Holy shit." Molochim whistled. "Ho-lee shit. You have no idea what happened, do you?"

"You obviously do," she grated.

"Rahmgoth has been stuck in here with me. For, like, six

thousand years or thereabouts, it's hard to keep count, ever since he got put on ice. But about a week ago things started feeling weird, and now you're *here*, which as best I can figure means he's *up there*."

"Up *where*?"

"Back where you were." Molochim waved his fingers. "In your body, type of thing. He doesn't have one of his own anymore."

"You're kidding."

"'Fraid not."

"That pervert is walking around in *my* body?" Lina bristled. "What if he does something awful to it? What if he—"

"Your body's probably safe," said Molochim. "I'd worry more about everyone else's. Rahmgoth's a fuckin' lunatic. But forget that for a second—don't you understand what this means?"

"No!" Lina shouted.

"The sword. He got to you through the sword, that makes it a gate, a metaphysical channel to this space."

"What the *fuck* does that mean?"

"It means there's a *way out of here*." Molochim's eyes gleamed bright and not, in Lina's opinion, entirely sane. *Though I'm not in the best of states to judge.* "I just don't understand why. Usually He wants the people he put in here to fuckin' stay put . . ."

He stopped in mid sentence, and put up a hand when Lina tried to interject. "Shh."

"What?"

"I thought . . . *down!*"

"*What*?"

Molochim was already moving, flinging his cigarette to one side and jumping for the underbrush. Lina turned around first, to see what he'd been looking at, and froze like a deer in the lights of a tractor-trailer. The oncoming beast reminded her vaguely of a Tyrannosaur—two big hind legs and a massive head that seemed to be mostly teeth—but it had four huge, clawed arms that jutted from behind its shoulder blades and folded in, like a spider's. Its skin was covered in whitish fur, liberally stained with black and red. When it saw her, it emitted a bloodcurdling shriek and charged, covering ground at an unbelievable rate.

Lina felt her hand go for the sword at her side, but of course it wasn't there. That cost her another moment, so her attempt to dive aside was not fast enough. One of the taloned feet caught her in the stomach with the force of a jackhammer, flinging her forward. She rolled to a halt a little further on, lying sideways on the forest floor. The razor-sharp claw had laid open her stomach from hips to breastbone; Lina felt a hot bloom and pieces of something wet and sticky underneath her. Her next breath was a bubbling agony.

The creature was on her in an instant, putting one foot on her hip with a *crunch* of bone. The huge head came down, and for a moment she thought it was going to swallow her whole. Instead, the circle of teeth closed on her left shoulder and side, pulling upward with irresistible force. Flesh and bone gave way with a sick, tearing sound, and she got a brief glimpse of her own hand sticking out between the thing's teeth before her arm disappeared into the creature's gullet. A last twist of its foot ground her shattered hip further into the dust, and then the thing was bounding off, thundering past her and farther into the forest.

The pain was indescribable. Lina wanted to scream, but her mouth was filled with blood. She couldn't move, couldn't breathe, couldn't feel her own heart beat, couldn't even close her eyes, which were left staring at the twisted wreckage of her intestines. She waited to die—she *had* to die—*this can't just go* on . . .

"I told you to fuckin' duck," came Molochim's voice, from far away. "Now look what happened. Fuck, I've seen chopped liver that was more appetizing."

Leave me alone, she wanted to shout. *I'm dying—fucking die already!* The agony continued unabated.

"The thing is, you're not going to die. You're not even really hurt."

Fuck *you*. *I'm hurt* . . .

"It's all in your mind, see. I know you probably don't believe me, but I fuckin' suggest you start trusting me real fast."

It tore off my arm *and he's going on like it never happened.*

"Look at it this way," said Molochim, leaning closer. "Either you listen to me, or you get to spend the *next* six thousand years decomposing and feeling every last fuckin' second of it. So pull yourself together, all right? Just close your eyes . . . well, maybe not. Just fuckin' think, hard. You're not hurt. You're *not* hurt. You're just lying there, on the ground, like you just woke up from a nap. Got it?"

I'm not *hurt. I'm not . . . it fucking* hurts . . . *damn him* . . . Lina wanted to cry, but she couldn't do that either. *Sylph . . . help me. Mom . . . someone . . . please . . .*

"You're not hurt," Molochim repeated, like a mantra. "You're *not* hurt. You're not hurt."

Lina grabbed at the sound of his voice, like a lifeline. *I'm not hurt. I'm not. I'm not. I'm not. I'm not.*

And then, much to her surprise, she wasn't. The agony faded as though it had never been. She tried to move her arm, and found it back in its place, her gray sweatshirt without even a bloodstain. Lina sat up and patted her stomach, which was perfectly intact.

"See?" said Molochim. "Was that so hard?"

I'm not . . . hurt . . .

Tears welled up. She couldn't have stopped them, even if she'd wanted to; Lina curled up on the forest floor and cried deep, choking sobs. Molochim sat next to her, looking deeply uncomfortable.

"Sorry. Probably should have fuckin' warned you a bit earlier, right? It's hard, I forget these things." He extracted the pack of cigarettes and tapped one out. "Are you sure you don't want one? It'll make you feel better, I swear."

*   *   *

RAHMGOTH FELT IT WHEN THE DEMONS ARRIVED, SORT OF A

tickle at the back of his skull that bore the unmistakable finger-
print of Rathmado's power. The Magus had been as good as his
word in every particular, but Rahmgoth had been starting to
wonder whether his "plan" would ever materialize.

He was sitting in one of the citadel's chambers with Loquiana, Roswell's assistant. With every day that passed since the
battle, Roswell seemed to think less highly of the Liberator and
her army; now he didn't even bother to meet personally, but left
it up to his smug subordinates. His people had been tightening their hold on the city; there had been riots, Marlowe had
reported, but they'd been put down with a minimum of bloodshed. On the whole, Stonerings seemed to be settling down
under its new ruler—*probably no one could be as bad as the Archmagus.*
And Roswell would provide stability, which was what the merchants and farmers really wanted.

Rahmgoth smiled to himself. *I hate stability.*

". . . while we appreciate the role you and your men played
in the liberation of this city," Loquiana was saying, "providing
your supplies is starting to become a burden. The Governor has
instructed me to ask for a timetable for your departure."

"In other words," said Rahmgoth, "you're sick of feeding us
and you want us gone."

Loquiana gave him a cold smile. "To put it bluntly, yes."

Rahmgoth got to his feet, slowly, and stretched. He could
feel the kinks popping in Lina's shoulders.

Loquiana stood as well. "Don't think you can intimidate
me. The Governor is perfectly aware of your strengths and
weaknesses."

"You know what the best part of this is, you stupid bitch?"
said Rahmgoth, half to himself. "You just have *no* idea what's
going on."

Loquiana went blank for a moment, and then her face
clouded as her brain caught up with her ears. "You—"

That was all she got out. Rahmgoth's sword flashed from its
sheath, crackling with white fire, and carved her neatly in half.

Loquiana stayed upright for one more precarious moment, then toppled with a double thump. Blood sprayed briefly in the air, and Rahmgoth let it spatter over him, savoring the warmth.

There was a shout from outside, followed by an agonized scream. He gave it a moment longer, then walked calmly to the door and out into the corridor. There had been four guards outside—now two of them were on the floor, unmoving, and a third was screaming as a demon pulled his limbs off one by one.

The demon was roughly man-shaped, with a massive, furry torso that looked like it belonged to a bear. In the place of arms it had two massive pincers, like a crab's; one of these held the guard by the throat while the other snipped off his arms at the shoulders. When the thing caught sight of Rahmgoth it crushed the man's throat with a casual squeeze and flipped him over its shoulder, then turned and lumbered forward. Rahmgoth waited a moment, then struck. The demon blocked the strike with one chitinous claw and shrieked in surprise as the blade carved through without pause and decapitated it with a gush of dull green ichor.

The last guard, a woman, was backed against the wall and about two seconds from gibbering. Rahmgoth grabbed her roughly by the shoulders.

"Look at me!"

The soldier blinked and focused. "L . . . Lina. The Liberator."

"Listen carefully. We're under attack. There are demons in the citadel."

"D . . . Demons . . . how?"

"Vilvakis, of course." Rahmgoth shook his head. "There's no time. Sound general assembly. I want *everyone* out of the building."

"But . . . the demons—"

"Leave the demons to me." He let a little white fire crawl over the sword.

The guard appeared to be regaining her senses. "What about the general?"

"Is he in here?" *As if I didn't know.*

"In the throne room. He's got guards."

"Not enough. I'll get him out."

"Alone?"

I'm going to need witnesses. "Have a squad meet me in the main hall. Now go!"

The woman nodded frantically and set off down the corridor at a jog. Rahmgoth went the other way, heading straight for the main hall of the citadel. Along the way he met another group of frantic guards and directed them outside. A few seconds later another demon lunged from a side passage. This one was worm-like, supporting itself with tendrils that drilled into the wall like roots. Rahmgoth chopped it to bits. It was still moving afterward, so he incinerated it in a wash of white flame.

This is fun. He giggled to himself as he stalked the blood-soaked corridors. The demons had gone through Roswell's men like reapers through a wheat field, and bodies were everywhere. A whole gaggle of merchants, no doubt come to protest some of the taxes Roswell had levied, had been chopped into sausage. The creature responsible was just beyond, a six-armed monstrosity with swords instead of hands. Rahmgoth fenced with it for a few moments before slamming a shoulder into what passed for its face and slicing it down the middle while it was stunned.

Killing demons is so . . . unsatisfying. Because, of course, they were from below, and only existed in this world due to Rathmado's power; they didn't provide the rush he normally associated with slaughter. He passed a wounded guard, crawling determinedly down the corridor despite an awful wound in her belly, and paused to put his sword through the back of her neck. He took a deep breath as power flowed into him.

"What are you doing?" Another pair of soldiers had rounded the corner just in time to see. "She—"

"Bad timing," Rahmgoth growled, and charged. A moment later two more bodies lay in the gore-spattered hallway.

The main hall was only a little further on. He found almost a score of guardsmen waiting for him. A demon had come rampaging in from a side passage and killed one of them, but the rest had managed to pin the beetle-like creature to the wall with their spears. Three or four of them jumped at the sound of his approach; a man in a sergeant's uniform, who seemed to be in charge, breathed a sigh of relief and stepped forward.

"You're coming with me to get the general?" said Rahmgoth, before the man could speak.

"Y . . . yes."

"Then follow me. Time is short."

He headed for the "throne room," a large chamber Roswell had adapted for holding audiences. Apparently Lady Fell hadn't needed one. It wasn't far from the main hall, and luckily for the hapless guards they encountered no resistance along the way. Rahmgoth was almost disappointed.

"There," said the sergeant unnecessarily, and pointed. Big wooden double doors had been smashed down and then trampled by something with a lot of weight behind it. Rahmgoth nodded and gestured the men forward, stalking through the rubble with spearmen on either side of him.

The room beyond was a bloody ruin. Roswell's bodyguards had at least put up a fight, but they'd been no match for the demons. Rahmgoth spotted the broken body of the general himself at the foot of the throne, and smiled slightly. *Perfect.*

The throne was occupied by another monster, this one a snake-like creature whose tail forked into three and ended in wicked blades. It was wrapped around the chair and raised its head when they entered, as if in greeting. Its voice was a hissing babble that only Rahmgoth understood.

"Greetingsss, Veritasss. You have ssslain many of my kin today. Know that you have my enmity."

"I care little for your kin and less for your enmity," he replied. The guards looked at him, surprised; they could only hear half the conversation.

"I have heard talesss of you. One who fought, and wasss betrayed. We need not be enemiesss. Come, let usss feassst together on these humansss."

Rahmgoth raised his blade. "This is my only answer."

"Then I have been sssummoned to my death." There was resignation in the serpent's eyes. "Neverthelessss . . ."

It darted forward, much faster than he'd expected, feinting a snap with its jaws before twisting into a lash of the triple tail. Rahmgoth threw himself to the floor and rolled. He felt distant pain as one of the barbed tips scored a line down the side of his face, and the swipe caught the guardsman who'd been standing to the left of him and slammed him into the wall hard enough to crack bone. The one on the right thrust his spear at the serpent's head; the demon easily dodged the clumsy strike and bit the shaft of the spear in two with a crunch, and the man danced backward.

Rahmgoth stayed low as the other guards charged, rage at the death of their leader temporarily overwhelming common sense. The three-pronged tail cracked like a whip, and the three leading soldiers jerked, impaled through the chest. In the moment of distraction that provided, Rahmgoth rolled to his feet and slammed his sword down, white power slashing across an arc bigger than the physical blade. It chopped through the serpent's midsection and left its tail twitching on the floor. The rest of the demon squirmed desperately, leaking fluids from one end, but it wasn't nearly fast enough. Rahmgoth put his boot on it, to stop its writhing, and obliterated its head with a swing and a blast of power.

There was a pause.

"The general is dead," said Rahmgoth, with what he hoped was the appropriate solemnity. "Find anyone still alive and bring them outside. I would speak to all of you."

The sergeant, who was among the living by the expedient of remaining near the back, straightened up and saluted. "Yes . . . yes, *sir*!"

✳   ✳   ✳

GENERAL ASSEMBLY MEANT EVERYONE. ALL THE MEMBERS of Roswell's army, formerly Gargorian's army, were drawn up in the square outside the main citadel building. Nervous unit commanders had the spearmen in ranks, and small groups of archers had their bows trained on the doors. Beyond the packed ranks of soldiery were the curious civilians who'd heard the ruckus or the rumors and had come for a look. *So much the better.*

Rahmgoth strode out of the gate, bleeding from the scratch on his cheek and coated from head to toe in blood and demonic fluids. He made his way to the tallest of the rubble piles that his attack on the city had left, most of which had yet to be cleaned up. It was the work of a moment to scramble to the top, perched on a wooden beam from the blasted door in the outer wall.

The civilians were talking to one another, but Roswell's men were silent, and all eyes were on the solitary figure. Guards were filtering out of the keep, the men who'd followed him to the throne room, and he heard a half-dozen whispered, urgent conversations.

He cut them off. "General Roswell," he said, subtle power throwing his voice across the courtyard, "is dead. He and the men defending him were cut down by demonic invaders."

The word *demonic* ran through the crowd like wildfire.

"Demons," he said, feigning weariness, "have a master. A summoner. The demon is the sword, but the identity of the wielder is clear enough."

He was silent a moment, hoping someone would make the suggestion. Inevitably, the shout came from somewhere and was quickly taken up by a dozen throats. "Vilvakis! Vilvakis!"

"Archmagus Vilvakis," Rahmgoth agreed. "The Magio Obliterator. Master of demons, and the *last* of the Archmagi." He held up his hands. "The General wanted to rule this city— justly, peacefully. Outside the tyranny of the Archmagi. He and I agreed that it is not enough to liberate, to cast down the oppressors, but that something must be raised in their place. To that end we had a plan. He would remain here, with you, and my army would proceed to Adriato and the final set of victims."

Rahmgoth took a deep breath. "My friends, that plan is dead. Vilvakis's demons are *here*. Can his legions be far behind? The Archmagi have no concept of liberation; all they see is a vacuum, an *opportunity* for more power. The Magio Obliterator must be destroyed if any of us are to *ever* see peace.

"Vilvakis has thrown down the gauntlet." He raised his bloodstained sword, and arcs of white lightning flashed from the tip to the tops of the walls. Thunder roared and raged, but Rahmgoth's voice rose above it all to a resounding boom. "I have *answered*. And now . . . will you?"

The screams of assent from the soldiers drowned out even the thunder. Rahmgoth lowered his sword, and smiled.

WHAT WOULD SYLPH DO?

It was a question Lina often asked herself, at least when her little sister wasn't around to tell her.

Sit up, stop crying, figure out what's going on. That's what Sylph would do. Lina doubted she'd be quite as capable. *But I have to* try.

She uncurled a little and wiped her eyes. Molochim, sitting against a nearby tree with the ever present cigarette in his hand, looked up expectantly.

"Feeling better?"

She sniffed and nodded. "I'm sorry. I didn't mean . . . you didn't have to just sit there."

He looked away. "It's not like I've got anything else to do."

"Okay." Lina sat up and tested her arm, which felt fine. "*Why* do I feel better? When that thing . . ." She flinched at the memory. "I thought I was going to die."

"Not here." He shook his head. "I told you, this isn't really a place. It's not . . ." He seemed to be struggling for words. "It's not *big* enough for anything real, right?"

"What was that thing?"

"That was a demon by the name of Hikano. He has also been in here for what you might call a long time, and these days it's better to just stay out of his way."

"But, if it's not real . . ."

"It's all, like, filters. Metaphor. He rips you to shreds because he thinks he can and because you agree he can."

"I didn't *agree*."

Molochim shrugged and took a drag. "It's hard to focus when you're scared."

"Okay." She tried to parse this. "Okay, okay, okay. This is a kind of prison for souls?"

"Something like that."

"How did you get here?"

"He killed me, of course."

"Like He killed Rahmgoth." Lina closed her eyes. "Why could I see Rahmgoth's memory?"

"Rahmgoth was the most powerful one in here, by a fuckin' long shot. He kind of—warped the place, around himself. Six thousand years is a long time, right? And even with him gone the space remembers. Or possibly he warped *us*, and we remember. But either way you see his memory because he's spent so much damn time thinking about it it's practically written on the walls." He took another drag. "Rahmgoth likes to *brood*, if you take my meaning."

"How many people are there in here?"

"You've met 'em all, now. Me, Hikano, Rahmgoth, and the girl. And now you."

"The girl. Who is she?"

"Fucked if I know. Presumably someone He iced, who knows why. She just got here."

"Just got here?"

"Maybe three years back?" He met Lina's incredulous stare. "I *told* you we've been here a while. But she never talks to anybody, she just runs away. There's fuckin' power there, though. There's a whole cluster of *her* memories on the other side of Rahmgoth's castle."

"Castle?"

Molochim pointed. Lina could just about make out a dark, craggy shape, rearing against the sky and occluding some of the stars.

"He lives in there?"

"It sort of grew up around him."

Lina blinked, then shook her head. "Never mind. Here's the important question—how do I get *out* of here?"

"Out?" Molochim blew a cloud of smoke. "Wouldn't be much of a fuckin' prison if you could get out, would it?"

"Rahmgoth did."

"Only because he had someone on the outside helping him. Someone built a gate into the Pit."

"We should be able to get out the same way, right?"

"In theory. If you have a plan I'd like to hear it, 'cause I got shit."

"I . . ." Lina hesitated. *I'm not good at plans.* She wished Sylph was there, or Marlowe even, someone she could depend on. *If Sylph* was *here she'd tell me to stop whining.* "I don't know."

"And there we are."

There was a long pause. Molochim took his cigarette between two fingers and stubbed it out on the ground, then pulled out another and lit it with a flick of his fingers.

"I think I'm going up there."

"Up where?" He followed her gaze to the distant castle. "Up *there*? Why?"

"There might be something he left behind, something we can use to follow him."

"That's probably a bad idea. His memories are thick as fuckin' flies in there, and most of them are pretty unpleasant."

She shrugged. "Do we have anything else to do?"

He took another drag. "No, I suppose we fuckin' don't. But I still think this is a bad idea."

"Stay here, then."

Molochim laughed. "Come on, I'll show you the way."

✳   ✳   ✳

"An excellent performance," Rathmado murmured, "if I do say so myself."

Rahmgoth sat lazily in his saddle, letting the horse take its own pace. The Magus rode at his side, and a half-dozen horsemen from the Liberator's army followed a few steps behind. Inside the city things had descended into chaos, but little by little Roswell's army was trickling out; he'd set Marlowe to dealing with them.

Marlowe. Rahmgoth snarled to himself. *The way he looks at me—we're going to have to have a* talk *with Marlowe.*

"Thank you," he said to Rathmado. "I thought so too."

The Magus gestured to his cheek. "Will you be keeping the scar?"

"Yeah." Rahmgoth rubbed the scabbed cut. "It'll make me look a little tougher."

"Indeed." After a moment, "And you remember the next step?"

"Of course. But if they don't take your bait, things are going to get ugly."

"Worried?"

"Just don't get in my way," Rahmgoth growled.

"They'll take it," Rathmado predicted. "Trust me."

The Magus hadn't been wrong yet. Rahmgoth squinted; he could make out the encampments of the Steelbreaker tribe up ahead, and their outer pickets were just coming into view. Three barbarian horsemen were converging on their little group.

"Who rides?" called the nearest, when they got close.

"I am the Liberator," Rahmgoth said, putting one hand on the sword. "I demand an audience with the Steelbreaker."

"The Steelbreaker tribe has had enough dealing with the

Liberator and her minions," spat one of the barbarians. "Go back to your army."

"You have had *no* dealings with me," said Rahmgoth. "But I imagine you watched the battle at Stonerings, which means you have some idea what I'm capable of. I'm here to see the Steelbreaker. Either you take us to him, or . . ."

He didn't finish, and he saw from their expressions that he didn't have to. The leader, to save face, said, "Then we will take you to the Steelbreaker, and he will decide your fate."

Rahmgoth gave him a humorless smile. "Lead the way."

They rode through the barbarian camp, which by now was well-established; rude lanes had been cleared through the drifts of tents, and hundreds of barbarians, men and women, were going about their business. Many stopped to look at the outsiders, but without much curiosity. *Apparently only the scouts know who I am. Or who Lina is, anyway.*

The Steelbreaker was sitting outside a larger-than-normal tent, set round with animal hides. He was a middle-aged man, tall and broad shouldered, and nursing a wound on his left side. Behind him was a hastily assembled leader's council: two old men, a young woman, and a crone.

"The Steelbreaker," Rathmado murmured. "It looks like the position has seen some contention."

Rahmgoth grunted. Sylph's ambush had chopped the head off the Steelbreaker tribe, and since they'd done nothing since then it seemed likely that they were having trouble getting their leadership sorted out. *Maybe we can fix that.*

"Liberator," said the Steelbreaker, standing despite an obvious stab of pain from his side. "Greetings. I apologize if my men spoke to you roughly."

"Rough speech does not bother me." Rahmgoth glanced at Rathmado, who nodded and faded into the background.

"I am Yoruul, of the Quickfire family. Now the uncontested leader of the Steelbreaker tribe."

"And I am Lina Walker, the Liberator," said Rahmgoth.

"And what do you want with me, Liberator? My people toil under no tyrant."

"I wanted to enquire what the great Steelbreaker tribe planned to do next. Run back to the hills, with your tails between your legs?"

The old men bristled, but Yoruul looked surprisingly unconcerned. "So the women have advised me. They say this war is one we would be better off without."

"And the men?"

"Once you and your army leave, they would have us descend on Stonerings. My people have often longed to loot the great fortress-cities of the south, and I think this General Roswell would not be able to stop us."

"General Roswell is dead," said Rahmgoth, "and his army gone as an independent force. They will accompany the army of the Liberator when we leave the city. Stonerings, if you want it, will be yours for the taking."

There was a pause. One of the old men whispered something to the crone. Yoruul kept smiling, and eventually said, "A lie. You would not abandon the people you fought for."

"My duty is to depose the Archmagi, not to rule the world. And, frankly, I thought better of your tribe. Sacking a defenseless city is an option fit for cowards and thieves."

That got through to him. Yoruul leaned forward. "You would have us return empty-handed?"

"Let me present a third possibility." Rahmgoth smiled broadly. "Come with me."

"The Steelbreakers want no part of your madness."

"But do the Steelbreakers want a part of Adriato? Vilvakis rules from the richest city in the world. It makes Stonerings look like a bunch of mud huts. Come with me, take Adriato, and your names will be spoken for a thousand years."

"You treated the inhabitants of Stonerings softly. There was no plunder to be had, and we will not accept your charity."

"You will earn what you take. Roswell wanted Stonerings

intact in return for his help, and he earned it. Now he is dead at the hands of cowards, and we march to avenge him. The time is right for your people."

"What if you lose? You could lead us all to our doom."

"That is a risk we all must take, of course. But you know what happened at Stonerings." Rahmgoth fingered the sword. "Do you *really* expect me to lose?"

He watched the Steelbreaker's face as emotions played across it, and saw the moment the man made his decision. *We've got him.*

"I will have to discuss your offer with the leaders of the other families," he said, in a tone of voice that meant it would be a formality. One of the old men stepped forward to speak, but Yoruul silenced him with a wave. "When do you march?"

"Two days time. Can you be ready?"

"If we choose to accompany you, we will be ready."

"Good." Rahmgoth couldn't resist a parting shot. "After my younger sister defeated the Steelbreaker so easily, I doubted there were any warriors left in the tribe. I am glad to see that I was mistaken."

Yoruul spun and went into his tent, the other clan leaders piling in behind him. Rahmgoth collected his own astonished bodyguards and led them back to the horses.

"Once again," said Rathmado, when they were riding, "you impress me."

"I'm not a child who needs constant praise, Magus." He lowered his voice. "Besides, I was manipulating mortals five thousand years before you were born. Don't presume to instruct me."

"Of course not," said Rathmado. "I'm just . . . pleased, that things are going according to plan."

Rahmgoth nodded. "After we take Adriato, we'll have the third geist." There was a dark hunger in his voice. "And then . . ."

"Then, my friend, you shall have your revenge."

*   *   *

It had been Sylph's idea to follow the road. Heraan's natural instinct was to sneak into Vilvakis's territory through the back country, but since the whole plan relied on the three of them not being noticed, Sylph had decided it would be better to put it to the test sooner rather than later. *Yahvy will be the hardest to pass off, but she can't be the only woman with a bandaged face out there.*

Now, staring at the checkpoint outside the little border town, Sylph was feeling decidedly less sanguine. She checked the pistol, snug in its holster at the small of her back and covered by her cloak. She'd been able to manufacture a third gun during the trip, so all three of them were now armed. Not unexpectedly, Yahvy had instantly taken to the weapon and practiced as much as she could without drawing attention.

The geists were in her innermost pocket, the metal cool against her skin through the thin fabric. She let Heraan take the lead; he'd taken off his uniform in favor of some brightly colored civilian clothes and a heavy cloak. The swords were strapped to the horses, not an unusual precaution, especially riding as they were on the edge of rumors of war.

The checkpoint consisted of a couple of squads of crossbowmen on either side of the road, and two mounted soldiers talking to people as they went past. From there the road went through the open town gate, over a small stone bridge, and further into Vilvakis's territory. They'd crossed the actual border some time ago; Sylph had been able to feel when they entered the outermost of Vilvakis's Circles. It was an odd, dead feeling compared to being outside. *The Circle draws all the power into the geist, so I'm not surprised.*

The soldiers were not what she'd expected. Gargorian's Diamond Guard had been impressive, but the rest of his men just wore leather and carried spears. Similarly, Lady Fell had focused her attention on the nigh-invincible Clockwork Legion and left her spearmen and archers lightly equipped. But each of

Vilvakis's men had a full breastplate gleaming in bronze and inlaid gold. They also sported blazing red cloaks and helmets with plumes of red-dyed horsehair. One of them carried a banner on which a rearing stallion was picked out in silver thread on black; the others had crossbows and long-swords. All in all they were the most impressive military force Sylph had seen since her arrival, though their spotless cleanliness was almost unreal; it was as though they'd just stepped out of a parade.

She'd hoped there would be a crowd and they could slip by without attracting notice, but only one wagon passed through while they were in sight. The soldier with the banner stood aside while the other horseman waved the wagon through, then settled back into a lazy slouch. He raised a hand as the trio approached.

"Hold!" He nodded to Heraan, who he apparently assumed was in charge. "Where are you coming from?"

Sylph had gone over the script with both of them. The idea was to lie as little as possible, and thus reduce the chances of being caught.

"Stonerings, sir," said Heraan.

"There's an army at Stonerings," said the soldier, frowning.

"Yes, sir. My family and I escaped just before they got there, sir. The stories we heard . . . I've got two daughters, sir, and I didn't want to take my chances, if you take my meaning. And I've got a brother in Adriato, works for a merchant, and I thought—"

"Enough." The man held up a hand. "Is there any news from the city?"

"I'm afraid not, sir. We've been keeping our heads down; I haven't talked to anybody for a week now. You never know, sir, and me with these daughters . . ."

The soldier eyed Sylph and Yahvy.

"Your daughters? What happened to that one?"

"Bit by a horse, sir," said Heraan, letting his eyes fall. "No one'll marry her, looking like that, so I was hoping to take her to

Adriato and get her into a trade . . ."

The man rolled his eyes as Heraan prepared to launch into another story. "Fine, fine. Move along. This road will take you all the way to Adriato."

"Thank you, sir, and White Lady bless you."

"Indeed." The soldier turned around and rode back to his checkpoint. Sylph managed to keep silent until they were well past, riding toward the little town that had grown up around the bridge, then she burst out laughing.

"What's the matter, ma'am?" said Heraan, in the same servile tone he'd adopted with the guard. "Have I done something wrong? You know I'm always willing to accept ma'am's corrections."

Sylph kept laughing as Yahvy rode up, smiling, and rapped Heraan on the back of his head with her knuckles.

"Ouch!" he said in a more normal voice. "What was that for?"

"Get me into a *trade*?" said Yahvy.

"Think I overdid it?"

Sylph smiled. "I think you got it right. Nobody's going to mistake the three of us for leaders in the Liberator's army."

"Perfect." Heraan stretched. "What do you two say to an inn tonight? My back could use a break from sleeping by the road."

"Could use some better food too."

Sylph looked at the sun, which was a couple of hours from the horizon. *We could probably make a few more miles tonight, but . . .* She shrugged. "Sounds good to me. I wouldn't mind a bath."

"Me too," said Heraan.

"I *meant* for you." She broke down laughing again, and trotted ahead while Heraan gave chase in mock indignation.

✳   ✳   ✳

LATER THAT NIGHT, THE GUARDS STOPPED ANOTHER LONELY rider. This one was shrouded in a dark cloak, and had been galloping for some time; his mount was winded and blowing. He slowed to a walk as the checkpoint approached.

"In a hurry, are we?" said the soldier. He was bored and eager for his shift to be done—another hour at most.

The stranger reached into his cloak and removed a folded leather case, which he flipped open to reveal to linked iron rings. "Inner Circle."

The soldier snapped to attention. "Sir!"

"I've an important message for Adriato. I'll need provisions and a fresh mount."

"At once, sir!" The guard beckoned frantically to a subordinate, who rushed off. The stranger got down from his horse, gave the exhausted animal a gentle pat on the nose, and accepted a water skin from one of the guards. He drank noisily and drained the skin before the other soldier returned with a new horse.

"Here you are, sir!"

"My thanks." The stranger swung himself into the saddle and kicked the beast into motion. The soldiers watched him go.

"Looks like he's going to gallop the whole way. What do you think he's carrying?"

"News about the war, most likely."

"Think we'll march?"

"Bet your ass," said the lead guard. "It'll make a nice change too."

"I don't know," said the other, shaking his head. "You hear stories. The Liberator . . ."

"She's been awful good against rabble." He smiled under his plumed helmet. "I'd like to see how she stands up to a *professional* army."

19

chapter nineteen

IT SEEMED TO LINA THAT NOT ENOUGH TIME HAD PASSED for them to reach Rahmgoth's castle, but they were there none the less. Molochim had muttered something about time and distance being transitory and looked away; she was increasingly convinced that he was making it up as he went along. He'd been getting more and more nervous as they got closer.

"Listen, Lina," he said, "I really think this is a bad fuckin' plan, okay? Let's go somewhere else. I can show you—"

"What? Can you take me to where the girl stays?"

"No. It's past the castle."

Lina stared at him. "Couldn't we go . . . around . . . the castle?"

"No. It's *past* the castle."

They looked at each other in mutual incomprehension. Lina finally shrugged. "In that case, there's nothing else to do here. Besides, what are you so afraid of? If we can't really be hurt and we can't die?"

Molochim said nothing, just took a long drag on his cigarette and moped behind her, angrily. The castle was on a hill, and she'd found a little track that seemed to lead in the right direction; it switchbacked across the slope, each ridge lined with dense, dead trees. She kept glancing upward; the castle loomed against the stars, an arched, gothic construction covered in pointlessly complex crenellations and unnecessarily spiky towers. But there was also something *off* about it that she couldn't quite put her finger on.

Some time later—there was no obvious method of marking time, since the stars didn't move and the sun never came up—she rounded the last line of trees, with Molochim in tow. The castle . . .

. . . the castle gleamed in the light of the sun, as if it were made entirely of glass. It was a fairy tale castle, like some enormous wedding cake, slim white spires poking skyward to catch the light. From the tallest spike whipped a banner, depicting the sun resting in two cupped hands. Lina, staring up from ground level, tried to get a sense of the distance; the flag had to be the size of a carpet to be visible.

She blinked, and found that it made no difference; the scene did not vanish. The hillside was gone, the creepy trees were gone, the night was gone, and Molochim was gone. Instead there was blazing day, and a castle all in white.

People were moving at the base of the walls. She saw Molochim, no cigarette, his suit as pure white as the driven snow; he stood like a soldier at ease, with his hands clasped behind his back. Next to him was the man whose death she'd watched a thousand times during her descent. *Rahmgoth.*

Opposite the pair were three other men, all tall and blond and stern-faced. They wore identical flowing white robes, as though it were some sort of uniform. The one in the center stepped forward and spoke in a commanding voice.

"You will open the gates."

"No," said Rahmgoth.

"I order you . . ."

He sneered. "By whose authority are you giving me orders?"

"I serve the Throne!"

Molochim stepped forward. "But His challenge to the Throne has gone unanswered. Until it is resolved, how dare you wield authority in the White Lady's name?"

"If you do not open the gates," said the other, "we will bat-
ter them down."

"And so His prediction comes to pass," Rahmgoth sneered.
"The Veritas divided."

"Only because of His treachery!"

The man lunged for Rahmgoth, but Molochim stepped between them. For a moment the two figures wavered, and Lina
got the strange impression that they were at the same time men
and giant creatures, armored in gold and clashing with swords
made of pure radiance. A single note rang out, high and pure,
and then Molochim stood over his opponent's crumpled corpse.

One of the other men stepped back, aghast. "Molochim . . .
you . . ."

"He would have done the same to me," he said with confidence. "And none of you can understand the wonders He has
shown us. We walk like *gods*, brothers, and no one dares oppose
us! And through all this the Throne has remained silent."

"Leave off, Molochim," said Rahmgoth. "They would not
have sent anyone who could be convinced." He stepped forward, and smiled like a wolf. "We'll have to kill them all . . ."

. . . and Lina snapped back to reality. *Whatever that is.*

The castle—the dark, brooding hulk of a castle—stretched
before her up into the night sky. But she could see that its outlines were the same as the one in her vision, with the brilliant
whites darkened to black and red and the graceful spires replaced by squat, spiked towers. There was no banner flying
from the heights.

"What was that?" she said.

"A memory. This fuckin' place is full of them."

"I saw *you* there. And you killed someone . . ."

Molochim said nothing.

"What were you talking about? What's the Throne?"

He spat his cigarette over the edge of the hill and extracted
another from his coat pocket. His fingers trembled as he lit it.

"Memories. All just fuckin' memories."

"But—"

"Things I don't *want* to remember. Fuck." He looked around. "We shouldn't be here. *I* shouldn't be here."

"I'm going inside," said Lina. She stalked toward the castle. A few moments later, there was a disappointed "fuck" from Molochim, and he hurried to catch up.

✳   ✳   ✳

"WE NEED TO TALK," MARLOWE SAID.

Rahmgoth grimaced. By the amount of sunlight coming in through the tent flap, it was just after dawn. Too late to pretend to be asleep. He'd been avoiding this confrontation out of respect for Rathmado's request, but it seemed there was nothing to do but try and go through with it—he sneered—*diplomatically*.

"Come in, then," he snapped. The flap rustled.

"Lina . . ." Marlowe stopped. "Are you all right?"

Rahmgoth looked up at him. "I'm fine."

"You're still wearing your armor."

"I didn't get much sleep, if that's what you mean." He sighed. "If you came here to say something, then say it."

"Lina, what's *wrong* with you?" He moved closer. "I've tried to talk a dozen times in the last week or so, and you keep chasing me away. I know Sylph's gone off somewhere—is that it?"

"We have a war to run, Marlowe."

"We've always had a war to run. I don't remember it making you so angry."

He moved even closer, and when Rahmgoth did nothing Marlowe reached to put his arms around him. At that point it was too much to bear. Rahmgoth managed to restrain himself and merely elbow the cavalryman in the gut, leaving him wheezing and staggering as Rahmgoth slipped away.

"Don't touch me," he spat. "Marlowe . . ." He fought the urge to send brilliant fire through the man. *Rathmado says we still need him.* "Your devotion to the cause is appreciated. But as far as our personal relationship . . . that was a mistake. It is ended, do you understand?"

There was a long moment while Marlowe regained his breath. "A mistake?" he said, finally.

"Yes."

"I see." He straightened up. "I suppose you won't even tell me why?"

"It wasn't the sort of thing I should have gotten involved in in the first place."

He nodded, and swallowed. "Well. As you say, we have a war to run. I came here to tell you that one of Vilvakis's armies has taken the field, as we expected. We'll meet them before noon."

"Excellent." Rahmgoth paused. "Was there anything else?"

"No," said Marlowe. "I guess not."

* * *

"LINA!"

Rahmgoth looked around and found Melfina hurrying in his direction. He nodded at the girl and continued toward the rocky outcrop that was the closest thing he'd been able to find as a vantage point. Melfina fell into step alongside, but said nothing while Rahmgoth raised the spyglass to look down at the opposing army.

Clever little things, these spyglasses. Humans were always so desperately clever, to make up for their inherent inferiorities. He focused, and the columns of troops a half mile away were suddenly easily visible. They were almost entirely mounted, save for a few regiments of archers, and their discipline was visible even at this distance; the horses maintained perfect formation, as though they were on parade. All the soldiers were armored in a red and gold, and the horses were barded to match. Dozens of banners fluttered bravely.

"Impressive," said Melfina, shading her eyes with one hand.

They certainly look *impressive enough. But there aren't nearly enough of them.* His count put enemy numbers at a little over three thousand. After incorporating Roswell's troops and volunteers from Stonerings, the army of the Liberator was more than twice that number. *Not counting three thousand Steelbreakers.* They were a half-day behind, and Rahmgoth had decided to proceed without them. Yoruul possessed a dangerously over-inflated sense of self-importance, and Rahmgoth wanted it made clear that the barbarians were far from essential.

He lowered the spyglass. "You wanted something?"

"Y . . . yes." The girl seemed taken aback. "I'm sorry. I was just wondering . . . no one seems to have seen Fah since Stonerings, and I'm worried about her."

"You shouldn't be," said Rahmgoth smoothly. He'd been wondering when this question would come up. "There's more to winning a war than just the battles, and some missions are easier alone. Fah is where she's needed most."

Melfina nodded vigorously. "I thought it was something like that. It's just . . . you know . . ."

"I understand," said Rahmgoth, and smiled.

"I'd better get back to my men." She took a last look at the enemy army. "They don't know what they're up against, do they?"

"Apparently not."

Melfina scrambled down off the rocks, and Rahmgoth watched her go. Something about the way she walked caught his eye. *There's another toothsome morsel. Rathmado would probably be mad if I touched her. We could always have another "special mission" . . .*

"My lady!" said a messenger from below. "They've requested a parlay."

"Why not? Let's hear what they have to say."

VILVAKIS'S GENERAL WAS, OF COURSE, EVEN MORE IMPRESsively armored than his soldiers. Rahmgoth was surprised he could even move under all the precious metals. He certainly hadn't been able to get on his horse without assistance. Rahmgoth had mounted so he could talk without looking *up* at him, but he still felt practically undressed in his light leathers.

In fact, he mused, the general under all that gold armor looked the faintest bit like Rahmgoth, that is, like Rahmgoth's *real* body, not this pathetic human's. Though his real body had been dust for six thousand years, he could still feel the pain where the traitor's sword plunged into his heart. He bared his teeth.

Lightbringer. I'm coming for you.

"Well met!" said the general, bringing Rahmgoth back to the present. He was an older man, with a big mustache and enormous sideburns that made it look as though his actual face were being devoured by some hairy parasite. That the whole mess was crammed in under a plumed helmet did not improve the image. "You must be the so-called 'Liberator'."

"Yes," said Rahmgoth. "I'll thank you not to use the term lightly."

"As you say. May I have your name, then?"

"Lina Walker."

He nodded. "I am General Borson of the Golden Brigade. I am ready to hear your demands."

"Demands?" Rahmgoth was at a loss for words.

"When *civilized* men make war on one another, the proper thing to do is to present one's demands at the outset."

"Does this mean you have demands for me?"

"You're the aggressor," said Borson patiently. "Therefore, you have the demands."

"Ah." Rahmgoth thought for a moment. "In that case, I demand that the Archmagus Vilvakis surrender and present himself to me, along with his geist."

Borson sputtered. "That's absurd!"

"You're the one who asked."

"You mean . . ." He stared at Rahmgoth, then began to chuckle. "You mean you actually expect to *win*? To take Adriato? With . . . *this*?" He swept a hand around. "Savages and peasants with sticks!"

"I'm getting tired of this," Rahmgoth said dangerously.

"I led the Golden Brigade to meet your army because things have been quiet lately, and the men are hungry for glory. Three thousand versus six seemed like pretty fair odds. And I expected you to make *reasonable* demands."

"Like what?"

"Money, land, and so forth. If you beat me I'd be more than happy to grant them."

"If I beat you I'll be in a position to take whatever I want."

"You . . ." The general turned to one of the guards who'd followed him. "She really believes it. Absurd."

"Enough." Rahmgoth gestured. "Return to your army before you exhaust my patience entirely."

Borson turned his horse around and led his guards across the field, still unable to control his laughter. ". . . going to *win* . . . unbelievable . . ."

Rahmgoth looked around and found Marlowe at his side. "You heard?"

"I heard." If their conversation earlier had had any effect, the big cavalryman wasn't showing it. His eyes were on the enemy army.

"The man's an idiot."

"He's just playing by a different set of rules," said Marlowe. "I don't think they've had a real war here in a long time. Vilvakis's demons are the real power, and who would want to fight them?"

Rahmgoth smirked. "They're in need of a reminder, then."

✳   ✳   ✳

THE CITY OF ADRIATO WAS NESTLED IN A VALLEY ON ONE side of an long, narrow inlet. It had begun on the flat land close to the water and gradually spread up the slope as the pressure for space grew. The result was a city of terraces, flat ground that had been reclaimed from the bare rock. The top of the cliff and the other side of the inlet were occupied mostly by palatial estates; Sylph assumed those would be the citizens wealthy enough to afford having everything delivered by boat or up a narrow, winding stair.

There was a natural gap in the cliffs a few miles north of the city, and it was through this that the road ran before bending south and losing its identity as it joined up to a dozen smaller streets. This close there was a steady stream of traffic, mostly carts and lone riders rolling into the city. Farmers bringing their goods to market, merchants from the outlying towns coming in to load themselves down, and anyone else who wanted to buy or sell. Bleloth had been a fortress against the unforgiving wilderness, and Stonerings a glorified clearing house for grain and cabbages; Adriato was the first place Sylph had seen since leaving Earth that really *felt* like a city.

It was also *huge.* She had to keep tugging Heraan's sleeve to stop him from staring around with wide eyes. Yahvy had a better poker face, but Sylph was reminded that neither of her companions had ever seen so many people in one place. It was a bit overwhelming, particularly in terms of smell. While Adriato was blessed with a bay in which it could dump its sewage, the streets were still piled with horse dung. She noticed a number of restaurants and shops kept piles of burning wood in metal bins out front, presumably to provide a pleasant scent, but the effect in the street was to make things even worse.

Sylph rode next to Heraan and tried to whisper, but got no response. She ended up speaking normally, and even that was barely audible in the babble.

"Well, we made it."

Heraan nodded. "Easy enough. Now what?"

"First we find somewhere to stay, get something to eat, then run a little bit of reconnaissance. See how much of what we need to know is public knowledge."

"What do we need to know?"

"Mostly where we're going. With these . . ." She patted the

pocket that held the geists. ". . . a break-in won't be hard."

"Okay." Heraan paused. "Pick an inn."

They'd come to one of the city's major north-south thor-oughfares—there was one running down the center of every terrace, it seemed—and it was lined with hundreds of painted signs. Most of these seemed to be taverns, but a few advertised lodging as well.

Sylph picked one that looked respectable. There was a blue crab painted on the sign, and an actual blue crab over the door. At a nod from Sylph, Heraan led the way in with Yahvy bring-ing up the rear.

The inside was a lot nicer than Sylph had pictured. A uni-formed servant sat behind a polished hardwood desk, scratching at a ledger; corridors stretched back from the street, lined with rooms. A wide ballroom-style staircase led to the second floor.

Heraan stepped in front of the desk and cleared his throat. The flunky held up a finger for him to wait, finished writing, and closed the book with a snap.

"Yes?" He sounded irritated. "What do you want? If you're looking for work we've nothing to offer."

"We're looking for a room."

"Really?" He peered at them nearsightedly. Sylph was suddenly aware that they didn't exactly look like this establish-ment's typical customers, all the more so since they were still covered in dust from the road. "Are you sure you've come to the right place?"

Heraan had apparently caught on as well. They'd acquired some of Vilvakis's currency in the village they'd passed through, and it had proved easy enough for Sylph to duplicate. Heraan dug a purse from his belt and set it very deliberately on the desk, where it clinked. "It's been a long road, and we're tired. A room, please."

"Very good, sir," said the flunky, instantly attentive. "Would you like a mountain view, or ocean?"

"I don't care," said Heraan wearily. "Just—"

"And would sir care for a bath?"

"Yes!" said Sylph, over Heraan's shoulder.

There hadn't been a bath in the little border village, just a bowl of hot water and a towel. Since then there'd been even less, just the occasional icy stream Sylph was reluctant to stay in any longer than necessary. But the Blue Crab had a bath, an honest-to-God bath apparently carved from a single large chunk of marble. Servants filled it with water so hot it steamed while Sylph undressed behind a screen. Once they'd left, she poked her head out to make sure no one was watching before slipping carefully into the tub.

"Ahhh." She couldn't help sighing aloud. *Running water. Once this is over and I've got somewhere to settle down, I'm going to damn well invent running water. And indoor plumbing.* There was, in fact, a long list of modern comforts that she'd have to figure out once she had the time. *Though I guess there's something to be said for having a dozen servants waiting on you hand and foot.* Another servant had taken her clothes to be laundered, and replaced them with a fluffy towel. *I could definitely get used to this.*

She luxuriated a bit longer before remembering that she should probably be feeling guilty. *After all, Lina and the others are still living in tents and marching for miles a day, maybe fighting for their lives.* Surprisingly, that didn't produce more than a twinge. *They've got their part to do, and I've got mine. Mine just happens to include hot baths.*

And we're almost there. One more geist, one more Archmagus. She hadn't even checked to see if her search in Lady Fell's geist had found her mother. *Somehow I don't think it will. Rathmado needs that to hold over my head—he's got this all* arranged. What to do about that had been preying on her mind. *It depends upon what I find out from* Chronicles, *but suppose he does have something nasty in mind? Do I get rid of him? Kill him? Can I kill him?* He called himself a Magus, but he'd never demonstrated any powers that Sylph could remember other than an odd ability to vanish when he didn't want to be found. *Either he's a fraud, or he's just being cagey.* Somehow she suspected the latter.

Sylph submerged far enough to blow bubbles. *One more geist. I'll find Mom, and then I'll figure something out.* She hadn't really thought that far ahead. *How can I get her* out *of the geist? Build a body, I guess—or find one somehow—I'll figure it out.* She closed her eyes. *If no other options present themselves, I'll give her mine. Let Lina and Mom live together, and I'll go . . . wherever she went.* It wouldn't be so bad. *It's only what I deserve.*

"Sylph?" Heraan opened the door. "Are you in . . . here . . . ?"

He trailed off, and there was a moment of frozen time. She suppressed the urge to scream and jump out of the bath, which would have most likely resulted in a painful fall on the wet marble. Instead, Sylph took a deep breath and said, "Yes!"

"Ah." Heraan paused—he didn't seem to be able to take his eyes from her chest. "That is to say. I thought. Another room—"

"Would you turn *around*?"

"Right!" He spun. Sylph fought down a furious blush.

"What do you want?"

"I was just . . . I mean, I'm sorry. I didn't mean to . . . it was an accident—"

"I know! What do you *want*?"

"I was going to go out and look around," he said in one long breath. "Neither of you really knows your way around a place like this."

"And you do?"

"All cities are basically the same, and I spent a long time in Bleloth dealing with underworld types. I'll poke around and see if I can find out some of what I need to know. It can't hurt."

Sylph considered. "Okay. But be careful. And come back to get us before you do anything serious."

"Of course." He swallowed. "You . . . I mean . . . that is, you look very . . ."

She let him sputter out, and he eventually deflated.

"Sorry. I'm sorry. I'll head out, then . . ."

"Please," said Sylph. "And shut the door behind you."

Once he was gone, Sylph sat up a little and looked down at herself. *Not all that much to get embarrassed about, anyway,* she mused. *And I "look very" what? Naked?* She sank back down and blew more bubbles. *Stupid Heraan.*

✳   ✳   ✳

"My lord Archmagus," said the spymaster stiffly, "I apologize for disturbing you."

"That's all right." Vilvakis had a soft voice that only rarely showed the steel underneath. The Magio Obliterator was a hair under six feet tall and thin as a rail, dressed in well-cut black and gray. Short dark hair was swept back from a widow's peak, and he had just enough of a goatee to accentuate the lines of his face.

Vilvakis had had a long time to get his appearance just right. His person was meticulously groomed, down to his fingernails— at the moment, in fact, he was attending to that. A servant girl was, anyway, filing carefully. Like all of his personal body servants, she was a deaf mute, with her tongue and parts of her inner ear removed courtesy of the Archmagus's sorcery.

The spymaster, whose name was Razio, was a huddled form under a dark cloak in the corner of the room. He preferred to avoid the light, and Vilvakis was kind enough to allow him his little affectations.

"You asked to be informed," he continued, "when the Liberator's sister and her party entered the capital. They have."

"I see. Have they taken any action thus far?"

"They've established lodging, my lord, and her manservant is out on the streets." He didn't need to add, "he's being followed," and Vilvakis didn't need to ask; he trusted his people to do their jobs.

"Any idea what they're after?"

"He's being a bit cagey, lord, but he seems to be inquiring after your library."

"The library?" Vilvakis switched hands. "Why?"

"We don't know. Shall I have him captured and interrogated?"

"That would tip off the others. No, I think we'd do best to get them all at once. Plant a path to the library, let them get what they're looking for—there's nothing in there that can hurt us. Once we know, take them."

Razio nodded. "As you will, Archmagus."

"What news from the west?"

"Borson has led the Golden Brigade to engage the Liberator's army. So far, no word."

"I don't imagine he'll succeed." Vilvakis sighed. "It's so hard to keep an army in shape without a real enemy; I shall think of this as a necessary winnowing. Still, her response should be interesting. You've confirmed my orders to the Blue and Silver Brigades?"

"They're on their way, my lord."

"Excellent." He yawned. "Let me know when this Sylph is in custody. I want her undamaged, you understand?"

"Perfectly, Archmagus."

"Good. Go."

✳   ✳   ✳

THERE WAS A MOAT AROUND THE CASTLE, OR AT LEAST THE space for a moat. Lina peered over the side and found it dry but studded with moss-wrapped objects that looked suspiciously like bones. All in all, she decided she'd rather not climb through it; fortunately there was a drawbridge, which was down. The wood was splintered and rotten, but it took her weight sturdily enough.

Inside the curtain wall was a courtyard, cobblestones broken here and there by little clumps of plants. The keep was the only building, and that was small, only a couple of stories. Besides that, there was nothing in evidence, and *that* helped Lina put her finger on the thought she'd been trying to capture; in her admittedly limited experience, castles were full of *stuff*, since they were places for people to live as well as fortresses. Here there was nothing, no wooden buildings, no pens for horses or livestock, no gardens. It was almost like a full-scale model of a castle rather than the real thing, as though it were an exhibit at Disneyworld.

"It doesn't look too scary," she said, as much for her own benefit as Molochim's.

The young man looked around suspiciously. "The damn things wait until you're not looking. Then they jump on you."

"If they're just memories, I don't see what you're so afraid of."

"Lina, please." He lowered his voice. "Let's leave, okay? We can find another way out of this fuckin' place, I swear, but—"

"Why? Answer me, and I'll think about it."

He shook his head and said nothing. Irritated, Lina spun and took a step closer to the keep . . .

. . . and the courtyard suddenly expanded, cobblestones stretching away in all directions. The stones lost their curtains of moss, the clumps of grass disappeared, and the curtain wall grew and grew until Lina was standing at the center of the largest fortress she'd ever seen.

There was a huge crowd gathered, packed shoulder to shoulder around a wide circle of clear cobbles. They were human, *really* human, she sensed, not just human-shaped like Molochim, and while they seemed very attentive none of them looked happy. There were banners here and there, with the same cupped-hands-and-sun she'd seen before.

Alone, in the center of the clear space, was an old man in the robes of a priest. He was looking straight up, eyes closed. Lina glanced up, and found the sun nearing its zenith. A moment later a ray of light shot down from on high, there was a flash, and three massive figures stood before the priest. Two of them she recognized as Molochim and Rahmgoth, despite the fact that they appeared as ten-foot glowing apparitions in golden armor rather than in their human guises. The last was another being of the same stature, but no details were visible; as though, no matter how hard she tried, Lina's eye simply could not focus on him.

The priest dropped to his knees. "Almighty Veritas, we thank you for your mercy and for your protection against the minions of the Throne, and we exalt your glory above all things! Guide us to grace and deliver us from evil, and may your rule continue from now until the end of time. We ask you now for your judgment." He turned. "Bring forth the accused!"

A half-dozen people were pushed into a rough line by armed guards. There were three men, one of them so young he was really a boy, along with two older women and a girl of around Lina's age. It was this last that caught Lina's attention; she had red hair that fell like a curtain past her shoulders, and something in her bearing was profoundly different from the others.

Rahmgoth strode forward, and the priest scuttled out of the way, remaining a step behind the giant. The guards also backed away hurriedly, and the accused were trembling. When Rahmgoth finally stopped in front of the first man in line, the prisoner dropped to his knees and started babbling incoherently, begging for forgiveness.

"And?" said Rahmgoth, his voice a bass rumble.

"He is accused of theft and murder, almighty Veritas," said the priest.

"Look at me."

The man refused to look up, so Rahmgoth grabbed his head by the hair and hauled him to his feet. Wide, glowing eyes bored into the prisoner for a long moment. Then the giant tossed him to the cobbles and said, "Guilty."

"No!" the man screamed. "Please—"

He managed no more than that before he burned from the

inside out, flesh briefly turning incandescent before falling into dust. In less than a second there was nothing left of him.

The next man was accused of rape, and burned as well. One of the women was a thief, the other an adulteress; the former was incinerated, but Rahmgoth stared into the latter's eyes and pronounced her innocent. He sounded reluctant, but she thanked him profusely and fled into the crowd.

The boy was standing steel straight, gaze fixed straight ahead. He hadn't watched the others die, hadn't even flinched at their screams.

"He stands accused of breaking the arm of a blooded warrior," said the priest.

Rahmgoth fixed him with his unblinking gaze. Lina saw a trickle of urine run down the boy's leg and pool at his foot.

"Guilty," said the giant. The boy kept his teeth clenched as he turned to ash from the inside.

The girl was last; her eyes were wide as she watched the boy's demise, but she stood straight and was the only one to meet Rahmgoth's eyes of her own free will. She stared at him, defiantly, as the giant glanced to the priest.

"She stands accused," the priest whispered, "of consorting with the enemy."

Rahmgoth looked back at her.

"Guilty," he said.

The girl closed her eyes and flinched, waiting for white-hot death. When it didn't come, she opened them cautiously. The third figure, the one that wasn't really visible, had held up its hand. Rahmgoth turned, then bowed. The priest looked utterly confused as Rahmgoth took the girl by the shoulder and led her toward the other two giants . . .

. . . and then, in a flash, the dark courtyard and the night returned. Lina gasped for breath and stumbled back against a wall, the stone cool under her hands. Molochim shivered.

"What *are* you?" she asked, eventually.

"Veritas," said the young man quietly.

"Rahmgoth and . . . Him, as well?"

He nodded.

"And that's what you really look like?"

"Well, *really* is a term that's pretty fuckin' tough to define. To be honest I have no idea what you see when you look at me. *But,*" he raised his voice as she started to object, "yes, that's probably pretty close to what we look like to one another, which is about as good as you're going to fuckin' get."

"The three of you were . . . friends."

"More like companions." Molochim sighed. "Or, fuckin' soldiers maybe. He was always the leader—we never even thought about it. Just seemed natural. Until . . ."

"Until what?"

"Why do you care? What the fuck does it matter?" He rounded on Lina. "This is fuckin' idiotic, and I'm sick of it. There's nothing here, no way out. You're stuck here with me and Hikano and whoever the fuck the little girl is until the end of time, and there's nothing you can do about it."

Lina blinked. Part of her, an old part, wanted to break down and cry for Sylph or her mother or anyone else. Or just curl up in a cold corner and wait for death, or madness. *But that's not what Sylph would do.* So Lina took another deep breath, curled her hands into fists, and said, "Go, if you want."

"I . . ."

"Why won't you?" She took a step in his direction. "You've been following me ever since I got here—are you just bored?"

"Sure, it's been . . ."

"I don't think so," Lina interrupted. "I think that *you* think there is something here. A way out, maybe. But this place is infested with memories and you just don't want to think about them."

"Fuck you." His voice changed as he spoke, and all of a sudden Molochim *loomed*, topping Lina by an easy five feet. His armor glittered and sparkled, even in the dark, and over one shoulder was the hilt of a sword the size of a log. Power flowed from him like blood from an open wound, and the air took on the metallic smell of ozone. His voice boomed. "You will not speak to me that way."

Lina found herself thinking of the girl in the memory. She tried to stand just as straight, meeting Molochim's eyes defiantly. "I'm not afraid of you. You said it yourself: I can't die, I can't even be hurt unless I agree to it. So don't think you can scare me just by looking like that."

Molochim hesitated. Then, all at once, he snapped back to his human form, cigarette dropping from between nerveless fingers. He fell to his knees, put his face in his hands, and—to Lina's astonishment—started to cry.

＊　＊　＊

"ALL RIGHT, ALL *RIGHT*," SAID GENERAL BORSON, SHRUGGING off the hands of the guards. "You don't have to be rough."

Rahmgoth watched him with the air of someone examining an insect performing an amusing trick. He'd spent the battle with Orbaa's pike-men, who'd been in the thick of things. Or as thick as things had gotten, in any case. Borson had tried some sort of elaborate feint to get the Liberator's cavalry out of position, which Rahmgoth had ignored. After trading arrows for a while and ending up on the short end of the exchange, the Golden Brigade had charged across the field into a thicket of pikes.

I have to give Sylph credit for that. Assuming the pike-men were disciplined enough, cavalry charges just broke up against that impenetrable wall of spear-points. Vilvakis's troops had been no exception; they'd charged, regrouped, and charged again, each time leaving dozens of bodies at the feet of the pike-men. At that point, somewhat to Rahmgoth's astonishment, they'd surrendered.

"They're good, those long spears of yours," said Borson as though he didn't have two of them leveled at his back. "Wasn't expecting that. Is it some sort of western thing?"

"My sister invented it," said Rahmgoth.

"Well, they do a damn good job. I'll have to think about that for next time."

Next time? "General," said Rahmgoth, "I wonder if you quite understand—"

"Lina!" Marlowe waved him over. Rahmgoth arrived shaking his head.

"He's mad. They're all mad."

"Sort of." Marlowe gestured to the field of battle where the Golden Brigade had been gathered after being stripped of their horses and weapons. They were sitting or standing in small groups, chatting or joking—not exactly the look of a defeated army. *What in the name of the Throne is going on?*

"I've been talking to some of them," Marlowe continued. "Apparently they usually fight the other brigades—Blue and Silver—and this is the way it normally goes. A little bit of fighting, one army gains the advantage, and then the other side surrenders. The winners collect their compensation and everybody goes home."

Rahmgoth gave him a level look. "You're not serious."

Marlowe shrugged. "It makes sense, if you think about it."

"Don't they all work for Vilvakis?"

"Sort of. Apparently, he tolerates a little feuding as long as it stays small scale."

"This is completely insane. Look at them." He gestured to the mass of prisoners. "They expect me to *let them go?*"

"I'm not sure there's anything else we can do with them. We don't exactly have the supplies to keep three thousand prisoners."

"So *that's* why Borson's so sanguine," said Rahmgoth, mostly to himself. "He thinks . . . unbelievable. The arrogance of him." *Of the* mortal*!*

"Lina," said Marlowe, "I think we should . . ."

Rahmgoth spun. "We'll show them what war is about. Maybe next time they won't charge quite so boldly. Come with me."

He stalked back toward Borson with Marlowe in tow.

Orbaa's pikes were still in formation, with Orbaa himself standing by the prisoner. Borson favored Lina with a strained smile.

"How does this work? I don't know how you people handle prisoners. Is there a ransom to be paid, possibly?"

"There's a price," Rahmgoth growled, "for opposing the will of the White Lady."

"How much? My family will be glad to—"

"Marlowe," said Rahmgoth without looking around, "kill them all."

There was a moment of stunned silence.

"What?" Marlowe whispered.

"You heard me. Kill them all. It will be a lesson to the brigades that remain."

Borson had gone white under his mustache. "You . . . you can't be serious."

"Lina," said Marlowe, "I think that would be a bad idea."

"It's an order," Rahmgoth snapped. "Are you going to carry it out, or not?"

"You can't seriously expect me to—"

"You can't do that!" Borson interrupted, sputtering. "You're mad!"

"*You* are mad," said Rahmgoth, "and as I've won the battle I can do whatever I like. Marlowe?"

"The men won't do it."

"They'll do as they're told. And so will you."

Another silence, longer. Finally Marlowe said, "And you'll kill me if I don't?"

Yes. But Rahmgoth was aware of the eyes of a regiment of pike-men on his back. "No. I'll take away your command."

"Then that's what you'll have to do."

Rahmgoth sneered. "As you will. Orbaa!"

"Yes, lady!"

"Kill them all."

The commander of pikes saluted smartly. "*Yes,* lady!"

"No." Borson shook his head violently. "No, no, no. This

isn't war, this is madness!"

"This is the judgment of the White Lady!" said Rahmgoth, letting his voice boom all across the field. "Men and women who worked directly for the Archmagi deserve their punishment!"

"*No!*" Borson screamed. Rahmgoth rounded on him.

"And as for *you* . . ." He held out one hand. "You have also been judged, and found wanting."

White fire bloomed all over the general's body. He screamed in earnest, falling to his knees and scrabbling desperately at his face; Rahmgoth watched him burn with a satisfied smile. After a moment he closed his hand, and the fire winked out. Borson was still screaming; his clothes were in tatters, and his golden armor had slumped and run against his skin, which was little more than a blackened crisp. All his hair was gone, along with his once proud mustache.

"However," said Rahmgoth, still smiling, "as I need someone to deliver the news to the other brigades, you can keep your pathetic life." He turned to Orbaa. "See to it that he's delivered somewhere where Vilvakis's men will find him."

"Yes, lady!"

Marlowe, tight lipped, spun on his heel and walked away. On the field, pike-men spread out, drew their short blades, and waded into the mass of prisoners. The shrieks and wails began.

✳   ✳   ✳

"I think," said Heraan between bites, "that I've got something."

"Oh?" Sylph paused to devour the chunk of bread she'd been using to wipe up the gravy. The Blue Crab's meals were as luxurious as the rest of its facilities. Dinner had been roast boar, along with some kind of beef Sylph couldn't identify. Dessert was eels, which she was too chicken to try; Yahvy was sucking them down with enthusiasm, however.

"Well, I found out where the library is." Heraan leaned

back from the table. "But I also may have found a way in."

"That was fast. How?"

"Luck. One of the guys I was drinking with knows someone who pulls guard duty up there. He claims he can get us in—for a consideration, of course."

"Hmm." Sylph glanced at Yahvy. "What do you think?"

"Too easy." She severed the intact head of another eel and devoured the remainder. "Seems unlikely—been what, one day?"

"You think it's a trap, then?" Heraan asked.

"Maybe."

"That means Vilvakis knows we're here," he said.

"Not necessarily," Sylph pointed out. "It doesn't take an Archmagus to try to scam a couple of out-of-towners out of their cash."

"What do we do?"

Yahvy finished her eel with a belch. Sylph rolled her eyes and said, "I think we try it. We've come this far. If we pass on this just because it seems too easy, we may not get another chance."

"What if it *is* a trap?"

"Hopefully, they don't know what we're capable of." Sylph had made up a couple of additional surprises too. "We just have to be careful."

"Yahvy?" Heraan asked.

"Agreed." She licked her fingers. "Probably not Vilvakis; he'd come here, just take us. Simple crooks we can handle."

"He wants to meet me tonight."

"Did you warn him you'd have two more people?" Sylph asked.

"Yeah," said Heraan. "We've got an hour or so."

"Let me go check on some things." Sylph pushed her chair back and stood up.

"Are those new clothes you're wearing?"

About time he noticed, Sylph thought, then wondered why. "Y . . . yeah. I figured I should find something a bit more suited for the city." That had turned out to be pants of some fabric she couldn't identify and a loose fitting silk shirt; in Adriato the tailors used silk like it was cotton. The city's fashion tended toward overstatement; she'd managed to find something in a halfway reasonable light blue and not covered in sequins. She'd gotten her hair cut too, back up to where she liked it. *We haven't been in a city for a long time*, Sylph thought defensively. *And we had some free time.*

"Looks good," said Heraan.

"Thanks." Sylph smiled, and pounded up the stairs a little bit faster than necessary.

HERAAN'S CONTACT TURNED OUT TO BE A SMALL MAN WITH a face like a weasel, who gave his name as Kevin. He was dressed in the same kind of armor as the soldiers Sylph had seen before, although his had a silver cast rather than golden and seemed a lot shabbier; the horsehair plume in his helmet was frayed and in need of new dye, and his breastplate was covered with nicks and scratches.

The meeting place was the alley outside of a particular tavern, and they found it easily enough. Heraan and Yahvy had brought their swords, in addition to the pistols they had concealed; Sylph had her own gun and the geists in her pocket. Kevin was waiting when they arrived, pacing nervously up and down the alley and occasionally kicking at a stack of empty boxes.

"Falk!" he said, on sighting Heraan. "Thought you weren't coming."

Falk? Sylph supposed it was good practice not to use real names. *Although I hardly think anyone would recognize us here.*

"I'm here." He gestured to the two girls. "It's just the three of us."

"You've got the money?" said Kevin, too eagerly.

Heraan grimaced and tossed him a purse. When Kevin looked inside, he said, "That's half."

"Right." He clapped his hands together. "Well, no time like the present. Follow me."

They did, a few steps behind. Sylph whispered to Heraan, "Falk?"

"Sorry. I couldn't think of anything else."

She shrugged. Kevin was leading them toward the inlet, through a series of alleys and side streets rather than by the main thoroughfares. Adriato by night was a blaze of fires, from the lanterns that illuminated the streets to the braziers hanging from the walls of the shops, but very little of that light penetrated past the first row of buildings. There was enough to throw dark shadows, and apparently enough for Kevin to find his way. Sylph had to carefully avoid any number of boxes, barrels, and other bits of debris. Before long she saw the bulk of a curtain wall ahead.

"Is that Vilvakis's fortress?"

Kevin gave her a funny look. "It's the Archmagus's compound, yes. The library is just past that wall. Luckily, my friend was able to arrange to have duty on the back gate tonight."

Luckily. Sylph had a sour taste in her mouth. *But we've come this far . . .*

The back gate was a tiny wooden portal, sunk deep in the stone. Kevin gestured for the three of them to stay put and sidled up to it, giving the door the tiniest of knocks. An equally quiet knock answered.

"It's me. Open up."

Sure enough, someone pulled the bar and opened the door. Another guard, armor not quite so badly worn, waited inside.

"He'll take you the rest of the way," said Kevin. "And now . . ."

"Here," said Heraan, and another pouch of coins hit the man in the chest. "Remember to keep this quiet."

"Of course," said Kevin, backing away. "Of course."

Heraan was first through the gate, and Yahvy last. The new guard looked them over before shutting the door and replacing the bar. "Call me Gabe," he said. "Stay quiet, whatever happens. If we run into a patrol let me talk to them." He frowned seeing that Heraan and Yahvy were armed. "You're only going to the library, right?"

"We're not the trusting type," said Heraan, and Yahvy gave him her best glower. Gabe shrugged.

"Just remember that I can have a dozen guards here any-time I shout for them."

"Just lead the way."

Sylph wiped her palms on her pants, trying to get rid of the sweat. The compound, as Kevin had called it, was wide and low. There was no massive keep, just a series of well lit buildings stretching down to a private set of docks jutting into the ocean. Gabe headed straight for a two-story building with a vaulted roof. Despite his warning about patrols, they saw no one, and the door to the library stood open.

"Shouldn't someone be here watching?" whispered Sylph.

"I arranged it before I came to get you," Gabe said. "Now go inside. You've got two hours or so before shift change. After that you're on your own."

"Good." Heraan pushed the door open a little farther and peered inside. "It's dark."

"Here." Gabe shoved a lantern into his hand. Heraan opened the flap and played the light around inside, reveal-ing the outlines of a central hall with corridors radiating in all directions. He stepped inside, carefully, and Sylph followed. The floor was marble, and she had to shuffle to avoiding loud footsteps. Yahvy brought up the rear, and then Gabe closed the door behind them.

Closed the door . . .

"Heraan—" Sylph began.

"Far enough!" someone shouted, and a dozen lanterns opened at once. Sylph blinked in the sudden glare; there were two lights in each of the six corridors, and behind them she could see the outlines of men with spears. Heraan froze, halfway to the center of the room, as the guards advanced into a semicircle. One man stepped out in front of the lights, hand on his sword.

"Sylph Walker, I assume." He gave her a tight little smile. "It will go easiest on you if you surrender. I have orders to keep you intact, but that does not apply to your companions."

Yahvy had turned to try the door, but now she turned back. "Barred on the outside," she reported.

"It was a trap after all," said Sylph, curiously calm.

"Apparently. Though I don't see how they found us," Heraan said.

"Spies, maybe?" said Yahvy.

"Enough!" said the leader of the guards, annoyed. "Both of you put down your swords and step away from them, please. And no heroics. My men have crossbows."

That was true, Sylph saw. Her vision was clearing. There was a back rank, six men on their knees with bows leveled. In front of them—*call it twenty spearmen? Against three of us.* Her mouth went dry. *But they don't have a clue what we can do to them.*

"Do it," said Sylph. "Throw down your *swords*."

She hit the last word with as much emphasis as she dared, and hoped the pair of them understood. Amidst the clatter of blades hitting the ground, Sylph slipped a hand into her pocket, gripped, tugged a moment, and threw.

Metal skittered across the ground. As she'd hoped, all eyes turned to follow it. Sylph grabbed Heraan and Yahvy by the shoulder and dragged them both to the ground an instant before the grenade went off. It was louder than she'd imagined, especially in the enclosed space, and she felt a bite of pain as a hard marble shard scored her back. Sylph squirmed onto her stomach, drew her gun, and started firing.

Yahvy had the same idea, and Heraan was only a little bit slower. Sylph's throw had been excellent, and the crossbowmen were scattered like bowling pins. The leader and the rest of the spearmen were caught looking the wrong way. The first volley dropped most of them, and Yahvy nailed two that dove for the cover of the doorway. Oil spread from a shattered lantern and ignited with a *whoomph*, racing across the marble floor. A few of the soldiers were still groaning and moving feebly, but no one was standing. Sylph got to her feet and reloaded, surveying the destruction.

Hell yeah! She was embarrassed at her first thought—*those are* people *lying over there in* pieces—but adrenaline was already working its seductive spell. *They were going to kill us, so it's not like we had much choice.*

"Lady Almighty," said Heraan, climbing slowly to his feet. "Everybody okay?"

Yahvy nodded. She was looking at her pistol as though she'd just found the love of her life.

"Okay." Sylph tried to concentrate. "Someone has to have heard that, so we don't have much time. Let's find what we need and get out of here."

"What do we need?" asked Yahvy.

"A book called *Chronicles.*" Sylph peered down one of the corridors; it led to an oddly shaped room lined with floor-to-ceiling bookshelves. "But first I think we need a librarian."

They found one at the end of the second corridor, a young man who'd climbed under his desk and clapped his hands over his ears at the sound of the gunfight. Yahvy hauled him out into the open, and Sylph leveled her pistol.

"Please don't kill mc, I didn't do . . ."

"*Chronicles.* The book. Where is it?"

"Third shelf from the right, eye level. Please . . ."

"Got it," said Heraan, and tossed the book onto the desk. "What do we do with him?"

"Get him to sit in the corner," said Sylph, putting her gun down and flipping the book open. It looked like a copy of the one she'd read. She picked it up and turned when the *thwap-hiss* of crossbows came from the corridor. Heraan, outlined in the doorway with the hapless librarian, grunted and hit the floor. Yahvy immediately moved to the doorway. After a few more bolts flashed past and embedded themselves in the bookshelf opposite, she ducked out and fired back. Sylph heard screams and running feet.

"Heraan!"

"I'm okay." He was already sitting up, the bolt in one hand; the tip dripped blood. "Got my leg. I'll be okay."

"Out of the doorway!" snapped Yahvy. Heraan scrambled aside just in time. More crossbow bolts hissed by, one clattering off the marble floor. Yahvy's return fire raised havoc, and Sylph heard the soldiers retreat back to the main chamber.

Not far enough. The corridor was the only way out, and with no cover it was a deathtrap.

"Now what?" said Yahvy, putting in another clip.

"Do you have another one of those fireball things?" said Heraan.

"Grenades," said Sylph distractedly. "Yes, two more, but I don't think that's going to get us out of here."

"Not that way." Heraan pointed. In one corner the marble floor was interrupted by wood, with a metal handle. *Trapdoor!*

Sylph stalked over and hauled the terrified librarian to his feet. "Where does that go?"

"Outside. There's a . . . a pulley, it's for moving big stacks in or out—"

"I'll take it." She put him down, picked up the book . . .

. . . saw the little flicker in his eyes, and picked him up again. "What?"

"What do you mean?"

"Why can't I take the book out of here? There's some trick, isn't there?"

"I . . ." His courage drained away. "There's an enchantment on the book. If you take it out of the building, it'll burn, and you'll probably burn with it."

Sylph let him fall. "Shit." *Shit shit* shit. *Now what do we do?* She closed her eyes and reached toward the book, only to meet with a ward of appalling complexity. The threads of the spell were woven into the matter itself. Picking them out without destroying the thing would be a long, painful process.

"Take them a while to regroup," Yahvy observed.

"Right." Sylph turned. "Heraan, take the trapdoor, make sure the other end is clear. Yahvy, you stay by the door."

"What are you going to do?"

"Read really fucking fast. Go!"

✳   ✳   ✳

MOLOCHIM'S TEARS WERE SO UNEXPECTED THAT LINA wasn't sure how to react. Somehow putting an arm around him and saying, "There, there," didn't seem the thing to do.

Instead, she sat on the ground next to him and waited. After a few moments Molochim sat down himself, wiping his eyes on the sleeve of his cheap suit and fumbling his pack of cigarettes with his other hand. His fingers were shaking; Lina eventually took pity on him and took the pack. She gave him one back, and he lit it gratefully behind his cupped palm.

"You're going to have to talk to me eventually," she said. "If there's no way out of here, we're going to be stuck with each other for a long time."

He nodded, miserably, and wiped his eyes again. "I know."

They sat in silence for a while.

Molochim said, "Fuck. I'm sorry for breaking down like that." He sniffed. "Not exactly cool, right?"

"It's okay. I've had my share of uncool moments."

He took a long drag. "The hard part," he said, "is figuring out where to start."

"Are you dead?"

"Yes."

"Like Rahmgoth?"

"Yes."

"Am I?"

"No." He blew out some smoke, staring at his shaking fingers. "Your body still exists, your soul still exists. Rahmgoth's just temporarily evicted you."

"Okay." Lina paused. "So, what are you? 'Veritas' doesn't mean much to me."

"That's the part I'm trying to figure out where to start. I assume you've never heard of tiered reality and the energy slope and all that shit?"

"Yes. I mean, no. I haven't heard of them."

"'Cause explaining what a Veritas *is* is basically explaining where we come from, which is a little weird. So this probably is going to sound like it has nothing to do with anything, but bear with me."

"Okay."

Molochim leaned forward and sketched two circles in the dirt with his finger, one above the other. "This is, like, the universe. In a nutshell. This is the Source, which is where souls come from, and this is the Sink, which is where they go. It's a flow, right? Like a waterfall."

"If you say so."

"Like I said, bear with me. Think of it as a waterfall, but one of those ones with many levels. The water flows from the spring or whatever into the first pool, and from there into the second pool, and so on until it gets to the bottom. And it can split up along the way and go through whatever complex crap it wants, but it never goes back up. Get it?"

"I think I do."

He scratched a few lines between Source and Sink. "The universe is like that. You can think of the Source as being at the top—which is totally fuckin' inaccurate since we're not talking your usual spatial dimensions but rather some kind of energy-potential-doohickey—but in terms of the waterfall it's the top. The spring. And each world is like one of these ledges, where water pools up and then overflows and goes down to the next one."

"*Each* world? How many are there?"

"How the fuck should I know? A lot. The place you come from is called Omega, and it's right about here." He drew a line about three quarters of the way down. Lina thought about mentioning that she wasn't, in fact, from Omega, but decided that would just confuse matters. "Above this there's Earth and a bunch of little tiny places, which are mostly populated by mortals. And above *that* . . ." He drew another line, about one quarter of the way down. ". . . is a place called Ring. That's where I come from."

"I'm missing something." Lina stared at the diagram. "You're saying that *souls* flow from place to place? How?"

"When somebody's born, a soul flows in. When someone dies, a soul flows out."

"When someone on—Earth, say—dies, their soul flows down this slope?"

"Yeah."

"And comes here—to Omega, I mean—and a new baby is born? Does it end up as the same person?"

"Sort of. I mean, it *is* the same person, but they don't remember anything. And neither does anybody else."

"That *almost* makes sense." She thought for a moment. *Sylph said the geist gathered souls for the Archmagi.*

"The other thing that flows is energy," Molochim continued. "Energy starts at the Source too. A soul from a place like Ring has a lot of energy compared to one from Earth, and Omega is even farther down. That's why it's called the energy slope, right? As a soul loses energy it slides further and further until it gets to the Sink."

"Fair enough. What does that have to do with the Veritas?"

"That's the fuckin' tricky part. If you want to . . ." He waved a hand vaguely. "Blow stuff up, or make stuff, or whatever, the key is the relative energy of the world. The higher it is the more difficult things like that are. On Ring, we're just people— not mortals, but people. But if a Veritas were to go to Earth, he'd be like a god. The Earth is so low-energy compared to us that everything becomes easy."

"Why don't all the Veritas leave Ring?"

"It's not allowed."

"By who?"

"The Empty Throne. Sort of the ruling council. They claim the White Lady was a Veritas once, and that she left and will one day return, so they're sort of keeping the seat warm. And everything was going great until one Veritas got it into his head that they were wrong, and convinced two other very stupid Veritas to go with him down to Earth."

It wasn't hard a conclusion to jump to. "You mean L—"

"Shh!"

"I mean, Him," Lina corrected. "He broke the rules?"

"A lot fuckin' worse than that. It's not like the rules were never broken, but when the Throne came after people they'd run, or fight, or whatever. Like criminals. *He* stood up and said that there shouldn't *be* a rule, that it was wrong. He started a war against the Throne."

"What happened?"

Instead of answering, Molochim climbed wearily to his feet. "You want to go through the castle, right?"

"Yes," said Lina, taken aback.

"Then I might as well show you." He sighed. "Come on."

Lina stood, uncertainly, and followed.

✳ ✳ ✳

"She's gone mad," said Marlowe.

Daana gave him a look that said, "It took you long enough to figure that out," but said nothing.

"You've got to realize it too. What are we going to *do*?"

"Wait." She desperately wanted a drink, but Daana was already a little tipsy and didn't dare make it more than a little. *I guess I have a little bit of self-preservation left, after all.*

Marlowe got up, all nervous energy. He paced between one wall of the tent and the other. "Who are we waiting for?"

"Melfina, and one more person I think you should meet."

Melfina entered just at that moment. Her eyes were wide,

and she looked ready to bolt at any moment.

"Marlowe?" The girl shook her head. "I can't do this. We shouldn't be meeting like this."

"There's no crime in talking," said Daana.

"You saw what she did today," Marlowe cut in. "Lina needs our help."

"They were enemy soldiers."

"They had *surrendered*. Lady defend us." Marlowe turned and started pacing again.

Daana gave him a hollow smile. "You seem to be taking this rather personally, Marlowe. Is it because she kicked you out of her bed?"

Melfina blushed. Marlowe spun and said, "Forget about that. I thought I *knew* her, and now she's using my army to do things like this."

His army, Daana thought. *Conceited little bastard, isn't he?* She'd never liked Marlowe, and it was hard to pass up the opportunity to deflate him a little. *Even if he's right.*

"You two are the only ones left from before Bleloth," Marlowe said after he'd calmed down. "Heraan's gone, Yahvy's gone, I don't trust Orbaa anymore, and Fah just vanished."

"Lina said that Fah was off on a mission too."

"You believe that?" muttered Daana. The girl winced as though she'd taken a physical blow. Watching her was painful. *So damn naïve. She'll learn.*

There was a scratch at the tent flap. *Finally.*

"Come in," Daana said. "And sit down, Melfina."

She did, and the spy entered. Daana still didn't know his name; when she'd asked, he'd smiled and told her to call him Joker. He favored Marlowe and Melfina with his brilliant smile; it practically lit up the room.

"Well, well," he said. "This is certainly distinguished company. Commander of the Liberator's army—*ex*-commander, I should say, since she's assigned Orbaa that position now. And a captain of archers as well."

"And you are?" Marlowe demanded.

"He's a spy," said Daana bluntly. "For Vilvakis."

His eyes flicked to her. "That's a harsh way of putting it. You can call me Joker."

"A spy?" Marlowe's tone dropped. "What is he doing here?"

Joker spread his hands. "What do you *think* I'm doing here? My master has an obvious interest in stopping the Liberator's army before it gets any further. Because this is a civilized land, we'd prefer to do that with as little bloodshed as possible. I was as horrified by the aftermath of the battle as you were."

"It's not Lina's fault," said Melfina. "There's something wrong with her, I can tell. She was always a little . . . off, but while Sylph was here she stayed on top of it. I never should have let her leave."

"I think slaughtering three thousand helpless men and women is more than just a little *off*," said Marlowe. "She's sent away everyone who was close to her: Sylph, Fah . . ."

"And you," Daana murmured.

"And me!" Marlowe turned on her. "Is gloating about that really that important to you?"

Not that *important.* Daana smiled. "Just pointing it out."

"It's obvious what's wrong," Marlowe said, breathing hard. "The question is, what do we do about it?"

"Do about it?" Melfina looked uncomfortable. "We should . . . talk to her, maybe . . ."

"We should kill her," said Daana.

There was a pause.

"Don't look so shocked, Marlowe," she continued. "You know that's what you were thinking."

"I'll speak for myself."

"You're not serious," Melfina said. "Daana . . ."

"Of course I'm serious," Daana spat. "What else is going to work? Defeating Gargorian was all well and good. Lady Fell, perhaps that was justified. But where are we going now? None of us has been here. I didn't know anyone who'd *visited*

Vilvakis's domain until we got close to it. But she says we have to come here and fight and die to set these people free." *And the hell of it is, everyone else seems ready to go along with it. Because the White Lady told her it was okay.* Daana wanted to laugh, or cry. *Where was the White Lady when I needed her?*

"With respect," said Joker, "Lina appears to be laboring under a misconception. Vilvakis's people are happy. They have no desire for the kind of 'freedom' your army has brought to Stonerings and Bleloth."

"You want her dead?" Melfina turned to the spy. "You would, of course. Vilvakis would love it."

"He may be right," Marlowe said. "If that's the only way . . ."

"I don't *believe* you, Marlowe!" Melfina got to her feet. "You were in love with her!"

"I was." He looked down.

"And that's changed? Just because she won't let you fuck her? That's so Lady-damned important?"

Joker cleared his throat. "Perhaps I can offer an alternative."

Daana glanced at him sharply. "Alternative?"

"Because of my . . . ah . . . profession, I've acquired a certain skill with rare herbs. The proper potion will ensure that the Liberator is incapacitated, without actually killing her. She need only be kept out of action for a little while. Without her at the center, this army will melt away. Correct, Marlowe?"

"I wouldn't have thought so back at Stonerings. But after today . . ." He shook his head. "They can't be happy, blessing of the White Lady or no. And with Sylph gone, and Fah . . ."

"They'll come back eventually," said Melfina.

"I'm sure they'd agree with us, if they were here," Joker said smoothly. "Once the threat of a marauding army is gone, and things return to normal, the problem of Lina's . . . illness . . . can be addressed safely."

Daana was a little bit disappointed. *I wanted her dead.* But this was almost as good. *And when Sylph gets back, maybe we can arrange something extra.* "It makes sense to me."

Marlowe nodded slowly. "How soon can you provide this potion? And how do we get it to her?"

"Happily, I anticipated this development." Joker reached inside his coat and withdrew a vial of opaque glass.

"And you can guarantee our safety?" Marlowe said.

Joker nodded.

"You're just using us," said Melfina bitterly.

"Of course." The spy smiled. "I've already admitted my interest, and my master's. It simply seems to dovetail with your own rather nicely. As for delivery, slipping it into her food or drink will be sufficient. The dosage need not be large."

"That shouldn't be a problem." Marlowe took the vial, holding it between two fingers as though it were a dead fish. "When?"

"Tomorrow night," said Daana. "After that we break camp. I'm not sure when we'll have another chance."

"Thought about this already, have you?" He glared at her. "You two are lucky I didn't find you earlier."

"Now, now," said Joker. "Let's keep things friendly."

"I'm going back to my tent." Melfina got to her feet.

"I trusted you with this, Mel. I thought you'd understand," Marlowe began.

"I don't want to know. I just . . . don't." The girl slipped out through the tent flap with a rustle.

"Do we need to worry about her?" Joker asked Daana.

"No." Daana sighed. "She understands what needs to be done."

After the spy was gone, Marlowe turned to Daana.

"Vilvakis's assurances don't mean much to me."

I can't tell him that I just don't care anymore. "Do you have a suggestion?"

"I'll start working on a backup plan." He smiled. "Most of the regimental commanders will listen to me over Orbaa, especially if Lina's temporarily out of the picture. If we can keep the army together and withdraw back to Stonerings . . ."

Daana nodded dully as he went on. *Stonerings, Adriato, it's all the same.* She didn't think she'd see either. *I'm not sure I ever believed I would get away with this, in the end.*

*W*HAT *I* WOULDN'T GIVE FOR A *"F*IND*"* FUNCTION. S*YLPH* turned the pages of *Chronicles* feverishly, looking for . . . *something. I'm not sure. Something about Rathmado. Some* reason. *What happens to the Liberators?*

The book was divided into sections, and Sylph quickly re-alized each was punctuated by the arrival of a Liberator. She flipped to the end of the first and read:

"Jaen's army, fleeing Lady Fell's victorious forces, turned like a hound at bay on the banks of the river. Jaen prepared to personally lead a desperate defense while his men built rafts to ferry themselves across. But Lady Fell unleashed the Clockwork Legion, and none could stand before them. Jaen's magic was not sufficient, and he and his men were crushed under a torrent of steel . . ."

That makes sense. She paged back a little bit. *But what* made *him the Liberator?*

Words jumped out at her:

"And, on the advice of the Magus Rathmado, Jaen led his army in a wide arc, leaving behind enough force to confuse Ty-ramax's scouts. The Liberator's army fell on the Magio Creator from behind, and Tyramax and all his generals were slain. Jaen laid siege to Lastfort, and without the Archmagus's power the city could not hold . . ."

Rathmado. She searched, back and forward, for another mention. *He was there—six hundred years ago.*

Next section. A Liberator named Adam had overthrown a Magio Creator named Golaic, Tyramax's predecessor. She zeroed in on another fleeting reference—

"Adam sent emissaries to Lady Fell, and while he awaited their return he set about establishing a kingdom based in Lastfort, a land where there would be no Plague and justice would be applied equally to all. But the emissaries were never seen again, and Rathmado, chief among Adam's advisors, counseled that Lady Fell meant to make war against the fledgling nation. In this he was correct; when Adam led his armies west, Lady Fell and her Legion were waiting."

How many Liberators did Lady Fell kill?

"Sylph!" Yahvy shouted, from the doorway. "Getting ready again."

"Just a bit longer," said Sylph without looking up.

Rathmado again. Always advising the Liberator, always telling him to go west. To conquer—

"—Hayao, with a few companions, entered the territory of the Lady Fell with the intention of stealing the focus of her power. The sage Rathmado had advised him that without it her empire would crumble, and the Plague would be lifted from her lands. But the Archmagus's scouts found Hayao, and drove him toward the river. On the banks he locked blades with Lady Fell's general Corvid, and Corvid proved the better swordsman. Hayao fell by the banks, and his companions were cut down to a man."

Again. Rathmado . . .

"Que-Li's lover, Rathmado, had a thirst for conquest, and the Liberator felt obliged to provide for him. She set out with her armies before Stonerings had been fully pacified, and invaded the territory of Vilvakis, the Magio Obliterator. The Liberator's magic drove away the flights of demons Vilvakis sent to harass her, but when she reached Adriato the power of the Magio Obliterator destroyed Que-Li and her army, leaving only an abyss from which nothing could escape."

Her lover? Sylph tried to picture taking Rathmado to bed. *God! Maybe he looked . . . younger?*

A series of shots brought her back to the present. Yahvy was on one knee, aiming calmly and firing around the corridor. A couple of crossbow bolts hissed past, but neither came close. She ducked back to reload and caught Sylph's eyes.

"Not brave enough yet. If they rush, it's over. We need to go."

"A minute," Sylph pleaded. *If only I could take the damn thing* with *me.* But Vilvakis's ward made that impossible. She shuffled through the pages.

"Keston's army of half-men met the Liberator Callius at the foot of the mountain, and Keston took his opponent's head in single combat—"

Five Liberators. All five had gone west, and all five had died at the hands of the Archmagi. *Is that what I'm looking for? That we don't have a chance?*

She turned to the second-to-last section, looking for a passage she remembered. *There!*

"With the Magio Obliterator's body cooling on the field before him, the Liberator declared himself content. He tasked Garveh and Sulian with the creation of a new empire, stretching from Adriato to the edge of the Bone Sea.

"But the Liberator's Magus was not content. Hatred had long ago poisoned his heart, and he whispered in Erik's ear that his victory was incomplete as long as the true ruler of Omega drew breath. Sulian argued long and hard, but in the end Erik had grown greedy for further conquest. He turned his eyes to the east, to the Black Keep, and at Rathmado's urging entered the lands of the Lightbringer with a small force. On the banks of the river Loth he fought a battle with the Shadowcore, but the Liberator's magic proved enough to drive them away and his progress toward the Black Keep was unimpeded.

"Upon reaching the Keep, Erik found the doors open. He bade his companions remain, and entered with Rathmado at his side to slay the Lightbringer and deliver Omega from his tyranny once and for all."

"Damn it!" Sylph said aloud. *What* happened *to him?* There was one more section . . .

"Sylph!" Yahvy was backing away from the doorway. "Out of time!"

A tide of blue and black bodies was advancing down the corridor. *Things*—Sylph couldn't call them people—that looked like upright beetles, all spindly legs and armor plating. Each sported a pair of mandibles that were razor sharp on the inside, like scissors. Yahvy fired into their midst, but most of the bullets glanced off their armor and whined away; one of the creatures fell, spurting green from where one of its eyes had been.

I waited too long. The demons would be on them in a moment. No time to get to the trapdoor, no time to escape.

"Yahvy!" Sylph pulled her away. "Go!"

"You first!"

"Go!" She reached into her pockets and pressed the two metal spheres into Yahvy's hand. "They said they wanted me alive—I'll be fine—you get out of here!" *And get* those *out of here.*

Yahvy saw there wasn't time to argue. "Be back soon." She nodded curtly and headed for the trapdoor, and Sylph spun. The beetles had reached the end of the corridor; she drew her gun and charged the lot of them, firing wildly. A ricochet screamed past, but she paid it no mind, shooting until the gun clicked empty. At that point she was almost on top of the things, and much to their surprise she just kept running, pushing the front rank aside until she was in the midst of them.

Pay attention to me, *come on* . . .

Her limbs were seized and held with inhuman strength. Sylph jerked, trying to free herself, but only managed to hurt her shoulder as she was lifted from the ground to face one of the demons. It clicked and buzzed something unintelligible.

"F . . . fuck you." She wanted to do something, punch it maybe, but her arms were held fast. The beetle spread its mandibles and placed them very carefully on either side of her neck. She felt them, just barely tickling her skin. If the demon twitched, her head would be rolling on the floor.

They want me alive, the guard said so. These are his *demons, Vilvakis's, they can't just kill me. They can't.* Something shot out from the demon's head, a thin tube with a spike on the end.

Sylph felt it bite into the side of her throat—it stung more than it hurt—and the world suddenly swam before her eyes. She felt her arms jerk, and then darkness rolled over her like a tide.

20

chapter twenty

LINA PUSHED OPEN THE DOOR TO THE KEEP, WHICH gave a groan like a dying elephant and eventually stuck with a metallic crunch. Molochim peered nervously through the gap. The interior was one enormous room, lit only by starlight filtering in from the outside. The furniture had long ago been smashed; bits and pieces still littered the floor, covered by an accumulation of cobwebs and dust.

And that too, was strange when Lina thought about it. She hadn't seen any spiders in the Pit—no animals of any kind—and after six thousand years there shouldn't have been any bits of wood *left*, just green smears. *I think I'm getting the hang of this. Rahmgoth felt like he should be pacing through dark, dusty halls, and so here's a dark dusty hall, right on cue. That's how it works in here.*

"What happens next?" said Lina, as she eased her way past the door and into the room. "Li . . . I mean, *he* spared that girl who was supposed to be executed. What happened to her?"

"He fell in love with her," Molochim whispered, as though he didn't want to disturb something that slept. "A human. That was against the rules too."

"Really? He fell in love with a human?" Lina shook her head. "It doesn't sound . . . right. He had the humans *worshipping* him. Why would he fall in love with one?"

"Who knows if he really loved her?" Molochim took a drag

on his cigarette. "The thing about Lightbringer, the most important fuckin' thing is that nothing ever had just one level. The more complicated things got, the happier he was. And the *other* most important thing was that he loved flipping the bird at anyone who told him 'thou shalt not.' I don't know if he really loved her, but he sure as hell convinced himself he fuckin' did."

"That's romantic," said Lina. "Did she love him too?"

"Not at first. He had her locked up in His fuckin' castle; I'm not sure what He was expecting. But He would have laid the world at her feet if she'd asked Him to. Eventually they came to a kind of understanding."

"I get the feeling this isn't a story with a happy ending?"

"They killed her. The Throne. It wasn't about the fuckin' rules for them, not anymore. They just wanted Him gone."

"Oh." Lina swallowed. "And then?"

"It's in here somewhere."

Lina walked forward, slowly. There was a kind of throne—just a chair, really, but it was the only intact piece of furniture in the room—and she made her way to it. Halfway there she felt the familiar rush of memory, and the blasted hall became brilliant glass and marble, immaculate and brightly lit.

The girl was slumped in the throne, her head resting on one shoulder and her other arm dangling limply. She wore a powder-blue dress, most of which was ruined by blood flowing from a gaping wound just above her collarbone. Beautiful red hair fell in front of her face like a veil, and those intense eyes were blurry and vacant.

All this hit Lina like a punch to the stomach. There was something *familiar* about the dead woman. *I've seen this before.*

The blurred figure of the Lightbringer emerged from a stairway at the back of the room, leading down. Rahmgoth followed him carrying Molochim in his arms. Lina put her hand to her mouth; the Veritas's gray suit was covered in blood, and his breathing was fast and rattling. Lightbringer strode to the chair, and Rahmgoth set his companion down beside it.

"She's gone, lord," said Rahmgoth.

There was a moment of silence. Lightbringer turned to Molochim and said, "Who?"

"Yarifel," he croaked. "Carnadas. Torquai. Others."

"The Throne."

"Yes." Molochim coughed, his frame wracked with agony. "I fought."

"Why are you still alive?"

"They said . . . they would not kill, not for this war . . . would not sink to our level . . ."

Lightbringer turned to regard the corpse.

"She was human, lord. I suppose they didn't consider this 'sinking to our level'," said Rahmgoth. He took a deep breath. "Give me leave. I will show the Throne what war means. I will make them regret—"

"And what good is that?" said the Lightbringer. He walked to the chair and ran his fingers across the woman's face; closed her staring eyes with his index finger. "What good will it do?"

"There are others who are with us," said Rahmgoth. "We can bring down the Throne—"

"The Throne." Lightbringer gave a humorless chuckle. "We've been fighting the wrong enemy, my friend. Looking in the wrong place."

"Lord?" said Rahmgoth, confused. Lightbringer spun and went back to Molochim.

"She did not deserve to die," he said.

"No." Molochim took a bubbling breath.

"But, it is done," said Rahmgoth from behind him. "It cannot be undone. All that is left is revenge."

"No," said Lightbringer quietly. "Not revenge."

He drew his sword and got down on one knee, the point over Molochim's chest. The shattered Veritas closed his eyes as the blade flashed down . . .

"Molochim!"

. . . and Lina was standing in the dark, shattered hall.

Molochim leaned against one wall, breathing hard.

"He . . . he *killed* you?"

"Of course he fuckin' killed me. How do you think I ended up here?"

"Why?"

"Power. He needed power. Don't you get it? He wanted her *back*; he never cared about the war. It was just a game for him, something to occupy the fuckin' time; it can get so boring when you live forever. And then when he found something he really wanted they took it away from him. He tossed me in the Pit so that he could use my power."

"And Rahmgoth?"

"The same. You saw, before."

Lina remembered—

"We . . . would have won."

"Yes."

"You would have had . . . everything.*"*

"Not everything. You never understood, Rahmgoth. I never wanted to crawl back in, pull myself hand over hand up the slope . . . for what? There's nothing left for me there. I have nothing *without her."*

"But . . . You can't. It is . . . forbidden."

—Rahmgoth and Lightbringer.

"What did he mean," said Lina slowly, " 'forbidden'?"

"Returning the dead to life, bringing a soul back up the energy slope. It is forbidden."

"By the Throne?"

"*Not* by the Throne." Molochim steadied himself against the wall, discarded his cigarette and lit another. "Not by the Veritas. It's just . . . not allowed. The White Lady, the universe, whatever you want to call it, will not permit it. Anything else, but not that."

"Why?"

"How the fuck should I know? Go ask her."

"But, you're still alive." *And me.* She'd decided not to mention that.

"I'm fucking not. I *exist*, here in the Pit, but my real body died six thousand years ago. I told you, nothing in this place is real. That's why we can't leave—why I can't leave. Rahmgoth only managed it because he took *your* body."

"What happened to Him?"

"The White Lady created a prison for Him. Wove Him into the heartbeat of a world so that He could never escape."

"But He lives—"

"On Omega." Molochim took a drag. "Of course. The whole fuckin' place is His prison cell. See, *her* soul passed on, down toward the Sink. Maybe there's something after that, maybe there isn't. But now he's separated from her until the end of fuckin' eternity."

"That's awful."

"He *knew*. We all knew it was forbidden."

"Still . . ."

Molochim closed his eyes. "Forget it. It'd be hard for you to understand."

Suddenly Lina did understand; if not that, then something else. *He just watched himself get killed, again. Maybe felt it. I made him come here . . .*

There was a moment of silence.

"I'm sorry."

"For what?"

"That I kept asking questions. And for what I said earlier."

"Forget it," Molochim repeated. He put the cigarette aside and took a deep, clean breath. "Now you know."

Lina nodded. "What next?"

"You wanted to see where the girl lives, didn't you?" He pointed to the stairs at the back of the room. "It's through there."

"Are you coming?" She was a little hesitant. *If he doesn't . . .* She didn't know what she'd say to that.

He gave her a shaky smile. "Might as well, now that we're past that."

Lina smiled back. "Come on."

* * *

SYLPH OPENED HER EYES AT THE FEELING OF COLD WATER against her skin. Someone was holding her upright; she felt rough hands gripping her arms above the elbows. It was dark, and the two men in front of her were backlit shadows.

"Good morning," said the one on the left. He had a silky smooth voice. "Brutus?"

A fist like a cannonball slugged her in the stomach and Sylph doubled over, her mouth filling with bile. Whoever had been holding her from behind let go and she ended up on her knees, gasping for breath. A kick caught her in the shoulder, hard enough to send her sprawling across the floor like a rag doll. The next kick took her in the side of the head; stars flashed behind Sylph's vision, and it felt as though someone had driven a dagger into her skull. She half-expected, dreamily, to black out again. Instead, the same unseen hand took her by the collar and hauled her back to her feet, where she dangled limply.

"That was just to get everyone in the correct frame of mind," said the silky voice. "I am the Archmagus Vilvakis. *You* are the Magus Sylph Walker, sister to the Liberator Lina Walker. I know you left your army and came here in search of something *very important* . . ." He gave the words a nasty spin. ". . . and I think we can all guess what that might be. Don't bother to deny any of it."

Sylph couldn't have, even if she wanted to; her mouth was filling with blood, and it was all she could do not to swallow it. Her vision was still double.

"The fact that breaking into the library was the best you could manage speaks volumes for the incompetence of my *peers*." The Archmagus chuckled. "I really have no idea what you thought you could accomplish there, and frankly I don't care. There is only one thing I need from you."

He paused to let that sink in, then continued.

"You will not leave this dungeon alive. In the best case you will be given food and water and left to live out your days as my prisoner. This option is available only if you cooperate immediately. After that you will have to beg for a swift death. It may be granted if you tell me what I want and I'm feeling merciful. Otherwise . . ." He paused. "Well, Brutus is a man of many talents."

"So," said a rougher voice, "will you be telling the Archmagus what he wants to know?"

Sylph let the blood trickle from her mouth and spatter on the floor.

"You answer me," said the voice, "when I ask a question. One more time."

Sylph looked up at the looming shadow defiantly. Vilvakis sighed.

"As I suspected," the Archmagus said.

The other man grabbed her upper arm in one hand and her shoulder in the other and twisted. Something inside the joint went *crunch*, and Sylph's world went white with pain. She screamed, completely against her will. It just welled up inside her and went on and on until her throat was raw. It was a minute before she was aware of anything except agony; she found herself huddled against a stone wall, eyes overflowing with tears. Vilvakis, still just a blurry shadow, was standing over her.

"One more time," he said, "before I leave you for the moment. You know what I want to know." His voice dropped to a hiss. "Where are your friends? Where are the geists?"

He doesn't know. That meant that Yahvy, at least, had gotten away. *Probably both of them.* Sylph tried to cling to that thought. *He doesn't know.*

"I . . ." Her voice caught. "I don't know."

The Archmagus straightened. "Pity."

More blows out of the darkness. Sylph sank back against the wall, helpless to even raise her arms in resistance. All she could do was close her eyes and sink back into oblivion.

Yahvy.

Heraan . . .

*   *   *

SHE WOKE AGAIN TO THE CHILL OF DAMP AIR AGAINST HER bare skin. Her clothes were gone, and some kind of rope bit deep into her wrists and ankles. There was hot air coming from somewhere too, like someone's dry breath against the back of her neck.

"I want you to know," said the rough voice, "that it's nothing personal."

Brutus leaned into her field of vision. The light was better—he was a big man with a shaved head and so many scars he looked as though he'd been put together from scraps. One of his ears was gone entirely, with little more than a nub of scar tissue remaining. He smiled at her; half his teeth were gone, though those that remained were still white.

"I'd hate," said Sylph, and broke down coughing. Brutus waited patiently until she'd recovered. "I'd hate to think that it was something *personal.*"

"It's just my job." He shrugged. "You'll probably hate me anyway, but I thought you might like to know that."

"You have a really awful job."

"I don't know." He reached to one side, carefully, and came back with a metal platter on which were a number of long pieces of twisted metal, cruelly shaped hooks and barbs. The tips all glowed red hot, as though they'd just been removed from a furnace. "It has its moments."

The worst part, Sylph thought, *is the moment before it touches me. There'll be a moment of anticipation . . .*

There was a moment of anticipation, but she realized shortly thereafter that it hadn't been the worst part after all.

*   *   *

RAHMGOTH WAS UP LATE—HE DIDN'T REALLY NEED TO sleep, other than to let Lina's body rest—and was going over the map again. He was in a good mood. *Progress is quite satisfactory.* Two of Vilvakis's brigades, the Blue and the Silver, had been marching to engage the Liberator's army. Once news of the massacre had filtered out, they'd first stopped dead and then begun a measured retreat toward Adriato. *Running to the Archmagus.* It confirmed his assessment: they hadn't had a real war here in a long time. *Vilvakis and his demons protect them. Who would dare challenge the oldest Archmagus?*

Undoubtedly they'd prepare a defense. Vilvakis's powers as the Magio Obliterator were formidable. *But Sylph should be there by now, and if she gets her hands on the geist it's all over. And even if she fails, we have options.* Yoruul had been to see Rahmgoth just that morning, complaining that his Steelbreakers had not been allowed to cover themselves in glory. *They'll get their chance.*

Either way, the path to Adriato was now clear. Most of the towns they'd passed had capitulated without a fight, giving up the supplies the army needed to sustain its advance. The Blue and Silver Brigades had not been willing to scorch the earth behind them, and that meant the army of the Liberator would arrive on the capital's doorstep with a full stomach. Vilvakis would have to give battle. *Adriato couldn't stand a siege in any case, unless he was willing to let the civilians starve.* The city was reliant on food imports to survive.

Speaking of food. Lina's body was once again imposing its inconvenient demands. For the thousandth time Rahmgoth wondered how mortals managed to get anything done in the short time they had available, when their own bodies were constantly interrupting them with irrelevancies. It was necessary, this far down the energy slope; they couldn't simply live off background energy like a Veritas. *Still, you'd think something more efficient would have evolved.* He got up from the table and poked his head out the flap.

"I'm hungry," he said to one of the two guards on duty. "Have someone send my dinner."

It would be more satisfying to have them bring in a prisoner, preferably a tender young thing, so that Rahmgoth could devour her life. *But that would not be subtle.* He hoped Rathmado marked his restraint. *Only until we get the third geist. Then we won't need to bother with subtlety any longer.*

It didn't take the guard long to return with dinner, some cold meat, bread, and a skin of wine. The other guard lifted the flap with one hand while his partner was setting up the food and said:

"My lady, Captain Melfina is here to see you."

"Oh?" Rahmgoth sat back in his chair. "Send her in, I suppose."

He picked up the wineskin and uncorked it, pouring a measure into a glass. Melfina ducked through the flap, looking agitated. As he raised wineglass her face went white, and she dashed across the room. Before Rahmgoth could drink she grabbed for it, wrestling it from his surprised grip and dashing it against the table. Shards went everywhere, and Melfina clutched at her hand; blood and wine dripped from it in a steady patter onto the map.

Rahmgoth stared for a moment, trying to control himself. The scent—*blood. Blood. I* . . .

Melfina was breathing hard, and shaking as though she'd narrowly escaped death. With an effort of will, Rahmgoth closed his eyes and reined in his desire.

"I assume," he said, "that there's some reason for this?"

"I couldn't let them." The girl's eyes were filling with tears. "I thought about it, and I couldn't let them do it. Lina . . . please . . ."

"Poison?" Rahmgoth glanced at the wineskin. "Who?"

"I can't tell you. You'd just hurt them." Melfina tried to catch her breath. "You killed them all—why? I *know* you, Lina. You wouldn't do that, you saved Myris and the others . . ."

"It had to be done," Rahmgoth said. "To warn off the rest of Vilvakis's troops."

"Everyone says that. 'It has to be done'." Melfina was swaying. "They were saying . . . that you've gone mad . . ."

She collapsed, slumping forward onto the table before rolling off onto the floor of the tent. Rahmgoth jumped to his feet.

"Melfina?"

She gasped for breath, fast and shallow. "Poison. I cut . . . my hand . . . it must have . . ."

Rage flared in Rahmgoth. *How dare they?* "Who?"

"It's okay," said Melfina. "Just . . . put me to sleep . . ."

She closed her eyes. A moment later she took a deep breath, then stilled.

No. Rahmgoth snatched the sword from beside his chair, drawing his power from where it was still mostly imprisoned in the Pit. He reached out to the girl's body, feeling for the nasty, spiky touch of the poison. It wasn't hard to find; it had burned a path up her veins from the wound in her hand until it got to her heart. *Put me to sleep—not likely.* If he'd actually swallowed the stuff, Lina's body would have died so quickly Rahmgoth doubted he would have had time to react.

No time. White fire crackled, following the poison and scorching a path inside Melfina's body. He let the tiniest bit crawl across her heart, and the girl twitched as though she'd been struck by lightning. Another deep breath turned into a scream loud enough to hurt his ears.

She may not live. Rahmgoth wasted no time; he hauled Melfina to her feet, holding her by the collar. Her eyes blinked and focused on Lina's face.

"*Who?*" he growled.

Melfina closed her eyes again. "Marlowe. Daana . . ."

They dare! He let her fall. "Rathmado! *Rathmado!*"

The Magus must have already been on his way, since he entered only a moment later. "Lina. I heard—"

"Make sure she doesn't die," Rahmgoth grated. He picked

up the sword again and stalked toward the exit.

"That's compassionate of you," said Rathmado as he passed.

"She may not have said all she knows. There could be more of them."

"Ah."

Rahmgoth smiled to himself and slipped out into the night.

＊　＊　＊

Marlowe was pacing again. Daana wished he'd stop; she was surprised there wasn't a rut in the ground by now.

The tent flap rustled and they looked up, but it was only Joker. He gave them both a wide smile.

"It's done, then?" said Marlowe.

"Of course."

"Someone will suspect us," said Daana. "Someone *has* to."

"It won't matter. If Lina's out of the way half the army will follow *me*, whether she replaced me or not." Marlowe managed a tight smile of his own. "That should be enough to get us out of here."

"You remember our bargain," said Daana to Joker.

"Of course." The spy nodded. "Places are being prepared for you in Adriato as we speak. The Archmagus is most generous to those who have served him well."

"I'm not serving the Archmagus," Marlowe spat. "I'm doing this for my own reasons."

I'll bet you are, Daana thought.

"Where's Melfina?" Joker asked.

"In her tent, I assume," said Marlowe. "She didn't want to know about this."

"One of us should check on her," said the spy. "Just in case."

"It's too late for her to interfere by now," said Marlowe.

"Nevertheless . . ." Joker went to the tent flap, only to have it yanked out of his grip. He backed away, slowly.

Lina entered, a naked blade in one hand and a half-skin of

wine in the other, held carefully by the drawstring.

We're dead. Daana knew it as soon as she saw Lina's expression. *We're all dead.*

"What a nice little gathering," said Lina, in a too-calm voice. "And who might this be?"

Joker bowed. "It's nice to meet you, my lady. I've heard so much about you. My name is—"

Lina slashed sideways, blade alive with energy. Joker toppled, cut completely in half at the waist, his smooth voice tapering off into a gurgle. Blood spurted into the air.

"Oh, well." Lina stepped over his twitching legs. "Guess it doesn't matter now, does it?"

Marlowe backed away. "You have to understand, Lina. We meant the best—for everyone! After what happened to the Golden Brigade—you're not well. Can't you see that?"

"You decided to kill me?" Lina took another step forward.

"No! Just make you . . . sleep, for a while. I would have kept you safe—"

"*Liar.* Melfina got a bit of your 'sleeping potion' and it nearly stopped her heart."

Marlowe's eyes went wide. "Melfina . . . but . . ."

Joker. Daana looked at the spy's corpse. *He fucked us. Of course. Lina dies, he says he got the dosage wrong, leaves us for the wolves . . .*

I never really thought I was going to get out of this alive. She hadn't moved from her chair. *I just wanted to take something back before the end. Something for myself.*

Marlowe was still backpedaling, until he came to the edge of the tent. "Please. I don't . . . I didn't know. It was him—Joker—you have to believe me!" He sounded close to panic.

Lina stopped in front of him. "It doesn't matter whether I believe you or not. You're still a traitor."

"I'm sorry. Lady, Lina . . . I just . . ."

She raised the sword.

"Please!" Marlowe held up a hand. "You said you loved me. You *said* it. What happened?"

Lina lowered the blade and paused. A ray of hope entered the cavalryman's face. Then Lina smiled, as though at some private joke.

"I changed my mind." She rammed the sword to the hilt in his stomach. Marlowe groaned and slid off the blade when she stepped back; he sank to the floor, clutching his wound. Lina reversed her grip, took the sword in two hands, and shoved the point in just forward of his ear.

"And you, Daana?" Lina pulled the sword out with a jerk, clear fluid dripping from the end. "What was in it for you? Money? Power?"

"You killed him," said Daana calmly.

"Killed who?"

"Garot." Her knuckles clenched until they were white. "I begged him not to go—I *begged* him—but he couldn't turn you down. I never meant as much to him as your *cause*, and now you've taken even that and turned it into lies."

"Poor fool." Lina shook her head. "Not going to try to bargain with me?"

"Would it help?"

"Not really. I rarely make deals with mortals, and even more rarely keep to them."

Mortals?

Then Daana screamed as her body was consumed by white fire.

RATHMADO PICKED HIS WAY FASTIDIOUSLY PAST JOKER'S body. Rahmgoth was slumped in the chair Daana had been sitting in, absentmindedly pulling a cloth along his sword.

"What have I told you," said the Magus, "about being subtle?"

"Don't," said Rahmgoth warningly. "I was betrayed once, Rathmado. I *died*, and spent six thousand years in a solitary hell. I will not suffer it to happen again."

"All I meant was that we could have gotten information out of them."

"Forget them. In two weeks we'll be at Adriato, and we'll have the geists."

"True." There was a hint of anticipation in Rathmado's normally bland expression.

"Will the girl live?"

"Yes. Though it will be some time before she wakes."

"Just as well." Rahmgoth looked around. "Could you . . . ?"

"Clean up?" The Magus sighed. "Honestly."

∗   ∗   ∗

VILVAKIS'S STUDY WAS LAYERED IN RARE HARDWOODS AND gilt—tastefully ostentatious. The Archmagus sat at his monstrous desk, writing; he didn't look up when the door opened with a carefully oiled click.

"Brutus," he acknowledged.

Brutus shuffled uncomfortably. He didn't belong in the nicer sections of the keep; he was a man who was suited by nature to the dank stone of the dungeons. But he bowed and said, "Archmagus."

"Your progress?"

"None, my lord. She repeats that she doesn't know where the geists are."

Vilvakis continued writing. "And her state?"

"Getting worse, my lord, but she was a healthy one to begin with."

"Do you think she'll break?"

"Couldn't say, my lord. I wouldn't have credited her to last this long. It may be that she really doesn't know where her friends are hiding."

The Archmagus paused, dipped his pen in ink, and turned a fresh page. He tried to conceal his irritation; it would never do to be discomfited in front of an underling. The inability of his

spies to find where Sylph's two companions had gone was an irritation, but an unavoidable one—the Liberator's approach had
thrown the city into an uproar, and normally reliable sources
had gone to ground for the duration.

"Continue, then," Vilvakis said. "Either she'll confess something or die and save us the trouble of an execution."

"As you say, my lord."

"Will she last for another week?"

"Oh, certainly."

"Good."

"It occurs to me," said Brutus, "that she might be more coop-
erative if we started removing bits. A finger, perhaps, or an eye."

"Tempting, but no. I want her undamaged until after the
battle; we may need her. Once the other threat is dealt with you
can do as you like."

Brutus's head bobbed. "As you say, my lord."

"Was there anything else?"

"No, Archmagus." Brutus withdrew, and the door clicked
closed behind him.

IT HAD BEEN A WEEK. OR POSSIBLY LONGER, SYLPH WASN'T
sure; there were no windows in her cell, no light, nothing to mark
the passing of days. They gave her food and water while she was
unconscious, so she didn't even have the cyclical demands of
her body to rely on. There was only Brutus and his visits. In
between she lay in total darkness, listening to the rasping of her
breath and trying not to think.

He'd established a routine, early on. First she heard the
heavy clunk of the key in the lock, which was enough warning
for her to close her eyes against the relative brilliance of his
torch. He hung that on the wall, worked the bellows in the
corner for a moment, then opened the mouth of the furnace and
stuck the end of his bundle of tools in the coals.

While they heated, he cleaned her, wiping dried sweat and blood from her skin with a damp cloth. Then he would climb onto the table and rape her. Sylph kept her eyes squeezed shut, but she still felt him; the pale flab of his potbelly pressing against her breasts, the stink of his hot breath against her face, his little grunts and sighs.

Sylph had occasionally thought about being raped. It wasn't as though she'd had a sheltered upbringing. Early on, first her mother and then Lina had explained why it was important to avoid strange men and not walk down certain alleys after dark. But she'd never pictured it, never tried to imagine what it would be like. It had just been a threat, like the possibility of being mugged or murdered, something that preyed on the mind.

But now—it as was all she could do to sustain herself through it. In a horrible way she wanted it to continue, to go on for as long as possible, because when he was done taking his pleasure Brutus would heave himself off and go to the furnace to get his tools, now glowing a dull, horrible red. *As long as he's fucking me, he's not sticking hot needles under my fingernails.* There was an awful logic in that.

After he began his real work there was only agony, unending pain until consciousness mercifully fled. Every day the torturer found something new to try; every time Sylph thought she had found the worst pain there was, Brutus showed her differently.

And he asked only one question, over and over again. "Where are the geists?"

Sylph was aware, during the times her mind was her own, of the irony. She didn't know—*really* didn't know. *If I knew I would have told them by now.* She'd realized that on the fourth day. Her brave front, her resolve, everything had gone. *If it would stop the pain, I would have told them.*

But she didn't know, so Sylph could only scream. She arched her back, straining against the chains; she thrashed and sobbed and pissed on the table. Brutus was unmoved. Even his rapes were like some kind of automaton, ignorant or uncaring of the humanity of the battered flesh beneath him.

"I just want you to know," he said, "that it's nothing personal."

Sometimes, in the darkness, rage seized her. *I'll show you "personal." When I get out of here I'm going to kill him—I'm going to kill all of them.* Gunpowder and pistols were just the start. *The whole arsenal of the twentieth century. Artillery, machine guns, mustard gas, nerve toxin. I'm going to* fucking kill them all. She screamed, though her throat was already raw.

Worse than the rage was what came in between. A kind of indifference. *Resignation.* It seemed to come more and more frequently as the days wore on. It got harder and harder to re-member what it had been like *not* to be chained up and tortured, when her days hadn't ended with the coarse touch of her stink-ing jailor.

It was at those times that she cried, all alone in the dark. *Yahvy. Heraan. Lina, Mom, someone. Please. I can't take it. I can't take it, it* hurts *and I want to go home.*

She wondered if she was going mad. Wondered if that might not be for the best after all. *But what if, no matter how crazy I became, there's still a tiny little core of* self *trapped inside the screaming, thrashing mess?*

Mom, please.

I'm sorry. I'm so sorry.

But she'd had that thought a thousand times before, and she knew it didn't make any difference whether she was sorry or not.

THE TWISTED STAIRCASE THAT RAN DOWN FROM RAH-mgoth's keep bent and turned through solid rock for some time. The way was lit by torches that flared ahead of them and faded as they passed by; Lina was starting to get used to the way things functioned in the Pit, so this didn't surprise her. After what seemed like a long way, there was a doorway crudely hacked in the side of a cliff, and a path leading out into a forest much like the one they'd started out in.

She glanced at Molochim. "Have you ever been here before?"

"No. I just . . ." He gestured vaguely. "Felt it, you know? This is where the girl always runs off to."

"Hmm." Lina stepped out. There was a light from a little way off, shining through the trees. The path led in that direction, so she followed it until she came to a clearing.

Then she stopped and stared. So did Molochim.

"What in the name of the White Lady is *that*?" he said.

Lina blinked. What it *was* was obvious enough to her. It was a house, a cheap prefabricated thing with plastic white siding that had cracked and flaked away under the elements. There was a gravel driveway that ended in a badly overgrown little garden; next to that was a dirt patch and an extremely rusty frame for a swing, which hung forlornly by one chain. A couple of Barbie dolls, naked, had been buried to the waist in mud. One of them was missing an arm, and the other had had most of its hair chopped off with a pair of scissors.

The light they'd seen was coming from one window, through which Lina could also see the flicker of a television set.

That was all mundane enough. It was the fact that it was in the middle of a forest in a not-very-real dimension outside a spooky, gothic castle that was a little disturbing.

"It's a house," said Lina slowly. "And it looks like something from . . . where I come from." She looked at Molochim. "I thought you'd know about that sort of thing."

"I've been stuck here for six thousand years, remember."

"But . . ." She indicated the cigarette and the suit.

"Filters, remember? I have no idea what I look like to you. It's sort of a collaboration between us, right? Like speaking."

Lina decided to let it go. "Anyway. I recognize this. Not specifically, but . . . sort of."

"It's funny looking, I'll tell you that."

"Should we go inside?"

Molochim shrugged. "Why not?"

"It seems kind of . . . rude."

"You didn't have any problems walking into Rahmgoth's castle," Molochim pointed out.

Lina started to say that it was a *castle*, and somehow walking into a scary-looking fortress seemed like a much more normal thing to do than just barging into someone's house uninvited. She quickly decided that didn't make any sense, so she simply shrugged and started toward the house. Gravel crunched under her feet.

The door was open. There was a screen door too, with one of the screens missing and the other torn. Lina thumbed it open and held it so Molochim could come inside. Most of the house was a combination kitchen/living room, and a couple of doors at one end probably led to bedrooms. Like the outside, the place was a mess; the carpet might originally have been green, but it had faded to a kind of vomit-hued yellow. There was a couch, which was strewn with mismatched cushions, and a big leather recliner facing the TV. In the kitchen Lina could see a counter and a sink, both covered in dirty dishes.

Sitting in the recliner was the biggest, fattest man Lina had ever seen. He wore jeans with the button open and a T-shirt that didn't have a hope of covering his bulk; the hairy flab of his belly protruded between them, as though it were trying to escape. He was asleep, piggy little eyes closed; his breath whistled, and the jiggles of his stomach as it rose and fell made Lina feel nauseous. One hand was still locked around a can of beer, while the other dangled in a half empty bowl of bright orange cheese puffs.

The TV was on, but odd. Lina could make out blurry images if she looked hard enough: one man talking, two men shaking hands, a long shot of an audience. Laughter, then someone talking over what sounded like a bad PA system, enough to suggest language without actually being comprehensible. *Not exactly television*, she thought. *More like the* idea *of a television. Or the ghost of one.*

"I—" Molochim began.

"Shhh."

"Sorry." He lowered his voice. "This is really strange."

"I know."

The girl was there too, Lina realized. She was curled up on a corner of the couch, covered in a ratty brown blanket with only her eyes showing. At first Lina had mistaken her for another cushion. And there was something else; her eyes kept catching movement in the kitchen, but there was no one there . . .

"Well?" said Molochim. "Didn't you want to talk to her?"

"What about him?" Lina hissed back.

"He's not real. Can't you tell?"

"No." Lina closed her eyes and opened them again, as a test. "It all looks real to me."

The fat man grunted and opened his eyes, staring blankly at the TV set for a moment as though his brain needed time to get moving. Then he noticed the beer in his hand and brought it to his mouth automatically; once it was empty, he chucked the can across the room.

"Nora!" he said, voice halfway between a belch and a roar. "When's dinner?"

"Not for another half hour, dear," said a faint, quivering voice from the kitchen. Lina looked up in surprise. She could *just* discern the misty outlines of a woman standing at the sink; a moment later they were gone.

"Hrmph," the man said, resettling his bulk in the chair. Wooden slats groaned. He groped on one of the armrests and found nothing. "Chris, did you get me another pack of smokes?"

"I gave them to you this morning," said a small voice from under the blanket. "You smoked them all."

"So why the fuck didn't you get two?"

"You know your father needs two packs of cigarettes, dear," came the voice from the kitchen.

"You only gave me money for one," the girl said, quiet but somehow defiant.

"You've got money, don't you?" He leaned out of his chair and turned. "It would kill you to do something nice for your father? I swear to God, I support this goddamned family and this is the thanks I get."

"You're *not* my father," said the girl. She probably meant it to be inaudible, but the man had paused, out of breath, and the statement hung in the air like the slap of a dueling glove. The fat man started breathing hard.

"*What* did you say?"

"Nothing," the girl mumbled.

"I fucking heard you say *something*." He climbed out of his chair, something Lina wouldn't have laid odds on his being able to do. "Say it again."

"I didn't . . ."

He took a step toward the couch and shouted, "*Say it again!*"

The girl sat up, blanket falling away. Her eyes glittered with tears. "You're *not* my father!"

The fat man's face clouded, turning bright red with rage. When he took a threatening step in he direction, Lina swore the whole house shook.

"You ungrateful little *cunt*! This is what I get for feeding you . . ."

He raised his hand, but she was already moving, darting off the couch and headed for the door. A fist the size of a melon reached out, clumsily, but the girl had already slipped past Lina and Molochim and stepped through the space where the missing screen should have been.

"Come on," Lina said, slamming the screen door open.

Molochim trailed behind her. "You're going to have to explain all this to me at some point."

"After we catch her."

"Right."

*   *   *

Yoruul, the Steelbreaker, walked in a circle around Rahmgoth's tent with the air of a mother-in-law trying to find something to complain about. The center of the tent was occupied by a table covered by a map, and he eventually settled his gaze on this, stabbing a finger at the mark that showed the army's current position.

"Look how far we've come!" There was a little less than a week's worth of distance left to Adriato. "And we've had one battle. One! Over before my people even arrived. And since then you have *forbidden*"—he spat the word—"forbidden us to raze the little towns we pass."

"They supply us with food and water," said Rahmgoth.

"We should *take* what we need from them. Take their wealth too, and their women as our slaves." He gestured at the map dismissively. "I grow tired of this war, Liberator. You promised the Steelbreakers treasure and glory, and thus far we have found neither. Only endless marching through a rich land we are not *permitted* to touch."

"Adriato is the goal, Steelbreaker," said Rahmgoth. "I can't help the fact that Vilvakis is too cowardly to send his forces against us in the open field. Most likely, we will meet his two remaining brigades outside the walls of his fortress, and there will be battle that will be spoken of for a thousand years."

"And are your armies to once again hoard the glory for themselves?"

"Of course not." Rahmgoth spread his hands. "The Golden Brigade was too trivial, Yoruul. There was no glory to be claimed in destroying such pathetic opponents. Look how easily they surrendered! That is why I ordered my men to end their miserable lives."

"True." Yoruul paused. While Rahmgoth's massacre had caused some muttering amongst his own men, it had apparently been well received in the Steelbreakers' camp. The barbarians saw slaughter as a sign of strength. *Honestly, it's like fooling children.*

"Only a little while longer," Rahmgoth said. "There'll be

glory and loot to spare once we get to the city, I assure you."

"There had better be. Or—"

Yoruul never got to finish his thought; the pair was inter-rupted by a scream from outside. It went on and on, getting fainter for a while before suddenly dopplering upward and end-ing in a wet crunch. Then there were more shouts, and the hiss of longbows.

The barbarian's first instinct was to suspect his ally. He whirled and shouted, "Is this a trap?"

"We're under attack. Vilvakis's demons." *I didn't feel them coming.* That meant the Archmagus had exerted his power to blind his opponent's senses, which was a pretty sophisticated trick. *It also means he knows that I'm here, or someone like me. Hmm.* He grabbed the sword, drawing from the reserve of power still trapped in the Pit, and burst out through the tent flap with Yor-uul on his heels.

Outside there was chaos. A dozen demonic monstrosities the size of cows had burst from a low-hanging cloud. They had wide, membranous wings, and vicious claws. Half of them had man-aged to grab a soldier, and Rahmgoth was in time to see the last of these unfortunates released and tumble toward the ground.

In the meantime, a trio of four-legged, four-armed insec-toids were fighting their way to the command tent in a flurry of flashing claws. Yoruul had brought a score of his barbarians with him as bodyguards, and they'd taken it upon themselves to engage the demons; they were braver than Rahmgoth had expected, but they were still being chopped into meat. As he watched, one demon ran a barbarian through the chest with a pointed claw; a woman charged it while it was trying to rid itself of the twitching corpse, but it simply impaled her as well before scraping both bodies off against the ground.

Orbaa was just outside the tent, with a guard of two dozen scared-looking spearmen. "What are your orders?"

"Leave the ones on the ground to me," said Rahmgoth, unsheathing the sword. White fire sparkled. "Get the archers together and bring down those flyers; aim for the wings, understand? Once they crash get the pikes to chop them up." He noted the glazed look in Orbaa's eyes. "Pull yourself together! This is just a jab at our morale, not a real attack. There aren't enough of them."

"Y . . . yes, Liberator!"

Rahmgoth turned away. One of the three demons had noticed him and was bearing down with deceptive speed, four sword-like limbs outstretched. Rahmgoth shifted his grip on the sword and waited till the last moment. When the creature lunged, he jumped, thrusting the sword in front of him like a lance. It sank squarely between the middle two of its four eyes, and power flared. A moment later the demon's whole head came apart, blowing outward in a spray of brackish blood. Rahmgoth landed on its hindquarters and jumped again before the thing collapsed, landing near where the other two were just finishing with the Steelbreakers.

The nearest demon turned toward him, lashing out to keep him at bay while it changed its footing; that was a mistake, since Rahmgoth's blade crackled with white fire and his parry chopped one of the demon's arms in two. It screamed defiance, but he was able to dodge to its now-undefended side and drag his sword down the length of its flank; the creature staggered drunkenly and rolled over, crushing a tent beneath it.

The last creature backed away, all four arms raised. Rahmgoth didn't bother to close in, just raised a hand. When he closed it into a fist, white power punched up from the ground and consumed the monster in a torrent of fire. Rahmgoth opened his hand and the flames faded; he let out a deep breath, satisfied.

It's not quite the power I once had, but it's good enough. The girl's body was proving surprisingly durable, and he was able to channel quite a large portion of his energy. *This far down the energy slope, I am invincible. It's no surprise Lightbringer rules this world.*

The airborne demons were dying too, albeit more slowly. Half of them were already down and had become the center of struggling knots of pike-men. There were broken bodies everywhere, but more and more arrows were rising toward the creatures that remained. One more screeched and pinwheeled into the ground on one wing, and then the rest were fleeing, rising back into the clouds they'd emerged from. *Let them go. It's not as though Vilvakis is going to run out of demons.*

"By the White Lady," said Orbaa, jogging over. "That one worried me. Half the boys were so scared they weren't even shootin'." He glanced at the quickly fading remains of the three grounded creatures. "I can see you didn' need any help."

Rahmgoth smiled. "No. But it's kind of you to think of me." He turned to Yoruul. "You see, my friend? This is just a taste. When we arrive at Adriato, glory awaits us in plenty."

The barbarian had gone white—from watching the demons or seeing what the Liberator could do, Rahmgoth wasn't sure. *Either way is fine with me.*

"THE PROBLEM," SAID SYLPH, "IS THAT IT REALLY WAS MY fault. They say that guilt is pretty normal in these kinds of things; it's like the parent abandoning the child, so of course the child feels like its her fault. So you can imagine what it's like for me, since it actually was my fault."

She paused for a moment. The tabletop shivered as Brutus climbed onto it. Sylph closed her eyes.

"I was supposed to come right home after school. I always did. I mean, *always.* You might find this hard to believe, but I was a really good girl when I was eleven. Never missed a day of school in three years, not even when I had the flu. Mom worked all day, and so did Lina, so I was better off at school anyway. Nothing to do at home but watch daytime talk shows, and you know what that's like. Or, I guess you don't. It doesn't matter."

Pain screamed from her limbs as her abused body took his weight. It wouldn't have been comfortable if she'd been healthy, since Brutus was at least three hundred pounds, but now Sylph's skin was covered with half-healed wounds and burns, and her joints ached from immobility.

"But that day—one day—I wanted to stay after school. A couple of my friends were having a party or some bullshit like that. I didn't mean to stay so late, but by the time everyone left it was almost dark, and I was exhausted. It had been a long day, you know?"

Brutus grunted. She could feel him fumbling between her legs with fingers as fat as sausages, his skin cold against hers.

"I called Mom at work. I wasn't supposed to do that, either, but it was scary walking home in the dark. I was worried . . ." She swallowed, and blinked away tears. "Worried something bad might happen to me. Mom had been having a good day; she was working at Circuit City, and she must have sold something big or something. She said she'd take the rest of the day off and come pick me up."

He entered her. The first time it had hurt; now all she felt was numb. The torturer's potbelly pressed against her, and she got an unavoidable whiff of his breath, which smelled of stale wine and days-old fish. It made her want to vomit, but her throat was already raw from vomit and screaming, so she swallowed hard.

"I sat outside the school," she continued, "while all the other kids went home from their sports practices and clubs and so on. I watched the road I knew Mom would come down, waiting for each pair of headlights, watching to see if it could possibly be our old blue minivan. And each time the car didn't turn, or it came to pick up some other kid, and it just got darker and darker and later and later. I went back inside and called the store, but they said Mom had already left, so I went outside to wait some more.

"I wasn't worried at all. I remember that. You'd think I would have been worried, but I was just mad. I walked home, eventually, and I was so scared and angry I sprinted almost the whole way. And the whole time I was thinking, 'Damn it, can't you get anything right?' She wasn't even there when I got home;

no note, no dinner ready, nothing. Lina was working nights so I just had a bowl of cereal and watched TV until it was time to go to bed."

Her body jerked, involuntarily, in response to Brutus's movements. Sylph kept her head against the table and tried to concentrate on the specks of color that floated behind her eyes.

"They called me at four in the morning. I almost didn't answer. I remember thinking about whether it was worth getting out of bed for. Then they told me to stay right there, and a policeman came to pick me up. He told me the rest of the story. Mom came out of the store, on the way to the parking garage down the street. She turned a corner, crossed a street without looking both ways—she always told us to look both ways—and got hit by some hick with a pickup truck. Broken legs, ribs, blood everywhere."

She bit her lip as he put a hand on her shoulder, the one he'd nearly pulled out of its socket what seemed like an eternity ago. The blood was salty on her tongue.

"At the very moment I was walking home and thinking 'Can't you get anything right?', my mother was on the operating table with her chest opened up. They tried, but one of the broken ribs had nicked an artery near her heart, and in the middle of the surgery it just let go. And that was . . . ah . . . it. I didn't . . . ah . . . didn't have a mother anymore."

Brutus shuddered and sank down on top of her. Sylph took a deep breath.

"I've never told anyone, you know? Not even Lina. She thinks I was at home the whole time."

He rolled off of her, drying himself with a crusty towel before tossing it into the corner. The torturer redid the tie on his pants and bent over to check his instruments, pulling the bundle of thin metal tools carefully out of the fire.

"I can't take it anymore," said Sylph. "I'm going to die here, right?"

Brutus, laying out his tools on a platter, gave a quick nod.

"Then just kill me." Her eyes filled with tears. "Please. I deserve . . . I don't know what I deserve. But just kill me."

For a moment—a beautiful, awful moment—she thought she'd gotten through to him. But Brutus just shrugged and said, "Master's orders. It's nothing personal."

✳   ✳   ✳

THE FOREST OUTSIDE THE RUNDOWN PREFAB WAS DARKER than Lina remembered. She got a glimpse of the girl, darting behind a grove of dead trees, and took off in pursuit. She hadn't run very far when she lost sight of her quarry. Lina pounded a few more steps and then pulled up short, thinking.

Molochim puffed into the clearing after her, breathing hard.

"See what smoking does to you?" Lina said automatically.

"I'm already fuckin' dead."

"No reason not to stay in shape. Now be quiet."

He nodded, and she listened carefully. There was no wind, and none of the small noises she associated with a forest: no birds, no rustling leaves or babbling brooks. Nothing but Molochim's labored breathing, and a little extra noise . . .

She turned. "You can come out. We're not going to hurt you."

"I'm not hiding from *you*," said a child's voice from behind a fallen log. "Go away. He'll find me."

"We won't let him hurt you, either."

"He'll just hurt you too." But the girl poked her head out. Her hair was a mess, and her eyes were red where she'd been crying. "Who are you?"

"I'm Lina," said Lina gently. "And this is Molochim."

"Molockeem?" She giggled. "That's a strange name."

"What's your name?"

"Christina." The way she said it rang distant bells of familiarity in Lina's mind—an emphasis on the last syllable, daring anyone to try and shorten it.

"I think that's a pretty strange name," Molochim muttered.

Lina glared at him.

"Christina." Lina paused, not quite sure how to phrase what she wanted to ask. "What are you doing here?"

The girl's eyes went shifty for a moment. "Just . . . living. With my foster parents."

"What happened to your real parents?"

"Daddy died in the war," she said matter-of-factly. "And then Mommy got sick, and I asked her not to leave but she did anyway. So I got sent to live with Nora and Robert."

"Have they always lived here? In the forest, I mean."

Christina closed her eyes. "We've never moved. I moved once with Mommy; they took everything away in a big truck and then brought it back again. But . . ."

"But?" Lina prompted.

"I remember when there were other houses," she said in a small voice. "And I could walk to the store. And there were kids for me to play with. But around here there's just the castle and the . . . the scary place, and besides that . . ."

She is *a real person. I wonder how long she's been here?*

"*Chris!*" came a roar from behind them. "Chris! Get your ass in the house *right now*!"

"He's coming!" Christina ducked back behind the log. "Hide or he'll find us!"

"So help me, you little shit," the fat man roared, "if you don't come out right now I'm going to break every fucking bone in your body!"

Lina looked around, but she couldn't see him. Christina was vibrating with terror. At the sound of heavy, thudding footsteps, she bolted, springing up from behind the log and tearing off into the woods. Lina was about to run after her when Robert, the fat man, entered the little clearing.

He wasn't fat anymore; it was as though his bulk had migrated, building layer upon layer of muscle until he had legs like a couple of barrels and huge, hairy arms. He'd gotten taller too, and when he opened his mouth there was a hint of fangs.

"*Chris!*" the apparition screamed. "I'm going to find you, and when I do . . ." He took notice of the pair for the first time. "Where's Chris?"

Lina couldn't help backing away. She repeated, over and over, *He can't hurt me unless I let him. None of this is real.* But somewhat to her surprise Molochim stepped into the ogre's path. He was a good head and a half shorter than Robert.

"Go home," the Veritas said. "Christina doesn't want to go back."

"*She* doesn't get to decide. *I'm* her father." His eyes narrowed. "And who the *fuck* are you, you little . . . ?"

Molochim's figure blurred. A moment later he was once again a golden-armored giant, dwarfing Robert. One hand reached over his shoulder and drew a sword the size of a girder.

"*Go home*," he said, voice reverberating with authority.

Robert hesitated, spat a curse, and turned away. He quickly vanished into the dark forest, though Lina could hear his mutterings as he crashed through the bushes. Molochim sheathed his sword and snapped back into his human-sized form.

"That was impressive," said Lina.

He shrugged. "It was nothing. He was just a bully; all you have to do is stand up to them."

"Still. Thanks."

"Shouldn't we be following Christina?"

Lina nodded.

*   *   *

KURAI, THE BLACK MAGUS, UNTIL RECENTLY IN THE EMPLOY of the Lady Fell, was riding across Vilvakis's domain. He was uncomfortable—uncomfortable with riding, uncomfortable with the Archmagus Vilvakis, and most of all uncomfortable at being without the omnipresent power of a Circle underneath him.

As a Magus, Kurai drew his power from the limitless well of the Archmagi. *With the Circles scooping up all the souls, there's little enough left for the rest of us.* Without the blessing of the Archmagus, he was limited to what power he'd been able to store or scrounge; not nearly enough to travel as he normally preferred to, flowing like a formless shadow across the landscape.

Damn Vilvakis. The Archmagus had always been arrogant; his power was well established and he had no obvious rivals, which meant he thought himself beyond the services of a mere Magus like Kurai. Lady Fell and Gargorian had both been more than willing to provide power in exchange for his help, but from the moment he'd stepped across Vilvakis's outermost Circle he'd been able to feel the Archmagus's rejection. *And since Lady Fell's power is gone, that leaves me with few options.*

Kurai had the feeling that Vilvakis's arrogance would last right up until the moment Lina—*Lady damn her*—ran her demonic sword through his heart. While the prospect was not exactly upsetting, it meant that only one potential employer remained.

I could go to ground, I suppose. Wait until all this blows over and then gather the souls on my own, as they fall. The thought was not appealing. He'd grown accustomed to the easy flow of Lady Fell's power; in his early days, Kurai had lived outside the Circles, scrounging energy where he could find it, and he had no desire to return to that kind of life.

So. Lightbringer. The name carried a little thrill of nervous energy. *He knows what's happened to the Archmagi, what will happen to Vilvakis. I have no doubt he'll see the need for . . . assistance.* Just stepping onto the Lightbringer's territory would be enough, in any case—an implicit offer, made or rejected. *If he doesn't want me, I'll have more than enough time to hide.*

The horse veered to avoid a bump in the road, jolting Kurai in the saddle and shaking him away from his thoughts. He was taking the long route to avoid the Liberator and her army. *There's no hurry, after all.* Without Vilvakis's power he had no desire to confront Lina and whoever her mysterious backer was. *Once I have the Lightbringer behind me . . .*

The Black Magus smiled to himself, despite the bumpy ride.

chapter twenty-one

ARCHMAGUS VILVAKIS, THE MAGIO OBLITERATOR, stood alone on the plain outside Adriato. It was a strip of rolling grasslands just west of where the land descended to meet the inlet, a pleasant enough field that was soon to become a battleground. The army of the Liberator was less than a day away, or so the Archmagus's scouts had reported.

Still she comes on. Vilvakis shook his head. He wasn't sure if he should be impressed or horrified. He knew the Liberator hadn't gotten any good intelligence for days; his demons had made sure that none of her scouts had returned. She'd ignored the normal careful methods of war between the Archmagi, plunging recklessly onward without even stopping to break Vilvakis's Circles. There was certainly a conventional advantage to be had by doing this—given a few months, Vilvakis could raise a horde of conscripts to support his professional army—but charging straight as an arrow for Adriato meant the Liberator was now fighting on the Archmagus's ground, at the center of his power.

She'll just have to learn. Magic pulsed up through the ground, drawn from the geist that sat safely ensconced at the center of the Circles. Vilvakis shaped it, weaving raw energy into meticulously spun death, and when he was finished he left the ball of power to drift. There was a kind of string leading back to the Archmagus, a trigger. *It wouldn't do to be too close when it goes off.*

He sensed the arrival of Sakoth as he was finishing. The demon lord was followed by another stream of power, wherever he strode within Vilvakis's domain—a constant flow of energy and souls from the geist, payment for services rendered. The price was a steep one, but Vilvakis felt it was well worth it. Sakoth was the most powerful demon he'd encountered in more than three thousand years of trolling the lower worlds for servants, and the creature commanded the allegiance of a veritable legion.

Vilvakis looked up as the demon lord's shadow fell over him. Sakoth's form in this world was appropriately hideous: he was more than twenty feet high, a centauroid figure on four stubby legs plated with metal. His chest was a solid steel plate, on which arcane patterns crackled in letters of fire, and his two massive arms ended in fists the size of boulders. The demon's head had a mouth like a bear trap, and when he spoke it was possible to see the eternal flame that burned at the back of his throat; five free-floating eyeballs circled around his brow, their gaze harsh and unblinking.

"Setting a trap?" Sakoth's voice was a bass rumble, but he was surprisingly articulate for a demon.

Vilvakis nodded. "Take care that your people don't get caught in it."

"They will not." The demon looked at the horizon. "When is battle expected?"

"Tomorrow, assuming the Liberator continues on her present course."

"Good." He smiled, with a scream of twisting metal. "It has been too long."

"Remember that the Liberator is a Magus. The source of her power is still unknown, but . . ."

Sakoth waved a hand dismissively. "If need be, I will engage her myself."

Vilvakis nodded. "Excellent. She must be disposed of first of all."

"It will be a pleasure to devour such a soul."

"In that vein," said Vilvakis, "I trust my arrangements for your payment are satisfactory?"

"If they were not," said Sakoth with another bear trap smile, "I would already have taken your soul in exchange."

"I trust that will not be necessary."

"As long as the power flows, wizard. Now I must attend to my servants."

The demon vanished in a burst of fire, leaving behind a patch of scorched and blackened earth. Vilvakis's lip twisted.

" 'Wizard' indeed," he muttered. He stalked toward his army's camp, trailing the spell's trigger invisibly behind him.

SYLPH WAS TRYING TO FIGURE OUT HOW SHE COULD KILL herself. Strapped to the table, her options were limited. She'd tried swallowing her tongue but hadn't been able to discover the trick to it, and trying to stop her heart by sheer effort of will had been similarly unsuccessful. *The body lives on, mindlessly, even when it's nothing but a prison.* It was almost time for Brutus's visit, and then there would be nothing to do but bear the pain for another day, not because she was holding out for something, but simply because there was no other option.

I'm just tired. So goddamn tired. Sylph felt tears rising and tried to banish them. *What the fuck good does crying do? He doesn't care. Nobody cares.*

The key turned in the door's lock with a screech, and she saw Brutus's shadow stretch across the room. Sylph turned her head the other way; she wanted to scream, but that only made things worse. *I can't take this. I can't take another day.*

"Move," said another voice. Sylph's head snapped round. *Vilvakis? Has he come here to finally finish me off? Or . . .*

Light flared, painfully bright to Sylph's dark-adapted eyes. She moaned, involuntarily, and heard rapid footsteps.

"White Lady," someone said. It took Sylph a moment to identify the voice; it was Heraan, but cold with rage.

A dream? But she knew it wasn't. *I haven't dreamed since they put me in here.* She blinked and tried to focus; he was standing over her, bending down.

"Sylph?" he said quietly. "Can you hear me?"

"Yes," Sylph rasped. "The . . . the light . . ."

"Shit. Close that lantern!"

The light dimmed to a much more tolerable level. Heraan said, "We're getting you out of here. Does he have the keys to these cuffs?"

Sylph rolled her head from side to side. "No. Only Vilvakis."

"Shit," Heraan said again. "We'll have to cut them off."

"No." Sylph swallowed, despite the pain from her raw throat. "Yahvy?"

"Here," Yahvy said. Sylph wanted to jump and down and scream with joy, but she forced herself to speak slowly and carefully.

"Geist. Give me the geists."

"Heraan, cover him," said Yahvy. Sylph opened her hand, and a moment later felt the always-cool metal spheres pressed against her palm. She closed her fingers around them, savoring the first rush of power, then let her mind flow outward. The manacles holding her to the wooden table were old iron; Sylph let the geist's power bleed into them, just a little, and scramble their structure until they had the consistency of pudding. Then she pulled her limbs free, one by one, and curled up in the center of the table. Joints that hadn't bent in weeks screamed in agony, and Sylph clutched her knees in a silent ball of pain. She felt Yahvy's touch on her shoulder, and couldn't help but flinch. All she could think about was Brutus and his rough, probing fingers . . .

"Water," Sylph croaked. Yahvy put a skin to her mouth and tipped it up, and Sylph swallowed greedily. By the time it was half empty Sylph took it in her own hands, ignoring the protests of her elbows. She handed the skin back to Yahvy and managed to sit up, dangling her legs over the edge of the table.

"Can you walk?" Heraan asked. "Yahvy can carry you otherwise."

"I'll try." Slowly, painfully, she lowered herself to the floor. Her legs wouldn't bear her weight at first, and Yahvy had to catch her to keep her from falling. Sylph let herself rest for a few moments and tried again, and this time managed a few teetering steps.

Heraan opened the lantern a little bit. He had Brutus in one corner of the room, covering the torturer with a pistol. Yahvy dug through her pack and came up with a cloak, which Sylph wrapped around herself gratefully. She closed her hand even tighter around the geists, drawing strength from the flow of power. Her next step was better, and the next better still. She managed to make it to where Heraan was standing and look up at Brutus.

"Is he the one who did this to you?" said Heraan.

Sylph nodded, without looking away from the torturer. Brutus met her gaze with the same indifference with which he'd raped her. She would have liked to have seen fear, or anger, but there was just nothing there.

Heraan pulled another pistol from his belt and handed it to her, butt first. "You probably want to do it, then."

She took the gun and aimed it right between the torturer's eyes. He stared back at her, and she tried to project the same indifference, the absolute absence of interest in the feelings of another human being. But she couldn't do it; rage boiled up, deep inside, and came frothing to the surface in a wave.

"I'm sorry about this," Sylph grated. "It's nothing personal."

She lowered her aim to his crotch and fired three times. Then Brutus screamed, curling up around his own private pain in a spreading pool of blood. Heraan winced, but Yahvy nodded appreciatively. Sylph handed the gun back.

"I'm sorry we took so long," Heraan said. "We had to lay

low. They almost caught us, and there was nothing we could do . . ."

Sylph waved a hand. "It's okay."

"It's not okay. We . . . *I* . . . left you behind to be tortured and Lady knows what else . . ."

"I told you to." Sylph swallowed again. The water had helped, but her throat was still ragged.

Heraan was in tears. "Sylph . . ."

"Enough." Yahvy pushed past him to the door. "Still need to get out of here."

"Right." Heraan wiped his eyes. "There's fewer guards around, and no demons; that's how we managed to get in. Vilvakis has taken his army into the field. Lina's only a couple of days from laying siege to this place. So all we need to do is get out of the castle and find somewhere to hide, and join up with the army once she gets down here."

"No." Sylph was thinking furiously, but her brain didn't seem to be in complete working order yet. *Ten minutes ago I was trying to figure out a way to kill myself.* She wanted her sister and a nice soft bed, so she could curl up in someone's arms and never leave again. "I've got a better idea."

"Sylph," said Heraan. "Don't tell me you're thinking of something—"

"Stupid," Yahvy finished. She smiled at Sylph. "Good to have you back."

Sylph smiled back, despite the pain from the sores on her lips. "It's . . . good to see you." She turned to Heraan. "You too. Thank you."

"I . . ." He blushed a little, and shook his head. "What did you expect? We couldn't just leave you in here."

"What's the stupid plan?" asked Yahvy.

Sylph was filled with a strange determination. She could barely walk, and every movement brought pain from a half-dozen wounds. Inside she was still numb, broken. But she could keep smiling.

"The geist," she whispered. "We're going to get the geist."

* * *

LINA KEPT CATCHING GLIMPSES OF CHRISTINA AS SHE FOUGHT her way through the woods. The girl was changing before her eyes, growing up at a furious pace. Her hair got longer and longer, until it hung halfway down her back like a beautiful red curtain, and her height shot up like a weed. She spent a moment as a gawky, awkward adolescent; then she disappeared behind a tree and by the time Lina got another look Christina was nearly her own age and had become a very pretty young woman. The ratty clothing she'd worn earlier had gone, replaced by a green-and-white vest and slacks.

She crested a little rise and looked down. Apparently she didn't like what she saw, but it was too late. Christina tried to turn back, but something pulled her down the slope and out of sight. Lina cursed under her breath and quickened her pace, scrambling on her hands and knees to get through a tight spot near the top before finally making her way into a clear space. Molochim was right behind her—she heard a rip as his suit got caught on something and gave way—and when she tried to stop he kept moving and bowled into her. Lina lost her footing and started to slide. On the other side of the little hill there was only more of the gray mist that she'd seen throughout the forest. And then . . .

This time she was ready for the transition, but the scene was so achingly familiar it made her want to cry. It was a supermarket, complete with slightly sticky floors, overactive air-conditioning, and the vaguely musty, wet smell of the produce. Someone crooned unintelligibly over the PA system, and the shelves were stacked high with boxes of stuff whose labels were only a blurred mess. *The idea, but not the substance.*

Molochim appeared behind her, putting a hand on her shoulder to steady himself. He looked around, surprised.

"This is new. Also from your world, I take it?"

"Yeah," said Lina.

"Any idea why?"

"I think," she said, "that these are memories. Like Rahmgoth's. When he was stuck in here, that's all he did, right? Live out his memories over and over again. These are *her* memories."

"That makes sense." Molochim glared at the rip in his sleeve, and the fabric wove itself back together. "But I'm surprised they formed around her so quickly. She hasn't been here very long."

"I know." Lina looked around. "There's something wrong. It feels like she's stuck here. If Rahmgoth could relive his memories, why didn't he pick happier ones?"

"Because he was insane," said Molochim bluntly. "He was obsessed with what—He, you understand—with what He did to him."

"Right," said Lina. It felt right, anyway. What she'd seen in Rahmgoth's castle had the feeling of someone going over and over how he'd been wronged, until he drove himself mad. "Is Christina insane too?"

"I don't know."

"Come on." Lina had spotted the girl at the checkout counters.

There were a few people in line, faceless blurs that made Lina queasy if she looked at them for too long. Christina was behind the counter, scanning and bagging with a fierce intensity rather than the listlessness Lina usually associated with supermarket cashiers.

The first customer was clear, unlike the rest: a hawk-faced man in his early twenties with a leather jacket and an expensive looking haircut. He said something to Christina that Lina was too far away to hear, but the girl broke out laughing. Lina frowned.

"Who's this guy?"

"How should I know?" said Molochim. "Someone from her memory, presumably."

Lina pushed her way closer, shoving a couple of the blobs out of the way, until she was close enough to hear what was going on. The guy had his elbows on the counter, watching Christina scan his stack of nondescript boxes.

"What are you doing here, anyway?" he said.

"Have to pay the bills," she said. She didn't look up.

"It just seems like you could do better." He smiled. "A pretty girl like you."

God, thought Lina, *what a jackass.* He was handsome enough in a bland sort of way, especially when he smiled. *But still!*

Christina turned to him. "Your total is seventy-five dollars and eighteen cents, sir."

He swiped a credit card. When she presented him with the receipt, he signed it and added something else. *Probably a phone number.*

"Be careful," the guy said, "or you're going to be stuck here forever."

"Have a nice day," Christina said, with a plastic smile. He sighed and walked away; she stared after him just a bit longer than she should have, and put the receipt next to the register, instead of in the drawer.

"You're not seriously going to fall for that?" Lina said.

The whole scene shimmered, as though it were being projected onto a soap bubble. Christina blinked and looked around, a little bit dazed.

"That guy," Lina repeated. "You're not going to fall for a line like that?"

"What choice did I have?" she said. The supermarket vanished with a pop, and Christina, Lina, and Molochim were once again standing in the mist shrouded forest. "I was working two jobs, every hour I could get my hands on, and it *still* wasn't enough. Just building up debt, little by little. It was like I was bailing water as fast as I could and sinking anyway."

"That still doesn't mean you should be hanging around with a scumbag."

"I was eighteen! And Tom was good looking and rich and he *cared* about me!"

"You're still eighteen," Molochim pointed out.

"I'm not . . ." Christina looked down at herself. "What the hell? What's wrong with me?"

"Memories," Lina said quickly. "You're trapped in your memories."

"Then I'm getting out of here." She started to walk back up the slope, toward the house where Robert lurked. Lina grabbed her sleeve.

"*Not* that way. There's nothing good that way."

"But I don't . . ." Christina looked over her shoulder, nervously. "I can't . . . I mean . . . I don't want to go the other way. I don't *want* to . . ."

She tried to pull away, but Lina stood firm. The girl's body jerked as though in pain, and she put her hands over her eyes.

"Lina," said Molochim, "do you have any idea what you're doing?"

"Not really. But if she's really from my world, we may need her to get out of here."

"That's a little slim."

Lina had to admit that was true. *I can't just leave her, though.*

Christina stood up, suddenly, and tugged her arm away from Lina's grip. The scene shimmered and changed. All at once they were in an tastefully decorated upscale apartment. Tom, the guy from the supermarket, sat on a color-coordinated leather sofa with his feet on the coffee table and a wineglass between his fingers. He was wearing an elegant suit. Christina, on the other hand, was now wearing a clean skirt and a blouse with no visible stains and still obviously feeling out of place.

"Would you stop walking back and forth?" he asked, smiling. "You'll wear a hole in my floor."

She started, then blushed and shook her head. "Sorry. I'm sorry."

"And stop apologizing for everything." He got up, retrieving another glass of wine from the table, and held it out to her. "You really just need to relax."

Christina considered for a moment, then took the glass and downed half of it in one swallow.

"Very good. Now try sitting down."

She giggled. "I'm sorry. I just don't get to do this kind—"

"I know. Didn't I say to stop apologizing?"

She open her mouth—to apologize again, Lina thought—then stopped herself and flopped onto the couch.

"Much better," said Tom, sipping from his own glass.

"You said there was something on your mind?"

"Yes." He folded his hands in his lap. "Christina, I wanted you to know that you are the most amazing girl I've ever met."

She blushed deeper. "I . . ."

"And I was wondering if you'd mind terribly if I kissed you."

There was a long moment of silence.

"I really don't like this guy," Lina whispered to Molochim.

The Veritas shrugged. "Don't ask me. I never understood human mating rituals."

Christina leaned forward. Tom put an arm around her, and their lips met.

They watched for a while.

"It's about time for this to fade out," Lina commented. Tom was sliding his hand up Christina's thigh, and she was pressing herself against him enthusiastically. His other hand fumbled at the buttons on her blouse. Lina glanced at Molochim, who was watching with interest. She sighed, stepped up to the couch, and poked the girl in the shoulder. Tom seemed to freeze in place, and once again the environment took on the subtle feeling of unreality.

"You," said Christina, after she'd focused. "Still? You had to interrupt the only good part."

"Good part of what?" Lina leaned forward. "You're just going around in circles. You realize that, right?"

"I'm just . . ." Christina shook her head, fighting to clear it.

"I'm not. I mean. This isn't real . . . I don't quite understand, but . . ."

"She's stuck," said Molochim. "The memory won't let go."

"I can't do this," said Christina. She fell to her knees. "Not again. Please . . ."

With another little *pop*, the apartment vanished.

*　*　*

"As I said," Rahmgoth deadpanned, "there will be glory in plenty."

The day had dawned bright and clear. Rahmgoth's forces had separated into their formations the previous night, when it became clear that Vilvakis intended to offer battle. He'd expected as much; a siege would be messy, and the Archmagus almost certainly planned to rely on his demons and sorcery as much as his conventional forces. *Which is absolutely fine with me.* He smiled to himself. *I'm sure his demons have told him that I'm out of the ordinary by now, but there's nothing in this world that can match the power of a Veritas.*

He looked over the enemy forces through Sylph's spyglass and was pleased to note that they were deploying dismounted. The last battle had showed the deadly efficiency of the pike blocks against charging cavalry, and Vilvakis wasn't taking any unnecessary risks with his elites. Like the Golden Brigade, the Blue and Silver both looked very impressive; rank after rank of spearmen and archers, heavily armored and led by officers with magnificent flags snapping in the morning breeze. By comparison the army of the Liberator looked shabby and haphazard, but its morale was high. *We also have half again as many men.*

That was counting the Steelbreakers, of course. The tribesmen held the center of the line, mostly mounted and obviously itching for action. Yoruul wasn't the only one who'd chaffed during the long, boring march across Vilvakis's domain, and now the barbarians were eager to get to grips. Rahmgoth had deployed his pikes along their flanks with the archers nearly on the main line; he didn't expect Vilvakis to come and get them. *He's much too smart for that.* And when the demons turned up it wouldn't matter where they were positioned.

Yoruul stood at his side, watching Rahmgoth stare into the spyglass with benign incomprehension. When the Liberator finally snapped the thing shut, the barbarian looked up.

"Are the Steelbreakers ready?"

"Of course," Yoruul said. "We've been ready for weeks."

"This is your chance. I trust you will not disappoint."

"Whether or not the Liberator is disappointed," the barbarian sneered, "is of little consequence to us. Just be sure to remember your promises, once we have won this battle for you."

When the battle was over, Rahmgoth decided, he was going to have Yoruul killed at some length. He gave the Steelbreaker a smile. "You may give your men the signal to attack."

"At last." Yoruul unsheathed his sword and held it over his head, the steel flashing in the sun. Three thousand barbarians roared simultaneously, until the tumult seemed as though it would shake the field itself. The Liberator's army answered with its own cry, but Vilvakis's forces were silent as horses started to pound across the no-man's-land.

Rahmgoth turned to his runners. "Tell the archers to open fire. Concentrate on the flanks."

Soon arrows were hissing back and forth. Vilvakis's army had its own archers, and while their weapons lacked the range of Sylph's alloy longbows, they were more than adequate to reach into the mass of screaming barbarians bearing down on their center. Rahmgoth saw riders fall, horses rearing or shying away; the bodies were instantly swallowed up and crushed as the charge went on. The Steelbreakers had their own set of tactics for this kind of situation, Yoruul had informed him, a massed charge to open a hole in enemy lines, after which the army would break into small groups to chase down fleeing foes. It fit well enough into Rahmgoth's plan, so he hadn't objected.

The demons are the real battle, in any case. He loosened the sword in his scabbard. All the rest of this was simply window dressing; Vilvakis knew no conventional army could hope to oppose Rahmgoth's power. *The question is, how long before he shows his cards?*

THE ARCHMAGUS VILVAKIS WATCHED THE BARBARIAN horde approach his lines from a hill safely out of bowshot. The demon lord Sakoth stood behind him, and the human troops gave the demon a wide berth. That would have made it difficult to give commands, but Vilvakis had no commands to offer; the generals of the Blue and Silver Brigades knew their business, and in any case theirs was not the important part of the battle.

The tiny string—the trigger—was still wrapped around his finger. Vilvakis watched the lead horsemen cross the place he'd been standing the evening before. *A little bit farther. It's a blessing they're so tightly packed.*

A little bit farther—the grassy field was being pounded into mud by the passing hooves—*just a little more*—

Now.

His finger twitched, sending a pulse of power running down the trigger line. The spell, held in a kind of stasis, was suddenly completed. Magic started to fall inward, a tiny sphere of power that quickly got much smaller until the center was crushed out of existence entirely, becoming an incomprehensible point of nothingness. Then the motion reversed, and the hungry void started to expand.

"This," Vilvakis whispered, "is the power of the Magio Obliterator." He was breathing hard. "Sakoth, have your people charge as soon as the spell clears."

"As you say, wizard," the demon rumbled.

Vilvakis's disciplined troops maintained their order, even as arrows started falling among them. At this distance the arrows lacked the force to punch through their gilded armor, and Rahmgoth was contemplating ordering the archers closer when he felt the ripple of power.

So, he's finally taken the field. But it was just a ripple, not the torrent he expected from a demonic summoning.

A tiny black spot bloomed, near the center of the charging Steelbreakers. It looked as though it was about the size of a man's head. Rahmgoth watched one of the barbarians gallop into it, unable to turn in time, and start screaming as her arm and part of her shoulder simply vanished into the darkness.

"Tell your men to get away from it!" Rahmgoth shouted to Yoruul. But there was no way for the Steelbreaker to get a message to his people, even if he'd been paying attention. The barbarian was mesmerized by the black spot—now the size of a man, the size of a horse, and growing at a ferocious pace—

The tide of darkness shot outward, a solid sphere of black that swallowed men and horses without a trace. On all sides the barbarians shouted and screamed and tried to turn away, but it was moving far too quickly for that now. It sliced outward faster than a horse could gallop, until it was so wide that almost the entire charge had vanished inside it. The edge brushed Vilvakis's own lines, and a few luckless soldiers of the Blue Brigade stumbled inside as well. Then, finally, the expansion slowed and stopped. For a moment the sphere of darkness stood still. Then it began to contract even more rapidly, until there was nothing left but a tiny black dot that vanished in a roar of thunder.

What it left behind was—nothing. The edges were littered with organic wreckage, men and horses who'd *almost* made it and had only part of their bodies devoured by the shadow. The ground itself had vanished, leaving a smooth, steep-sided crater. A few Steelbreakers had made it away, or reined in their horses in time, but in a few seconds the better part of three thousand men and women had vanished without a trace.

Rahmgoth stood stock still for a moment, plans running through his mind at high speed. Beside him, Yoruul fell to his knees. Vilvakis's lines were parting to pass a cavalry charge, but even at this distance Rahmgoth could see flames around the horses' hooves and the riders' lances. *Demons.* He shook himself and started sprinting for the front lines.

✳　✳　✳

"THIS IS THE WAY?" ASKED YAHVY.

Sylph didn't trust herself to speak, so she simply nodded. Her breath rasped in her throat. Heraan, bringing up the rear, looked on with concern.

"This is a bad idea, Sylph. You're . . ."

She waved a hand, gulping air. "I know. But we're not going to get another chance."

"Yahvy and I could go alone . . ."

"Not leaving her again," said Yahvy flatly. She came to the corner of a building and peeked around.

As Heraan had promised, Vilvakis's compound was almost deserted—they'd sprinted across the open spaces between the low, square buildings without seeing anyone except a few guards in the distance. Thus far, no one had challenged them.

"Two," Yahvy said, leaning back. "Ready?"

"You're sure this is the place?" Heraan said to Sylph.

"Yes." The building looked like all the others—it might as well have been a barn or an equipment shed, albeit with stone walls—but Sylph could feel the steady pulse of energy from deep inside. This close it was impossible to mask the geist, and Vilvakis apparently hadn't even made the attempt. *There'll be guards, and not just humans.* And every step she took felt like there were razors inside her knees.

Sylph shook her head. *Lina is about to fight a battle, maybe fighting already. And without me there to help against Vilvakis . . .* Maybe the sword's power would be sufficient and maybe it wouldn't, but

Sylph couldn't take the chance. *If we can get to the geist, we can stop him cold.*

"Three, two, one," Yahvy counted. She and Heraan stepped around the corner at the same moment and each fired twice; Sylph heard two bodies hit the floor in quick succession.

"Come on. Anybody who heard that is on their way." Heraan offered his arm to Sylph, but she waved him off. Walking was an effort, but in a way it felt good, any movement felt good after so long on the table. *Right about now Brutus would be just finishing up, and getting ready to start with the irons.* She shivered involuntarily, and wished she could shoot him again.

The building had a thick oaken door, which was locked. Sylph put her hand to it and melted the iron into a puddle, and the door swung open. Two guards on the other side were busy setting up a table as a makeshift barricade and obviously hadn't expected anyone to come through so quickly. Yahvy dropped them both with two quick shots.

"Not exactly unguarded, then," said Heraan. He grunted and pushed the table into place so it blocked the now-lockless door.

"There'll be a demon here somewhere," Sylph said. "Maybe a few."

"That's cheering." Heraan looked around. The inside of the building was as utilitarian as the outside—a corridor running just inside the wall, with a door about halfway down. "Is that the way?"

"Yes." She could feel the geist, just on the other side of the wall. The feeling was more powerful than the one she'd had under Stonerings—*is Vilvakis's geist that much bigger? Or maybe he's drawing power from it?*

The next door was also locked. Sylph reached out to it, a nearly automatic gesture by now, and sent a wave of power into the steel. It melted, but something else reacted as well; she felt something inside react, drawing off the energy she'd used to power itself . . .

"Get back!" Sylph stumbled away from the door; Yahvy grabbed her by the shoulder and pulled her backward, and Heraan jumped behind them. The door crackled and spat, seething with arcs of black lightning. A moment later it vanished, shrinking down to a point and then disappearing with an echoing boom. It had taken a good chunk of the surrounding wall with it, and Sylph had a reasonable idea what would have happened had she been standing nearby.

"What in the Lady's name was that?" asked Heraan.

"Booby trap." Sylph closed her eyes, trying to keep her heart from racing. "Vilvakis must have left something behind. When I touched it, it went off." *I wonder how he managed that? I only seem to be able to affect things within arm's reach.* Obviously the Archmagus knew a few tricks.

"Great." Yahvy let go of Sylph. "Safe now?"

"I . . . think so." She quested out into the doorway with a tendril of power, but found nothing. "Be careful."

"You can say that again." Heraan advanced cautiously. "There's some kind of bridge—looks like water down below. A little island or something at the center."

Sylph nodded and climbed to her feet with some difficulty. Heraan had a pained look, watching her, but said nothing. He slipped through the shattered doorway, and she followed.

The room beyond was indeed occupied by a pool of still water, with an arched stone bridge stretching from the doorway to a circular patch of bare rock. There the light glinted on something metallic—it was hard to see, but Sylph didn't need to. *That's the geist.* And she could feel power pouring out of it, a stream that spread out through the Circles toward wherever Vilvakis was. *He must be drawing energy. That means he's already fighting. We don't have much time.*

"That's it?" said Heraan.

Sylph nodded.

"I'll go across. Yahvy, cover me from here."

"Right." Yahvy dropped into a crouch, gun raised, and

Heraan started across the bridge. He'd gotten almost halfway when there was a disturbance in the water.

Sylph saw it first, a dark shape that rose toward the surface deceptively fast.

"Heraan, watch out!"

He looked around and saw the thing breach the water. A great mass of green flesh slammed upwards; Heraan fired a couple of shots, neither of which came close, and then it was on top of him. It slid across the bridge and carried him with it into the water. Sylph got a brief glimpse of an eye the size of a watermelon, struggling to focus on her.

"Heraan!" Yahvy fired, two bullets burying themselves in the green stuff with little *pock pock* noises. The creature didn't seem to care; it slipped off the bridge, back into the water, and sank like a stone. Heraan went with it, thrashing desperately as the ripples closed over him.

BY THE TIME RAHMGOTH HAD DESCENDED FROM THE LOW hill he'd made his vantage point, the front lines of the Liberator's army were in chaos. The demons were shrouded in preternatural smoke, making it difficult to see exactly how many there were; they'd hit one of the pike regiments with a head-on charge and left nothing behind but scorched grass and broken bodies. The archers immediately behind the pikes had broken—Rahmgoth had passed them on his way down, streaming toward the rear despite their captain's entreaties. A few recognized the Liberator and tried to turn their fellows around, but he waved them off. *With all the time I've spent on these men, it'd be a shame to waste them.*

He plunged into the cloud of smoke at a run, looking for the demons. A dull red glow led the way; he caught up to one as it circled its horse, seeking another victim. The thing could have been mistaken for a human wearing full plate, from afar, but close up Rahmgoth saw that the armor was in fact the creature's metallic skin. It was also far too large: seven feet tall at least, and broader than a human would be, giving the appearance of squatness. Its mount was a jet black stallion whose hooves were sheathed in crackling flames.

The *power* of the thing hit Rahmgoth like a punch in the stomach. *Vilvakis summoned* this?

Nevertheless, he pressed the attack. The demonic steed roared a warning, but Rahmgoth drew his sword and brought it around in a complete arc well before he reached the creature, sending a whip of white fire crackling outwards.

The horse was caught in the flank, and blood sprayed as it collapsed; the demon itself, moving far more quickly than its bulk should have allowed, rolled out of the saddle and hit the ground in a crouch. Rahmgoth twisted his sword and sent the whip of flame after it, but the creature yanked a double-handed battleaxe from where it hung over one shoulder and swung it into the line of magic as though felling a tree. The white energy flickered and dissipated.

The thing spared a moment to look at its dying mount, then turned its eyes back to Rahmgoth.

"He had been with me a long time," it said in a deep, buzzing voice. "You will pay for that, mortal."

"Be careful who you call 'mortal'," Rahmgoth grated.

The demon tilted its head, quizzically. "My master warned me of one such as you."

Rahmgoth bared his teeth. "Did he tell you to run away?"

"A fine jest." The demon hefted its axe. "The *Sakoth'Brae* flee from nothing. He instructed us to take special care to grant you a painful death."

"Remind me to thank him."

Rahmgoth closed the distance, throwing another wave of white energy at the demon with a slash of his blade. The creature blocked once again, but that kept it occupied until Rahmgoth was within striking range; he feinted left and went right, hoping to outmaneuver his larger opponent's clumsy battleaxe. The demon, however, didn't go for the bait; it smashed his blade aside with a gauntleted fist and bulled forward with an unstoppable downward slice. Fire bloomed in the axe's wake, and Rahmgoth ducked aside just in time.

White fire squirmed on the demon's hand where it had touched the sword, but it quickly guttered out and left behind only a few burned patches. Rahmgoth retreated, thinking, and the creature staggered after him. Its movements were far from graceful, but it possessed enormous strength; Rahmgoth doubted his sword could turn a blow from the heavy axe.

Let's try something else. He gave more ground, a little faster, and let the demon lumber into a slow run. It came on with its blade raised high; when it got close enough, he dug his feet in and reversed direction, slipping under the stroke as it came down and bringing his own weapon around in a backhand slice into the thing's knee.

Rahmgoth was used to the empowered blade slicing through solid matter like water, but this felt as though he'd swung it into a steel wall. He nearly lost his grip, and something in his wrist crunched. But white power crackled off the sword, and the demon's metallic skin exploded. It bellowed and toppled forward, the slow, awful collapse of a giant tree that ended with an earth shaking concussion when it hit the ground. Rahmgoth ended up in a crouch, holding the sword awkwardly in his off hand. The demon struggled to rise, but its right leg was in tatters below the knee.

Rahmgoth got to his feet, breathing hard. *Damn this body.* It was so easy to forget its limitations.

"When we are finished with you," said the demon, "you will be *begging* for death."

"You don't seem to be in any position to be making threats." He circled the fallen creature cautiously, and eventually decided that finishing it off, tempting as it might be, was too risky. *Better see if there are any more of them . . .*

He turned and found himself face to face with another black

horse, little trickles of smoke issuing from its nostrils. Another demon, nearly identical to the first, sat atop it. Rahmgoth backed away hastily and raised the sword, despite the protests from his wrist.

"One more?" He forced a smile. "Come on, then."

The demon was motionless. On either side of it the smoke swirled, revealing another horse and rider. Then another, and another, until five of the things stood in a rank. All had axes over their shoulders and lances leveled, the tips red with flames.

Rahmgoth kept his sword up, defiant. *But five of them . . .* He let power bleed into his voice, until it would carry across the battlefield, and shouted, "*Rathmado!*"

The center demon urged its mount a little closer.

"*Rathmado!*"

There was no response. Rahmgoth grimaced and waited for their charge.

✳   ✳   ✳

ANOTHER APARTMENT MATERIALIZED AROUND LINA. THIS one was much shabbier, and obviously the domain of at least one child; there were the telltale finger paintings hung on the refrigerator and cereal ground into the carpets. Christina stood in the kitchen, under a flickering fluorescent light, drumming her fingers on the stained whiteboard table and obviously trying to control herself. At the sound of a door opening she strode into the hall and took a position blocking the front entrance; Tom, at the door to a bedroom, paused.

She looked older, while he was much the same. Same elegant attire, the same gentle smile that looked so ready to pull back into a sneer. Lina and Molochim were behind him, looking over his shoulder. Lina felt like punching him in the back of the head.

Tom sighed. "Christina, please tell me you're not going to do this."

"To do what?" Her tone was low and dangerous.

"Make a scene."

"Oh, no." Her hands tightened into fists. "The father of my children is walking out without leaving me so much as a *card*, why would I make a scene?"

"We've been over this."

"In the sense that you lecture me, then ignore everything I have to say."

"I don't think either of us did much listening—"

She cut him off. "*Stop* trying to sound reasonable, you weaselly little *fuck*."

"Calling me names is not very productive."

"How can you be so goddamn cool about this?" She was vibrating with rage, and looked to be on the brink of tears. "Do you not have a *drop* of human feeling?"

"Chris, I don't think—"

"Don't call me Chris," she snapped. "Has the thought that you might have just a little bit of *responsibility* occurred to you?"

He was tired of arguing. "Get out of my way, please."

"There's a little girl asleep in there. What do I tell her when she asks about her father?"

He took a step forward, but she moved to stay in his way.

"*Answer* me. What do I say?"

There was a pause before Tom answered in a whisper. "Tell her he's dead. Tell her he ran off, that he's the biggest jackass on the face of the earth and she should kill him if she ever meets him. Tell her he went missing in the Bermuda Triangle and is out voyaging with Captain Kirk. Tell her whatever you want. I don't give a *fuck*, do you understand?"

She finally broke down in tears. "You . . ." Christina seemed unable to think of a sufficiently nasty epithet. "You *bastard*."

"Get out of the way, Christina."

He stepped forward again, until he was practically on top of her. She looked up at him and defiantly spread her arms. Tom sighed theatrically.

"This is ridiculous. Do you want me to hit you, is that it? So that you can call the police? I'm not going to."

"I . . ."

"You can hit me, if it will make you feel better. Here." He ducked until his face was about at her level.

"Like hell it would make me feel better."

Tom shrugged, and was caught off guard when her fist smashed him on the side of the jaw and sent him sprawling against the wall. Christina raised her hand, her knuckles white.

"However," she grated, "who knows when I'll get the chance to do it again."

"Fine." He got back to his feet. "Is that enough drama for one day?"

He pushed past her, and this time she let him, standing perfectly still as he brushed by and wrenched open the hall door. Despite his demeanor, either her words or the punch had gotten to him; he closed the door too hard, and it bounced off the stopper and shuddered back into the room. His retreating footsteps echoed down the hallway.

Lina realized she was crying along with Christina, and ran a sleeve across her eyes. Molochim looked at her, awkwardly, and put a hand on her shoulder.

"I'm okay." Lina sniffed. "It's just . . . not the sort of thing someone should go through, you know?"

"Not really," Molochim admitted.

They stepped aside as Christina shuffled past, headed for the other bedroom. Lina stepped behind her as she opened the door, torn between her instinct to put an arm around the crying woman and a desire to keep watching. She settled for staying close as Christina entered what was obviously a child's bedroom, went over to the tiny bed and knelt beside it. There was a little girl in the bed, though between the dark and the sheets it was hard to make out more than that.

"I knew," Christina whispered to the sleeping girl. "It had to happen, sooner or later. He's . . . himself. A goddamn stupid moth . . ." She cut off and bowed her head. "My father left me too, you know? I was younger than you. And my mother—I begged her and begged her. I wish I hadn't. She was so sick, and then to listen to me there just begging and pleading with her not to leave—that was terrible. I didn't know any better."

Christina sat with her head on the bed for a long time, and cried. Eventually, she wiped her eyes, which didn't help much, and spoke with quiet determination.

"Never again. Never, never, never." She ran a hand over the girl's arm, and the child shifted in her sleep. "I will never leave you behind, Lina. I swear to God Almighty." It was almost a plea. "Never." She let her head drop back to the covers, her voice muffled. "Never . . ."

"Hey," said Molochim, "did you hear . . . ?"

"Yes," Lina said.

"But she has the same name . . ."

He stopped as Lina reached out and took Christina's hand. The woman looked up, surprised, and got back to her feet; the apartment, and the sleeping girl, took on the now-familiar soap bubble texture of strained reality.

It's not possible. Lina stared. *I mean, the hair is the same. But she's . . . different.* Younger. The girl in the bed couldn't have been more than four. *Not just that . . . I would recognize . . .*

Lina took a shaking breath.

"Mom?"

✳   ✳   ✳

Yahvy rushed to the edge of the bridge, then danced back as another rope of rubbery green emerged. It stayed above the water for a moment, a pillar of gently oozing flesh, then dropped back down.

How many are *there?* The pool didn't look big enough for more than a few.

"Sylph!" Yahvy threw herself flat as she shouted, and Sylph

did likewise, the impact bruising her abused skin. Two green tentacles arced overhead, through the space where she'd been standing. She wriggled away before they landed on the bridge with a wet *slap*, then slithered back into the depths.

"We have to get Heraan out of there." Sylph rolled to the edge of the bridge. "Yahvy, stay away from the water."

"Right." Yahvy holstered her gun and drew her sword. *Probably a smart move; the edge might be more effective.* The creature seemed to be little more than a blob of slime. *Maybe there's only one, with a lot of tentacles, like a squid.*

She squirmed a little bit over the edge and looked down. There was a mass of green, deep underneath, and she could just make out Heraan's wriggling form, covered in tiny tendrils. *It looks like it's trying to absorb him. More like an amoeba, then?*

Sylph closed one hand around the geists. Power filled her; power alone wasn't enough to repair her exhausted body, but for the moment it lent her strength. There would be a price later. Another tendril slammed out of the water toward Yahvy, who dodged and took a slice at it. The blade caught and stuck in the green stuff and was yanked from her hands. *So that's no good, either.*

Sylph dipped one finger in the water, delicately. Then she closed her eyes, and concentrated. *It should be simple enough, heat and state change.*

Feathery branches of frost shot through the water, followed by a nearly solid cloud of ice. It happened so fast the surface was perfectly preserved, every ripple and drop frozen in time. A handful of tiny pebbles of ice, thrown into the air by the tentacle, clattered on the suddenly solid surface. The walls of the pool crunched and groaned as the expansion slammed into them, and sprays of pulverized ice rose from the sides, where the pressure had ground it against solid rock.

The one tentacle caught above water thrashed and spasmed, but Yahvy had already retreated out of reach. Sylph pulled her hand back, leaving a patch of bloody skin behind where her

finger had touched the ice. She could still see the demon, a blob
of shadows in the depths of the giant ice cube. *I have to move fast.*
She scrambled out onto the slippery surface, ignoring a shout
from Yahvy, until she was directly over the thing.

"Get ready to help me out!" She hoped Yahvy would pick
up on what to do. Once Sylph was directly over the creature,
she bent down and laid her hand on the ice, and the geists' power flared. Another state change, this time the other way; ice
flashed into chilly steam in a neat circle around her, and Sylph
descended as her magic bored a hole. She heard Yahvy above
her, clattering across the ice, but Sylph was focused on her goal
below. The creature loomed larger, holding the trapped Heraan
atop it; in a few more seconds she'd reached him, and the bore
exposed dozens of tiny green tendrils. Sylph pulled them off
until she could work Heraan's body free; his skin was blue with
cold, and horribly clammy.

Now to get out of here. She looked up. Yahvy's hands were
reaching down, as though in answer to her prayers. Sylph
grunted as she propped Heraan against the wall of the bore
and put his hands into Yahvy's. He started to ascend, jerkily,
and Sylph turned her attention to climbing the wall of ice. It
was easier than it sounded. She used the geists to carve herself
handholds, little knobs she could get a firm grip on despite the
slippery surface. When she was halfway there, Yahvy reached
down for her and pulled her up the rest of the way.

Yahvy had planted her sword in the ice—a network of cracks
radiated from the blade—and had been using it as an anchor.
Sylph nodded to her, exhausted.

"Look . . . after Heraan." She was breathing hard and
ragged.

"What . . . ?"

It's not over. She felt the ice shiver. The demon's strength was
colossal, enough to shatter the entire pool of ice and drop the
three of them into a sea of razor-edged shards. *Maybe. I have to
stop it.* She knelt by Heraan, feeling along his belt, and smiled

when she found what she wanted. *My last grenade. Thank God he didn't use it.*

"Get back to the bridge." Sylph slithered over to the bore, pulled the pin on the grenade, and let it fall right into the demon's exposed maw. Then she ran for it—as best she could, on the ice—and had just managed to throw herself onto solid stone when the thing went off. A column of flame roared out of the hole in the ice, throwing fragments across the room.

And if that doesn't kill it, we're screwed. Sylph waited, but there was no more shaking, just the creaks and groans of the ice. She let out a deep breath and fell back onto the rock.

"Sylph?" said Yahvy worriedly. "Okay?"

No. She hurt all over: half-healed wounds, burns, bruises from Brutus's not-so-tender affections. There was blood on the index finger of her left hand where it had touched the ice, and more cuts and bruises from climbing through it. As adrenaline and the power of the geists faded away, Sylph felt as though there was nothing left inside her.

"I'm okay," she said. "Just . . . tired. What about Heraan?"

"Alive, but cold," Yahvy said.

"We should get him out of here." *There was something else.* She blinked. *Oh, yes.*

Sylph struggled to her feet—the bridge was rimed with frost, which made for treacherous footing—and worked her way to the little island in the center. Vilvakis's geist lay on its own tiny pedestal, a little metal marble. Water had splashed over it during the fight, and now steam rose gently from a little circle of rock.

Sylph reached down, wincing at the heat of the thing, and picked it up. She felt the stream of power strain and snap.

And that's it. She dropped the geist into the pocket with the other two, heard them click together. *As easy as that?*

✳ ✳ ✳

DAMN RATHMADO. HE CAN'T LET THIS HAPPEN; HE NEEDS ME

still, I know it. I will *have my revenge!*

The five demons had dismounted after they'd seen what had happened to the sixth's horse, unwilling to risk their precious steeds. They hardly needed to. Rahmgoth faced five axes, a circle of blackened, glowing steel, and his own blade seemed pathetically small in comparison.

To let them come at him all together would be suicidal. So, as they tensed to charge, Rahmgoth raised his blade and ran at the demon on the far left. He sent a pair of white-hot streams of power into the creature, forcing it to parry and take a step backward. Rahmgoth jumped, white energy crackling at his feet—Lina's legs protested, but he ignored the pain and found purchase halfway up the demon's body, perched on a steel arm. Before it could shake him off he raised his blade in two hands and stabbed viciously into the center of the creature's ornate faceplate. Power warred against power. Rahmgoth's knuckles went white against the hilt as he drove it through the demon's head almost by force of will alone.

The thing staggered back, and Rahmgoth rode it to the ground, freeing his sword with an effort. The other four were lumbering in his direction, and he moved to back away and let them string out. Before he could get clear of the stricken demon, however, one of its arms shot out and closed a steel grip around his ankle. He fell badly, and felt something in that joint let go with an agonizing wrench. He whipped the sword around and into the demon's wrist, but without leverage the blade glanced off the absurdly hard steel, raising sparks.

Rahmgoth knew he wouldn't get a second try. Four shadows loomed around him, axes raised in a headsman's two-handed grip.

"The *Sakoth'Brae* do not fall so easily," said one.

Rahmgoth gripped the sword a bit tighter. "I've been dead once already. When next I return for revenge, I'll make sure to add you to my list."

The demons stopped. For a moment Rahmgoth thought his

words had affected them, somehow, but their heads had turned, as though they were all listening to words he could not hear.

"WIZARD," SAID SAKOTH, IN HIS DEEP, RUMBLING VOICE.

"One moment." Vilvakis was trying to take stock of the battlefield. The charge of Sakoth's minions had shattered the Liberator's center, and the girl herself was still engaged there, if the clouds of smoke were any evidence. But each flank of the army had rallied around their damnable archers, and they continued to rain death onto Vilvakis's forces. The Blue Brigade had hunkered down behind their shields and whatever cover they could find, waiting for the demons to finish the battle; the Silver had staged a halfhearted charge across the no-man's-land and were being cut down by the score.

The Archmagus was displeased. The death of the Liberator would end the war, but the time spent to rebuild his brigades would be considerable.

"*Wizard*," said Sakoth.

"I am an Archmagus," Vilvakis said irritably as he turned to face the demon.

"Archmagus, then." Sakoth's bear trap mouth stretched into a grotesque parody of a smile. "Your payment has ceased."

"What? That's not possible." He reached through the Circles for the power of his geist and found nothing but a void. The flow of power and souls to Sakoth was gone. "That's not possible!"

"Archmagus," Sakoth said, "I hunger."

"Wait." Vilvakis backed away. "Wait—there's some mistake—I'll make it up to you. Double the payment. Triple . . ."

Sakoth lashed out, obscenely fast. The Archmagus had time for one last, desperate scream before he disappeared down the demon lord's gullet.

22

chapter twenty-two

CHRISTINA LOOKED AROUND, FRANTICALLY, WITH THE air of a rabbit caught in an arc light. Lina tensed, in case she decided to run for it.

"What?" she said, finally. "What do you mean?"

Lina put her hand on her chest. "It's me, Lina."

"No." Christina shook her head. "That doesn't make any sense. Lina's over . . . there . . . and Tom just walked out . . ." Her eyes were filled with tears.

The more Lina watched, the more she was convinced. The woman in front of her looked a little different, and Lina's mother had never called herself Christina, but there was something in the way she held herself that was familiar. *But what's* wrong *with her?*

"Mom, it's *me*. Listen. None of this is real, you have to understand. It's just memories. You can't—"

"No," Christina mumbled. She looked around again and this time started to run, back toward the ridge where her foster father waited.

Lina pounded after her, catching one of her arms and bringing her up short. The forest reappeared as the apartment vanished with a *pop*, and her feet dug for purchase in the damp earth.

"Wait. Mom . . . Christina . . ."

"Let *go* of me!" The tone was suddenly so familiar that it was hard for Lina not to obey. "I have to go back—I can't go *that* way. I can't!" Her voice rose to a wail.

"Molochim, help me!"

The Veritas, who had been watching quietly, tossed his cigarette away. "What do you want me to do?"

"Hold her!" Christina's struggles were becoming more frantic.

Molochim shrugged and walked over, putting one hand on each of the woman's shoulders. Lina let go, tentatively, and Christina twisted against the Veritas's unbreakable grip but couldn't get free. She put her shoulder into Molochim, but he didn't budge; after a few more tries, she sank to the ground defeated. Christina covered her eyes and sobbed.

Something about seeing her mother bawling like a little girl made Lina uncomfortable, and she looked away. "Molochim, what's wrong with her?"

"I'm not sure. I'm not exactly a fucking expert on human psychology."

"You're an expert on this place. At least, you know more about it than me. Take a guess?"

"Hmm." He lit another cigarette, crouching in front of Christina in case she made another break for it. "I don't know, but it feels like she's not all there."

"You mean she's crazy?"

"Not crazy. More like—you know—not *all* there. Like not all of her is sittin' here in front of us."

"Where's the rest?"

He pointed in the direction the little girl had called scary, the opposite of the way Christina had been trying to run. "Best guess is that way."

"But why would she run away from that?"

"Don't know. Maybe there's something in the rest of her memory she'd rather forget. Fuck knows we all have stuff like that."

Lina felt a stab of sympathy for the Veritas. *I did kind of drag him into this.* "What do we do?"

"What do you want to do?"

"I want her to be normal again!"

"Oh." He bent down and took Christina's arms; she jerked away, but his grip didn't budge. "Want me to carry her?"

"You think we can just carry her?"

"Sure. See, you keep thinking of this as a real place. *None* of this is fuckin' real. It's just kind of a projection our minds have ginned up to keep from thinking about the fact that we're dead, or disembodied in your case. The trick is to take advantage of it, fuckin' turn things around, right? So if I pick her up—sorry about that, try not to thrash so much—and drag her toward the physical embodiment of things she doesn't want to think of, I'm forcing her to think of them."

"No," Christina said. "No, no, no. Please . . . not there . . . let me go back . . ."

Her voice was heartbreaking. Lina offered her a hand, and she grasped it desperately.

"We'll beat it, whatever it is." She squeezed her mother's hand. "Whatever's out there can't be *that* bad."

Molochim opened his mouth to offer his observations on that subject, caught Lina's expression, and wisely closed it again. He hoisted the still-struggling woman over one shoulder with an arm wrapped around her waist. "Lead the way."

Lina reluctantly let go of her hand and started to pick a path through the forest. It didn't take very long before things started to change. The shadows shifted, and the omnipresent half-light took on a red tinge, making it look as though the entire forest had been drenched in blood. After another few steps Lina realized she was starting to feel an echo of Christina's terror, a sick emptiness in the pit of her stomach. *We have to be almost there.* She gritted her teeth and kept walking; Molochim followed, apparently not bothered.

A last row of bushes formed the border of a small clearing,

which was completely bathed in the infernal red glow. The source was a ball of eerily liquid looking crimson, hovering a few feet above the ground. It was five or six feet across and filled with swirling shades of red, and bright enough that all the shadows in the clearing pointed away from it.

"Any idea what *that* is?" said Lina, her voice shaking.

"Nope." Molochim took a pull on his cigarette. "It looks like there's something inside."

Lina stared. *There* is *something inside.* Visible only in glimpses, as though it were rolling slowly in its vermilion bath. It was hard to make out shapes, but suddenly Lina was struck by a dull certainty.

"That's her in there, isn't it?"

Molochim nodded slowly. "Could be."

"How do I get her out?"

"Remember, none of this is real. Whatever you do is just an expression of the fuckin' imposition of your will, right?"

"In other words," Lina said, "I should try the direct approach."

"Sure." He sat Christina on the ground, keeping his hands on her shoulders. She'd stopped squirming; her eyes were locked on the red sphere, wide and terrified.

Lina stepped closer. The feeling of horror got worse, but somehow she could tell that it wasn't real, something imposed from the outside to keep her away. It made it a little bit easier; she managed to keep it under control until she was right next to the thing. When she tried to touch it, however, her arms simply wouldn't respond.

"I can't do it."

"Sure you can." Molochim shifted his cigarette to his hand and gestured to for emphasis. "It's not real, remember?"

It's not real. Lina tried again, this time with her eyes closed. *None of this is real—this isn't really my arm, not really my fingers. This thing*—the surface was *warm* and organic under her skin—*isn't real, either. It's like a little blister in someone's mind.* She remembered Christina's eyes. *It hurts, but sometimes you have to deal with a blister before it gets worse.*

Lina pressed inward. Fluid inside the ball went *glonk*, and the wall resisted a little; it was like pressing into a stiff balloon. She pushed harder, and it started to deform around her fingers.

Christina screamed. *I'm sorry.*

Lina thrust her hand forward, and the thing tore open. Blood, as dark as wine, rushed out to cover her in a wave.

✳　✳　✳

THE IRONY OF IT, SYLPH THOUGHT, *IS THAT IF THEY TRIED TO stop us now I don't think we could put up much of a fight.*

Heraan could barely walk, and Sylph's energy was finally giving out; between them they could just about stumble forward slowly, with Yahvy holding an arm around Sylph's shoulder to steer. A squad of guards—*hell*, one *guard*—would have presented serious problems.

But there weren't any, or at least none prepared to stop them. The castle was in chaos; Sylph had managed to glean that the Liberator had defeated Vilvakis in the field, and that the Archmagus was either dead, captured, or fleeing. The one thing everyone agreed on was that the Liberator's army was coming to seize the city. A grizzled old scout, his young daughter under his arm, swore up and down that the Liberator had promised the city to her barbarian allies and that they were about to be unleashed.

That, at least, Sylph wasn't worried about. *Lina would never do something like that.* Once they passed through the now-open, unguarded doors of the fortress and into the city proper, she started to breathe a little bit easier. There were still soldiers all around, but they were as panicked as the civilians. Everyone seemed to want to run, but no one was quite sure where. The docks, to the south and east, were packed; every available ship was getting ready to head out to sea.

Sylph wanted to tell everyone to relax, that the Liberator

wasn't as bad as they'd heard—rumor had her committing a wide variety of horrible crimes, including slaughtering a whole brigade of prisoners—but most people weren't in the mood to hear it. So she just kept walking, up the thoroughfares and the gentle slope and toward the edge of the river valley.

Her theory was that they'd eventually run into Lina's advancing troops. Sylph desperately wanted to stop and rest, but with chaos and rioting breaking out in the city it didn't seem like a particularly good idea. *Besides, I won't feel safe until I have my own people around me again.*

Near the northeast edge the city emptied out very quickly, since that was the sector everyone was scrambling to get away from; Sylph expected to see cavalry rounding the next bend at any moment, from the way the civilians were acting, but in fact they'd almost made it to the top of the valley before they ran into a patrol of three soldiers and a sergeant on foot with bows.

Two of them covered the trio while the other two approached. The sergeant said, "The road is closed this way. You'll have to go back."

Closed? That made a little bit of sense. *She'd hardly want civilians running around if there was a possibility of more fighting.* Sylph stepped forward and waited for him to recognize her. When he didn't, she said, "We're with the Liberator's army."

He shook his head. "I'm sorry. I was given explicit instructions to allow no one from the city . . ."

At this point his subordinate's eyes widened, and he leaned forward and whispered ferociously in his sergeant's ears. The man listened without changing his expression.

"You're Sylph?" he said, finally. "My apologies. I've only been with the army since Stonerings."

Sylph gave him a weary smile. "Don't worry about it, sergeant. I assume the rule doesn't apply to us, then?"

"I'll have to escort you in, my lady."

"That's fine."

A messenger was dispatched and quickly returned with

horses. Yahvy sat double with Sylph, and one of the soldiers rode with Heraan; it was only a short ride to the edge of the camp, but Sylph was profoundly glad to be off her feet. Dismounting was a bit painful—it stretched some of her recent scars—but she was almost in tears at the sight of her old familiar tent.

It's over. The change had been so abrupt it was hard to accept. *This morning I was trying to find a way to kill myself. And now I'm back.* "Lina. Tell Lina I need to see her."

"Yes, lady," said one of the soldiers.

"Yahvy, can you take Heraan to the hospital?"

She nodded. "You'll be okay?"

"For the moment. I just need to sleep."

Once the two of them were gone, Sylph stumbled into her tent. She made the mistake of sitting down on the camp bed, and ended up lying on her stomach, breathing the familiar scent of freshly washed sheets. The temptation to close her eyes and simply drift away was almost unbearable.

I need to see Lina first. The soldiers would have said something if she'd been killed or even badly hurt, but somehow Sylph needed to confirm it with her own eyes. She rolled over, found a pitcher of iced water at the bedside, and guzzled most of it; the rest she splashed against her face, feeling the sting where it touched a multitude of cuts and bruises.

A few minutes later, the tent flap rustled.

"Come in."

Lina entered. She had a length of wood under one arm as a kind of crutch, and one of her wrists was heavily bandaged. Her armor was spattered liberally with blood, and the sword still hung at her side.

"Lina!" Sylph sat up suddenly. "What happened?"

Lina shrugged, and winced at the pain the movement produced. "Demons. Vilvakis's best, of course."

"Are you okay?"

"I'm not going to be sprinting anytime soon, but I'll survive." Lina peered at Sylph. "And what about you? You don't look so good."

"I'm . . ." Sylph hesitated. "Not okay. I'll survive." She hastily shifted on the bed. "Here, sit down."

"Thanks." Lina made her painful way over and sat down, gingerly. Sylph couldn't help staring at her, and her eyes filled with tears. Lina saw, and smiled. "Did you miss me?"

She's changed. Gotten harder. Sylph couldn't decide if that was a good thing or a bad thing. *I wonder what's happened to her?*

"More importantly," Lina said, leaning closer, "did you get it?"

"Get what?"

"The geist!" Lina said impatiently.

Sylph stared. Deep in her mind, a horrible suspicion unfolded, and she knew exactly who to blame.

Rathmado.

※　※　※

Lina sputtered; she hadn't closed her mouth fast enough and had gotten a swallow of the stuff pouring out of the bubble. It was blood-warm and salty; she spat hastily and ended up trying to cough the rest of it out. The floor of the clearing was completely soaked, and she was covered from head to toe.

A woman's body slid out of the disintegrating blister while Lina was choking, landing heavily on the sodden grass. Christina's eyes snapped to it, as steady as though her gaze was a steel rod. The blood-slicked body started to glow a faint yellow, and a matching glow came from behind Christina's eyes. By the time Lina raised her head, the body's radiance was so strong it was difficult to look at. There was a enormous *crack*, like the snap of a ruler, and when the light cleared the body was gone and Christina was lying on the ground curled into a tight ball.

Lina's first thought was, *Dear God, what did I do?* She wiped the blood away from her eyes and crawled away from where the bubble had been hovering. Grass squelched under her knees. Molochim hurried to her side and helped her up, which was not easy given how slippery she'd become; by the time she was on her feet the front of his suit was badly stained. He glared at it.

"Sorry," Lina said.

"You just have to concentrate." And the stains vanished, between one instant and the next. Lina stared down at her own soaked outfit and focused her mind. She opened her eyes and found herself clean and stain free. *That's all it takes?* She shook her head. *More important things to deal with now.*

Christina had uncurled a little, and Lina hurried to her side. She knelt as the woman sat up, and Lina saw that her face had changed. Christina was now, unmistakably, her mother. Lina couldn't help but throw herself forward into a hysterical hug.

"Mom!"

"L . . . Lina?" Christina blinked, then wrapped her arms around Lina just as tightly. Her voice was choked. "Are you real?"

Lina felt like giggling hysterically. "I think so."

There was a long silence. Lina knew that it wasn't real—her body, her mother's, none of it—but the woman hugging her was warm and *alive* and for the moment that was all that mattered.

Christina pulled back. "What are you doing here? Are you dead too?" Her eyes narrowed. "If you killed yourself over me, I will give you *such* a smack . . ."

"No, I'm not dead. Well," Lina said reflectively, "actually I guess I *am* dead, but that doesn't matter really. Sylph . . ."

"Sylph's dead too?"

Lina nodded.

"What happened?"

"I was driving, and the car skidded on some ice . . ."

"Where?"

"Route twelve."

"Didn't I always say that was dangerous?" Christina gave her a shaky smile.

"It wasn't my fault. There was some old guy in the road, and I was trying not to run him over."

"God. I never thought . . ."

"Mom. Mom, it's okay. I'm here, and Sylph is here, and now we've found you. It's all going to be okay."

"We're all dead, how can it possibly be okay? This place is—I don't know. Awful."

"I know." Lina looked around; the woods of the Pit managed to look, if anything, more oppressive than usual. "We're getting out of here. Back to Omega. That's where Sylph is."

Christina sat back. "You've gotten taller."

"Yeah."

"How long has it been?"

"Close to three years."

"Three years." Her voice cracked. "Three years."

"Mom? What's wrong?"

"Nothing." Christina wiped away tears. She looked around, and appeared to notice Molochim for the first time. "Who's this young man?"

"I'm not young," he said, smiling.

"Not exactly a man, either." Seeing Christina's surprised look, Lina continued, "Not like that. Anyway, his name is Molochim. He's a . . . friend of mine."

Molochim bowed. "Hello, Christina."

"Rose," she corrected.

"Rose?" Molochim looked at Lina questioningly.

"That's what *we* always called her," Lina said.

"I used to be called Christina." She paused. "How does he know that?"

"We . . . saw a few things." Lina stopped, not quite sure how to explain.

"This place," said Molochim, "is too fucking small for us, right? And after you get stuck here for a while it starts to resonate. For some reason the strongest resonance for you was your childhood—fuck if I know why—so we had to walk through half of it on the way here. Or, rather, a fuckin' filter-modulated representation there of, sort of thing."

There was a pause.

Christina pointed at Molochim. "Is he insane?"

"No. At least," Lina smiled, "I think he's sane and there's fuck-all for anyone else around here to say that I'm wrong."

"Language," Christina warned automatically.

"Sorry." Lina leaned forward. "Do you remember what happened after you got here?"

Christina closed her eyes and thought. "A little. I remember the pain, and then I was falling. The forest. I figured out I was dead pretty quickly, and after that . . ." She stopped.

"What?" Lina prompted gently.

Her mother took a deep breath. "I just couldn't stop thinking about you and Sylph. And about how *stupid* I was—I just stepped in front of the thing. I even saw it in time. I remember thinking, 'Oh, he'll have to stop.' And then, *wham*, smear on the pavement. And the two of you, by yourselves . . ."

The back of Lina's mind echoed with her mother's voice. *"Never again. I will never leave you behind, Lina. I swear to God Almighty. Never. Never . . ."*

Christina hid her face behind her hands. Lina hesitated, then hugged her again, feeling the dampness of tears on her shoulder.

"I'm sorry," her mother whispered. "I'm so sorry."

"You have nothing to be sorry for."

"I left you behind."

"You died, Mom. You don't get a choice in that kind of thing. It's not the same."

Christina took a deep breath. "When I was a little girl, and my mother died, I hated her for it. I didn't understand why she had to leave."

"Mom . . ."

"If you hate me . . ." She swallowed. ". . . it's okay. Honestly."

"Never," Lina whispered. "Never, never, never."

It was a long time before they separated again, mother and daughter both wiping their eyes. Eventually Lina said, "Was that asshole Tom really my father?"

"You saw that?" Christina blushed, which to Lina looked so incongruous she had to laugh. "Yes, he was. You don't look much like him. I was pregnant with Sylph when he left, and I didn't hear from him again for two years. Then he wanted to get involved in your lives again, and I told him to get lost. I thought he might come after us, so I moved and changed my first name, just to be safe. I didn't want you two to have anything to do with him." She shook her head. "It was probably the wrong decision. His family had money. However much of a jerk he was to me, he might have been better for you two . . ."

"Mom." Lina put a hand on her shoulder. "I think you did the right thing."

"Thanks."

Molochim cleared his throat, and both women looked up.

"I'm sorry," Christina said. "I didn't mean to just leave you sitting there."

"It's not like there's much else to do," he said dryly.

"You can call me Christina," she said. "It's the name my mother gave me. And I don't suppose I have to worry about Tom anymore."

"Nope." Lina got to her feet and stretched. *I haven't slept in ages. Or eaten, or even had any water for that matter.* Apparently those things were unnecessary in the Pit, because she felt better than she had in a long time. "Molochim, we're getting out of here. I'm taking Mom and we're going back to Omega to find Sylph. Do you want to come?"

"Of course." He paused. "Any idea how?"

Lina raised one finger, opened her mouth, thought for a moment, then closed it again and scratched her chin.

✳   ✳   ✳

I NEVER TOLD LINA ABOUT THE GEISTS. SHE BROUGHT ME THE first one, but I never told her what they are or what to call them.

Sylph swallowed and tried to stay calm. *It could be innocent. Maybe she just talked to Rathmado, and he told her the story.*

Or . . .

"I got it," Sylph said slowly.

Lina exhaled. "Thank God. We were worried that Vilva-kis might have gotten away with it."

"We?"

"Marlowe and I," Lina answered smoothly. *I certainly never told Marlowe. And I doubt Rathmado would have. So where does that leave me?*

This isn't Lina. The thought was somehow a relief. *I didn't want to think she cared more about the geist than she did about me. No one should be that hard.*

But I have to make sure.

Sylph leaned back against the bed and closed her eyes. It wasn't difficult to feign exhaustion. "All this is hard to believe, isn't it?"

"What?"

"You know." Sylph raised an arm and waved. "All this. Two little girls beating the three most powerful people in the world."

"I suppose." Lina stretched a little. "It just goes to show you can get used to anything."

Sylph chuckled. "True enough. Do you remember when Mom took us to that amusement park last year? And I didn't want to go on the roller-coaster?"

Lina hesitated just a fraction too long; Sylph could almost see the wheels turning behind her eyes, trying to figure out if the question was a trap. In the end she apparently decided to play it safe.

"I'm not sure I was there. What'd she say?"

Got her. "She told me that if I didn't try it, I'd never get used to it." Sylph lay back flat on the bed. "Sometimes I feel like roll-er-coasters would have been good training for all of this."

Somewhat to Sylph's surprise, Lina fell back as well and cuddled up beside her. "No kidding. We've been running since we hit the ground." She paused, then put her arm around her sister. "It's good to have you back, Sylph. I was . . . worried about you."

The body pressing against Sylph was her sister, and the hug was nothing she hadn't done a thousand times before, but suddenly the whole situation seemed slimy and *wrong*. Lina was pressing against her a little too tightly; one of her hands had crept onto Sylph's chest, sliding up to her breasts . . .

Sylph suddenly felt other hands on her breasts, big, callused hands, and a fishbelly-pale gut pressing against her stomach. It was an effort not to scream; instead she rolled toward Lina, retrieved her gun from where it had fallen beside the bed, and pressed it into her sister's stomach just below the bellybutton. Lina froze at the feeling of cool metal against her skin.

"My mother died more than two years ago," Sylph said calmly. "So who the *fuck* are you, and what have you done with my sister?"

She wasn't really sure what to expect—hysterical denial, metamorphosis to a hideous demonic form, or something similar. Instead Lina just sat up, pointedly ignoring the gun, and said, "Are you going to shoot me?"

"If I have to. But not before you answer my question."

"I'd recommend against it. This *is* your sister's body; I'm just borrowing it for a while. If you put a hole in it I imagine she'd be a bit angry with you."

Sylph sat up too, keeping the gun trained. "We'll see. Now answer the question."

"My name is Rahmgoth." Lina put a hand on her sword, as though for reassurance. "Lina is in storage for the moment."

"Why?"

"Rathmado felt having me as his Liberator would improve our chances. After all, we share a goal."

"Bring her back," said Sylph coldly. "Now."

"I'm afraid that's not possible."

"Bring her back or I'm going to strap you to a table and pick you out of her brain with my bare hands." As threats went, it left something to be desired. Lina—Rahmgoth—just smiled.

"Let me make a counter offer. Give me the geists. Once Rathmado and I are finished, we'll let you have your sister back."

Sylph shook her head. "There's no way I could trust you."

Rahmgoth watched her for a moment, then shrugged. "I suppose not. I would have liked to do it the easy way. Guards!"

There was movement at the tent flap, and a moment later Orbaa entered, holding a loaded crossbow. Three more soldiers followed him, taking up positions to Rahmgoth's right.

"Orbaa," Sylph grated, "get Marlowe."

Orbaa hesitated. "I guess you haven' heard? Marlowe tried to betray the Liberator."

"That's ridiculous. I said get him."

"I'm afraid," Rahmgoth said, "that his punishment has already been carried out."

"You killed him?" Sylph closed her eyes. "You did, didn't you. God." *I never should have left. I never should have left her.*

"He was a traitor," Orbaa said.

"Listen to me very carefully," said Sylph. "This is *not* Lina. Would the Liberator do this? She's been taken over by . . . an evil spirit, or something. We've got to restrain her until we can get rid of it . . ."

Rahmgoth gave her a tiny smile. "I fear that we've found the source of the treason. Power corrupts, you see. And Sylph has the power of three Archmagi, more power than any human should have." She turned back to Sylph. "Give me the geists."

Sylph said nothing, thinking desperately.

"You can't win," said Rahmgoth. "You're not going to shoot me, no matter what. Whereas, while I would rather not, I *will* shoot you. Give me the geists."

Sylph suddenly recalled Vilvakis. *"Where are the geists?"* And afterwards a thousand years of pain and violation . . .

"No." Sylph straightened. "If you're going to shoot me . . ."

"Shoot her," Rahmgoth snapped.

Sylph turned her gun on the soldiers and fired once as she threw herself flat. The shot went safely wide, but the flash and the bang threw off their aim. Four bolts *hiss-whapped* into the bedstead, one of them missing her side by only a hair. Just an instant later there was another shot and one of the soldiers fell with a gurgle. Yahvy ripped the tent flap aside, already taking aim at another crossbowman. He dove in time to take the bullet in the shoulder and went down in a spray of blood.

Orbaa and the last remaining soldier drew their swords, but Rahmgoth was faster. One of Lina's hands rested on the hilt of her sword, and a whip of white flame lashed across the room into Yahvy's gun, sending it flying against one wall of the tent in two pieces.

Yahvy didn't even hesitate. She drew her own sword in a fraction of a second and steel rang on steel as she engaged the guard. He gave ground rapidly, tripped over one of his fallen companions and took a lunge through the throat. Then Yahvy back pedaled to avoid Orbaa's attack, and blades clashed again.

"Sylph!" Yahvy shouted. "Run!"

Sylph was struggling back to her feet, trying to find a clear shot at Orbaa. Before she got one, Rahmgoth drew the sword and stepped into the fray, his swing a curtain of white fire that cut Yahvy's blade in half in one unstoppable stroke. He stopped the sword an inch from her throat, then looked back at Sylph.

"Last chance, Sylph. Give me the geists and no one else has to die today."

Orbaa backed away from Yahvy and advanced on Sylph, sword raised. "Drop the weapon."

Sylph tensed. Her body was exhausted, and she was sure she wasn't thinking clearly. *There has to be someway out of this, something I'm not seeing. I don't want anyone else to die—I don't want to shoot my own men. But once Rahmgoth has the geists I'm as good as dead.*

Everyone in the room froze as Rahmgoth suddenly screamed.

✳   ✳   ✳

"THE TRICK," LINA SAID SLOWLY, "IS TO TURN THINGS around, right? Since all of this"—she waved a hand—"is a metaphor created by the interaction of our minds with the Pit, we can exploit properties of the metaphor to make it do what we want."

"What?" said Christina.

"How so?" asked Molochim.

"Mom," Lina turned to her, "when you got here, what's the very first thing you remember?"

"Falling. And I saw . . . I'm not sure what. Someone getting killed."

"Rahmgoth's memory. I saw it too. So if we got in by falling, that means that the exit is up there!" She pointed at the sky.

"That almost makes sense," said Molochim. "If someone drilled a hole in the Pit, there'd have to be a way back out. And if Rahmgoth got out . . ."

"We should be able to." Lina beamed.

"Or you should, at least," the Veritas said. "Your mom and I don't have bodies to go back to."

"We'll figure something out," said Lina. "My sister's a . . . Magus, or whatever."

"I told you the fuckin' story, right? The only person who ever brought somebody back to life was Lightbringer, and look what happened to him! It's *forbidden*, the White Lady won't allow it."

"We'll figure something out," Lina repeated. Her good mood was suddenly unquenchable. *I've got Mom and I'm getting out of here. And so is she, whatever Molochim says.*

"Excuse me," Christina said. "Can I ask a question?"

"Go ahead," Lina said.

"I'm not going to pretend I understand what you've been talking about, but if the way out is up *there*, then how are we going to get to it?"

That stumped Lina too, but only for a moment. She smiled again. "Another thing Molochim taught me. None of this is real." She bent down, and put her hands flat against the grass. "All it is is what we make it. You might want to hang on, this could get bumpy."

She couldn't be sure it was going to work. But it *felt* right. She thought about how things were, and then about how they *ought* to be, and tried to develop a rock hard certainty that they could change. *This place is made of nothing but the interactions of our minds, and what's left over from whomever came before. The forest, the ground, the castle, all that must come from Rahmgoth. The house and the apartments came from Mom. Hell, she even managed to split herself in two rather than be stuck remembering that she'd left us behind. If they can do all that, this should be easy.*

"Lina . . ." began Molochim carefully.

The earth shook.

Not a big tremor, not at first, but it didn't stop. A grinding, crunching sound that Lina felt as much as heard, coming up through the soles of her shoes. Before long the ground was moving visibly, and a neat circle that took up most of the clearing was marked off by boiling earth. Bits of grass and dirt shot up in a fountain.

Now, Lina thought, *up!*

A column of stone rose with the trio atop it, fast enough to press Lina against the grass. She shouted with the sheer exhilaration of it; the air whipped past, and she heard her mother scream. Hastily Lina reached out and grabbed her hand, slowing the column's breakneck ascension to a more stately rise.

"Sorry. You okay?"

"I'm fine." Christina took a deep breath. "It just startled me." Her eyes were drawn upward, and Lina followed her gaze. "Look!"

The sky was getting closer the higher they went. The stars were showing definite parallax, as though they were nothing more than lights mounted on some impossibly high vaulted ceiling. Lina carefully edged to the side of their platform and looked down. The ground was already a green-brown blur far, far below, but something closer caught her attention and she backed away.

"Molochim! That . . . thing . . ." *Hikano*, her memory supplied. *A demon.* "Hikano's down there!"

"Hikano?" Molochim smiled. "Glad to hear it. I won't be sorry to leave *that* behind."

"Not *all* the way down there. It's climbing the tower!"

"Oh, *fuck*." He raced to the side and looked down. The huge thing had somehow gotten a grip on the ascending spire, four clawed arms digging into the rock and letting it climb like a squirrel. Its huge doglike hind legs scrabbled for purchase, but it was making remarkably fast progress. Lina and Molochim backed away.

"We have to get out of here." Molochim looked around at the clearing; small, flat, with nowhere to hide. "Lina, can you get us *off* this thing?"

"It can't hurt us, can it?" Lina said. "Not permanently, I mean."

"He wants out, the same as we do. Do you want *that* loose in your body? If it gets to the exit . . ."

"The hell with *that*," Lina growled. "Mom, stay here. Molochim, watch out for her, would you?"

"I don't need watching out for," said Christina, "and would someone please tell me . . . *what the hell is that?*"

Hikano crawled over the lip of the still-ascending platform, levering himself up with two massive arms. It roared in triumph, focusing tiny bloodshot eyes on the three of them. Lina stood directly in its path, her arms crossed and her heart pounding. *I survived last time, but fuck did that hurt.* Her hands tightened into fists. *Remember.*

"It's all, like, filters. Metaphor. He rips you to shreds because he thinks he can and because you agree he can."

I just have to disagree with it. Looking up at the demon's looming bulk, that seemed easier in theory than in practice. Thankfully, she didn't have much time to think about it. Hikano roared again and charged, mouth wide open and obviously intending to swallow Lina whole.

She braced herself and, at the last moment, extended her arms to grab the monster's jaws. Its charge stopped dead; she didn't so much as slide on the grass, while Hikano's taloned feet dug huge rips in the earth. The demon thrashed in a frenzy, trying to close its jaws or bull her aside, but Lina kept it fixed in place as though she were wired to the ground.

I just have to disagree.

"I think," she whispered to the demon, "that we are all getting just a little bit tired of you."

She spread her arms wider. Hikano screamed, this time in pain, as its jaw was forced open wider than it was ever meant to go. Lina took a step forward and kept pushing as the demon's claws dug into the ground, kept pushing until she heard a horrible *crack*. Then she pulled, and with a crunch and the sound of tearing gristle the demon's whole lower jaw came away in her hand. Hikano staggered backward, hands clawing at its face in disbelief, and it was easy enough for Lina to step forward, put a hand on its chest, and push.

The demon's scream dopplered into the distance as it went over the side, vanishing long before it hit the ground, who knows how far below. Lina watched for a moment, then tossed its lower jaw after it and turned back to Molochim and Christina.

"Well, there's that taken care of."

They gaped at her.

"What?"

Christina shook her head and pointed upwards. "We're there."

Lina looked up. The ceiling—a wall of solid black rock—was only a few feet overhead. There was a star a little way away, a giant circle of light that looked as though it had been painted onto the stone. Directly above her there was a fissure, a narrow crack through which she saw a trickle of daylight.

"Okay." Lina took a deep breath. "Okay, okay. I just have to go up there?"

"I *think* so," Molochim said. "I've never seen anything like this."

"That's good to know," Christina said faintly. "I'd hate to think this was an everyday thing."

"I'll be back," Lina said. "I swear to . . . whomever. I *will* get you out of here. Okay?"

Molochim shrugged, but Christina nodded fervently.

"Molochim, can you take care of her until then?"

"Lina! I don't need . . ." said Christina, but the Veritas nodded.

"Thanks," Lina said. "For everything."

He reached into the pocket of his battered suit, pulled out a mostly empty pack of cigarettes, and extracted one with a deft tap. It ignited on its own as he held it between two fingers.

"Any time."

Lina closed her eyes, took one last breath, and reached up toward the fissure. There were plenty of handholds, and she managed to wedge herself solidly into the rock and slowly work her way up. The light glittered, tantalizingly within reach, and she stretched out a hand to it . . .

✳   ✳   ✳

A LANDSCAPE, ALL IN WHITE, AND ONE MAN STANDING ALONE in the midst of the snow.

Rahmgoth's head snapped round. "You!"

Lina dropped lightly to the ground, looked around, and smiled. "I'm back . . . here?"

"What are you doing here?" He took a threatening step forward.

"I'm taking back my mind."

"You let me in. You *handed* me the door, used enough of my

power to create a bridge. I intend to stay."

"And I won't let you." Lina concentrated and *pushed*, and she felt Rahmgoth respond.

"You're going to fight me?" He sneered. "I am a Veritas, little girl."

Lina didn't respond, just pressed him harder. The white snowfield faded as the comforting layers of metaphor and allegory were stripped away, leaving only the primal conflict of two minds in one body. It was a deeply unnatural situation, and Lina could feel her body's agony. The sensation was distant, as though she were swathed in cotton wool, but she relished the feeling. It was *real*, and she pressed near it. Rahmgoth gave ground, and she felt his astonishment. Then she felt him reach back into the Pit; power flowed through, and his attack redoubled.

There must be something of him left down there. It made sense—*his memories, his castle.* Lina pushed herself, spending every reserve she had in an assault that left the Veritas in baffled retreat. But it wouldn't last. In a few moments, the power flowing up from the Pit would overwhelm her.

✳   ✳   ✳

RAHMGOTH—LINA—FELL TO HIS KNEES, CLUTCHING HIS head. Orbaa turned and said, "Lina?"

That was his last mistake. Sylph fired twice, and he spun with the impact and hit the ground with a thump.

"What's happening?" Yahvy said.

"I have no idea." Sylph stepped closer to Lina's body, still covering her with the pistol. "Lina? Can you hear me?"

"Sylph." The word forced itself out, as though Lina spoke only with great effort.

"Lina? Or Rahmgoth?"

"No time." Lina's breathing was harsh. "The Pit . . . stop him."

"The Pit?" Sylph glanced at Yahvy, who could only shake

her head in confusion. "Lina, I don't . . ."

"The *sword.* Take it . . ."

Lina's head snapped around, as though she'd been slapped. She stumbled away from Sylph, toward Yahvy, one white-knuckled hand wrapped around the sword's hilt. When she raised her head, Rahmgoth was once again in charge; Sylph saw it in her eyes, now that she knew what to look for.

"We tried . . . the easy way," he said, with some effort. "Now . . . you die. Rathmado . . . will be . . . disappointed."

He raised the blade, and white fire coruscated along its length. Sylph flicked her eyes past Lina's body, caught Yahvy's gaze, and nodded ever so slightly.

Rahmgoth slashed, a ribbon of white fire rippling outward at head height. Sylph hit the ground just in time, landing awkwardly on one shoulder which spiked in crimson agony. The energy wave took out the back wall of the tent and one of the poles, and the whole structure creaked and began a slow collapse. Rahmgoth spun in Yahvy's direction, but not fast enough; the Circle Breaker caught him with a low tackle from behind, bearing him onto Sylph's bed.

Sylph sprang up and added her weight to Yahvy's, keeping Lina's body pinned by the simple expedient of sitting on the small of her back. Yahvy shifted and clawed at the hilt of the sword, but Lina's grip was too sure. White fire growled, and Sylph heard Rahmgoth's muffled laughter.

We've got to get it away from her . . .

Yahvy pushed herself back to her feet, then threw herself forward. Her knee, precisely placed, came down on Lina's outstretched forearm with all Yahvy's weight behind it. Sylph heard the *snap* of bone, and Lina's fingers spasmed; Yahvy swept the sword out of her reach.

❋   ❋   ❋

"You're done, girl." Rahmgoth had pressed Lina to

the outer reaches of her mind. Beyond was on a great void, and being pushed there meant oblivion. The power flowing from the Pit made the Veritas unstoppable.

Lina gritted her teeth—or would have, had she had teeth to grit—and fought a desperate defense. *Sylph, come on . . .*

The *snap* echoed through the non-space like the shattering of worlds. Lina screamed in agony, and felt Rahmgoth do the same; a moment later, the stream of power from the Pit stretched and died.

Rahmgoth had been preparing for a final assault. With all his reserves behind him, he could have ended Lina once and for all; without them, just for a moment, he was exposed.

Lina went on the attack without wasting a breath, tearing through Rahmgoth's mind and soul. He reeled and fell back, trying desperately to organize a defense, but there was no time. Lina hounded him across the mindscape until he was pressed against the same ultimate boundary.

There were no final words—Lina wouldn't have paused to give them. But she felt from Rahmgoth, to the last, a deep, abiding hatred. It made it easier to press the final attack home.

✳   ✳   ✳

LINA'S THRASHING HAD STOPPED.

Sylph leaned close to her sister's ear. "Lina?"

"I'm here," Lina said, muffled by being face down in the bed.

"Really?" Sylph felt tears welling up. She felt completely spent. If Lina had grabbed the sword and skewered her, Sylph couldn't have lifted a finger. "Lina?"

"Yeah."

Sylph shifted, slowly, and Lina rolled over. When she moved her arm, it shifted in an extremely unnatural direction, and she screamed.

"Get someone!" Sylph shouted at Yahvy, who nodded and sprinted from the room. Lina had made it onto her back, breathing hard.

"Sylph," Lina said between gritted teeth, "I think my arm is broken."

"I know. It was Yahvy."

"Ah."

There was a moment of silence. Sylph felt tears flowing freely down her cheeks.

"At times like this," she said, with the last of her rationality, "one of us usually collapses crying into the other's arms." Sylph took a deep breath. "And . . . I was wondering if it could be me."

"I'm not sure I want to move," said Lina, "so go ahead."

Sylph buried her face in her sister's chest and sobbed, breathing in great gulps. Lina raised her good arm and put a hand on Sylph's shoulder.

chapter twenty-three

AFTERWARD, **S**YLPH FELT LIKE SLEEPING FOR A SOLID week. She knew there were nightmares waiting, that Brutus's cold hands were hovering somewhere in the dark recesses of her mind, but curled up in Lina's embrace kept all that at bay. Her sister's arms—*well*, Sylph thought with a bit of guilt, *arm*—were the antidote for everything she'd suffered, if there could be such a thing. Sylph wanted to stay in a warm little ball forever, or at least until she stopped hurting.

That was not to be, of course. As always, there were things to be attended to. At the very least Lina's arm needed a healer's attention. Yahvy had returned fairly quickly with someone from the hospital, and they'd gotten the break bandaged and splinted with only a little bit of screaming from Lina. According to the healer it was a clean break and would probably heal quickly; later, when they'd crawled back into bed, Sylph touched the geists and took a look with her eyes closed. Healing flesh or even bone was out of the question—the human body was such a complex mechanism the thought made her dizzy—but she was able to reinforce the splinting with a few pins around the bone itself, to make sure it stayed in place.

By the following morning, Lina was no longer in horrible agony every time she moved, and Sylph's total exhaustion had been reduced to a bone deep weariness, along with a myriad aches and pains. By unspoken agreement they spent the whole day in bed, with soldiers bringing in food and water. Yahvy visited, briefly, to assure Sylph that nothing had gone horribly wrong; she'd managed to assemble enough troops to officially accept the surrender of the city of Adriato. In Vilvakis's absence the captain of his palace guard had assumed command and managed to keep the city from self-destructing.

Sylph had Yahvy send a runner to retrieve *Chronicles* from the library, then retreated back into her tent—a new tent, actually, given that Rahmgoth had destroyed the previous one—and went back to sleep. The sisters didn't talk much, and Sylph was happy with that, but in the time that they were awake Lina gave at least a partial recounting of what had happened to her. And, curled up together afterward, she couldn't seem to stop her thoughts from running ahead.

Mom is alive.

Well, no. But still in existence. Still herself, even if she is stuck in some prison dimension. Absurdly, she felt a little jealous of Lina— *though I wouldn't want to surrender my body to Rahmgoth, either.* There was so much she needed to talk to her mother about.

But there were other matters. *Rahmgoth was locked up in the Pit until someone let him out. That sword*—it was tucked away under the bed—*is a gate into that place, a little chink in the wall.* Where it had come from originally was a matter for speculation. *But I know who gave it to us.*

Rathmado. Her teeth ground. *He lied to me from the start. All of it—finding my mother, his absurdities about Destiny—it was all* bullshit. *And he's done it before.* He'd been at the side of every previous Liberator, prodding them to fight and conquer and ultimately challenge the Lightbringer. *He's been at this a long time. Why?* It was one of many questions she couldn't answer. *What does he get out of it?*

The story of the Lightbringer that Lina had sketched out matched with what Sylph had so briefly read in the last chapter of *Chronicles. "A love beyond death."* First he declared war on the Throne, for *daring to interfere in his business. Then when they killed her, he went against the laws of the universe itself.* Or the White Lady—Lina hadn't been exactly clear. After all this Sylph wouldn't have been surprised to find out that the White Lady had a literal, physical existence. *And she created this whole world just to imprison him.*

The next morning, Sylph forced herself out of bed bright and early and had the soldiers bring hot water to wash. It was beyond paradise to finally be *clean*, after weeks of having her own blood and filth swabbed off by Brutus's washcloth. Getting back into proper clothes was similarly heavenly. Her hair was so tangled that she seriously considered just hacking it all off, but an hour's work with a comb and a basin restored it to a state where she could tie it back. Once all that was done, she helped Lina with her own ablutions, working around the splint and sling. Then Sylph sent for Yahvy, who in turn sent for Rathmado.

The Magus entered with his usual smile. Sylph had set up two chairs for herself and Lina, and Yahvy was standing silently near the door; half a regiment of guards were within earshot, waiting for a signal or a shout. Sylph was well aware that she had no idea of the extent of Rathmado's powers, and she wasn't taking any chances. *Of course, if it comes to that, the geists are more likely to be useful than any number of swords.* She had one hand in her pocket, shuffling the metal spheres round and round.

"Sylph," the Magus said, "it's such a relief to see that you've returned safely." He gave her a low bow. "And my lady the Liberator. I hadn't heard about your . . . injury."

"Tell me," Sylph said quietly, "do you remember someone named Erik?"

Rathmado blinked. "I know a great many people. I'm sure there have been a few with that name."

"This one was special. You were an . . . advisor, of sorts."

The Magus fell silent.

"You took him all the way to the Black Keep, to the Lightbringer's doorstep." Sylph let her smile fade. "This was thirty-five hundred years ago, so I'm not surprised if you can't recall. Lady Fell has been a real obstacle for you, hasn't she? She killed Jaen, and Adam, and Hayao. Vilvakis killed Que-Li and Callius. But Erik made it all the way."

She reached into her pocket and removed the geists, holding them loosely in her palm. "Like we have. Tell me, Rathmado, what happened to Erik?"

Still he said nothing. Sylph closed her hand around the geists.

"*Damn* you and your 'Destiny.' *I have done nothing that has not been done before!*"

Sylph took a deep breath.

"In case you were thinking of trying anything, Yahvy is behind you. You're familiar with my new weapons? Your magic may make you immune to bullets, but I suspect not."

She watched his eyes. There was only a tiny flicker—to Lina for an instant, then back again—but it was enough. *Bastard. He expects Rahmgoth to come to his rescue.*

"Now. Start talking, beginning with why I should let you live."

"If you kill me," Rathmado said calmly, "your mother will be trapped in the Pit forever."

How did he know Lina told me where she was? "Why?"

"Do you think bringing someone back to life is easy? Only one person has ever managed it, but it wasn't for lack of trying. Lightbringer knows the secret. Ask your sister if you don't believe me."

"Lightbringer isn't going to tell me, with or without you."

"Not if he has any choice in the matter, no."

"Even if I wanted to force that information out of him," Sylph said, "why do I need you?"

"Without me you don't have a chance." The Magus permitted himself a tiny smile. "As you said. I've been fighting the Lightbringer for more than thirty-five hundred years. I've learned a thing or two in that time."

"You're bluffing." It was more a hope than an observation. If

Rathmado was afraid, he hid it well. He wasn't even sweating.

"You really think I'd go to all this trouble if I didn't have a way to win? I am many things, Miss Walker, but not a fool."

"Why?" Lina blurted out. "What do you have against him?"

Rathmado stared at her for a moment. "Astonishing," he said eventually. "A Veritas defeated by a human. I wouldn't have believed it."

"Answer the question," Sylph snapped.

"Does it really matter?" the Magus said. "You wouldn't believe me."

"Try me."

"You read the *Chronicles*, I assume. I should have had it destroyed, but I admit to a touch of sentimentality."

"I read it," said Sylph.

"And you understand what happens—it's a *cycle*. The Liberator arrives and tries to defeat the Archmagi—eventually, he or she dies, and it's not long before someone else picks up where the last tyrant left off."

"Because of *you*. You push the Liberators toward Lightbringer."

"Oh, certainly. I create them in the first place." He eyed the two of them. "Don't look so shocked. Without Rahmgoth and the sword, would the two of you have even survived your first night? I simply wait for a powerful enough Magus and then . . . adjust matters appropriately." He paused. "But that's besides the point. Think about the other side of the cycle. Who do you think sets the Archmagi back up again? Who created the geists?"

Sylph mulled that for a moment. "You're saying it was Lightbringer?"

"Of course. This world was created for him, as a prison, but it's still a world like any another. The people on it don't deserve to have their entire way of life twisted to serve his needs."

"What needs?" Lina asked.

"You haven't figured that out?" Rahmgoth raised an eyebrow.

"Power, of course. The Circles of the Archmagi gather the power that flows down the energy slope, funneling it and the souls that come with it into the geists. Lightbringer created the geists for that purpose, and then set up the Archmagi as . . . administrators, of sorts. They squabble and fight, but he doesn't care as long as the Circles are maintained. And every time I knock them down he sets them back up again, like bowling pins."

"What good does the power do him?" Sylph couldn't help but ask, though she didn't like the way the tone of the discussion had changed; it felt like Rathmado was doling out patient explanations to unruly children. "What does he want?"

"The same thing any prisoner wants. He thinks that if he gathers enough energy, he'll be able to break out of the prison and challenge the White Lady."

"And that's why you're fighting him? Because you feel *sorry* for the people of Omega?" Sylph snorted.

The Magus shrugged. "I said you wouldn't believe me. Simply toppling the Archmagi is not enough. As long as the Lightbringer stands, this world will always be twisted to suit his will. I've dedicated my life to ending his."

"Even if it means destroying mine," Sylph said. "Even if it means replacing Lina with a *thing* like Rahmgoth."

"I was in need of allies. Rahmgoth may have been insane, but his hatred of the Lightbringer was as great as mine. I thought that having him on our side would prove more useful than having Lina."

"And my mother?"

"I anticipated that I could find myself in need of a suitable . . . lever. So I took the precaution of securing her. You should thank me. She would have been difficult to locate otherwise."

"Enough."

Rathmado fell silent. Sylph closed her eyes and sat back, idly shuffling the geists with a series of dull metallic clicks.

"Now what?" Lina said.

"Now we take the army and march on the Black Keep,"

the Magus said. "We defeat the Shadowcore and kill the Light-bringer. End this tyranny forever."

"You expect us to go along with that?" Lina asked. "After—"

"Lina." Sylph raised a hand. Her sister quieted. "Yahvy, take Rathmado back to his tent. I want him under guard every minute of every day, with hourly checks. If the slightest thing goes wrong I want to know about it. Understood?"

"Understood," said Yahvy. "Come."

"It's not necessary," said the Magus. "I will give you my word."

"Don't make me express how little your word means to me," Sylph snarled. "Now, get out of my sight."

She was silent while Yahvy escorted Rathmado through the tent flap. Once they were gone, Sylph turned to Lina.

"Well?"

"He was right. I don't believe him," Lina said.

"I certainly don't believe that he's doing it out of the good-ness of his heart," Sylph said. She sighed. "I'm just worried that he may be right."

"About Lightbringer?"

"Yeah. Given what you told me, it makes as much sense as anything else I've heard."

"So what? We've set the people free. You were the one who kept telling me we weren't supposed to be ruling them."

"These are the problem." Sylph held out the geists. "As long as I have these, there will be no more Archmagi. If Rath-mado is right, it follows that Lightbringer will eventually come and collect them."

Lina nodded, slowly.

"And then there's Mom," Sylph said.

"I promised her I'd get her out of there," Lina said.

"I know."

"Can't you . . . magic up a body for her?"

"No. A human being is too complex; metal and diamond and so forth are all Tinkertoys by comparison to anything organic. Besides, I wouldn't know how to get her out of the Pit and into whatever body I made."

Lina looked down.

"Even then," Sylph said, "we'd still be stuck here in Omega."

"What?"

"Lightbringer knows a lot of secrets. You told me the story; one of them is *how to travel between worlds*. If Rathmado is right—if we really can beat him, make him tell us what he knows—we might be able to go home."

It was a thought Sylph hadn't even articulated until that moment. She hadn't dared. But somehow this felt like the right time to voice the possibility.

"What are you saying?" Lina asked. "That we should do what he says?"

"I don't like it any more than you do, but we may not have a choice."

"That's fine for *us*. What about everyone else? Are you going to ask the soldiers to fight and die for this?"

Sylph hadn't thought about that. "I . . . don't know. If Rathmado's right about the Lightbringer . . ."

"If!"

They fell silent. Sylph sorted through her thoughts. Among them were a few blood-soaked plans, conceived in the darkness and pain of Brutus's torture chamber.

"I want Mom back," she said eventually, her voice small.

"Me too."

"And I want to go home."

"Me too."

✳   ✳   ✳

"ALL RIGHT," SAID SYLPH. "WHAT NEEDS TO BE DONE?"

Heraan, newly released from the hospital tents, snapped off a salute.

"And stop doing that."

He smiled. "As you wish."

"Heraan . . ."

"Fine, fine. Okay, first thing: some of the regimental commanders want to meet with you. The provisional head of the government in Adriato wants to know what we're doing next; I'm a little curious about that myself, to tell you the truth. There's a bunch of prisoners from Vilvakis's army and the city guard. Since . . ." He paused. ". . . since Rahmgoth apparently ordered the execution of a number of prisoners, people are a bit concerned."

"Let them go, all of them."

"But . . ."

"And send a messenger to Adriato. I can't say exactly where we're going next, but we won't be staying here. So whoever this provisional governor is he's free to do what he likes. How badly were we hurt in the battle?"

"Not badly at all, except for the Steelbreakers. One pike regiment was apparently broken by demons, but the Liberator . . . ah . . . Rahmgoth dealt with them before they could do any more damage."

"And the Steelbreakers?"

"They're getting ready to leave. What's left of them, mostly women and children."

Sylph closed her eyes. Rahmgoth's use of the barbarians as cannon fodder was inexcusable, but there was nothing that could be done about it. *Just another crime to lay at his door. At least they didn't get a chance to pillage the city.* "Are the regimental commanders ready to see me?"

"They should be."

"Good. I have a proposition to lay out."

She followed Heraan to the command tent, where the map table had been cleared away in favor of a semicircle of chairs. The commanders of the army of the Liberator were gathered there, and Sylph realized with a start she recognized almost none of them. *Orbaa, Garot, Marlowe—all gone. Melfina's still unconscious*—though the healers said she was doing well—*and Yahvy's off organizing things as best she can.* That left an even dozen hard-eyed men and women, some veterans who'd accompanied the army all the way from Bleloth, others soldiers from General Roswell's ranks. They seemed suspicious of her. *And no wonder. They've only ever taken orders from Rahmgoth.* The hard core of the force Sylph had built was gone.

It makes my choice easier, really.

"Ladies and gentlemen," Sylph said. "You probably know who I am. And I'm sure you're all wondering what comes next."

There was some muttering to that effect. Sylph continued, "I have a choice for you, for everyone who fought under the Liberator's banner. The war is over, and we were victorious. The Archmagi have fallen and may not rise again. You will no longer have to suffer the Plague; no more tributes to the Archmagi lest your children be stillborn.

"But the Liberator believes—I believe—that we are not finished. We have defeated the manifestations of evil, but the source remains. To the east lies the Black Keep, the fortress of the Lightbringer. My intention is to travel there and bring him down."

Half a dozen people started to talk at once, Heraan among them. Sylph held out her hands.

"Please, let me finish. I know how dangerous this is, which is why I won't be taking an army. Lina and I are looking for volunteers—a few hundred, no more—to come with us. The rest of you will be free to return home, or to stay here if you choose. I've sent a message to the guards in Adriato. In exchange for our mercy on the city and its people, rewards will be paid to our soldiers out of Vilvakis's personal treasury. There will be enough there for everyone."

One of the commanders, a young woman with a thick white scar that crawled along her collarbone like a caterpillar, got out of her seat. "Attacking the Black Keep is suicide! The Liberator can't possibly be serious. Even the Archmagi were human, but the Lightbringer . . ."

"They told me attacking Gargorian was suicide," Sylph said reasonably. "Confronting the Clockwork Legion was suicide. Going to Adriato alone was suicide." She winced a little at that last, but continued, "By all rights I should have been dead a long time ago. The Liberator believes that the White Lady has chosen her for this task, and I have faith." It wasn't exactly the truth, but it was close enough. *At least we're not telling them to come and die for us.*

"Of course it will be dangerous," said a stout older man. "It's been danger every step of the way! But the Liberator has always seen us through. She has promised us—"

"This time we promise nothing," Sylph said quickly. "Most of those who come with us, perhaps all, will not return. We may not return. The Liberator and I will think no less of anyone who stays behind. We *want* you to stay behind, as a reward for loyal service."

There was silence. Sylph cleared her throat.

"No one has to decide immediately. I ask that you pass this offer on to your men, and make sure to include the particulars. We're leaving in two days' time."

Heraan followed Sylph when she turned and left the command tent. She said, "Where's Yahvy?"

"Back by the supply train, I think."

"Good. I need to make sure we're well provisioned."

They walked for a way and found that the cooks were already preparing for lunch. Several whole pigs and sections of cow cooked over a crackling bonfire, juices sizzling as they dripped onto the flames. Yahvy was nowhere in evidence, but one of the butchers said she'd gone to chase down an errant wagonload of horseshoes and would return shortly, so Sylph and Heraan settled on one of the logs near the fire to wait.

The warmth felt good, and Sylph let her mind wander. She could feel the information propagating through the camp as the commanders told their men and it spread from there with the speed of rumor. *Hopefully enough of them will be willing to come along.* At the same time, she wished they would all just go home. *This time, it really might be a suicide mission.* But there was no getting around the fact that they needed men. According to Rathmado, the Black Keep was protected by the fanatical Shadowcore knights, who were at least several thousand strong. It was a big enough risk not taking the whole army. *If things go right, we won't need them.*

She became aware of Heraan at her shoulder, brooding to himself. Sylph said, "So? Do you have somewhere to go home to?"

"No. Not really. I suppose I could go back to Bleloth."

"You could stay here in Adriato, then. We'd make sure . . ."

"I'm going with you, Sylph."

She nodded. Sylph hadn't really expected him to say otherwise. "Even though it's dangerous?"

"You'll need everyone you can get. Especially if this plan works out as well as the last one." He looked over at her. "Sorry. I shouldn't have said that."

"It's okay." Sylph drew her knees in and put her chin on them, staring into the flames. There was a pause as the bonfire spat and crackled.

"I never thanked you," Heraan said.

"For what?"

"For saving my life, of course. In the room with the geist."

"I nearly froze you to death."

"Considering the alternatives, I'm grateful anyway."

"Well," said Sylph, smiling, "then you're welcome. After what you saved me from, it seemed like the nice thing to do."

Heraan laughed, looked at her face, and quieted. Sylph hadn't been glaring, at least not consciously, but obviously he saw something there that bothered him.

"I have to say this," Heraan said. "Or I know that I'll regret it."

"Heraan . . ."

"It's the last thing I can remember thinking, under the ice. That I wanted to tell you."

"Tell me?"

"I think I'm in love with you."

Sylph, to her own astonishment, blushed. "Ah. I mean . . ." All she could think, incongruously, was, *I think he's a little bit old for me.*

"You're the bravest woman I've ever met. Certainly the smartest. And . . ." He sighed, and shook his head. "I don't know. It just hit me when I thought I was going to die. When we were in Adriato, beforehand, you seemed so happy; I'd never seen you like that. And then when we broke into the dungeon . . ." His voice got thick. "If you hadn't shot him, I would have killed him with my bare hands. Seeing you like that was like having my heart ripped out. The only thing I could think was that I wanted to pick you up and take you away and never let anyone hurt you ever again."

"Heraan." Sylph paused, not sure what else to say.

He took a deep breath. "I'm not sure how you feel. I just had to get that out, you know?"

She turned to him, and their eyes met. Part of Sylph wanted nothing more than to lean forward and fall into his arms, or maybe kiss him; another part wanted to run away, put her head under a pillow, and pretend none of this had ever happened. She was barely even aware that he was reaching out until his fingers brushed her cheek.

"I just want you to know that it's nothing personal." And a cold hand against her cheek, rubbing her breasts, a fishbelly-pale gut pressed against her stomach . . .

She didn't realize she'd moved, just heard the *crack* as she knocked his hand away. Sylph leapt to her feet, breathing hard and her heart suddenly racing.

"I'm sorry," said Heraan. "I shouldn't have . . . I'm sorry. Lady. Sylph, I didn't mean to—"

"It's okay," said Sylph, more for her own benefit than his.

"It's *okay*. I'm okay."

"Forget it." He shook his head violently. "Forget all of it. Okay?"

"No." She saw him looking away and caught his eye. "*No*, Heraan. It's not that. It's just . . . you touched me, and it felt . . ." Sylph closed her eyes. "I'm the one who should be sorry. It's not your fault."

"I shouldn't have touched you."

"I need to think about this. Please?" Her voice had turned pleading. "It's not you. I just . . . I can't . . ."

"I understand." Heraan got to his feet as well. "It's okay, Sylph. Honestly."

"Really?" She found her eyes damp. "Please don't just say that and stay angry at me."

"I'm not angry at you." He smiled. "My hand hurts a little bit, but I'm not angry."

Sylph smiled back, out of relief. She rubbed the back of her hand, which stung a bit. "Mine too."

There was another pause.

"Sylph!" said Yahvy, from the other side of the bonfire. "Been looking for you."

Sylph held Heraan's gaze a moment longer, then tore herself away.

✳   ✳   ✳

LINA WENT TO THE HOSPITAL, TO SEE MELFINA.

The girl looked terrible. It had only been a week, but she'd lost an alarming amount of weight; it seemed like there was nothing left of her but skin and bones. According to the healers, something had *burned* in her veins, and her heart strained and juddered in her chest. They'd done their best, but it was Rathmado who'd kept her alive.

Her face had sunk, and the orbits of her eyes protruded; her cheekbones looked like daggers, and her skin was as white as

s h i n i g a m i 607

death. Only the slow rise and fall of her chest told Lina she was merely unconscious. But the healers insisted she was improving; they'd been able to get her to drink honeyed water, and whatever internal wound had been bleeding had apparently stopped.

That's one thing I have to thank Rahmgoth for, anyway. She could remember what her body had been doing while her mind had been stuck in the Pit. It was like a vast tract of unexplored wilderness in the back of her mind, a place she was frightened to venture. But she knew he'd ordered Rathmado to save the girl. *Only because he wanted information out of her.*

It was hard *not* to remember. *I have to face it, sooner or later.* Lina knew Rahmgoth had done some ugly things, but she didn't want to know the details. *I don't have much of a choice. I can't keep avoiding them forever.*

She sat at the edge of Melfina's bed and let her mind's eye drift back, with her chin held in her hands. Images flickered— white fire, blood, and a hatred powerful beyond all reason, fuelled by betrayal.

. . . and a last kiss, a girl's body pressed against her own, twitching in its death throes. Her last breath. And the power *that flowed . . .*

"God." Lina's fingers stiffened into claws against her cheeks. She felt the bite of pain where her fingernails broke the skin, but only distantly.

It wasn't me. It wasn't me. My body, my face, but it wasn't me. That didn't help much, not when she could remember the feeling of Fah pressed against her, or the taste of Marlowe's blood. Remember looking at Sylph, and wanting to kiss her and slowly strip off her clothes, then her skin . . .

It wasn't me. Lina wanted to scream. *Rahmgoth. It was Rahmgoth. I didn't do anything.*

"Lina?" said a weak voice. Lina looked up to find Melfina's eyes open.

"Mel?" Lina swallowed with an effort. "You're awake?"

"Are you okay? You're . . . bleeding."

Lina wiped a hand across her forehead and found it stained

crimson from many small cuts. "I'm fine. How are you feeling?"

"Better." Melfina coughed. "I didn't expect to live."

"You cut yourself," Lina recalled slowly. "Poison, intended for me."

"They said it would just put you to sleep," the girl said, "but I don't think I ever really believed it. Marlowe said that you'd gone mad. And there was someone there from Vilvakis . . ."

"I remember," Lina said.

"I had to make sure. Because I knew you would . . ." The girl stopped and looked away.

Lina was silent.

"I just didn't want anyone to get hurt," Melfina said. "I couldn't find a way out. Marlowe said you were crazy, and Daana hated you for what you'd done to Garot. I couldn't let you find out about them, but I couldn't let them hurt you. So when I saw the wine, I thought that would be . . . easier."

Lina gulped for breath. She couldn't have spoken, even if she'd wanted to; her throat was too thick.

Melfina glanced at her. "Did you . . . kill them?"

Lina nodded.

The girl closed her eyes. "And you're going to kill me too."

"No."

"It's okay." Melfina looked up at Lina again. "I'm glad you waited until I woke up. I wanted to talk to you again."

Lina wanted to explain. About Rahmgoth, about everything. *It wasn't me.* But somehow she couldn't bring herself to say it. Instead, she leaned forward until she was almost lying on Melfina's cot, her head against the girl's side. The sheet under her rapidly became wet with tears.

"I'm sorry," Lina whispered. "I'm sorry. I'm sorry."

Slowly, Melfina raised her hand—the fingers were like sticks—and ran it through Lina's hair. The Liberator kept crying.

✳   ✳   ✳

"Two hundred men?" Rathmado lay on the cot in the plain tent Sylph had provided him, hands crossed behind his head. "That's absurd."

Sylph rubbed her hands on her pants, a little nervously. There was something about Rathmado; he was unarmed, unarmored, in a tent surrounded by guards, but he still managed to project a worrisome bravado. She got the feeling that he stayed only because it would be more trouble to break free.

"Trust me," Sylph said.

"You've got the army here, why not use it?"

"Because I don't trust you, and if this is all some scheme to get me killed I'd like as few people to be involved with it as possible."

"To get you *killed*? That would be a bit of a waste of effort on my part at this point, wouldn't it?"

That was true. *He needs something from me. If he's a Magus, why not use the geists himself?*

"That's not the point. I need to know what to expect once we cross into the Lightbringer's domain."

"But with only two hundred men—"

"Answer the question, Rathmado."

He sighed. "Very well. At the borders, the land is much like what we've seen around Adriato, but as we progress toward the Black Keep the Lightbringer's hunger for energy has blighted it. Within his Fourth Circle, his need for power is so strong that *nothing* can be born, not even animals or plants. So the center of the place is a wasteland of sand and rock."

"Fourth Circle? How many does he have?"

"Nine. And the innermost is . . . unique."

"We'll cross that when we get there. So we'll need enough food and water to see us through, and we can't count on forage once we're close. What else?"

"The Shadowcore. You fought them once already."

"When?"

"When we first confronted Lady Fell's army."

Sylph thought back and remembered a legion of cavalry emerging from the woods, charging and dying in silence, overrunning her pikes through sheer force of will until they were killed to the last man. "What were they doing there?"

"Presumably Lightbringer had sent them to reinforce Lady Fell. He likes to play games with the Archmagi, make sure no one gets strong enough to destroy the others."

"How many men does he have?"

"A few thousand; no one really knows. He recruits them from the surrounding areas as a kind of personal guard and a way to intervene in world affairs without showing himself."

"All cavalry?"

"Yes."

"Good." Sylph smiled to herself. *That, at least, I can handle.* "Here's the really important question. Why do you think we have a chance?"

"We won't even get through the Shadowcore with two hundred men."

"Leave that to me. What happened to Erik?"

Rahmgoth looked disgruntled, but finally said, "We made it to the Black Keep itself, after smashing through the Shadowcore. What I found when I got there is that the Lightbringer's physical body is locked in the Keep's inner sanctum, behind a powerful barrier, so he could send his magic against us without risking himself. Erik was a Magus, like you, and with the power of the geists he was able to fight back, but by then the Shadowcore had regrouped and attacked us from behind. Ultimately he fell in battle, and I was forced to flee."

"And this time?"

"I know how to pierce his barrier. We can press home our attack against Lightbringer himself, instead of battling his minions while he finds a way to destroy us."

"Why haven't you done it already?"

"I haven't been able to find a Liberator strong enough." He smiled. "Someone who lost to the Archmagi could never defeat the Lightbringer. But now I have you."

"You mean Lina."

He put on a condescending expression. "Lina was a convenient host for Rahmgoth. You are the Liberator, Sylph. The geists are yours, and the power is yours."

Sylph wasn't in the mood to argue the point. *It doesn't matter anyway.* "How certain are you that you can get us through this barrier?"

"Certain." He watched her expression. "Come now. My life will be on the line as well, won't it?"

Sylph harrumphed and left the tent. Yahvy was standing outside with a cluster of guards. Sylph nodded to them and said, "Make sure he stays put. Yahvy, walk with me a moment?"

They ambled away, heading in the general direction of the rest of camp.

"How many volunteers do we have?"

"Two hundred fifty-seven," said Yahvy. She gave a half-smile. "Mostly women."

"I'm surprised there's that many. You made sure they all know the deal?"

Yahvy nodded. "They *believe.* Lina says Lightbringer will fall. So they follow."

"And you? I don't suppose there's any way I could talk you out of it?"

Yahvy barked a laugh. "Think I'd leave you now?"

"I didn't think so."

"Besides. Want to see what you're cooking up for us." The Circle Breaker's eyes gleamed. Sylph had observed, privately, that Yahvy seemed to have a positive fascination with her new weapons. *She certainly took to the pistol quickly.*

"I'm still putting it together. According to Rathmado, we've got a way to go before we get to Lightbringer's territory."

Yahvy paused, then said, "Trust him too much."

"I don't trust him at all." Sylph sighed. "He's just the only source of information we've got." She'd made some quiet inquiries, but no one in Adriato knew *anyone* who'd gone east and come back, and Vilvakis's library had yielded nothing substantial. Mostly the citizens didn't even think about it, as though the land just ended at the border of Vilvakis's territory. Unlike the Archmagi, Lightbringer didn't seem interested in expanding his domain; his nine Circles had been constant for as long as anyone could remember. *Probably since Rahmgoth led Erik to his death.*

They walked in silence for a while. Sylph looked around, to make sure no one could overhear, then said, "Can I ask you a . . . personal question?"

Yahvy nodded.

"It's just . . . it's not the kind of thing I feel like talking to Lina about. I'm not sure she'd know, to tell the truth."

The Circle Breaker nodded again and made a "get on with it" gesture.

"You and Orbaa were . . ." She searched for a word. ". . . lovers."

"Yes."

"And after you got hurt, he left you. And back in the tent, when he was threatening me, you had to shoot him."

"Yes."

Sylph paused. "Was it worth it? The first part, I mean. Falling in love. It must have hurt a lot, later."

Yahvy looked up, pensively. "Not love, really. After fighting, blood's up, you need someone. I do, anyway. So did he. Just . . . worked out." She shrugged. "Never expected more."

"Ah."

"Heraan's different."

Sylph's head snapped around. "What? I mean . . . how did . . . I don't know what you're talking about."

"Obvious." Yahvy snorted. "He looks like a puppy someone kicked."

"That bad?"

Yahvy nodded, and Sylph sighed.

"Do you love him?" Yahvy asked, after a while.

"I don't know." She closed her eyes. "I don't . . . think so.
I've never been in love with anyone before."

"Like him, then?"

"I guess."

"Fuck him, then."

Sylph turned beet read. "Yahvy!"

"Might die tomorrow. Regret it if you didn't."

"I can't."

"Just because you're not sure it's love . . ."

"Not that." Sylph crossed her arms, hugging herself. "I just
. . . can't."

There was an uncomfortable silence.

"Sorry," Yahvy said quietly. "Wasn't thinking."

"It's okay." Sylph took a deep breath. "I'm okay. I asked
for your advice."

"Not sure you should be asking me. Not a great track record."

They'd arrived at Sylph's tent. "In any case . . . you've got
the supply situation in hand?"

"Easily. There's too few men to defend without guns."

"I'll make sure we've got enough weapons, don't worry."

"Excellent."

"Until tomorrow morning."

Yahvy paused, as though there was something she wanted
to say, but ultimately turned away in silence. Sylph sighed and
slipped into her tent, collapsed on the bed, and went to sleep almost immediately.

✳   ✳   ✳

LINA WATCHED, HER SISTER AT HER SIDE, AS THE ARMY OF
the Liberator broke up for the last time.

They'd divided everything up among the men, with everyone getting an equal share. Even without the food, water, horses,
and fodder Sylph's small force was taking for itself, that amounted
to quite a bit. Weapons and armor, miscellaneous supplies, gold

from Gargorian's treasury and Stonerings's vaults. Lina had overheard a half-dozen plans, from gathering settlers to found a new city in the north to forming a mercenary company. The idea that the Archmagi were gone, and the people now had the freedom to move and live and have children wherever they wanted was starting to sink in. It made Lina smile to see it.

Maybe we've accomplished something after all. She could still feel the marks on her face and the blood on her hands. *After everything.*

The largest parting was also the hardest to watch. The Steelbreakers had done their best to pack up their camp, but a heartbreakingly large number of tents had simply been abandoned where they stood; both the owners and their horses were gone, and there was no way to carry them. What was left was mostly elders and children, along with some women and a few warriors who had escaped the holocaust on the battlefield. Rahmgoth and Rathmado had used the barbarians sorely, and Lina had tried desperately to think of someway to repay what had been done, but they wouldn't even speak to her.

She had seen a few of the tribe's women go to the great pit where Vilvakis's spell had gone off with a wrapped bundle. By the last rays of the setting sun, one of the eldest had pulled out a grinning, gleaming skull polished to a dull sheen. With apparent ceremony she'd tossed it in, and Lina heard it bounce and clatter before finally coming to rest. She'd asked about that too.

"Yoruul," the old woman had said quietly. "Afterward he took his life in shame. He would have wanted to stay with his warriors."

And Lina could get no more than that. Now she watched them leave, and tried not to think about the husbands, wives, and children in their distant home who did not yet even know of their loss.

"Come on," said Sylph. "Time to mount up."

Lina took a deep breath and followed her. The greatly reduced army headed east, a long snake of supply wagons surrounded by a thin, ragged line of horsemen. Horsewomen mostly, Lina had discovered. After Sylph's speech, only the most dedicated had volunteered, and the fanatic gleam in their eyes made Lina uncomfortable. *But we need them, of course. How many times have I made that excuse?* The train started east, while every other group went in the opposite direction.

It wasn't long before Lina fell into the by now familiar rhythm of travel—ride, camp, sleep, pack, and ride again. What felt odd was not having Marlowe at her side, but she stomped down heavily on that thought. *It's not my fault. Whatever my memory says.*

It was hard. Every time she tried to think about him, guilt threatened to overwhelm her so she couldn't really find a way to mourn. *He was my lover, after all, and now he's dead one way or the other.* Riding left her with long stretches of time to be alone with her thoughts, so Lina did her best to stay in conversation. She talked to Yahvy about the trivialities of supply and command; the Circle Breaker lacked Marlowe's talent for organization, but seemed to be able to manage a smaller force.

Sylph had become a recluse once again, living in a wagon she'd appropriated for her own use and emerging only infrequently for food and water. Lina recognized the signs; her sister was hard at work, and she made sure Sylph wasn't disturbed more than absolutely necessary.

Melfina recovered to the point where she was able to sit ahorse and eat solid food, and Lina spent an increasing amount of time riding with her. Something unspoken seemed to have passed between them. Neither mentioned what had happened to Marlowe and Daana, but with Melfina Lina didn't feel it hanging over her like she sometimes did with the others. The girl had gained back some of the weight she'd lost, but not all of it. She was still painfully thin, and sometimes Lina found Melfina staring at her, her eyes fever bright.

And, in the meantime, the land rolled on. The eastern half of what had been Vilvakis's domain was a mixture of lush grassland and patchy forest, and was apparently completely abandoned. Yahvy sent scouts ranging ahead to look for game to add to their food stores, and none of them ever reported seeing another human being. After a week they came to a river, whose name no one even knew. It was low and easily forded, though bringing the wagons across was a hassle as always. On the other side the land grew harsher; the trees vanished, and they entered a vast plain of scrub grass and gently rolling hills.

After another week, Sylph emerged from her wagon and announced that, according to Rathmado, the border of the Lightbringer's domain was no more than a few days away. She brought out her new weapons, and under Yahvy's watchful eye the soldiers began training; once they got over their shock at the ungodly racket, they seemed to take to them. Lina kept her eye on Sylph. Her little sister wasn't getting enough sleep, running herself ragged to produce guns and ammunition out of thin air. Lina worried but said nothing. *We may need all this soon enough.*

All through the journey, she'd kept the sword at her side. The feeling she got from it had changed; the rage that had powered Rahmgoth was fading away, and when she put her hand on the hilt she felt something of her mother's closeness. And Molochim—Lina found herself missing the foulmouthed, chain-smoking Veritas.

They crossed the border into the Lightbringer's domain, according to Sylph, early one cloudy morning. Nothing looked different, but Lina convinced herself that she could feel it—a sick feeling, deep in her gut. The mood of the party changed, grew darker. Cheery banter faded away during weapons training, replaced with a grim-eyed determination. As they traveled farther east, the scrub plain got rockier and more unpleasant, broken by large patches of hard-packed dry mud.

Eventually they came to a vast stretch of the stuff, cracked and brittle underfoot with no vegetation in sight. Yahvy made camp on the edge, a little earlier than usual; before the sun had set, her scouts returned with the news that the Shadowcore was camped out in the dry expanse, more than three thousand strong.

* * *

IT HAD BEEN A LONG RIDE, A LONG, DULL RIDE, AND KU-
rai was unaccustomed to long stretches of boredom. He passed
the time by capturing small creatures from the lands he passed
through and using what little power he could muster to dissect
their innards without ever breaking the skin. It was interesting
to see how much could be cut away before life fled, but ultimately he was simply killing time. *Among other things.*

He'd been able to *feel* it when Vilvakis fell; the whole Circle
flared in agony and then went dark. The power that had been
there, inaccessible, was just gone. Kurai simply smiled to himself and rode on. *Good riddance. I knew he wouldn't stand a chance
against the Liberator.* The demon—or whatever it was—that was
backing her had considerable energy and skill. *And Lady knows
Vilvakis's conventional army has never been worth much. If his demons fail
him, he has nothing left to rely on.*

In fact, the Archmagus's fall made Kurai all the more confident that the Lightbringer would accept his services. *He must see
that he needs me, now. He can't allow this to go on.*

Crossing the outermost of the Lightbringer's Circles was
like walking into an electrical storm. There was nothing physical—no line on the ground, no fortresses guarding the edge of the
Lightbringer's domain—but the sheer *power* hit him like a sledge-
hammer. *An implicit offer, made and accepted.* He reined in his horse
and got down, carefully; he had the feeling that if he brushed
against anything too quickly, sparks would erupt from his flesh.

Lightbringer. He took a deep breath and drew energy from
the Circle, felt the cool darkness of shadow rise up and surround
him. *My new master.*

There was a summons—nothing so direct as actual words,
but somehow all the more powerful for it. *Come.* It would have
been impossible for Kurai to resist, even if he'd wanted to. *Come.
To the Black Keep, and the Liberator. Come.*

24

chapter twenty-four

*T*HE DUST, SYLPH THOUGHT, *IS DEFINITELY GOING TO BE A problem.* She kicked idly at the parched ground, and each blow raised a tiny plume. Thousands of horses at a gallop was going to raise quite a cloud. She'd spent a few hours before dawn devising a filter, just a tight-meshed fabric that could be worn like a mask, and making a few hundred for her troops to use. *They should have goggles too.* But there was no time; the scouts reported the Shadowcore had startled marshalling at dawn, and there were other preparations to be made.

She shaded her eyes against the morning sun and looked down her line. The wagons were well back, along with the horses. *Don't want any of them to run off.* Her paltry two hundred were busily locking tripods into place and setting up their weapons just as they'd been drilled. Here and there Sylph saw an anxious face, but mostly they had a serene confidence. Quite a few glanced back where Lina sat on her horse. Sylph thought her sister looked a little uncomfortable, but Lina was doing her best to look Liberator-like.

If this goes bad somehow, they won't have time to break and run. The Shadowcore were mounted lancers. If they reached the line, they'd ride over it without breaking a sweat. *So, it just has to work.* She grinned at herself. *Come on, Sylph. Getting nervous now?*

Though I do wish we had a little more time. She'd been studying the reports of what Vilvakis had done to the Steelbreakers and trying to work out *how*; action-at-a-distance remained impossible for her, no matter how much power she drew from the geists. She'd made some progress after a conversation with Rathmado. *I think the trick is to set the thing up beforehand, and then leave a thread back to it. Like laying out a powder trail.* But she had nothing she was ready to use in battle. *Too bad. Using Vilvakis's trick on the Shadowcore would be poetic justice.*

Rathmado arrived behind her, accompanied by a half-dozen guards and wearing his usual enigmatic smile. That was another thing she was unsure of; he'd asked to observe, and she'd agreed, mostly because she felt like showing him firsthand what her creations could do. The Magus had remained stubbornly pessimistic about their chances, until Sylph felt like reminding him that he would die too, if things went wrong. *Probably he wouldn't,* she thought sourly. *You don't get to be three thousand years old by getting killed in little scraps like this one.*

"Ready," said Yahvy, behind her.

"Ammunition distributed?" Sylph asked.

"No problems." Yahvy looked across the field, and pointed out a rider galloping closer in a cloud of dust. His arms were waving. "They're coming."

"Good. Remember we want to maximize the shock. Hold your fire until about five hundred feet. And make sure the front of the column goes down—"

"I know," said Yahvy, with her half-smile.

Sylph subsided, and went back to peering across the flats. The dust cloud that heralded the enemy's approach was soon visible, spreading out across the horizon like a shroud. It caught the sun from the east, and glowed from within with an awful, sullen light. It was some time before the tiny figures at the base of the cloud were visible, a shapeless mass of blurred gray horsemen.

"How far do you make that?" Sylph asked after a while.

"Half mile." Yahvy turned to listen to a messenger for a moment, then whispered something back. The girl ran off.

"Moving quickly."

A few friendly horsemen returned, dust rising from their hooves, scouts clearing the field before the battle. Sylph couldn't take her eyes from the Shadowcore; their dust cloud spread until it encompassed half the sky, and under its cover the dark figures seemed to be multiplying. *How many* are *there?* It was possible to make out a few of them clearly, through breaks in the dust: black horses, each bearing a heavily armored lancer. They were already coated with the ubiquitous grit. *I wouldn't want to be riding at the back of that formation.*

"Twelve hundred," said Yahvy. "Thousand."

Sylph's mouth was dry. *No matter how many times I do this, I can't get used to it.* The shadow of the dust cloud reached out across the flats to engulf her soldiers, who suddenly seemed pitiful compared to the oncoming tide.

"Eight hundred."

The Shadowcore advanced from a trot to a gallop, leaving their cloud behind them. The clatter of hooves was already deafening.

"Six hundred." Yahvy judged her moment carefully. Beside her stood one of the messengers, chosen for her good lungs. Just when Sylph was about to say something, Yahvy prodded the girl in the side.

"Open *fire!*"

For all the tests and training they'd gone through, the noise was still a surprise. It hit Sylph like a brick wall, and she took an involuntary step back and slapped her hands over her ears. It didn't help. Fifty tripod-mounted machine guns, each spitting several hundred rounds a minute, made a racket that seemed to bypass hearing and smash into her like a punch to the gut.

It had to be worse for the soldiers on the line, but they didn't budge. Each gun was manned by a team of three, one to aim and two to keep the ammunition feed running. As long as more bullets were threaded into the hopper, the things would keep firing almost indefinitely; Sylph was relatively pleased with the design. It wasn't exactly elegant, and she was sure there were a few innovations used in the modern world she hadn't thought of. On the other hand, the barrels and moving parts could be made of diamond or other ultra-dense material, impervious to heat and wear.

The effect was everything she could have hoped for. The center of the Shadowcore charge simply disintegrated under the hellish maelstrom of fire, men and horses falling like stalks of wheat before the scythe and fouling the gallop of those behind them. Yahvy watched with a careful eye as the shooting swept out toward the flanks. She pointed to a concentration and sent runners to the section commanders, communicating by gesture since any speech would have been inaudible.

The worst part was that the enemy was not giving up. The five hundred feet separating the Shadowcore from their enemies had stretched to infinity, a space filled with so much hot lead that no horseman could cross it. But time and again they reformed in the dust cloud and charged, splitting into two, three, or even more columns in a desperate attempt to reach their tormentors. Every path was blocked, and the rain of bullets continued. Before long, the farthest extent of each sally was marked by piles of bodies.

Sylph wasn't sure how long it was before the Shadowcore finally quit the field. It seemed like consciousness itself dissolved in a sea of staccato blasts, drowning out even the cries of the dying. When, at last, the firing sputtered to a halt, the silence rang in her ears like church bells. No one spoke, up and down the line. The soldiers just stared, stunned by the carnage they had wrought.

Heraan hurried over to Yahvy and Sylph from where he'd been waiting, down by the line. Sylph glanced at him, but her eyes were drawn back to the killing field like lead filings to a magnet. Mercifully, the dust cloud was rolling forward to obscure the worst.

"Glad to be on *your* side," Yahvy commented, finally.

"Yeah." Heraan watched the dust close in and shook his head. "For all that they just saved our lives, those things are horrible."

"I know." Sylph closed her eyes for a moment and took a deep breath. Already the air tasted of grit, with the slight metallic tang of blood. "With any luck we won't have to do this again."

She looked around and caught Rathmado's eye. The Magus was staring at the guns, and his usual smile had faded. When he saw Sylph watching him, he turned with a snarl and stalked back to the tents, his guards racing to keep up.

Yahvy chuckled. "Think you made him mad."

"I wonder why?" Heraan mused. "Since he wants Light-bringer brought down . . ."

"I suspect it has more to do with him being wrong," Sylph said. That fit with what she knew of the Magus's personality, but it still seemed off somehow. *I've never seen him get so emotional.*

"What now?" Yahvy asked.

"Put scouts out, but everyone else can rest until after mid-day. Then I'd like to get moving. The farther from here we get, the better."

"Agreed," Heraan murmured.

AFTER THE BATTLE, FOR A WHILE AT LEAST, THE CAMP FELT numb. Lina watched as the soldiers trickled back from the bat-tlefield in groups of three or four, many of them leaning on one another or walking slowly, like drunks. It was some time before conversation started to rise, but once it did the funereal air was quickly dispelled. As food was distributed from the supply wag-ons, muted talks turned to shouts and cheers.

And why not? We won the battle. The Shadowcore were just faceless figures on horseback, encased in steel. *It's hard to think of them as human.*

Lina didn't have much of an appetite herself, but she sat

down to tear at a hunk of bread in the hopes of getting Melfina
to do the same. The girl followed her like a hungry shadow,
and refused to eat or sleep unless her Liberator did. Even then
she sometimes forgot; Lina had to ask for Melfina's ration herself. The girl chewed a strip of dried meat absentmindedly, lost
in thought.

Once the mundane work of packing up the camp was complete, the little army made a wide detour around the field where
the battle had taken place. Sylph said nothing about it, but it was
obvious that she didn't relish the prospect of walking through
Shadowcore bodies piled knee deep. The vast stretch of plant-
less hard-pack extended as far as anyone had been able to scout
to the east, north, and south; by that evening Lina had realized
that it wasn't just an isolated patch, but the beginning of the
dead lands around the Black Keep itself.

*It's all very well for Rathmado to talk about how nothing can grow,
but until you see it for yourself it's hard to believe.* She spent some time
that night walking the camp perimeter. The ground was absolutely dead—not a weed, not an ant, not even a scraggly bunch
of grass. Lina tried looking up at the stars instead, only to find
that those were disappearing too, one by one, starting at the
eastern horizon.

The explanation became clear once the sun rose. The
sky was black with thunderheads, and the only light that filtered though was a dull, washed-out gray. The storm waited
all day and broke just after dark with a stupendous detonation
of thunder, followed by a massive downpour. Lina lay in bed
and waited for it to pass. The lightning was bright enough to be
seen through the fabric of her tent as a dull glow, and the booms
shook the cup on her bedside table.

Thunderstorms had always been a mixed bag for her. Sylph
had been terrified of them for years, and every time one blew
into town it meant she'd run for Lina's room and hide under the
covers of her sister's bed, pressed up against Lina's side. At the
time Lina had found it something of a nuisance. *Now it seems kind*

of nostalgic. She wanted something warm to press herself against, but she avoided the thought. Eventually Lina drifted into an exhausted, fitful sleep, while thunder and lightning still raged overhead.

By morning the storm had abated a little, but the rain continued. The dry, cracked ground soaked it up like a sponge and turned into a nasty cauldron of mud that got worse as the day went on. Sylph got the column moving, though it was Yahvy who did most of the riding back and forth in the wet to get the wagons in line. It took longer than usual, and they lost even more time trying vainly to find a dry spot to camp. Eventually the exhausted soldiers simply threw cloth on the ground and pulled sopping blankets over themselves, while a lucky few took shelter in the lee of the wagons.

That was only the beginning. The rain didn't let up that day, or the next, or the next. The little column slogged resolutely eastward, with nothing but clouds visible from horizon to horizon. Every day the mud got a little deeper, the going got a little harder, and there was more bad news from the drovers—the constant pounding weakened the canvas tops of the wagons, and the rainwater had already ruined a few loads' worth of stores. Heraan, who'd assumed the task of quartermaster, calculated and recalculated the supplies remaining; every day, each meal was just a little bit smaller than the day before.

They lost the first wagon a week after the rain began. The wheels slipped on a hidden slope and the whole thing tipped up onto one side, rapidly becoming embedded in unshiftable mud. Yahvy set some of the soldiers to digging, but the slime flowed back faster than it could be removed, and eventually Sylph gave the order to abandon the load.

Lina was riding next to the second wagon that went down. One minute it was sloshing through the mud, wheels throwing wide splatters of dirt in both directions; the next the front of the thing was sinking, and the still-harnessed horses were whinnying in terror.

Soldiers converged on the stricken vehicle from all sides, but Lina was already there, urging her horse alongside and grabbing one of the lines that secured the canvas top. With that as a handhold she managed to swing across to the wagon and work her way to the driver's seat. A young woman was screaming, high and shrill, and Lina heard the sound of horses foundering in the mud.

"Cut the traces!" someone yelled. Overhead, thunder rolled, as though attracted by the drama.

The front of the wagon had sunk far enough that the back end was starting to rise clear of the mud. *It must be a sinkhole, the edge of some deep pool, maybe a lake before all the rain.* Lina worked her way down, closer to where the black sludge was bubbling up around the wood; she found a young man clinging to the edge of the top, with his hand reaching into the muck. The other driver, the woman, was only visible from the waist up—she stretched desperately and churned the mud around her, but couldn't get a foothold.

"Sara!" the man shouted.

"Help! *Help!*"

He leaned a bit farther in and managed to grab her hand. When he tried to pull, however, his boot tore through the wagon roof and his foothold there gave way. Lina threw herself forward and managed to grab the soldier's boot before both of them disappeared into the abyss. The wagon shifted with a *crunch*, now almost vertical and descending fast.

"You have to . . ." Lina sputtered as she got a faceful of churning mud. "You have to pull her out *now!*" She was trying to climb, but the weight of both soldiers was far too much for her to lift. Either the man didn't hear her or couldn't comply; the woman's scream was cut off as her head sank below the surface. He kept a firm grip on her hand, but Lina's grip on him was weakening. *I can't get a good purchase . . . too much mud . . .*

She gave another tug, and something gave way; one of her own boots slipped free of the wagon, and Lina was falling. She made a grab for the man's boot and missed, and ended up flopping heavily into the mud just short of where the wagon was disappearing. A half-dozen soldiers threw ropes to her, and with some effort she was able to haul herself out of the pool. Others tossed lines to the beleaguered drivers, but since the man refused to let go of his companion's hand he had no leverage to pull himself clear. By the time Lina was back on her feet the wagon, drivers and all, had vanished under the surface of the mud pool.

*   *   *

"Sylph?"

Sylph didn't look up; she couldn't afford to. Instead, she very carefully unraveled the material she had been attempting to create, piece by piece. Only once it was safely dissolved and the power dissipated did she dare pay attention to anything else.

"You know," she said, "barging in here is a very good way to get us all killed."

"Sorry," said Lina.

Sylph took in her sister's state. Lina was crusted with mud from head to toe, her hair hanging in a solid lump against her back. "Have you been swimming?"

"Trying not to. One of the lead wagons just went down a sinkhole, drivers included."

Oh. All of a sudden Sylph felt like an idiot. "Ah. Sorry."

"I tried . . ." Lina's voice broke, and she took a deep breath. "I'm not sure how much longer we can keep going if this rain keeps up."

"According to Rathmado it's just a bit farther."

"According to Rathmado." Lina glanced around to make sure the Magus wasn't in evidence. "Has it occurred to you that he could be purposely leading us out here to die?"

"Of course it has," Sylph said. "But what am I supposed to do, turn around and go back?"

"Is there anything you can do with the geists?"

"I might be able to clear us a dry space, but it wouldn't last. And I couldn't keep it up while we moved."

"Then why not clear a space and hunker down? Wait for the rain to stop?"

"That assumes it will," Sylph said.

"It has to stop *some*time."

"Rathmado says this whole place is under Lightbringer's control. That this is another way he's trying to stop us."

Lina stared at Sylph for a moment, then rolled her eyes. "Great. Just great." She staggered over to one of the wagon's two chairs and collapsed into it, sending mud everywhere.

"Lina? Are you okay?"

"Not really." She sighed. "It felt like we were so *close*. After the Shadowcore I didn't think there was much that could get in the way. But this . . ."

"I know. But we're almost there."

"We hope."

"Take solace in the fact that if we're not, I'll let you take it out of Rathmado's hide."

Lina managed the ghost of a smile. "That sounds oddly appealing."

"How's Melfina doing?"

"Worse. She's got a nasty cough. I've got one of the healers keeping an eye on her, but she says there's not much that can be done in this damp."

Sylph looked down. "I'm sorry."

"I should have left her behind. Should have forced her to stay."

There was a moment of silence before Lina rose with another squelch.

"I hope you're right," she said.

"Have Yahvy pull the scouts in. The Shadowcore certainly won't attack in all this, and they can help probe for sinkholes."

"Good idea." Lina moved to the door, then looked back

curiously. "What are you working on, anyway?"

"Sort of a backup plan. Vilvakis inspired me."

"Ah." Lina thought about that for a moment. "I hope we don't have to use it, then."

"So do I."

✳   ✳   ✳

IN HER WAGON, SYLPH WAS SHIELDED FROM THE WORST OF the rain. She felt a little guilty about that; Lina was out there with the men; so were Yahvy and Heraan. *But there's no point in my getting wet, just on principle. I've got things to work on.* The idea of keeping a thread of power—just enough to prevent a spell from collapsing into its final configuration—had proved to be very effective. Sylph was trying to think of something worthwhile to do with it that wouldn't get her killed. *It's great if you can leave it on the battlefield and get the enemy to run into it, but I'm not sure how I'd use it otherwise.*

She let the days roll by, without much to distinguish one from the other; soldiers brought food, and she slept when she was tired. Otherwise there was just the work and the endless drumming of rain on the canvas. It wasn't much lighter during the day than at night, so the only way Sylph knew the difference was when the wagon stopped rocking, meaning they'd settled down to camp.

I should be out there. Lina had sounded exhausted. *Everyone must be. Yahvy's been running herself ragged. And Heraan . . .*

There was the gentlest of knocks at the door. Everyone had taken to heart Sylph's instructions about not being disturbed. This time there was nothing sensitive going on, however, so she made her way to the door and undid the latch. In passing, she noted that the rocking of the wagon had stopped. *I didn't think it was time to camp yet.*

Heraan entered, rain dripping from his cloak. "Sylph? Are you busy?"

"Not at the moment. Why?"

"There's something outside that you should see."

She nodded. "Give me a second."

Finding all her gear took a bit—jacket, shoes, cloak, and so on—since she'd scattered things all over the wagon. Heraan waited in the doorway, ignoring the rain; he was soaked anyway. Sylph stepped off the wagon and into six inches of mud. Heraan held out his hand to help her down; without thinking, Sylph flinched away from his touch. He withdrew his hand and stepped away, looking down.

Idiot, Sylph thought as she squelched down from the wagon. *You could let him help you—he'd just hold your hand, for God's sake!* But somehow the idea made her skin crawl. *I should put up with it, for his sake.* Heraan's expression was unreadable, hidden in the shadow of his cloak as he trudged through the mud to the front of the column.

"Careful," he muttered, as they passed the last of the wagons. "We almost lost a scout in a sinkhole earlier."

Sylph nodded, but her attention was already captured by a huge shape up above, shining in the gloom with tiny flashes of reflected lightning.

"What *is* that?"

"Hoping you would know," said Yahvy. She was mounted, her horse struggling as much as the humans in the muck.

"We need to get closer," said Sylph.

"Are you sure it's safe?" Heraan asked.

"No. But we're not going to find out by sitting here." And Sylph had an inkling; the lightning's flash lit up something that looked metallic, shining like liquid mercury. She sloshed forward, with a nervous Heraan in tow and Yahvy to one side. A few moments later her suspicion was confirmed.

"Yahvy, go and get Rathmado."

Yahvy hesitated, then nodded and turned back to the camp.

"Do you know what it is?" Heraan asked.

"I can take a guess." Sylph stared up. The thing was a cylinder of gleaming metal, hovering perhaps ten feet off the ground. She guessed it was a couple of feet across, and it extended as far as she could make out in the direction perpendicular to their path. *A line. But not much of a barrier. Except* . . . She stared at the thing, and tried to convince herself that she was imagining the slight curvature. *Not a line but a* circle.

"Ah," said Rathmado, behind her. "I'd thought we were almost there."

"This is one of Lightbringer's Circles, isn't it?" Sylph said.

"His First Circle, to be precise." Rathmado had somehow managed to avoid the crushing exhaustion that burdened everyone else. His guards had been reduced from six to four, then to two, simply because every hand was needed to keep the wagons moving.

"Wait," said Heraan. "The Circles aren't actual *things*, are they? I thought you only needed a few nodes to keep one up."

"Why does it look like the geists?" Sylph said. She brought the little metal balls out for inspection. They appeared to be of an identical material, with the slickness of mercury in a solid form; water rolled off them as though they'd been oiled.

"As you've probably guessed," Rathmado said, "the Lightbringer's First Circle serves a similar purpose. That is, it stores the souls and energy he has collected. Presumably, since his domain is so much larger and older, he found the smaller form . . . inadequate."

"So this whole thing is to store his power? How far does it go?"

"All the way around the Black Keep, at a radius of twenty miles or so. It means the hardest part of the journey is over."

"If this thing holds Lightbringer's power," Heraan said, "why don't we just destroy it?"

"You're welcome to try," Rathmado snapped. "If it was that easy I would have done it thirty-five hundred years ago. Magic won't touch it, and even the toughest steel barely scratches the surface. Perhaps if we had a hundred years and ten thousand men we might be able to break through."

"Can we just move past it, then?" said Sylph.

"Of course."

Hesitantly, Sylph walked forward. She put the geists back in her pocket before crossing the Circle. As she passed underneath, she felt something hard under her boots rather then the soft squelch of mud. The muck receded the further she went, until she was standing on what looked like smooth black tile which stretched as far as she could see to the east. Another step, and . . .

What the hell? It took her a moment to realize what had happened—the omnipresent rain had stopped. Sylph spun and found that it was still raining *behind* her; there was a curtain of water, parallel to the First Circle, and beyond that the black flagstones were bone dry.

As she watched, Rathmado stepped through the curtain, accompanied by his two amazed minders. He raised an eyebrow.

"I suppose even the Lightbringer is not fond of getting wet?"

It took a little more than an hour to get everyone through, and the caravan had to be left behind; the wagons wouldn't fit without being broken down and rebuilt on the other side. Sylph immediately called a halt to the day's marching and gave the order to set up camp just inside the dry area. It was still *cold*, and the clouds blackened the sky; while relief from the constant pounding was wonderful, it would be days before anyone was really dry again.

Or would be if I don't do anything about it. Sylph wandered off as the camp was going up, found a nice clean stretch of tile, and dropped to her knees so she could put her hands flat on the ground. She reached for the power of the geist and explored cautiously into the stone. Somewhat to her surprise, it was just ordinary rock—manufactured by magic, certainly, but otherwise unremarkable. *Perfect.*

She drew power, just a trickle at first, from the geist's near-limitless well. *Gently, gently. We wouldn't want to melt anything.*

For a few moments, nothing happened. Then, gradually, the stone began to steam. Sylph kept her hands where they were so she could enjoy the warmth; it felt like a boulder that had been soaking in the sun all day. After who knows how long trudging through the rain and the mud, it was heavenly. Sylph wanted to lie on her back and let her body soak up the heat the way the tiles had. Instead, she got to her feet and called Yahvy over.

"Problem?" she said, and then walked into the wall of heat. Yahvy closed her eyes in a kind of ecstasy. "Oh."

"I thought this might help," said Sylph.

"Think you're right."

"Call people over once the camp is done, would you?"

Yahvy nodded and headed reluctantly back into the cold. Then Sylph walked to the center of her little paradise and lay down on her back. After a moment she got up again and stripped off her sodden things—cloak, jacket, thick outer shirt, and so on—and lay back in just thin cotton undergarments.

Ah.

When she opened her eyes again she realized she'd fallen asleep, because the whole warm stretch was filled with soldiers. Most of them had followed Sylph's example and stripped down to underwear, and a few had gone even farther than that. It made Sylph blush, and that made her smile. *Somehow it still makes me blush, after everything.*

Heraan was sitting nearby, cross-legged, staring at her. When Sylph sat up he started and looked resolutely away. Unfortunately the direction he chose to look in contained a half-dozen female soldiers in the act of disrobing, so he snapped his gaze back to Sylph and then down at the tiles.

"I'm sorry. I just wanted to make sure you were okay, and I didn't have the heart to wake you."

"It's okay."

"You didn't . . ." He looked at her again, then looked away. "I didn't quite realize, I mean."

Sylph had to look down at herself before she realized what

he was talking about. She was covered in tiny scars—*the width of a knife blade*—that clustered all over her body like the residue of some strange disease, most obvious wherever the skin was palest.

"It's okay," Sylph repeated, then took a deep breath. "Well. Not really. But I'm alive."

"I shouldn't have left you behind," he said.

"If you hadn't, you'd be dead and I'd *still* be in there."

There wasn't a good response to that, of course, but Heraan's expression told Sylph he was trying to think of one.

I should just reach out and touch him. Just a touch. Her heart thumped a little faster at the idea. *It would be good for us. Good for him and good for me, I mean. I . . .*

"It's nothing personal." And cold, clammy fingers . . .

Damn *him.* She felt tears suddenly come into her eyes. *God* damn *him.* She sat with her hands in her lap, trembling.

"I hope I'm not interrupting anything," Rathmado said. He'd lost his last two guards, who were presumably among the crowd of happy, under-clothed people. *Not that two guards would have a hope of stopping him if he tried anything,* Sylph thought wearily.

"Not at all."

Somewhat to her surprise, the Magus took a seat beside her, opposite Heraan. He stared too; while Heraan's eyes made her feel warm and a little giggly, Rathmado's gaze took her back to the dungeon and Brutus. Sylph suddenly wanted to cover herself in the thickest blanket she could find. Instead, she did her best to ignore him.

"Heating the rocks." He shook his head. "I must say it never would have occurred to me."

"Did Erik's army have to slog through this stuff as well?" Sylph asked.

"Yes. We lost several thousand men to pneumonia and the mud before we were done."

"You might have warned me."

"I warned you to take more men."

"We beat the Shadowcore," said Heraan, "in case you didn't

notice. Sylph's machine guns cut them down to size."

"Down to size. Indeed." Rathmado sighed. "I'm warning you now, in any case. The Shadowcore—what's left of it—has certainly reformed by now. I doubt they'll try to stop us here; my guess is they'll try to get to the Black Keep before we do. It's imperative that we get there first, and I believe we can. They won't have fared well in the mud either."

Sylph felt her good mood fading away. *It was nice to forget, just for a minute, that the world is full of people trying to kill me.* "Understood."

"It might be best—"

"*Understood*, Rathmado. We'll get there first."

He paused, then got to his feet. "As you say."

Heraan watched him go. "I still don't trust him."

"I never trusted him."

There was a long silence, but not an unpleasant one.

Heraan sighed. "What are we doing here, anyway?"

"Do you really want to know?"

"Sure."

Sylph looked around, but no one was listening. She closed her eyes.

"I've only ever told one person this, and later I had to shoot him. There's probably a lot you won't understand, but bear with me."

Heraan nodded.

"It has to do with my mother." Sylph took a deep breath. "I was supposed to come right home after school. I always did. I mean, *always* . . ."

✳   ✳   ✳

THERE WAS ONE MORE LITTLE TASK. SYLPH DID IT ALONE, in the dead of night, once the army had retired to their tents; the perimeter guards let her through without a second thought. If the Liberator's younger sister wanted to go out and fiddle around underneath the creepy floating ring for an hour or so, they weren't going to ask any questions.

Sylph preferred it that way. Her test had confirmed what Rathmado had said about the First Circle; it was impervious to magic, and almost indestructible. *If it ends up coming to this . . .* She didn't like to think what that would mean. *But it would be stupid not to set it up. Just in case.*

It stayed at the back of her mind all the next day, the trigger for the spell trailing out behind her, like a string tied to her finger.

✳   ✳   ✳

RIDING ACROSS THE BLACK TILES WASN'T LIKE RIDING DOWN a dirt road. Lina's horse didn't make friendly *clip-clop, clip-clop* noises; horseshoes and stone met with an awful *clack, clack, clack* that was enough to turn the brain to mush after a few hours.

Sylph's sauna had done wonders for morale. Lina had to admit that she'd been tempted to pull off the last few sodden bits of cotton herself. Melfina rode beside her, still pale and coughing but much improved from a few days before. So she claimed, anyway. But she wasn't happy with the way Melfina's whole frame shook when she coughed, or how she sometimes swayed in her saddle.

In the morning, with the army warm and dry, Sylph had announced that they were going to try and make it to the Black Keep as soon as possible. Without the wagons, there was no way to transport the heavy guns and their ammunition—much of it had been ruined anyway, by the rain and the mud—so the army broke the supply train apart and loaded themselves down with as much food as they can carry. Leaving that much firepower behind made Lina uneasy, but aside from spending a week or two lifting wagons there wasn't another option. About half the troops had rifles; Sylph hadn't been able to manufacture enough for everyone.

The hard tile was tough on the horses. Between the mud and thrown shoes during the ride, their supply of remounts had dwindled, and a few soldiers were already riding double. The mounts would pay for that, eventually, but in the meantime they'd made good progress under the gray, grumbling sky and by midday they saw the bulk of the Keep ahead.

It wasn't as impressive as Lina had imagined. She'd been picturing some Gormenghastian monstrosity, a mass of dark stone and hulking, spiked towers. Instead, there was a cube, blotting out a perfectly square chunk of horizon. It was hard to get a sense of perspective, but as they got closer Lina realized it wasn't even particularly large—the size of a small apartment building, maybe. Making out any details on the surface was difficult, but there were no obvious gates.

Another hour brought the group to the base. Lina dismounted while the soldiers spread out to set up a perimeter, pushing her way through lines of blowing, exhausted horses until she found Sylph, Yahvy, Heraan and Rathmado standing in front of a featureless black wall.

"I suppose it makes sense," Sylph was saying. "It's not like he needs a bunch of soldiers or servants, so why build a big castle?"

"The Shadowcore have their own barracks outside the dead zone," Rathmado agreed. "The Black Keep is for the Lightbringer alone."

"So this is the barrier?" Sylph said.

The Magus nodded. "Give me a moment to prepare, and I will break through."

"Sylph," Lina said. "We just heard from the rearguard; the Shadowcore is coming up behind us."

"Damn it. I was hoping they were a bit farther behind. How many?"

"Six or seven hundred at least, maybe up to a thousand. As far as we can tell they're not mounted."

"They must not have wanted to risk too many horses in the mud." Sylph flashed a smile. "Overconfident, aren't they?"

Lina smiled back, but she wasn't sure she felt it. *He doesn't have to be* over*confident, with five times our numbers.* The last massed Shadowcore charge had been broken up by Sylph's machine guns, but those were gone. In the rush to get the heavier weapons done Sylph hadn't turned out as many rifles and pistols as she might have. Most of their infantry was equipped, but Lina wasn't at all sure it would be enough. *Maybe. They won't have horses.*

"We must not be disturbed once we enter," Rathmado hissed. "If we fail to defeat the Lightbringer, all is lost. You must remember that."

"Yeah." Sylph was clearly chewing on a decision she didn't want to make.

"Go," Lina said. "You go inside with Rathmado. We won't let the Shadowcore pass."

"Wait a minute." Sylph shook her head. "I'm not just going to *leave* you here, Lina. We'll beat the Shadowcore first, and Rathmado can breach the barrier afterward."

"There is no *time!*" said the Magus. "Every minute we delay is a minute he will use against us. Do you really think that thunderstorms are the worst things he can summon?"

"She's right," said Heraan. "Be honest. How much good would any of us do in there?"

"None whatsoever," Rathmado snapped.

Sylph turned on him. "Enough! I won't be your damned puppet."

There was a pause. The Magus bowed his head. "I apologize. But I still must insist. I will break the seal, and the two of us will challenge the Lightbringer. Lina and the others should remain here, to protect the entrance against the Shadowcore."

"But . . ." Sylph looked from Rathmado, to Lina, to Heraan. And finally to Yahvy, who closed her eye and nodded grimly.

"What are you so worried about?" asked Heraan, with a cheerfulness that was obviously forced. "We beat them already. This should be simple."

"Go," said Yahvy. "We'll be fine."

After a long moment, Sylph sighed and turned to Rathmado. "Have it your way. Open the gate."

"As you wish."

❋   ❋   ❋

IT WASN'T THAT SYLPH WAS AFRAID LINA WOULD GET KILLED.

Well, that's not exactly true. The thought of that, after everything, was so terrible she couldn't even entertain it. *But it's not that I'm not* confident.

It was something else. A reluctance to let Lina out of her sight, even for a moment. *I feel like something awful will happen if we split up again.* But they were right, Yahvy and Heraan and Rathmado were right—no one else could help against the Light-bringer, and they needed everyone they could muster against the Shadowcore.

Word had gone out, and the army was busily arranging itself into a defensive formation. The Shadowcore was still out of sight, but the scouts were steadily trickling back in with reports. It wouldn't be more than another half hour.

I should have built more rifles. There were some among the army, but not enough. *Rifles, pistols, grenades—there wasn't any* time. *Well,* she thought guiltily, *there was. But I wanted to have insurance.*

Rathmado was standing very still, and Sylph felt the power blowing off him like waves of heat. The Black Keep, when she'd risked a tiny probe, felt like nothing she'd touched before; not the deep complexity of real matter or the simple feel of magically created stone, but something else entirely. *As though it weren't really a physical object at all.* The barrier was a crackling, vicious thing in her mind, and the thought of trying to break through it made her break out in a cold sweat.

But that was exactly what Rathmado was doing, coldly and methodically. She felt it fighting back, waves of power reaching out to burn the Magus to a crisp, but every time he pushed them back and continued his slow, determined cutting.

"Almost," said Rathmado, his voice betraying not a hint of effort. "This time . . ."

"Heraan." It seemed suddenly important that she see him one more time. Sylph darted off down the lines until she found him, organizing a squad into firing position. He looked up, instantly worried, when she called his name.

"Sylph! Is something wrong?"

"No!" *Not wrong. I just feel . . . I don't even know. Maybe I'm afraid.* "I thought . . . I wanted, before I went inside . . ."

He smiled. "Be calm, Sylph. It'll be okay."

"Heraan." She didn't know what she wanted to say, but one of her hands went out of its own accord, lifted his gloved fingers and held them to her face. Sylph's skin crawled, and thoughts of Brutus bloomed in the back of her mind, but she suppressed them viciously and held the pose for a moment longer. Heraan blinked, and smiled again.

"Sylph!" Rathmado called. "Quickly!"

"I'll see you later," Heraan said.

"Later." Sylph nodded. She turned back and ran for the Keep. On the way she caught Lina's eye as her sister walked back toward the front line with Melfina hovering behind her. There, at least, no words were needed; all Sylph had to do was nod, and get a nod in return.

Be safe. Please.

COME. KURAI FLOWED ACROSS THE MUDDY, RAIN-BLASTED terrain in the midst of a comforting shadow, slipping lightly above the muck. He had about as much choice in the matter as a branch being swept over a waterfall, but that was nothing new. *Come.*

Soon. He focused on anticipation. *Soon, Liberator. This time your demon will not save you.*

The First Circle of the Lightbringer and the dry tile beyond made Kurai pull up short. He stepped out of the shadow and onto solid ground. The Black Magus looked around, carefully. There was no one in sight, but judging by the muddy trail an army had recently passed eastward. *The Shadowcore. I must make sure to be there for the battle.*

"Oh," said an unfamiliar voice, "you'll be there."

The Black Magus whirled. "Who . . . ?" He paused. "My lord?"

"None other," the voice said, speaking from thin air. "I'm glad you made it so far, Kurai."

"It will be an honor to serve you, my lord." *And to give that girl what she deserves.*

"I'm glad you think so." There was a touch of humor in the voice. "And to make sure you succeed . . ."

Kurai gasped as power flooded up from the ground, through the Circle, power beyond anything he'd dreamed, beyond the petty trickle the Lady Fell had been willing to allow him. He gloried in it, lost himself in the flow. *She won't have a prayer.*

And then—too late—came the realization that something else was flowing in, riding the current of energy into his mind. Something big, and old, and angry. Kurai lashed out, desperately, but his newfound power obeyed only the newcomer. The Black Magus fell to his knees and screamed, alone in the vast expanse of ebony tile.

"Lightbringer!" he managed, in the moments before his mind was overwhelmed. "You . . . can't . . ."

Then the last vestige of Kurai was gone, and the demon roared triumphant. Power crackled, and his body jerked as the spirit inside it squirreled around and found that things were not to its liking. With a wet tearing of cloth, the body began to *change*, expanding and unfolding like some monstrous spider. The legs thickened and raised a low, hunched frame, and an extra pair of arms sprouted from the shoulder blades in a welter of blood. The face lost any semblance of humanity; the eyes shrank back in their sockets and the mouth extended into a snout filled with viciously sharp teeth.

In a few moments the transformation was complete. The demon Hikano, free at last from the Pit where it had been imprisoned for so long, screamed defiance into the semidarkness. Then, following a mental prod, it lumbered away with a speed surprising in a beast so large. Hikano ran east, toward the Black Keep.

Come.

∗   ∗   ∗

INSIDE THE BLACK KEEP WAS A LONG CORRIDOR, THE FLOOR done in the same featureless black tile as the ground outside. Sylph followed Rathmado through the hole in the wall—after taking down the barrier, opening up a hole in the physical surface had been trivial—and lit a torch she'd grabbed from the supplies. The light it threw was twisting and shadowy, but Rathmado seemed confident. He strode down the corridor without a second look, and Sylph hurried to keep up with him.

The walls were carved with deep bas-reliefs. A variety of scenes were depicted, mostly battles, in realistic and gruesome detail. The figures appeared to move on their own as the light from the torch passed over them, and Sylph swore she saw some of the tiny faces grimace or scream in agony. In between the combats were more abstract murals, the most common depicting a dozen spheres in circular orbits around a central point, like a miniature solar system. In the center, instead of the sun, were the mandibles of a disturbingly realistic spider; sometimes its furry legs reached out to touch the spheres, drawing them into its poisonous embrace.

Also repeated, over and over, was the symbol Lina had described flying above the Lightbringer's keep: two cupped hands with a glowing sun hovering between them.

"What does Lightbringer have in the way of guardians?"

Sylph fingered the grip of her pistol, though she suspected the geists were far more likely to be effective.

Rathmado shook his head. "Nothing. Why would he bother? He doesn't expect anyone to be able to breach the barrier."

"Does he know we're here?"

"Of course. He knows everything that happens this close to the center of his domain."

"So where is he?"

Rathmado pointed, and Sylph raised her torch. The corridor ended up ahead in a massive stone door. It was also elaborately carved: men and women, viewed from above, all raising their hands as if in prayer. The scene was so realistic Sylph found herself dizzy with vertigo for a moment, as though she were going to fall among them. Where the handle should have been there were more hands, reaching out; Rathmado stepped up to these and grabbed hold, pulling hard. The door swung back silently.

Beyond was darkness, but only for a moment. As the door opened, a soft light filled the room, emanating from the base of the walls. Once again the stone was carved, so delicately it might have been frozen flesh. This time, however, there was just one face repeated over and over on every wall. A woman's face, always the same woman and always with a different expression. She laughed, smiled, cried, gasped, screamed in terror and closed her eyes in ecstasy.

There was only one break in the faces: another door in the far wall, offset from the one they'd entered through. This one was unadorned except for a handle in the center, but it was enormous, stretching all the way up to the thirty-foot ceiling. Beside the door was a throne, also made of rock; the arms were carved to resemble the arms of a woman, with her palms up and her fingers splayed. Her shoulders formed the back, but above them, where her head should have been, there was again the hairy, bulbous figure of a spider, its fangs reaching down where the occupant would sit.

Would sit. The throne was empty.

Sylph let the torch fall and took a step forward. Just one. Her footstep echoed, unnaturally loud, and took a long time to fade away. When Rathmado padded to the throne, even his soft steps were magnified until they sounded like the susurration of insects.

Sylph looked from the throne to the thousands of faces and shivered. "Where is he?" She nodded at the still-closed door. "Through there?"

Rathmado did not immediately respond. Instead, he made his way to the base of the throne and stretched out a hand to touch it. His fingers traced a careful path across the stone woman's palm and along her fingers, caressing cold rock with the gentleness of a lover. Then he turned around, smiled grandly, and sat down, resting his hands on the arms of the throne so his fingers interlaced with hers.

"Welcome, Miss Walker," he said. He waved a hand. "How do you like the place?"

25

chapter twenty-five

LINA PACED BACK AND FORTH, HER BOOTS *CLOMPING* ON the black tile. Half the time she was happy for the delay, any delay; the other half she wished the Shadowcore would hurry up and *attack* already. *The waiting is killing me.*

Her little army was arranged in two lines in front of the breach Rathmado had made in the Black Keep. The first line consisted of everyone who had a rifle and had managed to hang on to it during the long, slow slog through the mud. Behind them was a second line of soldiers with pistols and swords. Lina and Heraan had come up with as much of a plan as they could manage, given the circumstances; the riflemen were supposed to break and reform behind the second line if the Shadowcore made it into melee range.

If that happens, we're all dead. But Lina didn't want to say that in front of the troops, didn't even really want to think about it. *All we have to do is hold out through the first charge. If they don't get to us then, they never will. And once Sylph deals with Lightbringer it'll all be over.*

And then . . .

"Lina?"

Lina looked and found Melfina standing at her side. The girl had found a pistol. Frankly, Lina thought she didn't look well enough to stand, but she'd insisted on being a part of the defense. *There's nowhere safe to hide, anyway.*

"What's wrong?"

Melfina gave a little shrug, with her eyes staying on the ground. Ever since Lina had made it back to her body, Melfina had been less of a friend and more of a worshipper. It wasn't a transformation Lina was happy with.

"Mel," Lina repeated. "What's wrong?"

"I'm afraid," Melfina said quietly.

Lina didn't laugh, but the thought occurred to her. *Of course you're afraid.* Everyone was afraid, but no one showed it. Looking down the lines of soldiers, young women clutching their rifles like lifelines and a few men sharpening swords or otherwise killing time, Lina didn't see a single one who looked afraid. *But they all are. I am. It just feels like we've gone beyond it, somehow. There's no* point *to being afraid, there's nothing we can do. The Shadowcore will kill us, afraid or not, if we don't stop them.*

And, she had to admit, there was a certain amount of fanaticism involved. The soldiers who'd followed Sylph from Adriato had been those most convinced of Lina's semi-divinity. The power of the White Lady had chosen the Liberator, and that would take care of everything. *I wish I could believe that.*

Lina tried to put on a comforting face. "I know. I'm afraid too. But . . ."

"You don't understand," said Melfina. "Everyone's dead. Marlowe, Daana, Kiry, Safael, *everyone.* Yahvy won't talk to me the way she used to. And Sylph went in to fight Lightbringer. I thought . . . I cut my hand and I thought . . ." She coughed, and swayed, and Lina held out a hand to steady her. "I thought I would be dead too," she continued in a whisper. "And now I'm not. So I'm scared."

"Of what?"

"That you'll die too," Melfina said. "And leave me behind. Please don't."

Lina nodded. "I won't."

"You promise? You won't . . . leave . . . without me?"

"I won't. I promise."

Melfina wrapped herself around Lina. "Thank you."

Lina was trying to think of something else to say, something comforting, when she became aware of another sound; a low thud, and then another. Metal on stone. *Footsteps.* All in sync, and getting closer. Up and down the line, soldiers stopped what they were doing and turned to watch. The riflemen shouldered their weapons and waited. Yahvy was in charge of that line, standing in the center with a rifle of her own. The thin line of swordsmen in the second rank, led by Heraan, looked a little more nervous. *They won't even get to fight unless things are going really badly.*

The Shadowcore appeared a little bit at a time. The sky was still overcast, and Lina had no idea whether it was morning or evening. The gloomy light glinted, first on spearheads and helmets, then on rank after rank of polished black armor. They marched in a column forty men wide, advancing with lockstep discipline, identical and featureless behind their ebony armor and blank visors. Lina found herself wondering if they were really men in there at all, or automatons. *Or just empty suits, animated by magic.*

"Aim!" Yahvy screamed, as the Shadowcore closed. The idea was to begin with a single, concentrated volley, hoping that enough carnage at once would make them break and run. And, Lina suddenly knew, it wasn't going to work. *They'll fight to the last, the very last.* She wanted to scream for everyone to run for their lives; knew it would be suicidal, and kept silent. The long snake of the Shadowcore column seemed endless. She'd faced bigger armies, of course, but never with so few at her side.

We'll stop them. We have to.

"Fire!"

Melfina gripped Lina's arm very tightly as a hundred rifles roared at once. It seemed like they couldn't miss in that big pack of targets; some of the black-armored soldiers toppled silently, but the column clanked on.

"Fire! Again!" Bullets cracked and whined through the air. The whole front rank of the Shadowcore was down, but the rest simply came on over the bodies. Lina could already see that they weren't dropping fast enough. *God. It's going to be a massacre . . .*

"Fire at will!" As the enemy approached, Yahvy called for the rifles to pick their own targets and shoot as fast as possible. As though they'd understood the command, the massed ranks of the Shadowcore broke into a jog, then into a run. The rapid cracks of the rifles merged into a syncopated roar, and Lina watched the approaching army shrink even as it got closer. But every time a man fell, those around him simply closed the gap. No one screamed in pain or shouted a battle-cry; there was only the footsteps on stone and the blasts of the guns.

"Wait," Yahvy was saying. "Wait . . . wait . . . grenades!"

Two dozen softball-sized spheres flew, skittering across the tile and detonating almost simultaneously at the leading edge of the Shadowcore. There was a bass *thump*, and for a moment the black-armored soldiers vanished in a wall of smoke rose from where they'd been standing. A ragged cheer went up from the Liberator's army—until the first enemy soldier stumbled through the cloud. Someone shot him down, but by then another had emerged, and another, and the charge continued. The rifles started up again, but it was obvious the Shadowcore was not going to be stopped.

This is unreal. Lina watched with a curious calm. One enemy limped forward, missing a foot; another had lost an arm to an explosion, but had his sword drawn in the other and pressed on toward the Liberator's line. *They just won't stop.*

"Ready!" This time it was Heraan shouting. The riflemen stepped back, and the second line moved forward. The first of the charging soldiers was only fifty feet away. "Charge!"

He led by example, sword in hand. A crowd of soldiers, more of a mob than an organized regiment, followed. Yahvy, always game for a fight, had traded her rifle for a pistol and short-sword and followed at the trailing edge. It was hard to see how many Shadowcore had made it through the smoke and the explosions, and Lina was starting to hope again. *If they have to be cut down to the last man, that's the way it'll be. We can still beat them.*

Her troops fired pistols as they charged, at point-blank range, but the thick black armor seemed to absorb most of the effect. A few dark soldiers went down, but they were so close there was no time for a second shot. The two armies met, and blackened steel clashed with flashing blades up and down the line. Neither side could stay together as a unit, and the battle dissolved into the chaos of a hundred individual swordfights and duels. Lina saw Heraan meet the first of the Shadowcore, batting aside the soldier's heavier blade and firing a pistol point-blank into his faceplate; the man fell, blood streaming through shattered steel. Yahvy stopped short of contact, shooting with deadly accuracy.

But, after a few moments, Lina could see the difference in quality beginning to tell. Her soldiers were dedicated, but they were also exhausted and stripped of any armor heavier than cloth. Against that were the men of the Shadowcore, clad head to toe in plate and wielding heavy long-swords against the Liberator's army's short blades. Sprays of blood and screams of agony filled the air.

Lina watched a trio of young women go up against a single Shadowcore soldier. Two split off to circle him while the third tried to parry his initial charge, but he forced her blade aside with contemptuous ease and carved her open from collarbone to bowels. The other two barely scratched his armor. He turned to engage one, parrying her increasingly desperate strokes until he found an opening and ran her through the throat. She fell, gurgling, as the last woman managed to find a gap in the man's plate and slide her blade between his ribs. She was trying to work it free when another black-armored soldier came up from behind and put his sword clean through her stomach.

It's not going to work. Lina felt numb. *All this way. I led them all this way, to die here.* Melfina still held her arm, and Lina looked down at her and smiled dreamily. *I won't leave you behind, I promise. We're all going to die . . .*

* * *

SYLPH THOUGHT FOR A MOMENT. THEN SHE RAISED HER pistol, aimed at Rathmado's smug face, and fired three times.

The Magus—the Lightbringer—didn't even flinch. The bullets simply burned in mid-flight as though they had been made of magnesium, three brief aquamarine flares that left nothing behind. Sylph lowered the gun.

"How refreshingly . . . direct of you." Rathmado smiled wider.

"I always wondered what would happen if I did that." Sylph shrugged. "Now I know."

There was a pause.

"Well?" he prompted. "What do you think?"

"Of the Keep? It's creepy." She shook her head. "I should have known."

"Oh?"

"Lina and I . . ." She paused. "We *died*, back on Earth. When we first got here I didn't know anything, but now . . . people don't just come back to life, even here on Omega. No one can bring someone back to life. It's *forbidden*."

"Except for someone who has already been punished." He spread his hands. "Ironic, isn't it? Only the bound can act freely."

"Why?"

"Why what?"

He's playing with me. Trying to make me mad. Sylph took a long breath. "Why all of this? Why the Liberators? Or was all that a lie too?"

"Oh, it's all true. I made the Liberators, I trained them, I set them at the throats of the Archmagi and marched them across the world until they made it here, or died."

"You said the Lightbringer sets the Archmagi back up again."

"I do that too. It's a shame, but I've found that the only amusing games are the ones where I'm playing both sides."

"Games?" Sylph clenched her hand into a fist. "That's what this is? Just a game?"

Lightbringer watched her gleefully. "That would make you really angry, wouldn't it? If I told you this was all just a game, that I played with people's lives like a kid playing with his blocks, setting them up and knocking them down again with no rhyme or reason."

"These are *real* people . . ."

Rathmado waved a hand. "Don't play high and mighty with me. You know that's not what bothers you. You just can't stand the thought that there might not be a *reason*. That your life, and the lives of everyone around you, are just toys in the hand of a mad godling with more power than sense. That there's really no greater purpose behind it all." He tilted his head. "Am I wrong?"

"And?" Sylph managed. "Is there?"

He lowered his hands. "A purpose? Of course. I am many things, Sylph Walker, but mad is not one of them. I have a purpose. Everything I do—everything I am—is devoted to it."

"The girl." Sylph looked at the thousand faces on the walls. "You still love her?"

"Beautiful, isn't she?" the Lightbringer sighed. "And I do. But I'm afraid that's not it."

"Then what?"

He put his hands behind his back and adopted a thoughtful pose. "When I was imprisoned here, I spent almost a century in a rage. I destroyed indiscriminately, boiled the seas and tore down the mountains and generally threw quite a tantrum. Afterward I cooled down a bit, and I spent some time thinking about what had happened. And finally—this took some time, you understand—I came to the conclusion that I was wrong. That I had always had been."

"That's it?" Sylph was incredulous. "You're *sorry*? You

twisted the lives of everyone on Omega because you're sorry for what you did?"

"Sorry?" He frowned. "Why would I be sorry?"

"But you said—"

"I said I was wrong. I had been aiming too low." His smile returned. "Lina told you the story, didn't she? The one she heard from dear old Molochim."

"She did," Sylph said guardedly.

"I thought," he said, tapping one finger on the woman's stone palm. "I thought that my enemy was the Throne. The Empty Throne of the Veritas. They prance around like they run the universe, telling me what I can and can't do. Live a neat, quiet life, but never go down and watch the humans, never teach them all the wonderful things we know, show them the wonderful things we can do. I took the name Lightbringer to spite them; I was going to be the one who brought the light of the Veritas into the darkness of the lower universe. In fact, I think I did a lot of it to spite the Throne, until I met her.

"And do you know what I found out then, Miss Walker?"

Sylph's mind had already raced ahead to that conclusion. "The Throne isn't running the universe after all. And there are rules that you shouldn't break just out of spite."

"She's waiting, down at the bottom. The Sink. Every soul that issues forth from the raging torrent of creation, every soul that flows through the myriad worlds, ultimately finds its end there. And *she* is waiting for them, like a trapdoor spider at the bottom of its pit. Like the Archmagi with their Circles."

"You mean . . . the White Lady?"

"Of course." He waved a hand. "I had been fighting the wrong people all along. She's the real enemy, the only enemy, the enemy of all that lives. She waits at the bottom and consumes the energy of every soul that ever will be. And that's why it's forbidden to bring someone back to life; it reverses the flow, you see? She doesn't like that at all."

"You want to fight the White Lady?" asked Sylph. She

raised an eyebrow. "I thought she was some kind of god."

"Power, Sylph. All that matters is power. I want to free all the realms from her embrace. Then the dead can return, and I will be with my beloved again." He locked gazes with her. "So what I told you was true, from a certain point of view."

He's mad. There was certainly an odd gleam in Rathmado's eye. "That still doesn't explain any of this. If you're going to fight the White Lady, go and do it. Why bother creating the Archmagi and then having them overthrown?"

"I am *imprisoned*. Don't you remember?"

Then it clicked, finally. Sylph dug in her pocket and produced the geists, holding them in the palm of her hand. "You can't use these, can you?"

"It would be a poor prison if they left me with the key, wouldn't it?" He gestured with one hand. "I can collect power of my own—and oh, how I have collected power—but I cannot bring it to bear on breaking free. And similarly, I am prevented from accessing power collected by others. A delightful conundrum, don't you think? Almost as though she were taunting me."

"So you set up the Archmagi and the geists. The Circles, to gather falling souls. And every so often you pick some poor human . . ."

He raised one finger. "More like, every so often a human comes along who is truly extraordinary. I can reach out to your Earth, a little, enough to feel what I need, and to be ready when the circumstances are right. And yes, I find them and guide them, as I guided you, to reclaim the geists from the Archmagi."

"But it's also a test, right?" Sylph shook her head bitterly. "You had to make sure I was good enough to risk your precious power on. Que-Li, Hayao, all the rest since Erik didn't measure up."

"You have to admit I gave you more than a fair chance. Without the sword you wouldn't have lasted a day. And then I generously provided Lady Fell with a legion of Shadowcore, so she could be enough of a threat to Gargorian to force him to divert his forces."

"Your *sword* possessed my sister!"

"Ah." He shrugged. "Rahmgoth hated me like poison, but he had his place. I thought having him along would prove an appropriate help to you."

"Tests." Sylph's knuckles were white with anger on the grip of her pistol. "All of this."

"And you passed them all. You planned for me, fought for me, killed for me. Schemed for me, built for me. You were raped and tortured, for me. And none of it broke you." He took a deep breath. "I've been waiting a long time for you, Miss Walker. Almost three thousand years."

"And after that you think I'm going to *help* you? I came here to kill the Lightbringer, and I plan on doing it."

"No, you didn't." Rathmado leaned forward and steepled his hands. "You came here to find your mother and bring her back to life. And that part was true too. Only the Lightbringer knows how to do that particular trick. So, yes, you're going to help me. I don't think you have much of a choice."

✳   ✳   ✳

THE ROUGHLY LINE-SHAPED SKIRMISH HAD CONTRACTED down to a knot. Lina, Melfina, and the small group of riflemen that remained unengaged had retreated until their backs were pressed against the outer wall of the Keep, taking shots at Shadowcore soldiers who broke far enough away from the melee to offer a clear target. The smoke was working against them, however, and for the moment the Shadowcore seemed content to finish off the remnants of the line they'd surrounded. Lina saw Yahvy in the center, and kept getting brief glimpses of Heraan amid an ever-shrinking group of struggling forms surrounded by a sea of black armor.

This is horrible. It was like having a front row seat at an execution; half the troops weren't even shooting anymore, just numbly looking on. More Shadowcore soldiers poured out of the smoke every second, so many that it was clear they couldn't be stopped. *There was nothing we could have done.* Lina straightened up. *We got here first, at least. And if Sylph and Rathmado stop the Lightbringer, maybe this will all have been worthwhile.*

She drew the sword, the straight, plain blade Rathmado had left for her on the top of a little hill outside Gargorian's territory, half a world away and a lifetime ago. It was the gate to the Pit, she knew now. *Molochim is in there, and Mom. I wonder if I'll go back there when I die?* There would be no getting out this time, no body to return to, but all in all Lina thought she wouldn't mind. *But I doubt it. Molochim said that Lightbringer personally grabs the people he wants.*

"What are you doing?" Melfina whispered.

"I'm going to help Yahvy and Heraan," Lina said.

"They'll kill you!"

"They'll kill me anyway."

"But you promised . . ."

"I'm not leaving you behind." Lina managed a shaky smile. "Come on."

Slowly, Melfina let go of Lina's arm and drew her pistol, hugging the gun to her chest. Lina patted her gently on the shoulder and looked back at the battle. Of the Liberator's army there was almost nothing left, a dozen soldiers at the center of a press of black steel. Yahvy and Heraan fought back-to-back in the center, moments from being overwhelmed. *So I don't get to save them, even for a little while.* She raised the sword, hoping against hope that white fire might light her way one more time, but Rahmgoth's power was gone. *He would be more useful here than I am.*

Then she screamed, as loud as she could, and charged.

The battle-cry distracted the Shadowcore for a moment, and Heraan took advantage of the lull to spear a soldier through the lungs and kick him back into the press. The next moment he was faced by two armored fighters, heavy swords hacking through his desperate parries; he took a wound to the leg and vanished into the press as he collapsed. Yahvy, somehow noticing amid the shouts and clashes of steel, whirled and tried to hack her way to him; she cut down two Shadowcore before one of the black-armored soldiers ran her through from behind.

Lina, halfway to the battle with what remained of her little army at her back, caught Yahvy's eye. Even spitted on a blade, the Circle Breaker managed a smile; one hand gripped the sword where it emerged from her stomach, while the other darted under her coat. Lina frantically reversed course when she saw a half-dozen metal spheres fall free; she skidded on the tile and tackled Melfina flat. They hit the ground hard enough to bruise, and there was one moment of peace. Lina felt the cold of the stone underneath her, even through her clothes; she felt how light and frail Melfina had become. Lina thought of Yahvy and squeezed her eyes shut.

The grenades all went off at once, turning the center of the Shadowcore line into shrapnel that blew outward with devastating effect. The tightly packed group of armored warriors was blown apart, and those farther away were knocked off their feet, a ripple that spread from where the battle had been like an opening flower. Lina felt a wash of hot air pass over her, and a fragment of hot metal *pinged* off the stone by her ear.

Afterward, she didn't bother getting up. She heard the shouts of the riflemen, and the *crack* of bullets passing overhead. It didn't seem to matter. Melfina wrapped her arms around Lina's neck and seemed content to lie in silence. The noises of battle drifted away. *Maybe we're going to live, after all.* It didn't seem *fair. Not when I've already accepted everything, not after Yahvy and Heraan are gone. I can't . . .*

It was a new sound that made her raise her head, a footstep deeper and louder than the clank of any armored boot, along with the flat click of claws on tiles. And then, again, the *cracks* of rifles. Then screams.

Lina rolled over and looked up; her breath caught in her

throat. *Hikano.* She remembered grabbing the demon's jaw in her hands, the euphoria she'd felt when its bones crunched and tendons tore. *He's come back to get me.*

The Lightbringer. He controlled the Pit. *He let him* out, *just to kill me?*

One way or another, the creature was bearing down on her. It shrugged off rifle bullets like pinpricks, batting aside soldiers foolish enough to stand in its way. White fur rippled as it charged, huge, floating strides covering ground at an unreal pace.

Lina found energy from somewhere, dragged herself to her feet. She pulled Melfina along behind her. She didn't have a plan, just a blind impulse to flee; before long the wall of the Black Keep loomed up in front of her. She found the breach Rathmado had blown in the wall, reached for it, and yanked her hand back as energy crackled and spat in her path. *Lightbringer must have repaired the barrier.* She turned around.

Hikano had stopped, not twenty feet away. Its huge, toothy mouth hung open, and its breath steamed in the chill air. Tiny red eyes were focused on Lina, and she could almost feel its hate.

Lina pushed Melfina to one side, gently.

"It wants me. It might vanish afterward . . . or leave you alone, or something . . ."

"No!" It was a scream. "You promised!"

"Sylph will take care of you, Mel. Please . . ."

"*No!*" Melfina broke free of Lina's grip, stepped between her and the monster with her pistol raised. Hikano advanced another step, and the ground seemed to tremble. Melfina fired, just once.

In a perfect world, Lina thought, *she would find some weak spot. Some chink in its armor. The thing would just collapse, and then Yahvy and Heraan would turn out to be okay after all, and Sylph would beat the Lightbringer and we'd all go home. In a perfect world—*

—the bullet whined away into oblivion. Hikano brought one claw around in a brutally fast arc, knocking Melfina off her feet and flinging her against the wall hard enough that Lina heard the crunch, saw the spray of blood. The girl flopped onto her face and didn't stir.

Lina raised her sword, then cast it aside with a tired sigh. It clanged and clattered on the stone.

She raised her arms.

"Fine. If you want me, here I . . . *oof* . . ."

One of the claws shot out and grabbed her, so tight that she couldn't draw a breath. Something in her body snapped with a *crack*, but Lina was beyond feeling the pain. A curious calm came over her as the demon lifted her completely off the ground and its jaws gaped wide.

"Don't worry," said a familiar voice. "I'll be there to catch you when you fall."

"I COULD THREATEN YOU TOO," RATHMADO MUSED. "I can't use my power to get free, but I can certainly use it to blow you into a greasy smear. Does that make any difference?"

"What exactly do you want me to do?"

"Open that door," he said.

Hesitantly, Sylph closed her hand around the geists and extended a probe at the door. When she made contact she had to stifle a gasp. It felt like a huge, tangled ball of yarn or a twisted cobweb; hundreds of tiny, shimmering threads stretching in all directions. And in the center, like the spider or the unexpected knitting needle, was the Lightbringer, his essence, the center of his power. The threads wrapped him like a cocoon, keeping him suspended and impotent. *No wonder he can't get loose.* It would be like a thrashing fly in a spider's web. *No matter how much power he applies, he just doesn't have the leverage. But . . .*

There was a kind of pulse, a throbbing that ran along the threads at regular intervals. *A heartbeat.* Sylph thought back to what Lina had told her.

"She buried you in this world," Sylph said slowly. "Down at

the bottom, nice and tangled up so you couldn't get out."

"It would take a genius of a wizard to undo," Rathmado agreed. "And a lot of power. Thousands of years, billions of souls."

"But it's all knotted up. I couldn't do it without cutting the threads, and that would mean—"

He cut her off. "Of course. This place is a prison; the only way out is for it to be unmade."

"What happens to all the people?" She caught his blank expression. "You haven't even thought about that. It doesn't matter to you, does it?"

"Not in the slightest. You should stop pretending that it matters to you."

"It does!" Sylph felt her voice quiver. "I'm not going to get my mother back if it means killing tens of thousands of people!"

"No? What about Lina?" The Lightbringer smiled. "We may be just in time, if you hurry."

He waved a hand, and a glowing oval formed in the air beside him. Sylph saw the outside of the Black Keep as though she were looking through a camera. Dead Shadowcore lay everywhere, especially around a deep crater where fires still burned. But dominating the center of the scene was a monster, a four-armed lizard-thing with an enormous maw reminiscent of a furred tyrannosaurus. Sylph just had time to recognize Lina, held tight in one of its claws, before the creature lifted her to its jaws. It tugged, ripped and tore, like a dog worrying a rubber bone; when it pulled its claw away, arterial blood spurted from a headless corpse. Bones crunched when the demon took another bite.

"Oops," said Rathmado, and giggled. "Just a bit too late."

Sylph fell to her knees, geists in one hand and the gun in the other. She couldn't look up at the horrible portal. *I suppose he could have faked it. But . . . no, it's not his style.* Besides, in her heart of hearts she knew what came next.

"Hikano has come in very useful, over the years. Its anger is a thing to behold." Rathmado shook his head. "It's a shame, but . . . I think there's still time after all."

He raised one hand, and there was a flash of light. When it cleared he was holding the sword, the sword he'd given Lina, the key to the Pit where Sylph's mother was held. *And now* . . .

"I've taken the liberty of trapping her in here," said Rathmado. "I'm afraid that *some* of what I told you earlier was a lie. In the geist, or in my own First Circle, the souls are too closely packed to return to life. They blur together, you see, and it's hard to extract any coherent sense of self. But in the Pit things are different." He shrugged. "It's your choice, Miss Walker."

There was a long silence.

"And that's it?" Sylph said, in a whisper. "I break the seal and destroy the world, and you bring Mom and Lina back to life. What happens to the three of us?"

"I'll find someplace to put you, since this world will cease to exist." Rathmado leaned forward. "Once I defeat the White Lady, there will be no limits to my power."

"How can I trust you?"

"You can't. But what choice do you have? If you refuse, I kill you now. That would be too bad. I'd have to wait another six hundred years or so for someone else to come along. But there's no second chance for you, Sylph Walker. You die. And your mother and Lina are trapped in the Pit for me to play with as long as I want. And," his grin turned wolfish, "I have a lot of patience when it comes to that sort of thing."

"How do you bring someone back to life? A person is much too complex to build piece by piece."

"I'm surprised you haven't worked that out. It's easy if you have a complete soul; it *knows* what its body should look like, down to the last molecule. You provide the power, and it provides the direction. You just have to let the soul choose its own natural shape."

Slowly, painfully, Sylph got back to her feet. She met Rathmado's eyes, and he must have seen the defiance there, because he laughed.

"Oh, is that how it is? Now that you've 'wrested the secret out of me,' as it were, you'll challenge me and resurrect them yourself?" He snorted. "You have the geists, little girl, but I have all of the First Circle to draw on. Don't force me to hurt you to prove my point."

Sylph took a deep breath.

"It's an interesting thing," she said. "The difference between a real thing and something created by magic. A real thing has more . . . complexity, you might say. Energy, bound up in its creation. If you arrange things in the right way you can get them to give back more energy then you put in. It doesn't work that way with magic."

Rathmado stared, at a loss. Sylph continued.

"We spent a night camped under your First Circle. It's damn near indestructible, isn't it? We could barely scratch the thing."

"Ah!" The Lightbringer snapped his fingers. "I see. You've left something back there, one of your 'machines,' no doubt. I was impressed with the gambit you used to defeat the Clockwork Legion. And now you hope you'll be able to somehow destroy the Circle and bring me down." He smiled broadly. "You are to be commended for thinking ahead, but I'm afraid there's nothing in your arsenal that can do the job. You're welcome to try, of course."

Sylph nodded. "I did a lot of thinking while I was in Vilvakis's dungeon. In between the rape, the red hot knives, and so on." She clenched her fist on the gun again. "Things have changed, back on Earth. We've learned a few more tricks."

"Obviously."

"One of them has to do with certain rare metals." Sylph looked up at him, and forced a smile. "They object to being *squeezed*."

She let go of the string that she'd been tugging since the night before, a gesture as easy as parting her thumb and forefinger. All the hard work was already done. Now all she had to do

was watch the magic whip away, coiling out into the darkness at
the speed of light—

*   *   *

—AND, IN THE SHADOW OF THE HOVERING FIRST CIRCLE,
the rest of the spell waited. At the center was a little sphere of
metal—*real* metal, not magically created forgeries, painstaking-
ly extracted grain by grain from the soil, the rocks, the water.
Sylph had been gathering it ever since Vilvakis, all through the
march across the Lightbringer's domain. Magic helped, as always; it meant she could dispense with the clumsy centrifuges
and separators, explosives and timers. Just a little ball of metal,
and a spell wrapped around it. The string whipped back, vanished, and an instant later the spell started falling inward, a
sphere attempting to become a point.

There was a little ball of metal in the way, suddenly subject to enormous pressure. It compressed, falling along with the
spell, and deep inside little bouncing pieces of nothing suddenly
found their world ripe with targets. A critical threshold was
reached, passed, and the tiny ball was still shrinking as energy
bloomed at its heart.

All this happened in a fraction of a second. An outside ob-
server would have seen nothing, had no warning. Just a tiny
point of light expanding outward, as fast as thought. The First
Circle shimmered as it was plunged into a furnace the likes of
which Omega had never seen; it resisted for only a moment, then
shattered like glass. A thousand shards were dark spots against
the fireball for another fraction of a second before it gobbled
them up.

Then there was only the light, and behind it a shockwave
harder than steel expanding at the speed of sound. And, rising
above it all, the beginnings of a mushroom cloud.

*   *   *

SYLPH KEPT HER EYES ON THE LITTLE VIEWING PORTAL.
The demon, Hikano, was still visible. A second after she'd let
go of the thread, the whole field of view flashed with a light so
brilliant she couldn't bear to look. It washed over Hikano and
dissolved the creature in a bath of atomic fire, then assaulted
the barrier that surrounded the Keep. Sylph heard the distant
crackle rise to a roaring fury.

And Lightbringer screamed.

"What have you done?"

She felt him reach out to the Circle, as Sylph had so often
reached for the geists, and the flood of raw power that answered
almost flattened both of them. It was gushing from the Circle
like blood from a wound, or water from a broken main—too
strong to control. Trying to do magic with a flow like that was
like trying to fly a kite in a hurricane, but that didn't stop him
from trying, flailing desperately at the torrent.

Sylph didn't even try. She just raised her gun and pulled the
trigger, kept pulling it until the pistol clicked empty. For a moment Rathmado stood, animated by sheer rage, still groping for
the magic that would save him.

Then he collapsed with a double thump, lying in a bloody
heap beside his throne.

Sylph let the gun fall from numbed fingers—it clattered
on the floor—and walked to the throne in a daze. The magical storm was passing, the souls falling *en masse* off of Omega
entirely and flowing down to their ultimate fate. *The Sink. The
White Lady.* She looked up at the throne and the horribly realistic spider's head that topped it, and shivered.

Still moving without conscious thought, Sylph reached down
and picked up the sword. She reached inside it, carefully, and almost immediately felt what it contained. A gateway to another
world, or a hole in this one. It was like encountering a gap where
her probing hand expected solid ground. *The Pit.*

By now the storm had burned itself out, the entire First

Circle evaporated like smoke. An eerie silence filled throne room. And something had changed in the Black Keep, as though air that had been still for centuries was suddenly stirred by a breath of hot wind. Sylph took a deep breath and smelled the tang of ozone.

I did it. That was just beginning to sink in. *It really worked. It really* fucking *worked!* That was her first thought, which made her feel guilty when all the rest caught up with her. Sylph leaned back against the wall, resting the point of the sword on the ground, and cried.

❋   ❋   ❋

EVENTUALLY SHE WIPED HER EYES AND STRAIGHTENED UP.

Later. There'll be time for that later. I've got work to do.

She reached out, and the geists responded eagerly. With their power behind her, Sylph plunged her metaphorical hand into the Pit. There were three souls within—the third was Molochim, according to Lina's story—and it wasn't hard to distinguish him from the two she wanted. Once they were in hand, she pulled them through to Omega.

And that's all it takes? Once she'd seen how the Pit was connected to Omega, traveling between worlds didn't seem difficult at all. *Just a little push* that *way, and that's all it takes?*

She released her grip on the two souls and let them float free for a moment. Without a physical form, they would drift through the world and on down toward the Sink; instead, Sylph started feeding them power. *Enough power to climb the energy slope, enough power to rebuild their bodies.* It wasn't so hard, after all, if you knew precisely what bit went where.

Two bodies took shape, hanging in the air in front of her. They solidified from the inside out: bones and cartilage, muscles and sinew, with blood vessels burrowing through it all like worms. Lungs and intestines, eyes and brain, plucking the necessary elements out of the air. *There's not much to us at all, when you think about it. Carbon, hydrogen, nitrogen, oxygen. It just needs to be put together like a jigsaw.*

She tried to keep her mind off of what *else* she could feel. Cold tendrils, slithering across her skin and binding her in place. The trap finding a new victim.

Skin, pink and new. Sylph looked away—*are they somehow less naked now than without skin?*—until clothes started to form. Lina was dressed in her old sweatshirt, Sylph was amused to note, and her mother's hair slithered down her back in a long red wave.

Almost as one, they opened their eyes.

"Sylph?"

Lina took a deep breath. "I knew it! I knew she'd do it!"

Sylph let go, letting them fall gently to the ground. Lina ran forward and wrapped her arms around her sister, holding so tight Sylph thought she would suffocate.

"I *knew* it. I told Mom that we'd be seeing you soon and I *knew* you'd do it!"

Sylph ran her hand through her sister's hair, absentmindedly, and looked up at her mother.

"Hi, Mom." Her voice cracked. "It's been a while."

"Sylph?" She looked around at the throne room, with all its horrible faces on the walls. "Is this real? Or am I dreaming again?"

"It's real," said Lina, a bit muffled. "Or as real as things get around here, anyway."

"Ah." Her mother ran the back of her hand across her eyes. "I . . . never expected to see you again."

"Me either." Sylph swallowed past the lump in her throat.

There was an awkward pause, and then they both spoke simultaneously.

"Mom . . ."

"Sylph . . ."

Lina looked from one to the other.

"If you want to hate me," said Sylph in a small voice, "it's okay."

Her mother blinked. "I was going to say that."

"Why would I hate *you*?"

"Because I left you girls behind."

Lina giggled. "Neither one of you blames the other, okay? Now, would you hug each other already?"

Sylph stepped forward, tentatively, then just fell into her mother's embrace. It was warm, and safe, and everything she remembered.

"Sylph," her mother whispered. "My Sylph."

"Now we can go home." Lina's voice was shaking. "We can all go home, and all of this will be over. Right?"

For a moment Sylph said nothing. Then she let go of her mother, and nodded. Lina hugged her again.

"Then what are we waiting for?"

"Nothing," said Sylph. She reached into her pocket and retrieved the geists, the little metal spheres clicking against one another in her hand. "Stand back, okay?"

Mother and daughter did so. Without looking, Lina held out her hand; without looking, her mother took it.

Just a little push. Sylph took a deep breath. *That way.* It wasn't a direction she could point to, but one she could *feel*. And all it took was power. A *lot* of power, but she had three thousand years' worth in the geists.

Lina raised her free hand and looked at it in wonder. She and her mother were fading, becoming translucent. Lina giggled again, then looked up at Sylph.

"Wait." Her voice was fading too. "Wait . . . Sylph! You're not . . ." Lina's eyes went wide. "You can't! You brought us back to life!"

"I'm imprisoned," said Sylph, with a wan smile.

"No!" Lina fought free of her mother's hand and ran to Sylph, but her arms were already immaterial and passed right through her sister. "I won't go without you! You can't . . . Sylph . . ."

"You're not going without me," said Sylph. "You're going

ahead of me." She caught her mother's eye. "I *will* be back, you understand? I don't care how long it takes. I'll invent immortality, time travel, whatever it takes. I will be *back*, and we'll all be together on Earth. Like we should have been."

"Lightbringer tried for six thousand years! Sylph, you *can't*. Please!"

"I'll wait for you," her mother said.

"Mom!" Lina wailed.

"I don't really understand," she said. "But Sylph is ten times as smart as that guy ever was. So we'll be waiting."

Sylph nodded. The two figures faded into twinkling motes, and were gone.

I'll find them. Sylph meant every word she'd said. *Lina won't forgive me, otherwise. It may take a while, but I'll find them.* Still, it was a shame she'd have to miss their arrival on Earth. *I'd give anything to see the look on Lina's face when she finds out I filled her pockets with diamonds.*

And that's everything. Her eyes fell on the sword. *Almost everything.*

This time reaching inside was easier; only one soul remained. She let it assemble, looking away until the clothes appeared.

Molochim was a young man in a gray suit, with a cigarette hanging from between his fingers.

"You're Sylph?"

She nodded.

"You don't look much like your sister."

Sylph shrugged. "And you're Molochim?"

"The one an' only."

"So?" Sylph suddenly felt very tired. "As long as I'm playing Wizard of Oz, what about you? Want to go back to Ring, or wherever it is you came from?"

Molochim looked at her for a long moment.

"Rahmgoth," he said finally, "never really got it. He was angry at Lightbringer, angry at me, angry at the Throne. But he never *thought* about it, never fuckin' sat down for a minute and questioned. And Lightbringer, he never second guessed himself. Never, ever. That was what made him so scary. He was always ready to take them on—the Throne, the White Lady, whomever. I guess that makes me the fuckin' intellectual of the group. I spent a long time thinking about it—not much else to do, stuck in the fuckin' Pit, right?—and I came to some conclusions."

"Oh?"

"I was wrong, and they were right. The Throne, the White Lady. It's a hard thing to say, but sometimes it's gotta be fuckin' said. We were wrong to mess around in the lower worlds, act like gods just because we'd been born higher up. It doesn't make us any better than them. Didn't give me the right to do what I did."

"I wondered," Sylph said. "Everyone in the Pit seemed to have gone crazy. Mom reverted to her childhood, Rahmgoth built a fortress of his hatred, and Hikano just went nuts. But not you. Why?"

"It was my punishment. Not fair, maybe, and certainly not delivered by the right person. But I deserved it."

"Do you want to go back to Ring? Have you served your time?"

"Nah. It's been six thousand years. I don't think I'd fit in." He took a long drag on the cigarette, gagged, and tossed it to the floor while he coughed violently. "*Fuck*. Is *that* what the damn things taste like in real life?"

Sylph couldn't help but smile. "Where do you want to go?"

"Who knows?" He tilted his head. "What about you?"

"I'm breaking out of here."

"Lightbringer tried that."

"I know. I'm smarter than him."

After a moment, Molochim laughed. "You know, I really fuckin' believe that. You need any help?"

"Help . . ." She paused. "Why?"

He shrugged. "I just got out of one prison. What's one more?"

*   *   *

A WHILE LATER, SYLPH WAS ALONE IN THE THRONE ROOM.
Molochim had wandered off, to gawk at the mess her bomb had
made of the surrounding area. Sylph considered warning him
the air was probably toxic, but decided the Veritas probably
wouldn't be bothered.

So. She closed her eyes. *Think about getting out of here.*

On the other hand, it would probably be best to rest for a
while. *I have all of eternity, after all.* Just running head on at the
problem wouldn't accomplish anything. *Build my strength back up,
plan out an attack. There's nothing to be gained from just leaping into
things. Rest comes first.*

She sat uncomfortably on Lightbringer's throne. In one
hand she held the geists, passing them idly through her fingers;
the clicking of metal on metal was the only sound in the room.

Rest, Sylph. Rest.

Sylph opened her eyes.

Okay, that's probably long enough. She jumped down from the
throne and stuffed the geists in her pocket. *Time to get started.*

End

Don't miss Django Wexler's other novel from
Medallion Press, "**Memories of Empire**"

chapter *1*

"The fundamental flaw in their culture is a certain
stubbornness, a continued resistance to the world as
it is. The clearest example is their religion, worshipping ghosts six thousand years dead, but this trait
runs throughout their entire culture. It makes them
fearsome in times of strength but pathetic in times of
weakness, and it leaves them unable or unwilling to
adapt to changing conditions . . ."

–Kabiru Shun, *The Fall of the Sixth Dynasty*

THERE'S ALWAYS ONE perfect moment, when the mind has just
awoken and consciousness has yet to fully engage—still
half-wrapped in dream, eyes open but uncomprehending, until
the weight of the world crashes down with all its harsh reality.
That moment, Veil had decided, was something to be savored.
It slipped away all too quickly. The very act of thinking about it
kicked her mind into action, and what had been mere patterns
of light and shadow resolved into familiar objects. She managed
one clean breath, held it for one perfect moment.

Then memory returned, and Veil settled in for a nice long
scream.

ONE MAN. IT didn't seem possible.

The scream was very uncharacteristic of Veil. She was not, as a rule, a person who screamed or cried or threw tantrums. Growing up in Kalil's massive household had taught her a number of important lessons about life, and not the least of these was that screaming and crying rarely accomplished anything.

But, in this case, she felt she deserved a good scream. It helped to burn off tension, that was the main thing, and, once she was done, she was able to look at the situation with a great deal more equanimity. Under other circumstances she might have been worried about her reputation, but since there wasn't another human being for at least fifty miles in any direction that was also not a concern.

The sun was up, having just cleared the eastern horizon, and was beginning to make itself felt. The day promised to be a scorcher—the sky was blue from edge to edge, not even a wisp of cloud to blunt the heat. Veil could feel the sand, gritty and cold against her back, but already starting to drink in the sun's rays. In a few hours it would be too hot to touch.

Mahmata lay on top of her, and blood from the wound in the fat woman's belly had crusted over Veil's legs. Once she was done screaming, Veil set about freeing herself. This took some time, since Mahmata was quite fat and Veil might have described herself, charitably, as 'wiry.' Eventually, though, she managed to wriggle out from underneath the corpse and survey what was left of the camp.

Most of Bali's men were sprawled on a blood-soaked stretch of sand halfway to the bluff. Low as it was, it was the only decent shade for miles; it was no surprise they'd run into someone. That was where they'd confronted the stranger, and it didn't look like any of them had gotten more than two steps. Veil wandered over to inspect them, in a stunned state of idle curiosity. Dead bodies didn't bother her—the spirits were gone, after all, settling into the Aether or snapped up as food for something bigger and meaner.

So what was left to be afraid of? They were all dead—seven men. Vosh, who'd boasted so around the campfire, hadn't even gotten his sword out of its scabbard. Vosh had voted to pass Veil around at night, as a kind of bonus for the guards. Thankfully Bali had overruled him—apparently her virginity was worth more than a sellsword could offer—but Veil gave Vosh's corpse a kick anyway and felt a little better.

The other slaves had died, too, tied together and unable to even run. Veil hadn't known the pair of dark-skinned aborigines very well, since they spoke no Imperial and only a few broken words of Khaev, but fair-haired Silel had come from a clan to the west of Kalil's. Veil had gotten to know her in a month of traveling—a pretty, empty-headed thing. It was no wonder her father had gotten rid of her; still, she hadn't deserved to be slashed open like a Mourning fowl, spilling purple and black on the sands. Veil looked at her a moment, and shook her head. In clan lands the corpse would already be covered with flies, or torn apart by coyotes, but nothing lived in the high desert. Not even insects.

Bali, himself, had gotten the farthest. She assumed he'd started to run as soon as his sellswords started falling like trees in a sandstorm, but he'd made the mistake of stopping at his pack to dig out his purses. She found him there, slumped over his gold, run through from behind. Blood had coated the open purse and dulled the gleam of the coins.

She thought about kicking Bali, too, but he was so pathetic in death that adding further insult to his corpse seemed point-less. Instead she bent down to look in the purse. It was filled to bursting, a not-inconsiderable load for a grown man and a hope-less encumbrance for a girl of fifteen. She reached in, delicately, and extracted two fat golden eyes. That had been the slave-price Bali paid her father; more than the usual one-six he paid for children, she remembered, because there was a shortage of virgin girls in Corsa and the brothels were paying double.

Veil tucked the coins into the pocket of her ragged shorts and sat down heavily on the already-warming sands, trying to decide whether or not she wanted to die.

Even that was a bit egotistical, she had to admit.

It's not as though I have much of a choice. A hundred miles from home, in the middle of the trackless high desert, with no food and no water other than what she might salvage from the wreckage of the camp. The right thing to do, the logical thing, would be to lie down in the sun, enjoy the warmth, and slowly wither to a mummified corpse. Either that or, if she was feeling brave, borrow a dagger from one of the guards and end it herself. *That would be the logical choice. No food, no water, no help, no chance.*

On the other hand, why not? Veil's life had ended two months ago, when Kalil lost a war against Siorn and came up short on the reparations. *And yet, I'm still here. Might as well make the most of it. What's the worst that happens, I die in the desert?*

She permitted herself a tight, sarcastic grin and went about stripping the bodies. She acquired a white cloth robe, suitable for desert wear, from Mahmata; it was a bit used and had a bloody hole through the middle, but Veil felt she wasn't in a position to pick and choose. From Silel, after a brief internal struggle, she took shoes — real bound-leather shoes, better by far for loose sand than the sandals Veil was wearing. The two biggest water skins — which Bali had been carrying — she hoisted over one shoulder. The little canteens that everyone had carried she drained, drinking until she squelched at the edges. There was no food— presumably the stranger had taken it. Veil shrugged. *If I live long enough that food becomes an issue, I'll have gotten farther than I expected.*

She hesitated over the last item. It seemed pointless, really— there wasn't a human for miles and miles, except for maybe the stranger, and there were no animals in the high desert. Nevertheless, she finally unstrapped Vosh's short sword and slung it awkwardly over her other shoulder. It was only a piece of pointed steel, but it made her feel better.

That left one last choice to make. *Which direction to go?*

Two options presented themselves. She could backtrack, heading west toward the Red Hills and home. That did not sound promising—the hills themselves were rife with bandits and rebels, and soldiers hunting both. Not to mention it was at least two weeks' walk through the high desert that way. *And if I turned up again at Kalil's door, what would he do? Probably chastise me for being disobedient and sell me to the next caravan that passed by, counting himself lucky to get paid twice for the same girl.* Veil's memories of her father were understandably colored by recent events, but, even in the past, Kalil had not been the kindliest of men. Not that he'd been particularly cruel, either—he didn't have time, with seven wives and uncounted children to manage, and there had been nannies and tutors to dispense the punishments. But she remembered him as distant, and cold.

Still, she hesitated. There was someone at home who would welcome her. *Kyre.* He was her truebrother, sharing both a father and a mother, born almost two years to the day before her. He'd cried, a little, when Kalil announced that she was to be sold. Afterwards, as she'd sat on her bunk in stunned silence, he'd kissed her lightly on the cheek and told her not to worry. *Kyre would be happy to see me.*

The other choice was south. The trail was clear enough, for the moment, a line of footprints running straight as an arrow across the sand. The first wind would obliterate them, but the baking air had barely stirred. The stranger had gone that way.

Bali had been heading vaguely south, she knew. There were oases, and little towns where you could buy water. She'd searched his body for a map, but either the slaver had navigated by memory or the stranger had taken it; probably the former, since Bali was— had been—only barely literate. Go south far enough, and the desert ran out. The city of Corsa was out there, somewhere. Every vile, nasty story Veil had ever heard had been set in Corsa; apparently the place was populated entirely by slavers and pirates, and operated beyond the reach of Khaev law.

It was ultimately curiosity that helped her to make up her

mind. *One man against seven.* Her memories of the fight were confused, a blur of blood and flashing steel, but she remembered the stranger. All in black, and he'd moved like a phantom. *He won't last, in the heat. He'll have to rest. I can catch up with him, and he has the food.* He'd killed everyone, even the women and slaves. *He didn't kill me.* In all likelihood, he hadn't even noticed her—Mahmata had fallen on top of her, and Veil had fainted. *But, still . . .*

The sun had climbed higher, and the sand was getting hot. Veil struggled to her feet, water skins clonking heavily against her breast, and started south. *One step at a time, one foot after the other.*

JUST AFTER MIDDAY, when the sun was at its hottest, she finally caught sight of him.

The air felt like it had been cooked, so dry she could feel her skin cracking every time she moved. It was like the inside of the bakery, back home, when she was standing next to the oven and feeling the waves of heat it threw off; except here the oven was the whole world, and she couldn't duck outside the hut for a quick break. Everything Veil wore—her new boots, her flimsy shirt—was soaked in sweat.

Her burden felt heavy, so heavy. Taking the sword had been a mistake. Just carrying the water was hard enough; the sword flapped against her back at every step, as though chastising her for her errors. She couldn't summon the energy to reach back and get rid of the damn thing, either. It would have meant putting everything down to rearrange the straps, and if she stopped walking, Veil was certain she wouldn't start again.

The dunes went on forever. At the crest of each one, she felt as though she could see to the end of the world—the desert receded eternally to the blue-hazed horizon. Only on her right, in the east, was anything else visible: the dim shapes of the Cloudripper range rode like ghosts on the edge of vision.

By chance, she crested a dune at the same moment he did. A tiny black ant, ten or twenty dunes ahead, crawling across the boiling sands. Veil stopped and shouted herself hoarse, trying to get his attention, but if the ant shifted in its progress she couldn't see it. She spent the next hour damning him in every way she could think of, coming up with creative torments the spirits of the Aether could subject his soul to before devouring it utterly. She saw him again a couple of hours later, a bit closer than she remembered—this time, when she shouted, the distant speck definitely paused for a moment to look back at her. Then he continued on his way, unconcerned. Veil rasped her tongue over cracked lips, took a swallow of precious water, and started down the dune.

Memories of Empire

django wexler

Available Now
ISBN#1932815147
Silver Imprint
US $14.99 / CDN $19.95
Fantasy

7

MORE THAN MAGICK

Rick Taubold

What if you were told you have a power you don't know about? What if you were told that you have to use it to save the universe from a major baddie? What if no one will tell you how you are supposed to do this?

A recent college graduate, Scott Madison is half-heartedly considering his future when he reads an ad on the dorm bulletin board. He ends up taking the job with Jake Kesten, Martial Arts expert and Ph.D. math whiz, and finds himself busting computer hackers for the government. It's an interesting job, if a little rough at times. Still, it's just a job.

Then Jake and Scott get a visit from what, apparently, is an old friend of Jake's — Arion. Scott thinks Arion dresses a little funny, what with the robes and all. But then Arion proclaims himself an Adept at Magick. Before Scott can even roll his eyes, he finds himself whisked away to another world where he joins his fellow adventurers, all plucked as unceremoniously from their own home worlds. Their mission? To save the Elfaeden and their friends, the Crystal Dragons. Their secret weapon? Scott Madison. Who is about to discover that there is something, indeed, **MORE THAN MAGICK.**

ISBN#0974363987
ISBN#9780974363981
Gold Imprint
US $6.99 / CDN $8.99
Available Now
www.ricktaubold.com

THE CARDINAL'S HEIR
JAKI DEMAREST

Cardinal Richelieu is dead, a victim of poison. The throne of France, which he has long protected, is once more unstable as rival factions vie for power. But the Cardinal has appointed two heirs: one to his religious position, and one to head the elite spy ring that has maintained France's fragile political balance.

Francoise Marguerite de Palis, the Cardinal's lovely but low born niece, is devastated by her uncle's murder and vows revenge, which she sets out after immediately. Though the task is daunting, she at least has some formidable tools at her command. Not only is she now the head of the Cardinal's Eyes, but is arguably the most powerful Sorciere in all France. Shapeshifting into her character Biscarrat, notorious swordsman, she sets out to find her uncle's murderer. But with an unexpected ally.

Handsome and dashing Jean de Treville, head of the King's Musketeers, is saddened to learn of the Cardinal's death, though both headed groups not generally fond of one another. Sadness turns to stunned amazement, however, when he learns who has been appointed to lead the Cardinal's spy ring . . . and who is also, in fact, the swordsman who has bested him on numerous occasions. Not to mention the beautiful, and untouchable, wife of Court favorite, Antoine de Palis.

But just as there is more, much more, to the enchanting Francoise, so is there more than simple murder afoot. Side by side, Francoise and Jean descend into a maelstrom of magic as they battle another powerful Sorcier, and enter a bloody race to obtain a fabulous jewel. And the throne of France hangs in the balance, supported only by the magic and mastery of . . .

The Cardinal's Heir

ISBN#1932815104
ISBN#9781932815108
Gold Imprint
US $6.99 / CDN $8.99
www.jakidemarest.com

For more information

about other great titles from

Medallion Press, visit

www.medallionpress.com